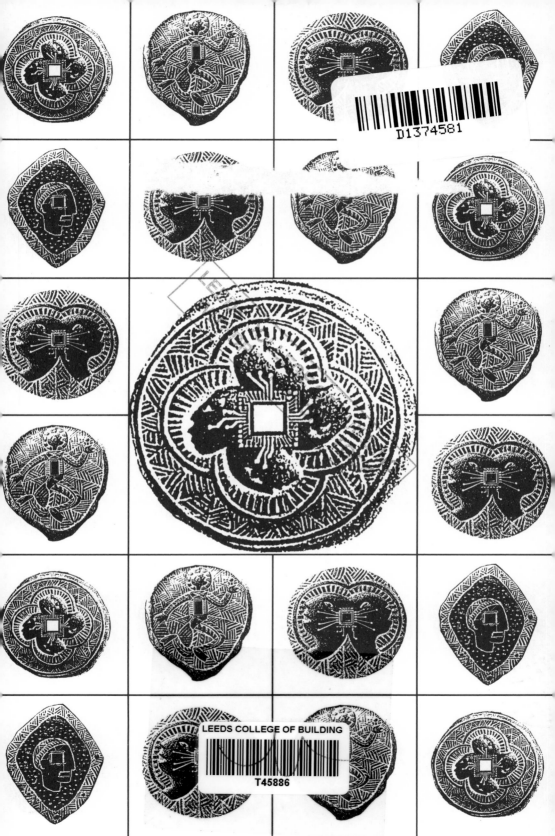

Otherland

Also from Legend by Tad Williams:
TAILCHASER'S SONG

MEMORY, SORROW AND THORN
THE DRAGONBONE CHAIR
STONE OF FAREWELL
TO GREEN ANGEL TOWER

OTHERLAND

Volume One: CITY OF GOLDEN SHADOW

Tad Williams

LEGEND

Published by Legend Books in 1996

An imprint of Random House UK Limited
20 Vauxhall Bridge Road, London SW1V 2SA

An imprint of Random House UK Limited

Random House Australia (Pty) Limited
16 Dalmore Drive, Scoresby, Victoria, 3179

Random House New Zealand Limited
18 Poland Road, Glenfield
Auckland 10, New Zealand

Random House South Africa (Pty) Limited
PO Box 2263, Rosebank 2121, South Africa

Random House UK Limited Reg. No. 954009

ISBN 0099683016

Printed and bound in Great Britain by
Mackays of Chatham PLC, Chatham, Kent

*This book is dedicated to my father, Joseph Hill Evans,
with love.*

*Actually, Dad doesn't read fiction, so if someone doesn't tell
him about this, he'll never know.*

Acknowledgments

This has been a hideously complicated book to write, and I am indebted to many people for their assistance, but especially the following, who either provided desperately-needed research help or waded through another giant-economy-sized Tad manuscript and had encouraging and useful things to say afterward:

Deborah Beale, Matt Bialer, Arthur Ross Evans, Jo-Ann Goodwin, Deborah Grabien, Nic Grabien, Jed Hartman, John Jarrold, Roz Kaveney, Katharine Kerr, M. J. Kramer, Mark Kreighbaum, Bruce Lieberman, Mark McCrum, Peter Stampfel, Mitch Wagner.

As always, many thanks are due to my patient and perceptive editors, Sheila Gilbert and Betsy Wollheim.

For more information, visit the Tad Williams web site at:

http://www.tadwilliams.com

Author's Note

The aboriginal people of Southern Africa are known by many names—San, Basarwa, Remote Area Dwellers (in current government-speak), and, more commonly, Bushmen.

I freely admit that I have taken great liberties in my portrayal of Bushman life and beliefs in this novel. The Bushmen do not have a monolithic folklore—each area and sometimes each extended family can sustain its own quite vibrant myths—or a single culture. I have simplified and sometimes transposed Bushman thoughts and songs and stories. Fiction has its own demands.

But the Bushmen's old ways are indeed disappearing fast. One of my most dubious bits of truth-manipulation may turn out to be the simple assertion that there will be *anyone* left pursuing the hunter-gatherer life in the bush by the middle of the twenty-first century.

However I have trimmed the truth, I have done my best to make the spirit of my portrayal accurate. If I have offended or exploited, I have failed. My intent is primarily to tell a story, but if the story leads some readers to learn more about the Bushmen, and about a way of life that none of us can afford to ignore, I will be very happy.

Contents

Third

ANOTHER COUNTRY

Fourth

THE CITY

Foreword

It started in mud, as many things do.

In a normal world, it would have been time for breakfast, but apparently breakfast was not served in hell; the bombardment that had begun before dawn showed no signs of letting up. Private Jonas did not feel much like eating, anyway.

Except for a brief moment of terrified retreat across a patch of muddy ground cratered and desolate as the moon, Paul Jonas had spent all of this twenty-fourth day of March, 1918, as he had spent the three days before, and most of the past several months—crouched shivering in cold, stinking slime somewhere between Ypres and St. Quentin, deafened by the skull-rattling thunder of the German heavy guns, praying reflexively to Something in which he no longer believed. He had lost Finch and Mullet and the rest of the platoon somewhere in the chaos of retreat—he hoped they'd made it safely into some other part of the trenches, but it was hard to think about anything much beyond his own few cubits of misery. The entire world was wet and sticky. The torn earth, the skeletal trees, and Paul himself had all been abundantly spattered by the slow-falling mist that followed hundreds of pounds of red-hot metal exploding in a crowd of human beings.

Red fog, gray earth, sky the color of old bones: Paul Jonas was in hell—but it was a very special hell. Not everyone in it was dead yet.

In fact, Paul noted, one of its residents was dying very slowly indeed. By the sound of the man's voice, he could not be more than two dozen yards away, but he might as well have been in Timbuktu. Paul had no idea what the wounded soldier looked like—he could no more have voluntarily lifted his head above the lip of the trench than he could have willed himself to fly—but he was all too familiar with the man's voice, which had been cursing, sobbing, and squealing in agony for a full hour, filling every lull between the crash of the guns.

All the rest of the men who had been hit during the retreat had shown the good manners to die quickly, or at least to suffer quietly. Paul's invisible companion had screamed for his sergeant, his mother, and God, and when none of them had come for him, had kept on screaming anyway. He was screaming still, a sobbing, wordless wail. Once a faceless doughboy like thousands of others, the wounded man now seemed determined to make everyone on the Western Front bear witness to his dying moments.

Paul hated him.

The terrible thumping roar subsided; there was a glorious moment of silence before the wounded man began to shriek again, piping like a boiling lobster.

"Got a light?"

Paul turned. Pale beer-yellow eyes peered from a mask of mud beside him. The apparition, crouched on hands and knees, wore a greatcoat so tattered it seemed made from cobwebs.

"What?"

"Got a light? A match?"

The normality of the question, in the midst of so much that was unreal, left Paul wondering if he had heard correctly. The figure lifted a hand as muddy as the face, displaying a thin white cylinder so luminously clean that it might have dropped from the moon.

"Can you hear, fellow? A light?"

Paul reached into his pocket and fumbled with numbed fingers until he found a box of matches, miraculously dry. The wounded soldier began howling even louder, lost in the wilderness a stone's throw away.

The man in the ragged greatcoat tipped himself against the side of the trench, fitting the curve of his back into the sheltering mud, then delicately pulled the cigarette into two pieces and handed one to Paul. As he lit the match, he tilted his head to listen.

"God help me, he's still going on up there." He passed the matches back and held the flame steady so Paul could light his own cigarette. "Why couldn't Fritz drop one on him and give us all a little peace?"

Paul nodded his head. Even that was an effort.

His companion lifted his chin and let out a dribble of smoke which curled up past the rim of his helmet and vanished against the flat morning sky. "Do you ever get the feeling. . . ?"

"Feeling?"

"That it's a mistake." The stranger wagged his head to indicate the trenches, the German guns, all of the Western Front. "That God's away, or having a bit of a sleep or something. Don't you find yourself hoping that one day He'll look down and see what's happening and . . . and do something about it?"

Paul nodded, although he had never thought the matter through in such detail. But he had felt the emptiness of the gray skies, and had occasionally had a curious sensation of looking down on the blood and mud from a great distance, observing the murderous deeds of war with the detachment of a man standing over an anthill. God could not be watching, that was certain; if He was, and if He had seen the things Paul Jonas had seen—men who were dead but didn't know it, frantically trying to push their spilled guts back into their blouses; bodies swollen and flyblown, lying unretrieved for days within yards of friends with whom they had sung and laughed—if He had seen all that but not interfered, then He must be insane.

But Paul had never for a moment believed that God would save the tiny creatures slaughtering each other by the thousands over an acre of shell-pocked mud. That was too much like a fairy tale. Beggar boys did not marry princesses; they died in snowy streets or dark alleys . . . or in muddy trenches in France, while old Papa God took a long rest.

He summoned up his strength. "Heard anything?"

The stranger drew deeply on his cigarette, unconcerned that the ember was burning against his muddy fingers, and sighed. "Everything. Nothing. You know. Fritz is breaking through in the south and he'll go right on to Paris. Or now the Yanks are in it, we're going to roll them right up and march to Berlin by June. The Winged Victory of Samo-whatsit appeared in the skies over Flanders, waving a flaming sword and dancing the hootchy-coo. It's all shit."

"It's all shit," Paul agreed. He drew once more on his own cigarette and then dropped it into a puddle. He watched sadly as muddy water wicked into the paper and the last fragments of tobacco floated free. How many more cigarettes would he smoke before death found him? A dozen? A hundred? Or might that one be his last? He picked up the paper and squeezed it into a tight ball between his finger and thumb.

"Thanks, mate." The stranger rolled over and began crawling away up the trench, then shouted something odd over his shoulder. "Keep your head down. Try to think about getting out. About really getting *out.*"

Paul lifted his hand in a farewell wave, although the man could not see him. The wounded soldier topside was shouting again, wordless grunting cries that sounded like something inhuman giving birth.

Within moments, as though wakened by demonic invocation, the guns started up again.

Paul clenched his teeth and tried to stop up his ears with his hands, but he could *still* hear the man screaming; the rasping voice was like a hot wire going in one earhole and out the other, sawing back and forth. He had snatched perhaps three hours of sleep in the last two days, and the night fast approaching seemed sure to be even worse. Why hadn't any of the stretcher teams gone out to bring back the wounded man? The guns had been silent for at least an hour.

But as he thought about it, Paul realized that except for the man who had come begging a light, he had not seen anyone else since they had all fled the forward trenches that morning. He had assumed that there were others just a few bends down, and the man with the cigarette had seemed to confirm that, but the bombardment had been so steady that Paul had felt no desire to move. Now that things had been quiet a while, he was beginning to wonder what was happening to the rest of the platoon. Had Finch and the rest all fallen back to an earlier series of scrapes? Or were they just a few yards down the line, hugging the depths, unwilling to face the open killing ground even on a mission of mercy?

He slid forward onto his knees and tipped his helmet back so it would not slide over his eyes, then began to crawl westward. Even well below the top of the trench, he felt his own movement to be a provocative act. He hunched his shoulders in expectation of some terrible blow from above, yet nothing came down on him but the ceaseless wail of the dying man.

Twenty yards and two bends later, he reached a wall of mud.

Paul tried to wipe away the tears, but only succeeded in pushing dirt into his eyes. A last explosion echoed above and the ground shook in sympathy. A gob of mud on one of the roots protuding into the trench quivered, fell, and became an indistinguishable part of the greater muddiness below.

He was trapped. That was the simple, horrible fact. Unless he braved the unprotected ground above, he could only huddle in his sealed-off section of trench until a shell found him. He had no illusions that he would last long enough for starvation to become a factor. He had no illusions at all. He was as good as dead. He would never again listen to Mullet complaining about rations, or watch old Finch trimming his mustache with a pocketknife. Such small things, so homely, but he already missed them so badly that it hurt.

The dying man was still out there, still howling.

This is hell, nor am I out of it . . .

What was that from? A poem? The Bible?

He unsnapped his holster and drew his Webley, then lifted it toward his eye. In the failing light the hole in its barrel seemed deep as a well, an emptiness into which he could fall and never come out—a silent, dark, restful emptiness. . . .

Paul smiled a bleak little smile, then carefully laid the pistol in his lap. It would be unpatriotic, surely. Better to force the Germans to use up their expensive shells on him. Squeeze a few more working hours out of some mottle-armed *fraulein* on a factory line in the Ruhr Valley. Besides, there was always hope, wasn't there?

He began weeping once more.

Above, the wounded man stopped screeching for a moment to cough. He sounded like a dog being whipped. Paul leaned his head back against the mud and bellowed: "Shut it! Shut it, for Christ's sake!" He took a deep breath. "Shut your mouth and *die,* damn you!"

Apparently encouraged by companionship, the man resumed screaming.

Night seemed to last a year or more, months of darkness, great blocks of immovable black. The guns sputtered and shouted. The dying man wailed. Paul counted every single individual object he could remember from his life before the trenches, then started over and counted them again. He remembered only the names of some of them, but not what the names actually meant. Some words seemed impossibly strange—"lawn chair" was one, "bathtub" another. "Garden" was mentioned in several songs in the Chaplain's hymn book, but Paul was fairly certain it was a real thing as well, so he counted it.

"Try to think about getting out," the yellow-eyed man had said. *"About really getting out."*

The guns were silent. The sky had gone a slightly paler shade, as though someone had wiped it with a dirty rag. There was just enough light for Paul to see the edge of the trench. He clambered up and then slid back, laughing silently at the up-and-down of it all. *Getting out.* He found a thick root with his foot and heaved himself onto the rim of the earthwork. He had his gun. He was going to kill the man who was screaming. He didn't know much more than that.

Somewhere the sun was coming up, although Paul had no idea where exactly that might be happening: the effect was small and smeared across a great dull expanse of sky. Beneath that sky, everything was gray. Mud and water. He knew the water was the flat places, so everything else was mud, except perhaps for the tall things. Yes, those were trees, he remembered. Had been trees.

Paul stood up and turned in a slow circle. The world extended for only a few hundred yards in any direction before ending in mist. He was marooned in the center of an empty space, as though he had wandered onto a stage by mistake and now stood before a silent, expectant audience.

But he was not entirely alone. Halfway across the emptiness one tree stood by itself, a clawing hand with a twisted bracelet of barbed wire. Something dark hung in its denuded branches. Paul drew his revolver and staggered toward it.

It was a figure, hanging upside down like a discarded marionette, one leg caught in the high angle of bough and trunk. All its joints seemed to have been broken, and the arms dangled downward, fingers reaching, as though muck were heaven and it was struggling to fly. The front of its head was a tattered, featureless mass of red and scorched black and gray, except for one bright staring yellow eye, mad and intent as a bird's eye, which watched his slow approach.

"I got out," Paul said. He lifted his gun, but the man was not screaming now.

A hole opened in the ruined face. It spoke. *"You've come at last. I've been waiting for you."*

Paul stared. The butt of the gun was slippery in his fingers. His arm trembled with the effort of keeping it raised.

"Waiting?"

"Waiting. Waiting so long." The mouth, empty but for a few white shards floating in red, twisted in an upside-down smile. *"Do you ever get the feeling. . . ?"*

Paul winced as the screaming began again. But it could not be the dying man—*this* was the dying man. So . . .

"Feeling?" he asked, then looked up.

The dark shape was tumbling down the sky toward him, a black hole in the dull gray air, whistling as it came. The dull thump of the howitzer followed a moment later, as though Time had turned and bitten its own tail.

"That it's a mistake," said the hanging man.

And then the shell struck, and the world folded in on itself, smaller and smaller, angle after angle creased with fire and then compressed along its axes, until it all vanished.

Things became even more complicated after Paul died.

He *was* dead, of course, and he knew it. How could he be anything else? He had seen the howitzer shell diving down on him from the sky, a wingless, eyeless, breathtakingly modern Angel of Death, streamlined and impersonal as a shark. He had felt the world convulse and the air catch fire, felt his lungs raped of oxygen and charred to cracklings in his chest. There could be no doubt that he was dead.

But why did his head hurt?

Of course, an afterlife in which the punishment for a misspent existence was an eternally throbbing headache might make a sort of sense. A horrible sort of sense.

Paul opened his eyes and blinked at the light.

He was sitting upright on the rim of a vast crater, a surely mortal wound ripped deep into the muddy earth. The land around it was flat and empty. There were no trenches, or if there were, they were buried under the outflingings of the explosion; he could see nothing but churned mud in any direction until the earth itself blurred into gray-gleaming mist along the encircling horizon.

But something solid was behind him, propping him up, and the sensation of it against the small of his back and his shoulder blades made him wonder for the first time whether he had anticipated death too soon. As he tilted his head back to look, his helmet-brim tipped forward over his eyes, returning him to darkness for a moment, then slid down over his face and onto his lap. He stared at the helmet. Most of its crown was gone, blasted away; the torn and tortured metal of the brim resembled nothing so much as a crown of thorns.

Remembering horror tales of shell-blasted soldiers who walked two dozen yards without their heads or held their own innards in their hands without recognizing what they were, Paul shivered convulsively. Slowly, as though playing a grisly game with himself, he ran his fingers up his face, past his cheeks and temples, feeling for what must be the pulped top of his own skull. He touched hair, skin, and bone . . . but all in their proper places. No wound. When he held his hands before his face, they were striped with as much blood as mud, but the red was dry already, old paint and powder. He let out a long-held breath.

He was dead, but his head hurt. He was alive, but a red-hot shell fragment had ripped through his helmet like a knife through cake frosting.

Paul looked up and saw the tree, the small, skeletal thing that had drawn him across no-man's land. The tree where the dying man had hung.

Now it stretched up through the clouds.

Paul Jonas sighed. He had walked around the tree five times, and it showed no sign of becoming any less impossible.

The frail, leafless thing had grown so large that its top was out of sight beyond the clouds that hung motionless in the gray sky. Its trunk was as wide as a castle tower from a fairy story, a massive cylinder of rough bark that seemed to extend as far downward as it did up, running smoothly down the side of the bomb crater, vanishing into the soil at the bottom with no trace of roots.

He had walked around the tree and could make no sense of it. He had walked away from the tree, hoping to find an angle from which he could gauge its height, but that had not assisted his understanding either. No matter how far he stumbled back across the featureless plain, the tree still stretched beyond the cloud ceiling. And always, whether he wanted to or not, he found himself returning to the tree again. Not only was there nothing else to move toward, but the world itself seemed somehow curved, so that no matter which direction he took, eventually he found himself heading back toward the monumental trunk.

He sat with his back against it for a while and tried to sleep. Sleep would not come, but stubbornly he kept his eyes closed anyway. He was not happy with the puzzles set before him. He had been struck by an exploding shell. The war and everyone in it seemed to have vanished, although a conflict of that size should have been a rather difficult thing to misplace. The light had not changed in this place since he had come here, although it must have been hours since the explosion. And the only other thing in the world was an immense, impossible vegetable.

He prayed that when he opened his eyes again, he would either find himself in some sort of respectable afterlife or returned to the familiar misery of the trenches with Mullet and Finch and the rest of the platoon. When the prayer had ended, he still did not risk a look, determined to give God—or Whoever—enough time to put things right. He sat, doing his best to ignore the band of pain across the back of his head, letting the silence seep into him as he waited for normality to reassert itself. At last, he opened his eyes.

Mist, mud, and that immense, damnable tree. Nothing had changed.

Paul sighed deeply and stood up. He did not remember much about his life before the War, and at this moment even the immediate past was dim, but he did remember that there had been a certain kind of story in which an impossible thing happened, and once that impossible thing had proved that it was not going to *un*-happen again, there was only one course of action left: the impossible thing must be treated as a possible thing.

What did you do with an unavoidable tree that grew up into the sky beyond the clouds? You climbed it.

It was not as difficult as he had expected. Although no branches jutted from the trunk until just below the belly of the clouds, the very size of the tree helped him; the bark was pitted and cracked like the skin of some immense serpent, providing excellent toeholds and handholds. Some of the bumps were big enough to sit on, allowing him to catch his breath in relative safety and comfort.

But still it was not easy. Although it was hard to tell in that timeless, sunless place, he felt he had been climbing for at least half a day when he reached the first branch. It was as broad as a country road, bending up and away; where it, too, vanished into the clouds, he could see the first faint shapes of leaves.

Paul lay down where the branch met the trunk and tried to sleep, but though he was very tired, sleep still would not come. When he had rested for a while, he got up and resumed climbing.

After a while the air grew cooler, and he began to feel the wet touch of clouds. The sky around the great tree was becoming murkier, the ends of the branches obscured; he could see vast shadowy shapes hanging in the distant foliage overhead, but could not identify them. Another half hour's climbing revealed them to be monstrous apples, each as large as a barrage balloon.

As he mounted higher, the fog thickened until he was surrounded by a phantom world of branches and drifting, tattered clouds, as though he clambered in the rigging of a ghost ship. No sound reached him but the creaking and scratching of bark beneath his feet. Breezes blew, cooling the thin sweat on his forehead, but none of them blew hard enough to shake the great, flat leaves.

Silence and shreds of mist. The great trunk and its mantle of branches above and below him, a world in itself. Paul climbed on.

The clouds began to grow even more dense, and he could sense the light changing; something warm was making the mists glow, like a lantern behind thick curtains. He rested again, and wondered how long it would take him to fall if he were to step off the branch on which he sat. He plucked a loose button from his shirt cuff and let it drop, watching it shiver down the air currents until it vanished silently into the clouds below.

Later—he had no idea how much later—he found himself climbing into growing radiance. The gray bark began to show traces of other colors, sandy beiges and pale yellows. The upper surfaces of the branches seemed flattened by the new, harsher light and the surrounding mist gleamed and sparkled as though tiny rainbows played between the individual drops.

The cloud-mist was so thick here that it impeded his climb, curling around his face in dripping tendrils, lubricating his grip, weighting his clothes and dragging at him treacherously as he negotiated difficult hand-to-hand changeovers. He briefly considered giving up, but there was nowhere else for him to go except back down. It seemed worth risking an unpleasantly swift descent to avoid the slower alternative which could lead only to eternal nothingness on that gray plain.

In any case, Paul thought, if he was already dead, he couldn't die again. If he was alive, then he was part of a fairy tale, and surely no one ever died this early in the story.

The clouds grew thicker: the last hundred yards of his ascent he might have been climbing through rotting muslin. The damp resistance kept him from noticing how bright the world was becoming, but as he pushed through the last clouds and lifted his head, blinking, it was to find himself beneath a dazzling, brassy sun and a sky of pure unclouded blue.

No clouds above, but clouds everywhere else: the top of the great frothy mass through which he had just climbed stretched away before him like a white meadow, a miles-wide, hummocked plain of cloud-stuff. And in the distance, shimmering in the brilliant sunlight . . . a castle.

As Paul stared, the pale slender towers seemed to stretch and waver, like something seen through the waters of a mountain lake. Still, it was clearly a castle, not just an illusion compounded of clouds and sun; colorful pennants danced from the tops of the sharp turrets, and the huge porticullised gate was a grinning mouth opening onto darkness.

He laughed, suddenly and abruptly, but his eyes filled with tears. It was beautiful. It was terrifying. After the great gray emptiness and the half-world of the clouds, it was too bright, too strong, almost too real.

Still, it was what he had been climbing toward: it called to him as clearly as if it had possessed a voice—just as the dim awareness of an inescapable *something* awaiting him had summoned him to climb the tree.

There was the faintest suggestion of a path across the spun-sugar plain, a more solid line of whiteness that stretched from the tree and meandered away toward the distant castle gate. He climbed until his feet were level with the top of the clouds, paused for a moment to revel in the strong, swift beating of his heart, then stepped off the branch. For a sickening instant the whiteness gave, but only a little. He windmilled his arms for balance, then discovered that it was no worse than standing on a mattress.

He began to walk.

The castle grew larger as he approached. If Paul had retained any doubts that he was in a story and not a real place, the ever-clearer view of his destination would have dispelled them. It was clearly something that someone had made up.

It was real, of course, and quite solid—although what did that mean to a man walking across the clouds? But it was real in the way of things long believed-in but never seen. It had the shape of a castle—it was as much a *castle* as something could ever be—but it was no more a medieval fortress than it was a chair or a glass of beer. It was an *idea* of a castle, Paul realized, a sort of Platonic ideal unrelated to the grubby realities of motte-and-bailey architecture or feudal warfare.

Platonic ideal? He had no idea where that had come from. Memories were swimming just below the surface of his conscious mind, closer than ever but still as strangely unfocused as the many-towered vision before him.

He walked on beneath the unmoving sun, wisps of cloud rising from his heels like smoke.

The gate was open but did not seem welcoming. For all the diffuse glimmer of the towers, the entranceway itself was deep, black, and empty. Paul stood before the looming hole for some time, his blood lively in his veins, his self-protective reflexes urging him to turn back even though he knew he must enter. At last, feeling even more naked than he had beneath the hail of shellfire which had begun the whole mad dream, he took a breath and stepped through.

The vast stone chamber beyond the door was curiously stark, the only decoration a single great banner, red embroidered with black and gold, that hung on the far wall. It bore a vase or chalice out of which grew two twining roses, with a crown floating above the flowers. Below the picture was the legend *"Ad Aeternum."*

As he stepped forward to examine it, his footsteps reverberated through the empty chamber, so loud after the muffling cloud-carpet that it startled him. He thought that someone would surely come to see who had entered, but the doors at either end of the chamber remained shut and no other sound joined the dying echoes.

It was hard to stare at the banner for long. Each individual thread of black and gold seemed to move, so that the whole picture swam blurrily before his eyes. It was only when he stepped back almost to the entrance that he could see the picture clearly again, but it still told him nothing of this place or who might live here.

Paul looked at the doors at either end. There seemed little to choose between them, so he turned toward the one on the left. Though it seemed only a score or so of paces away, it took him a surprisingly long time to reach it. Paul looked back. The far portal was now only a dark spot a great distance away, and the antechamber itself seemed to be filling with mist, as though clouds were beginning to drift in from outside. He turned and found that the door he had sought now loomed before him. It swung open easily at his touch, so he stepped through.

And found himself in a jungle.

But it was not quite that, he realized a moment later. Vegetation grew thickly everywhere, but he could see shadowy walls through the looping vines and long leaves; arched windows set high on those walls looked out on a sky busy with dark storm clouds—quite a different sky than the shield of pure blue he had left beyond the front gate. The jungle was everywhere, but he was still *inside,* even though the outside was not his own.

This chamber was larger even than the huge front hall. Far, far above the nodding, poisonous-looking flowers and the riot of greenery stretched a ceiling covered with intricate sharp-angled patterns all of gleaming gold, like a jeweled map of a labyrinth.

Another memory came drifting up, the smell and the warm wet air tickling it free. This kind of place was called . . . was called . . . a conservatory. A place where things were kept, he dimly recalled, where things grew, where secrets were hidden.

He stepped forward, pushing the sticky fronds of a long-leafed plant out of his path, then had to do a sudden dance to avoid tumbling into a pond that the plant had hidden. Dozens of tiny fish, red as pennies heated in a forge, darted away in alarm.

He turned and moved along the edge of the pond, searching for a path. The plants were dusty. As he worked his way through the thickest tangles, powdery clouds rose up into the light angling down through the high windows, swirling bits of floating silver and mica. He paused, waiting for the dust to settle. In the silence, a low sound drifted to him. Someone was weeping.

He reached up with both hands and spread the leaves as though they were curtains. Framed in the twining vegetation stood a great bell-shaped cage, its slender golden bars so thickly wound with flowering vines it was hard to see what it contained. He moved closer, and something inside the cage moved. Paul stopped short.

It was a woman. It was a bird.

It was a woman.

She turned, her wide black eyes wet. A great cloud of dark hair framed her long face and spilled down her back to merge with the purple and iridescent green of her strange costume. But it was no costume. She was clothed in feathers; beneath her arms long pinions lay folded like a paper fan. Wings.

"Who's there?" she cried.

It was all a dream, of course—perhaps just the last hallucinatory moments of a battlefield casualty—but as her voice crept into him and settled itself like something that had found its home, he knew that he would never forget the sound of it. There was determination and sorrow and the edge of madness, all in those two words. He stepped forward.

Her great round eyes went wider still. "Who are you? You do not belong here."

Paul stared at her, although he could not help feeling that he was doing her some insult, as though her feathered limbs were a sort of deformity. Perhaps they were. Or perhaps in this strange place he was the deformed one.

"Are you a ghost?" she asked. "If so, I waste my breath. But you do not look like a ghost."

"I don't know what I am." Paul's dry mouth made it hard to speak. "I don't know where I am either. But I don't feel like a ghost."

"You can talk!" Her alarm was such that Paul feared he had done something dreadful. "You do not belong here!"

"Why are you crying? Can I help you?"

"You must go away. You must! The Old Man will be back soon." Her agitated movements filled the room with a soft rustling. More dust fluttered into the air.

"Who is this old man? And who are you?"

She moved to the edge of the cage, grasping the bars in her slender fingers. "Go! Go now!" But her gaze was greedy, as though she wished to make him into a memory that would not fade. "You are hurt—there is blood on your clothing."

Paul looked down. "Old blood. Who are you?"

She shook her head. "No one." She paused and her face moved as though she would say something shocking or dangerous, but the moment passed. "I am no one. You must go before the Old Man returns."

"But what is this place? Where am I? All I have are questions and more questions."

"You should not be here. Only ghosts visit me here—and the Old Man's evil instruments. He says they are to keep me company, but some of them have teeth and very unusual senses of humor. Butterball and Nickelplate—they are the cruelest."

Overwhelmed, Paul suddenly stepped forward and grasped her hand where it curled around the bars. Her skin was cool and her face was very close. "You are a prisoner. I will free you."

She jerked her hand away. "I cannot survive outside this cage. And you cannot survive if the Old Man finds you here. Have you come hunting the Grail? You will not find it here—this is only a shadow place."

Paul shook his head impatiently. "I know nothing of any grail." But even as he spoke he knew it was not the full truth: the word set up an echo deep inside him, touched parts that were still out of his reach. *Grail.* Something, it meant something. . . .

"You do not understand!" the bird woman said, and shining feathers ruffled and bunched around her neck as she grew angry. "I am not one of the guardians. I have nothing to hide from you, and I would not see you . . . I would not see you harmed. Go, you fool! Even if you *could* take it, the Old Man would find you no matter where you went. He would hunt you down even if you crossed the White Ocean."

Paul could feel the fear beating out from her, and for a moment he was overwhelmed, unable to speak or move. She was afraid for him. This prisoned angel felt something . . . for *him.*

And the grail, whatever it might be—he could feel the idea of it, swimming just beyond his grasp like one of the bright fish. . . .

A terrible hissing sound, loud as a thousand serpents, set the leaves around them swaying. The bird woman gasped and shrank back into the center of her cage. A moment later a great clanging tread sounded through the trees, which shivered, stirring more dust.

"It's him!" Her voice was a muffled shriek. "He's back!"

Something huge was coming nearer, huffing and banging like a war engine. A harsh light flickered through the trees.

"Hide!" The naked terror in her whisper set his heart hammering. "He will suck the marrow from your bones!"

The noise was becoming louder; the walls themselves were quivering, the ground pitching. Paul took a step, then stumbled and sank to his knees as terror fell on him like a black wave. He crawled into the thickest part of the undergrowth, leaves slapping against his face, smearing him with dust and damp.

A loud creak sounded, as of mighty hinges, then the room was filled with the smell of an electrical storm. Paul covered his eyes.

"I AM HOME." The Old Man's voice was loud as cannonfire and just as boomingly inhuman. "AND WHERE IS YOUR SONG TO GREET ME?"

The long silence was broken only by that hiss like escaping steam. At last the bird woman spoke, faint and tremulous.

"I did not expect you back so soon. I was not prepared."

"AND WHAT DO YOU HAVE TO DO BESIDES PREPARE FOR MY RETURN?" More crashing footsteps sounded as the Old Man moved nearer. "YOU SEEM DISTRACTED, MY NIGHTINGALE. HAS BUT-TERBALL BEEN PLAYING ROUGHLY WITH YOU?"

"No! No, I . . . I do not feel well today."

"I AM NOT SURPRISED. THERE IS A FOUL SMELL ABOUT THE PLACE." The ozone stench grew stronger, and through his laced fingers Paul could see the light flickering again. "AS A MATTER OF FACT, IT SMELLS LIKE A MAN."

"H–how . . . how could that be?"

"WHY DO YOU NOT LOOK ME IN THE EYE, LITTLE SONGBIRD? SOMETHING IS AMISS HERE." The steps grew closer. The floor shuddered, and Paul could hear a discordant creaking like a bridge in high wind. "I BELIEVE THERE IS A MAN HERE. I BELIEVE YOU HAVE HAD A VISITOR."

"Run!" the bird woman screamed. Paul cursed and staggered to his feet, surrounded by head-high branches. A vast shadow hung over the room, blocking the soft gray light from the windows, replacing them with the stark blue-white of its own nimbus of sparks. Paul flung himself forward, smashing through the clinging leaves, his heart beating like a greyhound's. The door . . . if he could only find the door again.

"SOMETHING SCURRYING IN THE SHRUBBERY." The titan's voice was amused. "WARM FLESH . . . AND WET BLOOD . . . AND CRISP LITTLE BONES."

Paul splashed through the pond and almost lost his balance. He could see the door, only a few yards away, but the great clanking thing was just behind him.

"Run!" the woman pleaded. Even in his terror he knew that she would suffer some dreadful punishment for this; he felt that he had somehow betrayed her. He reached the door and flung himself through, skidding and then rolling on the smooth stone floor. The huge gate stood before him, and thank God, thank God, it was open!

A hundred steps, maybe more, difficult as running in treacle. The whole castle shook beneath his pursuer's tread. He reached the door and flung himself through and out into what had been sunlight, but was now twilight-gray. The topmost branches of the great tree stood just above the edge of the clouds, a seemingly impossible distance away. Paul bolted toward it across the field of clouds.

The thing was pushing through the door—he heard the great hinges squeal as it forced its way. Lightning-scented air billowed past him, almost knocking him off his feet, and a great roar filled the sky: the Old Man was laughing.

"COME BACK, LITTLE CREATURE! I WANT TO PLAY WITH YOU!"

Paul sprinted across the cloud-trail, his breath scorching in his lungs. The tree was a little closer now. How fast would he have to climb down to move beyond the reach of that terrible thing? Surely it couldn't follow him—how could even the great tree bear the weight of such a monstrosity?

The clouds below his feet stretched and jounced like a trampoline as the Old Man stepped from the castle. Paul tripped and fell forward; one of his hands came down to the side of the trail, pushing through the cloud surface as through cobwebs. He scrambled to his feet and sped forward again—the tree was only a few hundred paces away now. If he could only. . . .

A great gray hand as big as a steam shovel curled around him, a thing of cables and rivets and rusting sheet iron. Paul screamed.

The clouds fell away as he was jerked high into the air, then turned to dangle in front of the Old Man's face. Paul screamed again, and heard another cry, dim but mournful, echo from the distant castle—the keening of a caged bird.

The Old Man's eyes were the vast cracked faces of tower clocks, his beard a welter of curling, rusted wire. He was impossibly huge, a giant of iron and battered copper pipes and slowly turning wheels that steamed at every crack, every vent. He stank of electricity and grinned a row of concrete tombstones.

"GUESTS MAY NOT LEAVE BEFORE I CAN ENTERTAIN THEM." Paul felt the bones of his skull vibrate from the power of the Old Man's voice. As the great maw opened wider, Paul kicked and struggled in the cloud of choking steam. "TOO SMALL TO MAKE MUCH OF A MEAL, REALLY," said the Old Man, then swallowed him.

Shrieking, Paul fell down into oily, gear-grinding darkness.

"**Q**uit that, you bloody idiot!"

Paul struggled, but someone or something was holding his arms. He shuddered and went limp.

"That's better. Here—have a little of this."

Something trickled into his mouth and burned down his throat. He coughed explosively and struggled to sit up. This time he was allowed to. Someone laughed.

He opened his eyes. Finch was sitting beside him, almost on top of him, framed by the mud of the trench top and a sliver of sky.

"You'll be all right." Finch put the cap back on the flask and stowed it in his pocket. "Just a bit of a knock on the head. Sad to say, it's not enough to get you home, old man. Still, Mullet will be pleased to see you when he gets back from shifting his bowels. I told him you'd be fine."

Paul leaned back, his head full of muddled thoughts.

"Where. . . ?"

"In one of the back trenches—I think I dug this bastard myself two years ago. Fritz suddenly decided the war wasn't over yet. We've been pushed quite a way back—don't you remember?"

Paul struggled to hold onto the diminishing tatters of his dream. A woman with feathers like a bird, who spoke of a grail. A giant like a railroad engine, made of metal and hot steam. "And what happened? To me?"

Finch reached behind him and produced Paul's helmet. One side of the crown was dimpled inward. "Piece of shrapnel. But not enough to get you shipped back. Not very lucky are you, Jonesie?"

So it had all been a dream. Just a hallucination after a minor head wound. Paul looked at Finch's familiar face, his grayshot mustache, the weary eyes behind steel-rimmed spectacles, and knew that he was back where he was supposed to be, sunk once more in the mud and the blood. Of course. The war went on, uncaring of the dreams of soldiers, a reality so devastating that no other reality could compete.

Paul's head ached. He reached up to rub his temple with a dirty hand, and as he did so something fluttered from his sleeve into his lap. He looked quickly at Finch, but the other man was rooting in his bag, hunting a tin of bully beef, and had not seen.

He lifted the object and let it catch the last rays of the sun. The green feather sparkled, impossibly real, impossibly bright, and completely untouched by mud.

First:

UNIVERSE
NEXT DOOR

pity this busy monster,manunkind,

not.   Progress is a comfortable disease:
your victim(death and life safely beyond)

plays with the bigness of his littleness
—electrons deify one razorblade
into a mountainrange;lenses extend

unwish through curving wherewhen till unwish
returns on its unself.
                          A world of made
is not a world of born—pity poor flesh

and trees,poor stars and stones,but never this
fine specimen of hypermagical

ultraomnipotence.   We doctors know

a hopeless case if—listen:there's a hell
of a good universe next door;let's go

                                    —e. e. cummings

CHAPTER 1

Mister Jingo's Smile

NETFEED/NEWS: *Failed Chip Leads to Murder Spree*
(*visual: Kashivili at arraignment in body restraints*)
VO: Convict Aleksandr Kashivili's behavioral chip suffered an unexpected failure, authorities said today after the mod-paroled Kashivili—
(*visual: scorched shopfront, parked fire trucks and ambulances*)
—killed 17 restaurant customers in a flamethrower attack in the Serpukhov area of Greater Moscow.
(*visual: Doctor Konstantin Gruhov in university office*)
GRUHOV: "The technology is still in its early stages. There will be accidents. . . ."

One of the other insructors pushed open the cubicle door and leaned in. The noise of the corridor swept in with him, louder than usual.

"Bomb threat."

"*Again?*" Renie set her pad down on the desk and picked up her bag. Remembering how many things had gone missing during the last scare, she retrieved the pad before walking into the hallway. The man who had told her—she could never remember his name, Yono Something-or-other—was several paces ahead, vanishing into the river of students and instructors moving leisurely toward the exits. She hurried to catch him.

"Every two weeks," she said. "Once a day during exams. It makes me crazy."

He smiled. He had thick glasses but nice teeth. "At least we will get some fresh air."

Within minutes the wide street in front of Durban Area Four Polytechnic had become a sort of impromptu carnival, full of laughing students glad to be out of class. One group of young men had tied their coats around their waists like skirts and were dancing atop a parked car, ignoring an older teacher's increasingly shrill orders to cease and desist.

Renie watched them with mixed feelings. She, too, could feel the lure of freedom, just as she felt the warm African sun on her arms and neck, but she also knew that she was three days behind grading term projects; if the bomb scare went on too long, she would miss a tutorial that would have to be rescheduled, eating up more of her rapidly-dwindling spare time.

Yono, or whatever his name was, grinned at the dancing students. Renie felt a surge of annoyance at his irresponsible enjoyment. "If they want to miss class," she said, "why the hell don't they just skip out? Why play a prank like this and make the rest of us—"

A flash of brilliant light turned the sky white. Renie was knocked to the ground by a brief hurricane of hot, dry air as a tremendous clap of sound shattered glass all along the school facade and shivered the windows of dozens of parked cars. She covered her head with her arms, but there was no debris, only the sound of people screaming. When she struggled to her feet, she could see no sign of injuries on the students milling around her, but a cloud of black smoke was boiling above what must be the Admin Building in the middle of the campus. The campanile was gone, a blackened, smoking stump of fibramic skeleton all that remained of the colorful tower. She let out her breath, suddenly nauseated and light-headed. "Jesus Mercy!"

Her colleague clambered to his feet beside her, his dark skin now almost gray. "A real one this time. God, I hope they got everyone out. They probably did—Admin always clears first so they can monitor the evacuation." He was speaking so rapidly she could hardly understand him. "Who do you think it was?"

Renie shook her head. "Broderbund? Zulu Mamba? Who knows? God damn it, that's the third in two years. How can they do it? Why won't they let us work?"

Her companion's look of alarm deepened. "My car! It's in the Admin lot!" He turned and ran toward the explosion site, pushing his way through lost-looking students, some of whom were crying, none of whom seemed in any mood for laughing or dancing now. A security guard who was trying to cordon off the area shouted at him as he ran past.

"His *car?* Idiot." Renie felt like crying herself. There was a distant ululation of sirens. She took a cigarette out of her bag and pulled the flame-tab with trembling fingers. They were supposed to be noncarcinogenic, but right at the moment she didn't care. A piece of paper fluttered down and landed at her feet, blackened along its edges.

Already, the camera-drones were descending from the sky like a swarm of flies, sucking up footage for the net.

She was on her second cigarette and feeling a little steadier when someone tapped her shoulder.

"Ms. Sulaweyo?"

She turned and found herself confronting a slender boy with yellow-brown skin. His short hair curled close to his head. He wore a necktie, something Renie had not seen in a few years.

"Yes?"

"I believe we had an appointment. A tutorial?"

She stared. The top of his head barely reached her shoulder. "You . . . you're. . . ?"

"!Xabbu." There was a clicking sound in it, as though he had cracked a knuckle. "With an X—and an exclamation point when the name is written in English letters."

Light suddenly dawned. "Ah! You're . . ."

He smiled, a swift crease of white. "One of the San people—what they sometimes call 'Bushman,' yes."

"I didn't mean to be rude."

"You were not. There are few of us left who have the pure blood, the old look. Most have married into the city-world. Or died in the bush, unable to live in these times."

She liked his grin and his quick, careful speech. "But you have done neither."

"No, I have not. I am a university student." He said it with some pride, but a hint of self-mockery as well. He turned to look at the drifting plume of smoke. "If there will be a university left."

She shook her head and suppressed a shudder. The sky, stained with drifting ash, had gone twilight-gray. "It's so terrible."

"Terrible indeed. But fortunately no one seems badly hurt."

"Well, I'm sorry our tutorial was prevented," she said, recovering a

little bit of her professional edge. "I suppose we should reschedule—
let me get out my pad."

"Must we reschedule?" !Xabbu asked. "I am not doing anything. It
seems that we will not get back into the university for some time.
Perhaps we could go to another place—perhaps somewhere that sells
beer, since my throat is dry from smoke—and do our talking there."

Renie hesitated. Should she just leave the campus? What if her department head or someone needed her? She looked around at the
street and the main steps, which were beginning to resemble a combination refugee center and free festival, and shrugged. Nothing useful
would be done here today.

"Let's go find a beer, then."

The train to Pinetown was not running—someone had jumped or
been pushed onto the tracks at Durban Outskirt. Renie's legs were
aching and her damp shirt was stuck to her body when she finally
reached the flatblock. The elevator wasn't running either, but that was
nothing new. She trudged up the stairs and dumped her bag on the
table in front of the mirror and stopped, arrested by her reflection.
Just yesterday a colleague at work had criticized her short, practical
haircut, saying that a woman as tall as Renie should try to look more
feminine. She scowled and examined the dust streaked down her long
white shirt. When did she have time to make herself pretty? And who
cared, anyway?

"I'm home," she called.

No one answered. She poked her head around the corner and saw
her younger brother Stephen in his chair, as expected. Stephen was
faceless behind his net headset, and he held a squeezer in each hand
as he tilted from side to side. Renie wondered what he was experiencing, then decided it might be better if she didn't know.

The kitchen was empty, nothing in sight that looked like a hot meal
being prepared. She cursed quietly, hoping it was just because her
father had fallen asleep.

"Who's there? Is that you, girl?"

She cursed again, anger rising. It was clear from his slurred tone
that her father had found something besides cooking to while away
his afternoon. "Yes, it's me."

After a rattling thump and a sound like a large piece of furniture
being dragged across the floor, his tall shape appeared in the bedroom
doorway, swaying slightly.

"How come you so late?"

"Because the train's not running. And because someone blew up half the university today."

Her father considered this for a moment. "Broderbund. Those Afrikaaner bastards. For sure." Long Joseph Sulaweyo was a firm believer in the indelible evil of all white South Africans.

"Nobody knows yet. It could have been anyone."

"You arguing with me?" Long Joseph tried to fix her with a baleful stare, his eyes red and watering. He was like an old bull, she thought, enfeebled but still dangerous. It tired her out just looking at him.

"No, I'm not arguing with you. I thought you were going to make dinner for once."

"Walter come by. We had a lot of talking to do."

Had a lot of drinking to do, she thought, but held her tongue. Angry as she was, it wasn't worth going through another evening of shouting and broken crockery. "So it's up to me again, is it?"

He swayed again, then turned back into the darkness of his bedroom. "Suit yourself. I'm not hungry. I need some rest—a man needs his sleep." The bedsprings rasped, then there was silence.

Renie waited a moment, clenching and unclenching her fists, then stalked over and pulled the bedroom door closed, trying to make herself some room, some free space. She looked over at Stephen, still rocking and jiggling in the net. He might as well be catatonic. She slumped into a chair and lit another cigarette. It was important to remember her father as he had been, she reminded herself—as he still occasionally was—a proud man, a kind man. There were some people in whom weakness, once it had appeared, grew like a cancer. Mama's death in the department store fire had found and revealed that weakness. Joseph Sulaweyo no longer seemed to have the strength to fight back against life. He was letting it all go, slowly but surely disconnecting from the world, its pains and disappointments.

A man needs his sleep, Renie thought, and for the second time that day, she shuddered.

She bent down and tapped the *interrupt* button. Still faceless in his headset, Stephen spasmed in indignation. When he did not lift the insectoid visor, Renie held the button down.

"What for?" Stephen was already demanding before he had finished pulling the headset free. "Me and Soki and Eddie were almost to the Inner District Gateway. We've never gotten that far before!"

"Because I made you dinner, and I want you to eat it before it gets cold."

"I'll wave it when I'm done."

"No, you won't. Come on, Stephen. There was a bomb at school today. It was frightening. I'd like to have your company over dinner."

He straightened, the appeal to his vanity effective. "Chizz. What'd you make?"

"Chicken and rice."

He made a face, but was seated and pushing it into his mouth before she returned from the kitchen with a glass of beer for herself and a soft drink for him.

"What blew up?" He chewed rapidly. "People killed?"

"No one, thank God." She tried not to be disheartened by his clear look of disappointment. "But it destroyed the campanile—you remember, the tower in the middle of the campus."

"Chizz major! Who did it? Zulu Mamba?"

"No one knows. But it frightened me."

"A bomb went off in my school last week."

"What? You never said a word about that!"

He grimaced in disgust, then wiped grease from his chin. "Not that kind. In SchoolNet. Sabotage. Someone said that some guys from Upper Form did it as a graduation prank."

"You're talking about a system crash on the net." She wondered for a moment if Stephen understood the difference between the net and real life. *He's only eleven,* she reminded herself. *Things outside of his narrow circle aren't very real yet.* "The bomb that went off at the Poly today could have killed hundreds of people. Killed them dead."

"I know. But the blowdown on SchoolNet killed a lot of Crafts and even some high-level Constellations, backups and all. They'll never come back again either." He reached out for the rice dish, ready for seconds.

Renie sighed. Crafts, Constellations—if she were not a net-literate instructor herself, she would probably think her brother was speaking a foreign language. "Tell me what else you've been doing. Have you read any of that book I gave you?" For his birthday, she had downloaded, at not inconsiderable cost, Otulu's *Marching Toward Freedom,* the best and most stirring work she knew on South Africa's fight for democracy in the late twentieth century. As a concession to her young brother's tastes she had purchased the expensive interactive version, full of historical video footage and stylish "you-are-there" 3D reenactments.

"Not yet. I looked at it. Politics."

"It's more than that, Stephen. It's your heritage—it's our history."

He chewed. "Soki and Eddie and me almost made it into the Inner District. We got this flowpast off a guy in Upper Form. We were almost downtown! Open ticket!"

"Stephen, I don't want you trying to get to the Inner District."

"You used to do it when you were my age." His grin was insolently disarming.

"Things were different then—you can get arrested these days. Big fines. I'm serious, boy. Don't do it." But she knew the warning was useless. Might as well tell children not to swim in the old fishing hole. Stephen was already nattering on as though she hadn't said anything. She sighed. From the level of excitement, she knew she was in for a forty-minute discourse, full of obscure Junior Netboy argot.

". . . It was chizz major sampled. We dodged three Bullyboxes. But we weren't doing anything wrong," he said hurriedly. "Just tapping and napping. But it was so flared! We met someone who got into Mister J's!"

"Mister J's?" This was the first thing she hadn't recognized.

Stephen's look suddenly changed; Renie thought she saw something flicker behind his eyes. "Oh, just this place. Kind of like a club."

"What kind of club? An entertainment place? Shows and stuff?"

"Yeah. Shows and stuff." He toyed with his chicken bone for a moment. "It's just a place."

Something thumped on the wall.

"Renie! Bring me a glass of water." Long Joseph's voice sounded groggy and stupid. Renie winced, but went to the sink. For now, Stephen deserved something like a normal home life, but when he was finally out on his own, things would change around here.

When she got back, Stephen was finishing his third helping, but she could tell by his jittering leg and half-out-of-the-seat posture that he was aching to get back to the net.

"Not so fast, young warrior. We've barely had a chance to talk."

Now something almost like panic flashed across his face, and Renie felt her stomach go sour. He was definitely spending too much recreation time plugged in if he was so desperate to get back. She would make sure he spent some time out of the house. If she took him to the park this Saturday, she could make sure he didn't just go over to a friend's, plug in, and spend the whole day lying on the floor like an invertebrate.

"So tell me more about the bomb," Stephen said suddenly. "Tell me all about it."

She did, and he listened carefully and asked questions. He seemed so interested that she also told him about her first meeting with her student !Xabbu, how small and polite he was, his odd, old-fashioned style of dress.

"There was a boy like him in my school last year," Stephen said. "But he got sick and had to leave."

Renie thought of !Xabbu as he had waved good-bye, his slender arm and sweet, almost sad face. Would he, too, get sick somehow, physically or spiritually? He had said that few of his people did well living in the city. She hoped he would prove an exception—she had liked his quiet sense of humor.

Stephen got up and cleared away the dishes without being asked, then plugged in again, but surprisingly accessed *Marching Toward Freedom,* disengaging from time to time to ask her questions about it. After he finally went to his room, Renie read term papers for another hour and a half, then accessed the newsbank. She watched reports about a variety of faraway problems—a new strain of the Bukavu virus forcing quarantines in Central Africa, a tsunami in the Philippines, UN sanctions on the Red Sea Free State, and a class-action suit against a child-care service in Jo'Burg—and the local news as well, including lots of footage about the bomb at the college. It was strange to be on the net, watching in 360-degree stereoscope the same thing she had seen with her own eyes that morning. It was hard to tell which experience was more convincingly real. And these days, what did "real" mean anyway?

The headset began to feel claustrophobic, so she pulled it off and watched the rest of the news she wanted to see on the wallscreen. Full surround was a bit of a busman's holiday for her anyway.

It was only after she had made everyone's lunch for the next day, then set her alarm and climbed into her own bed, that the feeling which had nagged her all evening finally surfaced: Stephen had manipulated her somehow. They had been talking about something and he had changed the subject, then they had never got back to it. His subsequent behavior alone had been suspicious enough to suggest that he was avoiding something.

She couldn't for the life of her remember what they had been discussing—some netboy larking, probably. She made a mental note to speak to him about it.

But there was so much to do, so very much to do. And never enough hours in the day.

That's what I need. She was bleary with approaching sleep: even her thoughts felt heavy, like a burden she ached to put down. *I don't need more net, more full-surround realism, more pictures and sounds. I just need more time.*

"Now I have seen it." !Xabbu contemplated the apparently distant white walls of the simulation. "But I still do not understand precisely. You say this is *not* a real place?"

She turned to face him. Even though she herself was only vaguely human in appearance, beginners were comforted by retaining as many of the forms of normal interaction as possible. !Xabbu, in this beginner's simulation, was a gray human-shaped figure with a red "X" across his chest. Even though the "X" was a normal part of the simuloid, Renie had inscribed a complementary scarlet "R" across her own figure—again, anything to make the transition easier.

"I don't mean to be rude," she said carefully, "but I'm really not used to having this kind of session with an adult. Please don't be offended if I tell you something that seems very obvious."

!Xabbu's simuloid had no face, hence no facial expression, but his voice was light. "I am not easy to offend. And I know I am an odd case, but there is no net access in the Okavango Swamps. Please teach me what you would teach a child."

Again Renie wondered what !Xabbu wasn't telling her. It had become clear in the past few weeks that he had some kind of weird connections—no one else would be jumped into the Polytechnic's advanced networker program without any background. It was like sending someone to a Johannesburg University literature course to learn their ABC's. But he was smart—very smart: with his small stature and formal manner, it *was* tempting to think of him as a child or some kind of idiot savant.

Then again, she thought, *how long would I survive naked and unarmed in the Kalahari? Not bloody long.* There was still more to living in the world than net skills.

"Okay. You know the basics about computers and information processing. Now, when you say 'Is this a real place?' you're asking a very difficult question. An apple is a real thing, yes? But a *picture* of an apple is not an apple. It looks like an apple, it makes you think about apples, you can even choose one pictured apple over another in terms of which might taste better—but you can't taste either of them. You can't eat a picture—or at least, it isn't like eating a real apple. It's only a symbol, no matter how realistic-looking, for a real thing. Got that?"

!Xabbu laughed. "I understand you so far."

"Well, the difference between an imagined something—a concept— and a real thing used to be fairly straightforward. Even the most realistic picture of a house was only an image. You could *imagine* what it would be like to go inside it, but you couldn't actually go inside it. That's because it didn't fully replicate the experience of going into a real house, with all that entails. But what if you *could* make something that felt like a real thing, tasted like it, smelled like it, but wasn't that thing—wasn't a 'thing' at all, but only a symbol of a thing, like a picture?"

"There are places in the Kalahari Desert," !Xabbu said slowly, "where you see water, a pool of sweet water. But when you go to it, it is gone."

"A mirage." Renie waved her hand and a pool of water appeared at the far side of the simulation.

"A mirage," !Xabbu agreed. He seemed to be ignoring her illustration. "But if you could touch it, and it was wet—if you could drink it, and quench your thirst—then would it not *be* water? It is hard to imagine something that is real and not real."

Renie led him across the bare white floor of the simulation to the pool she had conjured. "Look at this. See the reflections? Now watch me." She knelt and scooped water with her simuloid hands. It ran out between her fingers, drizzling into the pool. Circular ripples crossed and recrossed each other. "This is a very basic setup—that is, your interface equipment, the goggles and sensors you just put on, are not very advanced. But even with what we have, this looks like water, does it not? Moves like water?"

!Xabbu bent and ran his gray fingers through the pool. "It flows a little strangely."

Renie waved her hand. "Money and time make it more realistic. There are external simulation rigs so well made that not only would this move just like real water, but you would feel it, cold and wet on your skin. And then there are 'cans'—neurocannular implants— which you and I won't get to use unless we wind up working for the top government labs. They let you pour computer-simulated sensations directly into your nervous system. If you had one of those, you *could* drink this water, and it would feel and taste just like the real thing."

"But it would not quench my thirst, would it? If I did not drink real water, I would die." He didn't sound worried, just interested.

"You would indeed. It's a good thing to remember. A decade or two ago you used to hear about a netboy or netgirl dying every couple of weeks—too long under simulation, forgot they needed real food and real water. Not to mention ordinary things like pressure sores. Doesn't happen much anymore—too many safeguards on the commercial products, too many restrictions and alarm routines on net access at universities and in business."

Renie waved her hand and the water disappeared. She waved again and a forest of evergreen trees suddenly filled the empty space around them, reddish rippled bark rising in tall columns and a blur of dark leafy greenness high above. !Xabbu's sudden intake of breath gave her a childish satisfaction. "It's all down to input and output," she said. "Just as someone used to sit in front of a flat screen and punch in instructions on a keyboard, now we wave our hands in a certain way and do magic. But it's not magic. It's just input, just telling the processing part of the machinery what to do. And instead of the result appearing on a screen in front of us, we receive the output as stereoscopic visuals—" she indicated the trees, "—sound—" she gestured again; a whisper of birdsong filled the forest, "—and whatever else you want, limited only by the sophistication of your processing machinery and your interface equipment."

Renie tweaked up a few details, placing a sun in the sky above the filigree of branches, carpeting the forest floor in grass and small white flowers. When she had finished, she spread her hands in a little flourish. "See, you don't even have to do all the work—the machines tidy up the details, angles and length of shadows, all that. This stuff is easy. You've already learned the basics—you'll be doing this yourself in a matter of weeks."

"The first time I watched my grandfather make a fishing spear," !Xabbu said slowly, "I thought that was magic, too. His fingers moved so fast that I couldn't see what they did, chip here, turn there, twist the cord—then suddenly there it was!"

"Exactly. The only difference is that if you want to make the best fishing spears in *this* environment, you have to find someone who'll pay for it. VR equipment starts with the simple stuff everyone has at home—everyone outside the Okavango Swamps, that is—" She wished he could see she was smiling; she hadn't meant the remark to be offensive. "But to get to the top of the line, you have to own a diamond mine or two. Or a small country. But even at a backwater college like this, with our creaky old equipment, I can show you many things."

"You have showed me many things already, Ms. Sulaweyo. May we make something else now? Might I make something?"

"Creating in VR environments . . ." she paused, trying to decide how to explain. "I can show you how to do things, make things—but you wouldn't really be doing the work. Not at this level. You'd just be telling some very sophisticated programs what you wanted and they'd give it to you. That's fine, but you should learn the basics first. It would be as if your grandfather did all but the last stroke of work on the spear and gave you that to do. You wouldn't have made it, and you wouldn't really have learned how to make one of your own."

"So you are saying that first I need to hunt the right kind of wood, learn how to see and shape the spearhead, how to decide where to put the first chip." He spread his simuloid arms in a comical way. "Yes?"

She laughed. "Yes. But as long as you realize there's a lot less dramatic work to be done before any of this is useful, I'll show you how to make something."

Under Renie's patient instruction, !Xabbu rehearsed the hand movements and body positions that commanded the microprocessors. He learned quickly, and she was reminded again of how children learned the net. Most adults, when confronted with a new task, tried to think their way through it, which often took them down blind alleys when their logical models failed to match the new circumstances. But for all his obvious intelligence, !Xabbu took to VR in a far more intuitive way. Instead of setting out to make a particular thing, and then trying to force the machinery to enact his ideas, he let the microprocessors and the software show him what they could do, then continued in the directions that interested him.

As they watched his first attempts to control shape and color appear and then disappear in midair, he asked her: "But why all this labor and expense to . . . *counterfeit*—is that the word? Why should we counterfeit reality at all?"

Renie hesitated. "Well, by learning to . . . counterfeit reality, we can make things that cannot exist except in our imaginations, just as artists have always done. Or make something to show what we would like to create, as builders do when they draw a plan. But also, we can create for ourselves an environment that is more comfortable in which to work. Just as this program takes a hand gesture—" she waved her arm; a puff of white appeared in the sky overhead, "—and makes a cloud, it can take the same hand gesture and move a large amount of information from one place to another, or go and find some other information. Instead of hunching at a keyboard or a touchscreen, as we used to do, we can sit or stand or lie down, point or wave or talk. Using the machines on which our lives depend can be made as easy as . . ." She paused, trying to find a simile.

"As making a fish spear." His voice was oddly inflected. "So we seem to have come in a full circle. We complicate our life with machines, then struggle to make it as simple as it was before we had them. Have we gained anything, Ms. Sulaweyo?"

Renie felt obscurely attacked. "Our powers are greater—we can do many more things. . . ."

"Can we talk to the gods and hear their voices more clearly? Or have we now, with all these powers, *become* gods?"

!Xabbu's change of tone had caught her off-balance. As she struggled to give him a reasonable answer, he spoke again.

"Look here, Ms. Sulaweyo. What do you think?"

A small and somewhat hard-angled flower had poked up from the simulated forest floor. It did not look like any flower she knew, but it had a certain vibrancy she found compelling; it seemed almost more a work of art than an attempt to imitate a real plant. Its velvety petals were blood red.

"It's . . . it's very good for a first try, !Xabbu."

"You are a very good teacher."

He snapped his clumsy gray fingers and the flower disappeared.

She turned and pointed. A shelf of volumes leaped forward so she could read the titles.

"Shit," she whispered. "Wrong again. I can't remember the name. *Find anything with 'Spatial development' or 'Spatial rendering' and 'child' or 'juvenile' in the title.*"

Three volumes appeared, floating before the library shelves.

"Analysis of spatial rendering in juvenile development," she read. "Right. *Give me a list in order of most occurrences of . . ."*

"Renie!"

She whirled at the sound of her brother's disembodied voice, exactly as she would have in the real world. "Stephen? Where are you?"

"Eddie's house. But we're . . . having a problem." There was an edge of fear.

Renie felt her pulse speed. "What kind of problem? Something at the house? Somebody giving you trouble?"

"No. Not at the house." He sounded as miserable as when he'd been thrown in the canal by older kids on his way home from school. "We're on the net. Can you come help us?"

"Stephen, what is wrong? Tell me right now."

"We're in the Inner District. Come quick." The contact was gone.

Renie pressed her fingertips together twice and her library disappeared. For a moment, while her rig had no input to chew, she hovered in pure gray netspace. She quickly waved up her basic starting grid, then attempted to jump straight to her brother's present location, but she was blocked by a No Access warning. He *was* in the Inner District, and in a subscription-only area. No wonder he hadn't wanted to stay in contact very long. He had been running up connection time on someone else's tab—probably his school's—and any large access group kept an eye open for just such leakage.

"God *damn* that boy!" Did he expect her to hack into a big commercial system? There were penalties for that, and some of them could involve jail time for trespassing. Not to mention what the Polytechnic would think if one of its instructors were caught in that kind of under-graduate foolery. But he had sounded so frightened. . . .

"Damn," she said again, then sighed and started working on her alias.

Everyone entering Inner District was required to wear a simuloid: no invisible lurkers were allowed to trouble the net's elite. Renie would have preferred to have appeared in the bare minimum—a face-less, sexless object like a pedestrian on a traffic sign—but a rudimentary sim bespoke poverty, and nothing would attract attention faster at the Inner District Gateway. She settled for an androgynous Efficiency sim that, she hoped, had just enough in the way of facial expression and body articulation to make her appear some rich net baron's errand-runner. The expense, filtered through several layers of accounting, should wind up in the backwaters of the Polytechnic's operating budget; if she could get in and out fast enough, the amount shouldn't attract anyone's attention.

She hated the risk, though, and hated the dishonesty even more. When she found Stephen and dragged him out again, she was going to give him a serious scorching.

But he had sounded so frightened. . . .

The Inner District Gateway was a glowing rectangle set in the base of what appeared to be a mile-high wall of white granite, daylit de-spite the lack of a visible sun anywhere in the bowl of simulated black sky. A swirl of figures were waiting to be processed, some wearing wild body shapes and bright colors—there was a particular type of lurker who stood around the Gateway despite having no hope of entry, as though the Inner District were a club that might suddenly decide the house wasn't interesting enough that night—but most were as functionally embodied as Renie, and all of them were constrained to approximately human dimensions. It was ironic that where the concentration of wealth and power on the net were greatest, things slowed down to something like the restrictive pace of the real world. In her library, or in the Poly's information net, she could jump with a single gesture to any place she wanted, or just as quickly construct whatever she needed, but the Inner District and other centers of influence forced users into sims, and then treated the sims just like real people, herding them into virtual offices and checkpoints, forcing them to idle for excruciatingly long periods of time while their connection costs mounted and mounted.

If politicians ever find a way to tax light, she thought sourly, *they'll probably set up waiting rooms for sunbeam inspection, too.* She took up a position in line behind a hunched gray thing, a lowest-order sim whose slumped shoulders suggested an expectation of refusal.

After what seemed an insufferable wait, the sim before her was duly rejected and she at last found herself standing before one of the most cartoonish-looking functionaries she had ever seen. He was small and rodent-faced, with a pair of old-fashioned glasses pinching the end of his nose and a pair of small, suspicious eyes peering over them. Surely he must be a Puppet, she thought—a program given the appearance of humanity. No one could look so much like a petty bureaucrat, or if they did, would perpetuate it on the net, where one could appear as anything he or she desired.

"Purpose in Inner District?" Even his voice was tight as kazoo music, as though he spoke through something other than the normal orifice.

"Delivery to Johanna Bundazi." The chancellor of the Polytechnic, as Renie knew, kept a small node in the Inner District.

The functionary looked at her balefully for a long moment. Somewhere processors processed. "Ms. Bundazi is not in residence."

"I know." She *did* know, too—she had been very careful. "I've been asked to hand-deliver something to her node."

"Why? She's not here. Surely it would be better to send it to the node she is currently accessing." Another brief moment. "She is not available at the moment on any node."

Renie tried to keep her temper. This *must* be a Puppet—the simulation of bureaucratic small-mindedness was too perfect. "All I know is that I was asked to deliver it to her Inner District node. Why she wants to make sure it has been directly uploaded is her affair. Unless you have contrary instructions, let me do my job."

"Why does the sender need hand-delivery when she's not accessing there?"

"I don't know! And you don't need to know either. Shall I go back, then, and you can tell Ms. Bundazi you refused to allow her a delivery?"

The functionary squinted as though he were searching a real human face for signs of duplicity or dangerous tendencies. Renie was glad to be shielded by the sim mask. *Yeah, go ahead and try to read me, you officious bastard.*

"Very well," he said at last. "You have twenty minutes." Which, Renie knew, was the absolute minimum access time—a deliberate bit of unpleasantness.

"What if there are return instructions? What if she's left a message dealing with this, and I need to take something else to somewhere in the District?" Renie suddenly wished this were a game and she could lift a laser gun and blast the Puppet to shards.

"Twenty minutes." He raised a short-fingered hand to stifle further protest. "Nineteen minutes, fifty . . . six seconds, now—and counting. If you need more, you'll have to reapply."

She began to move away, then turned back to the rat-faced man, occasioning a grunt of protest from the next supplicant, who had finally reached the Holy Land. "Are you a Puppet?" Renie demanded. Some of the others in line muttered in surprise. It was a very rude question, but one that law mandated must be answered.

The functionary squared his narrow shoulders, indignant. "I am a Citizen. Do you want my number?"

Jesus Mercy. He was a real person after all. "No," she said. "Just curious."

She cursed herself for pushing things, but a woman could only take so much.

Unlike the careful mimicry of real life elsewhere in the Inner District, there was no illusion of passing through the gate: a few moments after her admission was confirmed Renie was simply deposited in Gateway Plaza, a huge and depressingly Neofascist mass of simulated stone, a flat expanse which appeared to be the size of a small country, surrounded by towering arches from which spoke-roads radiated into the distance in a deceptively straightforward-seeming way. It was an illusion, of course. A few minutes' walk down one would get you somewhere, but it wouldn't necessarily be anywhere you could see from the Plaza, and it wouldn't necessarily be a broad straight avenue, or even a street at all.

Despite its immense size, the Plaza was more crowded and more rambunctious than the waiting area beyond the Gateway. People here were *inside,* even if only temporarily, and it lent a certain air of purpose and pride to their movements. And if they had the leisure to travel through the Plaza at all, to imitate real life to that extent, they probably had good reason to feel proud: the lowest-level admittees like herself weren't given the time for anything but instantaneous travel to and from their destinations.

It was a place worth lingering in. The actual citizens of the Inner District, those who had the money and power to commandeer their own private space in this elite section of the net, did not have the same restraints on their sims as visitors. In the distance Renie could see a pair of naked men with incredibly bulging muscles who also both happened to be bright candy-apple red and thirty feet tall. She wondered what the upkeep on *those* must have been, just in taxes and connection costs alone—it was much costlier to move a nonstandard body through the simulations.

New rich, she decided.

On the few other occasions she had managed to get into Inner District—usually hacking in as a student netgirl, but twice as someone's legitimate guest—she had been delighted just to sightsee. Inner District was, of course, unique: the first true World City, its population (simulated though it might be) was made up of planet Earth's ten million or so most influential citizens . . . or so the District's clientele clearly believed, and they went to great lengths to justify that contention.

The things they built for themselves were wonderful. In a place without gravity or even the necessity of normal geometry, and with highly flexible zoning laws in the private sectors, human creative ingenuity had flowered in most spectacular ways. Structures that would have been buildings in the real world, and thus subject to mundane laws, could here dispense with such irrelevant considerations as up-and-down and size-to-weight ratios. They needed only to serve as nodes, and so blazing displays of computer design appeared overnight and often disappeared as quickly, wild and colorful as jungle flowers.

Even now she paused for a moment to admire an impossibly thin, translucent green skyscraper rising high into the sky beyond the arches. She thought it quite beautiful and unusually restrained, a knitting needle of solid jade.

If the things they built for themselves were spectacular, these denizens of the innermost circle of humanity, the things they made *of* themselves were no less so. In a place where the only absolute requirement was to exist, and only budget, good taste, and common courtesy limited invention (and some District habitués were notoriously long on the first and short on the other two), just the passersby promenading along the major thoroughfares made for an endless and endlessly varied show. From the extremes of current fashion—elongated heads and limbs seemed to be a current trend—to the replication of real things and people—Renie had seen three different Hitlers on her first trip to the District, one of them wearing a ballgown made of blue orchids—on out to the realms of design where the fact of a body was only a starting point, the District was a nonstop parade. In the early days, tourists who had bought their way in with a holiday package had often sat at sidewalk cafes gawping for hours until, like the most junior of netboys, their real meat bodies collapsed from hunger and thirst and their simulations froze solid or winked out. It was easy to understand why. There was always one more thing to see, one more fabulous oddity appearing in the distance.

But she was here today for only one purpose: to find Stephen. Meanwhile, she was running up a bill on the Poly's account, and she had now incurred the wrath of a nasty little man at the Gateway. Thinking of this, she programmed Chancellor Bundazi's delivery for *Entry plus 19 minutes,* since she knew Mister "I am a Citizen" would be checking up. The delivery was actually a piece of department mail addressed to the Chancellor, one of no import. She had swapped its bill of lading with something actually addressed for hand-delivery to one of Ms. Bundazi's other nodes, and she hoped the resultant confusion would be blamed on the mail room—actually a two decades out-of-date electronic mail system—which certainly could never be blamed too much. Trying to get something through the Poly's internal delivery system was like trying to push butter through stone.

After a moment's examination of Stephen's message coordinates, Renie jumped to Lullaby Lane, the main thoroughfare of Toytown, a backwater sector which housed the smaller and less successful creative firms and merchants, as well as the residential nodes of those clinging to Inner District status by their fingernails. A subscription to the Inner District net was very expensive, and so were the creative fashions necessary to retain one's place among the elite, but even if you couldn't afford a new and exotic sim every day, even if you couldn't afford to redesign your business or personal node every week, just keeping Inner District residency was still major social cachet in the real world. These days, it was often the last pretension that the downwardly mobile would relinquish—and they did not give it up easily.

Renie could not immediately locate the signal source, so she slowed herself down to what would have been a walking pace, except her stripped-down sim did nothing as expensively, uselessly complicated as walking. Toytown's fringe status was apparent everywhere around her. Most of the nodes were functional in the extreme—white, black, or gray boxes that served no other purpose than to separate one struggling Citizen's enterprise from another's. Some of the other nodes had been quite grand once, but now their styles were hopelessly outdated. Some were even beginning to disappear, the more expensive visual functions sacrificed so the owner could cling to the space. She passed one large node, built to resemble something out of Fritz Lang's *Metropolis*—ancient Science Fiction had been a District fad almost a decade ago—which was now entirely transparent, the great dome a polyhedral skeleton, all its detail work gone, its once-magnificent colors and textures switched off.

There was only one node on Lullaby Lane that looked both contemporary and expensive, and it was very near the source-point of Stephen's message. The virtual structure was a huge Gothic mansion covering an area the size of a couple of real-world city blocks, spiky with turrets and as labyrinthine as a termite nest. Colored lights flashed from the windows: deep red; dull chalky purple; and seizure-inducing white. A thick rumble of music advertised that this was some kind of club, as did the shifting letters that moved along the facade like gleaming snakes, spelling out in English—and apparently also in Japanese, Chinese, Arabic, and a few other alphabets— "MISTER J'S." In the midst of the writhing letters, appearing and then immediately vanishing as though the Cheshire Cat were having an indecisive day, was a vast, toothy, disembodied grin.

She remembered the name of the place—Stephen had mentioned it. This was what had drawn them into the Inner District, or at least into this part of it. She stared, appalled and fascinated. It was easy to see its allure—every carefully shadowed angle, every light-leaking window screamed out that here was escape, here was freedom, especially freedom from disapproval. Here was a haven where everything was permitted. The thought of her eleven-year-old brother in such a place sent a cold bolt of fear up her spine. But if that was where he was, that was where she would go. . . .

"Renie! Up here!"

It was a quiet cry, as though from somewhere close. Stephen was trying to narrowcast, but he didn't realize there was no such thing as narrowcasting in the District, unless you could pay for privacy. If someone wanted to hear, they'd hear, so speed was the only thing that mattered now.

"Where are you? Are you in this . . . club?"

"No! Across the street! In the building with the cloth thing on the front."

She turned to look. Some distance down, on the opposite of Lullaby Lane from Mister J's, was what looked like the shell of an old Toytown hotel—a soothing simulation of a real-world resting place designed for District tourists, a spot to receive messages and plan day trips. They had been more popular in the early days, when VR was a slightly intimidating novelty. This one's heyday was obviously long over. The walls had lost color definition and were actually erased in some spots. Over its wide front door hung an awning, unmoving when it should have undulated in a simulated breeze, dulled like the rest of the structure to a state of minimal existence.

Renie moved to the doorway, then, after a brief survey suggested there was no longer anything in the way of security, moved inside. The interior was even more forsaken than the exterior, time and neglect having reduced it to a warehouse of phantom cubes stacked like discarded toy blocks. A few better-manufactured sim objects had maintained their integrity, and stood out in eerie contrast. The front desk was one of these, a shimmering block of neon blue marble. She found Stephen and his friend Eddie behind it.

"What the hell are you playing at?"

Both of them were wearing SchoolNet sims, scarcely even as detailed as hers, but she could still tell from Stephen's face that he was terrified. He scrambled up and grabbed her around the waist. Only the hands of her sim were wired for force-feedback, but she knew he was squeezing hard. "They're after us," Stephen said breathlessly. "People from the club. Eddie has a blanket shield and we've been using that to hide, but it's just a cheap one and they're going to find us soon."

"Since you told me you were in here, anyone who cares around here knows it, too." She turned to Eddie. "And where in God's name did you get a blanket? No, don't tell me. Not now." She reached down and carefully dislodged Stephen. It was strange to feel his slender arm between her fingers when she knew that their true bodies were on opposite sides of town in the real world, but it was that sort of miracle that had led her to the VR field in the first place. "We'll talk later—and I've got *lots* of questions. But for now we'll get you out of here before you get us all sent before a magistrate."

Eddie finally spoke. "But . . . Soki. . . ."

"Soki what?" Renie said impatiently. "Is he here, too?"

"He's still in Mister J's. Sort of." Eddie appeared to have run out of nerve. Stephen finished for him.

"Soki . . . he fell into a hole. Kind of a hole. When we tried to get him out, these men came. I think they were Puppets." His voice trembled. "They were real scary."

Renie shook her head. "I can't do anything about Soki. I'm running out of time and I'm not going to trespass in a private club. If he gets caught, he gets caught. If he tells who was with him, then you'll have to face the music. Netboy lesson number one: you get what you deserve."

"But . . . but they might hurt him."

"Hurt him? Scare him, maybe—and that's no more than you lot deserve. But no one's going to hurt him." She grabbed Eddie, so she now held both boys by the arm; back in the Poly's processors, her escape algorithm added two. "And we're going to . . ."

There was a thunderous crash nearly as loud as the bomb at the Poly, so loud that at the apex of its roar Renie's hearplugs could not deliver it and went mercifully silent for an instant. The front of the hotel dissolved into swirling motes of netstuff. A huge shadow loomed between them and the Toytown street, something far bigger than most normal sims. That was about all she could tell: there was something about it, something dark and arrhythmically wavery in its display pattern, that made it almost impossible to look at.

"Jesus." Renie's ears were ringing. That would teach her to leave the gain up on her plugs. "Jesus!" For a moment she stood frozen as the shape loomed over her, a brilliantly realized abstract expression of the concepts Big and Dangerous. Then she squeezed the boys tightly and exited the system.

"We . . . we got into Mister J's. Everybody does it at school."

Renie stared at her brother across the kitchen table. She had been worried for him, even frightened, but now anger was pushing the other emotions aside. Not only had he put her to a great deal of trou-

ble, but then it had taken him an hour longer to get home from Eddie's flatblock than it had taken her to return from the Poly, forcing
her to wait.

"I don't care if everybody does it, Stephen, and I seriously doubt
that's true anyway. I'm really scorched! It's illegal for you to enter the
District, and we truly couldn't afford the fines if you got caught. Plus,
if my boss finds out what I did to get you out, I could get fired." She
leaned forward and grabbed his hand, squeezing until he winced. "I
could lose my job, Stephen!"

"Shut up, there, you fool children!" their father called out from the
back bedroom. "You making my head hurt."

If there had not been a door between them, Renie's look might have
set Long Joseph's sheets on fire.

"I'm sorry, Renie. I'm really sorry. Really. Could I try Soki again?"
Without waiting for permission, he turned to the wallscreen and told
it to call. No one answered at Soki's end.

Renie tried to rein in her temper. "What was this about Soki falling
down a hole?"

Stephen drummed his fingers nervously on the table. "Eddie dared
him."

"Dared him to do what? Damn it, Stephen, don't make me drag
this out of you word by word."

"There's this room in Mister J's. Some guys from school told us
about it. They have . . . well, there's things in there that are real chizz."

"Things? What things?"

"Just . . . things. Stuff to see." Stephen wouldn't meet her eyes.
"But we didn't see it, Renie. We couldn't find it. The club is major big
on the inside—you wouldn't believe it! It goes on *forever!*" For a moment his eyes sparkled as, remembering the glory that was Mister J's,
he forgot that he was in serious trouble. A look at his sister's face
reminded him. "Anyway, we were looking and looking, and we asked
people—I think they were mostly Citizens, but some acted really
weird—but no one could tell us. Then someone, this far major fat guy,
said you could get in through this room down in the basement."

Renie suppressed a shiver of distaste. "Before you tell me any more,
young man, I want one thing clear. You are *never* going back to this
place again. Understand? Look me in the eye. *Never.*"

Reluctantly, Stephen nodded. "Okay, okay. I won't. So we went
down all these windy stairs—it was like a dungeon game!—and after
a while found this door. Soki opened it and . . . fell through."

"Fell through what?"

"I don't know! It was just like a big hole on the other side. There was smoke and some blue lights down deep inside it."

Renie sat back in her chair. "Someone's nasty, sadistic little trick. You all deserved to be scared, but I hope it didn't scare him too much. Was he using bootleg SchoolNet equipment like you two?"

"No. Just his home setup. A cheap Nigerian station."

Which was what their own family owned. How could kids be poor and still be so damn snobbish?

"Well, then there won't have been much vertigo or gravity simulation. He'll be fine." She stared narrowly at Stephen. "You did hear me, didn't you? You're never going there again, or you will have *no* station time and no visits to Eddie or Soki forever—instead of just for the rest of the month."

"What?" Stephen leaped up in outrage. "No net?"

"End of the month. You're lucky I haven't told Dad—you'd be getting a belt across your troublesome black behind."

"I'd rather have that than no net," he said sullenly.

"You'd be getting both."

After she sent Stephen grumbling and complaining to his room, Renie accessed her work library—making sure that her inbox contained no memos from Ms. Bundazi about defrauding the Poly—and called up some files on Inner District businesses. She found Mister J's, registered as a "gaming and entertainment club" and licensed strictly for adult visitors. It was owned by something called the "Happy Juggler Novelty Corporation," and had first been opened under the name "Mister Jingo's Smile."

As she waited for sleep that night, she was visited by images of the club's ramshackle facade, of turrets like pointed idiot heads and windows like staring eyes. Hardest of all to escape was the memory of the huge mobile mouth and rows of gleaming teeth that squirmed above the door—a gateway that only led inward.

CHAPTER 2

The Airman

NETFEED/MUSIC: Drone "Bigger Than Ever."
(visual: one eye)
VO: Ganga Drone music will be "bigger than ever" this year, according to
one of its leading practitioners.
(visual: half of face, glinting teeth)
Ayatollah Jones, who sings and plays neuro-cithara for the drone group Your
First Heart Attack, told us:
JONES: "We . . . it's . . . gonna be . . . big. Mordo big. Bigger than . . ."
(visual: fingers twining—many rings, cosmetic webbing)
JONES: ". . . Than ever. No dupping. Real big."

Christabel Sorensen was not a good liar, but with a little practice she was getting better.

She wasn't a bad girl, really, although once her fish died because she forgot to feed him for a bunch of days. She didn't think of herself as a liar either, but sometimes it was just . . . easier not to tell. So when her mother asked her where she was going, she smiled and said, "Portia has Otterland. It's new and it's just like you're really swimming except you can breathe and there's an Otter King and an Otter Queen. . . ."

Her mother waved a hand to halt the explanation. "That sounds

sweet, darling. Don't stay at Portia's too long—Daddy's going to be
home for dinner. For once."

Christabel grinned. Daddy worked too much—Mommy always said
so. He had an important job as Base Security Supervisor. Christabel
didn't know exactly what it meant. He was sort of a policeman, except
with the army. But he didn't wear a uniform like the army men in the
movies.

"Can we have ice cream?"

"If you come home in time to help me shell the peas, then we'll
have ice cream."

" 'Kay." Christabel trotted out. As the door resealed behind her with
its familiar sucking sound, she laughed. Some noises were just funny.

She knew that the Base was different than the kind of towns that
people lived in on net shows, or even in other parts of North Carolina,
but she didn't know why. It had streets and trees and a park and a
school—two schools, really, since there was a school for grown-up
army men and army women as well as one for kids like Christabel
whose parents lived on the Base. Daddies and Mommies went off to
work in normal clothes, drove cars, mowed their lawns, had each
other over for dinners and parties and barbecues. The Base did have a
few things that most towns didn't have—a double row of electric
fences all the way around it to keep out the crowdy hammock city
beyond the trees, and three different little houses called checkpoints
that all the cars coming in had to drive past—but that didn't seem
like enough to make it a Base instead of just a normal place to live.
The other kids at school had lived on Bases all their lives, just like her,
so they didn't get it either.

She turned left on Windicott Lane. If she had really been going to
Portia's, she would have turned right, so she was glad the street corner
was out of sight of her house, just in case her mother was watching.
It was strange telling Mom she was going one place and then going
somewhere else. It was bad, she knew, but not *really* bad, and it was
very exciting. She felt all trembly and new every time she did it, like
a shiver-legged baby colt she had seen on the net.

From Windicott she turned onto Stillwell. She skipped for a while,
being careful not to step on any of the sidewalk cracks, then turned
onto Redland. The houses here were definitely smaller than hers.
Some of them looked a little sad. The grass was short on the lawns
like everywhere else on the Base, but it looked like it was that way
because it didn't have the strength to grow any higher. Some of the
lawns had bare spots, and lots of the houses were dusty and a bit

faded. She wondered why the people living in them didn't just wash them off or paint them so they'd look like new. When she had her own house someday, she would paint it a different color every week.

She thought about different colors of houses all the way down Redland, then skipped again as she crossed the footbridge over the creek—she like the *ka-thump, ka-thump* sound it made—and hurried down Beekman Court where the trees were very thick. Even though Mister Sellars' house was very close to the fence that marked the outskirts of the Base, you could hardly tell, because the trees and hedges blocked the view.

That had been the first thing that attracted her to the house, of course—the trees. There were sycamores in the backyard of her parents' house, and a papery-barked birch tree by the front window, but Mister Sellars' house was absolutely *surrounded* by trees, so many of them that you could hardly see that there was a house there at all. The first time she had seen it—helping Ophelia Weiner look for her runaway cat Dickens—she had thought it was just like something in a fairy tale. When she came back later and walked up the twisty gravel driveway, she had almost expected it to be made out of gingerbread. It wasn't, of course—it was just a little house like all the others—but it was still a very interesting place.

And Mister Sellars was a very interesting man. She didn't know why her parents didn't want her to go to his house anymore, and they wouldn't tell her. He was a little scary-looking, but that wasn't his fault.

Christabel stopped skipping so she could better appreciate the crunchy feeling of walking down Mister Sellars' long driveway. It was pretty silly having a driveway at all, since the big car in his garage hadn't been moved in years. Mister Sellars didn't even go out of the house. She'd asked him once why he had a car and he had laughed kind of sad and said it came with the house. "If I'm very, very good," he had told her, "someday they may let me get into that Cadillac, little Christabel. I'll close the garage door real tight, and drive home."

She thought it had been a joke, but she didn't really get it. Grown-up jokes were like that sometimes, but then grown-ups seldom laughed at the jokes that Uncle Jingle did on his net show, and those were so funny (and kind of naughty, although she didn't know why exactly) that Christabel sometimes almost wet her pants from laughing.

To find the doorbell she had to push aside one of the ferns, which had practically covered the front porch. Then she had to wait a long time. At last Mister Sellars' strange voice came from behind the door, all hooty and soft.

"Who is it?"

"Christabel."

The door opened and wet air came out, along with the thick green smell of the plants. She stepped inside quickly so Mister Sellars could shut it again. He had told her the first time she came that it was bad for him if he let too much of the moisture out.

"Well, little Christabel!" He seemed very pleased to see her. "And to what do I owe this enchanting surprise?"

"I told Mommy I was going to Portia's to play Otterland."

He nodded. He was so tall and bent over that sometimes when he nodded like that, up and down so hard, she was worried he might hurt his skinny neck. "Ah, then we can't take too long having our visit, can we? Still, might as well do it up right and proper. You know where to change. I think there's something there to fit you."

He rolled his wheelchair back out of her way and she hurried down the hall. He was right. They didn't have very long, unless she wanted to risk having her mother phone Portia's to hurry her back to the peas. Then she'd have to think of a story about why she didn't go play Otterland. That was the problem about lying—if people started checking up, things got very complicated.

The changing room was, like every room in the house, full of plants. She had never seen so many in one place, not even at Missus Gullison's house, and Missus Gullison was always bragging about her plants and how much work they were, even though a little dark-skinned man came two times a week to do all the clipping and watering and digging. But Mister Sellars' plants, although they got plenty of water, never got clipped at all. They just *grew*. Sometimes she wondered if they would fill the whole house someday, and the funny old man would have to move out.

There was a bathrobe in just her size hanging on the hook behind the door. She quickly took off her shorts and shirt, socks and shoes, and put them all in the plastic bag, just as Mister Sellars had shown her. As she bent over to put the last shoe in, one of the ferns tickled her back. She squealed.

"Are you all right, little Christabel?" called Mister Sellars.

"Yes. Your plant tickled me."

"I'm sure it did no such thing." He pretended to be angry, but she knew he was joking. "My plants are the best-behaved on the Base."

She belted the terrycloth bathrobe and stepped into the shower thongs.

Mister Sellars was sitting in his chair next to the machine that put all the water in the air. He looked up as she came in and his twisted face moved in a smile. "Ah, it's good to see you."

The first time she had seen that face she had been frightened. The skin was not just wrinkled like on Grandma's face, but looked almost melted, like the wax on the side of a burned-down candle. He had no hair either, and his ears were just nubs that stood out from the side of his head. But he had told her, that first time, that it was all right to be scared—*he* knew what he looked like. It was from a bad burn, he said—an accident with jet fuel. It was even okay to stare, he had told her. And she had stared, and for weeks after their first meeting his melted-doll face had been in her dreams. But he had been very nice, and Christabel knew he was lonely. How sad to be an old man and to have a face that people would point at and make fun of, and to need to be in a house where the air was always cool and wet so that his skin didn't hurt! He deserved a friend. She didn't like telling lies about it, but what else could she do? Her parents had told her not to visit him anymore, but for no good reason. Christabel was almost grown-up now. She wanted to know reasons for things.

"So, little Christabel, tell me about the world." Mister Sellars sat back in the streaming mist of the moisture machine. Christabel told him about her school, about Ophelia Weiner who thought she was really special because she had a Nanoo Dress that she could change into a different shape or color by pulling on it, and about playing Otterland with Portia.

". . . And you know how the Otter King can always tell if you have a fish with you? By smelling you?" She looked at Mister Sellars. With his eyes closed, his bumpy, hairless face seemed like a clay mask. As she wondered if he had fallen asleep, his eyes popped open again. They were the most interesting color, yellow like Dickens the cat's.

"I'm afraid I don't know the ins and outs of the Otter Kingdom very well, my young friend. A failing, I realize."

"Didn't they have it when you were a boy?"

He laughed, a soft pigeon-coo. "Not really. No, nothing quite like Otterland."

She looked at his rippled face and felt something like the love she felt for her mother and father. "Was it scary when you were a pilot? Back in the old days?"

His smile went away. "It was scary sometimes, yes. And sometimes

it was very lonely. But it was what I was raised to do, Christabel. I knew it from the time I was . . . I was a little boy. It was my duty, and I was proud to perform it.'' His face went a little strange, and he bent over to fiddle with his water machine. "No, there was more to it than that. There is a poem:

> ". . . Nor law, nor duty made me fight,
> Nor public men, nor cheering crowds,
> A lonely impulse of delight
> Drove to this tumult in the clouds;
> I balanced all, brought all to mind,
> The years to come seemed waste of breath,
> A waste of breath the years behind
> In balance with this life, this death."

He coughed. "That's Yeats. It's always hard to say just what makes us choose to do something. Especially something we're afraid to do."

Christabel didn't know what yates were, and didn't understand what the poem meant, but she didn't like it when Mister Sellars looked so sad. "*I'm* going to be a doctor when I grow up," she said. Earlier in the year she'd thought she might be a dancer or a singer on the net, but now she knew better. "Do you want me to tell you where I'm going to have my office?"

The old man was smiling again. "I'd love to hear about it—but aren't you running a little late?"

Christabel looked down. Her wristband was blinking. She jumped up. "I have to go change. But I wanted you to tell me more of the story!"

"Next time, my dear. We don't want you to get into trouble with your mother. I'd hate to be denied your company in the future."

"I wanted you to finish telling me about Jack!" She hurried into the changing room and put her clothes back on. The plastic bag had kept them dry, just like it was supposed to.

"Ah, yes," Mister Sellars said when she returned. "And what was Jack doing when we stopped?"

"He climbed up the Beanstalk and he was in the Giant's Castle." Christabel was faintly offended that he didn't remember. "And the Giant was coming back soon!"

"Ah, so he was, so he was. Poor Jack. Well, that's where we shall begin when you come back to visit me next time. Now, on your way."

He carefully patted her head. The way his face looked, she thought it might hurt his hand to touch her, but he always did it.

She was most of the way out the door when she remembered something she wanted to ask him about his plants. She turned and came back, but Mister Sellars had closed his eyes again and sunk back into his chair. His long, spidery fingers were moving slowly, as though he were finger-painting on the air. She stared for a moment—she had never seen that before and thought maybe it was some special exercise he had to do—then realized that clouds of steam were drifting past her into the hot afternoon air. She quickly went out again and pulled the door closed behind her. The exercises, if that was what they were, had seemed private and a little of creepy.

He had been moving his hands in the air like someone who was on the net, she suddenly realized. But Mister Sellars hadn't been wearing a helmet or one of those wires in his neck like some of the people who worked for her Daddy. He had just had his eyes closed.

Her wristband was blinking even faster. Christabel knew it would only be a few more minutes before her mother called Portia's house. She didn't waste time skipping as she went back over the footbridge.

CHAPTER 3

Empty Signal Gray

NETFEED/NEWS: Asia's Leaders Declare "Prosperity Zone"
(visual: Empress Palace, Singapore City)
VO: Asian politicians and business leaders meeting in Singapore, led by aging
and reclusive Chinese financier Jiun Bhao and Singapore's Prime Minister
Low—
(visual: Low Wee Kuo and Jiun Bhao shaking hands)
—agreed on a historical trade agreement which Jiun calls a "Prosperity
Zone" that would give Asia an unprecedented economic unity.
(visual: Jiun Bhao, supported by aides, at press lectern)
JIUN: "The time has come. The future belongs to a united Asia. We are full
of hope, but we know there is hard work ahead. . . ."

It stretched before them from horizon to horizon, its millions of by-ways like scratches on glass under extreme magnification—but in every one of those scratches, lights flickered and minute objects moved.

"There cannot be any place so big!"

"But it's not a *place*, remember—not a real place. The whole thing is just electronic impulses on a chain of very powerful computers. It can be as big as the programmers can imagine."

!Xabbu was silent for a long moment. They hung side by side, twin stars floating in an empty black sky, two angels gazing down from heaven at the immensity of humankind's commercial imagination.

"The girl arose," !Xabbu said at last. *"She put her hands into the wood ashes. . . ."*

"What?"

"It is a poem—or a story—made by one of my people:

"The girl arose; she put her hands into the wood ashes; she threw the ashes up into the sky. She said to them: 'The wood ashes which are here, they must together become the Milky Way. They must lie white along the sky. . . .'"

He stopped as if embarrassed. "It is something of my childhood. It is called 'The Girl of the Early Race Who Made the Stars.' Being here, what you have done—they brought it back to me."

Now Renie was embarrassed, too, although she was not quite sure why. She flexed her fingers to take them instantly down to ground level. Lambda Mall, the main tradeground of the entire net, surrounded them completely. The Mall was a nation-sized warren of simulated shopping districts, a continent of information with no shore. Millions of commercial nodes blinked, shimmied, rainbowed, and sang, doing their best to separate customers from credits. The intricate web of virtual thoroughfares surged with sims of every visual type, every level of complexity. "It *is* a huge place," she said, "but remember that most people never bother with high-level overviews like the one we just had—they just travel directly to wherever it is they want to go. If you tried to visit every node on the net, or even just every node in this Mall . . . well, it would be like trying to call every single address in the Greater Beijing Directory. Even all these—" she indicated the crush of sims moving around them in endless parade, "—are just a tiny fraction of the people who are using the Mall right now. These are just the folk who want to have the visual experience of browsing and people-watching."

"The visual experience?" !Xabbu's gray simuloid swiveled to watch a flock of Furries push through the crowd, cartoon-voluptuous females with animal heads.

"Like you're doing now. There's plenty to see. But it's much faster just to go directly to what you want. When you're using the regular computer interface, do you read the name of every file in storage?"

!Xabbu was slow to respond. The Furries had met a pair of snake-headed men and were going through an elaborate ritual greeting which featured a great deal of sniffing. "Go to what I want?"

"I'll show you. Let's say we want to . . . I don't know, buy a new data pad. Well, if you know where the electronics district is, you could go there directly and *then* physically move around—people spend a lot of money trying to make their commercial nodes attractive, just like in the real world. But let's say you don't even know where the district is."

He had turned to face her. His gray face with its vestigial features caused her a moment of anxiety. She missed his animation, his smile: this was like traveling with a scarecrow. Of course, she herself must not look any more pleasant. "But it's true," he said. "I do not know where the electronics district is."

"Right. Look, you've spent a lot of time in the past few weeks learning to find your way around the basic computer setup. The only difference here is that you're *inside* the computer—or apparently so."

"It is hard to remember that I have a real body, and that it is back at the Polytechnic—that I am *still in* the Polytechnic."

"That's the magic." She made her voice smile since she couldn't do much with her face. "Now, do a search."

!Xabbu moved his fingers slowly. A glowing blue orb appeared in front of him.

"Good." Renie took a step closer. "No one can see that but you and me—that's part of our interaction with our own computer at the Poly. But we're going to use our computer to access the Mall's service directory." She showed him the procedure. "Go ahead and bring up the list. You can do voice commands, too, either offline, where no one will hear them but you, or online. If you keep an eye open here in the Mall, you'll see lots of people talking to themselves. They might just be crazy—there are more than a few—but they may also be talking to their own systems and not bothering to keep it private."

The orb spat out a list of services, which hovered in midair as lines of fiery blue letters. Renie adjusted the list to sunset red, more readable against the background, then pointed at those listed under *Electronics*. "There you go. 'Personal access devices.' Click it."

The world immediately changed. The open spaces of the Mall's public area were replaced by a long wide street. The simulated buildings on either side loomed high into the false sky, each one a riot of color and movement, the outside displays as colorful and competitive as tropical flowers. *And we're the bees,* she thought to herself, *with pollen credits to spread around. Welcome to the information jungle.* She rather liked the metaphor. Maybe she would use it in one of her lectures.

"Now," she said aloud, "if you had found a particular store in the services directory, we could have beamed straight there."

"Beamed?" !Xabbu's head was tipped back on his simulated neck. It reminded her of how amazed she'd been by the displays when she had first traveled on the net.

"It used to be an old science fiction term, I think. Kind of a net joke. It just means to travel directly instead of going the long way 'round, RL-style. RL means 'real life,' remember?"

"Mmmmm." !Xabbu seemed very quiet and withdrawn. Renie wondered if she'd shown him enough for a first visit—it was hard to know what an adult mind would make of all this. Everyone she knew had started net-riding in childhood.

"Do you want to go on with our simulated shopping trip?"

!Xabbu turned. "Of course. Please. This is all so . . . astonishing."

She smiled to herself. "Good. Well, as I said, if we wanted a particular store, we could have beamed directly to it. But let's browse."

Renie had been a professional for so long that the thrill of what was possible had worn off. Like her little brother, she had discovered the net at much the same time as she discovered the real world, and learned her way around both long before adolescence. Stephen was still interested in net for net's sake, but Renie was well past the sense-of-wonder stage. She didn't even like shopping, and whenever possible just reordered from an existing account.

!Xabbu, however, was a child in these virtual realms—but a man-child, she reminded herself, with a sophisticated and adult sensibility, however primitive her city-dweller prejudices made his background seem—so it was both refreshing and a little horrifying to accompany him on this maiden voyage. No, more than just a little horrifying: seeing it through his eyes, Lambda Mall seemed so huge and loud, so *vulgar. . . .*

!Xabbu stopped in front of one store's outside displays and gestured to see the full advertisement. Renie didn't bother. Although his sim was standing motionless before the shop's coruscating facade, she knew that he was currently in the middle of a family melodrama in which the crusty but benign father was slowly being brought around to the joys of purchasing a Krittapong Home Entertainment Unit with multiple access features. She watched the Bushman's small sim speaking and reacting to invisible presences and again felt a slightly shamed responsibility. After a few minutes, !Xabbu shook himself all over like a wet dog and stepped away.

"Did tight-fisted-but-basically-kindly Dad see the error of his ways?" she asked.

"Who were those people?"

"Not people. On the net, real people are called 'Citizens.' Those were Puppets—constructs which look like people. Invented things, just like the stores here and even the Mall itself."

"Not real? But they talked to me—answered questions."

"Just a slightly more expensive form of advertising. And they aren't as smart as they act. Go back and ask Mom about the Soweto Uprising or the second Ngosane Administration. She'll just tell you all over again about the joys of Retinal Display."

!Xabbu thought this over. "They are . . . like ghosts, then. Things with no souls."

Renie shook her head. "No souls, that's true. But 'Ghost' means something else on the net. I'll tell you about it one day."

They continued along the street, floating forward at walking speed, a comfortable pace for browsing.

"How can you tell the difference?" !Xabbu asked. "Between Citizens and Puppets?"

"You can't always. If you want to know, you ask. By law, we all have to respond—constructs, too. And we all have to tell the truth, although I'm sure that law gets broken often enough."

"I find that thought . . . upsetting."

"It takes some getting used to. Well, we're pretending to shop, so let's go on in—unless something in the advertising offended you."

"No. It was interesting. I think Dad should get more exercise. He has an unhealthy face."

Renie laughed as they stepped through into the store.

!Xabbu gaped. "But it is just a tiny space seen from outside! Is this more visual magic?"

"You must remember, none of this is real in the normal sense. Frontage space on the Mall is expensive so the exterior displays tend to be small, but the commercial node itself isn't *behind* it as it would be in a real market. We've just moved into another location on the information network, which could be right next to the Polytechnic's janitorial services, or a children's adventure game, or the banking records for an insurance company." They looked across the large and expensive-looking shop. Quiet music was playing, which Renie promptly blocked—some of the subliminals were getting very sophisticated and she didn't want to discover when she went offline that she'd bought herself some expensive gadget. The walls and floor space of the simulated store were covered with tasteful abstract sculptures; the products themselves, displayed atop low pillars, seemed to glow with their own soft inner light, like holy relics.

"Do you notice there are no windows?"

!Xabbu turned to look behind him. "But there were several on either side of the door where we came in."

"Only on the outside. Those were showing us the equivalent of a page in a printed catalog—easy to do. Far more difficult and expensive, not to mention distracting to potential customers, would be to show what was going on in Lambda Mall outside the facade. So, on the inside, no windows."

"And no people, either. Is this store, then, an unpopular place?"

"It is all a matter of choice. I didn't change the default setting when I came in. If you remember your computer terminology from last week, 'default' . . ."

". . . Is the setting you get unless you specify otherwise."

"Exactly. And the default in this kind of store is usually 'alone with the merchandise.' If we want, we can see any other customers who themselves choose to be seen." She made a gesture; for a brief moment a half-dozen sims flashed into sight, bending over one or another of the pillars. "And if we want, we could be visited by a shop assistant immediately. Or, if we hover around long enough, one will eventually appear anyway, just to help us toward a decision."

!Xabbu moved across the floor to the nearest gently-gleaming device. "And these are representations of what this company sells?"

"Some of what they sell. We can change the display, too, or see only the things we're interested in, hovering in front of us. We can even eliminate the showroom and view them only as text, with descriptions and prices. I'm afraid that's what I tend to do."

!Xabbu chuckled. *"The man who lives beside the water hole does not dream of thirst."*

"Another of your people's sayings?"

"One of my father's." He reached his blunt-fingered hand toward one of the pads, a thin rectangle small enough to fit in a simulated palm. "Can I pick this up?"

"Yes, but it will only feel as realistic as your own equipment allows it to feel. I'm afraid the sims we're wearing are pretty basic."

!Xabbu turned it in his hands. "I can feel the weight of it. Quite impressive. And look at this reflection across its screen! But I suppose this is no more real than that water you created my first day in simulation."

"Well, somebody spent more time working on that than I did on my puddle."

"Good afternoon, Citizens." An attractive black woman a few years younger than Renie appeared beside them. !Xabbu started guiltily and she smiled. "Are you interested in personal access devices?"

"We are merely looking today, thank you." Renie examined the perfect, just-ironed crease of the woman's pants and her flawless white teeth. "My friend . . ."

"Are you a Citizen or a Puppet?" !Xabbu asked.

The woman turned toward him. "I am a type-E construct," she said, her voice still as warm and soothing as when she had greeted them, "respondent to all UN codes for retail display. If you wish to deal with a Citizen, I will be happy to summon one now. If you have a complaint about my performance, please indicate and you will be connected with . . ."

"No, no," Renie said. "There's no need. My friend is on his first trip to Lambda Mall and was just curious."

The smile was still in place, although Renie fancied it was a bit stiffer than before. But that was silly—why should a Puppet be programmed with hurt feelings? "I am glad I could answer your question. Is there anything else I can tell you about this or any of Krittapong Electronics' other fine products?"

Out of an obscure sense of guilt, she asked the saleswoman—the *Puppet* saleswoman, she reminded herself, a mere piece of code—to demonstrate the pad for them.

"The Freehand is the latest in portable access data units," the Puppet began, "with the most sophisiticated voice recognition of any pad in its price range. It also allows the preprogramming of hundreds of different daily tasks, a smart phone-filtering service, and a wealth of other extras that have made Krittapong Asia's leader in consumer data-manipulation products. . . ."

As the Puppet described the voice recognition features for !Xabbu, Renie wondered whether it was a coincidence that this particular salesperson appeared as a black woman, or whether it had been summoned up tailor-made to match her own net index and address.

A few minutes later they were outside again, standing in the simulated street.

"Just for your information," she said, "it isn't really polite to ask if people are Citizens or not. But unless you specifically request a live human being, most of the salespeople in stores will be Puppets."

"But I thought you said that it was the law. . . ."

"It is the law. But it's a social thing—a little delicate. If you're talking to a Citizen and you ask them that question, then you're implying that they're . . . well, boring enough or mechanical enough to be artificial."

"Ah. So one should only ask if one is reasonably certain that the person in question is a Puppet."

"Or unless you really, really need to know."

"And what might cause such a need?"

Renie grinned. "Well, if you were falling in love with someone you met here, for instance. Come on, let's find a place to sit down."

!Xabbu sighed and straightened up. His gray sim had been sagging in its chair.

"There is still so much I do not understand. We are still in . . . on . . . the Mall, are we not?"

"We are. This is one of its main public squares."

"So what can we hope to do at this place? We cannot eat, we cannot drink."

"Rest, to begin with. VR can be like long-distance driving. You don't *do* much, but you still get tired."

As blood was red and wet in whichever artery it flowed, so, too, the crowd in the teeming streets seemed identical in its sheer variety to any other in Lambda Mall. The fraction of the Mall's visitors that floated, walked, or crawled past Café Boulle seemed no different than what Renie and !Xabbu had seen upon first entering the commercial sector, or in the streets of the electronics district. The most basic sims, which usually represented the most infrequent visitors, stopped frequently to rubberneck. Other, more detailed sims were covered in bright colors and traveling in groups, dressed up as though for a party. And some wore sophisticated rigs which would have been right at home in the poshest sectors of the Inner District, sims like handsome young gods which turned virtual heads everywhere they passed.

"But why is it a café? Why not a resting-house, or some such?"

Renie turned back to !Xabbu. The slope of his shoulders indicated fatigue. She would have to take him offline soon. It was easy to forget what a staggering sensory experience a first visit to the net could be. "Because 'Café' sounds nicer. No, I'm teasing. For one thing, if we had the equipment for it, we *could* eat and drink here—or at least feel like we were doing so. If we had the implants some rich people have, we could taste things we've never tasted in the real world. But even a real café serves more than just food and drink." She made a gesture and they were surrounded by the gentle sounds of a Poulenc string quartet; the noise of the street dropped to a low murmur in the background. "We are essentially renting a place where we can *be*— somewhere we can stop and think and talk and admire the parade without obstructing a public thoroughfare. And unlike a real restaurant, once you've paid for your table your waiter is always available, but only when you want him."

!Xabbu settled back. "It would be nice to have a beer."

"When we go offline, I promise. To celebrate your first day on the net."

Her companion watched the street life for a while, then turned to survey the Café Boulle itself. The striped awnings fluttered, though there was no wind. Waiters and waitresses in clean white aprons strode among the tables balancing trays stacked improbably high with glasses, although very few of the customers seemed to have any glassware in front of them. "This is a nice place, Ms. Sulaweyo."

"Renie, please."

"Very well. This is a nice place, Renie. But why are so many tables empty? If it is as inexpensive as you said. . . ."

"Not everyone here chooses to be seen, although they cannot simply be invisible without some indication." She pointed to a perfect but deserted simulation of a black cast-iron table with a vase of exquisite daisies in the center of the white tablecloth. "Do you see the flowers? How many other empty tables have them?"

"Most of them."

"That means someone is sitting there—or occupying the virtual space, more accurately. They just choose not to be seen. Perhaps they are secret lovers, or their sims are famous and readily recognizable. Or perhaps they merely forgot to change the default setting from the last people who sat there."

!Xabbu contemplated the empty table. "Are we visible?" he asked at last.

"Oh, yes. I have nothing to hide. I did put a mute on our conversation, though. Otherwise we'd be surrounded by hawkers as soon as we leave, waiting to sell you maps, instruction manuals, so-called 'enhancement packages'—you name it. They *love* first-timers."

"And that is all most people do here? Sit?"

"There are various kinds of virtual performances going on, for those who are not interested in watching the crowd. Dancing, object-creation, comedy—I just haven't requested access to any of them. Do you want to see one?"

"No, thank you, Renie. The quiet is very nice."

The quiet lasted only a few more moments. A loud detonation made Renie shout in surprise. On the street outside the café the crowd swirled and scattered like a herd of antelope fleeing a lion's charge.

Six sims, all muscular males dressed in martial leather and steel, stood in the open space, shouting at one another and waving large guns. Renie turned up the volume so she and !Xabbu could hear.

"We told you to stay off Englebart Street!" one of them bellowed in the flat tones of American English, lowering his machine gun so that it jutted from his waist like a black metal phallus.

"The day we listen to Barkies is the day pigs fly!" another shouted back. "Go on back to your Hellbox, little boy."

An expanding star of fire leaped from the muzzle of the first man's gun. The *phut-phut-phut* sound was loud even through the damped audio in Renie's hearplugs. The one who had been told to stay off Englebart Street was instead abruptly spread all over the thoroughfare in question, bright blood and intestines and bits of meat flung everywhere. The crowd gave a collective shout of fear and tried to push back even farther. More guns flashed, and two more of the muscular men were smashed down onto the street, oozing red from scorched black holes. The survivors lifted their weapons, stared at each other for a moment, then disappeared.

"Idiots." Renie turned to !Xabbu, but he had vanished, too. A moment's worry was eased when she saw the edge of his gray sim poking out from behind the chair. "Come back, !Xabbu. It was just some young fools larking around."

"He shot that man!" !Xabbu crept back into his seat, looking warily at the crowd which had rolled back over the spot like an incoming tide.

"Simulation, remember? Nobody really shot anybody—but they're not allowed to do that in public areas. Probably a bunch of school kids." For a worried moment she thought of Stephen, but such tricks were not his style. She also doubted he and his friends could get access to such high-quality sims. Rich punks, that was what these had been. "And they may lose their access privileges if they get caught."

"It was all false, then?"

"All false. Just a bunch of netboys on the prank."

"This is a strange world indeed, Renie. I think I am ready to go back now."

She had been right—she had let him stay too long. "Not 'back,' " she said gently. "Offline. Things like that will help you remember this isn't a real place."

"Offline, then."

"Right." She moved her hand and it was so.

The beer was cold, !Xabbu was tired but happy, and Renie was just beginning to unwind when she noticed that her pad was blinking. She considered ignoring it—the battery was low, and when the power faded, strange things often happened—but the only priority messages were those from home, and Stephen would have returned from school a few hours ago.

The beerhall's node was not working, and her battery wasn't capable of boosting her signal enough to use it from the table, so she apologized to !Xabbu and went out to the street in search of a public node, squinting against the late-afternoon glare. The neighborhood was not a good one, loose bits of plastic crinkle blowing like autumn leaves, empty bottles and ampoules in discarded paper bags lying in the gutter. She had to walk four long blocks before she found a node, defaced with graffiti but in service.

It was strange being so close to the well-manicured grounds of the Poly and yet in another world, an entropic world in which everything seemed to be turning to dust and litter and flakes of dried paint. Even the little lawn around the public node was only a phantom, a patch of baked earth and skeletal brown grass.

She jiggled the pad's access jack in the node until she made something resembling clean contact. The booth was voice-only, and she listened to her home phone pulse a dozen times before someone answered.

"What you want?" her father slurred.

"Papa? My pad was showing a message. Did Stephen call me?"

"That boy? No, little girl, I call you. I call you to say I won't put up with no nonsense no more. A man got a right to some rest. Your brother, he and his friends make a mess, make too much noise. I tell him to clean up the kitchen, he say it's not his job."

"It's *not* his job. I told him if he cleaned his room—"

"None of your lip, girl. You all think you can talk back to your father like I'm nobody. Well, I throw that upstart boy out, right out for good, and if you don't get home and clean this place up, I throw you out, too."

"You *what?* What do you mean, threw him out?"

There was a sly, pleased sound to Long Joseph's voice now. "You hear me. I throw his skinny behind out of my house. He want to play silly buggers with his friends and make noise, he can live with his friends. I deserve some peace."

"You . . . you. . . !" Renie swallowed hard. When her father got into these moods, he was just itching for conflict; smashed and self-righteous, he would carry it on for days if she fought back. "That wasn't fair. Stephen has a right to have friends."

"If you don't like it, you can go, too."

Renie hung up the phone and stared for long moments at a stripe of cadmium yellow paint splashed across the face of the node, the long tail of a graffiti letter so arcane that she couldn't make it out. Her eyes filled with tears. There were times she understood the violent impulses that made the netboys blow each other to shreds with make-believe guns. Sometimes she even understood people who used real guns.

The jack stuck in the public node when she pulled it out. She stared at the snapped wire for a moment, swore, then threw it down on the ground where it lay like a tiny stunned snake.

"**H**e's only eleven! You can't throw him out for making noise! Anyway, he has to live here by law!"

"Oh, you going to call the law on me, girl?" Long Joseph's undershirt was stained at the armpits. The nails on his bare feet were yellow and too long. At that moment, Renie hated him.

"You can't *do* that!"

"You go, too. Go on—I don't need no smart-mouth girl in my house. I told your mama before she died, that girl getting above herself. Putting on airs."

Renie stepped around the table toward him. Her head felt like it might explode. "Go ahead, throw me out, you old fool! Who will you get to clean for you, cook for you? How far do you think your government check will go without me bringing home my salary?"

Joseph Sulaweyo waved his long hands in disgust. "Talk that shit to me. Who brought you into this world? Who put you through that Afrikaaner school so you could learn that computer nonsense?"

"I put *myself* through that school." What had started as a simple headache had now transmuted into spikes of icy pain. "I worked in that cafeteria cleaning up after other students for *four years.* And now I have a good job—then I come home and clean up after you." She picked up a dirty glass, dried residue of milk untouched since the night before, and lifted it to smash it on the floor, to break it into the thousand sharp fragments she already felt rattling in her own head. After a moment, she put it down on the table and turned away, breathing hard. "Where is he?"

"Where is who?"

"God *damn* it, you know who! Where did Stephen go?"

"How should I know?" Long Joseph was rooting around in the cupboard, looking for the bottle of cheap wine he had finished two nights before. "He go off with his damn friend. That Eddie. What you do with my wine, girl?"

Renie turned and went into her room, slamming the door shut behind her. It was impossible to talk with him. Why did she even try?

The picture on her desk showed him over twenty years younger, tall and dark and handsome. Her mother stood beside him in a strapless dress, shielding her eyes from the Margate summer sun. And Renie herself, age three or four, was nestled in the crook of her father's arm, wearing a ridiculous bonnet that made her head look as big as her entire body. One small hand had wrapped itself in her father's tropical shirt as if seeking an anchor against the strong currents of life.

Renie scowled and blinked back tears. It did no good to look at that picture. Both of those people were dead, or as good as dead. It was a dreadful thought, but no less true for its horror.

She found a last spare battery in the back of her drawer, slotted it into the pad, and phoned Eddie's house.

Eddie answered. Renie was not surprised. Eddie's mother Mutsie spent more time out drinking with her friends than home with her children. That was one of the reasons Eddie got into trouble, and though he was a pretty good kid, it was one of the reasons Renie was not comfortable with Stephen staying there.

God, look at yourself, girl, she thought as she waited for Eddie to fetch her brother. *You're turning into an old woman, disapproving of everyone.*

"Renie?"

"Yes, Stephen, it's me. Are you okay? He didn't hit you or anything, did he?"

"No. The old drunk couldn't catch me."

Despite her own anger, she felt a moment of fright at hearing him talk about their father that way. "Listen, is it all right for you to stay there tonight, just till Papa calms down? Let me talk to Eddie's mother."

"She's not here, but she said it was okay."

Renie frowned. "Ask her to call me anyway. I want to talk to her about something. Stephen, don't hang up."

"I'm here." He was sullen.

"What about Soki? You never told me if he came back to school after—after you three got in that trouble."

Stephen hesitated. "He was sick."

"I know. But did he come back to school?"

"No. His mama and dad moved into Durban. I think they're living with Soki's aunt or something."

She tapped her fingers on the pad, then realized she had almost cut the connection. "Stephen, put the picture on, please."

"It's broken. Eddie's little sister knocked over the station."

Renie wondered if that was really true, or if Stephen and his friend were into some mischief they didn't want her to see. She sighed. It was forty minutes to Eddie's flatblock by bus and she was exhausted. There was nothing she could do.

"You phone me at work tomorrow when you get home from school. When's Eddie's mama coming back?"

"Soon."

"And what are the two of you going to do tonight until she gets back?"

"Nothing." There was definitely a defensive note in his voice. "Just do some net. Football match, maybe."

"Stephen," she began, then stopped. She didn't like the interrogatory tone of her own voice. How could he learn to stand on his own two feet if she treated him like he was a baby? His own father had wrongfully accused him of something just hours earlier, then thrown him out of his home. "Stephen, I trust you. You call me tomorrow, hear?"

"Okay." The phone clicked and he was gone.

Renie plumped up her pillow and sat back on her bed, trying to find a comfortable position for her aching head and neck. She had planned to read an article in a specialist magazine tonight—the kind of thing she wanted have under her belt when career review time came around—but she was too drained to do anything much. Wave some frozen food and then watch the news. Try not to lie awake for hours worrying.

Another evening shot to hell.

*   *   *

"You seem upset, Ms. Sulaweyo. Is there anything I can do to help you?"

She took an angry breath. "My name's Renie. I wish you'd start calling me that, !Xabbu—you make me feel like a grandmother."

"I am sorry. I meant no offense." His slender face was unusually solemn. He lifted his tie and scrutinized the pattern.

Renie wiped the screen, blotting out the schematic she had been laboring over for the last half hour. She took out a cigarette and pulled the tab. "No, I'm sorry. I had no right to take my . . . I apologize." She leaned forward, staring at the sky blue of the empty screen as the smoke drifted in front of it. "You've never told me anything about your family. Well, not much."

She felt him looking at her. When she met it, his gaze was uncomfortably sharp, as though he had extrapolated from her question about his family to her own troubles. It never paid to underestimate !Xabbu. He had already moved past the basics of computing and was beginning to explore areas that gave her other adult students fits. He would be constructing programmer-level code soon. All this in a matter of a few months. If he was studying at night to make such a pace, he must be going without sleep altogether.

"My family?" he asked. "That means a different thing where I come from. My family is very large. But I assume you mean my mother and father."

"And sisters. And brothers."

"I have no brothers, although I have several male cousins. I have two younger sisters, both of whom are still living with my people. My mother is living there, too, although she has not been well." His expression, or the lack of it, suggested that his mother's illness was nothing small. "My father died many years ago."

"I'm sorry. What did he die of? If you don't mind talking about it."

"His heart stopped." He said it simply, but Renie wondered at the stiffness of his tone. !Xabbu was often formal, but seldom anything but open in his conversation. She put it down to pain he did not wish to share. She understood that.

"What was it like for you, growing up? It must have been very different from what I knew."

His smile came back, but only a small one. "I am not so certain of that, Renie. In the delta we lived mostly outdoors, and that is very different, of course, from living beneath a city roof—some nights since I came here I still have trouble sleeping, you know. I go outside and sleep in the garden just so I can feel the wind, see the stars. My landlady thinks I am very strange." He laughed; his eyes almost closed. "But other than that, it seems to me that all childhoods must be much alike. I played, I asked questions about the things around me, sometimes I did what I should not and was punished. I saw my parents go to work each day, and when I was old enough, I was put to school."

"School? In the Okavango Swamps?"

"Not the sort you know, Renie—not with an electronic wall and VR headsets. Indoor school was much later for me. I was taken by my mother and her relatives and taught the things I should know. I never said that our childhoods were identical, only much alike. When I was first punished for doing something I should not have, it was for straying too near the river. My mother was afraid that crocodiles might take me. I imagine that your first punishments were incurred for something different."

"You're right. But we didn't have any electronic walls in *my* school. When I was a little girl, all we had were a couple of obsolete microcomputers. If they were still around, they'd be in a museum now."

"My world has changed also since I was a young child. That is one of the things that brought me here."

"What do you mean?"

!Xabbu shook his head with slow regret, as though she were the student rather than he, and she had fastened onto some ultimately unworkable theory. When he spoke, it was to change the subject. "Did you ask me about my family out of curiosity, Renie? Or is there some problem with yours that is making you sad? You do seem sad."

For a moment she was tempted to deny it or to push it aside. It didn't feel proper for a teacher to complain to a student about her home life, even though they were more or less the same age. But she had come to think of !Xabbu as a friend—an odd companion because of his background, but a friend nevertheless. The pressures of raising a little brother and looking after her troubled and troublesome father had meant that her friends from university days had drifted away, and she had not made many new ones.

"I . . . I do worry." She swallowed, disliking her own weakness, the messiness of her problems, but it was too late to stop. "My father threw my little brother out of the house, and he's only eleven years old. But my father's got it into his bloody mind to take a stand and he won't let him back until he apologizes. Stephen is stubborn, too—I hope that's the only way he's like Papa." She was a little surprised at her own vehemence. "So he won't give in. He's been staying with a friend for three weeks now—three weeks! I hardly get to see him or talk to him."

!Xabbu nodded. "I understand your worry. Sometimes when one of my folk has a dispute with his family, he goes to stay with other relatives. But we live very close together, and all see each other often."

"That's just it. Stephen's still going to school—I've been checking with the office—and Eddie's mother, this friend's mother, says he's okay. I don't know how much I trust *her*, though, that's part of the problem." She stood up, trailing smoke, and walked to the far wall, just needing to move. "Now I'm going on and on about it again. But I don't like it. Two stupid men, one big, one little, and neither one of them is going to say he's wrong."

"But you said your younger brother was *not* wrong," !Xabbu pointed out. "If he were to apologize, it is true that he would be showing respect for his father—but if he accepts blame that is not his, then he would also be submitting to injustice to maintain the peace. I think you are worried that would not be a good lesson."

"Exactly. His people—our people—had to fight against that for decades." Renie shrugged angrily and stubbed the cigarette out. "But it's more than politics. I don't want him to think that might makes right, that if you are pushed down yourself, it's acceptable then to turn around and find someone weaker *you* can push down. I don't want him to end up like . . . like his. . . . "

!Xabbu held her gaze. He seemed capable of finishing the sentence for her, but didn't.

After a long pause, Renie cleared her throat. "This is a waste of your tutorial time. I apologize. Shall we try that flowchart again? I know it's boring, but it's the kind of thing you're going to have to know for exams, however well you're doing with everything else."

!Xabbu raised an inquiring eyebrow, but she ignored it.

!Xabbu was standing at the edge of a sharp spur of rock. The mountainside stretched away beneath him, a curving, glass-smooth free fall of shiny black. In his outstretched palm lay an old-fashioned pocket watch. As Renie stared, !Xabbu began to take it apart.

"Move away from the edge," she called. Couldn't he see the danger? "Don't stand so close!"

!Xabbu looked up at her, his eyes crinkled into slits, and smiled. "I must find out how it works. There is a ghost inside it."

Before she could warn him again, he jerked, then held up his hand wonderingly, like a child; a drop of blood, round as a gem, became liquid and flowed down his palm.

"It bit me," he said. He took a step backward, then toppled over the precipice.

Renie found herself staring down from the edge. !Xabbu had vanished. She searched the depths, but could see nothing but mists and long-winged white birds, who circled slowly and made mournful sounds, *te-wheep, te-wheep, te-wheep*. . . .

She surfaced from the dream, her heart still pounding. Her pad was beeping at her, quiet but insistent. She fumbled for it on the night table. The digital numbers read *2:27 a.m.*

"*Answer.*" She flicked the screen upright.

It took her a moment to recognize Stephen's friend Eddie. He was crying, his tears a silver track on his blue-lit face. Her heart went cold inside her chest.

"Renie. . . ?"

"Where's Stephen?"

"He's . . . he's sick, Renie. I don't know. . . ."

"What do you mean, 'sick'? Where's your mama? Let me talk to her."

"She's not here."

"For God's sake. . . ! How is he sick, Eddie? Answer me!"

"He won't wake up. I don't know, Renie. He's sick."

Her hands were shaking. "Are you sure? He's not just sleeping very deeply?"

Eddie shook his head, confused and frightened. "I got up. He's . . . he's just lying there on the floor."

"Cover him with something. A blanket. I'll be right there. Tell your mother when she . . . shit, never mind. I'll be right there."

She phoned for an ambulance, gave them Eddie's address, then called a cab. While she waited, fever-chilled with worry, she scrabbled in her desk drawers for coins to make sure she had enough cash. Long Joseph had burned out their credit with the cab company months ago.

Except for a few dimly-lit windows, there was no sign of life outside Eddie's flatblock—no ambulance, no police. A sliver of anger pierced Renie's fear. Thirty-five minutes already and no response. That would teach them all to live in Pinetown. Things crunched under her feet as she hurried across the entranceway.

A handwritten sign said the electronic lock on the main door was

out of service; someone had since removed the whole latching mechanism with a crowbar. The stairwell stank of all the usual things, but
there was also a scorched smell, faint but sharp, as of some long-ago
fire. Renie took the stairs two at a time, running; she was gasping for
breath when she reached the door. Eddie opened it. Two of his
younger sisters sheltered behind him, eyes wide. The apartment was
dark except for the jittery light of the wallscreen's static. Eddie stood,
mouth working, frightened and prepared for some kind of punishment. Renie didn't wait for him to think of something to say.

Stephen lay on his side on the living-room carpet, curled slightly,
his arms drawn against his chest. She pulled the threadbare blanket
away and shook him, gently at first, but then with increasing force as
she called his name. She turned him onto his back, terrified by the
slackness of his limbs. Her hands moved from his narrow chest to the
artery beneath his jaw. He was breathing, but slowly, and his heartbeat also seemed strong but measured. She had been forced to take a
first-aid course as part of her teaching certificate, but could remember
little beyond keeping the victim warm and administering mouth-to-
mouth. Stephen didn't need that, at least not as far as she could tell.
She lifted him and held him tight, trying to give him something, anything, that might bring him back. He seemed small but heavy. It had
been some time since he had let her clutch him this uninhibitedly.
The strangeness of his weight in her arms made her suddenly feel cold
all over.

"What happened, Eddie?" Her heart felt as though it had been beating too fast for hours now. "Did you take some kind of drugs? Do
some kind of charge?"

Stephen's friend shook his head violently. "We didn't do anything!
Nothing!"

She took a deep breath, trying to clear her head. The apartment
looked a surreal shambles in the silver-blue light, toys and clothes and
unwashed dishes on every surface: there were no flat planes anywhere. "What did you eat? Did Stephen eat anything you didn't?"

Eddie shook his head again. "We just waved some stuff." He
pointed to the packaged dinner boxes, not surprisingly still out on the
counter.

Renie held her cheek close to Stephen's mouth just to feel his
breath. As it touched her, warm and faintly sweet, her eyes filled with
tears. "Tell me what happened. Everything. God damn it, where is
that ambulance?"

According to Eddie, they truly had done nothing much. His mother had gone out to her sister's, promising to be home by midnight. They had downloaded some movies—the kind Renie wouldn't let Stephen watch at home, but nothing so horrible she could imagine it having a physical effect on him—and made dinner. After sending Eddie's sisters to bed, they had sat up for a while talking before putting themselves to bed as well.

". . . But I woke up. I don't know why. Stephen wasn't there. I just thought he went to the bathroom or something, but he didn't come back. And I kind of smelled something funny, so I was afraid maybe we'd left the wave on or something. So I went out . . ." His voice hitched. He swallowed. "He was just lying there. . . ."

There was a knock at the unlatched door, which swung open. Two jumpsuited paramedics entered like storm troopers and brusquely took Stephen from her. She felt reluctant to let him go to these strangers, even though she herself had summoned them; she released some of her tension and fear by letting them know what she thought of their response time. They ignored her with professional elan as they quickly checked Stephen's vital signs. The clockwork performance of their routine ran down a bit as they discovered what Renie already knew: Stephen was alive but unconscious, and there was no sign of what had happened to him.

"We will take him to the hospital," one of them said. Renie thought he made it sound like a favor.

"I'll go with you." She didn't want to leave Eddie and his sisters alone—only God knew when their useless mother might turn up—so she called another cab, then wrote a hasty note explaining where they were all going. Since the local cab company was unfamiliar with her father, she was able to use a card.

As the paramedics loaded Stephen's gurney into the white van, she squeezed her brother's small, unmoving hand and leaned to kiss his cheek. It was still warm, which was reassuring, but his eyes were rolled up beneath his lids like those of a hanged man she had once seen in a history lesson. All she could see of them by the dim streetlights were two slivers of gray, screens showing an empty signal.

CHAPTER 4

The Shining Place

NETFEED/ARTS: TT Jensen Retrospective Begins
(visual: "Two-Door Metal Flake Sticky," by Jensen)
VO: . . . Based on car-chase images from 20th Century Films, the staged
"sudden sculpture actions" of fugitive San Francisco-based artist Tillamook
Taillard Jensen require the presence of unwitting participants, including this
legendary three-vehicle, multiple fatality for which the reclusive Jensen is
still being sought by authorities . . .

Thargor sat and nursed his mead. A few of the inn's other patrons inspected him when they thought he wasn't looking, but quickly glanced away when he returned their stares. Dressed from throat to toes in black leather, with a necklace of razor-sharp *murgh* teeth rattling on his chest, he didn't look like the sort of person they wanted to offend, even inadvertently.

They were wiser than they knew. Not only was Thargor a mercenary swordsman renowned throughout the Middle Country for his quick temper and quicker blade, but he was in an even fouler mood than usual. It had taken him a long time to find The Wyvern's Tail, and the person he had come to the inn to meet should have arrived when the last watch was called—quite some time ago. He had been forced to sit and wait, both his temper and his rune-scribed broadsword Lifereaper too large for this low-ceilinged public house. On top of everything else, the mead was thin and sour.

He was inspecting the serpent's nest of white scars on the back of his broad fist when someone made a just-standing-here noise behind him. The fingers of his other hand tightened around Lifereaper's leather-wrapped hilt as he turned his head and fixed the nervous inn-keeper with sharp, ice-blue eyes.

"Pardon me, sir," the man stuttered. He was large but fat. Thargor decided he would not need his runesword even if the man intended violence—not that his bulging eyes and pale cheeks suggested he did—and lifted his eyebrow in inquiry: he did not believe in wasting words. "Is the mead to your liking?" the innkeeper asked. "It's local. Made right here in Silnor Valley."

"It's horse piss. And I wouldn't want to meet the horse."

The man laughed, loudly and nervously. "No, of course not, of course not." The laugh ended up rather like a hysterical giggle as he eyed Lifereaper in her long black scabbard. "The thing is, sir, the thing is . . . there's someone outside. Said he wants to speak to you."

"To me? He gave you my name, did he?"

"No, sir! No! Why, I don't even know your name. Don't have the slightest idea what your name is, and no interest in finding out." He paused for breath. "Although I'm sure it's a very respectable and eu-phonious name, sir."

Thargor grimaced. "So how do you know he wants to speak to me? And what does he look like?"

"Simple enough, sir. He said 'the big fellow'—begging your pardon, sir—'the one dressed in black.' Well, as you can see, sir, you're the biggest fellow here, and that's black you're dressed in, right enough. So you can understand . . ."

A raised hand stilled him. "And. . . ?"

"And, sir? Ah, what he looks like. Well, that I couldn't rightly tell you, sir. It was shadowy, it was, and he was wearing a hooded cloak. Probably a very respectable gentleman, I'm sure, but what he looks like I couldn't tell you. Hooded cloak. Thank you, sir. Sorry to bother you."

Thargor frowned as the innkeeper hurried away, scuttling rather impressively for a man of his bulk. Who could be outside? The wizard Dreyra Jarh? He was said to travel anonymously in this part of the Middle Country, and certainly had a bone or two to pick with Thargor—the affair of the Onyx Ship alone would have made them eternal enemies, and that had merely been their latest encounter. Or could it be the haunted rider Ceithlynn, the banished elf prince? Although not a sworn enemy of Thargor's, the pale elf certainly would be looking to settle some scores after what had happened during their journey through Mithandor Valley. Who else might come looking for the swordsman in this unlikely place? Some local bravos he had offended? He had given those cutthroats a terrible thrashing back at the crossroads, but he doubted they would be ready for another go-round with him quite yet, even from ambush.

There was nothing to do but go and see. As he rose, leather trews creaking, the patrons of The Wyvern's Tail studiously examined their cups, although two of the braver tavern wenches watched him pass with more than a little admiration. He tugged at Lifereaper's pommel to make sure she sat loosely in her scabbard, then walked to the door.

The moon hung full and fat over the stableyard, painting the low roofs with buttery light. Thargor let the door fall shut behind him and stood, swaying a little, pretending to be drunk, but his hawklike eyes were moving with the precision he had learned during a thousand nights like this, nights of moonlight and magic and blood.

A figure detached itself from the shadow of a tree and stepped forward. Thargor's fingers tightened on his sword hilt as he listened for any faint sound that might betray the position of other attackers.

"Thargor?" The hooded figure stopped a few paces away. "Hell, man, are you drunk?"

The mercenary's eyes narrowed. "Pithlit? What are you up to? You were supposed to meet me an hour ago, and inside at that."

"Something . . . something happened. I was delayed. And when I arrived here, I . . . I could not go inside without drawing too much attention. . . ." Pithlit swayed, and not in feigned drunkenness. Thargor crossed the distance between them in two swift strides and caught the smaller man just before he collapsed. Hidden by the loose fabric, a dark stain had spread across the front of Pithlit's robe.

"Gods, what happened to you?"

Pithlit smiled weakly. "Some bandits at the crossroads—local bravos, I think. I killed two of them, but that was four too few."

Thargor cursed. "I met them yesterday. There were a dozen to begin with. I am surprised that they are back to work so soon."

"A man has to earn his imperials, one way or the other." Pithlit winced. "It was a last stroke just as I broke away. I do not think it is mortal, but by the Gods, it hurts!"

"Come, then. We will get that tended to. We have other business this full moon night, and I need you beside me—but afterward we will do a magic trick, you and I."

Pithlit grimaced again as Thargor set him on his feet once more. "A magic trick?"

"Yes. We will go back to that crossroads and turn four into none."

As it turned out, Pithlit's wound was long and bloody but shallow. When it was bandaged, and the little man had downed several cups of fortified wine to make up for the lost blood, he pronounced himself ready to ride. Since the hard physical work of the night's planned business was to be Thargor's, the mercenary took the thief at his word. While the moon was still rising in the sky, they left The Wyvern's Tail and its rustic patrons behind.

The Silnor Valley was a long narrow crevice that wound through the Catspine Mountains. As he and Pithlit coaxed their horses up the slender mountain track out of the valley, Thargor reflected that a cat would have to be malnourished indeed to have a spine so bony and sharp-knobbed.

What little life and noise there had been down in the valley seemed a lifetime away here in the heights. The woods were oppressively thick and silent: were it not for the bright moonlight, the swordsman thought, it would have been like sitting at the bottom of a well. He had been in more frightening places, but few as broodingly unpleasant as this part of the Catspine.

The atmosphere seemed to be weighing on Pithlit, too. "This is no place for a thief," he said. "We relish darkness, but only to hide us as we make our way toward glittering things. And it is nice to have somewhere to spend the ill-gotten gains afterward, and something to buy with them besides moss and stones."

Thargor grinned. "If we succeed, you may buy yourself a small city to play in, with all the toys and bright lights you wish."

"And if we do not succeed, I shall doubtless wish I were back facing the crossroads bandits again, wounded ribs and all."

"Doubtless."

They rode on for a while in near-silence, companioned only by the clip-clopping of their horses' hooves. The track wound up and around, through twisted trees and standing stones of odd shape upon whose surfaces the full moon picked out faint carvings, most of them incomprehensible, none pleasant to observe.

"They say that the Old Ones lived here once." Pithlit's voice was determinedly casual.

"They do say that."

"Long ago, of course. Ages ago. Not any longer."

Thargor nodded, hiding a thin smile at Pithlit's nervous tone. Of all men, only Dreyra Jarh and a few other sorcerers knew more of the Old Ones than Thargor, and no one was more feared by those atavistic deeps-dwellers. If the ancient race still maintained some outpost here, let them show themselves. They bled like any other creature—albeit more slowly—and Thargor had sent swarms of their kind to hell already. Let them come! They were the least of his worries tonight.

"Do you hear something?" asked Pithlit. Thargor reined up, quieting his mount Blackwind with a strong hand. There was indeed a faint sound, a distant piping swirl that sounded a little like . . .

"Music," he grunted. "Perhaps you shall have the entertainment you were bemoaning earlier."

Pithlit's eyes were wide. "I do not wish to meet those musicians."

"You may not have a choice." Thargor stared at the sky, then back at the narrow track. The otherworldly music faded again. "The trail to Massanek Coomb crosses here and leads in that direction."

Pithlit swallowed. "I knew I would have cause to regret accompanying you."

Thargor laughed quietly. "If yon pipers are the worst we hear or see tonight, and we find the thing we seek, you will curse yourself for even hesitating."

"*If*, swordsman. If."

Thargor turned Blackwind to the right and led Pithlit down the almost invisible trail into deeper shadow.

Massanek Coomb lay beneath the moon like a great dark beast, an ill-omened vale heavy with its own solitude. The very trees of the mountainside stopped at its edge as though they would not touch it; the grass that grew upon its ground was short and sparse. The Coomb was a scar in the woodland, an empty place.

Almost empty, Thargor noted.

At its center, partially obscured by rising mist, stood the great ring of stones. Inside the ring lay the barrow.

Pithlit tilted his head. "The music has stopped again. Why is that?"

"A man could go mad trying to make sense of such things." Thargor dismounted and looped Blackwind's reins around a tree branch. The charger had already turned skittish, despite a life spent treading paths no other horses knew. No point dragging him down closer to the place's center.

"A man could go equally mad trying to see the sense in this." Pithlit stared at the tall stones and shivered. "Defiling graves is a bad business, Thargor. Defiling the grave of an infamous sorceress seems to refute good sense entirely."

Thargor unsheathed Lifereaper. The runes glimmered silver-blue in the moon's cool light. "Xalisa Thol would have liked you much when she lived, little thief. I am told she kept a stable of small and well-made fellows like yourself. Why should she change her ways simply because she is dead?"

"Do not joke! 'Betrothed to Xalisa Thol' was a byword for a bad bargain—a few days of maddening bliss followed by years of hideous agony." The thief's eyes narrowed. "In any case, it is not me she will be meeting. If you have changed your mind, well and good, but I am not going inside in your place."

Thargor smirked. "I have not changed my mind. I but jested with you—I thought you rather pale, but perhaps it is the moonlight. Did you bring the Scroll of Nantheor?"

"I did." Pithlit rooted in his saddlebag and produced the object, a thick furl of cured hide. Thargor thought he could guess what sort of hide it might be. "I nearly wound up in the tusky jaws of a were-hog getting it," Pithlit added. "Remember, you promised that nothing would happen to it. I have a buyer waiting."

"Nothing will happen—to the scroll." Thargor took it in his hand, faintly but invisibly disturbed by the way the script seemed to writhe against his skin. "Now, follow me. We will keep you well away from danger."

"Well away from danger would mean out of these mountains altogether," complained Pithlit, but fell into step behind him.

The mist surrounded them like a crowd of importuning beggars, pawing at their legs with cold tendrils. The great stone circle loomed before them, casting broad shadows on the moonlit fog.

"Is any magical artifact worth such risk?" Pithlit wondered quietly. "What can the mask of Xalisa Thol be worth to you, who are no sorcerer?"

"Exactly what it is worth to the sorcerer who hired me to steal it," Thargor replied. "Fifty diamonds of imperial weight."

"Fifty! By the gods!"

"Yes. Now, shut your mouth."

Even as Thargor spoke, the strange music came to them again across the wind, a haunting, discordant skirl of pipes. Pithlit's eyes bulged, but he held his tongue. The pair strode forward between the nearest pair of standing stones, ignoring the symbols carved there, and stopped at the base of the great barrow.

The swordsman caught the thief's eyes once more, reinforcing the order of silence, then bent and put Lifereaper to work as though it were only a common farm tool. Soon Thargor had hacked away a wide stretch of turf. As he began to unpile the wall of stones that lay behind it a whiff of decay and strange spices rose from the opening. Up on the hill the horses nickered worriedly.

When he had cleared a hole big enough to accommodate his wide shoulders, Thargor waved for his companion to hand him the Scroll of Nantheor. As he unrolled it and whispered the words the sorcerer had taught him, words he had memorized but whose meaning he did not know, the painted symbols turned a gleaming red; at the same moment, a dim vermilion light was kindled in the depths of the barrow. When it died, and the glowing runes had also faded, Thargor furled the scroll and gave it back to Pithlit. He took out his flints and lit the brand he had brought with him—there had been no need for a torch beneath the bright moon—then eased himself down into the hole he had opened in Xalisa Thol's tomb. His last sight of Pithlit was of the nervous thief's silhouette limned by moonlight.

The first sight of the barrow's interior was both daunting and reassuring. At the far end of the chamber in which he stood, another hole—this one in the shape of an oddly-angled door—led down into further darkness: the great mound was only the antechamber for a far larger excavation. But Thargor had expected nothing else. His sorcerer-client's ancient book had described the place where Xalisa Thol had immured herself before lying down to die as "a labyrinth."

He lifted a small sack from his belt and spilled its contents into his palm. Glow-seeds, each one a small mote of light in this dark place, would serve to mark his path so that he would not wander below the ground forever. Thargor was among the bravest of men, but when the day of his death came, he wished it to be beneath open sky. His father, who had lived a life of near-slavery in the iron mines of Borrikar, had died in a tunnel collapse. It was a fearful and unmanly way to go.

As he pushed through the damp white roots that dangled from the ceiling, moving toward the door at the chamber's far end, he saw something strange and unexpected: a few paces to the right of the dark door something was flickering like a low fire, although it cast no light on the earthen walls. As Thargor watched, it flared into full radiance and became a hole in the air that seeped yellow light. He snarled and lifted Lifereaper, wondering if some magical spell had been laid

here to trick him, but his blade did not shimmer in his fist as she did
in the presence of sorcery, and the barrow smelled of nothing but
damp soil and the faint odor of mummification—neither unexpected
in a burial mound.

He paused, muscles tensed to iron-hardness, and waited for some
demon or wizard to step through this magical door. When nothing
emerged, he moved to the shining place and tested the opening with
his hand. It gave off no heat, only light. After looking around the
antechamber once more, just to be careful—Thargor had not survived
so many near-fatal adventures through carelessness—he leaned forward until he could gaze into the bright portal.

Thargor gasped in disbelief.

Long moments passed. He did not move. Nor did he show any sign
of life when Pithlit poked his head through the entrance hole and
called to him, quietly at first, but then with increasing volume and
urgency. The swordsman seemed to have turned to stone, a leather-
clad stalagmite.

"Thargor!" Pithlit was shouting now, but his companion gave no
sign of hearing. "The music is playing again. Thargor!" A moment
later, the thief became even more alarmed. "There is something coming into the chamber! The tomb's guardian! *Thargor!*"

The mercenary pulled himself back from the golden light, swaying
as though wakened from a deep sleep. Then, with Pithlit watching in
stunned horror, he turned to face the dessicated corpse of what had
been some great warrior shambling out of the darkened door at the
chamber's far end. Thargor's movements were slow and dreamy. He
had barely raised Lifereaper when the armor-clad mummy brought its
rusted battle-ax down on his head, splitting his skull to the first knob
of his spine.

Thargor fumbled in gray emptiness, Pithlit's astonished cries still
echoing in his memory. His own astonishment was no less.

I'm dead! I'm dead! How can I be dead?

It was beyond belief.

*That was a Lich. A stupid, sniveling Lich. I've killed thousands of them.
How could I get toasted by something as fringe as that?*

He searched wildly for a moment as the gray nothing washed over
him, but there were no solutions, nothing to be done. The damage
was too great. He exited, and was Orlando Gardiner once more.

*　　*　　*

Orlando pulled out his jack and sat up. He was so astounded by the turn of events that his hands moved in empty air for long moments before he unseeingly located—and then absently punched into shape—the pillows that cushioned his head, then reconfigured the bed so he could sit up. A cold sweat had pearled on his skin. His neck ached from being in one position too long. His head hurt, too, and the glare of midday through his bedroom window wasn't helping. He rasped a command and turned the window into a blank wall again. He needed to think.

Thargor is dead. It was so shocking, he found it hard to consider anything else, although there were many things to think about. He had made Thargor—he had made *himself* Thargor—with the labor of four long, obsessive years. He had survived everything, developing a facility that was the envy of players everywhere on the net. He was the most famous character in the Middle Country game, recruited for every battle, first choice for every important task. Now Thargor was dead, his skull crushed by a ridiculous low-level irritant—a Lich, for God's sake! The damned things were scattered around every dungeon and tomb in the simworld, cheap and ubiquitous as candy wrappers.

Orlando took a squeeze-bottle from his bedside and drank. He felt feverish. His head throbbed, as though the tomb guardian's ax had truly struck him. Everything had happened with such boggling abruptness.

That gleaming hole, that shining golden whatever-it-was—that had been something bigger, stranger by far than anything else in the adventure. In *any* adventure. Either one of his rivals had set the trap to end all traps, or something beyond his understanding had occurred.

He had seen . . . a city, a shining, majestic city the color of sunlit amber. It had *not* been one of the pseudo-medieval walled cities that dotted the simworld, the game territory known as the Middle Country. This vision had been alien but relentlessly modern, a metropolis with elaborately decorated buildings as tall as anything in Hong Kong or Tokyokahama.

But it was more than some science fiction vision: there had been something *real* about the place, more real than anything he had ever seen on the net. Set against the careful fractals of the game-world, it had glowed with its own splendid and superior presence, like a gemstone on a pile of dust. Morpher, Dieter Cabo, Duke Slowleft—how could any of Orlando's rivals have brought something like *that* into the Middle Country? Every spell-point in the world wouldn't allow you to alter the basics of a simplace that way. The city had simply

belonged to a level of reality higher than the game he had been playing. Higher even, it had almost seemed than RL itself.

That amazing city. It had to be a real place—or at least something
other than netstuff. Orlando had spent almost his whole life on the
net, knew it like a nineteenth century Mississippi pilot knew the big
river. This was something new, an entirely different order of experience. Someone . . . something . . . was trying to communicate with
him.

No wonder the Lich had been able to sneak up on him. Pithlit must
have thought his companion had gone mad. Orlando frowned. He
would have to call Fredericks and explain, but he wasn't quite ready
to rehash things with Fredericks yet. There was too much to think
about. Thargor, Orlando Gardiner's alter ego, his more-than-self, was
dead. And that was only one of his problems.

What was a fourteen-year-old kid supposed to do after he'd been
touched by the gods?

CHAPTER 5

A World Afire

NETFEED/NEWS: *Stuttgart Protest Memorial*
(visual: parade of people bearing candles)
VO: Thousands gathered in Stuttgart for a candlelight vigil to honor the twenty-three homeless people slain by German federal police in a riot over housing.
(visual: young man in tears, head bloodied)
WITNESS: "They had body armor. Big spikes sticking out. They just kept coming and coming. . . ."

Using a flat screen drove Renie crazy. It was like boiling water over an open flame to wash clothes. Only in a miserable backwater hospital like this. . . .

She cursed and pushed on the screen again. This time it shot right past the "S"s and into the "T"s before she could arrest the scroll's progress. It shouldn't be this hard to get information. It was cruel. As if the bloody quarantine wasn't hindrance enough!

Bukavu 4 information posters were everywhere in Pinetown these days, but most of them had been so densely covered with graffiti that she had never quite absorbed the content. She knew there had been outbreaks of the virus in Durban, and had even heard a pair of women talking about someone's daughter in Pinetown who had died of it after traveling in central Africa, but Renie would never have guessed

that the entire Durban Outskirt Medical Facility would be under official UN-mandated Bukavu Outbreak quarantine procedures.

If the disease is so damn dangerous, she thought, *then what are they doing
bringing sick people here who don't have it?* She was furious to think that
her brother, already struck down by some unknown illness, might be
exposed to an even worse contagion in the place she had brought him
for treatment.

But even as she raged, she knew the reasons. She worked for a
public institution herself. Funds were short—funds were *always* short.
If they could afford a hospital just to deal with Bukavu patients,
they'd have one. The hospital administrators couldn't be very happy
about trying to keep their normal operation running under quarantine
restraints. Perhaps there was even a very thin silver lining: Durban
still didn't have enough B4 cases to warrant devoting an entire hospital to their care.

That was small solace, though.

Renie finally got the ancient interface to stop on the "S"s and she
punched in her visitor code. "Sulaweyo, Stephen" was listed as "unchanged," which meant that she could visit him, at least. But seeing
Stephen these days was always heartbreakingly short of anything she
would have called a "visit."

A nurse reading from a pad briefed her as she struggled into an
Ensuit, although there was little he could tell Renie that she had not
gleaned from the single word on the monitor in the waiting room. She
had become so familiar with the litany she could have recited it herself, so she let the nurse go when he had finished, despite the urge to
hang onto any symbol of officialdom and beg for answers. Renie knew
by now that there were no answers. No detectable viruses—including,
thank God, no signs of the fatal disease that had forced the hospital
into such heavy-handed security. No blood clots or other blockages,
no trauma to the brain. Nothing. Just a little brother who hadn't
awakened for twenty-two days.

She shuffled along the passageway, holding her air hose to keep it
from catching on things. Groups of doctors and nurses—and possibly
other visitors as well, since everyone looked pretty much the same in
an Ensuit—hurried past her, making the same crackling and hissing
noises she made. It was a little like being in an old news video about
manned space exploration; when she passed a large window, she almost expected to look out and see the star-flocked depths of space
beyond, or perhaps the rings of Saturn. Instead, it was only another
ward full of tented beds, another campground of the living dead.

Renie was stopped twice on her way to the fourth floor and asked to produce her visitor's pass. Although both functionaries spent a long time examining the faint lettering—the effects of a dying printer exacerbated by perspex faceshields on the Ensuits—she was not angered by the delay. In a way, she found it vaguely reassuring to know that the hospital really did care about the security of their quarantine. Stephen had been stricken so quickly and thoroughly . . . and so mysteriously . . . that it almost seemed like an act of malice. Renie was frightened for her baby brother, frightened of something she could not explain. She was relieved to see that people were on guard.

Renie desperately wanted her brother to get better, but she was even more afraid of a turn for the worse. When she found him lying in exactly the same position as the day before, and all the monitors still locked on readings that were now as familiar as her own address, she felt both unhappiness and relief.

Oh, God, my poor little man. . . . He was so small in that big bed. How could a little tearaway like Stephen be so quiet, so still? And how could she, who had fed him, protected him, tucked him in at night, had in all ways except biology been a mother to him, how could she be so maddeningly unable to do anything for him now? It was not possible. But it was true.

She sat beside his bed and put her own gloved hand into the larger glove built into the side of the tent. She carefully maneuvered her fingers past the tangle of sensor wires radiating from his scalp, then stroked his face, the familiar and beloved line of his rounded forehead, his upturned nose. She was heartsick at being so completely separated from him. It was like trying to touch someone in VR—they might as well be meeting in the Inner District. . . .

A kindling of memory was interrupted by a movement at the doorway. Despite her own Ensuit, she jumped at the white apparition.

"Sorry to startle you, Ms. Sulaweyo."

"Oh, it's you. Any change?"

Doctor Chandhar leaned forward and surveyed the monitor dials, but even Renie knew there was no information to be had there.

"Much the same, it seems. I am sorry."

Renie shrugged, a resigned gesture belied by the heaviness in her gut, the warm imminence of tears. But crying was useless. All she would do was fog the faceplate. "Why can't anyone tell me what's wrong?"

The doctor shook her head, or at least moved the hood of her Ensuit from side to side. "You're an educated woman, Ms. Sulaweyo. Sometimes medical science does not have answers, only guesses. At the moment our guesses are not very good. But things may change. At least your brother's condition is stable."

"Stable! So is a potted plant!" Now the tears did come. She turned to face Stephen again, although at the moment she could see nothing.

A gloved, inhuman hand touched her shoulder. "I am sorry. We are doing all we can."

"What is that, exactly?" Renie struggled to keep her voice steady, but she could not help sniffling. How was a person supposed to blow her nose in one of these bloody suits? "Please tell me, what *are* you doing? Besides putting him in the sun and keeping him watered."

"Your brother's case is rare, but not unique." Doctor Chandhar's voice was pitched in the telltale *dealing with difficult family members* mode. "There have been—and are—other children who have fallen into this sort of comatose state without apparent cause. Some of them have spontaneously recovered, just woke up one day and asked for something to drink or eat."

"And the others? The ones who *didn't* just sit up and demand ice cream?"

The doctor removed her hand from Renie's shoulder. "We are doing our best, Ms. Sulaweyo. And there is nothing you can do except what you are doing—coming here so that Stephen can feel your touch and hear your familiar voice."

"I know, you told me. Which means I should be talking to Stephen instead of haranguing you." Renie took a shaky breath. The tears had stopped flowing, but her faceplate was still steamy. "I don't mean to take it out on you, Doctor. I know you've got a lot to worry about."

"This has not been a particularly good time, these past few months. I wonder sometimes why I picked a career with so much sadness in it." Doctor Chandhar turned at the doorway. "But it is good to make a difference, and sometimes I do. And sometimes, Ms. Sulaweyo, there are wonderful moments of happiness. I hope you and I can share one of those when Stephen comes back to us."

Renie watched the dim white form shuffle out into the corridor. The door slid closed again. The maddening thing was, although she was aching for someone to fight with, for someone to accuse, there was no one. The doctors *were* doing their best. The hospital, despite its limitations, had given Stephen almost every test that might help explain what had struck him down. None had. There were no answers. There was truly no one to blame.

Except God, she thought. *Perhaps.* But that had never done anyone much good. And perhaps Long Joseph Sulaweyo was not entirely without responsibility in the matter either.

Renie touched Stephen's face again. She hoped that somewhere deep inside that unresponsive body he could feel and hear her, even through two layers of quarantine.

"I have a book, Stephen. Not one of my favorites this time, but one of yours." She smiled sadly. She was always trying to get him to read African things—stories, history, folktales from the mixed tribal legacy of their family. She wanted him to be proud of his heritage in a world where such holdovers were fast disappearing, crushed in the inexorable, glacial flow of First World culture. But Stephen's tastes had never run that way.

She thumbed on her pad, then increased the size of the text so she could see it through brimming eyes. She blanked the pictures. She didn't want to see them, and Stephen couldn't. "It's *Netsurfer Detectives*," she said, and began to read.

" '*Malibu Hyperblock is completely sealed,*' *shouted Masker as he crashed through the door, letting his skimboard zoom off into the other room with none of his usual care. The Zingray 220 knocked several other boards loose as it tried to fit itself back into the rack. Masker ignored the clatter, more concerned with his news.* '*They've got bigmama Recognizers on every flowpoint.*'

" '*That's some vicious-bad wonton!*' *said Scoop. He left his holo-striped pad floating in midair as he turned to his excited friend.* '*I mean, there must be major trouble—double-sampled!*' . . .*"

"**I**f you would just go and see him!"

Long Joseph put his hands to his head as though to shut out the noise. "I did go, didn't I?"

"Twice! You've been twice—the day after I took him there and when the doctor made you come down for a conference."

"What more you want? He's sick. You think I should go down every day like you do, look at him? He's still sick. Visit him all you want, it don't make him better."

Renie seethed. How could anyone be so impossible? "He's your son, Papa. He's just a kid. He's all by himself in that hospital."

"And he don't know nothing! I went and talk to him, he don't know nothing. What good is all your talking, talking. . . ? You even read him books!"

"Because a familiar voice might help him find his way back." She paused and prayed for strength to the God of her trusting childhood—a kinder God than any she could summon belief for these days. "And maybe it's *your* voice he needs to hear most, Papa. The doctor said so."

His look became vulpine, his eyes darting to the side as though seeking escape. "What's that nonsense mean?"

"He had a fight with you. You were angry with him—told him not to come back. Now something has happened to him and maybe, somewhere down deep like a dream, he's scared to come back. Maybe he thinks you're mad at him and so he's staying away."

Long Joseph pushed himself up off the couch, frightened but trying to cover it with bluster. "That's . . . you can't talk to me like that, girl, and no doctor talks to me like that about my business either." He stamped his way into the kitchen and began to open cupboards. "A lot of craziness. Scared of me! I just set him straight. Didn't even lay no hand to him."

"There isn't any."

The cupboard-rifling noises stopped. "What?"

"There isn't any. I didn't buy you any wine."

"Don't tell me what I'm looking for!"

"Fine. Do what you like." Renie's head hurt, and she was so tired she didn't want to get out of her chair until the arrival of tomorrow morning forced her. Between working, commuting, and visiting Stephen, she was spending at least fourteen hours a day out of the house. So much for the Information Century—every time you turned around, you had to *go* somewhere, *see* someone, usually on aching feet because the bloody trains weren't running. The Cyber Age. What shit.

Long Joseph reappeared in the living room. "I'm going out. A man deserves some peace."

Renie decided to make one last try. "Listen, Papa, whatever you think, it would do Stephen good to hear your voice. Come with me to visit him."

He raised his hand as if to swing at something, then pressed it over his eyes for a long moment. When he took it away, his face was full of despair. "Go there," he said hoarsely. "So I should go there and watch my son die."

Renie was shocked. "He's not dying!"

"Oh? He jumping and running? He playing football?" Long Joseph stretched his arms wide; his jaw worked furiously. "No, he is lying in hospital just like his mama. You were with your grandmother, girl.

You weren't there. I sat there for three weeks and watched your mama all burned up in that bed. Tried to give her water when she cried. Watched her die slowly." He blinked several times, then abruptly turned his back on her, his shoulders hunched as though against the blow of a sjambok. His voice, when it came, was almost a different person's. "I spent . . . plenty of time in that damn hospital."

Stunned, her own eyes abruptly welling, Renie could not speak for a moment. "Papa?"

He would not turn to face her. "Enough, girl. I'll go see him. I'm his father—you don't need to tell me my job."

"You will? Will you come with me tomorrow?"

He made an angry sound in his throat. "I've got things to do. I'll let you know when I'm coming."

She tried to be gentle. "Please make it soon, Papa. He needs you."

"I'll see him, damn you—put on that foolish suit again. But don't tell me when to go." Still unwilling or unable to meet her eyes, he thumbed the door open and went lurching out.

Drained of energy, full of confusion, Renie sat for a long time staring at the closed door. Something had just happened, but she wasn't quite sure what it had been or what it had meant. For a moment she had felt something like a connection with the father she had known— the man who had labored so hard to keep the family together after his wife died, who had worked extra jobs and encouraged her studies and even tried to help Renie and her grandmother, Uma' Bongela, with little Stephen. But after her Uma' had died and Renie had become a grown woman, he had just given up. The Long Joseph she had known seemed completely lost.

Renie sighed. Whether that was true or not, she just didn't have the strength to deal with it right now.

She slumped deeper in the chair, squinting against the throb of her headache. She had forgotten to buy more painblockers, of course, and if she didn't take care of something, no one else was going to. She turned on the wallscreen and let the first thing she had cued up—a travelogue about holidays in Tasmania—wash over her, deadening her thoughts. For a brief moment she wished she had one of those expensive full sensory wraparounds, so she could *go* to that beach, smell the apple blossoms, feel the sand beneath her feet and the air of holiday freedom so expensively encoded into the program.

Anything to avoid the recursive memory of her father's hunched shoulders and of Stephen's sightless eyes.

* * *

When the beeping awoke her, Renie grabbed at her pad. Eight in the morning, but that wasn't her wake-up alarm. Was it the hospital?

"Answer!" she shouted. Nothing happened.

As she struggled into a sitting position, Renie finally realized that the noise was coming not from the phone but from the front door speaker. She pulled on a bathrobe and made her way groggily across the living room. Her chair was lying on its side like the dessicated corpse of some strange animal, victim of Long Joseph's late and drunken return. She leaned on the switch.

"Hello?"

"Ms. Sulaweyo? It is !Xabbu speaking. I am sorry to disturb you."

"!Xabbu? What are you doing here?"

"I will explain—it is nothing bad or frightening."

She looked around at the apartment, messy at the best of times, but now showing the effects of her cumulative absences. Her father's snores rumbled from his bedroom. "I'll be down. Wait for me."

!Xabbu seemed perfectly normal, except that he was wearing a very clean white shirt. Renie looked him up and down, confused and a little off-balance.

"I hope I am not disturbing you too much," he said, smiling. "I was at school early this morning. I like it when it is quiet. But then there was a bomb."

"Another one? Oh, God."

"Not a real one—at least, I do not know. But a telephone warning. They emptied the Polytechnic. I thought you might not know, so I decided I would save you a useless trip."

"Thank you. Hang on for a moment." She took out her pad and browsed the college system for mail. There was a general message from the chancellor declaring the Poly closed until further notice, so !Xabbu *had* saved her a trip, but she suddenly wondered why he had not merely called her. She looked up; he was still smiling. It was almost impossible to imagine deception lurking behind those eyes—but why had he come all the way out to Pinetown?

She noted the ironed creases in the white shirt and had a sudden disorienting thought. Was this romance? Had the little tribesman come out here to take her on some kind of date? She didn't know quite how she felt about that, but the word "uncomfortable" sprang to mind.

"Well," she said slowly, "since the Poly is closed, I guess you have the day off." Her use of the singular pronoun was intentional.

"Then I would like to take my instructor out for a meal. Breakfast?" !Xabbu's smile wavered, then flickered out, replaced by a look of disconcerting intensity. "You have been very sad, Ms. . . . Renie. You have been very sad, but you have been a good friend to me. I believe it is you who now needs a friend."

"I . . . think . . ." She hesitated, but could think of no good reason not to go. It was just half eight in the morning and the apartment seemed poisonous. Her little brother was lying in an oxygen tent, as unreachable as if he were dead, and the thought of being in the same kitchen with her father when he floundered to consciousness in a few hours made her neck and shoulders tighten like a pulled knot. "Right," she said. "Let's go."

If there was romance on !Xabbu's mind, he certainly didn't show it. As they walked down into Pinetown's business section, he seemed to be looking at everything but Renie, his half-closed eyes that could so easily look shy or sleepy flitting across peeling paint and boarded-up windows, watching rubbish blow down the wide streets like cartoon tumbleweeds.

"It's not a very nice part of town, I'm afraid."

"My landlady's house is in Chesterville," he replied. "This is a little more wealthy, although fewer people seem to be on the streets. But what astonishes me—and I must confess, Renie, horrifies me a little—is the *human-ness* of it all."

"What does that mean?"

"Is that not a word, 'human-ness'? 'Humanity,' perhaps? What I mean is that everything here—all of the city that I have seen since leaving my people—is built to block out the earth, to hide it from sight and mind. The rocks have been scoured away, the bush burned off, and everything has been covered with tar." He slapped his thong-soled foot against the cracked street. "Even the few trees, like that sad fellow there, have been brought here and planted by people. Humans turn the places they live into great crowded piles of mud and stone, like the nests termites build—but what happens when in all the world there there are only termite hills left but no bush?"

Renie shook her head. "What else should we do? If this were bush country, there would be too many of us to survive. We would starve. We would kill each other."

"So what will people do when they finally run out of bush to burn?" !Xabbu bent and picked up a plastic ring, an already unclassifiable remnant of the current civilization. He squeezed his fingers together and slipped it over his wrist, then held his new bangle up and examined it, a sour half-smile on his lips. "Starve then? Kill each other then? It will be the same problem, but first we will have covered everything with tar and stone and cement and . . . what is it called, 'fibramic'? Also, when the killing comes, there will be many more people to die."

"We'll go into space." Renie gestured toward the gray sky. "We'll . . . I don't know, colonize other planets."

!Xabbu nodded. "Ah."

Johnny's Café was crowded. Most of the customers were truck drivers starting their hauling day on the Durban-Pretoria route, big friendly men in sunglasses and bright-colored shirts. Too friendly, some of them—in the time it took to squeeze through to an empty booth, Renie received a proposal of marriage and several less honorable offers. She clenched her teeth, refusing to smile at even the most harmless and respectful of the flirts. If you encouraged them, it just got worse.

But there were things Renie liked about Johnny's, and one of them was that you could get real food. So many of the small restaurants and coffee shops these days served nothing but American-style convenience food—waved beefburgers, sausages in rolls with gluey cheese sauce, and of course Coca-Cola and fries, the wafer and wine of the Western religion of commerce. But somebody in the kitchen here—perhaps Johnny himself, if there was such a person—actually cooked.

Besides the cup of strong, driver-fuel coffee, Renie decided on bread with butter and honey and a plate of fried plantains and rice. !Xabbu let her order him the same. When the wide platter came, he stared at it in apparent dismay.

"It is so large."

"It's mostly starch. Don't finish it if you don't feel comfortable."

"Will you eat it?"

She laughed. "Thanks, but this is plenty for me."

"Then what will happen to it?"

Renie paused. Distant stepchild to the culture of wealth, she had never thought much about her own patterns of consumption and waste. "I'm sure someone in the kitchen takes home whatever's left over," she offered at last, and felt guilty and shamed even as she said it. She had little doubt that the onetime masters of South Africa had made the same excuse as they watched the remains of another Caligulean feast being cleared away.

She was grateful that !Xabbu did not seem inclined to follow up the question. It was at moments like this that she realized how different his outlook truly was. He spoke better English than her father, and his intelligence and quick empathy aided him in understanding many very subtle things. But he was *not* like her, not at all—he might have dropped in from another planet. Renie, again with an obscure feeling of shame, realized that she shared more of her fundamental outlook with a rich white teenager living in England or America than with this young African man who had grown up a few hundred miles away.

After he had eaten a few mouthfuls of rice, !Xabbu looked up. "I have now been in two cafés," he said. "This, and the one in the Lambda Mall."

"Which do you prefer?"

He grinned. "The food is better here." He took another bite, then poked at a glistening plantain with his fork, as if to make sure it was dead. "There is something else, too. You remember I asked about ghosts on the net? I see the life there, but I cannot *feel* it, which makes me uneasy in spirit. It is hard to explain. But I like this place much better."

Renie had been a net habitué for so long that she sometimes did indeed think of it as a place, a huge place, but just as geographically real as Europe or Australia. But !Xabbu was right—it wasn't. It was an agreement, something people pretended was real. In some ways, it *was* a country of ghosts . . . but all the ghosts were haunting each other.

"There *is* something to be said for RL." As if to prove it to herself, she lifted her mug of very good, very strong coffee. "No question."

"Now please, Renie, tell me what is troubling you. You said to me that your brother was ill. Is that it, or have you other problems as well? I hope I am not intruding too much."

Awkwardly at first, she described her last visit to Stephen and the latest version of her ongoing argument with Long Joseph. Once she began, it grew easier to talk, to describe the hopeless frustration of visiting Stephen every day when nothing ever changed, of the increasingly painful spiral of her relationship with her father. !Xabbu listened, asking questions only when she hesitated on the brink of some painful admission, but each time she answered the questions and found herself moving farther into revelation. She was not used to opening herself, to exposing her secret fears; it felt dangerous. But, as they dawdled through breakfast and the morning crowd slowly drifted out of the coffee shop, she also felt relief at finally being able to speak.

She was putting sweetener into her third cup of coffee when !Xabbu suddenly asked: "Are you going to see him today? Your brother?"

"I usually go in the evening. After work."

"May I come with you?"

Renie hesitated, wondering for the first time since they had sat down whether !Xabbu's interest was something other than mere comradeship. She lit a cigarette to cover the pause. Did he see himself becoming the man in her life, her protector? There hadn't been anyone significant since Del Ray, and that relationship (it was astonishing and somewhat frightening to realize) was years in the past. Except for brief moments of weakness in the small hours, she did not want anyone to take care of her. She had been strong all her life, and could not imagine giving responsibility over to someone else. In any case, she had no romantic feelings for this small young man. She looked at him for a long time as he, perhaps giving her a chance to do just that, examined the multicolored trucks ranked outside the dirty café window.

What are you afraid of, girl? she asked herself. *He's a friend. Take him at his word until he proves otherwise.*

"Yes, come along. It would be nice to have company."

He turned his gaze back to her, suddenly shy. "I have never been to a hospital—but that is not why I wish to accompany you," he said hurriedly. "I wish to meet your brother."

"I wish you *could* meet him, meet him the way he was . . . *is.*" She blinked hard. "I sometimes find it hard to believe he's in there. It's so painful to see him like that. . . ."

!Xabbu nodded solemnly. "I wonder whether it is more difficult your way, where your loved one is far from you. Among my people, the sick ones stay with us. But perhaps the frustration would be greater if you had to watch him always, every day, remaining in this sad state."

"I don't think I could take it. I wonder how the other families deal with it."

"Other families? Of the sick?"

"Of children like Stephen. His doctor said there were quite a few other cases."

Something like a shock ran through her as she realized what she was saying. For the first time in several days the feeling of helplessness, which even !Xabbu's patient listening had not much affected, suddenly receded.

"I'm not going to do it any more," she said.

!Xabbu looked up, startled by the change in her voice. "Not do what?"

"Just sit and worry. Wait for someone to tell me something, when I could be doing something myself. Why did this happen to Stephen?"

The little man was confused. "I am no city doctor, Renie."

"That's just it. You don't know. I don't know. The doctors don't know. But there are other cases—they said so. Stephen is being treated in a hospital that's under Bukavu 4 quarantine and the doctors there are being worked to exhaustion. Couldn't they have missed something? How much research have they had a chance to do? Real research?" She slid her card into the table, then thumbprinted the scuffed screen. "Do you want to come to the Poly with me?"

"But it is closed today."

"Damn." She replaced the card in her pocket. "That's all right—the net access is still available. I just need a station." She considered her home system and balanced the convenience against the likelihood that her father would just now be staggering out into the kitchen. Even if, against all odds, he was not hung over and foul-tempered, she knew that bringing !Xabbu home with her would mean she would be hearing about her "bushman boyfriend" for months.

"My friend," she said as she stood up, "we're going to visit the Pinetown Public Library."

"**W**e could get most of this off my pad," she explained as the chubby young librarian unlocked the net room, "or yours, for that matter. But we'd be getting text and flat pictures, and I don't like working that way."

!Xabbu followed her in. The librarian eyed the Bushman over the top of his glasses, shrugged, then strolled back to the desk. The few old men watching the news on kiosk screens had already turned back to the full-color footage of the most recent maglev train accident on the Deccan Plateau in India. Renie closed the door, shutting out the distractions of crushed metal, sacked bodies, and the reporter's breathless commentary.

She pulled a sad tangle of cables out of the storage cabinet, then searched through the obsolescent headsets until she found two that were in reasonable shape. She slid her fingers into the squeezers and keyed up net access.

"I see nothing," !Xabbu said.

Renie pushed up her helmet, then leaned over and tinkered with !Xabbu's faceplate until she found the loose connection. She pulled her own helmet back on and the gray of raw netspace surrounded her.

"I have no body."

"You won't. This is an information-only ride, and quite stripped down at that—no force-feedback, so no sensation of touching anything. This is about what you get on a cheap home system. Like the kind an instructor at the Poly can afford."

She tightened her fingers and the gray deepened into a blackness that, except for the absence of stars, might have been deep space. "I should have done this a long time ago," she said. "But I've been so busy, so tired. . . ."

"Done what?" !Xabbu's tone remained calm, but she could sense a little tension underneath the patience. Well, she decided, he would just have to hang on. He was riding in *her* car.

"Done a little research myself," she said. "Twenty-four-hour access to the greatest information system the world has ever known, and I've been letting someone else do my thinking for me." She squeezed and a ball of glowing blue light appeared, like a propane sun at the heart of an empty universe. "This unit should have a fix on my voice by now," she said, then calmly enunciated: *"Medical Information.* Let's get cracking."

After she had issued a few more commands, a supine human form appeared, hovering in the empty space before them, a strangely vacant figure as rudimentary as an inexpensive sim. Threads of light snaked through it, illuminating the circulatory system as a calm female voice described clot formation and subsequent oxygen deprivation to the brain.

"Like gods." !Xabbu sounded slightly perturbed. "Nothing is hidden."

"We're wasting time here," Renie said, ignoring him. "We know that there's no pathological indication in Stephen—even his brain chemical levels are normal, let alone anything as grossly obvious as a clot or a tumor. Let's get out of this Encyclopedia Britannica stuff and start looking for real information. *Medical journals, today's date to minus 12 months. Keywords, and/or—'coma,' 'children,' 'juvenile,'* what else? *'Brain trauma,' stupor'* . . ."

Renie had hung a glimmering time display just at the comfortable upper range of her vision. Most of the access calls were local, since most of the information was directly available on the main net info-banks, but some of the downloads were costing her, and the resource-starved Pinetown Library was going to add on a time-based surcharge. They had been online for over three hours, and she still had not found anything that made her feel the search had been worthwhile. !Xabbu had stopped asking questions at least an hour earlier, either over-whelmed by the dizzying, shifting displays of information or just bored.

"Only a few thousand cases like this all together," she said. "Every-thing else known causes. Out of ten billion people, that's not many. *Distribution map, reported cases in red.* Might as well look at that again."

The array of glowing lines dissolved and were replaced by a stylized globe of the Earth shining with inner light—a fruit, round and perfect, falling through emptiness.

And how could we ever find another planet like this? she asked herself, remembering what she had said to !Xabbu about colonization. *The greatest gift possible, and we have taken very poor care of it.*

A series of glowing scarlet dots appeared across the globe, spreading like mold as they replicated the chronological onset of incidents. The sequence showed no pattern that she could see, appearing in what seemed like random order all over the simulated Earth with no refer-ence to proximity. If it was an epidemic, it was a very strange one. Renie frowned. When all the dots were lit, the pattern still suggested nothing. The dots were thickest in the most populated areas, which was not surprising. In the First World countries of Europe, America, and the Pacific Rim, they were fewer in number, but scattered widely over the land masses. Across the Third World the spots clustered al-most entirely along the seacoasts and bays and rivers in hot red infes-tations that made her think of skin disease. For a moment she thought she might have discovered something, some link to polluted waters, discarded toxins.

"Environmental contaminant levels above UN-prescribed guidelines," she said. *"Purple."*

As the lavender dots ignited, Renie stared. "Shit."

!Xabbu's voice came to her from the darkness. "What is wrong?"

"The purple are sites of strong pollutant contamination. See how the coma cases are clustered along the sea coasts and rivers here and in southern Asia? I thought there might be a link, but that pattern doesn't hold true in America—half the cases are far away from any high contaminant levels. The First World doesn't have anywhere near as many cases, but I find it hard to believe there'd be two separate causes, one for them, one for us." She sighed. *"Purple off.* Maybe there *are* two separate causes. Maybe there are hundreds." She thought for a moment. *"Population density, in yellow."*

As the little yellow lights bloomed, she swore again. "That's what all the rivers and coastline cases were about—that's where most of the big cities are, of course. I should have thought of that twenty minutes ago."

"Perhaps you are tired, Renie," !Xabbu suggested. "It has been some time since you ate, and you have been working very hard. . . ."

"I'm just about to give up." She stared at the globe pocked with red and yellow lights. "But it's strange, !Xabbu. Even with population density, it still doesn't make sense. Almost all the cases in Africa, northern Eurasia, India are in heavily populated areas. But in the First World, they're a little thicker around the major metroplexes, but there are cases all over the place, too. Look at all those red dots across the middle of America."

"You are trying to find something that corresponds with the children who have gone into comas like Stephen's, yes? Some thing that people do or experience or suffer from which might have a connection?"

"Yes. But ordinary disease vectors don't seem to have anything to do with it. Pollutants don't either. There's no rhyme or reason I can see. I even thought for a moment it might have something to do with electromagnetic disturbances, you know, the kind you get from power transformers—but virtually all of India and Africa went through electrification years ago, so if EMD was causing these comas, why would they happen *only* in the urban areas? What do you get only around the urban metroplexes in the third world, but all over the first world?"

The globe hung before her, the lights mysterious as words written in an unknown alphabet. It was hopeless—too many questions, no answers. She began to key the exit sequence.

"Another way to think of it," !Xabbu said suddenly, "is what things do you *not* find in the places that city dwellers call ''undeveloped'?" There was a forcefulness to his tone, as though he were conveying important information, and yet he sounded strangely distant, too. "Renie, what do you not find in places like my Okavango Delta?"

At first she did not understand what he meant. Then something moved through her like a cold wind.

"Show me areas of net usage." Her voice was only a little shaky. *"Minimum one—no, two hours per day, per household. In orange."*

The new indicators sparked into existence, a swarm of tiny flames that turned the globe into a spherical conflagration. At the center of almost every bright smear of orange was at least one angry red spot.

"Oh, my God," she whispered. "Oh, my God, they match."

CHAPTER 6

No Man's Land

Her breath was like cinnamon. Her long-fingered hand on his breast seemed to weigh no more than a leaf. He kept his eyes closed, afraid that if he opened them she would vanish, as she had so many times before.

"Have you forgotten?" A whisper, faint and sweet as birdsong in a far-off wood.

"No, I haven't forgotten."

"Then come back to us, Paul. Come back to us."

As her sadness swept through him, he lifted his arms to clutch her. "I haven't forgotten," he said. "I haven't . . ."

An explosive crash jerked Paul Jonas upright. One of the German eleven-inchers had roared into life. The earth shook resentfully and the trench timbers creaked as the first shells struck, a quarter of a mile down the line. Very-pistol flares drifted across the sky, painting the shell trails bright red. A shimmer of rain spattered Paul's face. His arms were empty.

"I haven't . . ." he said stupidly. He held his hands before him and stared at the flarelit mud that covered them.

"Haven't what?" Finch was hunched a yard away, writing a letter home. Scarlet flickered across the lenses of his spectacles as he turned toward Paul. "Having a good one, were you? Was she pretty?" The force of his stare belied his light tone.

Paul looked away in embarrassment. Why was his comrade looking at him like that? It had just been a dream, hadn't it? Another one of those dreams that plagued him so insistently. A woman, a sorrowful angel. . . .

Am I going mad? Is that why Finch stares at me?

He sat up, grimacing. A puddle had formed beneath his boots as he slept, soaking his feet. If he didn't attend to them, he'd get trenchfoot. Bad enough to have people you didn't know and couldn't see tossing bits of exploding metal at you without having to watch your own extremities rot away before your eyes. He pulled off his boots and pushed them over to the tiny gas stove, tongues pulled down so they would dry faster.

But faster than never could still be awfully slow, he thought. The damp was an even more patient enemy than the Germans. It didn't take an evening off to celebrate Christmas or Easter, and all the guns and bombs the Fifth Army could deploy wouldn't kill it. It just seeped back in, filling trenches, graves, boots . . . filling people, too.

Trenchsoul. When all that makes you a person festers and dies.

His feet looked pale as skinned animals, ragged and soft; they were bruised blue along the toes where the blood wasn't circulating properly. He leaned forward to rub them and noted with a mixture of abstract interest and quiet horror that he couldn't feel either the toes or the fingers that squeezed them. "What day is today?" he asked.

Finch looked up, surprised by the question. "Strike me blind, Jonesie, how should I know? Ask Mullet. He's keeping track 'cause he's got leave coming."

On Finch's far side, Mullet's rounded bulk rose into view, a rhino disturbed at the waterhole. His close-cropped head turned slowly toward Paul. "What do you want?"

"I just asked what day it is." The bombardment had stuttered to a halt; his voice sounded unnaturally loud.

Mullet made a face, as though Paul had asked him the distance to the moon in nautical miles. "It's March twentieth, innit? Thirty-six more days until I go back to Blighty. What the hell do you care?"

Paul shook his head. It sometimes seemed that it had always been March, 1918, that he had always lived in this trench with Mullet and Finch and the rest of the grumbling remnants of Seventh Corps.

"Jonesie was having that dream again," Finch said. He and Mullet shared a brief look. They did think he was going mad, Paul was sure of it. "Who was she, Jonesie—that little barmaid from the *estaminet?* Or Missus Entroyer's little Madeleine?" He offered the names with his usual contempt for French pronunciation. "She's too young for you, old mate. Barely big enough to bleed, that one."

"For Christ's sake, shut up." Paul turned away in disgust. He picked up his boots and moved them so that each side would receive an equal proportion of the scant warmth from the primus stove.

"Jonesie's a romantic," Mullet brayed. He had teeth to complement his rhinoceroid physique—flat, wide, and yellow. "Don't you know that every man in the Seventh except you has had that Madeleine already?"

"I said shut up, Mullet. I don't want to talk."

The big man grinned again, then slumped back into the shadows beyond Finch, who turned to Jonas. There was more than a little anger in the slender man's voice as he said: "Why don't you just go back to sleep, Jonesie? Don't make trouble. There's plenty of that around already."

Paul took off his greatcoat, then pushed himself farther down the trench until he found a place where his feet would be less likely to get wet. He bundled the coat around his bare toes and leaned back against the duckboards. He knew he shouldn't get mad at his companions— hell, his friends, the only friends he had—but the threat of a last-ditch German assault had been hanging over all their heads for days. Between the constant barrages meant to soften them up, the anticipation of something worse to come, and the dreams that would not leave him alone . . . well, it was little wonder he felt like his nerves were on fire.

Paul stole a glance at Finch, who was bending over his letter again, squinting in the dim lantern light. Reassured, he turned his back to his trenchmates and pulled the green feather from his pocket. Although the Very-light was fading, the feather seemed to have its own faint radiance. He held it close to his face and breathed deeply, but whatever scent it had once held was gone, overwhelmed by the odors of tobacco, sweat, and mud.

It meant something, this feather, although he couldn't say what. He didn't remember picking it up, but it had been in his pocket for days. Somehow it reminded him of the angel dream, but he wasn't sure why—more likely the dreams were sparked by the possession of the feather.

And the dreams themselves were very strange. He remembered only fragments—the angel and her haunting voice, some kind of machine trying to kill him—but he felt somehow that even these fragments were precious, insubstantial good luck charms he could not afford to be without.

Clutching at straws, Jonas, he told himself. *Clutching at feathers.* He slid the shiny object back into his pocket. *Dying men think of funny things—and that's what we all are here, aren't we? Dying men?*

He tried to smooth the thought away. Such ruminations would not slow his tired heart or ease his trembling muscles. He closed his eyes and began the slow search for the path that would take him back down to sleep. Somewhere on the other side of No Man's Land, the guns began to roar again.

Come to us. . . .

Paul woke up as a great crash split the sky. The sweat that covered his forehead and cheeks was sluiced away by a sweeping wash of rain. The sky lit up, the clouds suddenly white at the edges and burning behind. Another powerful roll of thunder followed. It was not the guns. It was not an attack at all, but only nature pointing out heavy-handed parallels.

Paul sat up. Two yards away Finch lay like a dead man, his greatcoat pulled over his head and shoulders. A flare of lightning showed a row of sleeping forms beyond him.

Come to us. . . . The dream-voice still echoed in his ears. He had felt her again—so close! An angel of mercy, come to whisper to him, come to summon him . . . where? To heaven? Was that what it was, an omen of his coming death?

Paul put his hands over his ears as the thunder cracked again, but could not shut out the noise or ease the ache in his skull. He would die here. He had long been resigned to that miserable promise—it would be peace, anyway, a quiet rest. But now he suddenly knew that death would be no relief. Something worse waited for him beyond death's threshold, something far worse. It had something to do with the angel, although he could not believe any evil of her.

A fit of shivering racked him. Something beyond death was hunting for him—he could almost see it! It had eyes and teeth and it would swallow him down into its belly where he would be torn and chewed forever.

Terror climbed up out of the pit of his stomach and into his throat. As the lightning flashed again, he opened his mouth wide, then choked as water filled it. When he had spluttered it out again, he screamed helplessly, but his voice disappeared in the throbbing bellow of the storm. The night, the storm, the nameless terrors of dream and death, all closed in on him.

"Think about getting out," a voice in another half-remembered dream had urged him. *"About really getting out."* He clutched at that memory as at something warm. In that collapsing moment it was his only coherent thought.

Paul staggered to his feet and took a few steps down the trench, away from the rest of his platoon, then grabbed the rungs of the nearest ladder and climbed, as if to throw himself into enemy fire. But he was fleeing death, not running toward it. He hesitated at the top.

Desertion. If his comrades caught him, they would shoot him. He had seen it happen, watched them execute a red-haired Geordie who had refused to go over on a raid. The boy hadn't been more than fifteen or sixteen, lied about his age when he volunteered, and he had apologized and cried steadily until the rifle squad's bullets punched into him, changing him in an instant from a human being to a leaking sack of meat.

The wind howled and the rain flew horizontally before him as Paul pushed his head above the top of the trench. Let them shoot him, then—let *either* side shoot him if they could catch him. He was mad, mad as Lear. The storm had swept his senses away and he suddenly felt free.

Getting out. . . .

Paul stumbled off the top of the ladder and fell. The sky flared again. Great sagging coils of barbed wire stretched horizontally before him, running all along the front of the trenches, protecting the Tommies from German raids. Beyond that lay No Man's Land, and past that haunted place, as though a great mirror had been stretched across the Western Front, lay the dark twin of the British lines. Fritz had hung out his own wire, protecting the pits in which he crouched in his multiform sameness.

Which way to go? Which of two nearly hopeless alternatives to choose? Forward across the wasteland on a night when the German sentries and snipers might be huddled behind their walls, or back across his own lines toward free France?

The infantryman's inbred horror of the void between the armies almost ruled him, but the wind was wild and his blood seemed to respond to it, to urge a similar freedom from restraint. No one would expect him to go forward.

He ran blindly through the rain, bent like an ape, until he was a few hundred yards from his platoon's entrenchment. As he crouched before the wire and took his cutters from his belt, he heard someone laughing quietly. He froze in terror before he realized that the person laughing had been him.

The loose wire tore at his clothes as he pushed through, like the sentry brambles around a sleeping princess' castle. Paul flattened himself into the mud as another blaze of lightning turned the sky white. Thunder followed swiftly. The storm was coming closer. He crawled forward on knees and elbows, his head full of noise.

Stay in No Man's Land. Somewhere there will be a place to break out again. Somewhere. Stay between the lines.

The world was all mud and wire. The war in the heavens was only a faint imitation of the horror men had learned to make.

He couldn't find *up*. He'd lost it.

Paul rubbed at his face, trying to clear the muck from his eyes, but there was always more. He was swimming in it. There was nothing solid to push against, no resistance to tell him *here is the ground*. He was drowning.

He stopped struggling and lay with his hand cupped over his mouth to keep the mud out while he breathed. Somewhere far to his left a machine gun started up, its scratchy chatter a faint counterpoint to the wind and rumbling storm. He slowly tilted his head from side to side until the dizziness and confusion abated.

Think. Think!

He was somewhere in No Man's Land, trying to crawl south between the lines. The darkness striped by lightning and flares—that was the sky. The deeper darkness, giving light only from reflections in standing water, was the war-tortured earth. He, Private Paul Jonas, deserter, traitor, was clinging to that latter darkness like a flea on the back of a dying dog.

He was on his belly. No surprise there. He had been on his belly forever, hadn't he?

He dug in with his elbows and feet and pushed himself forward through the muck. The years' long bombardment had churned the mud of No Man's Land into a million peaks and troughs, an endless, frozen, shit-brown sea. He had been crawling through it for hours, awkward and mechanical as an injured beetle. Every cell in his body screamed for him to hurry, to get clear, to drag himself out of this no-place, this bleak and lifeless land, but there was no way he could move faster—to rise was to expose himself to eyes and guns on either side. He could only crawl, inch by miserable inch, groveling his way beneath shrapnel and storm.

Something hard was under his fingers. A flash of lightning revealed the skeletal head of a horse pushing up from the mud, like something born of sowing the Hydra's teeth. He jerked back the hand that had rested on its snout, on the stony teeth exposed behind shriveled lips. Its eyes were long gone, the sockets full of mud. A crooked fence of boards protruded from the earth behind it, the remains of the ammunition limber it had drawn. Strange to think—almost *impossible* to think—that this hellish place had once been a country road, a quiet part of quiet France. A horse like this would have clopped by with wagon in tow, taking a farmer to market, delivering milk or mail to village houses. When things made sense. Things *had* made sense once. He couldn't quite remember such a time, but he could not let himself believe anything else. The world had been an ordered place. Now country roads, houses, cart-horses, all the things that once had separated civilization from encroaching darkness were being crushed together into a homogeneous primordial ooze.

Houses, horses, people. The past, the dead. In the off and on glare of lightning he saw himself surrounded by the twisted corpses of soldiers—his fellow Tommies perhaps, or Germans: there was no way to tell. Nationality, dignity, breath, all had been ripped away. Like a Christmas pudding stuffed with shillings, the mud was salted with incomplete fractions of life—bits of arms and legs, torsos with extremities cauterized by shellblast, boots with feet still in them, rags of uniform glued to shreds of skin. Other, more complete bodies lay among the pieces, bomb-broken and flung like dolls, first swallowed by the ocean of viscous soil and then exposed by the driving rain. Eyes stared blankly, mouths gaped; they were drowning, all drowning in muck. And everything everywhere, whether it had once lived or not, was the same horrible excremental color.

It was the Slough of Despond. It was the ninth circle of hell. And if there was no salvation at the end of it, then the universe was a terrible, ill-constructed joke.

Shivering and moaning, Paul crawled on, his back against the angry sky.

A tremendous concussion knocked him down into the ooze. The ground lurched, engulfing him.

As he swam back toward the air, he heard another whistling shriek and the earth heaved again. Two hundred yards away the impact sent up a huge gout of mud. Small things hissed past. Paul screamed as field guns drumrolled behind the German lines, painting an arc of fire across the horizon that threw the vast field of mud spikes into sharp relief. Another shell struck. Muck flew. Something dragged a burning claw across his back, tearing shirt and skin, and Paul's scream climbed toward the thunder and then stopped as his face dropped into the mud again.

For a moment he was certain he was dying. His heart stuttered, beating so rapidly that it almost tripped over itself. He flexed his fingers, then moved his arm. It felt as though someone had opened him up and wiggled a knitting needle into his spine, but everything seemed to be working. He dragged himself forward half a yard, then froze as a shell crashed down behind him, blowing another great whirlpool of soil and body parts into the air. He could move. He was alive.

He curled up in a puddle of water and clasped his hands to his head, trying to shut out the maddening roar of the guns, louder by far than the thunder had been. He lay as motionless as any of the corpses littering No Man's Land, his mind empty of all but terror, and waited for the bombardment to abate. The earth rocked. Red-hot shrapnel buzzed over his head. The eleven-inch shells from the German guns kept coming down in mindless, jackhammer repetition—he felt their heavy tread as they walked their way from one side of the British trenches to the other, leaving behind craters, splinters, and pulverized flesh.

The excruciating noise would not stop.

It was hopeless. The bombardment would never end. This was the crescendo, the finale, the moment when the war would finally set the skies themselves on fire and the clouds would fall sparking and blazing from the heavens like burning curtains.

Get out or die. There was no cover here, nowhere to hide. Paul turned onto his stomach once more and began to slither forward as the earth bucked beneath him. Get out or die. Ahead, the ground sloped away to a lowland where once, years ago, before the shells had begun falling, a stream might have run. At the bottom lay a tongue of mist. Paul saw only a place to hide, a white murkiness that he could draw over him like a blanket. Hidden, he would sleep.

Sleep.

The single word rose in his battered mind like a flame in a dark room. Sleep. To lie down and shut out the noise, the fear, the unceasing misery.

Sleep.

He reached the top of the gentle slope, then tipped himself over and slithered downhill. All his senses were bent on the cool white fog lying at the bottom of the depression. As he crawled through the outlying layer of mist, the roar of the guns did seem to grow less, although the world still shuddered. He struggled forward until the fog closed above his head, shutting out the darts of red light crossing the sky. He was completely surrounded in cool whiteness. The hammering in his head quieted.

He slowed. Something lay before him in the murk—more than one thing—dark, oblong shapes scattered along the slope. He dragged himself forward, eyes painfully wide and smarting with dirt, trying to see what they were.

Coffins. Dozens of coffins were strewn along the hillside, some protruding from the sheared mud like ships breasting a wave. Many had spilled their occupants: pale winding sheets trailed down the shallow slope, as though the coffin owners too were fleeing the war.

The guns still boomed, but they were strangely muted. Paul drew himself into a crouch, staring, and something like sanity began to come back. This was a graveyard. The ground had fallen away, revealing an old burial ground, its markers long since smashed to flinders. The dead had been spat out by an earth now surfeited with death.

Paul pushed himself deeper into the fog. These corpses were now as homeless as those of his brothers above, a hundred tragic stories that would go unheard in the clamor of mass mortality. Here a mummified head sagged above the mud-spattered whiteness of a bridal dress, jaw dangling as though its owner called to the groom who had left her alone at Death's altar. Nearby, a small skeletal hand protruded from beneath the lid of a tiny coffin—Baby had learned to say byebye.

Paul's sobbing laughter almost choked him.

Death was everywhere, in uncountable variety. This was the Grim Reaper's wonderland, the dark one's private park. One sprawled skeleton wore the uniform of an earlier army, as though it crawled toward the muster bugle of the present conflict. A rotted winding sheet revealed two mummified children wrapped together, mouths round holes like hymn-singing angels on a sentimental card. Old and young, big and small, the civilian corpses had been cast forth in a macabre democracy to join the foreign strangers dying in throngs above, all to pass together into the blending mud.

Paul struggled on through the foggy village of dead. The sounds of war grew more distant, which drove him ever forward. He would find a place where the conflict did not penetrate. Then he would sleep.

A coffin at the edge of the ditch caught his eye. Dark hair trailed from it and wavered in the wind, like the fronds of some deep-sea plant. The lid was gone, and as he crawled nearer he could see the face of its female occupant nestled in the winding sheet, curiously undecayed. Something about her bloodless profile made him pause.

He stared. Quivering, he approached the coffin, laying his hands on the muddy box so he could draw himself up to crouch above it. His hand pulled down the decaying muslin.

It was her. *Her.* The angel of his dreams. Dead in a box, wrapped in a stained shroud and lost to him forever. His insides contracted—for a moment he thought he might fall into himself, shrink into nothingness like straw in a flame. Then she opened her eyes—black, black and empty—and her pale lips moved.

"Come to us, Paul."

He shrieked and leaped up, but caught his foot on the coffin handle and tumbled face-first back into the mud. He scrambled away, thrashing through the clinging muck like a wounded beast. She did not rise or follow, but her quiet, summoning voice trailed him through the fog until his own blackness swallowed him.

He was in a strange place, stranger than any he had yet seen. It was . . . nothing. The truth of No Man's Land.

Paul sat up, feeling curiously numb. His head still throbbed with the echoes of battle, but he was surrounded by silence. He wore a coating of mud inches thick, but the ground on which he lay was neither wet nor dry, neither hard nor soft. The fog through which he had crawled had thinned, but he could see nothing in any direction except pearl-white nothingness.

He rose on trembling legs. Had he escaped? The dead angel, the village of coffins—had those been a shell-shocked dream?

He took a step, then a dozen more. Everything remained as it was. He expected to see recognizable shapes appear through the mist at any moment—trees, rocks, houses—but the emptiness seemed to move with him.

After what seemed an hour of fruitless walking he sat down and wept, weak tears of exhaustion and confusion. Was he dead? Was this purgatory? Or worse, for one could at least hope to work one's way out of purgatory, was this where one went after death, to stay?

"Help me!" There was no trace of an echo—his voice went flatly out and did not return. "Help me, someone!" He sobbed again. "What have I done?"

No answer came. Paul curled up on the not-ground and pressed his face into his hands.

Why had the dreams brought him to this place? The angel had seemed to care for him, but how could kindness lead to this? Unless every man's death was kind, but every man's afterlife was unremittingly bleak.

Paul clung to the self-inflicted dark. He could not bear to see the mist any more. The angel's pale face appeared to his mind's eye, not cold and empty as it had been in the plundered graveyard, but the sweetly mournful visage that had haunted his dreams for so long.

Was it *all* madness? Was he even here in this place at all, or was his body lying in the bottom of the muddy trench or beside the other failures in the morgue of a field hospital?

Slowly, almost without his conscious attention, his hand stole across his muddy uniform blouse. As it reached his breast pocket, he suddenly knew what it—what he himself—sought. He stopped, terrified to move farther, for fear of what he might discover.

But there is nothing else left.

His hand dipped into the pocket and closed around it. When he opened his eyes, then brought it out into the dim light it shimmered, iridescent green.

It was real.

As Paul stared at the feather clutched in his fist, something else began to shimmer. Not far away—or what seemed, in this unfathomable place, not far away—the fog smoldered with a light like molten gold. He scrambled to his feet, fatigue and injuries almost forgotten.

Something—a kind of doorway or hole—was forming in the mist. He could see nothing within its circumference but shifting amber light that moved like oil on water, yet he knew with a sudden, unshakable certainty that there was something on the other side. It led to *somewhere else.* He stepped toward the golden glow.

"*What's your hurry, Jonesie?*"

"*Yes, you wouldn't run off without telling your mates, would you?*"

Paul stopped, then slowly turned. Coming forward out of the blanketing mist were two shapes, one large, one small. He saw something glint on one of the dim faces.

"F–Finch? Mullet?"

The big one honked a laugh. "We've come to show you the way home."

The terror that had dissipated now came flooding back. He took a step nearer to the golden glow.

"Don't do that!" Finch said sharply. When he spoke again, his tone was softer. "Come on, old mate, don't make it harder on yourself. If you come back peaceful-like—well, it's just shell shock. Maybe you'll even get a little time in hospital to pull yourself together."

"I . . . I don't want to come back."

"Desertion, is it?" Mullet came nearer. He seemed bigger than before, immensely round and strangely muscled. His mouth wouldn't close all the way because there were too many teeth. "Oh, that's very bad, very bad indeed."

"Be reasonable, Jonesie." Finch's spectacles threw back the light, obscuring his eyes. "Don't throw it all away. We're your friends. We want to help you."

Paul's breath grew short. Finch's voice seemed to pull at him. "But . . ."

"I know you've had a bad time," the small man said. "You've been confused. Felt like you were going mad, even. You just need rest. Sleep. We'll take care of you."

He did need rest. Finch was right. They would help him, of course they would. His friends. Paul swayed but did not retreat as they came nearer. The golden glow flickered behind him, growing dimmer.

"Just give me that thing in your hand, old mate." Finch's voice was soothing, and Paul found himself holding the feather out to him. "That's right, pass it here." The golden light grew fainter, and the reflection on Finch's spectacles grew fainter, too, so that Paul could see through the lenses. Finch had no eyes.

"No!" Paul staggered back a step and raised his hands. "Leave me alone!"

The two figures before him wavered and distorted, Finch growing even leaner and more spidery, Mullet swelling until his head disappeared down between his shoulders.

"You belong to us!" Finch shouted. He looked nothing like a man any longer.

Paul Jonas clutched the feather tightly, turned, and jumped into the light.

CHAPTER 7

The Broken String

NETFEED/NEWS: Fish-Killer Feared in Pacific
(visual: Scottish fishermen in port, emptying nets)
VO: The dinoflagellate parasite responsible for the North Atlantic die-off that
killed hundreds of millions of fish a decade ago has reappeared in mutated
form in some Pacific Ocean spawning grounds.
(visual: dead fish with severely ulcerated skin)
UN authorities fear that this version of the organism may be resistant to the
laboratory-constructed virus with which the dinoflagellate's reign of terror
was halted last time . . .

Stephen lay motionless, sunk in the smeary depths of the plastic tent like a fly entombed in amber. He had tubes in his nose, his mouth, his arms. He looked, Renie thought, as though he were slowly becoming part of the hospital. Another machine. Another appliance. She clenched her fists hard, fighting the swell of despair.

!Xabbu put his hands into the gloves attached to the tent wall, then looked up at her, asking permission. All she could do was nod her head. She did not trust herself to speak.

"He is very far away," the little man whispered. It was strange to see his light-skinned Bushman features peering from behind a plastic faceplate. Renie felt a pang of fear for him, a sudden spike that

punched through even the misery of seeing her brother's unchanged
state. VR, quarantine—every new experience she gave !Xabbu seemed
to demonstrate another way not to touch. Would it all sicken him?
Was his spirit already weakening?

She pushed the thought away. !Xabbu was the sanest, most well-
grounded person she knew. She was worrying because her brother
and her friend were much the same size, and both were sealed away
behind layers of plastic. It was her own helplessness pulling at her.
She moved forward and touched !Xabbu's shoulder with her gloved
hand. In a way, since he was touching Stephen, she was touching her
brother also.

!Xabbu's fingers traced the lines of Stephen's sleeping face, their
movements careful and precise in a way that suggested *doing* something rather than merely feeling, then moved down his neck to his
breastbone. "He is very far away," he said again. "It is like a powerful
medicine trance."

"What's that?"

!Xabbu did not reply. His hands remained on Stephen's chest, just
as hers stayed on the little man's shoulder. For long moments all the
parts of the small human chain were still, then Renie felt a gentle
motion: within the baggy confines of the Ensuit, !Xabbu had begun
to sway. Gentle sounds, like the sonorous hum and click of insects in
tall grass, rose and mixed with the mechanical noises of life support.
After a few seconds, she realized that !Xabbu was singing.

The little man was silent as they left the hospital. At the bus stop
he remained standing when Renie sat down, staring at the passing
cars as though looking for an answer to some difficult question in the
patterns of traffic.

"A medicine trance is not easy to explain," he said. "I have been to
city schools. I can tell you what they say—a self-induced hypnotic
state. Or I can tell you what I grew up with in the Okavango
Swamps—that the medicine man has gone to a place where he can
talk with the spirits, even the gods." He closed his eyes and was quiet
for a time, as though preparing for some trance state of his own. At
last he opened his eyes again and smiled. "The more I learn of science,
the more I respect the mysteries of my people."

A bus pulled up and disgorged a weary-looking group of passengers
who all seemed to hobble, shuffle, or limp as they made their way up
the ramp toward the hospital. Renie squinted at the bus until she

located the route number. It was not the one they wanted. Obscurely angry, she turned away. She felt unsettled, like the sky before a storm.

"If you mean that science is useless, I can't agree with you . . . unless you're talking about medical science, that is. Bloody worthless." She sighed. "No, that's not fair."

!Xabbu shook his head. "I do not mean that at all, Renie. It is hard to express. I suppose it is that the more things I read about the discoveries of scientists, the more I respect what my people already know. They have not come to these understandings in the same ways, in closed laboratories and with the help of thinking machines, but there is something to be said for a million years of trial and error—especially in the swamps or the Kalahari Desert, where instead of just spoiling an experiment, a mistake is likely to kill you."

"I don't . . . what understandings are you talking about?"

"The wisdom of our parents, grandparents, ancestors. In each individual life, it seems, we must first reject that wisdom, then later come to appreciate it." His smile returned, but it was small and thoughtful. "As I said, it is hard to explain . . . and you look tired, my friend."

Renie sat back. "I am tired. But there's lots to do." She moved, trying to find a comfortable position on the molded plastic bench. Whoever made them seemed to intend the things for something other than sitting: no matter how you arranged yourself, you were never quite comfortable. She gave up and slid forward to perch on the edge, then pulled out a cigarette. The flame-tab was defective, and she wearily groped in her bag for her lighter. "What were you singing? Did it have something to do with a medicine trance?"

"Oh, no." He seemed mildly scandalized, as if she had accused him of a theft. "No, it was merely a song. A sad song made by one of my people. I sang it because I was unhappy seeing your brother lost and wandering so far from his family."

"Tell me about it."

!Xabbu let his brown eyes drift to the crush of traffic once more. "It is a song of mourning for the loss of a friend. It is about the string game, too—do you know it?"

Renie held up her fingers in an imaginary cat's cradle. !Xabbu nodded.

"I do not know if I can make the exact words in English. Something like this:

> *"There were people, some people*
> *Who broke the string for me*

And so
This place is now a sad place for me,
Because the string is broken.
"The string broke for me,
And so
This place does not feel to me
As it used to feel,
Because the string is broken.

"This place feels as if it stood open before me
Empty
Because the string has broken
And so
This place is an unhappy place
Because the string is broken."

He fell silent.

"Because the string broke for me . . ." Renie repeated. The quietness of the sorrow, its very understatement, made her own feelings of loss come rushing up inside her. Four weeks—a full month now. Her baby brother had been sleeping for a month, sleeping like the dead. A sob shook her body and tears forced their way out. She tried to push the misery back, but it would not be suppressed. She wept harder. She tried to speak, to explain herself to !Xabbu, but couldn't. To her embarrassment and horror, she realized she had lost control, that she was having a helpless crying fit on a public bus bench. She felt naked and humiliated.

!Xabbu did not put his arms around her, or tell her over and over that things would be fine, that everything would work out. Instead, he seated himself beside her on the smooth plastic seat and took her hands in his, then waited for the storm to pass.

It did not pass quickly. Every time Renie thought it was over, that she had regained control over her emotions, another convulsion of misery broke across her and set her weeping again. Through tear-blurred eyes she saw another busload of passengers delivered to the curb. Several stared at the tall, weeping woman being comforted by a little Bushman in an antique suit. The idea of how odd she and !Xabbu must look tripped her up; soon she was laughing as well, although the weeping had not stopped or even weakened. A small, separate part of her that seemed to hover somewhere in the center of the maelstrom wondered if she would ever stop, or if she would instead be stuck here like a hung program, switching back and forth from hilarity to grief until the sky grew dark and everyone went home.

At last it ended—more from fatigue than any recovery of control, Renie noted with disgust. !Xabbu released her hands. She could not look at him yet, so she reached into her coat pocket and found a crumpled piece of tissue she had used earlier to blot her lipstick, then did her best to dry her face and wipe her nose. When she did meet her friend's eyes, it was with a kind of defiance, as though daring him to take advantage of her weakness.

"Is the sadness less painful now?"

She turned away again. He seemed to think it was perfectly natural to make an idiot of yourself out in front of the Durban Outskirt Medical Facility. Maybe it was. The shame had already diminished, and was now only a faint reproving voice at the back of her mind.

"I'm better," she said. "I think we missed our bus."

!Xabbu shrugged. Renie leaned over and took his hand in hers and squeezed it, just for a moment. "Thank you for being patient with me." His calm brown eyes made her nervous. What was she supposed to do, be proud of herself for breaking down? "One thing. One thing in that song."

"Yes?" He was watching her carefully. She couldn't undersand why, but she couldn't take the scrutiny. Not now, not with swollen eyelids and a running nose. She looked down at her own hands, now safely back in her lap.

"Where it said, *'There were people, some people, who broke the string for me'.* . . . Well, there *are* people—there must be."

!Xabbu blinked. "I do not understand."

"Stephen isn't just . . . sick. I don't believe that any more. In fact, I never really believed it, although I could never make sense out of the feeling. *Someone*—some people, like in the song—did this to him. I don't know who, or how, or why, but I know it." Her laugh was strained. "I guess that's what all the crazy people say. 'I can't explain it, I just know it's true.' "

"You think this because of the research? Because of what we saw in the library?"

She nodded, straightening up. She felt strength coming back. Action—that was what was needed. Crying was useless. Things had to be *done*. "That's right. I don't know what it means, but it has something to do with the net."

"But you said the net is not a real place—that what happens there is not real. If someone eats there, it does not nourish them. How could something on the net cause an injury, send a young child into a sleep from which he will not wake?"

"I don't know. But I'm going to find out." Renie suddenly smiled at how the most critical times in your life always threw you back onto clichés. That was the kind of thing people said in detective stories—it had probably been said at least once in the book she was reading to Stephen. She stood. "I don't want to wait for another bus and I'm sick of this bench. Let's go get something to eat—if you don't mind, I mean. You've wasted a whole day on me and my problems already. What about your work for class?"

!Xabbu showed her his sly grin. "I work very hard, Ms. Sulaweyo. I have already completed this week's assignments."

"Then come with me. I need food and coffee—especially coffee. I'll leave my father to fend for himself. It will do him good."

As she set off down the sidewalk, she felt lighter than she had for weeks, as though she had thrown off a soaking garment.

"There must be something we can learn," she said. "All problems have solutions. You just have to work at them."

!Xabbu did not reply to this, but sped his pace to keep up with her longer strides. The gray afternoon warmed as points of glowing orange bloomed all around them. The streetlights were beginning to come on.

"**H**ello, Mutsie. May we come in please?"

Eddie's mother stood in the doorway, looking from Renie to !Xabbu with a mixture of interest and suspicion. "What do you want?"

"I want to talk to Eddie."

"What for? Did he do something?"

"I just want to talk to him." Renie was beginning to lose her temper, which would not be a good way to start. "Come on, you know me. Don't keep me standing at your door like a stranger."

"Sorry. Come inside." She stepped aside to let them pass, then indicated the slightly concave sofa covered with a brightly-colored throw rug. Renie nudged !Xabbu toward it. Not that there would be anywhere else to sit—the apartment was as cluttered as the night Stephen had gotten ill.

Probably the same clutter, Renie thought, then chided herself for mean-spiritedness.

"The boy's taking a bath." Mutsie didn't offer to bring them anything, and didn't sit down herself. The moment hung awkwardly. Eddie's two sisters lay prostrated like worshipers in front of the wallscreen, watching two men in brightly-colored jumpsuits floundering in a vat of some sticky substance. Mutsie kept looking at it over her shoulder; she clearly wanted to sit down and watch. "I'm sorry about Stephen," she said at last. "He's a good boy. How is he?"

"Just the same." Renie heard the tightness in her own voice. "The doctors don't know. He's just . . . asleep." She shook her head, then tried to smile. It wasn't Mutsie's fault. She wasn't a great mother, but Renie didn't think what happened to Stephen had anything to do with that. "Maybe Eddie could come with me sometime to see him. The doctor said it would be good for him to hear familiar voices."

Mutsie nodded her head but looked uncertain. A moment later she went into the hallway. "Eddie! Hurry up, boy. Stephen's sister wants to talk to you." She emerged shaking her head, as though she had performed a difficult and thankless task. "He stay in there for hours. Sometimes I look around and say, 'Where is that boy? Is he dead or something?' " She stopped herself. Her eyes grew round. "Sorry, Irene."

Renie shook her head. She could almost feel !Xabbu's eyebrow lifting. She had never told him her real name. "It's okay, Mutsie. Oh, and I didn't introduce !Xabbu. He's my student. He's helping me do some research to see if we can find out something about Stephen's condition."

Mutsie cast an eye across the Bushman on her sofa. "What do you mean, research?"

"I'm trying to see if there's something the doctors missed—some article in a medical magazine, something." Renie decided to leave it there. Mutsie had no doubt already made up her mind who and what !Xabbu was to Renie: suggesting that they were trying to find out whether the net might have made Stephen ill would only make the story sound even more feeble. "I just want to do everything I can."

Mutsie's attention was drawn to the wallscreen again. The two men, covered with sticky ooze, were now trying to climb the sides of a rocking, transparent vat. "Of course," she said. "You do everything you can."

Renie reflected on the worth of this wisdom, coming from a woman who had once sent her children on the bus to her sister's house for the weekend without remembering that her sister had moved across Pinetown. Renie knew because the children had fetched up on her own doorstep and she had wasted an entire weekend afternoon tracking down the aunt's new address and delivering them to it.

Oh, yes, Mutsie, you and me, we do everything we can.

Eddie appeared from the back, hair wet and close to his head, wearing a pair of striped pajamas that were far too big: the cuffs, rolled several times, still dragged on the floor. His head was held low, as though he anticipated a whipping.

"Come in here, boy. Say hello to Irene."

" 'Lo, Renie."

"Hello, Eddie. Sit down, will you? I want you to answer some questions for me."

"People from the hospital asked him all kinds of questions already," Mutsie said over her shoulder. She sounded almost proud. "Some man come, he took the food out of the refrigerator, made notes."

"I have other things I want to ask about. Eddie, I want you to think very carefully before you answer me, okay?"

He looked to his mother, begging her further intervention, but she had already turned back to the wallscreen. Eddie sat down on the floor in front of Renie and !Xabbu. He plucked one of his little sisters' action figures from the threadbare carpet and began to twist it in his hands.

Renie explained who !Xabbu was, but Eddie didn't seem too interested. Renie remembered how she had felt in these situations at the same age, that adults were to be considered part of a shapeless enemy mass until proven otherwise.

"I don't blame you for anything, Eddie. I'm just trying to find out what happened to Stephen."

He still wouldn't look up. "He's sick."

"I know that. But I want to find out what made him that way."

"We didn't do anything. I told you that."

"Not that night, maybe. But I know you and Stephen and Soki were messing around on the net, going places you shouldn't go. I *know*, Eddie, remember?"

"Yeah." He shrugged.

"So tell me about it."

Eddie twisted at the doll in his hands until Renie worried that he might pull it apart—the damn things were expensive, and she ought to know, having supplied Stephen with more *Netsurfer Detectives* figures than she wished to count. "Masker" was particularly prone to damage, since he had a fragile, arch-exotic plastic hairstyle at least half his own height.

"Everybody else did it," he said at last. "We told you. Just tapping and napping."

"Everybody else did what? Got into Inner District?"

"Yeah."

"What about that place . . . Mister J's? Does everybody go there, too?"

"Yeah. Well, not everybody. A lot of the older guys talk about it."

Renie sat back, giving up on her attempt to force eye contact. "And a lot of them are probably lying. What have you heard about the place that made you want to go there?"

"What kind of place is this?" !Xabbu asked.

"Not very nice. It's on the net—a virtual club, like that place I took you is a virtual café." She turned back to Eddie. "What do the older kids say about it?"

"That . . . that you can see stuff there. Get stuff." He looked over at his mother, and even though she seemed enthralled with the two sticky men smacking each other with long glowing poles, he fell silent.

Renie leaned forward. "*What* stuff? Damn it, Eddie, I need to find out."

"Guys say that you can . . . feel things. Even if you don't have the flack."

"Flack?" A new netboy term. They changed so quickly.

"The . . . the stuff so you can touch what's on the net."

"Tactors? Sensory receptors?"

"Yeah, the good stuff. Even if you don't have it, there's things in Mister J's you can feel. And there's . . . I don't know. Guys say all kinds of. . . ." He trailed off again.

"Tell me what they say!"

But Eddie was clearly uncomfortable talking to an adult about back-room netboy gossip. This time it was Renie who turned to Eddie's mother for help, but Mutsie had relieved herself of responsibility and was not going to take it back.

Several other lines of questioning produced little new information. They had gone into the club in search of some of these whispered-about experiences, and to "see" things—Renie assumed it was por-nography of some kind, either sex or violence—but had instead gotten lost and wandered for hours through Mister J's. Parts of it had been very frightening and disorienting, others just interestingly weird, but Eddie claimed he could remember little of what they had actually seen. At last some men, including an unpleasant fat man—or a sim that looked like one—sent them downstairs to a special room. Soki had fallen into some kind of trap, and the other two had somehow escaped and called Renie.

"And you can't remember any better than that? Even if it might help Stephen get better again?"

For the first time all evening the boy met and held Renie's gaze. "I'm not dupping."

"Lying," she explained to !Xabbu. "I didn't say you were, Eddie. But I'm hoping you can remember a little better. Please try."

He shrugged, but now that she could see his eyes clearly, she saw something elusive in his gaze. *Was* she sure he was telling the truth? He seemed frightened, and they were long past the point when he should have feared punishment from Renie.

"Well, if you remember anything else, call me. Please, it's very important." She got up from the couch. Eddie started to move toward the hallway, head down again. "One other thing," she said. "What about Soki?"

Eddie turned to look at her, eyes wide. "He got sick. He's at his aunt's."

"I know. Did he get sick because of what happened when you were on the net together? Tell me, Eddie."

He shook his head. "I don't know. He didn't come back to school."

Renie surrendered. "Go on." Eddie, like a cork held underwater and then finally released, almost sprang from the room. Renie turned to Mutsie, who lay on the carpet beside her daughters. "Do you have Soki's aunt's number?"

Mutsie clambered to her feet, sighing heavily, as though she had been asked to carry several hundredweight of stone up the Drakensberg Mountains.

"Maybe it's around here somewhere."

Renie looked at !Xabbu to share her exasperation, but the little man was staring at the wallscreen in reluctant fascination, watching one of the sticky men trying to catch, kill, and eat a live chicken. The sound of audience laughter, captured and processed until it echoed like the roar of machinery, filled the small room.

The last classes of the day were being released into the halls. Renie watched the kaleidoscopic movement of color across the office windows as she reflected on human beings and their need for contact.

Back at the end of the previous century, people had been predicting that school would be uniformly taught over video links, or even that teachers might be replaced entirely by interactive teaching machines and hypertext infobanks.

Of course, people had been wrong about that sort of thing before. Renie remembered something one of her university instructors had told her: *"When they marketed frozen food a hundred years ago, the professional predictors said people would never cook again. Instead, thirty years later they were growing their own herbs and baking their own bread from scratch in well-to-do suburbs all over the First World."*

Similarly, it seemed unlikely that human beings would ever grow out of their need for personal contact. Live lectures and tutorials were not quite as large a part of the learning experience as they had once been, when books were the only form of stored information, but those who had claimed that such time- and resource-wasteful human contact would vanish had obviously been wrong.

One of Renie's pre-law friends from university had married a policeman. Before she and the friend lost touch she had gone to dinner with them a few times, and she remembered the husband saying much the same thing about criminology: no matter how many gadgets were invented for discerning truth, analyzers of heartbeat, brainwaves, voice stress, or electrochemical changes to the skin, police always felt most secure when they could look a suspect in the eye and ask questions.

So the need for real contact was universal, it seemed. However many changes had taken place in the human environment—most of them authored by humanity itself—the human brain was still much the same organ that everyone's ancestors had carried around the Olduvai Gorge a million years ago. It imported information and tried to make sense of it. There was no discrimination between "real" and "unreal," not at the most basic, instinctual levels of fear and desire and self-preservation.

Renie had begun pondering these things because of Stephen's friend Soki. She had reached his mother on the phone early that morning, but Patricia Mwete—whom Renie had never known well—was adamant that Renie should not come to the house. Soki had been sick, she said, and was just starting to get better. It would upset him. After a long and somewhat heated discussion, Patricia had finally agreed to let her talk to Soki on the phone when he got back from some undefined "appointment" that afternoon.

At first Renie's chain of thought had been prompted by the unsatisfactory nature of phone contact compared to an actual meeting, but now, as she considered the larger issues, she began to realize that if she continued to search for the cause of Stephen's illness, especially if it stemmed from his use of the net, she was going to be spending a great deal of time trying to separate unreality from reality.

Certainly it was impossible at this point to even think of sharing her thoughts with the authorities, medical or legal. VR had received alarmist press from time to time, especially in the early days—all new technologies did—and there were certainly cases of post-traumatic stress syndrome in users of extremely violent simulations, but none of the accepted case histories looked anything like Stephen's. Also, despite her own not-quite-definable certainty that something had happened to him online, there was no real proof in the correlation of net usage to incidence of coma. A thousand other factors could, and would, be suggested as equally likely to establish the pattern.

But the even more frightening thing was the idea of trying to establish truth on the net itself. A police detective with the full weight of law and training on her side would have trouble working through the masks and illusions that net users constructed for themselves, not to mention their UN-mandated privacy rights.

And me? she thought. *If I'm right, and that's where it takes me, I'll be like Alice trying to solve a murder in Wonderland.*

A knock at her office door interrupted the gloomy thoughts. !Xabbu poked his head in. "Renie? Are you busy?"

"Come on in. I was going to mail you. I really appreciate you spending so much time with me yesterday. I feel very bad about taking you away from your home and your studies."

!Xabbu looked slightly embarrassed. "I would like to be your friend. Friends help other friends. Also, I must confess to you, it is a strange and interesting situation."

"That may be, but you have your own life. Don't you usually spend your evenings studying in the library?"

He smiled. "The school was closed."

"Of course." She made a face and pulled a cigarette from her coat. "The bomb threat. It's a bad sign when they get so common that I don't even remember we had one until someone mentions it. And you know something? No one else did until you. Just another day in the big city."

There was another knock. One of Renie's colleagues, the woman who taught the entry-level programming classes, had come to borrow a book. She talked the whole time she was in the office, telling some drawn-out story about an amazing restaurant her boyfriend had taken her to. She left without ever looking at or addressing a remark to

!Xabbu, as though he were a piece of furniture. Renie was chagrined by the woman's manners, but the small man appeared not to notice.

"Have you thought any more about what you learned last night?" he asked when they had the office to themselves. "I am still not quite sure what you think could have happened to your brother. How could something unreal have such an effect? Especially if his equipment was very basic. If something was harming him, what would prevent him from taking off the headset?"

"He *did* take it off—or at least he didn't have it on when I found him. And I don't have an answer for you. I wish I did." The difficulty, perhaps even the ridiculous impossibility, of finding the answers to Stephen's illness on the net suddenly made her terribly weary. She ground out her cigarette and watched the last of the smoke twisting toward the ceiling. "This could all be the hallucinations of a grieving relative. Sometimes people need reasons for things, even when there are no reasons. That's what makes people believe in conspiracies or religions—if there's any difference. The world is just too complicated, so they need simple explanations."

!Xabbu looked at her with what felt to Renie like mild disapproval. "But there *are* patterns to things. Both science and religion agree on that. So what is left is the honorable but difficult task of trying to decide which patterns are real and what they mean."

She stared at him for a moment, surprised again by his perceptiveness. "You're right, of course," she said. "So, I suppose I might as well keep looking at this particular pattern and see if it means anything. Do you want to sit in while I call Stephen's other friend?"

"If it will not interfere."

"Shouldn't. I'll tell her you're a friend from the Poly."

"I hope I *am* 'a friend from the Poly.' "

"You are, but I'm hoping she'll think you're another instructor. You'd better take off that tie—you look like something out of an old movie."

!Xabbu looked a little disappointed. He was proud of what he saw as the formal correctness of his dress—Renie hadn't found the heart to tell him that he was the only person under the age of sixty she had ever seen wearing a tie—but he complied, then pulled over a chair and sat beside her, his back very straight.

Patricia Mwete opened the line. She regarded !Xabbu with open suspicion, but was mollified by Renie's explanation. "Don't ask Soki too many questions," she warned. "He's tired—he's been sick." She was dressed rather formally herself. Renie vaguely remembered that she worked in some kind of financial institution, and guessed that she had just come back from work.

"I don't want to do anything that will upset him," Renie said. "But my brother is in a coma, Patricia, and no one knows why. I just want to find out anything I can."

The other woman's worried stiffness eased a little. "I know, Irene. I'm sorry. I'll call him."

When Soki arrived, Renie was a little surprised to see how very well he looked. He hadn't lost any weight—he had always been a little on the husky side—and his smile was quick and strong.

" 'Lo, Renie."

"Hello, Soki. I'm sorry to hear you've been ill."

He shrugged. His mother, just offscreen, said something Renie couldn't hear. "I'm okay. How's Stephen?"

Renie told him, and most of Soki's good humor evaporated. "I heard about it, but I thought maybe it was just for a little while, like that kid in our form who got a concussion. Is he going to die?"

She recoiled a little at the bluntness of the question. A moment passed before she could answer. "I don't think so, but I'm very worried about him. We don't know what's wrong. That's why I wanted to ask you some questions. Can you tell me anything about the things that you and Stephen and Eddie were doing on the net?"

Soki looked at her a little strangely, surprised by the question, then launched into a long description of various legitimate and quasi-legitimate netboy meanderings, punctuated every now and then by sounds of disapproval from his temporarily invisible mother.

"But what I really want to know about, Soki, is the last time, just before you got sick. When you three got into Inner District."

He looked at her blankly. "Inner District?"

"You know what that is."

"Certain. But we never got in there. I told you we tried."

"Are you saying you *never* went into the Inner District?"

The look on his young face hardened into anger. "Did Eddie say we did? Then he's duppy—duppy major!"

Renie paused, taken aback. "Soki, I had to go in and get Eddie and Stephen out. They said you were with them. They were worried about you, because they lost you on the net. . . ."

Soki's voice rose. "They're dupping!"

Renie was confused. Was he putting this on just because his mother was around? If so, he was doing a very convincing job: he seemed genuinely indignant. Or had Eddie and Stephen lied to her about Soki being with them? But why?

His mother leaned into the screen. "You're getting him upset, Irene. Why are you calling my boy a liar?"

She took a deep breath. "I'm *not*, Patricia, I'm just confused. If he wasn't with them, why would they lie about it? It didn't get them off the hook—Stephen still lost his net privileges." She shook her head. "I don't know what's going on, Soki. Are you sure you don't remember any of this? About getting into Inner District, about going to a place called Mister J's? About falling through some kind of door? Blue lights. . . ?"

"I've never been there!" He *was* angry, angry and scared, but he still didn't seem to be lying. A few drops of perspiration had appeared on his forehead. "Doors, blue lights . . . I never. . . !"

"That's enough, Irene!" said Patricia. "Enough!"

Before Renie could reply, Soki suddenly tipped his head back and made a strange gargling noise. His limbs became rigid and his entire body began to tremble violently; his mother grabbed at his shirt but failed to hold him as he slid off the chair and fell to the floor, thrashing. Staring at the screen, helplessly transfixed, Renie heard !Xabbu gasp beside her.

"God *damn* you, Irene Sulaweyo!" Patricia shouted. "He was getting better! You did this to him! Don't you ever call this house again!" She knelt beside her son and cradled his twitching head. A froth of spittle had already begun to form on his lips. *"Disconnect!"* she shouted, and the padscreen went dark. The last thing Renie saw were the white crescents of Soki's eyes. His pupils had rolled up beneath the lids.

She tried to phone back immediately, despite Patricia's angry words, but the line at Soki's aunt's house was accepting no incoming calls.

"That was a seizure!" Her fingers trembled as she pulled the flametab on a cigarette. "That was a grand mal seizure. But he's not epileptic—damn it, !Xabbu, I've known that child for years! And I had to play chaperone on enough field trips for Stephen's schools: they always tell you if one of the kids has major health problems." She was furious, although she didn't know why. She was also frightened, but the reasons for that were clear enough. "Something happened to him that day—the day I went to get them out of the Inner District. Then later it happened to Stephen, but worse. God, I wish Patricia would answer my questions."

!Xabbu's yellow-brown skin was a shade paler than usual. "We spoke before of the medicine trance," he said. "I felt I was witnessing such a thing. He had the look of someone meeting the gods."

"That was no trance, damn it, and there weren't any gods involved. That was a full-blown seizure." Renie was ordinarily careful not to tread on the beliefs of others, but just now she had very little patience for her friend's sorcerous notions. !Xabbu, apparently not offended, watched her as she stood and began pacing, rattling with anger and upset. "Something has interfered with that child's brain. A physical effect in the real world from something that happened online." She went to the office door and pushed it shut: Soki's collapse had intensified her feelings of being shadowed by some nameless danger. A more cautious part of her protested that she was leaping ahead much too fast, making far more assumptions than could be scientifically safe, but she wasn't listening to that part of herself at the moment.

She turned back to !Xabbu. "I'm going there. I have to."

"Where? To the Inner District?"

"To that club—Mister J's. Something happened to Soki there. I'm almost certain that Stephen tried to sneak back in while he was staying at Eddie's."

"If there is something bad there, something dangerous . . ." !Xabbu shook his head. "What would be the point? What would the people who own this virtual club have to gain?"

"It may be a byproduct of one of their unpleasant little amusements. Eddie said they're supposed to have experiences for sale that transcend whatever equipment the users own. Maybe they've found some way to give the illusion of greater sensory receptiveness. They might be using compacted subliminals, ultrasonics, something illegal that has these terrible side effects." She sat down and began excavating the mess of papers on her desk in search of an ashtray. "Whatever it is, if I'm going to find out I'll have to do it myself. It would take forever to get anyone to investigate—UNComm is the world's worst bureaucracy." She found the ashtray but her hands were shaking so hard that she almost dropped it.

"But will you not be exposing yourself to danger? What if you are affected as your brother was?" The little man's usually smooth forehead was wrinkled in a deep frown of worry.

"I'll be a lot more alert than Stephen was, and a lot better informed. Also, I'll just be looking for possible causes—enough to build a case to take to the authorities." She crushed out the cigarette. "And maybe if I figure out what happened, we'll be able to find some way to reverse the damage." She curled her hands into fists. "I want my brother back."

"You are determined to go."

She nodded, reaching for her pad. She was filled with a high and even slightly giddy sense of clarity. There were many things to do— she had to construct an alias, for one thing: if the people who owned the club had something to hide, she would be foolish to walk in under her own name and index. And she wanted to do some more research into the club itself and the company that owned it. Anything she could learn before going in might improve her chances of recognizing useful evidence once she was on the inside.

"Then you should not go unaccompanied," !Xabbu said quietly.

"But I . . . hold on. Are you talking about *you?* Coming with me?"

"You need a companion. What if something were to happen to you? Who would take your story to the proper authorities?"

"I'll leave notes, a letter. No, !Xabbu, you can't." Her engine was running now. She was ready to move and this seemed a distraction. She didn't want to take the small man. Her entry would have to be illegal, for one thing; if she were caught, her crime would be seen as much worse if she had dragged a student along with her.

"Exams begin in two days." !Xabbu almost seemed to have sensed her thoughts. "After that, I will no longer be your student."

"It's illegal."

"There would be a presumption that, newcomer to the big city that I am, stranger to modern ways, I did not understand I was doing wrong. If necessary, I would help to support that presumption."

"But you must have your own responsibilities!"

!Xabbu smiled sadly. "Someday, Renie, I will tell you of my responsibilities. But at the moment I certainly have a responsibility to a friend, and that is very important. Please, I ask you this as a favor— wait until exams are finished. That will give you time to prepare, in any case. I am sure there are more questions to be asked before you confront these people directly, more answers to be sought."

Renie hesitated. He was right. At least a few days of preparation would have to be fitted in around her work schedule anyway. But would he be an asset or a liability? !Xabbu returned her gaze with nonchalance. For all his youth and small stature, there was something almost daunting about the Bushman. His calm and confidence were very persuasive.

"Okay," she said at last. Being patient took a tremendous effort of will. "If Stephen doesn't get any worse, I'll wait. But if you come with me, you do what I say while we're in there. Understand that? You're very talented for a beginner—but you *are* a beginner."

!Xabbu's smile widened. "Yes, teacher. I promise."

"Then get out of my office and go study for those exams. I have work to do."

He bowed slightly and went out, the door closing silently behind him. The displaced air stirred the remnants of her cigarette smoke. Renie watched them eddy across the light from the window, a swirl of meaningless, ever-changing patterns.

That night the dream came again. !Xabbu stood at the edge of a great precipice, examining a pocket watch. This time it had sprouted legs and was walking on his palm like a flat silver beetle.

Something hovered in the air beyond the edge of the cliff, obscured by the mist but moving closer. It was a bird, she thought when she first saw the wings. No, it was an angel, a shimmering, smoke-blue presence with a human face.

The face was Stephen's. As he drifted nearer, he called to her, but his voice was lost in the rush of the wind. She cried out, startling !Xabbu, who turned and took a step backward, then tumbled over the edge and vanished.

Stephen looked down at where the little man had fallen, then lifted his tearful gaze to Renie. His mouth moved again, but she still could not hear him. A wind seemed to catch him, spreading his wings and making his whole being ripple. Before Renie could move, he was swept away into the mist.

CHAPTER 8

Dread

NET FEED/NEWS: Police Kill 22 Cannibal Cultists
(visual: body bags being laid out in front of building)
VO: Greek military police gunned down 22 members of the controversial
"Anthropophagi" cult, reputed to engage in ritual cannibalism, in a firefight
that turned the center of Náxos into a war zone. One policeman was killed
and two others injured in the fierce exchange.
(visual: bearded man holding up bone, shouting at audience)
Pending identification of the bodies, some badly burned, it is not known
whether the group's leader, Dimitrios Krysostomos—shown here in footage
recorded covertly by a government informant— was one of those killed in the
assault on the Sakristos. . . .

He liked the way he was moving—a slow lope, like a leopard just before it sprang. He upped the volume and the shuddering drums were everywhere. He felt good. The soundtrack running on his internal system made it all . . . perfect.

Camera, camera, he thought, tracking the woman with his eyes. She had a rump, that one—it made him smile just to see its purposeful movements, and to accent the smile he called in a trumpet glissando, sharp and cold as a knife. The silvery tones made him think about his own blade, a flatbacked Zeissing tendon-cutter, so he pulled it out for a close-up look as the trumpet wailed, a slow dissolve that brought him up hard as a rock all over.

The woman jounced down the steps to the underground parking lot, hurrying a little. That fine rump bobbed, drawing his eyes away from the knife. Pale woman, rich and gym-slender, hair the color of sand, all trussed up in those fancy white pants. She hadn't seen him yet, but she must know he was following, some animal part of her that, gazellelike, could smell the danger.

She looked back when she hit the bottom of the stairs, and for a brief instant her eyes widened. She knew. As he stepped down into the shadowy stairwell, he accelerated the drums; they bounced around inside his head, battering his skull like boxing gloves against the heavy bag. But his stride did not increase—he was too much of an artist for that. Better to go slow, slow. He turned down the volume of the skittering drums to enjoy the inevitability of the unfolding climax.

A sneaky counter-rhythm crept into the mix, an off-balance wallop like a failing heart. She was nearing her car now, fumbling for the remote. He tuned his vision until the woman and her heat were the only thing that glimmered in the dark garage. He sped up, prodding the music along so that more horns came in and the beats overlapped, building toward a crescendo.

His fingers descended lightly, but the shock of his touch still made her shriek and drop her bag. Its contents spilled across the cement floor—sought-for remote, expensive Singapore data pad, tubes of lip-gloss like bullet cartridges. The tumbled bag retained a heat-trace of her hand, already fading.

Aggression fought with fear across her face—anger that someone like him should touch her, should make her spill her oh-so-private life on the floor. But as he moved to close-up on her face, his own mouth twisting in a grin, fear won out.

"What do you want?" The voice hitched, barely audible above the clamor rattling through the bones of his skull. "You can have my card. Here, take it."

He smiled, lazy, and the crescendo flattened out and held. The knife flicked up, pausing for a moment against her cheek. "What does Dread want? Your stuff, sweetness. Your sweet stuff."

Later, when he had finished, he slid the music down to a sunset diminuendo—chirping sounds like crickets, a mournful violin. He stepped over the spreading wetness and picked up her bank card, grimacing. What fool would take something like that? Only an outback idiot would fix the mark of Cain to his own forehead.

He lifted the blade and traced the word "SANG" across the card's hologrammed surface in lines of red, then dropped it beside her.

"Who needs VR when you got RL?" he whispered. *"Real* real."

The god looked down from his high throne in the heart of Abydos-That-Was, across the bent backs of his thousand priests, prostrated before him like so many turtles sunning on the Nile's bank, past the smokes of a hundred thousand censers and the glimmering light of a hundred thousand lamps. His gaze passed even into the shadows at the farthest reaches of his vast throne room and on through the labyrinth of passages that separated throne room from City of the Dead, but still he could not locate the one he sought.

Impatient, the god tapped his flail on the gilded arm of his chair.

High Priest Something-or-Other—the god could not be bothered with the names of all his underlings: they came and went like grains of sand in a windstorm—crawled to the dais on which the golden chair rested and rubbed his face against the granite tiles.

"O, beloved of shining Ra, father of Horus, Lord of the Two Lands," the priest intoned, "who is master of all the people, who makes the wheat to grow, who died but lives; O great Lord Osiris, hear your humble servant."

The god sighed. "Speak."

"O beautiful shining one, O lord of green things, this humble one wishes to tell you of a certain unrest."

"Unrest?" The god leaned forward, bringing his dead face so close to the prostrate priest that the old worthy almost wet himself. "In *my* kingdom?"

The priest sputtered. "It is your two servants, Tefy and Mewat, who trouble your worshipers with their evil behavior. Surely it is not your wish that they should make drunken riot in the priests' sanctuaries and terrify the poor dancers in such a distressing way. And it is told that they perform even darker acts in their private chambers." The old priest cringed. "I speak to you only of what others already say, O King of the Uttermost West, beloved and undying Osiris."

The god sat back, his mask concealing amusement. He wondered how long it had taken this nonentity to work up the courage to broach the subject. He briefly contemplated feeding him to the crocodiles, but could not remember if this High Priest was a Citizen or merely a Puppet. Either way, it seemed too much trouble.

"I shall consider this," he said, and raised the crook and the flail. "Osiris loves his servants, the greatest and the smallest."

"Blessed is he, our Lord of Life and Death," the priest gabbled, crawling backward. He made excellent time considering the indignity of his posture—if he was a Citizen, he had mastered his simulation skills well. The god decided it was good he had not fed this one to the crocodiles—he might prove useful someday.

As for the god's wicked servants . . . well, that was their job description, was it not? Of course, it was preferable that the pair be wicked somewhere other than in his favorite and most intricately-constructed sanctuary. Let them make their holidays in Old Chicago or Xanadu. Then again, perhaps more than mere banishment was in order. A little discipline might not go amiss where the fat one and the thin one were concerned.

He looked up from these thoughts at the brazen cry of a trumpet and the tattoo of a shallow drum from the rear of the throne room. Yellow-green eyes glowed in the shadows there.

"At last," he said, and crossed his emblems on his chest once more.

The thing that stepped out of the darkness, and before which the priests parted like the great river swirling around an island, appeared to be almost eight feet tall. Its handsome brown body was muscular, long-limbed and vital; but from the neck up it was a beast. The jackal head swiveled, watching the priests scurry aside. The lips curled back, showing long white teeth.

"I have been waiting for you, Messenger of Death," said the god. "Waiting too long."

Anubis dropped to one knee, a cursory gesture, then rose. "I had things to do."

The god took a calming breath. He needed this creature and its particular talents. It was important to remember that. "Things?"

"Yes. Just a few matters." The long red tongue emerged and swept over the muzzle. In the candlelight, traces of what looked like flecks of blood showed dark against the long fangs.

The god grimaced in distaste. "Your heedless pursuits. You risk yourself needlessly. That is not pleasing."

"I do what I do, like always." The wide shoulders shrugged; the bright eyes closed in a lazy blink. "But you have summoned me, and I have come. What do you want, Grandfather?"

"Do not call me that. It is impertinent as well as inaccurate." The old god took another deep breath. It was hard not to react to the Messenger, whose every movement reeked with the insolence of destruction. "I have discovered something of great importance. I seem to have an adversary."

The teeth flashed again, briefly. "You wish me to kill him."

The god's delighted laughter was entirely genuine. "Young fool! If I knew who he was and could set you upon him, then he would not be worthy to be called my adversary. He *or* she." He chuckled.

The jackal head tipped to one side, like that of a scolded dog. "Then what do you want of me?"

"Nothing—yet. But soon there will be dark alleys aplenty for you to haunt, and many bones for you to crack in those great jaws."

"You seem . . . happy, Grandfather."

The god twitched, but let it pass. "Yes, I am happy. It has been so long since I have been tested, since any but the most feeble have opposed me. The mere fact that one has risen against me and has trifled in even the smallest of my plans, is a delight. My greatest test of all is coming, and if there were no opposition there would be no art."

"But you have no idea who it is. Perhaps it is someone . . . *inside* the Brotherhood."

"I have thought of it. It is possible. Not likely, but possible."

The green-gold eyes flared. "I could find out for you."

The thought of unleashing this rough beast in that particular chicken coop was diverting but unworkable. "I think not. You are not my only servant, and I have subtler means of gathering information."

The jackal's tone became petulant. "So you called me away from other things merely to tell me that you have no tasks for me?"

The god swelled until his mummy wrappings creaked and snapped, growing until his deathmask face loomed far above the throne room floor. The thousand priests groaned, like sleepers beset with the same bad dream. The jackal took a step backward.

"*I call and you come.*" The voice boomed and echoed beneath the painted ceiling. "*Do not think that you are indispensable, Messenger!*"

Howling and clutching at his head, the jackal god fell to his knees. The moaning of the priests intesified. After what he deemed a suitable interlude, Osiris lifted his hand and the cry of pain died away. Anubis collapsed stomach-first to the floor, panting. Long moments passed before he dragged himself up onto his hands and knees. His trembling head bowed until the pointed ears brushed the steps before the throne.

The god resumed his normal size and surveyed Anubis' bent back with satisfaction. "But as it happens, I do have a task for you. And it does, in fact, concern one of my colleagues, but it is work of a less delicate nature than unmasking a secret adversary. My words of command are being sent to you even now."

"I am grateful, O Lord." His voice was hoarse and hard to understand.

The candles flared in the heart of Abydos-That-Was. The Messenger of Death received another commission.

Dread yanked the fiberlink from its slot and rolled off the bed onto the floor. Eyes clamped shut with pain, he crawled to the bathroom and groped for the rim of the tub, then vomited up the vat-grown kebab that had been his lunch. His stomach went on convulsing long after he had emptied himself. When it stopped, he slumped against the wall, gasping.

The Old Man had never been able to do *that* before. A painful buzzing here, a nasty splash of vertigo there, but never anything like that. It felt like a knitting needle had been pushed in one of his ears and pulled out the other.

He spat bile into a towel, then dragged himself erect and stumbled to the sink to wash the digestive fluids from his lips and chin.

It had been a long time since anyone had made him hurt like that. It was something to think about. Part of him, the squinting child who had first confronted the authorities after hitting another six-year-old in the face with a hammer, wanted to find out the old bastard's true name, track him to his RL hideaway, then razor him and pull his skin off string by string. But another part, the adult creature who had grown from that child, had learned subtlety. Both parts, however, admired the exercise of naked power. When he was on top someday, he would act no differently. Weak dogs became bones for other, stronger dogs.

Helpless rage was a hindrance, he reminded himself. Whoever the Old Man really was, going after him would be like trying to storm hell to throw rocks at the devil. He was a big wheel in the Brotherhood— maybe the biggest, for all Dread knew. He probably lived surrounded by over-armed bodyguards in one of those hardened underground silos so popular with the filthy rich, or on some fortified island like a villain in a Malaysian slash-and-smash netflick.

Tasting his own acids, Dread spat again. He must be patient. For the moment, anger was useless except as carefully-controlled fuel; it was far easier and smarter just to keep doing what the Old Man wanted. For the moment. There would be a day later on when the jackal would rise to its master's throat. Patience. Patience.

He lifted his head into the frame of the mirror and stared at his reflection. He needed to see himself clean again, hard, untouched. No one had made him feel this way for a long time, and the ones who had were all dead now. Only the first few had died quickly.

Patience. No mistakes. He steadied his breathing and straightened up, stretching the kinks from aching stomach muscles. He leaned forward, zooming into close-up, the hero looking back with dark flat eyes, swallowing his pain. Unstoppable. Music up. Coming back *strong*.

He stared at the puke-stained tub for a moment, then turned on the water, washing the vomit away in a swirl of brown. Edit that—edit the whole tub scene. Missed the point. *Unstoppable.*

At least this new job would be RL. He was tired of the costumed silliness of these rich fools, living out fantasies that would shame the lowest chargehead just because they could afford to. This task would have real risks, and it would end in real blood. That was worthy of him, at least, and of his special skills.

The target, though. . . . He frowned. Despite what he'd said to the Old Man, he wasn't crazy about being in the middle of one these Brotherhood feuds. Too unpredictable, like some net thing he'd seen back in school, kings and queens, scheming, poisoning. Still, such things had a hidden benefit. Let them all kill each other. It would just hasten the day when he could make things *happen*.

He rinsed his mouth again, then walked back to his bed. He needed his music—no wonder he felt off-balance. The soundtrack put everything into perspective, kept the story moving. He hesitated, remembering the agony the implants had so recently brought him, but only for a moment. He was Dread, and his chosen name was also his chosen game. *His*. No old man was going to frighten him.

He summoned up the music. It came without pain, a firm syncopation, quiet conga drums and dragging bass. He laid a series of sustained organ chords over them. Ominous but cool. Thinking music. Planning music. You'll-never-catch-me music.

Even now, that downtown parking garage must be full of police detectives, dusting, scanning, taking infrareds, wondering why the crime didn't show up on their closed-circuit camera-drones. All standing around examining the rags of white and red.

Poor pussy. And she hadn't wanted anyone touching her stuff.

Another one dead, they'd be saying. All over the net soon. He'd have to remember to watch some of the coverage.

Dread leaned back against the bare white wall as the music pulsed through him. Time to do some work. He summoned the information the old bastard had sent him, then called up some visuals, maps first, then LEOS scans and 3D blues of the target location. They floated in the air before him like heavenly visions against the background of the other white wall.

All his walls were white. Who needed pictures when you could make your own?

CHAPTER 9

Mad Shadows

NETFEED/ENTERTAINMENT: Concrete Sun *Highest Rated for May*
(visual: several explosions, man in white coat running)
VO: The series-ending episode of Concrete Sun *was the most watched net entertainment for the month of May—*
(visual: man in white coat kissing one-legged woman)
—appearing in sixteen percent of homes worldwide.
(visual: man in white coat carrying a bandaged dog through culvert)
The story of a fugitive doctor hiding out in the squatter city of BridgeNTunnel is the highest rated linear drama in four years. . . .

Renie turned her head sharply and the test pattern—an unending domino-row of grids in contrasting colors—jiggled. She grimaced. A touch against one of the dimples on the side of her headset brought up the pressure in the padding. She waggled her head; now the image stayed put.

She lifted her hands, then curled her right index finger. The front grid, a simple lattice of glowing yellow, remained where it was; all the other grids moved a little farther apart from each other, rippling out into the indeterminate distance, one full lockstep into infinity. She bent the finger farther and the distance between each grid shrank. She wagged the finger to the right and the entire array rotated, each a fraction of an instant behind the one before it, so that a neon spiral formed and then vanished as the grids came to rest once more.

"Now you do it," she told !Xabbu.

He carefully wove his hands through a complex series of movements, each of which marked different points of distance and attitude from the sensor affixed to the front of his visor like a third eye. The unending sequence of colored grids responded, spinning, shrinking, changing relationships like an exploding universe of square stars. Renie nodded in approval even though !Xabbu could not see her—the test pattern and the all-surrounding blackness were the only visuals.

"Good," she said. "Let's try out your memory. Take as many of those grids as you want—not from the front—and make a polyhedron."

!Xabbu carefully withdrew his selections from the array. As the rest moved to fill the vacated space, he stretched those he had chosen and folded them in half along the diagonal, then rapidly assembled the paired triangles into a faceted ball.

"You are getting *good*." She was pleased. Not that she could take too much credit—she had never taught anyone who worked as hard as !Xabbu, and he had a tremendous natural aptitude. Very few people could adapt themselves to the unnatural rules of netspace as quickly and completely as he had.

"Then may I put this away now, Renie?" he asked. "Please? We have been preparing all morning."

She flicked her hand and the test pattern disappeared. A moment later they stood facing each other in a 360-degree ocean of gray, sim to unprepossessing sim. She bit back a nettled reply. He was right. She had been delaying, going over and over her preparations as though this were some kind of combat mission instead of a simple trip into the Inner District in search of information.

Not that, strictly speaking, there *was* such a thing as a simple trip into Inner District for outsiders like them. There might very well be barriers they could not pass no matter how well prepared they were, but she did not want to be unmasked and ejected because of some stupid, preventable mistake. Also, if there *was* something illegal and dangerous going on in Toytown, discovery of her investigation would put the guilty ones on guard and perhaps even lead them to destroy evidence that otherwise might save Stephen.

"I did not intend to be rude, Renie." !Xabbu's sim lifted its simple hands in a gesture of peace; a rather mechanical-looking smile curled the corners of its mouth. "But I think that you, too, will be happier when we are doing something."

"You're probably right. *Disconnect and exit.*"

Everything vanished. She lifted the visor on her headset and the earnest but seedy ambience of the Poly's Harness Room surrounded her once more. The Bushman pushed up his own visor and blinked, grinning.

Reflexively, she began one final run through her mental checklist. While !Xabbu had finished his exams—which, the grapevine told her, he had handled with expected ease—she had created not just aliases to get them into the Inner District, but several backups as well. If things went badly, they could shuck off their first identities like old skin. But it had not been easy. Creating a false online identity was no different than creating one for RL, and was in many ways the same process.

Renie had spent a good portion of her time in the last few days hunting through backwater areas of the net. There were lots of vaguely unsavory people lurking in Lambda Mall's equivalent of dark alleyways for whom setting up false identities was everyday work, but ultimately she had decided to do it herself. If her investigations of the Inner District struck something important, the offended parties would go looking for the bootleg identity merchants first; not a one of them would take a stand for privileged information when their livelihood and perhaps even health was at stake.

So, pumped up on caffeine and sugar, smoking an endless chain of theoretically noncarcinogenic cigarettes, she had set off to do a little *akisu*, as the old-timers called it. She had worked her way through hundreds of obscure infobanks, copying bits and pieces as it suited her, inserting false cross-check data on the systems whose defenses were outdated or weak enough. She had created a reasonably solid false identity for both of them, and—she hoped—even some insurance if things went very wrong.

She had also learned a few things about Mister J's along the way, which was one of the reasons she had been drilling !Xabbu all morning. The Inner District club had a very dark reputation, and interfering with its operation might have some unpleasant real world repercussions. Despite her initial impatience, she was glad !Xabbu had talked her into waiting for him. In fact, even another week to prepare wouldn't have gone amiss. . . .

She took a breath. Enough. If she weren't careful, she would turn into one of those obsessive-compulsives who turned back five times to make sure the door was locked.

"Okay," she said. "Let's get going."

They made a few final tests of their harnesses, both of which hung
from the ceiling by an arrangement of straps and pulleys that would
allow their users freedom of movement in VR, as well as prevent them
from walking into real walls or hurting themselves with a fall. When
the pulleys had hauled them aloft, they dangled side by side in the
middle of the padded room like a pair of marionettes on the puppeteer's day off.

"Do what I say without questions. We can't afford to make mistakes—my brother's life could be at stake. I'll give you answers afterward." Renie checked one last time to make sure none of the wires
would be worked loose by the action of the harness straps, then pulled
her visor back down; the visuals flicked on and the gray sparkle of the
waiting net surrounded her. "And remember, even though the closed
band is provided by the Inner District, not the club itself, once we get
inside you'd better assume that *someone* is listening."

"I understand, Renie." He sounded cheerful, which was amazing
considering that she had already given him the eavesdroppers speech
twice before that morning.

She waved her hands and they went.

The crowd waiting at the Inner District Gateway was a brightly-
colored, noisy blur. As the clamor of their multilingual pleading thundered painfully in her ears, she realized that in her anxiety not to miss
any possible clues she had set the gain on her sensory inputs too high.
A flick of the wrist and a circled finger brought them down to a manageable level.

After a wait that had Renie bouncing in place with impatience, they
at last slid to the front of the line. The female functionary was polite
and seemed remarkably uninterested in making trouble. She examined their false identification, then asked if the reason for their visit,
submitted as part of the ID package, was still correct.

"It is. I'm examining an installation we've had a complaint about."
Renie's alias showed her working for a large Nigerian programming
company with !Xabbu as her trainee—a gear company which, she had
discovered, kept very sloppy records.

"And how much time will you need, Mister Otepi?"

Renie was astonished—actual kindness! She was not used to tracta-
bility from net bureaucrats. She eyed the smiling sim carefully, wondering if she were dealing with some new kind of hyper-actualized
Customer Service Puppet. "It's hard to say. If the problem is simple

enough, I may fix it myself, but first I must run it through its paces to find out."

"Eight hours?"

Eight! She knew people who would pay several thousand credits for that long a period of access to the Inner District—in fact, if she had any time left over when they finished, she was tempted to go find one of them. She wondered if she should try to get more—maybe this Puppet was broken, a slot machine that would just pay and pay—but decided not to press her luck. "That should be adequate."

A moment later they were through, floating just above ground level in monumental Gateway Plaza.

"You don't realize it," she told !Xabbu on their private band, *"but you've just witnessed a miracle."*

"What is that?"

"A bureaucratic system that actually does what it's supposed to do."

He turned to her, a half-smile illuminating the face of the sim Renie had arranged for the visit. *"Which is to let in two disguised people who are pretending to have legitimate business?"*

"Nobody likes a comedian," she pointed out, then exited from the private band. "We're clear. We can go anywhere we want to now, except private nodes."

!Xabbu surveyed the plaza. "The crowds seem different here than in the Lambda Mall. And the structures are more extreme."

"That's because you're closer to the center of power. People here do what they want because they can afford to." A thought came swirling up like a flake of hot black ash. "People who can get away with anything. Or think they can." Stephen was comatose in the hospital while the men who had hurt him enjoyed their freedom. Her anger, never completely cold, rekindled. "Let's go have a look around Toytown."

Lullaby Lane was far more crowded than the last time she had been there, almost choked with virtual bodies. Caught by surprise, Renie pulled !Xabbu into an alley so she could figure out what was happening.

The crowd flowed past the alley mouth in one direction, shouting and singing. It seemed to be a parade of sorts. The sims were embodied in a variety of bizarre ways, oversized, undersized, extra-limbed, even divided into unconnected body parts that moved like coherent wholes. Some of the revelers shifted and changed even as she watched: one violet-haired, attenuated figure wore enormous bat wings which dissolved into traceries of fluttering silver gauze. Many reformed themselves every few moments, extruding new limbs, changing heads, spreading and curling into fantastic shapes like boiling wax dumped in cold water.

Welcome to Toytown, she thought. *Looks like we arrived just in time for a reunion of the Hieronymous Bosch Society.*

She took the Bushman up to rooftop level where they could get a better view. Several in the crowd bore glowing banners proclaiming "Freedom!" or spelled it out above their heads in fire; one group had even turned themselves into a walking row of letters that spelled out "Mutation Day." Although most of the paraders' sims were extreme by design, they were also rather unstable. Some of them fell apart into unstructured planes and lines in a way that did not look intentional. Others flickered in midstep and occasionally disappeared entirely.

Home-cooked programming, she decided. *Do-it-yourself stuff.* "It's a protest, I think," she told !Xabbu.

"Against what person or thing?" He hung in the air beside her, a cartoon figure with a serious expression on its simple face.

"Embodiment laws, I would guess. But they can't be suffering much if they can afford to hang out here in the first place." She made a small noise of contempt. "Rich people's children complaining because their parents won't let them dress up. Let's go."

They beamed past the procession to the far end of Lullabye Lane where the streets were empty. Without the distraction of street theater the rundown quality of the neighborhood was immediately apparent. Many of the nodes seemed to have grown even more decrepit since her last visit; both sides of the street were lined with skeletal, colorless buildings.

A distant, skittery flare of music at last turned them toward a garish glow at the street's far end. In such dim surroundings, the awful, throbbing liveliness of Mister J's seemed even more sinister.

!Xabbu stared at the turreted sprawl and the giant carniverous grin. "So that is it."

"Private band," Renie snapped. *"And keep it there unless you have to answer a question from someone. As soon as you finish answering, switch back. Don't worry about being slow to respond—I'm sure they get lots of people in that place whose reflexes are not what they should be."*

They slowly floated forward, watching the club's facade gleam and squirm.

"Why are there no people about?" asked !Xabbu.

"Because this isn't a part of the Inner District that invites much sightseeing. People who come to Mister J's probably beam in directly. Are you ready?"

"I believe so. Are you?"

Renie hesitated. The question seemed flippant, but that was not the bushman's way. She realized she was wound tight and hard, her nerves thrumming. She took several deep breaths, willing herself toward calm. The toothy mouth over the doorway flapped its red lips as though whispering a promise. Mister Jingo's Smile, this place had been called. Why did they change the name but keep that horrid grimace?

"It is a bad place," !Xabbu said abruptly.

"I know. Don't forget that for a second."

She splayed her fingers. An instant later they were in a shadowy antechamber, a place with gold-framed carnival mirrors instead of walls. As she turned to survey the room, Renie could see that the latency—the tiny lag between initiation and action that characterized complex VR environments—was very low here, a quite passable mimicry of real life. The detail work was also impressive. Alone in the antechamber, they were not alone in the mirrors: a thousand reveling ghosts surrounded them—figures of men and women, as well as some more animal than human, all cavorting around the distorted reflections of their two sims. Their reflections appeared to be enjoying themselves.

"Welcome to Mister J's." The voice spoke oddly-accented English. There was no image to match it in any of the mirrors.

Renie turned to discover a tall, smiling, elegantly dressed white man standing close behind them. He lifted his gloved hands and the mirrors disappeared, leaving the three of them alone in a single pillar of light surrounded by infinite black. "So nice to have you with us." His voice crept in close, as though he whispered in her ear. "Where are you from?"

"Lagos," said Renie a little breathlessly. She hoped her own voice, processed an octave lower to match her masculine alias, did not sound as squeaky to him as it did to her. "We . . . we've heard a lot about this place."

The man's smile widened. He made a short bow. "We are proud of our worldwide reputation, and pleased to welcome friends from Africa. You are, of course, of legal age?"

"Of course." Even as she spoke, she knew that digital fingers were prying at the edge of her alias—but not prying too hard: deniability was all that a place like this needed. "I am showing my friend here some Inner District sights—he's never been before."

"Splendid. You have brought him to the right place." The well-dressed man was finished distracting them, which meant their indexes had been passed. He made a theatrical flourish and a door opened in the darkness, a rectangular hole that bled smoky red light. Noise spilled out, too—loud music, laughter, a wavecrash of voices. "Enjoy your visit," he said. "Tell your friends." Then he was gone and they were flowing forward into the scarlet glow.

The music reached out to gather them in like the pseudopod of some immense but invisible energy-creature. Blaringly loud, it sounded like the bouncy swing jazz of the previous century, but it had strange hiccups and slurs, secret rhythms moving deep inside like the heartbeat of a stalking predator. It was captivating: Renie found herself humming along before she could even make out words, but those came quickly enough.

> *"There's no call for consternation,"*

someone was singing urgently as the orchestra wailed and stomped in the background,

> *"A smiling face is invitation enough—*
> *No bluff!*
> *So bring your stuff to the celebration. . . ."*

The lounge was impossibly huge, a monstrous, red-lit octagon. The pillars that marked its angles, each one broad as a skyscraper, stretched up to disappear in shadow far above; the vertical rows of lights that trimmed them grew closer together and at last shrank into continuous lines of radiance as distance squeezed them. Up where even those lights failed, up in the unspeakable heights of the ceiling, sparking fireworks zigged and caromed endlessly against the blackness.

Spotlights wheeled through the smoky air, pushing fast-moving ellipses of brighter red across the velvet walls. Hundreds of booths sprawled between the pillars and filled the ringing balconies, which circled up at least a dozen floors before the swirling clouds of smoke made counting impossible. An almost endless mushroom forest of tables covered the shiny main floor, with silver clad figures speeding between them like pinballs off bumpers—a thousand waiters and waitresses, two thousand, more, all moving swiftly and frictionlessly as beads of mercury.

In the center of the enormous room the orchestra stood on a floating stage that sparkled and revolved like a sideways ferris wheel. The musicians wore black-and-white formal suits, but there was nothing formal about them. They were cartoonishly attenuated and two-dimensional. As the music squalled, their shapes wavered and flared like mad shadows; some grew until their rolling eyes peered directly into the highest balconies. Bright tombstone teeth snapped at the customers, who shrieked and laughed even as they scrambled for safer ground.

Only the singer, perched at the farthest edge of the circling stage in a filmy white dress, did not change size. As the shadowy musicians billowed around her, she glowed like a piece of radium.

> *"So toss away your trepidation,"*

she sang, her voice harsh yet somehow alluring, its quaver that of a child forced to stay up too late, watching the adults grow strange and drunken,

> *"Slip into some syncopation—no fuss!*
> *The bus*
> *Will pro-pel us to Party Station. . . ."*

The singer was only a spot of light in the midst of the cyclopean lounge and the crazily stretching orchestra, but for long moments Renie found that she could not see at anything else. Huge black eyes in a pale face made the woman look almost skeletal. Her fountain of white hair, half as tall as she was, combined with the white dress rippling beneath her arms to make her seem some kind of exotic bird.

> *"Sit right down—*
> *Lose that frown!*
> *Mingle with the Toast of Toytown!*
> *Pick a song,*
> *Sing along,*
> *All that's upright will turn out wrong. . . ."*

The singer swayed back and forth, buffeted by the pounding beat like a dove in gale winds. The great eyes were closed now in something that might be exultation but didn't seem like it: Renie had never seen a human being look quite so trapped, and yet the singer glowed, burned. She might have been a light bulb channeling too much juice, her filament an instant away from explosive collapse.

Slowly, almost unwillingly, Renie reached out for !Xabbu. She found his hand and closed her fingers on it. *"Are you okay?"*

"It . . . it is quite overwhelming, this place."

"It is. Let's . . . let's sit down for a moment."

She led him across the floor to one of the booths along the far wall—an RL journey that would have taken some minutes on foot, but which they made in seconds. All the musicians in the orchestra were singing now, clapping and hooting and stamping their mighty feet on the rocking stage; the music was so loud that it seemed the whole gigantic house might fall down.

> *"Free your heart of hesitation!*
> *Eves and Adams of every nation-state,*
> *Feel great!*
> *When they create a federation. . . ."*

The music swelled and the spotlights raced even faster, beams flickering across each other like fencers' foils. There was a cannonfire rattle of drums, a last explosive blare of horns, then the orchestra was gone. A hollow chorus of hoots and cheers wafted through the immense room.

Renie and !Xabbu had barely sunk into the deep velvet banquette when a waiter appeared before them, floating a few inches off the floor. He wore a chrome-colored, form-fitted tuxedo. His sim body appeared to have been modeled after some ancient fertility deity.

"Zazoon, creepers," he drawled. "What'll it be?"

"We . . . we can't eat or drink in these sims," Renie said. "Do you have anything else?"

He gave her an intensely knowing and slightly amused look, clicked his fingers, and vanished. A menu of glowing letters hung in the air behind him like a luminescent residue.

"There's a list labeled 'Emotions,' " !Xabbu said wonderingly. *" 'Sorrow: mild to intense,' 'Happiness: tranquil contentment to violent joy.' Fulfillment. Misery. Optimism. Despair. Pleasant surprise. Madness . . ."* He looked at Renie. *"What are these? What do they mean?"*

"You can speak on public band. No one will be surprised that this is new to you—or to me, for that matter. Remember, we're just a couple of backwoods boys from Nigeria, come to the virtual big city to see the sights." She changed over. "I suppose these are sensations that they simulate. Eddie . . . I mean that fellow we know—told us that they could give you sensory

experiences your equipment wasn't wired for. Or they claim they can."

"What should we do now?" In the midst of the immense room, the bushman's small sim looked even smaller, as though squeezed by the very weight of clamor and movement. "Where do you wish to go?"

"I'm thinking." She stared at the fiery letters hanging before them, a curtain of words that offered little privacy and no protection. "I'd like it to be a little less noisy, actually. If we can afford it, that is."

It was still the same booth, but its colors had become muted earth-tones, and it now sat in a small room along the Quiet Gallery. The arched doorway looked out on a wide blue pool set in the middle of stone cloisters.

"This is beautiful," said !Xabbu. "And we came here . . . just like that." He snapped his sim fingers, but they made no noise.

"And the money is flowing out of our account just like that, too. This has to be the only club in the VR world where it costs less to rent a back room than to turn the noise down at your table. I suppose they want to encourage people to use the services." Renie straightened herself. The pool was mesmerizing. Drops fell from the mossy ceiling, making circular ripples that spread and overlapped, throwing blurry reflections back against the torchlit walls. "I want to look around. I want to see what the rest of this place is like."

"Can we afford to?"

She flicked to private band. *"I put some credits in the account that goes with this alias, but not many—they don't pay teachers that well. But we're only paying for this because we requested it. If we just wander around—well, I think they have to warn us before they charge our account."*

!Xabbu's face stretched in a sim smile. *"You think the people who own this place capable of . . . of many things, but you do not suspect them of cheating their customers?"*

Renie didn't like discussing what she thought them capable of, even on private band. *"No one stays in business if they cheat everybody. That's a fact. Even one of those Broderbund-owned clubs on the Victoria Embankment—they may take a bit off the top, and deal to chargeheads and drug addicts in the back, but they still have to keep up pretenses."* She stood and switched back over. "Come on, let's have a look around."

As she and !Xabbu stepped through the arch onto the walkway that ringed the pool, a light began to glow deep beneath the placid waters.

"That way." She moved toward it.

"But . . ." !Xabbu took a step after her, then stopped.

"It's all illusion. Remember that. And unless they've abandoned the universal VR interface symbols, that shows us the way out." She took another step and hesitated, then bent her knees and dove. The descent took a long time. Back at the Poly her real body was being held horizontally, in harness, so she had no physical sensation of falling, but here in the Quiet Gallery she saw the glowing blue translucence come up to meet her, then saw her own splash create a vortex of bubbles around her. A circle of light glowed in the deeps. She headed toward it.

A moment later, !Xabbu was beside her. Unlike Renie, who had mimicked the head-forward, arms-outstretched posture of a diver, he sank downward while standing upright.

"What . . ." he began, then laughed. "We can talk!"

"It's not water. And those aren't fish."

!Xabbu chortled again as a great cloud of shimmering forms surrounded them, tails flicking, fins whirring like tiny propellers. One, its scales striped in bold patterns of black, yellow, and red, swam backward in front of the bushman, its nose almost touching his. "Wonderful!" he said, and reached toward it. The fish spun and darted away.

The doorway still glowed, but the water around them seemed to be getting darker. They had moved through into some other level of the pool, or rather of the simulation—Renie could see what looked like sea-floor below, rocks and white sand and waving forests of kelp. She even thought she saw a glimpse of something almost human sheltering in the forest's shadow-tangled depths, something with hands and fingers and bright eyes, but with the muscular tail of an ocean predator. Behind the splashing noises pumped into her hearplugs was a deeper noise, a kind of singing. She found it disturbing; with a gesture, she hurried them to the gleaming exit.

Up close, the ring was revealed to be a wreath of shining circles, each a different color.

"Pick one," she told !Xabbu.

He gestured and the red ring glowed more brightly. A calm, genderless voice murmured *"Inferno and other lower chambers,"* into their ears.

!Xabbu glanced at her; she nodded despite the sudden tingle of unease up the back of her neck. That would be the kind of place that would lure young boys like Stephen. !Xabbu touched the ring again and the whole wreath of circles turned molten red, then expanded, flowing over and past them so that for a moment they were in a tunnel of crimson light. When the glare had faded, they were still under water, although it now had a murkier cast. Renie at first thought the gateway had malfunctioned.

"Up there," said !Xabbu, pointing. Far above them hung another circle of light, this one a solid disk of red like a dying sun. "That is what the sky looks like from deep beneath the water." He sounded a little breathless.

"Then let's go." She wondered briefly what !Xabbu, a native of the shallow delta rivers and marshes, knew about deep water, then dismissed it. Maybe he'd been swimming in the Durban public pools.

They rose toward the red light, floating through more seaweed forests. These were black and thorny, drifting clumps of water brambles that sometimes blocked their view of the circle entirely and cast them into a strange undersea twilight. The water was cloudy, agitated by the steam vents which bubbled on the jagged ocean floor below them. All sign of where they had entered was gone, although she felt sure that if she and !Xabbu reversed direction, some indication of the route back into the Quiet Gallery pool would appear.

She fingered one of the barbed strands of kelp, marveling anew at how its rough, rubbery texture could be manufactured from unphysical numbers and yet, when transmitted to the tactors, the force feedback sensors in the glove of her simsuit, give every impression of palpable existence.

!Xabbu reached out and snatched at her arm, jerking her sideways. "See!" He sounded genuinely panicked. She looked down, following his pointing finger.

Something vast and dark was moving in the steaming depths. Renie could vaguely make out a smooth back and a strangely elongated head that seemed too big for the body, sliding along the rocky bottom near the spot where they had entered. The creature looked like some cross between a shark and a crocodile, but was far larger than either. The long, cylindrical body disappeared into the murk a dozen yards behind the questing muzzle.

"It smells us!"

She took his hand in hers and squeezed. "It's not real," she said firmly, although her own heart was beating very fast. The thing had ceased nosing at the vents and had begun lazily to move upward, its rising circular path taking it out of sight for the moment. She changed to private band. *"!Xabbu! Feel my hand? That's my real hand, under my glove. Our bodies are in the Harness Room at the Poly. Remember that."*

The eyes of !Xabbu's sim were shut tight. Renie had seen this before—a terrifying experience in a high-quality simulation could be just as overwhelming as in real life. She kept a tight grip on her friend's hand and accelerated their rise.

Something huge rushed through the spot they had just occupied, immense and swift as a maglev train. Her heart lurched. She had a brief glimpse of a gaping mouth full of teeth and a glinting eye as big as her head, then the dark shiny body was passing endlessly beneath them. She added more speed to their upward movement, then chided herself for doing just what she had warned !Xabbu against—using RL logic. *Just jump out, you fool! This isn't water, so you don't have to swim. Simulation or not, do you really want to find out what happens when that thing catches people?*

She gestured with her free hand and the red disk expanded dramatically; the surface seemed to fling itself down toward them. An instant later they were bobbing on a wide and unsettled lake in a chaos of steam and red rain. Still caught up in the experience, !Xabbu floundered, thrashing his arms in an attempt to stay afloat, though at that moment Renie's control rather than his own movements determined his position. A great shiny hump broke the surface, moving rapidly toward them. Renie squeezed !Xabbu's hand again and moved them instantaneously to the lake shore, two hundred yards distant.

But there was no shore. The crimson-lit water splashed against black basalt walls and then flowed *up,* hissing and boiling in great sheets to the stalactite-studded ceiling before drizzling back down in a continuous, smoking rain. Almost blinded, Renie and !Xabbu hung in place at the lake's edge being violently bumped against painfully well-simulated stone.

The hump splashed up into view again and this time kept rising until the head towered above the roiling steam as it wove from side to side, searching for its prey. Renie bobbed in place for a moment, stunned. What she had thought was a gigantic body was only the thing's neck.

The head moved closer, sluicing water like a dredging crane. *Leviathan,* she thought, remembering her mother's Bible readings, and felt a moment of superstitious fear, followed by a wave of hysterical mirth at the thought that a simple VR entertainment should surprise her so badly. The laughter died when !Xabbu's hands clutched at her shoulders and neck. Her friend was panicking.

"It's not real!" she shouted, trying to make herself heard over the roar of the boiling waters and the bubbling wheeze of the approaching beast, but the Bushman was caught up in his own private terror and did not hear her. The vast maw opened, looming through the spattering rain. Renie contemplated pulling the plug on the whole expedition, but they had learned nothing yet. Alarming though it was, this sort of thing was a roller-coaster ride for kids like Stephen—whatever had struck him down was nothing so obvious.

The walls of the great cavern were covered with upward-flowing cataracts, but there were dozens of places where crimson light gleamed through the sheets of water as though there were open spaces beyond. Renie picked one at random and moved them to it, even as the beast plunged its head downward, snapping at the emptiness where they had floated a moment before.

As they sped toward the glowing spot Renie saw that the cavern walls were lined with human forms, mouths agape, all writhing slowly just beneath the churning waters as though they had been partially absorbed by the stone. Fingers pushed through the cataracts, clawing toward her. The ceiling-bound water frothed from the stretching hands and dripped upward like strings of floating jewels.

Renie and !Xabbu splashed through a curtain of water and fell forward onto a stone walkway as Leviathan's disappointed bellow shook the walls.

"Inferno," said Renie. "They're playing games, that's all. It's supposed to be hell."

!Xabbu still trembled—she could feel his shoulder shaking beneath her hand—but had ceased thrashing. The face of his sim was inadequate to express what she guessed was going on behind it.

"I am ashamed," he said at last. "I have behaved badly."

"Nonsense." Her reply was purposefully swift. "It frightened *me*, and I do this for a living." Which was not quite true—very few of the VR environments she frequented had attractions of quite this order—but she didn't want the small man's spirit broken. "Join me on the other band. *That thing gives you some kind of idea of the programming and processing power they've got here, doesn't it?*"

!Xabbu would not be so easily mollified. *"I could not stop myself—that is why I am ashamed. I knew it was not real, Renie—I would not forget your teachings so easily. But when I was a child, a crocodile took me, and another took my cousin. I pulled free because it had a poor grip—I have the scars on my upper arm and shoulder still—but my cousin was not so lucky. When that crocodile was found and killed some days later, we found him in its belly, halfdissolved and white as milk."*

Renie shuddered. *"Don't blame yourself. God, I wish you'd told me about that before I dragged you into the pool. That's where VR can cause harm, and no one disputes it—where it touches on phobias or childhood fears. But because it's a controlled environment, they use it to cure those fears, too."*

"I do not feel cured," said !Xabbu miserably.

"No, I'm not surprised." She squeezed his arm again, then got to her feet. Her muscles were sore—just from the tension alone, she guessed. That and the pummeling !Xabbu had unwittingly given her. "Come on. We've burned an hour or so of our time already and we've barely seen anything."

"Where are we?" He, too, straightened and stood, then stopped as a sudden idea struck him. "Do we have to go out the same way when we leave?"

Renie laughed. "We most certainly do not. As a matter of fact, we can pull out directly any time we want. All you have to do is make the 'exit' command, remember?"

"I do now."

The corridor had been designed to carry on the motif of the boiling lake. The walls were the same black igneous stone, rough to the touch and dreary to look at. A sourceless red light suffused everything.

"We could wander aimlessly," she said, "or we can be a little more scientific about this." She paused for a moment, but saw nothing that looked suggestive. *"Options,"* she said, loudly and clearly. A tracery of burning lines appeared on the wall beside them. She studied the list, many of which were unpleasantly suggestive, and picked one of the most neutral. *"Stairs."*

The corridor wavered, then dropped away before them like water running down a drain. They stood on a landing in the middle of a wide, curving staircase that stretched away above and below, each step a massive slab of glossy black stone. For an instant they were alone; then the air flickered and they were surrounded by pale shapes.

"By my ancestors . . ." breathed !Xabbu.

Hundreds of ghostly figures filled the stairwell, some trudging wearily, many burdened by heavy bags or other burdens. Others, less substantial, floated in tatters above the steps like mist. Renie saw a variety of ancient costumes from many cultures and heard a whispering babel of different tongues, as though these shades were meant to represent a cross-section of human history. She gestured to raise the sound on her hearplugs, but still could not quite understand any of them.

"More lost souls," she said. "I wonder if someone is trying to send us a message. 'Abandon all hope, ye who enter here,' or something like that."

!Xabbu looked uncomfortable as he watched a beautiful Asian woman float past, her weeping head cradled carefully between the stumps of her wrists. "What shall we do now?" he asked.

"Go down." It seemed obvious. "You have to go down before you can come out—that's how these things always work."

"Ah." !Xabbu turned toward her, a sudden smile stretching his simulated face. "Such wisdom is not easily come by, Renie. I am impressed."

She stared at him for a moment. She had been talking about the endless dungeon games she had played as a netgirl, but she wasn't quite sure what *he* meant. "Come on, then."

She wondered at first whether there would be any resistance, or at least any scenarios to be played out, but the spirits of the staircase only eddied past on either side, as murmurously harmless as pigeons. One, a gnarled old man who wore nothing but a loincloth, stood stationary in the middle of the staircase, silently shaking with laughter or tears. Renie tried to walk around him, but his sudden convulsive movement brought him against her elbow; he instantly dissolved into smoky wisps, then reformed farther up the stairs, still bent, still shaking.

They walked for almost half an hour, companioned only by simulations of the restless dead. The staircase seemed endless, and Renie was considering choosing one of the doorways that led off each landing when she heard a voice cutting through the unhappy burble of the phantoms.

". . . Like a she-dog. Breathing hard, growling, foam on her lips— you shall see!"

The remark was followed by a chorus of raucous laughter.

Renie and !Xabbu rounded a bend. On the landing before them stood four men, all quite real, at least compared to the phantom bystanders. Three of them were dark-skinned, dark-haired demigods, tall and almost impossibly handsome. The fourth was not quite as tall but monstrously bulky, as though someone had dressed a hippopotamus in a white suit and given it a round, bald, human head.

Although his back was to them and their approach made no sound, the fat man turned to Renie and !Xabbu immediately. Renie felt the swift examination by his small bright eyes almost physically, like a series of probing finger jabs. "Ah, hello. Are you enjoying yourselves, gentlemen?" His voice was a work of genius, deep buttery tones like a viola da gamba.

"Yes, thank you." She kept a hand on !Xabbu's shoulder, uncertain.

"Is this your first time in the world-reknowned Mister J's?" asked the fat man. "Come, I am certain that it is—no need to be ashamed. You must join us, for I know all the ins and outs of this strange and wonderful place. I am Strimbello." He pushed the tip of his blunt jaw toward his breastbone in a minimal bow; his chins flattened and bulged like gills.

"Pleased to meet you," Renie said. "I am Mr. Otepi, and this is my business associate, Mr. Wonde."

"You are from Africa? Splendid, splendid." Strimbello beamed, as though Africa were a clever trick she and !Xabbu had just performed. "My other friends—what a day for new friends this has been!—are from the Indian subcontinent. Madras, to be specific. Please, may I introduce you to the brothers Pavamana."

His three companions gave fractional nods. They were practically triplets, or at least their sims were nearly identical. A lot of money had been spent on their handsome VR bodies. Renie decided that it was probably overcompensation—in RL, the Pavamana brothers were doubtless pockmarked and sunken-chested. "Pleased to meet you," she said. !Xabbu echoed her.

"And I was just taking these excellent fellows to see some of the Inferno's more *select* attractions." Strimbello lowered his voice and winked; he had more than a little of the carnival barker about him. "Would you care to join us?"

Renie suddenly remembered that Stephen had mentioned a fat man. Her heartbeat grew swifter. Could it all happen so quickly, so easily? But if opportunity was here, so was danger. "You are very kind."

She and !Xabbu shared a glance as they fell into step behind the other group. Renie lifted a finger to her lips, warning him not to say anything, even on private band. If this man was part of the inner circle of Mister J's, it would be folly to assume anything about his capabilities.

As they floated down the great staircase—Strimbello seemed uninterested in *arriviste* pursuits like walking—the fat man regaled them with stories about the various ghosts, or the people the ghosts represented. One of them, a Frankish knight from the Crusades, had been cuckolded in an admirably devious manner at which even Renie and !Xabbu had to laugh. Without changing tone, Strimbello then described what had happened afterward, and pointed out the two legless, armless figures worming along the stairs several paces behind the armored phantom. Renie felt sick.

The fat man lifted his broad arms and raised his hands, palms up. The whole company suddenly floated away from the staircase and around another bend in the cavern wall, which abruptly dropped away. They were hanging above a great emptiness, a miles-deep well. The stairway spiraled down around its perimeter, vanishing in the dim red glow far beneath them.

"Too slow," Strimbello said. "And there is much, much to show you." He gestured again and they were falling. Renie felt her stomach drop alarmingly—the visuals were good, but not *that* good, surely? Suspended in her harness and experiencing everything through the senses of her low-order sim, she should not be feeling this swift drop in such a . . . visceral way.

Beside her, !Xabbu had spread his arms as though to slow his descent. He looked slightly nervous, but there was a determined set to his narrow jaw that made Renie feel better. The little man was holding up well.

"We will, of course, land quite safely." Strimbello's round head seemed almost to blink like a lightbulb as the alternating levels of darkness and light strobed past. "I hope I don't sound patronizing, Mister . . . Otepi. Perhaps you have enjoyed such virtual experiences before."

"Nothing like this," said Renie truthfully.

Their fall ended, although they still hung in midair with a bottomless depth of well below them. At Strimbello's magisterial gesture they slid sideways through nothingness and alighted on one of the levels that ringed the pit like theater balconies. The Pavamana brothers grinned and pointed at the passersby. Their mouths moved without sound as they conversed on their own private band.

Doors were open all along the curving promenade, spilling noise and color and the sound of many voices and many languages, laughter, screams, and unintelligible rhythmic chanting. A variety of sims—mostly male, Renie could not help noticing; she suspected the few female shapes were part of the entertainment—moved in and out of the doorways and down the alleyways that radiated out from the central well. Some were embodied as handsomely as the Pavamana brothers, but many wore only the most basic forms: small, gray and almost faceless, they scuttled among their shining brothers like the pathetic damned.

Strimbello suddenly took her by the arm. His vast hand printed itself so powerfully on her tactors that she winced. "Come, come," he said, "it is time to see some of what you came here for. Perhaps the Yellow Room?"

"Oh, yes," one of the Pavamanas said. The other two nodded excitedly. "We have been told very much about that place."

"It is justifiably famous," said the fat man. He turned to Renie and !Xabbu, his sim face a perfect representation of shrewd humor. "And you are not to worry at the expense, my new friends. I am well known here—my credit is good. Yes? You will come?"

Renie hesitated, then nodded.

"So be it." Strimbello waved his hand and the promenade seemed to bend around them. A moment later they were in a long, low-ceilinged room lit in various unpleasant shades of ocher and acid-lemon. Throbbing music filled Renie's ears, a monotonous percussive thumping. The fat man was still gripping her arm firmly: she had to struggle to turn and look for !Xabbu. Her friend was behind the Pavamanas, staring around the crowded room.

The same mix of high- and low-quality sims that filled the promenade lined the tables of the Yellow Room, bellowing cheerfully at the stage which filled one end of the room, pounding with their fists until virtual crockery rolled and shattered on the floor. The bilious light gave their faces a feverish look. A woman—or what appeared to be a woman, Renie reminded herself—stood on the stage doing a jerky striptease timed to the swiftly lurching music. Renie was briefly reassured to see something so old-fashioned in its benign naughtiness until her she realized that what the woman was peeling off was not clothing, but skin. Already a ballet skirt of translucent, paper-thin, red-spotted flesh dangled from her hips. Worst of all was the look of resigned misery on the woman's—no, the sim's, Renie reminded herself—slack face.

Unable to watch, Renie looked around again for !Xabbu. She could see the top of his head past the Pavamanas, who were bobbing and elbowing each other like a slapstick comedy team. She stole another glance at the stage, but the wincing performer was now revealing the first layers of muscle flexing across her stomach, so Renie concentrated on the crowd instead. That did little to relieve her growing sense of claustrophobic discomfort: the simuloid faces of the audience were all wide soulless eyes and gaping mouths. This was indeed the Inferno.

A movement at the edge of her vision caught her attention. She thought Strimbello had been watching her, but when she turned, he appeared to be engrossed in the performance, his head nodding as if in proprietary approval, a tight smile pulling at the corners of his wide, wide mouth. Did he suspect, somehow, that she and !Xabbu were not what they professed to be? How could he? They had done nothing unusual and she had worked very hard on their aliases. But whatever he thought of them, he made her terribly uncomfortable. Whoever or whatever lived behind those small, hard eyes would be a very dangerous enemy.

The throbbing music died. Renie turned back to the stage as a blare of horns signaled the departure of the stripper. A few desultory handclaps followed her as she limped toward the back of the stage, trailing a bridal train of tattered, glistening flesh. A deep orchestral hum signaled the next act.

Strimbello leaned his huge head near. "Do you understand French, Mister Otepi? Hmmm? This is what you would call *'La Specialité de la Maison'*—the Yellow Room's signature attraction." He wrapped a large hand around her arm again and gave her a little shake. "You *are* of legal age, are you not?" He laughed suddenly, revealing broad, flat teeth. "Of course you are! Just my little joke!"

Renie sought !Xabbu, a bit desperately this time—they had to think about getting away from this man soon—but her friend was hidden by the three Pavamanas, who had leaned forward in unison to watch the stage, false faces rapt.

The deep rumble of the music changed, taking on a processional air, and a group of people walked out, all but one dressed in dark robes with hoods drawn up. The unhooded exception, Renie was surprised to see, was the pale singer from the lounge. Or was it? The face, especially the huge, haunted eyes, looked the same, but this one's hair was a great curling auburn cascade, and she also seemed taller and longer-limbed.

Before Renie could make up her mind, several of the robed figures stepped forward and grabbed the pale woman, who did not resist. The music shuddered and a quickening beat began to make itself felt beneath the humming chords. The stage lengthened like a protruded tongue. The walls and tables and even the patrons also reshaped themselves, flowing around the woman and her attendants until the room surrounded the strange tableau like a hospital operating theater. The acid glow dimmed until everything was in shadow and the woman's bone-white face seemed the only source of light. Then her robes were torn away, and her pale body leaped into view like a sudden flame.

Renie took a sharp breath. She heard louder, harsher inhalations on all sides. The young woman was not shaped like the dream-figure of male fantasy she would have expected in a place like this; her long, slender legs, delicate rib cage, and small mauve-tipped breasts made her seem little past adolescence.

The girl at last raised her dark eyes to look at the audience. Her expression was a mixture of reproach and fear, but something else lurked beneath, a kind of disgust—almost a challenge. Someone shouted at her in a language Renie didn't understand. Close behind, another customer laughed explosively. With no sign of physical effort, the robed figures grabbed at the girl's four limbs and lifted her from the floor. She floated between them, extended and glowingly pale, something pure to be marked or shaped. The music dropped to a low, anticipatory hum.

One of the dark figures twisted the girl's arm. She writhed, dull dark veins and the bunching of tendons suddenly visible beneath the translucent skin, but did not make a sound. The arm was twisted and pulled farther. There was a gristly noise as something tore and the girl cried out at last, a choking, drawn-out sob. Renie turned away, her stomach lurching.

It's only pictures, she told herself. *Not real. Not real.*

Shapes hunched forward on either side, craning for a better view. People were shouting, their voices already hoarse; Renie could almost feel a kind of collective darkness flowing from the watchers, as though the room were filling with poisonous smoke. More things were happening on the stage, more movements, more gasping cries. She did not want to look. The brothers from Madras were rubbing their hands back and forth on their impressively-muscled thighs. Strimbello, sitting next to Renie, watched the action with his small fixed smile.

It went on for long minutes. Renie stared at the floor, struggling against the urge to scream and run away. These people were animals—no, worse than animals, for what wild creature could dream of something so vile? It was time to take !Xabbu and get out. That wouldn't be enough to reveal their imposture—surely not all patrons of even as foul a place as this wanted to see these kinds of things? She started to rise, but Strimbello's broad hand pushed down hard on her leg, trapping her.

"You should not go." His growl seemed to push its way deep into her ear. "Look—you will have much to tell back home." He reached his other hand up and pulled her chin around toward the stage.

The girl's white limbs had been twisted into several impossible angles. One leg had been pulled to an obscene length, like a piece of taffy. The crowd was roaring now, so the girl's screams could no longer be heard, but her head snapped spastically from side to side and her mouth gaped.

One of the robed figures drew out something long and sharp and shiny. The clamor of the audience took on a different tone, a pack of dogs that had cornered some exhausted thing and now were baying for the kill.

Renie tried to pull away from Strimbello's implacable grip. A piece of something wet and gleaming flew past her, arcing out into the shadowed seats. Someone behind her caught it and lifted it to his expressionless sim face. He smeared it against his cheeks as though daubing a ceremonial mask, then pushed it into his idiot mouth. Renie tasted sour liquid as her stomach heaved again. She tried to look away, but all around her the patrons were lifting their hands, grabbing at other bits flung out from the stage. Horribly, she could hear the girl's shrieks even above the barking crowd.

She could not take this any longer—she would go mad if she remained. If a virtual object could burn, then this place should be burned to its dark foundation. She thrust her hand out toward !Xabbu, trying frantically to get his attention.

The little man was gone. The spot he had occupied behind the Pavamanas was empty.

"My friend!" She tried to tug herself free of Strimbello, who was unconcernedly watching the stage. "My friend is gone!"

"No matter," said Strimbello. "He will find something he likes better."

"Then he is a fool," chortled one of the Pavamanas, grinning like a lunatic. Simulated blood gleamed on his cheeks like an old courtesan's rouge. "There is nothing like the Yellow Room."

"Let me go! I have to find him!"

The fat man turned to look at her, his grin widening. "You are not going anywhere, my friend. I know *exactly* who you are. You are not going anywhere."

The room seemed to bend. His dark eyes held her, small holes that offered a glimpse into something dreadful. Her heart was thumping as it hadn't even in Leviathan's pool. She almost dropped offline before remembering !Xabbu. Perhaps he was caught somehow in the way Stephen had been caught. If she bailed out of the system, she might find him in the same deathlike trance that had claimed her brother. He was an innocent, as much so as Stephen. She couldn't abandon him.

"Let me go, you bastard!" she shouted. Strimbello's grip did not loosen. Instead he pulled her closer, dragging her into his wide lap.

"Enjoy the performance, good sir," he said. "And then you will see more—much more."

The crowd was shouting, an almost deafening roar of sound, but Renie could not think of the command to lower the volume. Something about the fat man submerged all her careful judgment in a flood of blind panic. She made a succession of gestures that accomplished nothing, then dredged up a command she hadn't used since her hacking days, splaying her fingers almost painfully wide and bowing her head.

For a moment the entirety of the Yellow Room seemed to freeze around her; a moment later, when it lurched back to life, she was several steps away from Strimbello, standing by herself on the floor before the stage. He stood, an expression of mild surprise on his broad features, and reached for her. Renie immediately moved herself out of the Yellow Room and onto the promenade.

Even the bottomless well looked normal compared to what she had left behind, but the Bushman's small sim was nowhere in sight. Strimbello would be on her in a moment.

"!Xabbu!" She shouted his name on the private channel, then boosted it and shouted again. "!Xabbu! Where are you?"

There was no answer. The little man was gone.

Second:

RED KING'S DREAM

. . . Long has paled that sunny sky:
Echoes fade and memories die.
Autumn frosts have slain July.

Still she haunts me, phantomwise,
Alice moving under skies
Never seen by waking eyes . . .

. . . In a Wonderland they lie,
Dreaming as the days go by,
Dreaming as the summers die:

Ever drifting down the stream—
Lingering in the golden gleam—
Life, what is it but a dream?

                              —Lewis Carroll

CHAPTER 10

Thorns

NETFEED/NEWS: Agreement Signed, But Mistrust Smolders in Utah.
(visual: men shaking hands in front of capitol building, Salt Lake City)
VO: A fragile three-way peace now exists between the Utah state government,
the Mormon Church, and the militant Mormon separatists known as the
"Deseret Covenant," but some question whether it can last without federal
involvement.
(visual: President Anford in Rose Garden)
The US government, citing the rights of states and cities to self-determination,
has so far declined to become involved, leading to complaints from some Utah
citizens that the Anford Administration has "reneged on the Constitution."
Others, however, applaud the Administration's hands-off approach.
(visual: Edgar Riley, Deseret spokesman, at press conference)
RILEY: "No government has a right to tell us what to do in God's country.
There are some warriors out here, hard men. If the state backtracks, we'll
just shut everything down from the borders in."

*T*hey come for you at dawn. It's Jankel, the nice one, and another named
Simmons or something—you haven't seen him much. They used to send
more than two, but times have changed. You haven't slept a wink, of course,
but they come in quietly anyway, as though they don't want to startle you
awake.

It's time, Jankel tells you. He looks apologetic.

You shrug off his extended hand and stand up—you aren't going to let someone else help you. You'll go on your own two legs if you can, but your knees are pretty weak. You've heard their footsteps in the corridor, phantom precursors, so many times through the long night. Now you feel gritty at the edges and blurry as a badly developed photograph. You're tired.

Sleep is coming, though. You'll sleep soon.

There's no priest or pastor—you told them you didn't want one. What kind of comfort could you get from some stranger babbling to you about something you don't believe in? Only Jankel to escort you, and Simmons or whatever his name is holding the door. Only a couple of low-wage prison bulls who need the overtime on a Sunday morning. They'll also pull a little bonus for doing this, of course, since it's one of the genuinely unpleasant jobs—no coercion of anyone but prisoners in the privatized penal system. Jankel must need the money with all those high-tax kids to feed. Otherwise, who else but a psychopath would sign up for this particular task?

The last walk. A shuffle, really, with those heavy-duty nylon restraints around your ankles. None of the things you've seen in flicks happen. The other inmates don't come to their bars to call terse farewells; most of them are sleeping, or pretending to sleep. You've been through this yourself when they took Garza. What could you say? And Jankel doesn't shout: Dead man walking! or any of that other stuff—never has. The closest he ever came was a quiet chat when you first came on the floor, where in best prison drama style he told you, If you work with me, everything'll be smooth—if not, you'll be doing some real hard time. Now he looks quiet and sorry, like he's taking someone else's dog, run over in the road, to the emergency veterinarian.

The place they take you isn't really a doctor's office—it is the death chamber, after all—but it has the look and smell of any prison surgery. The doctor is a small man—if he really is a doctor: you only need to be med-tech certified to perform an execution. He's obviously been waiting around about fifteen minutes longer than he wanted to with his morning coffee turning to acid in his stomach. He nods his head when you all come in, and a weird smile that's probably just dyspepsia and nerves plays across his lips. He nods again, then points a trifle shyly at the stainless steel table, just a regular examination table, with a little shrug as if to say, We wish it could be nicer, but you know how times are. . . .

The two guards each take an arm as you slide your backside onto the paper covering—they're helping you, really, making sure your trembling legs don't prompt an embarrassing collapse. They're helping, but their grips are very, very firm.

You lift your legs onto the table and let them ease you down onto your back. They begin to secure the straps.

Until this point, it could be any other visit to the prison doctor, except no one's talking. Not surprising, really—there's not much to say. Your condition has already been diagnosed, and it's terminal.

Dangerous. Useless bastard. Trouble. Poor self-control. Inconvenient to house and expensive to feed. The combination of symptoms has added up. The cure has been decided.

It's no use telling them you're innocent. You've done that for years, done it in every way possible. It hasn't changed a thing. The appeals, the couple of magazine articles—"Burying Our Mistakes" read one headline, appropriate to both prisons and hospitals—changed nothing in the end. The little kid in you, the part which had believed that if you cried hard enough someone would put it right, is gone now, rubbed out as efficiently and completely as the rest of you soon will be.

Some corporate officer is standing in the doorway, a sharkskin-gray shadow. You turn to watch him, but Jankel's hip is in the way. A brief splash of something cold in the crook of your elbow brings your eyes back to the doctor's pinched face. Alcohol? For what? They're swabbing your arm so you don't get an infection. A little prison humor, perhaps, more subtle than you would have expected. You feel something sharp slide though the skin, nosing for your vein, but something goes wrong. The doctor curses quietly—just a hint of panic underneath—and withdraws the needle, then probes for the vein again, once, twice, three more times without success. It hurts, like someone running a sewing machine up your arm. You feel something welling up in your chest that might be either a laugh or a long, bubbling scream.

You choke it down, of course. God forbid you should make a spectacle of yourself. They're only going to kill you.

Your skin has gone clammy all over. The fluorescents shimmer and swim as the spike of steel at last slides into its proper place and the doctor tapes it down. The other guard, Simmons or whatever his name is, leans over and tightens the strap so you don't jerk the needle free. They begin on the next needle.

There is something bewildering about this. It's the end of the world, but the people around you are acting as though they were performing some workaday job. Only the tiny beads of sweat on the doctor's upper lip and frowning forehead suggest otherwise.

When you have been trussed and lanced successfully, the gray suit in the corner of your vision moves forward. You haven't seen his face before, and you briefly wonder where he fits in the corporate hierarchy—is he an over-warden or an under-warden? Then you realize what kind of nonsense you're wasting your last moments on and feel a surge of dizzy disgust.

*This square-jawed white man mouths some suitably mournful platitudes,
then lifts a folder and reads out the penal corporation's indemnification, followed by their legal mandate to pump you full of sodium pentothal and then
potassium chloride until your heart stops beating and your brainbox goes flat-
line. They used to send a third fatal chemical down the pipe, too, but the
accountants decided that was gilding the lily.*

*The doctor has started the saline drip, although you feel nothing in your arm
except the discomfort of the needle and some stinging from the failed attempts.*

*Do you understand, son, the square-jawed white man asks you. Sure, you
want to snarl. You understand better than he knows. You understand that
they're just throwing out the trash and then recycling the empties. You'll be
more use to Society as ram-plugged hydroponic fertilizer than you ever were as
a mouth to feed in an expensive privatized cell.*

*You want to snarl, but you don't. For now, looking into the pale blue eyes of
this man, you realize in a way you haven't yet that you're really going to die.
No one is going to jump up from behind the sofa and tell you it was just a
joke. It's not a netflick either—no group of hired mercenaries is going to blow
down the prison doors and set you free. In a moment the doctor is going to
push that button and that bottle of clear liquid—they would be clear liquids,
wouldn't they, colorless, just like this square-jawed, flat-eyed white man they've
sent to read your death warrant—that bottle is going to start to bleed into the
main line. And then you're going to die.*

*You try to speak, but you can't. The cold has you shivering. Jankel pulls the
thin hospital blanket up to your chest, careful not to disturb the transparent
tube fanged into your arm like a long glass snake. You nod instead. By God,
you're not stupid. You understand the laws and how they work. If it hadn't
been one, it would have been another. They make those laws to keep people like
you away from what people like them have. So you nod, trying to say what
your dry tongue and constricted throat cannot: I know why you want me dead.
I don't need any more explanation than that.*

*The man in the gray suit smiles, a tight curved line, as though he recognizes
the look in your eyes. He nods to the doctor, just once, and then tucks his folder
under his arm and heads for the door, disappearing out of your sight beyond
the curving line of Jankel's blue trousers.*

*You have just met the Angel of Death. He was a stranger. He is always a
stranger.*

*Jankel gives your arm a squeeze, which means the doctor has turned the tap
on the second line, but you don't look up to meet the guard's eye. You don't
want your last sight on earth to be him. He's nobody—just a man who guarded
your cage. A decent guy for a keeper in a human zoo, maybe, but no more than
that.*

A short time passes—thick, sluggish time that nevertheless hurries. Your gaze slides up toward the flurorescent lights and they shimmer even more broadly than before. There are little fractures of color around the edges. Your eyes, you realize, are filling with tears.

At the same time, the room is growing warmer. You can feel your skin growing looser, your muscles unkinking. This isn't so bad.

But you're never coming back. Your heart speeds. They're pushing you out into the darkness. One passenger too many on the big ship, and you've drawn the short straw.

Some kind of animal panic races through you, and for a moment you strain against your bonds, or try to, but the whole thing is too far gone. A muscle twitches in your chest, that's all, a slow contraction like the early stages of labor. Like birth.

Wrong way, wrong way. You're going out, not coming in. . . .

The blackness is tugging you remorselessly, pulling you down, eroding your resistance. You're hanging by your fingernails over an ocean of warm velvet, and it would be so easy so easy so easy to let go . . . but there's something underneath all that softness, something harsh and final and oh so terrifyingly lonely.

Gone, the light almost gone, just a fast-disappearing smear. Gone, the light gone.

A soundless scream, a spark sizzling through a final instant before being swallowed by the cold darkness.

Oh, God, I don't want to

He was still shivering half an hour later.

"You're so scanny, Gardiner. Lethal injection—Jesus! You're a scan-master!"

Orlando looked up, trying to focus. The dark saloon was full of shadows and trailing mist, but his friend's broad silhouette was hard to mistake.

Fredericks slipped into one of the crooked high-backed chairs and perused the menu of experiences that flickered across the black table-top, an ever-changing abstract spiderweb of frost-white letters. He made a face of exaggerated disgust. The defiant lift to his shoulders made his sim appear even more chesty and musclebound than usual. "What is it with you and these fringe trips, Gardiner?"

Orlando could never figure why Fredericks liked bodybuilder sims. Maybe in RL he was a scrawny little guy. It was impossible to know, since Orlando had never seen his friend in the flesh, and at this point it would be embarrassing even to ask. Besides, Orlando himself was not innocent of image-tampering: the sim he was wearing was, as usual, a well-crafted product, although not particularly handsome or physically impressive.

"The death rides? I just like them." He was having some difficulty composing his thoughts, legacy of that last slide down into nothingness. "They . . . interest me."

"Yeah, well, I think they're morbid major." A line of tiny skeletons conga-danced across the tabletop in front of Fredericks, each one dressed in full Carmen Miranda drag; they strutted, hip-shook, then vanished in a sequence of pops as they tumbled over the edge. The place was full of the things—miniature skeletons playing fireman's pole on the swizzle sticks and skating on the ice trays, an entire skeletal army performing acrobatics on the vast chandelier. Some in tiny Stetsons and chaps even rode on the bats flittering in the shadows beneath the high ceiling. The decor of the Last Chance Saloon traded heavily on its virtual proximity to Terminal Row. Most of its habitués, however, preferred the mock-Gothic of the club to the more unpleasant and more realistic experiences on sale at the next site over.

"You did the airplane crash with me," Orlando pointed out.

Fredericks snorted. "Yeah. Once. You've been on that one so many times they probably have your seat permanently reserved." His broad sim face flattened out for a moment, as though somewhere the real Fredericks had withdrawn from the system, but it was only his software's inability to show sullenness—unfortunate, since Fredericks was prone to it. "That was the worst. I thought I was really going to die—I thought my heart was going to stop. How can you *do* that kind of shit, Gardiner?"

"You get used to it." But he hadn't, really. And that was part of the problem.

In the conversational lull that followed, the vast doors at one side of the saloon creaked open and a painfully cold wind swirled through the room. Orlando absently turned down his susceptibility; Fredericks, using a less expensive interface, didn't even notice. Something with glowing red eyes loomed in the open doorway, confettied with whirling snow. A few of the patrons nearest the door laughed. One very feminine sim screamed.

"Someone told me that they record those simulations from real people dying," said Fredericks abruptly. "They take 'em right off real people's interface rigs."

"Nah." Orlando shook his head. "They're just good gear. Well-written." He watched as the red-eyed thing grabbed the screaming woman and dragged her off into the snowy night. The doors creaked shut again. "What, they just sent somebody up fitted with a giga-expensive top-of-the-line teleneural recording rig, and it just happens to be running when a plane does a Manila? That's like a zillion to one chance, Frederico, and you wouldn't be getting it in some net arcade. Not to mention the fact that you can't record that kind of experience and play it back anyway, not like that. I've checked up on it, man. Real people recordings are just a jumble of stuff, a real monster mix. You can't interpret somebody else's experience through a different brain. It doesn't work."

"Yeah?" Fredericks did not sound entirely convinced, but he lacked Orlando's obsessive interest in VR and the net and generally didn't dispute him about such things.

"Anyway, that's not what I wanted to talk to you about." Orlando leaned back. "We've got more important things to deal with, and we need to talk in private. This place is dead, anyway. Let's go to my 'cot."

"Yeah. This place is dead." Fredericks giggled as two finger-length skeletons skittered across the table, playing frisbee with a bottlecap.

Orlando frowned. "That's not what I meant."

Orlando's electronic cottage was in Parc Corner, an upscale but Bo-hemian section of the Inner District inhabited mostly by well-to-do university students. His homebase in the virtual world was an almost stereotypical version of a boy's bedroom—the kind of room Orlando would have liked to have at home, but couldn't. A wall-wide screen showed a constant live video feed from the MBC Project, a vast swirl-ing desert of orange. Orlando's visitors had to squint to see the armies of little constructor robots moving through the haze of Martian dust. On the far wall a broad window looked down on a simulation of a late Cretaceous waterhole. It was pretty lively for over-the-counter wallpaper; at the moment, a young Tyrannosaurus was messily de-vouring a duck-billed Hadrosaurus.

The interior was modeled on the Scandinavian-style beach house Orlando's parents had rented when he was a child. He had been very impressed with the multitude of nooks, stairs, and partially-hidden alcoves, and if anything he had exaggerated the labyrinthine effect in his virtual reconstruction. Strewn everywhere about the multilevel space were souvenirs of his—and especially Thargor's—netgaming prowess. One corner of the room held a pyramid of simulated glass cases, each one containing a replica of the head of a vanquished enemy, rendered directly from a snapshot dump of the foe's final seconds whenever possible. At the summit of the pyramid Dieter Cabo's Black Elf Prince held pride of place, cross-eyed from the swordstroke that had just split his narrow skull. That battle had lasted three days, and had almost caused Orlando to fail his biology midterm, but it had been worth it. People in the Middle Country still spoke of the epic struggle with awe and envy.

Various other objects had niches of their own. There were cages of wrestling homunculi, the remnants of another enemy's misfired spell; the Aselphian Orb that Thargor had pulled from the brow of a dying god; even the skeletal hand of the wizard Dreyra Jarh. Thargor had not removed that himself, but he had filched it from a certain merchant of oddities only moments before its original (and somewhat irritated) owner arrived to reclaim it. Up the length of the staircase, in place of a banister, stretched the body of the unpleasant Worm of Morsin Keep. An hour wrestling with the thing in the Keep's brackish moat— and a certain respect for anything so stupid and yet so determined— had earned it a place in his collection. Besides, he thought it looked pretty detailed stretched out beside the stairs.

"I didn't think you'd want to talk about it." Fredericks slid down onto the broad black leather couch. "I figured you'd be really upset."

"I *am* upset. But there's more to this than Thargor getting killed. Much more."

Fredericks squinted. Orlando didn't know what his friend looked like in RL, but he was pretty sure he wore glasses. "What does that mean, 'more to this'? You impacted, Thargor got killed. What did I miss?"

"You missed a lot. C'mon, Fredericks, have you ever seen me do something like that? Someone hacked my venture. Somebody got at me!"

He did his best to explain the arresting vision of the golden city, but found it was almost impossible to find words that would explain how vibrantly, unbelievably *real* it had been. ". . . It was like, like—like if I tore a hole in that window," he gestured to the Cretaceous gnashing and squawking on the far side of simulated glass, "and you could see the real world behind it. Not a video picture of the real world, not even with the best resolution you can imagine, but the *real actual world.* But it was some place I've never seen. I don't think it's a place on earth."

"You think Morpher did it? Or maybe Dieter? He was really scorched over the Black Elf thing."

"Don't you get it? *Nobody* we know could do this. I don't know if

the government or Krittapong's top level research lab could do it."
Orlando began to pace back and forth across the sunken room. He felt
hemmed in. He made a quick gesture and the floorspace expanded,
moving the walls and Fredericks' couch several yards back.

"Hey!" His friend sat up. "Are you trying to tell me it was UFOs or
something? C'mon, Gardino, if someone was doing something that
weird on the net, it would be in the news or something."

Orlando paused, then shouted *"Beezle!"*

A door opened in the floor and a small something with rolling eyes
and too many legs leaped out and hurried toward him. It tumbled to
a stop by his feet, then tugged itself into an untidy heap and said, in
a raspy Brooklyn accent, "Yeah, boss?"

"Do a news search for me on the phenomenon I just described, or
any other major net anomalies. And find me the record of the final
fifteen minutes of my last Thargor game."

"Doing it now, boss." Another door opened in the floor and Beezle
popped into it. There was a cartoon-soundtrack noise of pots and pans
crashing and things falling, then the creature reappeared, limbs flailing, dragging a small black square as though it were the anchor off a
luxury liner. "Phew," the agent panted. "Lot of news to check, boss.
Wanna look at this while I'm searching? It's the game record."

Orlando took the small square and stretched; it grew to the size of
a beach towel and hung unsupported in space. He started to tilt it
toward Fredericks, then smiled. Even with as much time as he spent
on the net, he could still fall into a bit of RL-thinking when he was in
a hurry. VR didn't work that way: if Fredericks wanted to see the
sample, he'd see it no matter where he was sitting. But now he was
thinking about angles; he rapped on the square with his finger and it
expanded into the third dimension. "Run it, Beezle," he said. "Give
me a viewpoint from somewhere outside the characters."

There was a moment's pause as the processors reconfigured the
data, then the black cube was illuminated by the light of a torch flickering on two figures.

". . . Diamonds of imperial weight," he heard himself saying in his
deepened Thargor-voice.

"Fifty! By the gods!"

"Yes. Now, shut your mouth."

Orlando surveyed the scene critically. It was strange to stand on
the outside of Thargor like this, as though the barbarian were only a
character in a netflick. "Too early. I haven't even dug into the tomb
yet. *Forward ten minutes."*

Now he could see his alter-ego pushing through the upside-down thicket of roots, torch in one hand, runesword in the other. Suddenly, Thargor stood straight, Lifereaper lifted as if to ward off a blow.

"That's it!" said Orlando. "That's when I saw it! Beezle, give me POV so I can see the wall directly in front of Thargor."

The image blurred. An instant later, the viewpoint had moved to a place just behind the mercenary's right shoulder. The wall was fully visible, including the place where the burning crevice had appeared.

Except it hadn't appeared.

"What? This is scanny! Freeze it, Beezle." Orlando slowly rotated the shape, looking at the wall from different sides. His stomach lurched. "I don't believe this!"

"I don't see anything," said Fredericks.

"Thanks for pointing that out." Orlando made his agent change the viewpoint several times; he and Fredericks even froze the recorded simulation and entered it, but there was nothing out of the ordinary: Thargor was not reacting to anything visible.

"Shit." Orlando led his friend back out of the recording. "Let it run."

They watched in silence as Thargor leaned forward to stare at the still-unbroken wall. Then they heard Fredericks, as Pithlit the thief, shouting: *"There is something coming into the chamber! The tomb's guardian! Thargor!"*

"It didn't happen that fast, did it?" Fredericks sounded a little uncertain, but Orlando felt a surge of relief. He wasn't crazy after all.

"It sure as hell didn't! Look, here it comes." He pointed to the Lich shambling in from the edge of the cube, battle-ax flailing. "The whole sequence takes ten seconds, maybe, according to this. But you know it was longer than that, right?"

"Yeah. I'm pretty sure you were staring at that wall for a much longer time. I thought you'd had to break your connection, or the link had gone dead or something."

Orlando snapped his fingers and the cube vanished. "Beezle, investigate that section of the game record for editing or tampering of any kind. Check runtime discrepancies against the game clock. And send a copy to the Table of Judgment, noted as a possible improper character death."

The spidery agent popped into the room from out of nowhere and sighed deeply. "Jeez, boss, anything *else* you want me to do? I got the first download of search records."

"File 'em. I'll look at them later. Anything seriously interesting? Anything right on the nose?"

"Golden cities and/or super-real phenomena in virtual media? Not really, but I'm giving you everything I can find that's even a little warm."

"Good." Something was tugging at the back of Orlando's mind, a memory of the strange metropolis, its shining pyramids and towers of folded amber and gold leaf. At first it had seemed a personal vision, a gift for him alone—was he ready to give up on that possibility? "I changed my mind about the Table of Judgment. I don't want them involved—not yet, anyway."

Beezle grunted. "Whatever. Now, if you don't mind, I got work to do." The creature produced a cigar from out of the air, stuck it in one corner of its wide, wobbly mouth, then exited through a wall, ostentatiously blowing cartoon smoke rings.

"You gotta get another agent," said Fredericks. "That one's scanny, and you've had it for years."

"That's why we work so well together." Orlando crossed his legs Indian-style and floated half a yard up into the air. "The whole point of having an agent is that you don't need to worry about commands and stuff. Beezle knows what I mean when I say something."

Fredericks laughed. "Beezle Bug. That's so woofie."

Orlando glowered. "I named it when I was a kid. C'mon, we've got some weird stuff happening—*tchi seen* major sampled. Are you going to help me think, or are you going to sit there making stupid comments?"

"Sit here making stupid comments."

"Thought so."

Christabel's daddy and his friend Ron—but Christabel had to call him Captain Parkins—were sitting in the living room having a couple of jars. That's what they called it when they drank her father's Scotch and talked. But when her daddy drank some by himself or with Mommy, it wasn't called that. One of those grownup things.

She was wearing her Storybook Sunglasses, but she was having trouble paying attention to the story because she was also listening to the men. It was a treat for her daddy to be home in the daytime even on a Saturday, and she liked to be in the room he was in, even if he was talking to Captain Parkins who had a silly mustache that looked

like it belonged to a walrus. The two men were watching some football
players on the wall screen.

"It's a shame about that Gamecock kid, whatever his name was,"
her daddy said. "His poor parents."

"Hey, football's a dangerous game." Captain Parkins paused to
drink. She couldn't see him, because she was looking at Sleeping
Beauty on the Storybook Sunglasses, but she knew the sounds he
made swallowing, and she also knew his mustache would be getting
wet. She smiled to herself. "Most of them are ghetto kids—they'd
never get out otherwise. It's a calculated risk. Like joining the military." He laughed his loud ha-ha-ha laugh.

"Yeah, but still. It's a helluva way to go."

"What do you expect when you've got kids who are four hundred
pounds of muscle and can run like a sprinter? One of them hits you
and *pow*! Even with that new body armor, it's a wonder there aren't
more deaths."

"I know what you mean," her daddy said. "It's like they're breeding
them special in the inner city, extra-big, extra-fast. Like they're a
whole different species."

"I was in the National Guard during the St. Louis riots," said Captain Parkins. There was something cold in his voice that made Christabel squirm even across the room. "They *are* a whole different
species."

"Well, I wish the 'Heels would start recruiting a few more of them,"
her daddy said, laughing. "We could use some muscle on our defensive line."

Christabel got bored with listening to them talk about sports. The
only thing she liked were the names of the teams—Tarheels, Blue
Devils, Demon Deacons. They might have been from a fairy tale.

The picture of the handsome prince had been frozen for a little
while. She touched the earpiece and let it run. He was sliding through
a forest of bushes covered with thorns, big long sharp ones. Even
though she'd seen the story many times, she still worried that he
might get caught on one of them and really be hurt.

*"He made his way through the ring of thorns, wondering what might be
hidden inside,"* the voice said in her hearplug. She was only wearing
one so she could hear Daddy and his friend talk, so the voice was
quiet. *"Now you read the next part,"* it told her. Christabel squinted at
the lines of print that appeared beneath the thorns as though written
on a cloud of mist.

"Sev . . . several times he was snagged on the thorny branches," she read,

"and once he was ca . . . ca . . . caught fast so that he feared he might never escape. But he carefully pulled his shirt and cloak free. His clothes were torn, but he was not hurt."

"Christabel, honey, could you read a little more quietly?" her daddy called. "Ron doesn't know how that one ends. You'll spoil it for him."

"Funny. Very funny," said Captain Parkins.

"Sorry, Daddy." She read on, whispering, as the prince broke through a wall of cobwebs and found himself at the gate of Sleeping Beauty's castle.

"Oh, I've got a story about our little old friend," said Captain Parkins. "Caught him yesterday mucking about in the records for the PX. You'd think with the way he goes through food that he was trying to double his meals quota, but he was just trying to increase his allowance of a certain key product."

"Let me guess. Plant food? Fertilizer?"

"Even stranger. And, considering he hasn't been out of that place in thirty years, downright bizarre. . . ."

Christabel stopped listening because there were new words forming across the bottom of the Sleeping Beauty story. They were bigger than the others, and one of them was her name.

HELP ME CHRISTABEL, it read. SECRET DON'T TELL ANYONE.

As the word "SECRET" appeared she realized she was reading out loud. She stopped, alarmed, but Captain Parkins was still talking to her daddy and they hadn't heard her.

". . . I told the PX to refuse the order unless he could give them an acceptable explanation, of course, and I also asked them to reroute any unusual requests to me. Now what do you think he's after? Making a bomb? Spring cleaning?"

"Like you said, he hasn't been out in decades. No, I think he's just senile. But we'll keep an eye on him. Maybe I should drop by and check up—after I've shaken this cold. I'm sure that place incubates viruses like nobody's business."

Christabel was still reading the words in her Storybook Sunglasses, but she was reading them silently now, and holding her breath, too, because it was such a strange secret to have right next to her daddy. ". . . AND BRING THEM TO ME PLEASE HURRY DON'T TELL ANYONE SECRET."

The regular words came back, but Christabel didn't want to read about Sleeping Beauty any more. She took off her Sunglasses, but before she could stand up, her mother appeared in the living-room door.

"Well, you boys look comfortable," she said. "I thought you were sick, Mike."

"Nothing that a little football and a few judicious doses of single malt won't clear up right smart."

Christabel stood up and turned off the Sunglasses in case they started talking out loud and gave the secret away. "Mom, can I go out? Just for a minute?"

"No, honey, I've just put lunch on the table. Have something to eat first, then you can go. Ron, will you join us?"

Captain Parkins shifted in his chair and put his empty glass down on the coffee table. "I'd be delighted, ma'am."

Christabel's mother smiled. "If you call me ma'am, again, I'll be forced to poison your food."

"It'd still be an improvement over what I get at home."

Her mother laughed and led the men into the kitchen. Christabel was worried. The message had said hurry. But once lunch was on the table, no one went anywhere. That was the rule, and Christabel always obeyed the rules. Well, almost always.

She stood up, a stalk of celery in her hand. "Can I go out now?"

"If it's okay with your father."

Her daddy looked her up and down like he was suspicious. For a moment she was scared, but then she saw he was playing a joke on her. "And where are you taking that celery, young lady?"

"I like to eat it when I'm walking." She took a bite to show him. "I like to make it crunch when I walk, so it sounds like a monster going crunch crunch crunch stepping on buildings."

All the grownups laughed. "Kids," said Captain Parkins.

"Okay, then. But be back before dark."

"I promise." She scurried out of the dining room and took her coat down off the peg, but instead of heading directly for the front door she went quietly down the hall toward the bathroom and opened the cabinet under the sink. When she had filled her pockets, she moved as silently as she could back to the door. "I'm going now," she shouted.

"Be careful, little monster!" her mother called back.

Red and brown leaves were skittering across the front lawn. Christabel hurried to the corner. After peeking back to make sure no one was watching, she turned toward Mister Sellars' house.

Nobody answered when she knocked. After a few minutes she let herself in, even though it felt funny, like being a robber or something.

The wet, hot air pressed in all around her, so thick it seemed like something alive.

Mister Sellars was sitting in his chair, but his head was way back and his eyes were closed. For a moment she was sure he was dead, and was getting ready to be really scared, but then one eye opened like a turtle's eye, really slow, and he looked at her. His tongue came out, too, and he licked his ragged lips and tried to talk, but he couldn't make any sounds come out. He held his hand up toward her. It was shaking. At first she thought he wanted her to take it, but then she saw that he was pointing at her bulging pockets.

"Yes, I brought some," she said. "Are you okay?"

He moved his hand again, almost a little angry this time. She pulled the bars of her mother's face soap out of her coat and piled them in his lap. He began scratching at one of the bars with his fingers, but he was having trouble getting the wrapping off.

"Let me do it." She took the bar out of his lap and unpeeled it. When it lay in her hand, white and shiny, he pointed to a plate sitting on the table beside him. On the plate was a very old cheese—it was all dry and cracked—and a knife.

"You want some food?" she asked.

Mister Sellars shook his head and picked up the knife. He almost dropped it, his hands were shaking so much, but then he held it out to Christabel. He wanted her to cut the soap.

She sawed away at the slippery bar for some time. She had done soap carving in class, but it wasn't easy. This time she concentrated very hard, and at last she managed to cut off a piece as wide as two of her fingers side by side. Mister Sellars reached out a hand like a melted bird claw and took it from her, then popped it in his mouth and slowly began to chew.

"Yuck!" she said. "That's bad for you!"

Mister Sellars smiled for the first time. Little white bubbles were in the corner of his mouth.

He took the soap and the knife from her and began to cut himself more pieces. When he had swallowed the first and was about to put the second in his mouth, he smiled again and said: "Go get changed." His voice was weak, but at least he sounded like the Mister Sellars she knew.

When she returned wearing the terrycloth bathrobe, he had finished the whole first bar and had begun to cut up another.

"Thank you, Christabel," he said. "Zinc peroxide—just what the doctor ordered. I've been very busy and I haven't been getting my vitamins and minerals."

"People don't eat soap for vitamins!" she said indignantly. But she wasn't completely sure, because since she'd been in school she'd been getting her vitamins in a skin patch, and anyway maybe old people had a different kind of vitamins.

"I do," the old man said. "And I was very sick until you got here."

"But you're better now?"

"Much better. But *you* should never eat any—it's just for special old men." He wiped a smear of white from his lower lip. "I've been working very, very hard, little Christabel. People to see, things to do." Which was a silly joke, she knew, because he never went anywhere or saw anyone but her and the man who delivered his food, he'd told her that. His smile went away and his eyes started to close. After a moment, he opened them again, but he looked very tired. "And now that you've rescued me, perhaps you'd better head back home. I'm sure you had to make up some story about where you were going. I feel guilty enough about having you lie to your parents without getting you in trouble by keeping you too long."

"How did you talk to me in my Storybook Sunglasses?"

"Oh, just a little trick I learned when I was a young cadet." His head wobbled a little. "I think I need to sleep now, my friend. Can you let yourself out?"

She sat up straight. "I *always* let myself out."

"So you do. So you do." He raised his hand as if he were waving to her. His eyes closed again.

When Christabel had changed back into her clothes—they were damp, so she would have to walk around for a while before she went home—Mister Sellars was asleep in his chair. She looked at him carefully to make sure he wasn't sick again, but he was a much pinker color than he'd been when she arrived. She cut him off a few more pieces of soap, just in case he felt weak when he woke up again, then tucked his blanket close around his long thin neck.

"It's so difficult," he said suddenly. She jumped back, afraid she'd woken him up, but his eyes did not open and his voice was whispery and hard to understand. "Everything must be hidden in plain sight. But I despair sometimes—I can only speak to them in whispers, half-truths, bits of tattered poetry. I know how the oracle felt. . . ."

He mumbled a bit more, but she couldn't hear the words. When he got quiet and didn't say anything more, she patted his thin hand and left. A cloud of mist followed her out the front door. The wind on her wet clothing made her shiver.

An Oracle was a kind of bird, wasn't it? So was Mister Sellars dreaming about the days when he used to be an airman?

The leaves came swirling down the sidewalk past her, skipping and tumbling like circus acrobats.

His arms were pinioned. He was being jostled and pushed down a dark trail, sheer cliff faces looming on either side. He was being carried away, he knew, down into blackness and nothingness. Something important lay behind him, something that he dared not lose, but every moment the hands that clutched him, the shadowy forms on either side, were carrying him farther and farther away from it.

He tried to turn and felt a sharp pain in his arm, as though someone held a needle-bladed dagger against the flesh. The deeper darkness of the mountain pass was reaching out to enfold him. He struggled, ignoring the piercing agony in his arms, and at last managed to pull free enough to turn his head.

In the cleft behind him, nestled between the rocky slopes but miles away, lay a field of sparkling golden light. As he looked out from shadow, it burned in the distance like a prairie fire.

The city. The place where he would find the thing he had hungered for so long. . . .

The hands seized him and turned him back around, then shoved him forward. He still could not see who held him, but he knew that they were dragging him down into shadow, into emptiness, into a place where even the memory of the golden city at last would fade. He fought against his captors but he was held fast.

His dream, his one hope, was receding. He was being carried down helplessly into a black void. . . .

"Orlando! Orlando! You're having a bad dream. Wake up."

He struggled upward toward the voice. His arms hurt—they had him! He had to fight! He had to . . .

He opened his eyes. His mother's face hovered over him, shining faintly in the light from the window like a three-quarter moon.

"Look what you've done." Concern fought with annoyance in her voice; concern won, but just barely. "You've knocked all your things over."

"I . . . I was having a bad dream."

"As if I couldn't tell. It's that net, all day long. No wonder you have nightmares." She sighed, then bent and began picking things up.

A little anger pierced his lingering chill. "You think the net is the only reason I have nightmares?"

She paused, a wad of dermal patches filling her palm like fallen leaves. "No," she said. Her voice was tight. "No, of course I don't." She put the patches on his bedside table and bent to pick up the other things he had knocked over. "But I still think it can't be good for you to spend so much time plugged into . . . into that machine."

Orlando laughed. It was an angry laugh, and he meant it to be. "Well, everybody needs a hobby, Vivien."

She pursed her lips, even though it had been his parents' idea that he should call them by their first names, not his. "Don't be bitter, Orlando."

"I'm not." And he wasn't, really, he realized. Not like sometimes. But he was angry and frightened and he wasn't quite sure why. Something to do with the nightmare, the details of which were already beginning to evaporate—a feeling that something else was also slipping away from him. He took a breath. "I'm sorry. I'm just . . . it was a scary dream."

She set his IV stand back up straight—he had tipped it over against the wall with his thrashing—and checked to make sure the needle was still in place and secured. "Doctor Vanh says we can stop using this at the end of the week. That will be nice, won't it?" It was her way of apologizing. He tried to accept it in good grace.

"Yeah, that'll be nice." He yawned. "I'll go back to sleep. Sorry if I made a lot of noise."

She pulled the blanket back up to his chest. For a moment she rested her cool hand against his cheek. "We . . . I was just worried. No more bad dreams, now. Promise?"

He slid down, found the remote, and tilted the upper part of the bed to a more comfortable angle. "Okay, Vivien. Good night."

"Good night, Orlando." She hesitated for a moment, then leaned to kiss him before she went out.

For a moment he considered turning on his nightlight to read, then decided against it. Knowing that his mother had heard his distress from the other room made the darkness a little more comfortable than usual, and he had things to think about.

The city, for one thing. That preposterous place, of which no record seemed to remain in the Middle Country. It had invaded his dreams just as it had invaded Thargor's world. Why did something which was probably no more than a bit of signal interference, or at most a hacker's prank, seem so important? He had given up believing in far more practical types of miracles long ago, so what could this mirage possibly mean for him? Did it signify anything at all, or was it only a freak occurrence acting now as a magnet for his fear and largely-abandoned hope?

The house was quiet. Nothing short of an explosion would wake his father, and by now his mother would have slid back down into her own shallower and more restless slumber. Orlando was alone in the darkness with his thoughts.

CHAPTER 11

Inside the Beast

NETFEED/MUSIC: Christ Plays For Lucky Few
(visual: close-up of dog's head)
VO: Johann Sebastian Christ made a surprise appearance on a local net show
in his adopted hometown of New Orleans—
(visual: dog head, human hands)
—the first time the reclusive singer has been seen since the death of three
members of his musical group Blond Bitch in a stage accident last year.
(visual: man dancing in dog mask, flaming stage shown on wallscreen in
background)
Christ performed three songs for the astonished studio audience,
accompanying himself with a playback of the accident. . . .

Renie turned, frantically scanning the crowd that filled the terraces around the bottomless well. !Xabbu hadn't replied, but perhaps there was something wrong with his equipment. Perhaps he'd just gone offline, and there was something wrong with *her* equipment, which still registered a guest on her line. She prayed it was that simple.

The crush was insubstantial but still overwhelming. Laughing businessmen in smoothly tailored, blade-hard bodies bumped her aside as they passed, their first-class rigs and paid-up accounts generating an invisible but very real barrier between them and the hoi polloi. A few obvious tourists in rudimentary virtual forms moved aimlessly, overwhelmed, as the swirling traffic bounced them from one edge of the walkway to the other. Smaller forms, servitor creatures and agents, darted in and out of the throng, running errands for their masters. As far as Renie could tell, !Xabbu was not one of them, but her search was made more difficult by the unexceptional quality of the sim he had been wearing. There were at least two dozen quite similar figures within a short distance of her, gawking at the scenery while trying to stay out of the way of the big spenders.

Even if he were close by, without audio contact it was impossible to locate him quickly, and Renie knew she had only moments before Strimbello arrived. She needed to move, to get going—but where? Even if she ran far and fast, she couldn't hope to hide for very long within Mister J's from someone who was connected to the club. Besides, the fat man had announced that he knew her, knew who she truly was. Even now the club's management might be accessing her index, contacting the Poly to get her fired—who could guess?

But she could not afford those worries right now. She had to find !Xabbu.

Had he simply gone offline, disgusted by the Yellow Room's grotesque floor show? He might even now be loosening his straps in the Harness Room, waiting for her to return. But what if he hadn't?

A startled eddy of reaction passed over the faces around her. Most of the terrace crowd turned toward the door of the Yellow Room. Renie turned, too.

Something huge had appeared in the passage behind her, vast and round, wider than four or five normal sims and still growing. Its shaven head swiveled like the turret on a tank; black eyes like machine gun barrels raked the crowd, then locked on her.

The thing that called itself Strimbello smiled. "*There* you are."

Renie spun, took two swift steps, and flung herself over the rim of the well. Moving at top permissible speed, she dove downward through other, less hurried club patrons who floated like lazy fish. Her descent was still agonizingly slow—the well was a browsing device, not a thrill-ride—but she did not intend to outrun the fat man: he almost undoubtedly knew Mister J's far too well for that to work. She had simply moved out of his visual field for a moment, which she hoped would give her time to do something more effective.

"*Random,*" she commanded.

The well and its thousands of sims bobbing like champagne bubbles blurred and vanished, replaced a moment later by another crush of bodies, all naked this time, although some bore attributes she had never seen on a living human form. The light was directionless and low, the close-leaning walls velvety folds of uterine red. Throbbing music made her hearplugs almost bounce. A sim face, frighteningly imprecise, looked up from the nearest coil of forms; a hand snaked free and reached out to her, beckoning.

"Oh, no," she murmured. How many of these shapes were minors, children like Stephen, admitted with a smirk by the management and allowed to glut themselves on the filth of this place? How many disguised children had been present in the Yellow Room, for that matter? Nausea knotted her stomach. *"Random."*

A vast flat-walled space opened before her, its farther end so distant as to be nearly invisible. Gasflame blue letters appeared before her in a script she did not recognize, while a voice intoned words into her hearplugs that were equally incomprehensible. An instant later the whole picture shuddered as the translation software read her index and changed to English.

". . . Choose now whether you wish a team game or an individual competition."

She stood and stared as humanoid shapes snapped into existence just behind the blue-burning letters. They wore spiked helmets and shiny body armor; the eyes within the visors were only sparks.

"You have opted for an individual competition," said the voice with a faint note of approval. *"The game is creating your designated opponents now . . ."*

"Random."

She moved through the rooms faster and faster, hoping to lay down so many kinks in her trail that even if they tried to pin her location directly it would take Strimbello some time to find her. She jumped, and found . . .

A pool, surrounded by lazily swaying palm trees. Bare-breasted mermaids lounged on the rocks beside it, combing their hair as they swayed to languid steel guitar music.

She jumped.

A long table with one empty seat. The dozen men waiting there all wore robes; most also wore beards. One turned as she popped in, smiled, and cried, "Seat yourself, Lord."

She jumped again, and kept jumping.

A room full of blackness, with stars gleaming distantly up where the roof should be, and red-lit crevices in the floor. Somebody or something was groaning.

A thousand men with smooth heads like crash dummies, all dressed in identical coveralls, sitting on benches in two long rows, slapping each other.

A jungle full of shadows and eyes and bright, colorful birds. A woman in a torn blouse was tied to a tree. Oily red blossoms were piled around her feet.

A cowboy saloon. The bad guys wore nothing but spurs.

A ship's rocking cabin, oil lamps swinging, tankards waiting in the gimbals.

A glittering ballroom where all the women's faces were hidden behind animal masks.

A medieval inn. The fire burned high and something howled outside the tiny windows.

An empty park bench beside a streetlight.

A blast of throbbing noise and blinding glare that might have been a dance club.

A cave with wet walls, illuminated by strands like glowing spiderwebs that dangled from the ceiling.

An old-fashioned phone box. The receiver was off the hook.

A desert with walls.

A casino that seemed to inhabit the gangster era of Hollywood movies.

A desert without walls.

A chamber with an oven-hot floor and all the furniture made of metal.

A formal Korean garden, the bushes full of grunting naked shapes.

An open-air café beside the ruins of an ancient freeway.

A terraced garden jutting like a theater balcony from the side of a tall cliff. Beside it, a vast waterfall thundered down into the gorge . . . .

Dizzy, almost ill from the speed of her transitions, Renie paused on the terrace. She closed her eyes until the blur of colors stopped, then opened them again. A few of the dozen or so guests sitting at tables along the edge of the garden looked up incuriously, then turned back to their conversations and the spectacle of the waterfall.

"May I serve you?" A smiling, elderly Asian man had materialized beside her.

"I'm having trouble with my pad," she told him. "Can you connect me to your main switching center?"

"Done. Would you like a table while you conduct your business, Mister Otepi?"

Damn. She had stopped in one of the high-rent zones of the club. Of course they would have run her index as soon as she entered. At least they hadn't grabbed her; maybe Strimbello hadn't put out a general alert. Still, there was no sense pushing her luck. "Not yet, thank you. I may have to leave. Just a privacy shield, please."

The man nodded and then vanished. A circle of blue light appeared around her at waist level, demonstrating that she was shielded. She could still hear the roar of the great waterfall and watch it smashing down the rocks into the canyon, where it disappeared into a cloud of white spume; she could even see the other guests and hear the occasional snatch of conversation over the water noises—but they, presumably, could no longer see or hear her.

No time to waste. She forced herself to think calmly. She dared not leave unless !Xabbu had already gone offline, but if he had, she would have no way of knowing. If she stayed, she felt sure Strimbello would find her sooner rather than later. He might not have sounded a general alarm—even as an intruder, she was probably not very important in the larger scheme of things—but Strimbello himself, whether human or frighteningly realistic Puppet, did not seem the type to give up easily. She would have to find a way to stay inside the system until she either located !Xabbu or was forced to give up.

"Phone connect."

A gray square appeared before her, as though someone had taken a sharp knife to reality—rather, to imitation reality. She gave the number she wanted, then keyed in her pad's identification code. The square remained gray, but a small glowing dot appeared in the lower corner to tell her she'd connected with the one-shot access bank she'd prepared for just such an emergency.

"Carnival." She whispered, but it was only reflex: if the privacy shield was legitimate, she could scream the code word until her lungs ached without anyone hearing. If it wasn't, everything she had done was already known to her pursuers.

Nobody seemed to be watching. The access bank downloaded the new identity instantly. She was faintly disappointed that there was no sensation—surely shape-changing, a hallowed and ancient magical art, should feel like something? But of course her shape hadn't changed: she still wore the nondescript sim in which she'd entered, and behind that was still Irene Sulaweyo, teacher and part-time Net Bandit. Only her index was different. Mister Otepi from Nigeria had vanished. Mister Babutu from Uganda had taken his place.

She dissolved the privacy shield and surveyed the massive waterfall, the elegant formal garden. Waiters, or things that looked like waiters, were skimming from table to table like waterbugs. She could not hang about this place forever. In such a service-intensive sector of the club she would quickly attract attention again, and she did not want her new identity linked in any way with the old one. Someone would notice eventually, of course: she had entered as Otepi, and at the end of some arbitrary accounting period an expert system checking the records would notice that Otepi had never left. But that might be hours from now, or even days. A node with a turnover as large and constant as Mister J's would have a hard time locating the other half of the discrepancy, and with luck she would be long gone by the time they did. With luck.

With a word she shifted back to the main lounge, where she would pass unnoticed more easily in the large and active crowd. She was tired, too, and eager for the chance to stay in one place for a few minutes. But what about !Xabbu? He was so much less experienced. What effect would such stress be having on him if he wandered somewhere in this vast labyrinth, alone and frightened?

The lounge was still full of glaring lights and long shadows, of voices and wild music. Renie picked a bench sunk in the darkness at the base of one of the cyclopean walls and turned down the gain on her hearplugs. It was hard to know where to start. There were so many rooms here, so many public spaces. She herself had been in dozens, and she was sure she had only scratched the surface. And she could not even guess at how many people might be in the club—hundreds of thousands, perhaps. Mister J's was not a physical space. The only limitation was the speed and power of the equipment that lay behind it. Her friend could be anywhere.

Renie turned to look at the revolving stage. The pale singer and her goblinish band were gone. Instead, a group of elephants, normal in every detail except for their straw hats, sun glasses, and strangely spiky instruments—and of course the delicate rosy pink of their baggy skins—were churning out slow, thumping dance music. She could feel the jar of the bass even through her lowered hearplugs.

"Excuse me." One of the shiny-faced waiters hovered before her.

"Nothing but rent for me," she told him. "I'm just resting."

"Fine with me, sir, I assure you. But I have a message for you."

"For me?" She leaned forward, staring. She felt her skin tingle. "That's not possible." He raised an eyebrow. His foot tapped on air. Renie swallowed. "I mean, are you sure?"

If the waiter was playing a game with her on behalf of her pursuers, he was doing a very convincing job. He practically seethed with impatience. "Oh, sweeze. You are Mister Babutu, aren't you? Because if you are, the rest of your party wants to meet you in the Contemplation Hall."

She recovered herself and thanked him; an instant later he was gone, a vanishing huff of silver.

Of course, it *could* be !Xabbu, she thought. She had told him the names of both emergency identities, his and hers. Then again, it might just as easily be Strimbello or some other, less broadly-drawn functionaries, wishing to avoid a scene. !Xabbu or Strimbello, it had to be one or the other—Mister Babutu didn't really exist, so no one else would be looking for him.

What choice did she have? She couldn't ignore the possibility of finding her friend.

She picked Contemplation Hall out of the main menu and shifted. She thought she detected an almost infinitesimal hitch to the transfer, as though the system were experiencing unusually heavy usage, but it was hard to dispel the idea that the delay might mean she was going somewhere deep into the heart of the system, far from the metaphorical surface. Deep inside the beast.

The hall was a very striking conception, a sort of Classical folly writ large. Tall columns covered in flowering vines held up a huge circular dome, part of which had cracked and fallen away. White shards, some as large as a suburban house, glinted like bones along the base of the columns, tucked in threadbare blankets of moss. A bright blue sky striped with wind-tattered clouds showed through the hole in the dome and between the pillared arches on each side, as though the hall stood atop Mount Olympus itself. A few sims, most of them far in the simulated distance, strolled about the wide grassy space inside the ring of stone.

She did not like the idea of leaving the outer edge and moving into the open space, but if the club's authorities had summoned her to this place, it wouldn't matter whether she tried to be inconspicuous or not. She shifted toward the center and turned to gaze around her, impressed with the completeness of the design. The stones of the massive folly seemed convincingly old, surfaces shot with cracks, columns surrounded and overgrown with vegetation. Rabbits and other small animals moved across the hummocky ground, and a pair of twittering birds were building a nest on one of the shards of the tumbled dome.

"Mister Babutu?"

She whirled. "Who are you?"

He was a tall, lantern-jawed man, made to seem even bigger by his baggy dark suit. He wore a tall and scuffed black top hat; a striped muffler hung loosely around his long neck. "I'm Wicket." He smiled broadly, tipping the hat. The shabbiness of his attire sat oddly with his quick, vigorous movements. "Your friend Mister Wonde sent me. You got a message from him?"

Renie eyed him. "Where is he?"

"With some of my mates. Come on—I'll take you to him." He pulled something from inside his coat. If he saw Renie flinch at the movement, he showed no sign, but instead lifted the battered flute to his lips and played a few piping bars, something that she could not identify but which seemed familiar as a nursery rhyme. A hole opened in the grass between them. Renie could see steps leading down.

"Why didn't he come himself?"

Wicket was already in the hole to his waist, which left the top of his black stove-pipe at about Renie's eye level. "Not feeling well, I think. He just asked me to fetch you. Said you might ask some questions, and to remind you about some game with string."

The string game. !Xabbu's song. Renie felt a weight of worry lift from her. No one but the Bushman could know about that. Wicket's hat was just vanishing below the surface of the ground. She climbed down after him.

The tunnel seemed to be something from a children's book, the home of some talking animal or other magical creature. Although within moments she and Wicket had moved far below what should have been the surface, the tunnel wall was pierced with small windows, and out of each she could see a scene of artificial beauty—riverlands, meadows, wind-groomed forests of oak and beech. Here and there along the downward spiral of the steps were small doors no higher than Renie's knee, each with a knocker and minute keyhole. The urge to open one was powerful. The place was like some wonderful dollhouse.

But she could not pause to look at anything. Although she herself was forced to keep one hand on the curving banister, Wicket, despite his long legs and broad shoulders, bounced down the stairway ahead of her at a rapid pace, still blowing on his flute. After a few minutes he had vanished down the twisting stairwell. Only thin musical echoes proved he was still in front of her.

The stairwell wound down and down. Occasionally she thought she heard high-pitched voices from behind the doorways, or caught a glimpse of a bright eye peering out through a keyhole. Once she had to duck to avoid garrotting herself on a laundry line which had been stretched right across the stairwell. Tiny calico dresses, none bigger than a slice of bread, slapped damply against her face.

Down they went, still farther. More stairs, more doors, and the continuous trill of Wicket's elusive music—Renie felt the fairy-tale charm of the place beginning to pall. She craved a cigarette and a glass of beer.

She ducked her head again to go under a low spot in the stairwell, and when she raised it, the light had changed. Before she could react, her foot met resistance too suddenly, giving her a jolt that would have been painful if her body were not in harness back at the Poly. She had reached level ground.

Stretching before her, as if in continuation of the storybook theme, was a Mystery Cave, the sort of place which jolly children discovered in jolly stories. It was long and low, all stone and soft earth. The ceiling was whiskery with roots, as though the cavern were some hollow space beneath forest earth, but tiny lights twinkled amid the tangle. The dirt floor was covered with piles of strange objects. Some—feathers and shiny beads and polished stones—looked as though they had been collected and abandoned by animals or birds. Others, like a pit filled with the limbs and heads of dolls, seemed purposeful and somewhat overwrought, a university art project on corrupted innocence. Other objects were just incomprehensible, featureless spheres and cubes and less recognizable geometric shapes scattered across the earthen floor. Some of these even seemed to glow with a faint light of their own.

Wicket stood grinning before her. Even with his shoulders hunched, the top of his head loomed up among the twinkling fairy-lights. He lifted his flute and played again, doing a slow dance as he did so. There was something incongruous about him, some oddness that Renie couldn't quite name. If he was a Puppet, he was a work of real originality.

Wicket stopped and repocketed the flute. "You're slow," he said, mockery in his deep voice. "Come on—your friend's waiting."

He swept one hand to the side in a mock-formal bow and stepped back. Behind him on the far side of the long cavern, blocked from her sight until this moment, was the occluded glow of a campfire fenced by shadowy figures. Renie, again feeling the need for caution, moved forward. Her heart sped.

!Xabbu, or a sim that looked very much like his, was sitting in the midst of a group of much better-defined figures, all men in tattered finery similar to Wicket's. With his sketchy features and rudimentary body details, the Bushman seemed like nothing so much as a ginger-bread man.

More fairy tales. Renie was feeling a little punchy.

"Are you okay?" she asked on private band. *"!Xabbu! Is that you?"*

There was no reply, and for a moment she was certain she'd been tricked. Then the sim turned toward her, and a voice that, despite the distortion, was recognizably the Bushman's, said: "I am very glad my new friends have found you. I have been here such a long time. I was beginning to think you had left me behind."

"Talk to me! If you can hear me, just raise your hand."

The sim did not move, but sat regarding her with expressionless eyes.

"I wouldn't leave you," she said at last. "How did you end up here?"

"We found him wandering around, lost and confused." Wicket drew up his long legs as he seated himself beside the fire. "My friends and me." He pointed to the others in the circle. "That's Brownbread, Whistler, and Corduroy." His companions were fat, thin, and thinner still. None were as tall as Wicket, but all seemed otherwise quite similar, full of nudges and restless energy.

"Thank you." Renie turned her attention back to !Xabbu. "We must be going now. We're really quite late."

"Are you sure you wouldn't rather stay with us for a while?" Wicket spread his hands before the flames. "We don't get many visitors."

"I would like to. I'm very grateful for your help. But we are running up too much connect time."

Wicket raised his eyebrow as though she had said something faintly off-color, but remained silent. Renie leaned forward and put her hand on !Xabbu's shoulder, conscious that back at the Poly she must be touching his real body. Despite the low quality of the force-feedback, it certainly felt like her friend's narrow, birdlike physique. "Come along. Let's go back."

"I do not know how." There was only a little sadness in his voice, but a great lassitude, as though he spoke from the edge of sleep. "I have forgotten."

Renie cursed to herself and triggered the exit sequence for both of them, but as the cavern around her began to blur and fade, she could see that !Xabbu was not shifting with her. She aborted the exit.

"Something's wrong," she said. "Something is holding him here."

"Perhaps you'll have to stay a little longer." Wicket smiled. "That'd be nice."

"Mister Wonde can tell us some more stories," said Brownbread, pleasure evident on his round face. "I wouldn't mind hearing the one about the Lynx and the Morning Star again."

"Mister Wonde *can't* tell you any more stories," Renie said sharply. Were these men simple-minded? Or were they just Puppets, enacting some strange looped tableau that she and !Xabbu had stumbled into? "Mister Wonde has to leave. Our time is up. We cannot afford to stay longer."

Greyhound-thin Corduroy nodded his head gravely. "Then you must call the Masters. The Masters see to all comings and goings. They will put you right."

Renie felt sure she knew who the Masters were, and knew she did not want to explain her problem to the club's authorities. "We can't. There . . . there are reasons." The men around the fire frowned. If they were Puppets, they might at any moment trigger some automatic message of breakdown to the club's troubleshooters. She needed time to figure out why !Xabbu could not be removed from the net. "There is . . . there is someone very bad pretending to be one of the Masters. If the Masters are summoned, then this bad one will find us. We cannot call them."

All the men nodded now, like superstititous savages in some Z-grade netflick. "We'll help you, then," said Wicket enthusiastically. "We'll help you against the Bad One." He turned to his companions. "The Colleen. The Colleen will know what to do for these fellows."

"That's right." Whistler's lisp betrayed the origin of his name. He spoke slowly and wore a lopsided grin. "She'll help. But she'll want something."

"Who's Colleen?" Renie struggled with fear and impatience. Something was seriously wrong with her friend, the club authorities were searching for her, and Strimbello had said he knew who she really was, but instead of taking !Xabbu and getting the hell out, she was being forced to participate in some kind of fairytale scenario. She looked at the Bushman. His sim sat motionless beside the fire, rigid as a chrysalis.

"She knows things," said Brownbread. "Sometimes she tells."

"She's magical." Wicket waved his long hands as if to demonstrate. "She does favors. For a price."

Renie could not help herself. "Who are you? What do you do here? How did you get here?"

"Those are some very, very good questions," Corduroy said slowly. He seemed to be the thoughtful one. "We'd have to give a lot of gifts to the Colleen to get the answers to all those."

"You mean you don't know who you are or how you got here?"

"We have . . . *ideas*," Corduroy said meaningfully. "But we're not sure. We argue about it some nights."

"Corduroy is the best arguer," Wicket explained. "Mainly because everyone else gets tired and quits."

They had to be Puppets, these men, but they seemed somehow lost, remote from the rest of the club's bright glare and knowing blandishments. Renie felt a chill at the idea of constructs, bits of coded gear, sitting around a virtual campfire and arguing about metaphysics. It seemed so . . . lonely. She looked up at the glittering lights snarled in the tangle of roots above. Like stars. Little flames to ameliorate the darkness above, as a campfire stands sentinel against the darkness of earth.

"Okay," she said at last. "Take us to this Colleen."

Wicket reached down and plucked one of the burning brands from the fire. His three friends did the same, their faces suddenly full of solemnity. Renie couldn't help feeling that in some strange way this was all a game to them. She reached for the final piece of wood, but Corduroy waved his hand. "No," he said. "We always have to leave the fire burning. So we can find our way back."

Renie helped !Xabbu to his feet. He swayed slightly, as though almost fainting with weariness, but stood by himself when she took her hand away and turned to the men. "You said we'd have to take her a gift. I don't have anything."

"Then you must give her a story. Your friend Mister Wonde knows lots—he told us some." Brownbread smiled, remembering. "Good stories, they were."

Wicket took the lead, bending his neck to keep his head below the trailing roots. Whistler came last, holding his torch high so that Renie and !Xabbu were surrounded by light. As they walked, Renie experienced a faint blurring along the edges of her vision. She could never see it happening directly, but the place around them was changing. The feathery roots overhead became thicker and the tiny lights dimmed. The soft, loamy earth beneath their feet hardened. Before long, Renie realized that they were walking through a succession of caves with only the torches for light. Strange shapes covered the cavern walls, drawings that might have been done in charcoal and blood, primitive representations of animals and people.

They seemed to be moving downward. Renie reached out to !Xabbu, wanting mostly to be reassured of his presence. She was beginning to feel almost as much a part of this place as Wicket and the others. What section of the club was this? What was its purpose?

"!Xabbu, can you hear me?" There was still no response on private band. "How are you feeling? Are you okay?"

He was a long time answering. "I . . . I am having trouble hearing you. There are other presences, very close."

"What do you mean, other presences?"

"It is hard to say." His voice was listless. "I think the people of the Early Race are near. Or perhaps it is the Hungry One, the one burned by the fire."

"What does that mean?" She tugged at his shoulder, trying to break through his odd lethargy, but he merely tipped a little to one side and almost stumbled. "What is wrong with you?" !Xabbu did not answer. For the first time since she had found him, Renie began to feel truly frightened.

Wicket had stopped before a large natural archway. A chain of crudely-sketched eyes surrounded it, dark as bruises against the torchlit stone. "We must go quietly," he whispered, lifting a long finger to his lips. "The Colleen hates clatter." He led them under the arch.

The cavern beyond was not as dark as the corridor outside. At the far end, scarlet light glared from a crevice in the floor, staining the rising steam. Barely visible through the redshot mist was someone seated on a tall stone chair, still as a statue.

The figure did not move, but a voice filled the cavern, a throbbing, growling sound which, despite the clearly understandable words, sounded more like a church organ than human speech.

"Come forward."

Renie flinched, but Wicket took her arm and led her toward the crevice. The others helped !Xabbu over the rough ground. *It's the what's-it-called—the Delphic Oracle,* Renie thought. *Someone's been studying Greek mythology.*

The shape on the stone chair stood, spreading its cloak like the wings of a bat. It was hard to tell through the rough garment and obscuring steam, but it seemed to have too many arms.

"What do you seek?" The tolling voice came from everywhere at once. Renie had to admit the whole thing was impressively eerie. The question was, would going through this charade actually help?

"They want to leave," said Wicket. "But they can't."

There was a long moment of silence.

"You four must go. My business is now with them."

Renie turned to thank Wicket and his friends, but they were already hurrying back toward the cavern's entrance, jostling each other in their haste like a gang of kids who had just lit the fuse of a firecracker. She suddenly understood what had puzzled her about Wicket since the first meeting, and about his companions as well. They moved and spoke like children, not like adults.

"And what do you offer in return for my help?" asked the Colleen.

Renie turned. !Xabbu had slumped to the ground before the crevice. She squared her shoulders and made her voice as calm as she could. "They told us we could give you a story."

The Colleen leaned forward. Her face was veiled and invisible, but the shape beneath her robes, extra arms or no, was recognizably female. A necklace briefly caught the light as large pale beads glinted against the darkness of her breast. *"Not just any story. Your story. Tell me who you are, and I will set you free."*

The word gave Renie a moment's pause. "We simply wish to leave, and something is preventing us. I am Wellington Babutu, of Kampala, Uganda."

"Liar!" The word clanged down like a heavy iron gate. *"Tell me the truth."* The Colleen lifted hands clenched into fists. Eight of them. *"You cannot mock me. I know who you are. I know exactly who you are."*

Renie stumbled back in sudden panic. Strimbello had said that, too—was this all some game of his? She tried to take another step and found she couldn't, nor could she turn away from the crevice. The burning light was suddenly very bright; the red glow and the dark shape of the Colleen scratched against it were now almost the only things she could see.

"You will go nowhere until you tell me your true name." Each word seemed to have physical weight, a crushing force like a succession of hammer blows. *"You are in a place you should not be. You know that you have been caught. Everything will go better for you if you do not struggle."*

The power of the creature's voice and the constant serpentine movement of the arms silhouetted against the glare were strangely compelling. Renie felt an almost overwhelming urge to surrender herself, to blurt out the whole story of her deception. Why shouldn't she tell them who she was? They were the criminals, not she. They had harmed her brother, and God knew how many others like him. Why should she keep it secret? Why shouldn't she just scream out everything?

The cavern warped around her. The scarlet light seemed to burn at the bottom of a deep hole.

No. It's some kind of hypnosis, trying to break me down. I have to resist. Resist. For Stephen. For !Xabbu.

"*Tell me,*" demanded the Colleen.

Her sim still wouldn't retreat or turn away. The snakelike arms moved in ever swifter patterns, turning the glare from the crevice into a strobing succession of dark and light.

I must close my eyes. But she couldn't even do that. Renie struggled to think of something other than the shape before her, the demanding voice. How could they stop her even from blinking? This was only a simulation. It couldn't physically affect her, it had to be some kind of high-intensity hypnosis. But what did it all mean? Why "Colleen"? A maiden? A virgin, like the Delphic Oracle? Why go to such lengths just to terrify trespassers? It was the kind of thing you did to scare a child. . . .

Eight arms. A necklace of skulls. Renie had grown up in Durban, a town with a large Hindu population; she understood now what the thing before her was supposed to be. But people from other places might not understand the oracle's name, especially children. Wicket and his friends had probably never heard of the Hindu death goddess Kali, so they had come up with their own version.

Wicket, Corduroy—they weren't adults, she suddenly realized, they were children or childlike Puppets. That was why she had found them so strange. Here in this horrible place, children were being used to catch other children.

Then this monster thinks I'm a child, too! So did Strimbello! They had sniffed a false identity, but they had assumed Renie was a child sneaking through the club in adult guise. But if that was true, then Wicket and his cronies had delivered her to the process that had crippled Stephen and God knew how many others.

!Xabbu was still on his knees, staring helplessly. He, too, was caught—perhaps had been caught before she had ever found him, and was now as far gone as Stephen. He could not exit.

But Renie could, or at least she had been able to a few minutes before.

For a moment she stopped struggling against the invisible restraint. Sensing surrender, the dark shape of Kali expanded, looming now so that it filled her vision. The veiled face tilted forward, cloak billowing around it like a cobra's hood. The lights flashed. Words of warning, commands, threats, all cascaded over Renie, running together into a ragged drone so loud that it seemed to make her hearplugs vibrate.

"*Exit.*"

Nothing happened. Her sim remained frozen, an unwilling wor-
shiper at Kali's feet. But that made no sense—she had spoken the
codeword, her system was set for voice commands. There was no reason it shouldn't work.

She stared into a vortex of swirling red light, trying to hold concentration through the shattering, never-ending noise, struggling to block
out the panic and think. Any voice command should trigger her system back at the Poly . . . unless these people could somehow jam her
voice in the same way they had frozen her sim. But if they could do
that, why go to all the trouble to bring her to this particular place
when Strimbello could just have immobilized her in the Yellow Room?
Why put on such an elaborate show? They must need her here, isolated, exposed to this barrage of light and sound. It had to be hypnosis, some method using high-speed strobing and special sonics that
operated right at the nervous system level, something that cut in between her higher thought processes and her physical responses.

Which might mean that she hadn't spoken at all, but only thought
she had.

"Exit!" she screamed. Still, nothing happened. It was hard to concentrate, hard to feel her real body beneath the blinding, jaggedly
pulsating light and the painful hum of a million wasps in her ears.
She could feel her attacker ripping away at her shell of concentration,
the only thing protecting her from a tumble down into nothingness.
She could not keep it up much longer.

Dead Man's Switch. The words fluttered up, a few scraps of memory
shaken loose by the maelstrom. *Every system has a Dead Man's Switch.
Something to release you if you get into serious trouble, a stroke or something.
The Poly must have one.* It was so loud, so excruciatingly loud. Each
thought felt as slippery as an untanked goldfish. *Heart rate? Is the switch
hooked into the EKG monitor in the harness?*

She would have to assume it was—it was the only chance she had.
She would have to try to drive her pulse rate up beyond permitted
danger levels.

Renie let the fear she had been struggling to check finally burst free.
It was not difficult—even if she had guessed correctly, there was only
a very thin chance of this plan working. More likely, she would fail
and find herself sliding down a long tunnel into blackness, as Stephen
had done before her, a blackness indistinguishable from death.

She could not feel her physical body, which was no doubt hanging
uselessly beside !Xabbu's in the Harness Room. She was only eyes and

ears, battered to the edge of madness by the howling whirlwind of light that was Kali.

Unchecked and without outlet, desperation ran through her like some horrible silent electrocution. But it was not enough—she needed more. She thought of her heart and imagined it pumping. Now, letting her sheer fright color the image, she visualized it pounding ever faster, struggling to cope with an emergency for which evolution could never have prepared.

It's hopeless, she told herself, and pictured her heart shuddering, hurrying. *I'll die here, or fall down into madness forever.* The dark muscle was a shy, secret thing like an oyster ripped from its shell, struggling hopelessly to survive. Pumping hard, straining, losing the beat for a moment as the rhythms bounced awkwardly against each other.

Streaks of hot and cold went jagging through her, fear to the toxic level, shivers of helpless animal panic.

Racing, fighting, failing.

I'll be lost, just like Stephen, just like !Xabbu. Soon I'll be in the hospital, zipped into an oxygen-filled body bag, dead, dead meat.

Images began to flash before her eyes, leaping out of the kaleidoscopic display that filled her vision—Stephen, gray and unconscious, lost to her, wandering somewhere in an empty, lonely place.

I'm dying.

Her mother, shrieking in agony during her final moments, caught on the upper floor of the department store as the flames climbed hungrily upward, knowing she would never see her children again.

I'm dying, dying.

Death the destroyer, the great Nothing, the freezing fist that seized you and squeezed you, crushed you into dust that floated in the blank dark between stars.

Her heart stuttered, laboring toward failure like an overheated engine.

I'm dying I'm dying I'm dying I'm . . .

The world jerked and turned gray; light and dark were evenly smeared. Renie felt a sharp pain race down her arm, a streak of fire. She was in some between-place, she was alive, no, she was dying, she . . .

I'm out, she thought, and the idea rattled in her suddenly cavernous and echoing skull. The shrieking drone was gone. Her thoughts were her own, but even through the agony, a vast, adhesive weariness pulled at her. *I must be having a heart attack.*

But she had already determined her course before she had begun. She couldn't afford to think about what she was going to do, couldn't pay any attention to the pain—not yet.

"*Backtrack—last node.*" Her voice, though loud against the new stillness in her head, was only a dry whisper.

Even before the gray had finished forming, it was gone. The cavern surrounded her again, the red light blazing. Her position had changed; now she stood to one side of Kali, who was leaning forward over the hunched figure of !Xabbu like an interested vulture. The death goddess' arms were motionless, the maddening voice silent. Her veiled face pivoted toward the spot where Renie had reappeared.

Renie leaped forward and seized the Bushman's sim. Another jagged bolt of pain shot up her arm; she gritted her teeth and fought off a wave of nausea. "*Exit,*" she shouted, triggering escape for both of them, but aborted immediately when !Xabbu's part of the program didn't respond. Her stomach lurched again. The little man was still trapped, somehow, still hooked. She would have to find another way to get him out.

A shadow swung across her like a negative searchlight. She looked up to see the scarlet-limned figure of Kali looming above, arms spread wide.

"Oh, *shit.*" Renie tightened her grip on !Xabbu, wondering how lifelike this simulation was. Bracing herself against the inevitable pain, she straightened suddenly and put a shoulder into the oracle's midsection. There was no sensation of contact, but the creature slid back several feet into the middle of the steaming pit. The monster hung in midair, bathed in the red glow, feet flattened on nothing.

One of Kali's hands darted toward her own face and tore away the veil, revealing blue skin, a ragged hole of a mouth, a dangling red tongue . . . and no eyes.

It was meant to hold Renie until the visual tricks could start again. It might have worked before, but now she had no strength left to be startled. "I'm so tired of your goddamned game," she grunted. Black spots swam before her eyes, but she doubted they had anything to do with the programming in Mister J's jolly little hellhole. Dizzied, she turned her face away from the blind thing and heard the ululation beginning again.

Renie was having trouble breathing: her voice was faint. "Get stuffed, bitch. *Random.*"

The shift was suprisingly fast. The cavern dissolved, and for a moment a long dark hallway began to form before her eyes. She had a dim perception of a near-endless row of candelabra along the walls, each held by a disembodied hand, then she was suddenly shifted again—this time without her command and against her will.

This transition was not as smooth as the others. For several long instants her vision was nauseatingly distorted, as if the new location would not come into correct focus. She tumbled and felt soft earth—or the simulation of it—beneath her aching body. She kept her eyes closed and reached out until her fingers touched !Xabbu's silent, still form. It was hard to imagine moving another inch, but she knew she had to get up and start looking for ways to get them out.

"We have only moments," someone said. Despite its urgent tone, it was a soothing voice, pitched almost equally distant from the stereotypical extremes of both masculine and feminine. *"They will find it much easier to track you this time."*

Startled, Renie opened her eyes. She was surrounded by a crowd of people, as though she were an accident victim lying in a busy street. After a moment, she saw that the forms around her were gray and still. All except one.

The stranger was white. Not white as she was black, not Caucasian, but truly white, with the blank purity of unsmirched paper. The stranger's sim—for that was what it must be, since she was clearly still inside the system—was a pure colorless emptiness, as though someone had taken a pair of scissors and snipped a vaguely human-shaped hole in the fabric of VR. It pulsed and danced along its edges, never entirely at rest.

"Leave us . . . alone." It was difficult just to speak: she was short of air, and a bright fist of pain was squeezing inside her rib cage.

"I cannot, although I am a fool to take this chance. Sit up and help me with your friend."

"Don't touch him!"

"Stop being foolish. Your pursuers will locate you any moment now."

Renie forced herself up onto her knees and swayed for a moment, catching her breath. "Who . . . who are you? Where are we?"

The blankness crouched beside !Xabbu's unmoving form. The stranger had no face and no distinct shape; Renie could not tell what it was looking at. "I am taking enough risks already. I cannot tell you anything—you may still be caught, and it would mean death to others. Now, help me lift him! I have little physical strength and I dare not bring more power to bear."

Renie crawled toward the shapeless pair, and for the first time took

notice of her surroundings. They were in a kind of open grassy park,
pinned beneath dark gray skies, bounded by tall trees and ivy-choked
stone walls. The silent figures that surrounded them stretched away on
all sides, row after row; making the place seem a bizarre cross between
a cemetery and a sculpture garden. Each shape was that of a person,
some highly individual, some as featureless as the sims she and !Xabbu
wore. Each had been frozen in some moment of fear or surprise. Some
had stood a long time and like the deserted structures of Toytown had
lost their colors and textures, but most looked new-minted.

The stranger lifted its head as she approached. "When something
happens to one of the guests while they are online, their sim remains.
Those who own this place are . . . amused to keep their trophies this
way."

Renie put her arms under !Xabbu and lifted him into a sitting position. The effort made the edges of her sight go black for a moment; she
swayed, struggling to maintain consciousness. "I may be . . . having a
heart attack," she whispered.

"All the more reason to hurry," said the empty space. "Now, hold
him still. He is a long distance away, and if he doesn't return, you will
not be able to take him offline. I must send for him."

"Send for him. . . ?" Renie could barely form the words. She was
beginning to feel quite drowsy, and although a part of her was frightened by that, it was a small and diminishing part. This human-shaped
blankness, the strange garden—they were simply a few more complications to an already complex situation. Difficult to think about . . . it
would be easier simply to let herself roll down into sleep. . . .

"The Honey-Guide will fetch him back." The stranger held up the
blunt white shapes that were its hands as if about to pray, but kept
them a few inches apart. When nothing happened, Renie began gathering the energy to ask another question, but the featureless shape
had become as rigidly still as any of the trophy garden's other residents. Renie felt a cold pall of loneliness settle over her. Everything
was lost now. Everyone was gone. Why keep fighting, when she could
let go, could sleep. . . ?

There was a stirring between the stranger's hands, then a sort of
opening appeared there, a deeper nullity, as though something had
cast a shadow onto naked air. The darkness flicked, then flicked again,
then another white shape fluttered out of it. This smaller blank patch,
which was bird-shaped in the way the stranger was human-shaped,
fluttered onto the shoulder of !Xabbu's sim, then crouched there for a
moment, vibrating gently, like a newborn butterfly drying its wings.

Renie stared in lazy fascination as the tiny white shape slid close to !Xabbu's ear—or the rudimentary fold in his simulation that represented it—as if to share a secret. She heard a high-pitched trill, then the bird-thing leaped into the air and vanished.

The larger blankness abruptly shivered back into life. It leaped up and smacked its rudimentary hands together. "Go now. Hurry."

"But . . ." Renie looked down. !Xabbu was moving. One of his sim hands clenched fitfully, as though trying to catch something that had flown away.

"You can take him back now. And you must take this, too." The stranger plunged one arm inside itself, then pulled out something that glimmered with a soft amber light. Renie stared. The stranger reached and took her hand with its other arm, peeled open her clenched fingers, and dropped the object onto her palm. She wondered for a moment at the mundane and unremarkable touch of the ghostly presence, then looked down at what had been given to her. It was a round yellow gem, cut into hundreds of facets.

"What . . . what is it?" It was becoming hard to remember much of anything. Who was this gleaming white shape? What was she supposed to be doing?

"No more questions," it said sharply. "Go!"

Renie stared for a moment into the void where its face should be. Something swam through her mind, down deep, and she struggled to identify it.

"Go now!"

She squeezed !Xabbu a little tighter. He felt as slender as a child. "Yes. Of course. *Exit.*"

The garden popped like a soap bubble.

Everything was very dark. For a moment Renie thought they had become stuck in transition, until she remembered the headset. She lifted her arm, gasping at the painful effort, but managed to tip up her visor.

The view around her improved only a little; she still saw mainly gray, although now there were dark stripes as well. Then she understood that the blurry verticals around her were the straps of the Harness Room. She was hanging in place, swinging slightly. She turned. !Xabbu was dangling beside her, but it was the real !Xabbu in his real body. As she watched, he shivered convulsively and lifted his head, eyes rolling as he tried to focus.

"!Xabbu." Her voice sounded muffled. She was still wearing her hearplugs, but she couldn't work up the strength to lift her arm again. There was something she needed to tell him, something important. Renie stared at him, trying to remember, but her head was beginning to feel very heavy. Just before she gave up, it came to her. "Call an ambulance," she said, and laughed a little at the oddness of it. "I think I'm dying."

CHAPTER 12

Looking Through
the Glass

NETFEED/NEWS: *California's "Multi-Marriages" Now Law*
(*visual: two women, one man, all wearing tuxedos, entering Glide Memorial Church*)
VO: *Protestors howled outside as the first of California's newly legalized multi-partner marriages took place at a church in San Francisco. The man and two women said it was "a great day for people who don't have traditional two-person relationships."*
(*visual: Reverend Pilker at church rostrum*)
Not everyone agrees. The Reverend Daniel Pilker, leader of the fundamentalist group Kingdom Now, called the new law "indisputable evidence that California is hell's back door . . ."

Paul stepped through and out. The golden light faded and he was in emptiness again.

The mist stretched away in every direction, as heavy and empty as before, but there was nothing else. There was no Finch or Mullet either, which was a great relief, but Paul had been hoping that he would find something more on the other side of the glowing gateway. He wasn't quite sure what "home" meant, but in the back of his mind he had been hoping to find exactly that.

He sank to his knees, then lowered himself until he lay stretched on the hard and featureless earth. The mists swirled around him. He closed his eyes, exhausted, without hope or ideas, and for a while gave himself to the dark.

The next thing he was aware of was a quiet whispering, a thin papery sound that grew out of the silence. A warm breeze stroked his hair. Paul opened his eyes, then sat up, full of wonder. A forest had sprung into being around him.

For a long time he was content just to sit and stare. It had been so long since he had seen anything but blasted fields of mud that the sight of unbroken trees, of thickly tangled branches still bearing their leaves, soothed his spirit like a drink of water to a thirsty man. What did it matter that most of the leaves were yellow or brown, that many had already fallen to the earth and lay ankle-deep around him? Just the return of color seemed a gift beyond any price.

He stood. His legs were so stiff that they might have been things discarded by someone else that necessity compelled him to use. He took a great breath of air and smelled everything, damp earth, the scent of drying grass, even the faintest tang of smoke. The scents of the living world coursed through him so powerfully and so richly that it awakened hunger inside him; he suddenly wondered when he had last eaten. Bully beef and biscuit, those were familiar words, but he could not remember what the things they named were. In any case, it had been long ago and far away.

The warm air still surrounded him, but he felt a moment of inner chill. Where had he been? He had a memory of a dark, terrifying place, but what he had been doing there or how he had left had slipped from his mind.

The very lack of things to remember meant that their absence did not worry him long. Sun was filtering down through the leaves, making spots that swam like golden fish as the wind moved the trees. Wherever he had been, he was in a living place now, a place with light and clean air, a carpet of dry leaves, and even—he tilted his head—the distant sound of a bird. If he could not remember his last meal, well, that was all the more reason to find himself another. He would walk.

He looked down. His feet were shod in heavy leather shoes, which at least felt familiar and correct, but nothing else in his attire seemed quite right. He wore heavy wool stockings and pants that ended not far below his knee, as well as a thick shirt and waistcoat, also of wool. The fabric seemed strangely rough beneath his fingers.

The forest stretched away in all directions, revealing nothing that looked like a road or even a trail. He pondered for a moment, trying to remember which direction he had been traveling when he stopped, but that, too, was gone, evaporated as completely as the bleak mist, which was now the only thing that he remembered with certainty had existed before the forest. Granted an open choice, he noted the stretching shadows and turned to put the sun at his back. At least he would be sure of seeing his way clearly.

He had been hearing the intermittent birdsong for a long time before he finally saw its author. He was kneeling, freeing his stocking from a bramble bush, when something brilliant glided through a column of sunshine just ahead of him, a flash of green both darker and shinier than the moss crawling on the tree trunks and stones. He straightened, looking for it, but it had vanished into the shadows between trees; all that remained was a trill of piping music, just loud enough to claim a single echo for its own.

With a stiff tug he pulled himself out of the bramble bush and hastened in the direction the bird had gone. Since he had no path, he thought he might as well follow something pretty as plod on with no better destination in mind. He had been walking for what seemed hours and had seen no sign of change in the endless forest.

The bird never came close enough for him to see it completely clearly, but neither did it disappear from sight. It flitted from tree to tree, always just a few dozen paces ahead. On the few occasions where the branch it chose for a resting place was in sunlight, he could see its emerald feathers shining—an almost impossible glow, as though it blazed with some inner light. There were hints of other colors, too, a dusky purple like an evening sky, a hint of darker color along the crest. Its song also seemed somehow less than ordinary, although he could remember no other bird's song for comparison. In fact, he could remember very little about any other birds, but he knew that this was one, that its song was both soothing and alluring, and that was enough to know.

Afternoon wore on and the sun passed out from behind the gaps in the treetops, sliding toward the hidden horizon. He had long ago stopped worrying about what direction it shone, so caught up had he become in his pursuit of the green bird. It was only when the forest began to darken that he realized he was lost in a trackless wood with night coming on.

He stopped, and the bird alighted on a branch not three steps from him. It cocked its head—there *was* a dark crest—and gave voice to a

melodic trill that, though swift and bright, had something in it of a
question and something in it even less definable, but which made him
suddenly mournful for his lost memory, for his directionlessness, for
his solitude. Then, with a flip of its tail that revealed the midnight-
purple brushing underneath, the bird spread its wings and spiraled up
into the air to disappear among the twilight shadows. A last thread of
song floated down to him, sweetly sad, diminishing to nothing.

He sat down on a log and put his head in his hands, overcome with
the weight of something he could not define. He was still sitting that
way when a voice made him jump.

"Here, none of that. These are good solid oaks, not weeping wil-
lows."

The stranger was not dressed much differently than he, all in rough
browns and greens, but he wore a broad strip of white cloth tied
around one arm like a bandage or a token. His eyes were a strangely
feline shade of tawny yellow. He held a bow in one hand and a skin
bag in the other; a quiver of arrows stood up behind his shoulder.

Since the newcomer had made no hostile moves, he felt it safe to
ask him who he was. The stranger laughed at the question. "The
wrong thing to be asking here. Who are *you*, then, if you're so clever?"

He opened his mouth, but found he could not remember. "I . . . I
don't know."

"Of course not. That's the way of this place. I came in after . . . I'm
not certain, you know, I think it was a deer. And now I won't remember my name until I'm on my way back out again. Queer, this forest."
He extended the skin bag. "Are you thirsty?"

The liquid was sour but refreshing. When he had handed it back to
the stranger, he felt better. The conversation might be confusing, but
at least it was a conversation. "Where are you going? Do you know
that? I'm lost."

"Not surprised. As to where *I'm* going, it's out. Not a good place to
be after dark, these woods. But I seem to remember something just
outside the forest that feels like a good destination. Perhaps it will be
the kind of place you're looking for." The stranger beckoned. "In any
case, come along. We'll see if we can't do you some good."

He quickly rose to his feet, afraid that the invitation might be re-
scinded if he took too long. The stranger was already pushing through
a tangle of young trees which had made a hedge around the wreckage
of their toppled older relative.

They traveled for a while in silence as late afternoon twilight gradually deepened into evening. Fortunately, the stranger held down his

pace—he seemed like the sort who could have traveled much faster if he chose—and remained, even in the dying light, a dark shape only a few steps ahead.

At first he thought it was the night air, that the colder sharpness was bringing a different kind of sound to his ear, a different kind of scent to his nostrils. Then he realized that instead it was a different kind of thought that was suddenly drifting through his mind.

"I was . . . somewhere else." The sound of his own voice was strange after the long time without speaking. "A war, I think. I ran away."

His companion grunted. "A war."

"Yes. It's coming back to me—some of it, anyway."

"We're getting near the edge of the forest, that's the reason. So you ran away, did you?"

"But . . . but not for the normal reasons. At least I don't think so." He fell silent. Something very important was swimming up from the depths of his mind and he was suddenly frightened he might grab at it too clumsily and lose it to darkness once more. "I was in a war, and I ran away. I came through . . . a door. Or something else. A mirror. An empty place."

"Mirrors." The other was moving a little more quickly now. "Dangerous things."

"And . . . and . . ." He curled his fists, as though memory could be tightened like a muscle. "And . . . my name is Paul." He laughed in relief. "Paul."

The stranger looked back over his shoulder. "Funny sort of name. What does it mean?"

"Mean? It doesn't mean anything. It's what I'm called."

"It's an odd place you come from, then." The stranger fell silent for a moment, though his legs still carried him forward in long steps that had Paul hurrying to keep up. "I'm Woodling," he said at last. "Sometimes Jack-of-the-Woods, or Jack Woodling. That's my name because I do tramp all the woods near and far—even this one, though I don't like it much. It's a fearful thing for a man to lose his name. Although perhaps not so much so when the name doesn't mean aught."

"It's still a fearful thing." Paul was struggling with the new ideas that were suddenly skittering through his head like beetles. "And where am I? What place is this?"

"The Nameless Wood, of course. What else would it be called?"

"But where is it? In what country?"

Jack Woodling laughed. "In the king's land, I suppose. The *old* king's land, that is, although I trust you've got the sense not to call it that among strangers. You may tell Her Ladyship I said so, though, if you meet her." His smile blazed briefly in the shadows. "You must be from somewhere far away indeed, that you concern yourself with such schoolmasterish things as the names of places." He paused and pointed. "There it is, then, as I hoped it would be."

They had stopped on a high place at the edge of a narrow valley. The trees fell away down the gradually sloping hillside; for the first time Paul could see some distance in front of him. At the bottom of the valley, nestled between the hills, a cluster of lights gleamed.

"What is it?"

"An inn, and a good place." Jack Woodling clapped him on the shoulder. "You will have no trouble finding your way from here."

"But aren't you going?"

"Not me, not tonight. I've things to do and elsewhere to sleep. But you will find what you need there, I think."

Paul stared at the man's face, trying to make out the expression through the night-shadows. Did he mean more than he said? "If we are going to split up, then I want to thank you. You probably saved my life."

Jack Woodling laughed again. "Don't put such a burden on me, good sir. Where I go, I must travel light. Fare you well." He turned and moved back up the hillside. Within moments Paul could hear nothing but the leaves rustling in the wind.

The sign swaying in the wind over the front door named the inn "The King's Dream." It was crude, as though it had been put up hurriedly to replace some earlier insignia. The small figure painted below the name had his chin on his chest and his crown tipped low over his eyes. Paul stood for a moment just outside the circle of lantern glow puddled in front of the door, feeling the great trackless weight of the forest breathing like a dark beast at his back, then stepped foward into the light.

Perhaps a dozen people were ranged about the low-ceilinged room. Three of them were soldiers in surcoats as bloody-red as the joint that turned on a spit over the fireplace. The young boy tending the spit, so covered with soot that the whites of his eyes were startling, gave Paul a furtive look when he came in, then quickly turned away with an expression that might have been relief. The soldiers looked at Paul, too, and one of them inched a little way down the bench they shared, toward the place where their pikes leaned against the whitewashed clay wall. The rest of the denizens, dressed in rough peasant clothes, paid him the attention any stranger would receive, staring as he made his way to the landlord's counter.

The woman who waited for him there was old, and her white hair, disarranged by heat and sweat, looked something like the fleece of a sheep kept out on a bad night, but the forearms bared by rolled sleeves looked strong and her hands were pink, callused, and capable. She leaned on the counter in obvious weariness, but her gaze was shrewd.

"We've no beds left." She wore an odd smirk on her face which Paul could not immediately understand. "These fine soldiers have just taken the last of them."

One of the red-smocked men belched. His companions laughed.

"I'd like a meal and something to drink." A dim memory of how these things worked wriggled into Paul's thoughts. He suddenly realized he had nothing in his pockets but air, and no purse or wallet. "I have no money, I'm afraid. Perhaps I could do some work for you."

The woman leaned forward, inspecting him closely. "Where are you from?"

"A long way away. The other side of . . . of the Nameless Forest."

She seemed about to ask something else, but one of the soldiers shouted for more beer. Her lips thinned in annoyance—and, Paul thought, something more.

"Stay here," she told him, then went to deal with the soldiers. Paul looked around the room. The hearth urchin was staring at him again with an intensity that seemed closer to calculation than curiosity, but Paul was tired and hungry and did not much trust his own over-strained perceptions.

"Let's talk about work you might do," the woman said when she returned. "Follow me back here, where it's less noisy."

She led him down a narrow stairway to a cellar room that was clearly her own. The walls were lined with shelves, and they and every other surface were crammed with spools and skeins, jars and boxes and baskets. Except for the small pallet bed in the corner and a three-legged stool, the room looked more like a shop than a bedroom. The landlady sank onto the stool, fluffing her rough woolen skirt, and kicked off her shoes.

"I'm that tired," she said, "I couldn't stay on my feet a moment longer. I hope you don't mind standing—I've only the one stool."

Paul shook his head. His attention had been captured by a small, thick-paned window. Through the distorted glass, he could see water moving and glinting in the moonlight outside. The inn evidently backed on a river.

"Now then," the old woman's voice was suddenly sharp, "who sent you here? You're not one of us."

Paul turned around, startled. The landlady had a knitting needle gripped in her fist, and while she showed no immediate sign of getting up from the stool and coming after him with it, neither did she look particularly friendly.

"Woodling, his name was. Jack Woodling. I met him in the forest."

"Tell me what he looks like."

Paul did his best to describe what had been, after all, a rather nondescript man seen largely in twilight and later in darkness. It was only when he remembered the white cloth tied around his savior's arm that the woman relaxed.

"You've seen him, sure enough. Had he any message for me?"

He could not think of anything at first. "Do you know who 'Her Ladyship' would be?"

The woman smiled sadly. "No one but me."

"He said something about it being the old king's woods, though I shouldn't say that to anyone except Her Ladyship."

She chuckled and tossed the knitting needle into a basket with several dozen others. "That's my Jack. My paladin. And why did he send you to me? Where is this place you're from, beyond the Nameless Woods?"

Paul stared at her. There was something more than ordinary weariness in her features. Her face seemed almost like something that had been soft once, but had been frozen into harsh creases by some terrible winter. "I don't know. I . . . there's something wrong with me. I was in a war, that's all I remember. I ran away."

She nodded her head as if to the sound of an old familiar tune. "Jack would have seen that, all right. No wonder he took a shine to you." She sighed. "But I told you rightly enough earlier. I've no bed. The blasted robin redbreasts have taken the last of them, and with not so much as a copper to pay me for my trouble."

Paul frowned. "They can do that?"

Her laugh was rueful. "They can do that and more. This is not my land anymore, but hers. Even here, in my pitiful burrow, she sends her strutting fellows to mock me. She will not harm me—what use having won without the only person who can appreciate it?—but she will make me as miserable as she can."

"Who is she? I don't understand anything you're saying."

The old woman stood up, puffing out breath as she did so. "You're better off if you don't. And you're also better off not staying in this country long. It isn't very friendly to travelers any more." She picked her way through the sea of bric-a-brac, leading him back to the door. "I'd put you up here on my own floor, but that would only make those roundheads upstairs wonder why I'd taken interest in a stranger. You can sleep in the stable. I'll say you're going to do some hauling for me tomorrow, so you won't attract attention. I can at least give you food and drink, for Jack's sake. But you're not to mention to anyone that you met him, and certainly not what he said."

"Thank you. You're very kind."

She snorted, making her slow way up the stairs. "Falling to a low estate can do that—you see so much more of the world than you did before. You become very aware of how thin the line is, of how little safety exists."

She led him back up to the noisy common room where they were greeted by rude questions from the soldiers and the watchful eyes of the hearth boy.

A caged bird, a tall tree, a house with many rooms, a loud voice shouting, bellowing, crashing down on him like thunder. . . .

Paul came up from the dream like a drowning man, surfacing to the smell of damp hay and the noises of fretful horses. He sat up, trying to shake off the disorientation of sleep. The stable door was partway open, a shadow showing lightless against the slice of starry night.

"Who's there?" He fumbled for a weapon, an urging of some sunken memory, but came up with nothing but a handful of straw.

"Quiet." The whisperer was as nervous as Paul's stable mates. "It's only me, Gally." The shadow came closer. Paul could see that it was someone quite small. "The pot boy."

"What do you want?"

"Not to rob you, governor." He sounded aggrieved. "I'd of come in quieter than that, were the case. I come to warn you."

Paul could see the boy's eyes now, gleaming like mother-of-pearl. "Warn me?"

"Those soldiers. They've been drinking too much, and now they're talking of coming for you. I don't know why."

"The bastards." Paul climbed to his feet. "Did the lady send you?"

"Naw. Locked herself in her room for the night, she has. I heard 'em talking." He straightened up now as Paul moved toward the door. "Where you going to go?"

"I don't know. Back to the forest, I suppose." He cursed quietly. At least he had no possessions to slow his flight.

"Come on with me, then. I'll take you to a place. King's men won't follow you there—not after dark."

Paul paused, one hand on the door. There was indeed a soft clatter coming from the front of the inn across the courtyard, a noise very much like drunken men trying to move stealthily. "Why?" he whispered.

"Help you? Why not?" The boy grabbed his arm. "None of us much like them redbreasts. We don't like their mistress neither. Follow me."

Not waiting for Paul to reply, the boy slipped out the door and moved rapidly but quietly along the wall. Paul pulled the door closed and hurried after him.

Gally led him around the back of the stable, then stopped and touched a hand to Paul's arm in warning before leading him down a narrow stone stairway. The only light came from the half-moon. Paul nearly stepped off the stairs into the river before Gally took his arm again.

"Boat," the boy whispered, and guided Paul into a gently rocking shadow. When he was seated in the boat's damp bottom, his rescuer carefully lifted up a pole that had been lying on the tiny dock and pushed the little craft out onto the dark river.

From above them came the sudden gleam of an unhooded lantern and a clatter as the stable door was flung open. Paul held his breath until the noise of the soldiers' drunken disappointment faded behind them.

The trees on the near bank slid silently past. "Won't you get into trouble?" Paul asked. "Won't they blame you when they see you've gone?"

"The lady'll speak up for me." The boy leaned forward as if looking for some landmark in what to Paul was impenetrable night. " 'Sides, they were so knobknocked with drink, they didn't know where I'd got to anyway. I can just say I went to sleep in the washing hamper to get away from their noise."

"Well, I'm grateful. Where are you taking me?"

"To my place. Well, it's not just mine. We all live there."

Paul settled back. Now that his sudden rousing and narrow escape were behind him, he was almost enjoying the quiet of the night, the feeling of gliding along beneath another, larger river of sky. There was peace here, and companionship of a sort. "And who are 'we all'?" he asked at last.

"Oh, my mates," Gally answered with a hint of pride. "The Oyster-house Boys. We're the White King's men, every one of us."

They tied up the boat at a wide pier that jutted far into the river. The place where the pier touched the shore and the narrow stairs leading upward were lit by a single lantern which swayed gently in the quickening wind.

Paul looked up to the shadowy bulk on the headlands. "You live there?"

"Do now. It was empty for a while." Agile as a squirrel, Gally scrambled out of the boat and onto the pier. He reached down and pulled up a sack that Paul had not noticed. After he had set it down, he reached back a helping hand. "All the boats stopped here once on a time—men singing, bringing in the nets. . . ."

Paul followed him up the hillside. The stairwell had been cut into the solid rock and the steps were narrow and slippery with night dew; Paul found he could only climb safely by turning sideways, putting the length of his foot along each step. He looked down. The lantern was burning far below. The boat had drifted under the pier.

"Don't be so slow," Gally whispered. "We've got to get you inside. Few folk come down around here, but if her soldiers are a-hunting for you, we don't want no one seeing you."

Paul leaned in toward the hill, steadying himself against the steps above him, and made his way up as quickly as he could. Despite being burdened with a sack, the boy kept bouncing back down to urge him on. At last they reached the top. There was no lantern here, and Paul could see nothing of the building except a deeper darkness spread wide against the stars. Gally clutched his sleeve and led him forward. After a while Paul felt boards creaking beneath his feet. Gally stopped and knocked on what was unmistakably a door. A few moments later an apparition appeared at the height of Paul's knees, a gleaming, sideways rectangular face.

"Who's there?" The voice was almost a squeak.

"Gally. I've brought company."

"Can't let you in without the password."

"Password?" Gally hissed his disgust. "There wasn't no password when I left this morning. Open it up."

"But how do I know it's you?" The face, which Paul could now see was peering through a slot in the door, scowled in a laughable attempt at officiousness.

"Are you mad? Let us in, Pointer, or I'll reach through and knuckle your pate. You'll recognize that, right enough."

The slot clapped closed, then a moment later the door opened; a faint, fishy scent wafted out. Gally picked up his sack again and slid through. Paul followed him.

Pointer, a small pale boy, took a few steps backward, staring at the new arrival. "Who's he?"

"He's with me. He's going to spend the night here. What's this diddle about a password?"

"That was Miyagi's idea. Some strange folk been coming around today."

"And how was I supposed to know the password when I wasn't here?" Gally reached out and rubbed savagely at Pointer's unkempt hair, then pushed him ahead of them down the dark hallway. They followed the small boy into a wide, high-ceilinged room as large as a church hall. It was lit by only a few candles, so there were more dark places than light ones, but as far as Paul could see it was empty but for the clinging odor of dampness and river mud.

"All's well," Pointer sang out. "It's Gally. He's brought someone with him."

Dark shapes emerged from the shadows, first two or three, then many, like the fairy-folk appearing from their woodland hiding places. Within moments some three dozen children had crowded around Paul and his guide, staring solemnly, many wiping eyes still puffy from sleep. None were older than Gally; most were a great deal younger. There were a few girls, but the greatest number were boys, and all of them were dirty and starveling-thin.

"Miyagi! Why is there a password, and don't you think you might have told me?"

A small, round boy stepped forward. "It weren't meant to keep you out, Gally. There were some folk nosing around today we hadn't seen before. I made the little'uns keep quiet, and I told 'em all not to let anyone in who didn't say 'custard.' "

Several of the smaller children repeated the word, the excitement of a secret—or possibly a dim memory of the thing itself—clear in the hushed thrill of their voices.

"Right," said Gally. "Well, I'm here now, and this is my friend . . ." He frowned, rubbing the soot on his forehead. "What's your name, governor?"

Paul told him.

". . . Right, my friend Paul, and he's for the White King, too, so there's nothing to be afraid of. You lot over there, get more wood on the fire—it's cold as a brass monkey in here. Milady sent some cheese and bread." He dropped his sack on the floor. "You'll never learn all the names. Miyagi and Pointer you met. Chesapeake's over there, falling back asleep already, the lazy lummox. That's Blue—she's Pointer's sister—and that's my brother, Bay." The last-named, a skinny, snub-nosed child with curling red hair, pulled a horrible face. Gally aimed a mock-kick in his direction.

Paul watched the Oysterhouse Boys—and Girls—scatter in various directions, as Gally, a natural general, set them each tasks. When they were alone again, Paul turned to his guide and asked quietly: "What did you mean, I'm for the White King? I don't know anything about this—I'm a stranger here."

"That's as may be," said Gally, grinning. "But since you ran away from the Red Lady's soldiers, I don't think you'll be wearing *her* token, will you?"

Paul shook his head. "I don't know anything about that. I don't even know how I came to this town, this country. A man found me in the woods and sent me to the inn—fellow with strange eyes, named Jack. But I don't know anything about Kings or Queens."

"Jack sent you? Then you must have more to say than you're letting on. Did you fight with him in the war?"

Paul shook his head again, helplessly. "I fought . . . I fought in a war. But it wasn't here. I don't remember anymore." He slumped down onto the wooden floor and put his back against the wall. The excitement had worn off and he was exhausted. He had only managed a few hours' sleep before Gally had woken him.

"Well, never you mind, governor. We'll sort you out."

Gally handed out the bread and cheese, but Paul had eaten earlier, and although he was hungry again, he did not want to reduce the childrens' small portions any further. They looked so small and poorly nourished that he found it painful to watch them eat. Even so, they were remarkably well-behaved urchins, each waiting his or her turn for a mouthful of crust.

Afterward, with the fire blazing and the room warm at last, Paul was ready to go back to sleep, but the children were too excited by the night's events to return to bed.

"A song!" cried someone, and others took up the cry: "Yes, a song! Have the man sing a song."

Paul shook his head. "I'm afraid I don't remember any. I wish I did."

"No need to worry," Gally said. "Blue, you sing one. She's got the best voice, even though she's not the loudest," he explained.

The little girl stood up. Her dark hair hung in tangled knots around her shoulders, confined only by a band of soiled white cloth around her forehead. She frowned and sucked her finger. "What song?"

"The one about where we come from." Gally seated himself cross-legged beside Paul like a desert prince commanding entertainment for a foreign dignitary.

Blue nodded thoughtfully, took her finger from her mouth, and began to sing in a high, sweet, and slightly wavering voice.

> *"The ocean dark, the ocean wide*
> *And we crossed from the other side*
> *The ocean dark, the ocean deep*
> *Between us and the Land of Sleep*
>
> *"Away, away, away, sing O*
> *They called for us, but we had gone*
> *Away, away, away, sing O*
> *Across the sea we had to go . . ."*

Huddled with this small tribe, listening to Blue's voice float up like the sparks from the fire, Paul suddenly felt his own loneliness surrounding him like a cloud. Perhaps he could stay in this place. He could be a kind of father, make sure these children did not hunger, did not need to fear the world outside their old house.

> *"The night was cold, the night was long*
> *And we had no light but our song*
> *The night was black, the night was deep*
> *Between us and the Land of Sleep . . ."*

There was a sadness in it that Paul could feel, some note of mourning that sounded beneath the melody. It was as though he listened to the keening of a baby bird which had fallen from its nest, calling across the hopeless distance to the warmth and safety it had forever lost.

"We crossed the sea, we crossed the night
And now we search the world for light
For light to love us, light to keep
The memories of the Land of Sleep.

"Away, away, away, sing O
They called for us, but we had gone
Away, away, away, sing O
Across the sea we had to go . . ."

The song went on, and Paul's eyes began to sag closed. He fell asleep to the sound of Blue's small voice chiming against the night.

A bird was beating its wings against a windowpane, wingtips pattering against the glass in frantic repetition. Trapped! It was trapped! The tiny body, shimmering with green and purple, beat helplessly against the pane, rustling and thumping like a failing heart. Somebody must set it free, Paul knew, or it would die. The colors, the beautiful colors, would turn to ashy gray and then vanish, taking a piece of sun out of the world forever. . . .

He woke up with a start. Gally was kneeling over him.

"Quiet," the boy whispered. "There's someone outside. Might be the soldiers."

As Paul sat up the knocking came again, a dry sound that murmured through the vast Oysterhouse.

Perhaps, Paul thought, still tangled in the rags of his dream, *it's not soldiers at all. Maybe it's only a dying bird.*

"Get up there." Gally pointed to a rickety staircase leading up to one of the galleries. "Hide. We won't tell them you're here, whoever it is."

Paul mounted the squeaking stairs, which swayed alarmingly. Clearly it had been a long time since anyone so heavy had climbed them. The furtive knocking sounded again.

Gally watched until Paul had reached the shadowy upper reaches, then took a smoldering stick from the fire and crept toward the doorway. A thin blue light seeped in through the wide fanlight over his head. Dawn was approaching.

"Who's out there?"

There was a pause, as though whoever knocked had not truly expected an answer. The voice, when it came, was smooth and almost childishly sweet, but it raised the hairs on the back of Paul's neck.

"Just honest men. We are looking for a friend of ours."

"We don't know you." Gally was fighting to keep his voice steady. "Stands to reason there's no one here calls themself your friend."

"Ah. Ah, but perhaps you've seen him, this friend of ours?"

"Who are you, knocking on doors at such an hour?"

"Just travelers. Have you seen our friend? He was a soldier once, but he has been wounded. He's not right in the head, not right at all. It would be cruel to hide him from us—we are his friends and could help him." The voice was full of kind reason, but something else moved behind the words, something greedy. A blind fear gripped Paul. He wanted to scream at whatever stood outside to go away and leave him in peace. He put his knuckle between his teeth instead and bit down hard.

"We've seen nobody, we're hiding nobody." Gally tried to make his voice deep and scornful, with only middling success. "This is our place now. We are working men who must have our sleep, so be off before we set our dogs on you."

There was a murmuring sound from behind the door, a grumble of quiet conversation. The door creaked in its frame, then creaked again, as though someone had for a moment set a heavy weight against it. Struggling against his terror, Paul began to creep around the upper gallery toward the door so he could be close enough to help Gally if trouble began.

"Very well," the voice said at last. *"We are truly sorry if we have disturbed you. We will go now. Sadly, we must seek our friend in another town if he is not here."* There was another creak and the latch rattled in its socket. The invisible stranger continued calmly, as though the rattling were something quite unconnected. *"If you should happen to meet such a man, a soldier, perhaps a trifle confused or strange, tell him to ask after us in the King's Dream, or in other inns along the river. Joiner and Tusk, those are our names. We so badly want to help our friend."*

Heavy boots scraped on the doorstep, then there was a long silence. Gally reached up to open the door, but Paul leaned over the railing and signaled him not to touch it. Instead, he moved to where the gallery rail stood closest to the fanlight above the door, and leaned out.

Two shapes stood on the doorstep, both bundled in dark cloaks. One was larger, but otherwise they were little more than lumps of shadow in the gray before morning. Paul felt his heart speed even faster. He gestured frantically at Gally not to move. By the thin light, he could see some of the children were awake and peering out of various sleeping places around the Oysterhouse, their eyes wide with fear.

The smaller of the two shapes cocked its head to one side as though listening. Paul did not know why, but he was desperate that these people, whoever they were, should not find him. He thought his heart must be pounding as loud as a kettledrum. An image came bubbling up through his panicked thoughts, a picture of an empty place, a vast expanse of nothingness in which only he existed—he and two things that hunted him. . . .

The smaller figure leaned close to the larger as though whispering, then they both turned and made their way down the path and vanished in the fog that was drifting up from the river.

"Two of them, eh? Are those the strange folk you said you saw?"

Miyagi nodded vigorously. Gally screwed up his forehead in an awesome display of concentration. "I can't say as I've ever heard of such before," he said at last. "But there's plenty of strange folk coming through these days." He grinned at Paul. "No offense. But if they're not soldiers, they're spies or something like. They'll be coming back, I reckon."

Paul thought the boy was probably right. "Then there's only one thing to do. I'll go, then they'll follow after me." He said it briskly, but the idea of having to move on so soon made him ache. He had been foolish to imagine that he might find peace so easily. He could remember very little, but he knew it had been a long time since he had been somewhere he could call his home. "What's the best way out of this town? As a matter of fact, what's beyond this town? I have no idea."

"It's not so easy to travel through the Squared," said Gally. "Things have changed since we came here. And if you just set out, chances are you'll walk right into the Red Lady's soldiers, and then it'll be the dungeons for you, or something worse." He shook his head gravely and sucked his lip, pondering. "No, we'll need to ask someone who knows about things. I reckon we should take you to Bishop Humphrey."

"Who's that?"

"Take him to Old Dumpy?" Little Miyagi seemed amused. "That great bag of wind?"

"He knows things. He'll know where the governor here should go." Gally turned to Paul, as though asking him to settle an argument. "The bishop's a smart man. Knows the names of everything, even things you didn't think had names. What do you say?"

"If we can trust him."

Gally nodded. "He's a bag of wind, it's true, but he's an important man, so the redbreasts leave him alone." He clapped his hands for attention. The children gathered around him. "I'm taking my friend to see the bishop. While I'm gone, I don't want you lot going out, and I *certainly* don't want you letting no one in. The password idea's a good one—don't open the door to anyone, *even me,* 'less they say the word 'custard.' Got it? *'Custard.'* Miyagi, you're in charge. And Bay, wipe that grin off your fazoot. Try not to be an eejit just this once, will you?"

Gally led him out the back door, which opened onto the headlands and a pine forest that grew almost to the very walls of the Oyster-house. The boy checked carefully, then waved for Paul to follow him into the trees. Within moments they were tramping through a wood so dense that they could no longer see the large building just a few dozen yards behind them.

The morning fog was still thick and lay close to the ground. The woods were unnaturally silent; except for the sound of his own feet crunching across the carpet of fallen needles—the boy made almost no noise at all—Paul could hear nothing. No wind rattled the branches. No birds saluted the climbing sun. As they made their way beneath the trees with the mist swirling about their ankles, Paul could almost imagine that he was walking across clouds, hiking through the sky. The idea cast a shadow of memory, but whatever it was would not allow itself to be grasped and examined.

They had walked for what seemed at least an hour, the slope slanting downward more often than not, when Gally, who was several paces ahead, waved Paul to a halt. The boy silenced any questions by lifting his small hand, then lightfooted his way back to Paul's side.

"Crossroads lies just ahead," he whispered. "But I thought I heard something."

They made their way down the hillside until the land flattened and they could see a cleared place between the trees with a strip of reddish dirt road at its center. Gally led them alongside it with great caution, as though they paced the length of a sleeping snake. Abruptly, he sank to his knees, then reached up to pull Paul down, too.

They had reached the place where a second dusty road cut across the path of the first. Two signposts that Paul could not read pointed away in the same direction down the crossroad. Gally crawled forward until he could watch the spot from behind a bush, not fifty paces from the intersection.

They waited in silence so long that Paul was just about to stand up and stretch when he heard a noise. It was faint at first, faint and regular as a heartbeat, but it slowly grew louder. Footsteps.

Two shapes appeared out of the misty trees, coming toward them from the direction the two signs were pointing. The pair walked in an unhurried way, their cloaks dragging in the dew-sodden dust of the road. One of them was very large and moved with an odd shuffle, but both were familiar from the front porch the night before. Paul felt his gorge rise. For a moment he feared he would not be able to breathe.

The figures reached the center of the crossroad and paused for a moment in some silent communion before continuing in the direction from which Paul and Gally had come.

The mist eddied around their feet. They wore shapeless hats as well as the sagging cloaks, but still Paul could see the glint of spectacles on the smaller. The larger had a peculiar grayish cast to his skin, and appeared to be holding something in his mouth, for the jutting shapes that bulged his upper lip and pressed against his jaw were surely far too large to be teeth.

Paul clutched hard at the mat of needles, digging furrows in the ground with his fingers. He felt light-headed, almost feverish, but he knew that death was hunting for him on that road—no, something worse than death, something far more empty, grim, and limitless than death.

As if they sensed his thoughts, the two figures suddenly stopped in the center of the road, directly opposite the hiding place. Paul's pulse, already painfully fast, now rattled in his temples. The smaller figure bent down and craned its head forward, as though it had somehow become a different kind of creature, something more likely to go on four legs than two. It pivoted its head slowly; Paul saw the lenses spark, spark, spark as they caught light through the shadowing trees. The moment seemed to stretch endlessly.

The larger figure dropped a flat grayish hand onto its companion's shoulder and rumbled something—in his panic, Paul could only hear words that sounded like *"sealing wax"*—then set off down the road, waddling so slowly its legs might have been tied together at the ankles. A moment later the smaller straightened up and followed, shoulders up and head thrust forward in a sullen slouch.

Paul did not release the breath burning in his chest until the two shapes had vanished into the mist, and even then he lay unmoving for some time. Gally did not seem in a hurry to rise either.

"Going back to town, they are," the boy said quietly. "That's as well. Plenty to keep them busy there. All the same, I think we'll stay off the road." He scrambled to his feet. Paul got up and staggered after him, feeling as though he had almost fallen from some high place.

A short time later Gally cut across the road and led them down a smaller side road which wound through the trees and up a small rise. At the top of the hill, rising from a copse of birch trees, stood a very small castle whose central keep jutted like a pointed hat. The drawbridge was down, the front door—no larger than the door on an ordinary house—stood open.

They found the bishop sitting in the front room, surrounded by shelves of books and curios, reading a thin volume in the light that streamed in through the entrance. He fit his wide chair so snugly it was hard to imagine that he ever left it. He was huge and bald, with a protuberant lower lip and a mouth so wide that Paul felt sure he must have a greater than ordinary number of bones in his jaw. He looked up as their footfalls sounded against the polished stone floor.

"Hmmm. In the middle of my poetry hour, my all-too-brief moment for restful contemplation. Still and all." He folded the book closed and let it slide down to the place where the hemisphere of his belly met his small legs—there was nothing flat enough in the area to be called a lap. "Ah. The scullion lad, I see. Gally, is it not? Tender of the cookfire. What brings you here, pot urchin? Has one of your spitted carcasses suddenly called out for shriving? The fiery pit has a way of engendering such second thoughts. *Harrum, harrum.*" It took a moment before Paul realized that the hollow, drumlike sound was actually a laugh.

"I've come asking your help, Bishop Humphrey, true enough." Gally grabbed Paul's sleeve and tugged him forward. "This gentleman needed some advice, and I told him, 'Ask Bishop Humphrey. He's the cleverest man in these parts.' And here we are."

"Indeed." The bishop turned his tiny eyes to Paul, then after an instant's shrewd examination, let them slide away again. He never kept his gaze on anything for very long, which gave his conversation an air of distracted irritation. "A stranger, eh? A recent immigrant to our humble shire? Or perhaps you are a visitor of a more transient nature? Passing through, as it were? A peregrine?"

Paul hesitated. Despite Gally's assurances, he was not entirely comfortable with Humphrey. There was something distant about the man, as though something glassy and brittle stood between him and the outside world. "I am a stranger," he finally admitted. "I'm trying to leave town, but I seem to be caught in some trouble between the red and white factions—some red soldiers tried to harm me, though I did nothing to them. And there are other men looking for me as well, people I don't want to meet. . . ."

". . . So we need to reckon out the best way for him to get out of the 'Squared,'" Gally finished for him.

"The squared?" Paul was confused, but the bishop seemed to understand.

"Ah, yes. Well, what sort of moves do you make?" He squinted for a moment, then lifted to his eye the monocle which had been dangling on its ribbon down the expanse of his belly. In the bishop's pudgy fingers it seemed a mere chip of glass. "It's hard to tell, since you are an outsider like Gally and his tatterdemalions. Hmmmm. You have something of the kern about you, yet something of the horseman as well. You might be another thing entirely, of course, but such speculation as to locomotion would be fruitless for me—like asking a fish whether it would prefer to travel by coach or by velocipede, if you see what I mean. *Harrum, harrum.*"

Paul was lost, but he had been warned that the bishop was prone to talk. He put on an attentive look.

"Bring that over here, boy—the large one." Humphrey gestured. Gally sprang to do his bidding, tottering back with a leather-bound book almost as big as he was. With Paul's help, they opened it across the arms of the bishop's chair. Paul was expecting a map, but to his astonishment the open pages contained nothing but a grid of alternating colored squares, each one full of strange notations and small diagrams.

"Now then, let me see . . ." The bishop traced his way across the grid with a broad forefinger. "The most obvious course would seem to be for you to hasten here, catty-cornered to us. But then, I have always favored bold diagonals, at least since my investiture. *Harrum.* However, there have been reports of an unpleasantly savage beast in that vicinity, so perhaps that should not be your primary choice. But you are rather hemmed in at the moment. The queen has a castle not far from here, and I take it you would prefer not to meet with her minions, hmmm?" He turned a shrewd look on Paul, who shook his head. "I thought not. And the lady herself visits this area here with some frequency. She moves very swiftly, so you would do well not to arrange any long journeys through her favorite territory, even should she prove to be temporarily absent."

The bishop leaned back, making his sturdy chair squeak. He gestured for Gally to take the book away, which the boy groaningly did.

"I must cogitate," the fat man said, and let suety eyelids descend. He was silent for so long that Paul began to think he might have fallen asleep, and took the opportunity to look around the room. Beside the bishop's large collection of handsomely bound books there were also all manner of curious things lining the walls, bottles full of dried plants, bones, and even complete skeletons of unfamiliar creatures, bits of twinkling gemstone. All alone on one shelf stood a huge jar containing living insects, some that looked like crusts of bread, others that resembled nothing so much as puddings. As he watched the strange creatures climbing over each other in the stoppered jar, Paul felt a pang of hunger which was followed a moment later by a surge of nausea. He was hungry, but not that hungry.

"While there is a great deal to be said for the order which Her Scarlet Majesty has brought to us during this extended period of check," the bishop said abruptly, making Paul jump, "there is also something to be said for the more *laissez-faire* attitudes of her predecessor. Therefore, while I myself have excellent relations with our ruler—as I also did with the previous administration—I can understand that you may not be so fortunate." Humphrey stopped and took a deep draught of air, as though struck breathless by his own admirable rhetoric. "If you wish to avoid the attentions of our vermilion monarch, I suggest you must take the first alternative I proposed. You can then pass through that square and find yourself directly at the border of our land. The terrible beast said to inhabit the area is doubtless a phantasy of the peasantry, who are famously prone to enliven their dull and rusticated routine with such tales. I will draw you a map. You can be there before sunset. *Carpe diem,* young man." He spread his hands contentedly on the arms of his wide chair. "Boldness is all."

While Gally scurried to find the bishop's pen and paper, Paul seized the chance for information. He had been traveling in fog, figuratively and literally, too much of late. "What is the name of this place?"

"Why, it is sometimes referred to as the Eight Squared, at least in the oldest and most learned of tomes. But those of us who have always lived here do not often find cause to refer to it, since we are in the midst of it! Rather like a bird, do you see, when asked to define the sky. . . ."

Paul hurried to ask him another question. "And you were once on good terms with . . . the White King?"

"Queen. None of us have ever met the somnolent seigneurs of our humble territory—they are rather absentee landlords. No, it is the ladies, bless them both, who have traditionally kept the order within the Eight Squared while their husbands stayed close to home."

"Ah. Well, if you were on good terms with the White Queen, but the Red Queen now rules the land, how do you manage to be her friend as well?"

The bishop looked a trifle annoyed. "Respect, young man. In a single word, that is it. Her Scarlet Majesty relies on my judgment—and I am consulted on things secular as well as superworldly, I might add—and thus I am possessed of a rather unique status."

Paul was not satisfied. "But if the Red Queen finds you've helped me, despite the fact that her soldiers might have been looking for me, won't she be annoyed? And if the White Queen ever gains back her power, won't *she* be furious with you for being so close with her enemy?"

Now Humphrey seemed truly put out. His sparse eyebrows moved together and tilted sharply downward over the bridge of his nose. "Young man, it does not become you to speak of things beyond your expertise, whatever may be the current fashion. However, in the interest of beginning an education which you obviously sorely need, I will explain something." He cleared his throat just as Gally reappeared bearing a plume and a large sheet of foolscap.

"I found them, Bishop."

"Yes, that's fine, boy. Now hush." The bishop briefly fixed his small eyes on Paul before allowing them to roam once more. "I am a respected man, and I dare not, for the good of the land, throw my not inconsiderable weight behind either one faction or the other. For factions are impermanent, even ephemeral, while the rock upon which my bishopric is founded is made of the stuff of eternity. So, if I may create an analogy, my position is that of someone who sits upon a wall. Such a perch might seem dangerous to one who, without my experience and natural sense of balance, gazes up at me from below. In fact, to such a one, a man such as I might seem in imminent peril of a great . . . downfalling. Ah, but the view from up here, from *inside* here," he tapped his hairless head, "is quite different, I assure you. I am, as it were, made in the perfect shape for wall-sitting. My Master has designed me, as it were, to balance permanently between two unacceptable alternatives."

"I see," said Paul, who could think of nothing else to say.

The bishop appeared to be in a much better mood after explaining. He rapidly sketched a map, which he handed over with a flourish.

Paul thanked him, then he and Gally left the tiny castle and thumped back across the drawbridge.

"Leave the door open," Bishop Humphrey called after them. "It is too nice a day to miss, and after all, I need fear no one!"

Looking down as they thumped across the drawbridge, Paul saw that the moat was very shallow. A man could walk across it and barely get his ankles wet.

"I told you he'd have the answer you needed," Gally said cheerfully.

"Yes," said Paul, "I can see he's the kind of fellow who has answers to things."

It took most of the afternoon to walk back. By the time they reached the Oysterhouse, the sun had vanished behind the forest. Paul was looking forward to a chance to sit down and rest his legs.

The door swung inward on Gally's first knock.

"Curse those addlepates," the boy said. "Larking about and they don't remember a thing I've told them. Miyagi! Chesapeake!"

There was no answer but echoes. As Paul followed the boy down the hallway, the sound of their footsteps as stark as drumbeats, he felt a tightening around his heart. There was a strange smell in the air, a sea-smell, salty and unpleasantly, sweetly sour. The house was very, very quiet.

It was silent in the main room as well, but this time no one was hiding. The children lay scattered across the floor, some struck down and left to lie in strange postures like frozen dancers, others piled carelessly together in the corners, things that had been used and cast away. They had not merely been killed, but violated in some way that Paul could not completely understand. They had been *opened up*, shucked, and emptied. The sawdust on the floor had clumped in sodden red balls and still had not sopped up all the red, which gleamed, sticky-shiny in the failing light.

Gally fell to his knees, moaning, his eyes so wide with horror that Paul feared they might burst from his skull. Paul wanted to pull him away, but found he could not move.

Written on the wall above one of the largest piles, arching above the pale, spattered arms and legs and blind, wide-mouthed faces, smeared across the boards in sloppy scarlet letters, was the word "CUSTARD."

CHAPTER 13

Eland's Daughter's Son

NETFEED/INTERACTIVES: IEN, Hr. 4 (Eu, NAm)—"BACKSTAB"
(visual: Kennedy running across estate garden pursued by tornado)
VO: Stabbak (Carolus Kennedy) and Shi Na (Wendy Yohira) again try to
escape the fortress estate of the mysterious Doctor Methuselah (Moishe
Reiner). Jeffreys, 6 other supporting characters open. Flak to:
IEN.BKSTB.CAST

"Someone at the door downstairs." Long Joseph stood nervously in the doorway of her room, unwilling to enter the proximity of illness, even something as unlikely to be contagious as what he had been told was a 'breakdown due to stress.' "He says his name Gabba or something."

"It's !Xabbu. My friend from the Poly. You can let him in."

He stared for a moment, frowning, then turned and trudged away. He was clearly not happy about answering the door or taking messages for her, but in his own way he was doing his best. Renie sighed. In any case, she couldn't summon up the energy to be angry—suspicious and bad-tempered was just her father's way. To his credit, in the days she'd been home, he hadn't expected her to get up and fix him meals. Of course, his own contribution to the household hadn't grown much either. They were both eating a lot of cold cereal and waved Menu Boxes.

She heard the front door opening. She struggled upright in the bed and drank some water, then tried to fluff herself into some appearance of normality. Even if you'd almost died, it was embarrassing to have bed-hair.

Unlike her father, the Bushman came into the sickroom with no hesitation. He stopped a few feet away from her, which she guessed was more from some strange sort of respect than anything else. Renie reached out her hand to draw him closer. His fingers were warm and reassuring.

"I am very happy to see you, Renie. I have been worrying about you."

"I'm doing pretty well, actually." She squeezed his hand and released him, then looked around for something for !Xabbu to sit on. The only chair was covered with clothes, but he seemed content to stand. "I had to fight like hell to get them to send me home from the emergency room. But if I'd gone into hospital, I would have been stuck in quarantine for weeks."

She would also have been close to Stephen, but she knew that would have been a bittersweet proximity at best.

"You are best at home, I think." He smiled. "I know that amazing things can be done in a modern hospital, but I am still one of my people. I would become even more sick if I had to stay in such a place."

Renie looked up. Her father was back in the doorway, staring at !Xabbu. Long Joseph had a very strange expression on his face; when he saw Renie, it changed to something like embarrassment.

"I'm going over to see Walter." He showed her his hat as proof. He took a few steps away, then turned. "You be all right?"

"I'm not going to die while you're gone, if that's what you mean." She saw the closing-up of his face and regretted her words. "I'll be fine, Papa. Don't you and Walter drink too much."

Her father had been looking at !Xabbu again, but he scowled at Renie. It was not particularly unpleasant, more of a general-purpose scowl. "Don't you worry about what I'm getting up to, girl."

!Xabbu was still standing patiently when the door closed behind Long Joseph, eyes bright in his small solemn face. Renie patted the edge of the bed.

"Please sit down. You're making me nervous. I'm sorry we couldn't talk before, but the drugs I've been taking make me sleep a lot."

"But you are better now?" He scrutinized her face. "You look healthy in your spirit to me. When we first came back from . . . from that place, I was very frightened for you."

"It was an arrhythmia—not really a full-fledged heart attack. In fact, I'm feeling enough better that I'm beginning to get really angry. I saw them, !Xabbu, the bastards who run that place. I saw what they do in that club. I still don't have the slightest idea why, but if we weren't both this close—" she held up her fingers, "—to having the same thing happen as Stephen and who knows how many others, I'll eat my hat." !Xabbu stared at her, confused. Renie laughed. "Sorry. That's an expression that means 'I'm certain I'm right.' Haven't you heard it before?"

The Bushman shook his head. "No. But I am learning more all the time, learning to think, almost, in this language. Sometimes I wonder what I am losing." He finally sat down. He was so light Renie barely felt the mattress give. "What do we do now, Renie? If what you say is true, these are bad people doing very bad things. Do we tell the police or the government?"

"That's one of the reasons I wanted to see you—to show you something." She reached down behind her pillows feeling for her pad. It took her some moments to pull it from the gap between the mattress and the wall where it had been wedged. She was dismayed by how weak she still felt; even the small effort made her feel short of breath. "Did you bring the goggles? It's so much slower trying to work on a flat screen."

!Xabbu produced the cases stamped with the Polytechnic's logo. Renie took out both sets, neither much larger than a pair of sunglasses, found a Y-connector in the tangle of cables beside her, and jacked both the goggle-cable and a pair of squeezers into her pad.

When she handed one pair of goggles to !Xabbu, he did not immediately take them.

"What's wrong?"

He shook his head slowly. "I was lost, Renie. I failed you when we were in that place."

"We're not going anywhere near there—besides, this is just optical display and sound, anyway, not full wrap-around. We're just going to go visit the Poly's infobanks and a few other subnets. There's nothing to be afraid of."

"It is not so much fear that holds me back, although I would be a liar if I said I was not frightened. But there is more. There are things I need to tell you, Renie—things about what happened to me in that place."

She paused, not wanting to push him. Despite his facility, she re-minded herself, he was still very new to this—new to everything she took for granted, in fact. "I have things I need to show you, too. I promise you it will be no worse than working in the lab at the school. Afterward, I very much want to hear what you have to say." She of-fered the goggles again and this time !Xabbu accepted them.

The empty gray quickly became the ordered polygons of her per-sonal system—a simple array resembling a home office, far less so-phisticated than what she had available at the Poly. She had customized it with a few pictures on the wall and a tank of tropical fish, but otherwise it was a coldly functional environment, a system for someone who was always in a hurry. She couldn't see herself changing it any time soon.

"We were in that place for what, three hours? Four?" As she pal-pated the squeezers, one of the polygons became a window. After a moment, the Polytechnic's logo and advisory warning appeared. Renie keyed in her access code and immediately the library environment sprang into detailed existence. "Bear with me," she said. "I'm used to doing my work here with some kind of free-hand capabilities, but today we're stuck with these squeezer things, which are pretty basic."

It was strange to be moving through such a familiar and realistic environment but not being able to react directly to anything; when she wanted to manipulate one of the symbolic objects, instead of reaching out toward it, she had to think about the quite different things needed to key in a direction.

"This is what I wanted you to see," she said when she'd finally opened the information window she wanted, "—the Poly's records for that day." Lines of numbers rolled rapidly upward in front of them. "Here's the Harness Room prefix, all the connections. There we are, signing in. That's my access code, right?"

"I see it." Xabbu's voice was steady but distant.

"Well, scan this. That's our usage record. No connection except to the in-house school system."

"I don't understand."

"It means that, according to this, we never logged onto the net, never entered the commercial node called 'Mister J's' at all. Every-thing we experienced, the pool, that sea-monster, that huge main room, none of it happened. That's what the Poly's records say, anyway."

"I am confused, Renie. Perhaps I am still not as wise about these things as I believed myself to be. How could there be no record?"

"I don't know!" Renie played the squeezers. Inside the goggle-universe, the Poly's records disappeared and another window opened up. "Look at this—my own personal accounts, even the ones I set up just for this, are zeroed. None of the connection time was charged to me, to the school—anywhere! There's not a single record of what we did. Nothing." She took a breath, reminding herself to stay calm. She still got a little dizzy now and then, but was feeling stronger every day, which made the whole thing even more frustrating. "If we can't find the records, we can't very well make a complaint, can we? You can just imagine what the reaction of the authorities would be: 'That's a very serious charge, Ms. Sulaweyo, especially since you've apparently never used the node in question.' It would be useless."

"I wish I could make some suggestion, Renie. I wish there was some help I could give, but this is beyond my very young knowledge."

"You *can* help. You can help me try to find out what happened. I don't have much stamina, and I get tired if I have to stare at anything too long. But if you can be my eyes, we can try a few things I haven't had a chance to do yet. I'm not giving up that easily. Those bastards have hurt my brother, and they damn near got you and me, too."

Renie was leaning back against the pillows. She'd taken her medicine, and as usual it was making her sleepy. !Xabbu was sitting cross-legged on the floor, his eyes hidden by the goggles, his fingers moving with surprising fluency on the squeezer keys.

"There is nothing like what you describe," he said, breaking a long silence. "No loops, no repetitions. All the loose ends are, as you would say, tied up."

"Shit." She closed her eyes again, trying to think of another way through the problem. Someone had wiped out all record of what she and !Xabbu had done, then fabricated a new one and inserted it seamlessly into place. The time they had spent in the club, all of it, was now as insubstantial and unprovable as a dream.

"The thing that frightens me is not just that they've managed to do that, but the fact that they tracked back all my aliases and wiped them, too. There shouldn't be any way in hell they could do that."

!Xabbu was still moving through the data-world. The goggles looked like insect eyes on his narrow face. "But if they have found these false selves you constructed, can they not trace them back to you?"

"Yesterday I would have said 'Not in a million years,' but suddenly I'm not so sure. If they know it was someone at the Poly, they wouldn't have much trouble narrowing it down without even getting into internal records." She bit her lip, wondering. It was not a pleasant thought; she somehow doubted that the people who ran Mister J's would limit themselves to the kind of intimidation that came in a solicitor's letter. "I kept them as far from me as I could when I was setting up the aliases, went in through public nodes, everything I could think of. I never believed they could track me straight back to the Poly."

!Xabbu made a sudden noise, a small click of surprise. Renie sat up. "What?"

"There is something . . ." He paused and his fingers moved swiftly. "There is something here. What does it mean when an orange light flashes in your office? It is blinking like a lightning beetle! It just began."

"That's the antivirals kicking in." Renie leaned over, ignoring the moment of light-headedness, and picked the other pair of goggles up from the floor. She pulled the Y-connector tight between her and !Xabbu. "Someone's trying to get into my system, maybe." A shiver of unease moved through her. Had they tracked her already? Who *were* these people?

She was in the system's basic VR representation again, the three-dimensional office. A small vermilion dot was blinking on and off, a smoldering glow like a coal from a *braai*. She leaned and groped blindly across !Xabbu's knee, then tapped a couple of keys. Inside the virtual space, the dot of light exploded into a welter of symbols and text which filled much of the office.

"Whatever it is, it's already in the system, but it's still dormant. Probably a virus." She was angry that her system had been penetrated and perhaps hopelessly corrupted, but at the same time it seemed an oddly muted response from the kind of people who owned such a club. She set her Phage gear in search of the intruding code. It didn't have to hunt very long.

"What in hell. . . ?"

!Xabbu sensed her puzzlement. "What is wrong, Renie?"

"That's not supposed to be there."

Hanging in virtual space before them, rendered much more realistically than the planar office furniture, was a translucent, yellow-glinting, faceted object.

"It looks like a yellow diamond." An image, as tenuous as a dream, floated up to her—*a pure white shape, an empty person made of light*—then it was gone again.

"Is it a computer sickness? Is it something those people have sent?"

"I don't know. I think I recall something about it from just before we went offline, but it's all very confused. I don't remember much of what happened after I went back to the cave to get you." The yellow gem hung before her, staring back like an emotionless golden eye.

"I really must talk to you, Renie." !Xabbu sounded unhappy. "I must tell you about what happened to me there."

"Not now." She quickly threw her analyticals at the gem—or at what the gem represented. When the results came back a few moments later, surrounding the foreign object like a system of tiny text planets orbiting a diamond-edged sun, she whistled between her teeth in surprise. "It's code, but it's been compacted until it's tight as a drum. There's an amazing amount of information packed in there. If it is some kind of destructive virus, it's got enough information to rewrite a system much bigger than mine."

"What are you going to do?"

Renie didn't answer him for several long moments as she hastily checked back through her earlier connections. "Wherever it came from, it's attached itself to my system now. But I don't see any trace of it remaining on my part of the Polytechnic's net, which is just as well. God, the pad is bulging—I hardly have any memory left." She cut her connection to the school. "I don't think I can even activate this thing on my little system here, so maybe it's effectively neutralized, although I can't imagine why someone would set up a virus that downloads itself to a system too small for it to operate. For that matter, I can't imagine why anyone would make a virus that big—it's like trying to use an elephant to do surveillance in a phone booth."

She turned off her system and removed the goggles, then slumped back on her bed. Small spots of yellow light like the diamond's smaller cousins jittered before her eyes. !Xabbu took off his own goggles and looked at the pad with suspicion, as though something unpleasant might crawl out of it. He then turned his worried look onto her.

"You look pale. I will pour you some water."

"I have to find a system that's powerful enough to let the thing activate," Renie said, thinking out loud, "but that's not connected to any other system—something big and isolated, sterile. I could probably set that up in one of the labs at the Poly, but I'd have to answer a lot of questions."

!Xabbu carefully handed her a glass. "Should you not destroy it? If it is something that those people made, the people of that terrible place, it must be a dangerous thing."

"But if it came from the club, it's the only proof we've got that we were there! Even more important, it's code, and people who write high-level code have their own style, just like flick directors or artists. If we can figure out who writes the gear for Mister J's dirty side—well, it's a place to start, anyway." She drained the glass in two long swallows, amazed at how thirsty she was. "I'm not going to give up just because they frightened me." She let herself slump back against the pillows. "I'm not giving up."

!Xabbu still sat cross-legged on the floor. "So how will you do this if you do not use the school?" He sounded almost mournful, far more so than was appropriate for what he'd said, as though he were making small talk while saying good-bye to someone he did not expect to see again.

"I'm thinking. I have a couple of ideas, but I need to let them cook."

The Bushman was quiet, staring at the floor. At last he looked up. His eyes were troubled, his forehead wrinkled. Renie suddenly realized that a quite uncharacteristic gloom had been hanging over him since he had arrived.

"You said you wanted to talk to me about what happened."

He nodded his head. "I am very confused, Renie, and I need to speak. You are my friend. You have saved my life, I think."

"And you saved mine, and I know that for certain. If you had waited too long before getting help for me. . . ."

"It was not hard to see that your spirit was very weak, that you were very ill." He shrugged as though embarrassed.

"So talk to me. Tell me why *your* spirit is weak, if that's what is wrong."

He nodded, his expression solemn. "Since we came back from that place, I do not hear the sun ringing. That is what my people say. When you can no longer hear the sound the sun makes, your spirit is in danger. I have felt that way many days now.

"First I must tell you things about me you do not know—some of the story that is my life. I told you that my father is dead, that my mother and my sisters live with my people. You know that I have been to city schools. I am of my people, but I also have the language, the ideas of city-people. Sometimes these things feel like a poison inside of me, something cold that might stop my heart."

He stopped, drawing a deep, ragged breath. Whatever he was about to tell clearly pained him. Renie found that she was clenching her fists tightly, as though watching someone she loved perform a dangerous feat in a high place.

"There are very few of my people left," he began. "The old blood is mostly gone. We have married the taller people, or sometimes our women have been taken against their wishes, but there are fewer and fewer who look like me.

"There are fewer still who live in the old way. Even those who are of the true Bushman kind, of the pure blood, are almost all raising sheep or working in cattle stations along the edges of the Kalahari or in the Okavango Delta. That was my mother's family, a delta family. They had sheep, a few goats, they took fish from the delta and traded in the nearest town for things that they felt they needed—things our ancestors would have laughed at. How they would have laughed! Radios, someone even had an old television that worked on batteries—what are those things but the voices of the white man, and the black man who lives like the white man? Our ancestors would not have understood. The voices of the city drown out the sounds of the life my people once lived, just as they make it hard to hear the ringing of the sun.

"So my mother's family lived a life like many of Africa's poor black people, haunting the outside places of what had been their own lands. The whites do not rule in Africa now, at least they no longer sit in the offices of the Government, but the things they brought here rule Africa in their place. This you know, even living in the city."

Renie nodded. "I know."

"But there are still some of our people who live the old way—the way of the Early Races, the way of Mantis and Porcupine and Kwammanga the Rainbow. My father and his people lived this way. They were hunters, traveling in the desert where neither the white man nor the black man go, following the lightning, the rains, and the antelope herds. They still lived the life that my people have lived since the very first days of Creation, but only because there is nothing the city-folk want from the desert. I learned in school that there are still a few such places left in this world, a few places where no radios play, where no rolling wheels leave their tracks, but these places are shrinking away like water spilled on a flat rock that dries beneath the sun.

"But the only way my father's people could keep their life and hold on to the old ways was to stay far away from everyone, even those of our blood who had left the desert and the sacred hills. Once all Africa was ours, and we roamed it with the other first peoples, with the eland and the lion, the springbok and the baboon—we call baboons 'the people who sit on their heels'—and all the others. But the last remnants of our kind can live only by hiding. To them, the city-world is true poison. They cannot survive its touch.

"Many years ago now, before you or I were born, a terrible drought began. It hurt all the land, but most of all the dry places, the places where only my father's people lived. It lasted three full years. The great springbok herds deserted the land, the kudu and the harte-beeste, too, they all died or moved away. And my father's family suf-fered. Even the sipping wells, the places where only the Bushmen can find water, ran dry. The old people had already given themselves up to the desert that the younger ones might live, but now the young and strong were dying also. The children already born were weak and sickly, and no new children had come, since in a time of great drought our women are no longer fertile.

"My father was a hunter, in the early prime of his life. He traveled far across the desert, walking for days in search of anything that might help keep his family, his brothers and sisters, nieces and neph-ews, alive.

"But each time he went out he had to go farther in search of game, and each time there was less food to keep him alive as he hunted. The ostrich shells in which my people carry water were always nearly empty. The other hunters had no better luck, and the women worked all day long every day, digging for any roots that might have survived the terrible drought, collecting what few insects remained so that the children would have something to eat. At night they all prayed that the rains would finally come back. They had no happiness. They did not sing, and after a while they did not even tell stories. The misery was so great that some of my father's family suspected that the rain had finally left the earth and gone away forever to some other place, that life itself was ending.

"One day, when my father was on a hunting trip and had already been away from his people for seven days, he saw an impossible vi-sion—a great eland, the most wonderful of all creatures, standing at the edge of a desert pan, nibbling at the bark of a thorn tree. An eland, he knew, would provide days of food for his family, and even the water in the grass remaining in its stomach would help to keep the children alive a little longer. But he knew it was also a strange thing to see this single solitary beast. The eland does not travel in vast herds like the other antelope, but where he goes, his family goes, just as with our own people. Also, this eland was not sick, its ribs did not show, despite the terrible drought. He could not help wondering if perhaps this animal was a special gift from Grandfather Mantis, who had made the very first eland from the leather of Kwammanga's sandal.

"As he wondered, the eland saw him and darted away. My father gave chase.

"All of one day he followed the eland, and when at last it stopped to rest, he crept as close as he could, then daubed an arrow with his strongest poison and let it fly. He saw the arrow strike before the eland ran away. When he went to the place it had been, the arrow was not there, so his heart was full. He had struck what he shot at. He began to track it, waiting for the poison to take effect.

"But the eland did not slow or show any sign of weakness. All the next day he tracked it, but never came close enough to shoot another arrow. The eland moved quickly. My father's ostrich shells were empty and there was no more dried meat in his pack, but he had no time to search for water or hunt for food.

"Two more days he tracked the animal across the sands, by hot sun and cold moon. The eland ran ever southeast, toward the place where the desert ended in what had been a great swamp around a river delta. My father had never in his life been half so close to the Okavango—his people, who had once traveled a thousand miles every season, now kept to the most inaccessible inner reaches of the desert for their own safety. But he had become a little mad with hunger and weariness and fear, or perhaps a spirit was in him. He was determined that he would catch the eland. He now felt sure that it was a gift from Mantis, and that if he brought it back to his people, the rains would come.

"At last, on the fourth day after he had shot at the eland, he stumbled across the fringes of the desert, through the hills into the outer edges of the Okavango Swamp. But of course the swamp had also dried in the great drought, and so he found nothing but cracked mud and dead trees. But still he saw the eland running before him, as faint as a dream, and saw its track in the dust, so he went on.

"He walked all night through that unfamiliar place, the bones of crocodiles and fish showing white beneath the moon. My father's people lived in the old way—they knew every rock and mound of sand, every tree and thornbush of the desert in the way that city-people know the habits of their children or the furnishings of their houses. But now he was in a place that he did not know, and chasing a great eland that he believed was a spirit. He was weak and afraid, but he was a hunter and his people were in terrible need. He prayed to the grandmother stars for wisdom. When the Morning Star, who is the greatest hunter of all, at last appeared in the sky, my father prayed to him as well. 'Make my heart as your heart,' he asked the star. He was begging for the courage to survive, for he had grown very weak.

"As the sun rose up into the sky and began to burn the land again, my father saw the shape of the eland beside a stream of running water. The sight of so much water, and the spirit-beast so close at last, made my father's head hurt and so he fell to the ground. He crawled toward the eland, but his arms and legs grew weak and he could not crawl any farther. But as his senses fled from him, he saw that the eland had become a beautiful girl—a girl of our people, but with an unfamiliar face.

"It was my mother, who had gotten up early in the morning to walk to the water. The drought meant that even the great river delta was nearly dry, and she and her family had to travel a long way from their tiny village beside the road to draw water. My mother saw this hunter come from the desert and fall down in a swoon at her feet, and she saw that he was dying. She gave him to drink. He emptied her jug, then nearly drank the little stream dry. When he could walk, she took him back to her family.

"The older ones still spoke his language. While my mother's parents fed him, the grandparents asked him many questions, clucking to themselves in wonder at seeing a man of their own early memories. He ate, but did not say much. Although these people looked much like him their ways were strange, but he hardly noticed what they did. He had eyes only for my mother. She, who had never seen a man of the old ways, had eyes only for him.

"He could not stay. He had lost the eland, but he would at least take water back to his family and people. He was also uneasy with the strangers, with their box-that-spoke, with their strange clothes and strange language. My mother, who did not like or respect her own father because he beat her, ran away with my father, preferring to go to his people than to remain with her own.

"Although he did not urge her to leave her family, he was very happy when she came with him, for she was beautiful in his eye from their first meeting. He called her Eland's Daughter, and they laughed together, although at first they could not understand each other's speech. When at last, after a journey of many days, they found his people again, the rest of his family was amazed by his story and welcomed her and made much of her. That night thunder rang out over the desert and lightning walked. The rains had come back. The drought was ended."

!Xabbu fell silent. Renie waited as long as she could before speaking.

"And then what happened?"

He looked up, a small, sad smile playing about his lips. "Am I not tiring you with this long story, Renie? It is only my story, the story of how I came to be, and how I came here."

"Tiring me? It's . . . it's wonderful. Like a fairy tale."

The smile flickered. "I stopped because that was the happiest moment for them, I think. When the rains came. My father's family thought he had brought back the Eland's Daughter in truth, that he had brought luck back to them. But if I go on, the story grows more sad."

"If you want to tell me, I want to listen, !Xabbu. Please."

"So." He spread his hands. "For a time after that, things were good. With the rain's return came the animals, and soon things were growing again—trees were making new leaves, flowers were springing up. Even the bees returned and began to make their wonderful honey and hide it away in the rocks. This was truly a sign that life was strong in that place—there is nothing the Bushmen like so much as honey, and that is why we love the little bird called the Honey-Guide. So things were good. Soon after, my mother and father conceived a child. That was me, and they named me !Xabbu, which means 'Dream.' The Bushmen believe that life is a dream which itself is dreaming us, and my parents wanted to mark the good fortune that the dream had sent them. Others in the family also bore children, so my first few years were spent among companions of my own age.

"Then a terrible thing happened. My father and his nephew were out hunting. It had been a successful day—they had killed a fine big hartebeeste. They were happy because they knew that there would be a feast when they returned, and that the meat would feed their families well for several days.

"On their way back they came across a jeep. They had heard of such things but had never seen one before, and at first they were reluctant to go near it. But the men in it—three black men and one white, all tall, all dressed in city-clothes—were clearly in danger. They had the look of people who would die soon if they did not get water, so my father and his nephew went to them and helped them.

"These men were desert scientists from one of the universities—I would guess that they were geologists searching for oil or something else of value to city-people. Their jeep had been struck by lightning, so that both engine and radio were useless. Without help they would doubtless have died. My father and his nephew led them to the outskirts of the desert, to a small trading village. This they would not have dared to do, except that my father remembered he had left the desert once before without harm. My father planned to take them to the edge of the town and send them on their way, but as they all walked—very slowly, since that was as fast as the city-folk could go—another jeep came. This one belonged to government rangers, and although they used their radio to summon help for the men my father had rescued, they also arrested my father and his nephew for having killed a hartebeeste. The hartebeeste, you see, is protected by the government. The Bushman is not."

The uncharacteristic bitterness in his words made Renie flinch. "They arrested them? After they'd just saved those men? That's horrible!"

!Xabbu nodded. "The scientists argued against it, but the rangers were the kind of men who fear that they will get in trouble if they are seen to let some small thing pass, so they arrested my father and his relative and took them away. Just like that. They even took the hartebeeste as evidence. By the time my father and his nephew reached the town, it was a rotting carcass unfit to eat and was thrown away.

"The scientists were so ashamed that they borrowed another vehicle and went to tell my father's people what had happened. They did not find them, but they found another group of Bushmen, and soon my mother and the rest of the family heard what had happened.

"My mother, who if she had not lived in the city-world at least knew something of it, determined that she would go and argue with the government, which she thought of as a wise man with a white beard in a big village, and tell them they must let my father go. Although the rest of the family warned her not to do it, she took me and set out for the town.

"But, of course, my father had already been sent on to the city, far away, and by the time my mother could make her way there, he had already been convicted and sentenced for poaching. Both he and my cousin were put in prison, caged with men who had committed terrible crimes, who had shot their own families dead, had tortured and killed children or old people.

"Every day my mother went to beg for my father's freedom, taking me with her, and every day she was driven away from the court, and later the prison, with harsh words and blows. She found us a shack on the edge of the city, two walls of plywood and a piece of tin for a roof, and she scavenged in the rubbish heaps for food and clothing with the other poor people, determined that she would not leave until my father was free.

"I cannot even imagine what it felt like for her. I was so young that I did not really understand. Even now I have only the faintest memories of that time—a vision of the bright lights of a truck shining through the cracks between the boards, the sound of people arguing and singing loudly in other shacks. But it must have been a terrible time for her, alone and so far from her people. She would not give up. She was certain that if she could only find the right man—'the real Government,' as she thought of it—then eventually the mistake would be made right and my father allowed to go free.

"My father, who had even less knowledge of the city-world than she, grew sick. After a few visits he was not allowed to see my mother any more, although she continued to go to the prison every day. My father did not even know she was still in the city, only a few hundred yards from him. He and his nephew lost their happiness, lost their stories. Their spirits became very weak and they stopped eating. Soon, after only a few months in the prison, my father died. His nephew lasted longer. I am told that he was killed in a fight some months later."

"Oh, !Xabbu, how terrible!"

He raised his hand, as if Renie's cry of sympathy was a gift he could not accept. "My mother could not even take my father's body back to the desert. He was buried instead in a cemetery beside the shanty-town. My mother hung his ostrich-shell beads on a wooden stick for a marker. I have gone there, but I could not find his grave.

"My mother took me and started the long trip back. She could not bear to go to the desert again, to the place that meant my father to her, so she stayed with her own family instead, and that is where I was raised. Before too many more years she found another man, a good man. He was Bushman, but his people had left the desert long ago. He did not know the old ways and barely spoke the language. He and my mother had two daughters, my sisters. We were all sent to school. My mother demanded that we learn the city-ways, so that we could protect ourselves as my father could not do.

"My mother did not give up all contact with my father's people. When some of the farther-ranging bushmen came to the village to trade, my mother sent back messages. One day, when I was perhaps ten years old, my uncle came out of the desert. With my mother's blessing, he took me to meet my relations.

"I will not tell you the story of the years I spent with them. I learned much, both of my father and the world in which he had lived. I grew to love them, and also to fear for them. Even at that young age I could see that their way of life was dwindling away. They knew it themselves. I often think that although they never told me so—that is not my people's way—they hoped that through me they would save something of the wisdom of Grandfather Mantis, of the old ways. Like a man lost on an island who writes a letter and puts it in a bottle, I think they meant to send me back to the city-world with something of our people saved inside me."

!Xabbu hung his head. "And the first of my great shames is that for many years after I returned to my mother's village, I thought no more of it. No, that is not true, for I thought of my time with my father's people often, and always will. But I thought little of the fact that they would be gone someday, that almost nothing would be left of the old world. I was young and saw life as something limitless. I was eager to learn everything and afraid of nothing—the prospect of the city-world and all its wonders seemed far more intriguing than life in the bush. I worked hard in the small school, and a man who was important in the village took interest in me. He told a group called The Circle about me. They are people from all over the world who are interested in what city-folk call 'aboriginal cultures.' With their help I was able to gain a position at a school in the same city where my father died, a good school. My mother feared for me, but in her wisdom she let me go. At least, I think it was wisdom.

"So I studied, and learned of other kinds of life besides that led by my people. I became familiar with things that are as ordinary to you as water and air, but to me were at first strange and almost magical— electric light, wallscreens, plumbing. I learned about the science of the folk who had invented these things, and learned some of the history of the black and white peoples as well, but in all the books, all the netflicks, there was almost nothing about my own people.

"Always I returned to my mother's family when school was ended for the season to help with the sheep and set out the nets for fish. Fewer and fewer of those living in the old way came to the village to trade. As the years passed, I began to wonder what had happened to my father's people. Did they still live in the desert? Did my uncle and his brothers still dance the eland dance when they had killed one of the great beasts? Did my aunt and her sisters still sing songs about how the earth is lonely for the rain? I decided that I would go and see them again.

"And here is my second shame. Even though it had been a good year, even though the rains had been plentiful and the desert was friendly and full of life, I almost died while searching for them. I had forgotten much of what they had taught me—I was like a man who grows old and loses his vision, loses his hearing. The desert and the dry hills kept secrets from me.

"I survived, but only barely, after much thirst and hunger. It was a long time until I could feel the rhythm of life the way my father's family had taught me, before I could feel again the ticking in my breast that told me game was near, smell the places where water lay close beneath the sand. I slowly found the old ways, but I did not find my father's family or any other free Bushmen. At last I went to the sacred places, the hills where the people painted on the rocks, but there was no sign of recent habitation. Then I truly feared for my relations. Every year they had gone there to show their respect for the spirits of the First People, but they had not come for a long time. My father's people were gone. Perhaps they are all dead.

"I left the desert, but something in me had changed forever. I made a promise to myself that the life of my people would not simply disappear, that the stories of Mongoose and Porcupine and the Morning Star would not be forgotten, the old ways would not be swept away by the sand as the wind blows away a man's footprints after he has died. Whatever must be done to save something of them, I would do it. To accomplish this I would learn the science of the city-people, which I then believed could do anything.

"Again the people in The Circle were generous, and with their help I came to Durban to study how the city-people make worlds for themselves. For that is what I wish to do, Renie, what I *must do*—I must make the world of my people again, the world of the Early Race. It will never exist again in our time, on our earth, but it should not be lost forever!"

!Xabbu fell silent, rocking back and forth. His eyes were dry, but his pain was very clear.

"But I think that's a wonderful thing," Renie said at last. If her friend was not crying, she was. "I think that's the best argument for VR I've ever heard. Why are you so unhappy now, when you have learned so much, when you're so much nearer to your goal?"

"Because when I was in that terrible place with you, while you were struggling to save my life, I went away in my thoughts to another world. That is shameful, that I left you behind, but I could not help it, so that is not what makes me sad." He stared at her, and now she saw the fear again. "I went to the place of the First People. I do not know how, or why, but while you were experiencing all the things that you told to me in the emergency room, I was in another place. I saw sweet Grandfather Mantis, riding between the horns of his hartebeeste. His wife Kauru was there, and his two sons Kwammanga and Mongoose. But the one who spoke to me was Porcupine, his beloved daughter. She told me that even the place beyond the world, the place of the First People, was in danger. Before the Honey-Guide appeared to lead me back, she told me that soon the place where we were would become a great emptiness, that just as this city-world in which you and I sit had gradually overwhelmed my people in their desert, so the First People were being overwhelmed.

"If that is so, then it will not matter if I build my people's world again, Renie. If the First People are driven from their place beyond this earth, then anything I make will only be an empty shell, a beetle's hollow casing left behind when the beetle has died. I do not want to use your science simply to make a museum, Renie, a place for city-folk to see what was once alive. Do you understand? I want to make a home where something of my people will live forever. If the home of the First People disappears, then the dream that is dreaming us will dream us no more. The whole life of my people, since the very dawn of things, will be nothing but footprints vanishing under the wind.

"And that is why I can no longer hear the sun ringing."

They sat together in silence for a while. Renie poured herself another glass of water and offered some to !Xabbu, but he shook his head. She could not understand what he was saying, and a part of her was uncomfortable, as she was when her Christian colleagues spoke of heaven, or the Moslems spoke of the Prophet's miracles. But there was no ignoring the Bushman's deep unhappiness.

"I do not understand exactly what you mean, but I'm trying." She reached out and lifted his unresisting hand, squeezing his dry fingers in hers. "As you have helped me try to help Stephen, I'll do my best to help you—just tell me what I can do. You're my friend, !Xabbu."

He smiled for the first time since he had arrived. "And you are my good friend, Renie. I do not know what I must do. I have been thinking and thinking." He gently retrieved his hand and rubbed his eyes, his weariness very evident. "But we also have your questions to answer—so many questions the two of us have! What are we to do about the yellow diamond, that dangerous thing?"

Renie yawned, hugely and—to her—embarrassingly. "I think I may know someone who can help us, but I'm too tired to deal with it now. After I get some sleep, I'll call her."

"Then sleep. I will stay until your father returns."

She told him it was not necessary, but it was like arguing with a cat.

"I will give you privacy." !Xabbu stood up smoothly, a single motion. "I will sit in your other room and think." Smiling again, he backed out the door and pulled it closed behind him.

Renie lay for a long time thinking of the strange places they had both visited, places only linked because they had both been conceived in the human mind. Or so she believed. But it was hard to hold firmly to that belief when watching the deep longing and expression of loss on !Xabbu's serious, intelligent face.

She woke up, startled by the tall, dark figure bending over her. Her father took a hurried step back, as though he had been caught doing something bad.

"It's only me, girl. Just checking you all right."

"I'm fine. I took my medicine. Is !Xabbu here?"

He shook his head. She could smell the beer on his breath, but he seemed relatively steady on his feet. "He gone home. What, you making 'em line up now?"

She stared at him in puzzlement.

"Another man sitting in a car out in front when I got home. Big man, beard. He drove off when I walked up."

Renie felt a swift pang of fear. "A white man?"

Her father laughed. " 'Round here? Naw, he was black as me. Somebody for one of the other places, probably. Or a robber. You keep that chain on the door when I'm not around."

She smiled. "Yes, Papa." It was rare to see him so concerned.

"I'll see if there's something to eat." He hesitated in the doorway, then turned. "That friend of yours, he's one of the Small People."

"Yes. He's a Bushman. From the Okavango Delta."

There was a strange look in her father's eye, a small fire of memory. "They the oldest folk, you know. They were here even before the black man came—before the Xhosa, the Zulu, any of them."

She nodded, intrigued by the faraway sound of his voice.

"I never thought I'd see one of his kind again. The Small People. Never thought I'd see any more."

He went out, the distracted expression still on his face. He shut the door quietly.

CHAPTER 14

His Master's Voice

NETFEED/NEWS: Merowe To Face War Crimes Trial
(visual: Merowe surrendering to UN General Ram Shagra)
VO: Hassan Merowe, the outsted president of the Nubian Republic, will face
a UN tribunal for war crimes.
(visual: UN soldiers excavating mass graves outside Khartoum)
As many as a million people are thought to have died during the ten years
of Merowe's rule, one of the bloodiest in the history of Northeastern Africa.
(visual: Merowe's attorney, Mohammad al-Rashad)
RASHAD: "President Merowe is not afraid to stand before other world
leaders. My client singlehandedly built our nation from the smoldering ruins
of Sudan. These people all know that a leader must sometimes take a firm
stand during times of chaos, and if they claim they would have done
differently, then they are hypocrites. . . ."

A neon-red line crawled at the edge of his vision, as though one of his own ocular capillaries had suddenly become visible. The line wriggled and turned on itself, branching and then rebranching as the expert system which it symbolized did its work. Dread smiled. *Beinha y Beinha* were not trusting his promises on security—they wanted to know his virtual office as well as they knew their own. Not that he would have expected anything different. In fact, despite some successful past partnerships, he would have had serious doubts about hiring them again if they had taken him at his word.

Confident, cocky, lazy, dead. It was the Old Man's mantra, and a good one, even if Dread sometimes drew the lines in different places than the Old Man would. Still, he was alive, and in his kind of business that was the only measurement of success—there were no failures who were merely poor. Of course, the Old Man had something to show for his greater caution—he had been alive longer than his hired gun. A lot longer.

Dread augmented the field of abstract color outside the office's single window, then returned his own attention to the virtual white wall as the Beinhas' gear finished checking the security of his node. When it had satisfied itself, it disconnected, the red line vanishing from Dread's own monitor program and the Beinha twins immediately snapped in.

They appeared as two identical but almost featureless objects, seated side by side on the far side of the table like a pair of headstones. The Beinha sisters disdained high-quality sims for personal meetings, and no doubt regarded Dread's own expensive replication as a meaningless and flashy example of excess. He enjoyed the prospect of their irritation: noting the tics of other professionals, and even of his victims, was the closest he ever came to the fondness for the habits of friends that enlivened the existence of more mundane people.

"Welcome, ladies." He gestured to the simulated black marble table and the Yixing stoneware tea service, so important for doing even virtual business with Pacific Rim clients that Dread had made it a permanent part of his office environment. "Can I offer you anything?"

He could almost feel the annoyance that emanated from the twin shapes. "We do not waste our net time on amateur theatricals," one of them said. His satisfaction increased—they were annoyed enough not to hide it. First move to him.

"We are here to deal," said the other faceless shape.

He could never remember their names. Xixa and Nuxa, something like that, elfin Indio names quite out of character with their real selves, first given to them when they were the child stars of a Sao Paolo brothel. Not that it mattered whether he remembered or not: the two operated so much as a single entity that either would answer questions addressed to the other. The Beinha sisters considered names almost as much of a sentimental indulgence as realistic sims.

"Then we'll deal," he said cheerfully. "You reviewed the prospectus, of course?"

More irritation, revealed in the slight pause before reply. "We have. It can be done."

"It will not be easy." He thought the second had spoken, but they used the same digitized voice, so it was difficult to tell. The sisters had an effective act—they seemed to be one mind inhabiting two bodies.

What if it really is *only one person?* he suddenly wondered. *I've certainly never seen more than one of them at a time in RL. What if the whole "deadly twin" thing is just a marketing gimmick?* Dread put aside the interesting thought for later. "We are prepared to pay 350,000 Swiss credits. Plus approved expenses."

"That is unacceptable."

Dread raised an eyebrow, knowing his sim would mimic the effect exactly. "Then it seems we'll have to find another contracting agency."

The Beinhas regarded him for a moment, blank as two stones. "The job you wish done is only technically within the civil sector. Because of the importance of the . . . object you plan to remove, there would be many repercussions from the national government. Loss of the object would, in fact, have worldwide impact. This means that any contractors would have to prepare a greater degree of protection than is usual."

He wondered how much of their unaccented English was voice-filters. It was not hard to imagine a pair of twenty-two-year-old women—if his information on them could be trusted—purposefully shedding their accents along with everything else they had jettisoned on their way to becoming what they were.

He decided to poke them a bit. "What you're saying is, this not really a civilian job but a political assassination."

There was a long moment's silence. Mockingly, Dread brought up the background music to fill it. When the first sister spoke, her voice was as flat and inflectionless as before. "That is correct. And you know it."

"So you think it's worth more than Cr.S. 350,000."

"We will not waste your time. We do not want more money. In fact, if you sweeten the job for us with something else, we will ask only Cr.S. 100,000, most of which we will need for post-action protection and a cooling-off period."

Again the eyebrow lifted. "And what is this 'something else'?"

The second of the two shapeless figures laid spatulate hands on the tabletop. "We have heard that your principal has access to certain biological products—a large source of them in our own hemisphere."

Dread sat forward. He felt something tightening at his temples.

"My principal? I'm the only person you deal with on this contract. You're on very dangerous ground."

"Nevertheless, it is known you do a great deal of work for a certain group. Whether they are the ultimate source of this contract or not, they have something we want."

"We wish to start a side-business," said the other sister. "Something less strenuous for our old age than our current occupation. We think that wholesaling these biological products would be ideal, and we seek a way into the business. Your principal can grant us that. We seek a franchise, not a rivalry."

Dread considered. The Old Man and his friends, despite the immense influence they wielded, were certainly the object of many rumors. The Beinhas traveled in the sort of circles that would know much of the truth behind even the most horrifying and unprovable speculations, so their request didn't necessarily imply a breach of security. Even so, he did not particularly relish the thought of going to the Old Man with such an impertinent offer, and it also meant he would lose some of his control over his own subcontractors—not the sort of thing that suited his future plans at all.

"I think perhaps I should give this job to Klekker and Associates." He said it as lazily as possible—he was angry with himself at being caught off-balance. Second move to the Beinha sisters.

The first shape laughed, a snick of sound like a breadknife being drawn across someone's windpipe. "And waste months and credits while he does the backgrounding?"

"Not to mention trusting the job itself to his team of bravos," added the second, "who will come in like wild bulls and leave hoofprints and horn-scars on everything. This is our territory. We have contacts all over that city, and in some very useful sectors of it, too."

"Ah, but Klekker won't try to extort me."

The first placed her hands on the table beside her sister's, so that they seemed to be performing a seance. "You have worked with us before. You know we will deliver what you need. And unless you have changed mightily, *senhor*, you plan to play the role of foreman yourself. Whose preparations would you rather trust your own safety to— Klekker, working in a strange place, or us, performing in our back garden?"

Dread lifted a hand. "Send me your proposal. I'll consider it."

"It has just been transferred."

He curled his fingers. The office and the faceless sisters vanished.

* * *

He dropped his glass of beer to the floor and watched the last few ounces foam out onto the white carpet. Fury burned in him like a gutful of cinders. The Beinhas were clearly the right people for the job, and they were right about Klekker and his mercenaries, which meant he'd at least have to talk to the Old Man, tell him what the sisters had requested.

Which would mean going back to the mad old bastard on his knees, at least symbolically. Again. Just like that ancient advertising logo, the dog listening alertly to the radio or whatever it was. His master's voice. Down on all fours, like so many times in his childhood before he had learned to answer pain with pain. All those dark nights, screaming under the other boys. His master's voice.

He rose and paced back and forth across the small room, his hands fisted so tight his fingernails cut into his own flesh. Rage swelled inside him, making it hard to breathe. He had three more interviews to go that night, minor ones, but he didn't trust himself to handle them properly just now. The Beinhas had him where they wanted and they knew it. Ex-whores always knew when they had you by the balls.

Answer pain with pain.

He walked to the sink and filled his palms with cold water, then splashed it on his face. It matted his hair and dripped from his chin onto his chest, soaking his shirt. His skin felt hot, as though the anger within had heated him like an iron stove; he looked at himself in the mirror, almost expecting to see the water rising from him as steam. His eyes, he noted, were quite wide, so that a rim of white showed all the way around.

Relief, that was what he needed. A little something to soothe his thoughts, to cool the tension. An answer. An answer to his master's voice.

Through his small window he could see the saurian hump of the bridge and the vast scatter of shimmering lights that was Greater Sydney. It was not hard to look down on that pulse and glitter and imagine each light as a soul, and that he—like God in *His* high place— could just reach out and extinguish any one of them. Or all of them.

Before he could get any more work done, he decided, he would have to get a little exercise. Then he would feel stronger, the way he liked to feel.

He turned up his inner music and went to get his sharp things.

"I do not doubt it is true," said the god. "I ask is it *acceptable?*"

The rest of the Ennead stared back at him with the eyes of beasts.

Eternal twilight filled the broad windows of the Western Palace and steeped the entire room in a bluish light which oil lamps could not entirely dispel. Osiris lifted his flail. "Is it acceptable?" he repeated.

Ptah the Artificer bowed slightly, although Osiris doubted that Ptah's real-life counterpart had done anything like it. That was one of the advantages of the Brotherhood conducting its meetings on his own virtual turf—his governing systems could insert at least a modicum of courtesy. As if to prove that the bow had not been his own gesture, Ptah snapped back: "No, damn it, of course it's not acceptable. But this stuff is very new—you have to expect the unexpected."

Osiris paused before replying, allowing his anger to cool. Most of the other members of the Brotherhood's high council were at least as stiff-necked as he was; it would do no good to put them on the defensive. "I simply want to know how we can lose someone whom we ourselves placed in the system," he said at last. "How can he have 'disappeared'? We have his body, for God's sake!" He frowned at this accidental self-mockery and folded his arms across his bandaged chest.

Ptah's yellow face creased in a smile: he had a typical American disrespect for authority and no doubt thought Osiris' VR habitat grandiose. "Yes, we certainly do have his body, and if that was all we cared about, we could eliminate him at any time. But *you* were the one who wanted this particular addition, although I've never understood why. We're working in unknown territory here, especially with all the variables our own experiments have added to the mix. It's like expecting objects to behave the same way in deep space that they do back on Earth. It seems pretty damn unfair to blame my people when it goes a little flippy."

"This man has not been kept alive solely on a whim. I have good reasons, even though they are private." Osiris spoke as firmly and calmly as he could. He did not wish to appear capricious, especially in argument with Ptah. If anyone was likely to challenge his leadership in days to come, it was the American. "In any case, it is unfortunate. We are nearing the crisis point, and Ra cannot be kept waiting much longer."

"Jesus wept." Falcon-headed Horus banged a fist down on the basalt table. "*Ra?* What the hell are you talking about now?"

Osiris stared. The black, emotionless bird-eyes stared back. Another American, of course. It was like dealing with children—albeit very powerful children. "You are in my house," he said as calmly as he

could. "It would not harm you to show some respect, or at least courtesy." He allowed the sentence to hang in the air for a moment, giving
ample time for the various other Brotherhood members to think what
might harm Horus—to think of all the things an angry Osiris could do.
"If you would avail yourself of the information provided, you would
know that 'Ra' is my name for the final phase of the Grail Project. If
you are too busy, my system will be happy to translate for you so you
do not impede the flow of conversation during meetings."

"I'm not here to play games." The bird-headed god's bluster had
abated somewhat. Horus scratched his chest vigorously, making Osiris
wince with distate. "You're the chairman, so we play with your toys—
wear your sims, whatever, fair enough. But I'm a busy man, and I
don't have time to download your newest set of rules every time I
hook up."

"Enough squabbling." Unlike the others, Sekhmet seemed quite
comfortable in her goddess-guise. Osiris thought she would enjoy
wearing the lion's head in real life. She was a natural deity: no corrup-
tive notions of democracy had ever sullied her outlook. "Should we
eliminate this loose end, this 'lost man'? What does our chairman
want?"

"Thank you for asking." Osiris leaned back in his tall chair. "For
reasons of my own, I wish him to be found. If enough time goes by
without success, then I will allow him to be killed, but that is a clumsy
solution."

"Actually, it's not only clumsy," Ptah offered cheerfully, "it may not
be a solution at all. At this point, we might not be able to kill him—at
least not the part of him resident in the system."

A slender hand was lifted. The others turned, their attention drawn
by the rarity of Thoth having anything to say. "Surely things have not
gone so far already," he asked. His narrow ibis head nodded sorrow-
fully, the beak dipping down to his chest. "Have we lost control of our
own virtual environments? That would be a very distressing event. I
would have to think carefully before continuing my commitment. We
must have more control of the process than this."

Osiris started to reply, but Ptah leaped in quickly. "There are always
perturbations at the edge of any paradigm shift," he said. "It's like
storms on the edge of a weather front—we expect them as a generality
without being able to anticipate them exactly. I'm not worried about
this, and I don't think you should be either."

A fresh spate of argument broke out around the table, but this time

Osiris was not displeased. Thoth was of the careful Asian character
that did not like sudden changes or bold assertions, and almost certainly did not like American abruptness: Ptah had not done himself
any favors. Thoth and his Chinese consortium were a large and important power bloc in the Brotherhood; Osiris had been cultivating them
for decades. He made a note to contact Thoth privately later and deal
carefully with his concerns. Meanwhile, some of the Chinese tycoon's
irritation would undoubtedly localize around Ptah and his Western
contingent.

"Please, please," he said at last. "I will be happy to talk to any of
you individually who are worried about this. The problem, however
minor, has its source in my own personal initiative. I take complete
responsibility."

That at least silenced the table, and behind the emotionless sims,
behind the beetle mandibles, the masks of hippo, ram, and crocodile,
he knew that calculations were being made, odds were being reexam-
ined. But he also knew that his prestige was such that even self-
satisfied Ptah would not argue with him any further, at risk of seeming divisive.

Were it not for the Grail at the end of this long, wearisome road, he
thought, *I would happily see the whole of this greedy lot buried in a mass
grave. It is sad that I need the Brotherhood so badly. This thankless chairman-
ship is like trying to teach table manners to piranha.* Behind his corpse
mask, he smiled briefly, although the various teeth and fangs glinting
along the length of the table lent the image a certain unpleasant ring
of truth.

"Now, if we have dispatched other business, and if the problem of
our little runaway has been tabled for the time being, there is only
one other thing—the matter of our former colleague, Shu." He turned
to Horus with mock-conern. "You do realize that Shu is only a code-
name, another little bit of Egyptiana? A joke of sorts, actually, since
Shu was the sky god who abdicated the throne of heaven in favor of
Ra. You do understand that, General? We have so few living ex-
colleagues, I felt sure you would not require translation."

The falcon eyes glittered. "I know who you're talking about."

"Good. In any case, I took it as the sense of our last full meeting
that . . . Shu . . . has become, since retirement, a liability to the old
firm." He allowed himself a dusty chuckle. "I have initiated certain
processes designed to reduce that liability as much as possible."

"Say what you mean." Sekhmet's tongue lolled from her tawny muzzle. "The one you call Shu is to be killed?"

Osiris leaned back. "Your grasp of our needs is admirable, Madame, but overly simple. There is more to be done than that."

"I could have a black bag team on top of him in twelve hours. Clear out the whole compound, burn it to the foundations, take the gear back home for study." Horus lifted a hand to his hooked beak, an odd gesture that Osiris needed several seconds to decode. Back in RL, the general had lit himself a cigar.

"Thank you, but this is a weed whose roots go deep. Shu was a founding member of our Ennead—excuse me, General, of our Brotherhood. Such roots must be carefully uncovered and the whole plant taken in one reaping. I have initiated such a process and I will lay the plans before you at our next meeting." *With just enough obvious flaws in them to give imbeciles like you something to piss upon, General.* Osiris was impatient now for the meeting to end. *Then I will thank you for your clever suggestions and you will let me get on with the real business of protecting our interests.* "Anything else? Then I thank you for joining me. I wish you all good luck in your various projects."

One by one, the gods winked out, until Osiris was alone again.

The austere lines of the Western Palace had been transmuted into the lamplit homeliness of Abydos-That-Was. The scent of myrrh and the chants of the resurrected priests rose around him like the soothing waters of a warm bath. He dared not bring the full panoply of his godliness to the Brotherhood's gatherings—he was already regarded as slightly, although harmlessly, eccentric—but he was far more comfortable being Osiris now than the all-too-mortal man underneath, and he missed the comforts of his temple when he was forced to leave it.

He crossed his arms across his chest and called forward one of his high priests. "Summon the Lord of the Mummy Wrappings. I am ready now to grant him audience."

The priest—whether software or sim, the god could not guess and did not care—hurried away into the darkness at the back of the temple. A moment later the arrival of Anubis was proclaimed by a skirling fanfare. The priests fell back, pressing themselves against the temple walls. The dark jackal head was raised and alert as though testing the air. The god was not certain whether he liked this change from the Messenger's usual sullenness.

"I'm here."

The god stared at him for a moment. It was appropriate, this guise
he had chosen for his favorite tool. He had spotted the youth's potential quite early, and had devoted many years to raising him, not like a
son—heaven forbid!—but like a trained hound, shaping him to the
tasks for which he was best suited. But, like any spirited beast, this
one sometimes became overexuberant or even defiant; sometimes a
taste of the whip was necessary. But he had been giving Anubis more
than a taste lately, and that was unfortunate. Too much punishment
dulled its effect. Perhaps this was an occasion to try something a little
different.

"I am not happy about your South American subcontractors," he
began. The jackal head lowered slightly, anticipating a rebuke. "They
are impertinent, to say the least."

"They are, Grandfather." Too late Anubis remembered his master's
dislike of that particular honorific. The narrow muzzle flinched again,
ever so slightly.

The god pretended it hadn't happened. "But I know how such
things can be. The best are often ambitious in their own right. They
think they know more than those who employ them—even when
their employers have invested time and money in their training."

The sharp-eared head tilted, just like a real canine expressing puzzlement. Anubis was wondering what other message was being delivered here.

"In any case, if they are the best for the job, you must employ them.
I have seen their request, and I am now sending you the terms within
which you may bargain with them."

"You are going to deal with them?"

"We are going to hire them. If they fail to serve to our satisfaction,
they will, of course, not receive the reward they seek. If they do perform—well, I will consider at that time whether to honor the bargain."

There was a pause in which he could sense the messenger's disapproval. The god was amused—even murderers had a sense of propri-
ety. "If you cheat them, the word will travel very quickly."

"If I cheat them, I will be very sure to do it in such a way that no
one will ever know. If they happen to meet with an accident, for instance, it will be something so clearly not of our doing that you need
not worry about your other contacts taking fright." The god laughed.
"You see, my faithful one? You have not learned everything from me

yet after all. Perhaps you should wait a little longer before thinking to strike out on your own."

Anubis responded slowly. "And how do I know you will not some-day do the same to me?"

The god leaned forward to lay his flail almost lovingly against the jackal's sloping forehead. "Rest assured, my messenger, if I saw the need, I would. If you rely solely on my honor to protect you, you are not the servant in whom I wish to place my trust." Behind the mask, behind the complexity of instrumentation, Osiris smiled as he watched Anubis quite visibly consider whatever safeguards he had put in place to protect himself against his master. "But betrayal is a tool that must be used very discreetly," the god continued. "It is only because I am known for honoring my agreements that I could, if I wished, dispose of these overly-forward sisters. Remember, honor is the only really good disguise for an occasional act of dishonor. No one trusts a known liar."

"I observe and learn, O Lord."

"Good. I am glad to find you in a receptive mood. Perhaps you will give your careful attention to this as well. . . ?"

The god flicked his crook and a small box appeared in the air, hover-ing before his throne. Inside it was a grainy hologrammatic represen-tation of two men wearing disheveled suits, standing on either side of a desk. They might have been salesmen, except for the photographs spread across the desk's untidy surface.

"See the pictures there?" Osiris asked. "We are lucky the public constabulary's financial restraints mean they still rely on two-dimensional representations. Otherwise this might make for quite a dizzying effect—not unlike the mirrors in a barber shop." He ex-panded the cube until the figures were life-size and the photos could be easily viewed.

"Why are you showing me this?"

"Oh, come now." The god nodded and the two figures inside the cube sprang into life.

"*. . . Number four. No difference,*" the first man was saying. "*Except this time the writing was on the victim herself, not on something she was carrying.*" He pointed to one of the photos. The word "*Sang*" was printed in block capitals across her stomach, the bloody letters smearing into the greater redness below.

"*And still no hits on it? A name? A place? I assume we've given up on the possibiltiy of it being a reference to informing?*"

"*None of these peoples were informers. These are ordinary folk.*" The first cop shook his head in frustration. *"And once again we've got blurring on the surveillance cameras. Like someone took an electromagnet to them, but the lab says no magnet was used."*

"Shit." The second cop stared at the pictures. *"Shit, shit, shit."*

"Something'll come up." The first man sounded almost convincing. *"These blokes always screw up somewhere along the line. Get cocky, y'know, or they just get too crazy. . . ."*

The god gestured and the cube dwindled away to a spark. His long silence was alleviated only by the moans of the kneeling priests. "I have spoken to you about this before," he said at last.

Anubis did not reply.

"It is not so much the messiness of your compulsions that offend me," the god continued, allowing anger to creep into his voice for the first time. "All artists have their quirks, and I consider you to be an artist. But your methodology displeases me. You have consistently advertised your peculiar talents in a way that may eventually prove your undoing. They tested you repeatedly in those institutions, you know. Someday soon, even the plodding Australian police will make some connection there. But most unfortunate of all, you are advertising by your little signatures, however obliquely, something that is far more important to me than you are. I do not know what you think you know of my work, but the Sangreal is not a joke for you to snigger at." The god rose to his feet, and for a moment allowed a hint of something larger to smear itself around him, a blurring, lightning-charged shadow. His voice rumbled like a summer storm. *"Do not misunderstand me. If you compromise my project, I wll deal with you swiftly and finally. If such a situation comes to pass, whatever protections you think you have will blow away like straws in a hurricane."*

He allowed himself to settle back into his throne. "Otherwise, I am pleased with you, and it hurts me to upbraid you. Do not allow this to happen agin. Find a less idiosyncratic way to slake your compulsions. If you please me, you will find that there are rewards you cannot even *imagine.* I do not exaggerate. Am I understood?"

The jackal head wagged as if its owner were exhausted. The god looked for a hint of defiance, but saw only fear and resignation.

"Good," he said. "Then our audience is finished. I look forward to your next progress report on the Sky God Project. Next week?"

Anubis nodded but did not look up. The god crossed his arms and Death's Messenger disappeared.

Osiris sighed. The old, old man inside the god was weary. The interview with his underling hadn't gone too badly, but now it was time to talk to the dark one, the Other—the one creature in all the world that he feared.

Work, work, work, and none of it pleasant any more. Only the Grail could be worth such heartache, such suffering.

Death cursed sourly and got on with it.

CHAPTER 15

Friends in High Places

NETFEED/NEWS: Six Powers Sign Antarctica Pact
(visual: metal wreckage scattered across ice floe)
VO: The twisted wreckage of fighter jets will remain as a mute reminder of
the short-lived but disastrous Antarctic Conflict. Representatives of the six
powers whose disagreement over mineral rights began the conflict met in
Zurich to sign a treaty reestablishing Antartica as an international
territory. . . .

She met !Xabbu on the bus at Pinetown Station. He sprang from his seat when he saw her, as though she had fainted in the aisle instead of merely stopping to take a breath after climbing the steps.

"Are you all right?"

She gestured for him to sit, then slid into the seat beside him. "I'm well. Just a little short of breath. I haven't been getting around much lately."

He frowned. "I would have come to meet you."

"I know. That's why I wouldn't let you. You've been all the way out to my flatblock three times now since I had my . . . since I got ill. All I had to do was catch a local bus to get here. Ten minutes." !Xabbu, of course, had probably been on the bus almost an hour already; the service from Chesterville was not particularly fast.

"I am worried for you. You have been very poorly." His concerned look was almost stern, as though she were a child playing in a dangerous place. She laughed.

"I told you, it wasn't a full-blown heart attack, just a temporary arrhythmia. I'm okay now."

Renie didn't want anyone worrying over her, even !Xabbu. It made her feel weak, and she didn't trust weakness. She was also growing uncomfortable about the burden of responsibility she had dropped on her small friend. He had completed his course work, so he was not losing study time, but what money he had must be running out while she was using up an unconscionable amount of his energies. Only the fact that his safety, too, now seemed compromised had convinced her to drag him along on this errand.

But it was my problems that exposed him to danger in the first place, she thought miserably.

"What are you going to do now that you've finished the course?" she asked. "Are you going to do a graduate program?"

A certain melancholy crept over his delicate features. "I do not know, Renie. I am thinking . . . there are things I do not know yet. I told you something of my plans, but I see now that I am far from being ready to make them real. *Also* . . . " His voice dropped conspiratorially. He looked up and down the aisle of the bus as though checking for spies. "Also," he continued quietly, "I am thinking and thinking of the . . . experience I had. When we were in that place."

The rasp of gears changing as the bus cornered was deafening. Renie suppressed a smile. Any eavesdropper would have to be a lip-reader.

"If I can help in any way," she said, "please tell me. I owe you a lot. I could help you find a grant, maybe. . . ."

The Bushman shook his head vigorously. "It is not money. It is more difficult than that. I wish it *were* a city-problem—then I could ask my friends and find a city-answer. But in this place where I live now, I must discover the answer to this problem myself."

Now it was Renie's turn to shake her head. "I'm not sure I understand."

"Neither am I." !Xabbu smiled, banishing his own somber look, but Renie saw his conscious effort and felt a momentary pang of sadness. Was this what he had learned in Durban, and in the other places where what he called city-people lived? To dissemble, to hide his feelings and show a false seeming?

I suppose I should be grateful he's not that good at it. Yet.

The bus was climbing an overpass. !Xabbu was staring out the window and down at the riverine expanse of National Route 3, at the cars packed into it even in mid-morning like termites in a split log.

Suddenly uncomfortable with the symptoms of modern life she normally took for granted, Renie turned away to examine their fellow passengers. Most of them were older black women, heading for Kloof and the other wealthy northeastern suburbs to work as domestics, just as they and their predecessors had for decades, both before and after liberation. The chubby woman nearest her, head wrapped in a traditional but now slightly old-fashioned headscarf, wore a look that someone less familiar with it than Renie would have called blank. It was not hard to see how white South Africans in the old Apartheid days, facing that expressionless stare, would have projected onto it any emotions they wished—sullenness, stupidity, even the potential for murderous violence. But Renie had grown up around such women, and knew that the expression was a mask that they wore like a uniform. At home, or in the shebeen or teashop, they would smile and laugh easily. But working for the volatile whites, it had always been easier to show nothing. If you showed nothing, the white boss could not take offense, or feel pity, or—as was sometimes worse—presume to a friendship that could never really exist under such inequality.

Renie had white colleagues at the Poly, and some she even socialized with after work. But as Pinetown had become a mixed neighborhood, the whites that could afford to had moved out—out to places like Kloof and the Berea ridgetop, always to the high places, as if their black neighbors and coworkers were not individuals, but part of some vast dark tide drowning the lowlands.

If institutionalized racism was gone, the dividing wall of money was as high as it had ever been. There were blacks in all industries now, and at all levels, and blacks had held most of the top jobs in government since the liberation, but South Africa had never quite climbed out of its Third World hole, and the twenty-first century had not been any kinder to Africa than had the twentieth. Most blacks were still poor. And most whites, for whom the transition to black rule had not been anywhere near as bad as they had feared, were not.

As she looked around, Renie's gaze was arrested by a young man a few seats behind her. Despite the overcast day, he was wearing sunglasses; he had been watching her, but when his eyes—or his lenses—met her stare, he turned quickly to look out the window. She felt a moment of reflexive fear, but then she saw the shunt at the base of his skull, just peeping from beneath his cap, and understood. She turned away, clutching her bag a little tighter to her lap.

After a moment she cautiously turned to look again. The charge-head was still staring out the window, fingers jittering on the seatback in front of him. His clothes were wrinkled and sweat-stained at the armpits. The neurocannula was a township job and the insertion had been cheap and dirty—she could see a gleam of suppuration around the edge of the plastic.

A slight pressure on her leg made her jump. !Xabbu raised his eyes, questioning.

"It's nothing," she said. "I'll tell you later." She shook her head. There had been a chargepit in one of the flats when she and Stephen and her father had first moved in, and she had more than once encountered its zombie denizens in the stairwell. They were generally harmless—extended use of charge-gear with its high-speed strobing and infrasound tended to make a person uncoordinated and passive—but she had never been comfortable around them, however loopy and withdrawn they seemed. She had been violently pawed on a bus when she was a student by a man who clearly wasn't seeing her at all, but was reacting to some unimaginable vision induced by pounding his brain into jelly, and afterward she had never been able to laugh at chargeheads the way her friends did.

In fact, they had turned out not to be so harmless after all, but the police didn't seem capable of doing much, so after several of the older residents had been robbed and some of the flats had been burglarized, a vigilante group—her father had been part of it—had taken cudgels and cricket bats and kicked down the door. The skinny creatures inside had not put up much of a fight, but heads were still split and ribs were cracked. Renie had seen the chargeheads in nightmares for months after, tumbling down the stairs in slow motion, flapping their arms like drowning men and making hooting noises that sounded more animal than human. They had been almost incapable of defending themselves, as though this sudden eruption of anger and pain were only a further, if somewhat unsatisfactory, part of the charge.

Still in the midst of her idealistic student phase, Renie had been shocked when she discovered that her father and the other men had taken the equipment and gear they found there—cheap Nigerian stuff, mostly—and sold it, drinking up the returns over the succeeding week while retelling the story of their victory. As far as she knew, none of the building's robbery victims had ever received a share of the profits. Long Joseph Sulaweyo and the others had won the prerogative of conquerors, the right to divide the booty.

Actually, the effect she had suffered in Mister J.'s was not that different from charge, although far more sophisticated. Is that what they'd done? Found some way to hyperpower a charge high—supercharge it, as it were—then put in some kind of hypnotic shackle to keep the victims from breaking the loop?

"Renie?" !Xabbu patted her leg again.

She shook her head, realizing that she had been staring into space as fixedly as the man with the 'can in his head.

"Sorry. Just thinking about something."

"I would like to ask you about the person we are going to see."

She nodded. "I was going to tell you, I just got . . . sidetracked. She used to be a teacher of mine. At the University of Natal."

"And she taught you . . . what is your degree called? 'Virtual Engineering'?"

Renie laughed. "That's what they called it, all right. Sounds kind of quaint, doesn't it? Like being a Doctor of Electricity or something. But she was brilliant. I'd never met anyone like her. And she was a real South African, in the best sense of the word. When the rand dropped so badly all the other white professors—and even a lot of the Asian and black ones—were sending their CVs off to Europe and America, she just laughed at them. 'Van Bleecks have been here since the sixteenth century,' she always said. 'We've been here so long you can't pull the roots out. We're not bloody Afrikaaners—we're Africans!' That's her name, by the way—Susan Van Bleeck."

"If she is your friend," !Xabbu said solemnly, "then she will be my friend, too."

"You'll like her, I'm sure. God, I haven't seen her in person for a long time. It must be almost two years. But when I called her, she just said 'Come on up, I'll give you lunch.' Like I'd been dropping by every other week."

The bus was laboring now, climbing the steep hills into Kloof. The houses, so close together down below, seemed to be a little more snobbish here in the highlands, each keeping a careful distance from its neighbors, surrounding itself with a discreet drapery of trees.

"The smartest person I know," Renie said.

There was a car waiting at the bus station, an expensive-looking electric *Ihlosi*. Standing beside it, dressed in immaculate casual clothing, was a tall middle-aged black man who introduced himself as Jere-

miah Dako. He did not say much more before ushering Renie and
!Xabbu into the car's back seat. Renie suggested that one of them
could ride in the front, but the man's only reply was a chilly smile.
After her initial conversational volleys were returned with minimum
effort on his part, she gave up and watched the scenery slide by.

Uninterested in chitchat, Jeremiah did seem interested in !Xabbu,
or so Renie deduced from his frequent surveillance of the bushman in
his rearview mirror. He did not particularly seem to approve of the
little man's presence, although what she had seen of Mr. Dako did
not suggest he approved of much of anything. Nevertheless, his covert
attention reminded her of her father's reaction. Perhaps this man, too,
had believed the Bushmen to be only an old memory.

As they drove through the security gate (the swift way in which
Dako typed in the code and applied thumb to sensor showing the
smoothness of old routine) the house was suddenly visible at the end
of the long tree-lined street, like something out of a dream—tall,
clean, welcoming, and just as big as she remembered. Renie had visited Doctor Van Bleeck at home just a few times long ago, so she was
inordinately pleased to find it so familiar. Dako entered the semicircular driveway and stopped in front of the pillared porch. The effect of
its great size was mitigated by the lounger and lawn chairs scattered
about on either side of the front door. Susan Van Bleeck was sitting
on one of the chairs reading a book, her white hair bright as a candle-
flame against the dark background. She looked up as the car stopped,
then waved.

Renie threw open the car door, earning a sour look from the driver,
who had been about to open it. "Don't get up!" she cried, then hurried
up the steps and hugged her, secretly shocked at how small and birdlike the old woman felt.

"Get up?" Susan laughed. "You don't have *that* much time, do
you?" She pointed to the wheels on her chair, which had been obscured by the tartan blanket bundled over the doctor's knees.

"Oh, my God, what's wrong?" Renie was a little shocked. Susan
Van Bleeck looked . . . ancient. She had already been in her late sixties
when Renie had studied with her, so it wasn't entirely surprising, but
it was still unnerving to see what just two more years had done.

"Nothing permanent—well, that's a dangerous thing to say at my
age. Broke my hip, basically. All the calcium supplements in the world
won't help you if you go down the stairs arse-first." She looked past
Renie. "And this is the friend you said you might bring, yes?"

"Oh, of course, this is !Xabbu. !Xabbu, meet Doctor Van Bleeck."

The little man nodded and smiled gravely as he shook her hand. Dako, who had reappeared after parking the car off to one side of the driveway, muttered something as he walked past, apparently to himself.

"I'd hoped we could sit outside," said their host, frowning at the sky. "But of course the weather's being bloody." She lifted a frail hand to gesture at the cavernous porch. "You know how we Afrikaaners are—always out on the *stoep*. But it's just too cold. By the way, young man, I hope you're not planning to call me 'Doctor' all day. 'Susan' will do nicely." She pulled off the blanket and handed it to !Xabbu, who took it as though it were a ceremonial vestment; then without using any controls Renie could see, she turned the wheelchair toward the door and up and over a ramp built into the threshold.

Renie and !Xabbu followed her down the broad hallway. The wheels made squeaking sounds on the polished wooden floorboards as the doctor turned and rolled ahead of them into the living room.

"How does the chair work?" Renie asked.

Susan smiled. "Pretty slick, don't you think? It's quite clever, really. You can get the kind that's controlled directly from a shunt, but that seemed a little severe—after all, I intend to get out of the damn thing eventually. This one just works off skin-contact sensors reading my leg muscles. I flex, it goes. At first it had to be the old-fashioned, manually-operated kind so the bone could heal, but now I can use this as a form of physical therapy—you know, keep the leg muscles in some kind of shape." She gestured to the couch. "Please sit down. Jeremiah will bring in some coffee soon."

"I have to admit I was surprised to hear you were still at the University," Renie said.

Susan pulled a face like an extremely wrinkled child trying spinach for the first time. "God, what else would I do? Not that I'm in there often—about once a month, really, for something euphemistically called 'office hours.' Mostly I do consultation work right from here. But I do have to get out of this place occasionally. There's only so much solitude I can stand, and as you may have noticed, Jeremiah isn't the world's most energetic conversationalist."

As if demon-summoned by the sound of his name, Dako appeared in the doorway carrying a coffee service and cafetiére on a tray. He put it down and pressed the plunger—the doctor's appreciation of modern technology apparently did not extend to coffee-making—then left the room again, but not without another odd and slightly covert look at

!Xabbu. The Bushman, who was looking at the doctor's roomful of paintings and sculpture, seemed not to notice.

"He keeps staring," Renie said. "All the way up the hill he kept looking at !Xabbu in the mirror."

"Well, it might be that he fancies him," Susan said, smiling, "but I suspect it's a bit of a guilty conscience."

Renie shook her head. "What do you mean?"

"Jeremiah's a Griqua—wht they used to call a half-caste in the bad old days, although he's as black as anyone else. A couple of hundred years ago they drove the Bushmen out of this part of southern Africa. Violently. Horribly. It was a terrible time. I suppose the whites could have done more to stop it, but the hard truth is they saw more potential in the Griqua than they did in the Bushmen. Those were days when having any white blood at all made you better than someone with none—but still nothing like a white." She smiled again, rather sadly. "Do your people remember the Griqua with hatred, !Xabbu? Or are you from a different part of the country entirely?"

The little man looked around. "I am sorry, I was not listening carefully to what you were saying."

Susan gazed at him shrewdly. "Ah. You've seen my picture."

He nodded. Renie turned to see what they were talking about. What she had thought was merely the wallscreen above the fireplace was actually a photographic print almost three meters wide, bigger than any she had seen outside a museum. It showed a painting on a natural rock wall, a primitively simple and graceful work. A gazelle was described in just a few lines, a group of dancing human figures on either side of it. The rock seemed to glow with a sunset light. The paint looked almost fresh, but Renie knew it was not.

!Xabbu was staring at it again. He was holding his shoulders in a strange way, as though something might be stalking him, but his eyes seemed full of wonder rather than fear.

"Do you know where it's from?" Susan asked him.

"No. But I know it is old, from the days when we Bushmen were the only people in this land." He reached out a hand as if to touch it, though it was a good ten feet from the couch on which he sat. "It is a powerful thing to see." He hesitated. "But I am not certain I am happy to see it in a person's house."

Susan frowned, taking her time. "Do you mean a white person's house? No, it's all right. I understand—or I think I do. I don't mean it to give offense. It does not have religious meaning to me, but I think it's a beautiful thing. I suppose I get spiritual value from it, if that doesn't sound presumptuous." She stared at the photo as if seeing it anew. "The painting itself, the original, is still on a cliff face at Giant's Castle in the Drakensberg Mountains. Will it bother you to see it, !Xabbu? I could ask Jeremiah to take it down. He won't be doing anything else much for the next few hours, but he's getting a salary anyway."

The small man shook his head. "There is no need. When I said I was not comfortable, I was speaking of my own thoughts, my own feelings. Renie knows that I have many worries about my people and their past." He smiled. "Their future, too. Perhaps it is better that some people can see it here at least. Perhaps they will remember . . . or at least wish they could remember."

They all three drank their coffee for a while in silence, looking at the leaping gazelle and the dancers.

"Well," the doctor said at last, "If you still want to show me something, Irene, we should get to it or we will miss lunch. Jeremiah does not take kindly to alterations in the schedule."

Renie had not explained much on the phone. Now, as she began to tell Susan about the mystery file, she found herself revealing more than she had intended. The doctor, trying to get at the context, asked questions for which it was hard to find partial answers, and Renie soon discovered that she had told her old teacher almost everything except the name of the online club and the reason they had gone there in the first place.

Old habits die hard, Renie thought. Susan was looking at her expectantly, eyes bright, and it was possible to see not only the powerfully impressive woman she had been when Renie had first met her, but the sharp-witted and sharp-tongued girl she had been more than half a century ago. *I never could lie to her worth a damn.*

"But why in the name of God would anyone have a security system like that? What on earth could they be protecting?" The doctor's intent stare made Renie feel positively delinquent. "Have you gotten yourself involved with criminals, Irene?"

She suppressed a flinch at the hated name. "I don't know. I don't really want to talk about it yet. But if they're doing the kind of things I think they are, then the place should be burned out like a nest of poisonous snakes."

Susan sank back against the cushions of her wheelchair, her face troubled. "I'll respect your privacy, Irene, but I don't like the sound of this much. How did you get involved in such a thing?" She looked over at !Xabbu, as though he might be the cause.

Renie shrugged. "Let's say that I believe they've got something important to me and I want it back."

"Very well, I give up. I never had the patience for Miss Marple-ish guessing games. Let's see what you've got. Follow me."

She led Renie and !Xabbu down the hallway in her silent chair. What looked like an ordinary pair of French doors opened up to reveal a small freight elevator.

"Thank God I put this in for moving equipment," said the doctor. "Squeeze in tight, now. Since this hip nonsense, if I'd only had the stairs I wouldn't have been able to get down here for months. Well, maybe I could have made Jeremiah carry me. *There's* a picture."

The basement seemed to cover almost as much space as the house itself. A large part of it was taken up by the lab, which contained several rows of tables in typical laboratory array. "Mess and confusion," was how the doctor put it.

"I've got a clean standalone system already, and I've finished the antiviral work I was doing with it," she said. "We might as well use that. You'd probably just as soon watch this on a monitor screen, wouldn't you?"

Renie nodded emphatically. Even with Doctor Van Bleeck around to help, she wasn't going to put herself in a surround environment to explore whatever gift the Mister J's folks had sent her. Nobody got to play that trick on her twice.

"Okay, then. Fire up your pad and let's go. Load these, so I can run some diagnostics before we try to move it onto the new system."

After several minutes, the doctor dropped her squeezers onto her lap robe and made another of her childlike faces. "I can't get into the damn thing. But you're right, it's very strange. Doesn't seem to make much sense as an anti-intrusion device. How are you punishing someone if you Trojan Horse something onto their system too big to be activated? Ah, well. You might as well hook up."

Renie connected her pad to the doctor's dedicated machine. Things started to happen very quickly.

"It's transferring itself. The same way it downloaded onto my pad in the first place."

"But it's not sending a copy, the whole thing is *moving*." Susan frowned as she watched the diagnostics flutter through their various calculations. Renie almost felt sorry for all the doctor's specialist programs, as though they were living things, tiny little scientists wringing their hands and arguing with each other as they tried to classify a completely alien object.

"I know," Renie said. "It doesn't make sense . . . " She broke off, staring. The monitor screen was beginning to glow more brightly. The diagnostic level disappeared entirely, numbers and symbols and graphs vanishing as though burned away by fire. Something was forming on the screen.

"What in the hell is that?" Susan sounded irritated, but there was an edge of real disquiet in her voice.

"It's . . . a *city*." Renie leaned forward. A slightly hysterial laugh was building inside her. It was like stealing secret microfilm in some old spyflick and discovering it contained holiday snaps. "It's visual feed of some city."

"That's no place I've ever seen." Susan, too, was leaning forward, as was !Xabbu, standing behind her chair. The light from the monitor gilded their faces. "Look—have you ever seen cars like that? It's some kind of science fiction clip—some netflick."

"No, it's real." Renie couldn't say exactly how she knew, but she knew. If it had been a still photograph like Susan's cliff-painting, it would have been hard to tell. But movement increased the level of information to the eye—and the brain—exponentially; even the best effects people found moving objects harder to synthesize. Renie hadn't been in the VR business as long as Susan, but she had as good an eye as anybody, and better than most. Even in Mister J's, with the top of the line machinery they clearly had at their command, she had been able to spot subtle failures of coordination and naturalistic movement. But this city of golden towers, of rippling banners and elevated trains, had no such flaws.

"I think I have seen this somewhere," said !Xabbu. "It is like a dream."

Susan picked up her squeezers and made a few gestures. "It's just running on automatic. I can't find any information attached to it." She frowned. "I'll just . . . "

The picture vanished. For a moment the entire monitor went dark, then the screen came back up in a blizzard of flickering pixels.

"What did you do?" Renie had to look away—the juddering, sparkling light reminded her of the last unpleasant hour in the club.

"Nothing. The damn thing just turned itself off." Susan restarted the system, which came back up as if everything were normal. "It's gone."

"Turned itself off?"

"Gone. Gone! There's no trace of it at all."

Ten minutes later Susan dropped her squeezers again and rolled her chair back from the monitor. She had searched both her own computer and Renie's pad diligently, with no result. "My eyes hurt," she said. "Do you want a go at it?"

"I can't think of anything you haven't done. How could it just disappear?"

"Some kind of autophage. Played, then ate itself. Nothing left now."

"So all we had was some picture of a city." Renie was depressed. "We don't know why. And now we don't even have that."

"Ah, of course! I almost forgot." Susan pulled her chair back close to the screen. "I was taking a display sample when the thing went *kerploonk*—let's see what we got." She directed the machine's search. A few moments later the screen resolved into a gauzy golden abstract. "We got it!" The doctor squinted. "*Kak*. It was just losing resolution when I got the snapshot. My eyes aren't so good on close-up work, Irene. Can you see anything in it at all, or is it just random colored pixels?"

"I think so."

"There is a tower," !Xabbu said slowly. "There."

"Right. Then we'll need to move it onto the main system. Since I took the sample myself, we'll assume it's inert and therefore safe— although this whole thing has been strange enough to make me less than completely confident about anything. Ah, well." She had a quick talk with the household wiring; a few minutes later they were again staring at the golden smear, now stretched yards wide across the laboratory wallscreen.

"I have some image enhancement gear that might help," she said. "Some of the preliminary stages can work through while we have lunch—clean up the signal noise, rewind the de-resolution sequence as much as possible. Come along. Jeremiah's probably having a fit."

"!Xabbu?" Renie put her hand on his shoulder. The Bushman seemed entranced by the wallscreen image. "Are you okay?"

"This way, even distorted so, it still seems familiar to me." He stared at the shapeless swirls of amber, gold, and creamy yellow. "I have seen this somewhere, but it is not a memory so much as a feeling."

Renie shrugged. "I don't know what to say. Let's go have lunch. Maybe it will come to you."

He followed her almost reluctantly, stopping one last time in the elevator doorway to look back, his brow wrinkled in perplexity.

Susan had been right: Jeremiah was more than a little offended when the doctor and her guests trooped in twenty minutes late for lunch. "I did not poach the fish until I heard you coming," he said accusingly. "But I cannot promise anything about the vegetables."

In fact, the vegetables had survived very nicely, and the sea-bass was tender and flaky. Renie could not remember when she had eaten such a nice meal, and she took pains to tell Dako so.

His good humor slightly restored, the man nodded as he cleared the dishes. "Doctor Van Bleeck would rather have sandwiches every day," he said, an art dealer asked for paintings on black velvet.

Susan laughed. "I just never want to have to come upstairs and sit down when I'm working. The days when I don't work through lunch and sometimes dinner are the days I'm feeling my age. You don't want me to be old, do you, Jeremiah?"

"The doctor is not old," he said. "The doctor is stubborn and self-centered." He withdrew to the kitchen.

"Poor man." Susan shook her head. "He came to work for us when my husband was still alive. We used to have parties then, people from the university, foreign visitors. It was a more fulfilling household to run, I'm sure. But he's right—he doesn't see me most days after breakfast, unless there's some correspondence I have to sign. He leaves bitter little notes about all the things he's done that I haven't noticed. They make me laugh, I'm afraid."

!Xabbu had been watching Jeremiah with careful interest. "He is like my mother's brother, I think—a proud man who could do more than he is asked to do. It is not good for the spirit."

Susan pursed her lips. Renie thought the doctor might be offended. "Perhaps you are right," she said at last. "I have not set Jeremiah many challenges lately—I have rather drawn in on myself. But maybe that has been selfish of me." She turned to Renie. "He came to us at a time when things were still very unsettled, of course. He had been very poorly educated—-you do not know how lucky you are, Irene. The school system was already much better by the time you came along. But I think Jeremiah would have done well in any number of things, given the opportunity. He is an extremely quick learner and very thorough." The doctor looked down at her hands, at the silver spoon held in her gnarled fingers. "I had hoped his generation would be the last to grow up damaged by what we did."

Renie could not help thinking of her own father, floundering in an ocean invisible to everyone else, unable to find solid ground on which to stand.

"I'll think about what you said, !Xabbu." Susan put down her fork and briskly wiped her hands. "It is possible to get too set in one's ways. Anyway, let's go see what we can do with our mystery city."

The imaging programs had restored the shapshot to something like a recognizable picture. The substance of the city was now visible as a garden of fuzzy vertical oblongs and triangles, with impressionist smears representing the roads and elevated rails. Renie and the doctor began to correct small areas, adding detail from their own memory that augmented the general patterns imposed by the enhancement gear. !Xabbu proved particularly helpful. His visual memory was excellent: where Renie and Susan might remember that there had been windows in the flat plane of a wall, !Xabbu could often tell them how many there had been and which had been illuminated.

After more than an hour a picture had taken shape that was recognizably the golden city which had burned on the screen for a few brief moments. It was less sharply-defined, and there were areas in which the reconstruction was largely guesswork, but anyone who had seen such a place would recognize this as an image of it.

"So now we start searching." Susan tilted her head to one side. "Although it's still not quite right, somehow."

"It doesn't look real anymore," said Renie. "It's lost that *alive* quality. Of course it has—it's a flat, unmoving, totally rebuilt version. But that was part of the effect of the original. It was like looking through a hole in the computer at a real city."

"I suppose you're right. Still, it's the strangest damn place I've ever seen. If it's real, it must be one of those prefab fibramic monstrosities they string up overnight in the Indonesian Archipelago or somewhere like that." She rubbed at her knees. "These damn sensors are starting to chafe my legs. I'm afraid I'm going to have to call it a day, my dear. But I'll start searching for a good match off the specialist nets—you're not back at work yet, are you? Then you might as well let me do it. I've got at least three contracts I could charge it off to—multinationals with million human-hour datacomb projects who'd never notice a little extra connection time. And I've got a friend—well, an acquaintance—named Martine Desroubins, who's an absolute top-flight researcher. I'll see if she has anything to offer. Maybe Martine will even pitch in a little free help, since it's for a good cause." She looked at Renie, that shrewd, searching gaze again. "It *is* for a good cause, isn't it? This is something very important to you."

Renie could only nod.

"Right, then. On your way. I'll call you if I get any hits."

Dako met them outside the elevator on the main floor. As if by magic, he had the car waiting at the front door.

Renie hugged Doctor Van Bleeck and pressed a kiss against her powdered cheek. "Thank you. It's been wonderful to see you."

Susan smiled. "You didn't have to wait until you were being chased by VR terrorists to come visit me, you know."

"I know. Thank you so much."

!Xabbu shook the doctor's hand. She held on to him for a few moments, her eyes bright. "It's been a pleasure to meet you. I hope you will come again."

"I would like that very much."

"Good. It's settled." She rolled her chair onto the porch as they climbed into the car, then waved to them from the shadows of the porch as Dako swung around the long driveway and out onto the tree-lined road.

"You look very sad." !Xabbu had been staring at her for a long uncomfortable time.

"Not sad. Just . . . frustrated. Every time I think I might be getting somewhere with this, I run into a brick wall."

"You should not say 'I,' but 'we.' "

His liquid brown eyes rebuked her, but Renie could not even find the strength to feel guilty. "You've helped me a lot, !Xabbu. Of course you have."

"I am not speaking of me, but of you. You are not alone—look, today we have spoken to that wise woman, your friend, and she will certainly help us. There is strength in companionship, in family." !Xabbu spread his hands. "We are all of us small when set against the great powers, against the thunder or the sandstorm."

"This is more than a sandstorm." Renie fumbled reflexively for a cigarette, then remembered she couldn't smoke on the bus. "If I'm not completely crazy, this is bigger and stranger than anything I've ever heard of."

"But that is just the time when you must call on those who will help you. In my family, we say 'I wish baboons were on this rock.' Except that we call them 'the people who sit on their heels.' "

"Call who?"

"The baboons. I was taught that all the creatures who live beneath the sun are people—like us, but different. It is not a familiar way to think among city-folk, I know, but to my family, especially my father's family, all living things are people. The baboons are the people that sit on their heels. Surely you have seen them and know it is so."

Renie nodded, a little ashamed that she had only seen baboons caged in the Durban Zoo. "But why did you say you wished there were baboons on a rock?"

"It means that it is a time of great necessity and we need help. Usually, my people and the people who sit on their heels were not friends. In fact, long ago the baboons committed a great crime against our Grandfather Mantis. There was a great war between his people and theirs."

Renie could not help smiling. He spoke of these mythical beings, monkeys and mantises, as casually as if they were fellow students at the Poly. "A war?"

"Yes. It came of a long argument. Mantis was fearful that things would turn sour, so to be prepared he sent one of his sons to gather sticks to make arrows. The baboons saw this boy carefully choosing and gathering the wood and asked him what he was doing." !Xabbu shook his head. "Young Mantis was foolishly innocent. He told them that his father was preparing to make war against the people who sat on their heels. The baboons were enraged and fearful. They became more and more agitated, arguing among themselves, then at last they fell upon Young Mantis and killed him. Then, made bold by their easy victory, they took his eye and played with it, throwing it back and forth between them as though it were a ball, crying 'I want it! Whose turn is it?' over and over again as they fought for it.

"Old Grandfather Mantis heard his son crying out to him in a dream. He took his bow and ran so fast to the place that even the few arrows he carried rattled like wind in a thorn bush. He fought the baboons, and though he was far outnumbered, he managed to take from them his son's eye although he was badly wounded himself. He put it in his skin bag and fled.

"He took the eye to a place where water rose from the ground and reeds grew, and he put the eye in the water, telling it to grow once more. Many days he returned to find nothing had changed, but still he did not stop. Then one day he heard splashing, and found his child made whole again, swimming in the water." !Xabbu grinned, enjoying the happy moment, then his expression sobered. "That was the first battle in the war between the baboons and the Mantis people. It was a long and terrible fight, and both sides suffered many losses before it ended."

"But I don't understand. If that's the story, why would you say you want baboons to help you? They sound terrible."

"Ah, but they were only that way because they were frightened, thinking that Grandfather Mantis intended to make war on them. But the real reason we ask the baboons to help is an old story of my father's family. I fear I am talking too much, though." He looked at her from beneath his eyelashes with, Renie thought, a certain sly humor.

"No, please," She said. Anything was preferable to dwelling on her own failures as the bleak gray city rolled past the windows. "Tell me."

"It happened long ago—so long that I'm sure you would believe it to be a myth." He gave her a look that was mockingly stern. "I was told that the woman involved was my grandmother's grandmother's grandmother.

"In any case, a woman of my family whose name was N!uka became separated from her people. There had been a drought, and all the people had to go in different directions, all to search the farthest sipping holes. She and her husband went one direction, he carrying their last water in an ostrich egg, she carrying their young child upon her hip.

"They walked far but did not find water at the first or the second hole they tried. They moved on, but had to stop because of the darkness. Thirsty and hungry as well—for during a drought, of course, game is hard to find—they lay down to sleep. N!uka cradled her child close, singing so that he might forget the pains in his stomach.

"She awoke. The slivered moon, which inspired men of the Early Race to make the first bow, was high overhead, but it gave little light. Her husband sat upright beside her, his eyes wide and frightened. A voice spoke from the darkness beyond the last smoldering coals of their fire. They could see nothing but two eyes gleaming like cold, distant stars.

" 'I see three of you, two large, one small,' the voice said. 'Give me the small one, for I am hungry, and I will let the other two go."

"N!uka held her child close. 'Who is that?' she cried. 'Who is there?' But the voice only repeated what it said before."

" 'We will not do that,' her husband cried. 'And if you come near to our fire, I will shoot you with a poisoned arrow and your blood will turn sour in your veins and you will die.'

" 'Then I would be foolish to come to your fire,' the voice said. 'But I am patient. You are far from your people, and you must sleep sometime. . . .'

"The eyes winked out. N!uka and her husband were very frightened. 'I know who that is,' she said. 'That is Hyena, the worst of the Old Ones. He will follow us until we fall asleep, then he will kill us and devour our child.'

" 'Then I will fight him now, before weariness and thirst take all my strength away,' said her husband. 'But it may be my day to die, for Hyena is clever and his jaws are strong. I will go out to fight him, but you must run away with our child.' N!uka argued with him, but he would not change his mind. He sang a song to the Morning Star, the greatest of all hunters, then went out into the darkness. N!uka wept as she carried their child away. She heard a coughing bark—*chuff, chuff, chuff*!"—!Xabbu jutted his chin forward to make the noise, "and then her husband cried out. After that, she heard nothing. She ran and ran, urging her child to be silent. After a while, she heard a voice calling from behind her, 'I see two of you, one large and one small. Give me the small one, for I am hungry, and I will let the other one go.' She had a great fear then, for she knew that Old Hyena had killed her husband, and that soon he would catch her as well and kill both her and her child, and there were none of her people anywhere close that could help her. She was alone in that night."

!Xabbu's voice had taken on a strange cadence, as though the original tale in its original words struggled to make itself heard through the unfamiliar English tongue. Renie, who had been wondering a little uncomfortably whether her friend actually believed the story was true, suddenly had a kind of revelation. It was a story, no more, no less, and stories were the things people used to give the universe a shape. In that, she realized, !Xabbu was exactly right: there was little difference between a folktale, a religious revelation, and a scientific theory. It was an unsettling and oddly liberating concept, and for a moment she lost the track of !Xabbu's tale.

". . . Rising before her from the sand, three times her height. She climbed this stone, holding her child close against her breasts. She could hear Hyena's breathing, louder and louder, and when she looked back, she could see his great yellow eyes in the darkness, growing larger and larger. She sang again, 'Grandfather Mantis, help me now, Grandmother Star, help me now, send me strength to climb.' She climbed until she was out of Hyena's reach, and then huddled in a crack in the rock as he walked back and forth below.

" 'Soon you will be hungry, soon you will be thirsty,' Hyena called up to her. 'Soon your child will be hungry and thirsty, too, and will cry for sweet milk and water. Soon the hot sun will rise. The rock is bare and nothing grows upon it. What will you do when your stomach begins to ache? When your tongue cracks like the mud cracks?'

"N!uka felt a great fear then, for everything that Old Hyena said was true. She began to weep, crying 'Here is where I have come to the ending, here where no one is my friend and my family is far away.' She heard Old Hyena singing to himself below, settled in to wait.

"Then a voice said to her, 'What are you doing here on our rock?' A person came down from the top of the rock and it was one of the people who sit on their heels. In old times my family's people had been at war with the baboons, so N!uka was afraid.

"'Do not hurt me,' she said. 'Old Hyena has driven me here. He has killed my husband, and he waits below to kill me and my child.'

"This person looked at her, and when he spoke he was angry. 'Why do you say this to us? Why do you ask us not to hurt you? Have we ever offered you harm?'

"N!uka bowed her head. 'Your people and my people were enemies once. You fought a war with Grandfather Mantis. And I have never offered you friendship.'

"'Because you are not a friend does not make you an enemy,' said the baboon, 'and Hyena down below is an enemy to both of us. Come up to the top of the rock where the rest of my people are.'

"N!uka climbed up behind him. When she got to the top of the rock, she saw that all the baboons were wearing headdresses of badger hair and ostrich plumes, for they were having a celebration feast. They gave food to her and her child, and when everyone was full, one of the oldest and wisest of the people who sit on their heels spoke to her, saying, 'Now we must talk together, thinking of what we may do about Old Hyena, for just as you are trapped upon this rock, so are we, and now we have eaten all the food and drunk all the water.'

"They talked and talked for a long time, and the Hyena down below became impatient, and shouted up to them: 'I smell the people who sit on their heels and them, too, I will bite, and crack their bones in my jaws. Come down and give me the smallest, tenderest one, and I will let the rest of you go.' The old baboon turned to N!uka and said: 'There is a red flame that your people can summon. Summon it now, for if you can, there may be something we can do." N!uka took out her fire-starter and bent down low so the wind would not blow away the spark, and when she had made the red flames come, she and the baboons took a piece of stone from the great rock and put it in the fire. When it was hot, N!uka wrapped it in a piece of hide that the old baboon gave her, then she went to the edge of the rock and called down to Old Hyena.

" 'I am going to throw you down my child, because I am hungry and thirsty and the rock is bare.'

" 'Good, throw him down,' Hyena said. 'I am hungry, too.'

"N!uka leaned out and threw down the hot stone. Old Hyena leaped on it and swallowed it, hide and all. When it was inside his belly, it began to burn him, and he called out to the clouds, begging them to send rain, but no rain came. He rolled on the ground, trying to make himself vomit it up again, but while he was doing this, N!uka and the baboons came down from the rock and picked up more stones and killed Hyena with them.

"N!uka thanked the people who sit on their heels, and the oldest of those people said to her: 'Remember that when the greater enemy was before us both, we were your friends.' She swore that she would, and from that day, when danger or confusion is upon my family, we say: 'I wish baboons were on this rock.' "

Renie left !Xabbu in the Pinetown Bus Station with scarcely time to say good-bye, since her local was about to pull out. As the bus rolled down the ramp onto the busy rush-hour street, she watched the small young man standing beneath the overhang, scanning the schedule board, and again felt a rush of guilt.

He believes that baboons are going to come and help him. Jesus Mercy, what have I dragged him into?

For that matter, what had she gotten herself into? She seemed to have made some very powerful enemies, and for all that she had almost died, she had very little idea of what might be going on, and even less proof.

Make that no proof. Well, a blurry snapshot of a city, one copy on my pad, one on Susan's system. Try that with UNComm. "Yes, we think these people are murdering the minds of children. Our evidence? This picture of a lot of tall buildings."

There were quite a lot of people out on the streets around her neighborhood in the lowlands of Pinetown. She was a little surprised since it was a weeknight, but the people on the sidewalk definitely exhibited something of a carnival air, standing in knots in the center of the road, calling out to acquaintances, passing cans of beer around. When she dismounted the bus at the bottom of the hill, she could even smell smoke hanging sharp in the air, as though someone had been letting off fireworks. It was only when she had made her way halfway up

Ubusika Street and saw the lights of emergency vehicles flaring and dying against the side of the flatblock tower, the cloud of camera-drones hovering like flies in front of the flames, that she finally understood.

She was breathless and sweating when she reached the police cordon. A thick pall of smoke was funneling upward from the flatblock roof, a dark finger against the evening sky. Several of the windows on her floor were smashed and blackened as if by intense heat exploding outward; Renie's stomach contracted in fear when she saw that one of them was hers. She counted again, hoping she had been wrong but knowing she hadn't. A young black trooper in a visor held her back as she pressed against the temporary barrier, begging to be let through. When she told him she was a resident, he directed her to a mobile trailer at the far side of the parking lot. At least a hundred people from the flatblock, and two or three times that number of people from the surrounding area, were milling around in the street, but Renie didn't see her father among them. Suddenly, she was trying desperately to remember what he'd said he was going to do that day. Usually he was home by late afternoon.

There was too much of a crush around the trailer to talk to anyone official—dozens of voices were baying for attention, most desperate for news of loved ones, some just wanting to know what had happened or whether there would be insurance compensation. Renie was pushed and jostled until she thought she would scream from frustration and fear. When she realized that no one would notice if she *did* scream, she fought her way back out of the crowd. Her eyes blurred with tears.

"Ms. Sulaweyo?" Mr. Prahkesh, the small round Asian man who lived down the hall, took his hand from her arm as if surprised at himself. He was wearing pajamas and a bathrobe, but had pulled a pair of unlaced *takkies* onto his feet. "This is terrible, is it not?"

"Have you seen my father?"

He shook his head. "No, I have not seen him. It is too confusing here. My wife and daughter are somewhere here, because they came out with me, but I have not seen them since."

"What happened?"

"An explosion, I think. We were eating our meal, then *fooom!*" He clapped his hands together. "Before we knew what had occurred, there were people in the hallway shouting. I do not know what has caused it." He shrugged nervously, as though he might somehow be held responsible. "Did you see the helicopters? Many of them came, dumping foam on the roof and spraying it on the outside walls. I am sure it will make us all very sick."

Renie pulled away from him. She could not share in his alarmed but somehow excited mood. His family was safe, doubtless gossiping with other neighbors. Had everyone survived? Surely not, with damage of the sort she could see. Where was her father? She felt cold all over. So many times she had wanted him gone, wished him and his bad temper out of her life, but she had never thought it might come to this: seven-thirty in the evening, the street full of chattering voyeurs and shell-shocked casualties. Things didn't happen this suddenly, did they?

She stopped short, staring at the blackened row of windows. Could it have been her? Had something she'd done inspired a reprisal from the people at Mister J's?

Renie shook her head, feeling dizzy. Surely that was paranoia. An old heater, faulty wiring, someone using a cheap stove—there were any number of things that could cause this, and all of them far more likely than the murderous vengeance of the owners of a VR club.

A murmur of thrilled horror went through the crowd. The firefighters were bringing stretchers out of the front door. Renie was terrified, but could not simply wait for news. She tried to push back through the knot of onlookers, but passage was impossible. Squirming, applying an elbow when necessary, she worked her way out to the edge of the crowd, meaning to circle around and try to get near the front door from the other side of the cordon.

He was sitting on a curb beside an unoccupied police van, his head in his hands.

"Papa? *Papa!*"

She dropped to her knees and threw her arms around him. He looked up slowly, as though not sure what was happening. He smelled pungently of beer, but at the moment she didn't care.

"Renie? Girl, that you?" He stared at her for a moment, his reddened eyes so intent that she thought he might hit her. Instead, he burst into tears and wrapped his arms around her shoulders, pushing his face against her neck, hugging her so close she was almost throttled. "Oh, girl, I feel so bad. I shouldn't have done it. I thought you were inside there. Ah, God, Renie, I feel so bad, I'm so ashamed."

"Papa, what are you talking about? What did you do?"

"You were going out for the day. See your teacher-friend." He shook his head but would not meet her eyes. "Walter come by. He said, 'Let's just go out and have a little time.' But I drank too much. I came back, this whole placed burned up here, and I thought you were back and got burned up, too." He swallowed air, struggling. "I am so ashamed."

"Oh, Papa. I'm okay. I just got back. I was worried about *you*."

He took a deep, shuddering breath. "I saw the fire, burning the place up. Jesus save me, girl, I thought about your poor mother. I thought I lost you, too."

Renie was crying now, as well. It was a while until she could bear to let him go. They sat side by side on the curb, watching the last of the flames slowly wink out as the firefighters finished their job.

"Everything," said Long Joseph. "All Stephen's toys, the wallscreen, everything. I don't know what we gonna do, girl."

"Right now I think we need to go find some coffee." She stood up, then stretched out her hand. Her father took it and got to his feet, shaky and unstable.

"Coffee?" He stared at what had been their home. The flatblock looked like the site of a fierce battle that nobody had won. "I guess so," he said. "Why not?"

CHAPTER 16

The Deadly Tower Of Senbar-Flay

NETFEED/NEWS: Death of Child Called "Nanotech Murder"
(visual: school picture of Garza)
VO: Lawyers representing the family of fire victim Desdemona Garza called the lack of government oversight of chemical companies "a license to commit nanotech murder."
(visual: children in clothing store)
Garza, age seven, died when her Activex™ jacket caught fire. Her family maintains that the fatal fire was caused by the fabric's faulty nanoengineering. . . .

The lanterns of the Thieves' Quarter were dim and widely separated, as though a few glowing fish swam in the vast pool of night that drowned the criminal district of ancient Madrikhor. The city heralds, who never descended into the quarter, called the hour from the safety of the curtain wall. Hearing their cry, Thargor the swordsman stared sullenly at his cup of mead.

He did not look up at the sound of quiet footsteps, but his muscles tensed. His runesword Lifereaper's oiled length rested lightly in the scabbard, ready to leap forth at an instant's notice to deal death to anyone so foolish as to try a treacherous attack on the scourge of the Middle Country.

"Thargor? Is that you?" It was his sometime companion Pithlit, shrouded in a gray traveling robe to keep out the evening chill—and to hide his identity as well: the little bandit had dabbled too many times in the complicated politics of the Thieves' Guild, and currently was not entirely welcome in the quarter.

"Yes, it's me. Damn! What took you so long?"

"I was detained by other business—a dangerous commission." Pithlit did not sound very convincing. "But now I have come. Pray tell me our destination."

"Another ten minutes and I'd have left without you." Thargor snorted, then rose to his feet. "Let's go. And for God's sake, quit talking like that. This isn't a game any more."

"And we go to the house of the wizard Senbar-Flay?" Fredericks had not quite readjusted to normal speech.

"Damn right. He was the one who sent me into the tomb in the first place, and I want to know why." Orlando fought down his impatience. He would have preferred to jump directly to Flay's fortress, but the Middle Country simworld was rigorous about distances and travel times: unless you had a transportation spell to burn, or a magic steed, you went at RL pace. Just because he no longer wanted to slog through the game's normal complications didn't mean he could change the rules. At least his horse was the Middle Country's top-of-the-line model.

"But how can you be here at all?" Fredericks' voice had a worried edge. "You got killed. I mean, Thargor did."

"Yeah, but I decided to file a request for review after all. But Table of Judgment won't be able to find what I saw—that whole section of the game record is just gone—so the city will stay a secret."

"But if they don't find it, they'll just confirm Thargor's death." Fredericks spurred his horse forward—it had been dropping steadily behind Orlando's swifter Blackwind. "The Table will never overrule on your word alone."

"I know, scanboy. But while they're reviewing, Thargor is alive-until-proven-dead. And I can get around the Middle Country a lot faster and learn a lot more as him than if I had to start over as Wee Willie Winkle the Midget Mercenary or something."

"Oh." Fredericks thought about this for a moment. "Hey, that's major crafty, Gardino. Kind of like getting out on bail so you can prove you're innocent, like that Johnny Icepick flick."

"Kind of."

The city was quiet tonight, or at least the streets were, which was not surprising considering that it was time for end-of-semester exams in most places. Madrikhor, some journalist had once commented, was a bit like a Florida beach town: the population rose and fell with school vacations, peaking during summer, spring break, and Christmas. The New Year's Eve party in Madrikhor's King Gilathiel Square was not a great deal different than any end-of-season drunken orgy in Lauderdale, the writer had pointed out, except that in Florida fewer people had bat wings or carried battle-axes.

They rode out of the Thieves' Quarter and down the cobbled Street of Small Gods. Orlando deliberately made a wide detour around the Palace of Shadows. The PoS people were not real gamers, as far as he was concerned—they never seemed to *do* anything. They just hung around together and had parties, pretended to be vampires or demons, and did a lot of softsex and other things that they thought were decadent. Orlando thought they were basically pretty embarrassing. But if you wandered into their turf, you had to go through all kinds of bullshit to get out again. They had established ownership of their little piece of Madrikhor early in the history of Middle Country, and inside the Palace of Shadows—as well as in a few other private houses in the city—they made the rules and enforced them.

Fredericks had taken him to a PoS party once. Orlando had spent most of it trying not to stare at what people were doing, mostly because he knew they really wanted to be stared at and he didn't want to give them the satisfaction. He had met a fairly nice girl in a Living Dead sim—tattered shroud, pale rotting skin and deep-sunken eyes—and they had talked for a while. She had an English accent, but she lived on Gibraltar off the coast of Spain and wanted to visit America. She said she thought suicide could be an art form, which he thought was pretty stupid, but otherwise he had enjoyed talking to her, even though she had never heard of Thargor and in fact had never been anywhere in the Middle Country outside the Palace of Shadows. But nothing came of it, of course, although she acted like she would have liked to meet him again. After a couple of hours he had left and gone to The Garrote and Dirk in the Quarter to swap lies with other adventurers.

Lights were burning in the tallest tower of the Palace of Shadows as Orlando and Fredericks turned down Blind Beggar's Lane toward the river. Probably having one of their stupid initiations, he decided. He tried to remember the Living Dead girl's name—Maria? Martina?—but couldn't. He wondered if he might bump into her again sometime. Probably not unless he went back to the Palace, which effectively meant never.

Senbar-Flay's house was built on a jetty that stretched halfway out into the Silverdark River. It crouched above the murky water like a gargoyle, silent but watchful. Fredericks reined up and stared at it. It was hard to see his Pithlit-face on the dark embankment, but he didn't sound happy. "You've been here before, haven't you?"

"Once. Sort of."

"What does that mean?"

"He magicked me directly inside. He was hiring me for a job, remember?"

"So you don't know anything about his defenses? Hey, Gardiner, you may be dead, but I'm not. I don't want to get Pithlit killed off for nothing."

Orlando scowled. It was hard to resist drawing Lifereaper and brandishing it, the kind of thing he normally did when someone got fluttery in the middle of a dangerous quest, but Fredericks was coming along as a favor, after all. "Look," he said as calmly as he could, "I've knocked off places that make this look like a coat closet. Just hold your water."

Fredericks scowled back. "Do you even have a plan, or are you just going to pound your way in with your thick head? Gossip around the Quarter says he's got a watch-gryphon. You can't kill one of those things with anything short of nuclear weapons, Monsieur Le Scanmaster."

Orlando grinned, his bad temper washed away by the familiar bickering and the pleasure of doing what he did best. "Yeah, they're tough, but they're stupid. C'mon, Fredericks—what kind of thief are you, anyway?"

Things went smoothly enough at first. At Orlando's request, Fredericks had brought along a counteragent to the poisonous flowers in the wizard's garden and the four men-at-arms dicing in the gazebo had proved no match for barbarian Thargor's athletic runesword-swinging technique. The stone walls of the wizard's tower were smooth as glass, but Orlando, who had survived the most rigorous schooling in adventure that the Middle Country could offer, always carried plenty of rope. He flung a grappling hook over the fourth floor railing and soon was standing on the balcony's mosaic floor, helping Fredericks climb over.

"Couldn't you just have asked him why he sent you to that tomb?" The thief was wheezing very convincingly. Orlando guessed that Frederick's parents must have come through with the higher quality implant he had coveted for his birthday.

"Oh, *fenfen,* Fredericks, use your brain. If this was some kind of plot to get Thargor killed, I'm sure he'd tell me."

"Why should he be in on some plot? You don't even know who Senbar-Flay is."

"I don't *think* I know. But even if I don't know him, that still doesn't mean anything. Thargor's pissed off a lot of people."

Fredericks, or rather Pithlit, straightened up from breath-recovering position. "Thargor's pissing *me* off . . . " he began, but was interrupted by the abrupt appearance of a very large watch-gryphon.

The great beak glimmered in the moonlight; its tail lashed from side to side as it padded across the balcony, moving with the relaxed but steady tread of a cat heading toward a full supper bowl. "Thargor, 'ware the beast!" squeaked Fredericks, reverting to old habits under stress. Then, remembering: "It's a red one. The expensive kind. Not affected by magical weapons."

"It would be a red one," Orlando said sourly. He drew Lifereaper and dropped into a defensive crouch.

The gryphon stopped, its posture still deceptively casual—if anything about a lion-eagle mixture eight feet tall at the shoulder could be termed casual—and regarded them both with glassy, emotionless black eyes before it settled on tall Thargor as the one to be dealt with first. Orlando was disgusted: he had hoped it would at least make an initial move toward Fredericks, which would give him one clean shot at its rib cage. The creature twisted its neck to look at him sideways, since its aquiline head allowed it only very limited binocular vision. Orlando seized the opportunity and moved until he was directly in front of its beak again, then leaped forward, aiming for the throat.

The gryphon had better vision than he'd have wished, or better reflexes. It reared at his attack and swung a massive, taloned paw. Orlando dove, rolling beneath the terrible claws, took a two-handed grip on Lifereaper and jabbed as hard as he could into the beast's vitals. The sword clanked against scales and was turned aside.

"God *damn!*" He scrambled back under the paws again, just before the vast bulk could drop down and trap him. "The frigging thing might as well be wearing chain mail!"

"The rope!" shouted Fredericks. "Head for the rope!"

Orlando raised his sword again and began circling the gryphon. The creature's deep, rumbling growl sounded almost amused as it pivoted on its hindquarters, watching him. "No. I'm going to get inside this place."

Fredericks was jumping up and down beside the railing. "Damn it, Orlando, if you get killed again while you're on probation, you'll never get back into the game!"

"Then I guess I'd better not get killed. Now shut up and do something useful."

He flung himself to one side as the gryphon snatched at him again. The powerful claws snagged for a moment in his cloak and scored his side. Orlando was as good as anybody in the simworld at making conversation while fighting for his life, but there was a good reason he'd adopted Thargor's laconic barbarian style. Snappy repartee was for court duelists, not monster-fighters. Monsters didn't get distracted by chatter.

The red gryphon was slowly backing him toward the balcony railing, herding him with slashing nails and darting beak. Another few steps and he'd have nowhere to go.

"Orlando! The rope!"

He darted a glance over his shoulder. Escape was indeed only an arm's reach away. But if he gave up, then what? He could live without Thargor, work his way back up with another character, despite the dreadful loss of all the time he'd put in. But if he admitted defeat he might never learn anything more about the golden city. No gaming alter ego, not even one as much a part of him as Thargor, would ever haunt his dreams the way that wild vision had.

"Fredericks," he shouted. "Grab the rope and wrap it tight around the railing. Now!"

"It'll hold the way it is!"

Orlando cursed and danced back. The great red thing lunged forward another step, staying out of reach of Lifereaper. "Just do it!"

Fredericks worked frantically at the railing. Orlando swiped at the thing's eyes to distract it, but instead bounced his blade ringingly off its beak. Its head-darting counterattack almost took off his arm.

"I did it!"

"Now pull up the rest of it and throw it over the thing's neck. Right over, like I was standing on the other side waiting for it—instead of staring right up its nose." He fended off another sweep from a huge scarlet paw.

Fredericks started to protest, but instead hauled up the rope and flung it across the creature's shoulders in a loose coil. Startled, the gryphon raised its head, but the rope just snaked over the top of its mane and tumbled down onto the tiles a few yards from Thargor's left hand.

"Now do something to distract it!"

"Like what?"

"Damn it, Fredericks, tell it some knock-knock jokes! Anything!"

The thief bent and picked up a clay pot that stood near the railing, heaved it up over his head, then flung it at the gryphon. It smashed against the creature's ponderous rib cage; the gryphon hissed and darted its head to the side as though snapping at a flea. In the moment of its inattention Orlando jumped to his left and grabbed the coil of rope, then threw himself at the creature's neck just as it was turning back toward him. The beak scythed down. He sprawled onto the ground, still clutching the rope, and tumbled and crawled beneath the gryphon's neck. As he emerged from the other side the beast growled its displeasure at this irritatingly swift-moving enemy.

Before it could turn far enough to get at him, Orlando dropped Life-reaper to the tiles and sprang onto the gryphon's shoulder, grasping at the mane of blood-red bristles to pull himself up to bareback riding position. He dug his heels into its broad neck and yanked back on the rope as hard as he could, tightening it around the creature's throat.

I hope it doesn't think of rolling over on me . . . was the last coherent thought he had for some moments.

The great worm of Morsin Keep had been long and strong and slippery, and its death-battle against Thargor had possessed the added attraction of taking place underneath three fathoms of dirty water. Even Orlando, connoisseur of the game-world, had been impressed by the realism of the experience. Given the time to reflect now, he would have been similarly awed by the excellent way the gryphon's designers had managed to foresee his own somewhat dubious strategy, and had managed to program in a quite inspiring simulation of what it must feel like to simultaneously ride and strangle two tons of supernatural fury on the hoof.

Fredericks was a shouting blur. The entire balcony was little more than a vibrating smear. The thing beneath him was both frenetic in its movements and stone-hard: he felt like he was like trying to wrestle an angry cement mixer.

Orlando leaned in as close as he could, hugging the gryphon's neck even as he held the rope tight. He was in the one place its claws and beak could not reach, but the thing was doing its best to see he wouldn't stay there long. Every jerk, every convulsive shake, almost knocked him from his perch. The gryphon's thunderous growl did not sound amused any more, but neither did it sound like it was suffocating. Orlando wondered briefly if Red Gryphons, besides being immune to supernatural weapons, might not also breathe in some unusual way.

Just my luck. . . .

It bucked again. He realized it was only a matter of moments until its frantic struggling would dislodge him. For consistency's sake, Orlando said the prayer Thargor would have said as he took one hand off the rope and reached down to his boot, searching for his dagger. He tightened his legs around the creature's neck, wrapped his fingers more firmly around the rope, then gauged his moment and drove the knife into the gryphon's eye.

The rumbling snarl ripped upward into a screech. Orlando found himself flying through the air in a most convincing way. As he struck and rolled, the vast scarlet bulk of the gryphon toppled toward him, fountaining black blood.

"*Dzang*, man. *Ho dzang.* Utterly chizz. That was one of your best ever."

Orlando sat up. Fredericks stood next to him, his Pithlit-face wide-eyed with excitement. "Thank God I don't use regular tactors," he said, then groaned as Fredericks helped him up. "But I still wish I'd turned off the feedback. That hurt."

"But you wouldn't get credit for the kill if you did that."

Orlando sighed and looked at the gryphon. Dead, it seemed to take up even more room than before, sprawling across the tiles like an upended bus. "Frigging hell, Frederico, I got other things to worry about. I just want to get into that tower. If Thargor's gonna be declared dead, what does another notch mean?"

"Career statistics. You know, like an athlete or something."

"Jesus, you really scan. Come on."

Orlando picked Lifereaper out of the spreading puddle of dark blood, then wiped it on the corpse's hide before heading confidently toward the door at the back of the balcony. If there had been any more guards lurking, the commotion would surely have brought them by now.

The balcony opened onto the base of a wide stairway composed of writhing human forms. In the light from the wall sconces he could see a row of mouths opening and shutting along the banister. The murmur of their complaining voices filled the room. He would have been more impressed if he hadn't seen an advertisement for the Tortured Souls overlay in a gaming magazine a few weeks before. He curled his lip. "Typical wizard."

Fredericks nodded.

The stairs led up past several more floors, all full of snap-on wizard gear, much of it familiar and most of it fairly low-rent. Orlando decided that Senbar-Flay, whoever he was, had shot most of his allowance on the gryphon.

Shame about that, he thought. *Maybe it was insured.*

He didn't bother to search any of the lower rooms. Wizard-types, like cats, always opted for the highest perches, as if they had to look down on everyone else. Other than a squadron of large but somewhat sluggish guard-spiders, which Orlando easily dispersed with a few strokes from Lifereaper, they encountered no further opposition.

In the topmost part of the tower, in a great circular room with windows that overlooked Madrikhor in all directions, they found Senbar-Flay, asleep.

"He's not home," said Fredericks, half-relieved. The body was stretched out on a jet-black bier, and surrounded by something that would have looked like a glass box if it had been a bit more substantial. "Got wards around his body, too."

Orlando examined the wizard's inert sim. Senbar-Flay was as heavily robed as he had been at their first meeting, everything but his lidded eyes wrapped in metallic black fabric. He wore a goblin-skull helmet, although Orlando had real doubts the sorcerer had killed the goblin himself: the markets of Madrikhor's Merchant Row were full of such things, harvested by local adventurers and sold so they could improve their weaponry, their attributes, or buy a little extra online time. Adding a more exotic touch to the ensemble, the wizard's hands were gloved in human flesh—but, from the puckered stitching, it did not appear to be his own.

"Glory Hands," noted Fredericks. "I saw 'em in this shop in Lambda. Give you power over the dead, I think. What are you gonna do, Orlando? He's not here."

"I knew he wasn't here when the gryphon didn't bring him out. But this guy sent me down that hole and something weird happened to me there. I want answers." He reached into his pocket and brought out a small black circle the size of a poker chip. "And I'm gonna get 'em."

"What's that?"

"Wizards aren't the only people who can do magic." Orlando
dropped the circle onto the floor, then crouched and pulled at its edges
until it looked like a manhole the size of a dinner plate. "Beezle! Come
here!"

The shambling something with too many legs clambered up out
of the black circle. "Keep your shirt on, boss," it growled, "I'm here
already."

"What are you doing?" Fredericks was so shocked that Orlando
almost laughed—his friend sounded like an old lady. "You can't hack
that thing in here! No unregistered agents allowed in the Middle
Country!"

"I can do anything if I can make the gear work."

"But you'll be banned forever! Not just Thargor—*you!*"

"Only if somebody tells. And who would do that?" He fixed Fredericks with a stern look. "Now do you see why I'm not going to register
that kill?"

"But what if someone checks the record?"

Orlando sighed for the second time in fifteen minutes. These arguments with Fredericks could go on for days. "Beezle, pull this node
apart. Get me every piece of local information you can, but concentrate on communications in and out."

"Will do." The cartoon bug dropped back down into the hole, and
immediately the air filled with a ruckus of chainsaws and clawham-
mers.

Orlando turned back to his friend. "No one's going to check the
record unless Senbar-Flay asks them to, and he won't do that if he's
got something to hide."

"And if he doesn't have anything to hide?"

"Then I'll have to apologize, won't I? Or at least buy him a new
gryphon."

Orlando pulled opened the data window until it blocked his view of
Fredericks' frowning face. He opaqued the background, just to make
sure no disapproval leaked through, and studied the glowing characters Beezle was pumping out.

"His name's Sasha Diller. Never heard of him. You?"

"No." Fredericks sounded distinctly sullen, perhaps thinking of the
potential damage to his own Middle Country franchise if this affair
came to the attention of the Table of Judgment.

"Registered in Palm Beach Inner. Huh. I would've thought a rich kid would do better than this—everything except the watch-gryphon is strictly House of Gear." He let his eyes rove down the window. "Twelfth Level—like I couldn't guess. Calls in and out? Hardly any. A couple of codes here I don't recognize. Hmmm. He hasn't been around much lately." Orlando pointed at a section of the window, which reconfigured. He grunted in surprise.

"What?"

"He's been around exactly twice in the last six months. Two days in a row. The second was the one where he gave me the commission."

"That's weird." Fredericks looked down at Senbar-Flay's uninhabited body. "Why don't you just pump out the data you want? We should get out of here."

Orlando smiled. He knew his sim wasn't showing much of it—Thargor didn't smile very well. "Some thief you are. Is this how you act when you're on one of your little jobs? Like a kid sneaking down to rattle his Christmas presents?"

"Pithlit doesn't break the rules of the Middle Country." Fredericks' dignity was wounded. "He's not scared of anything, much—but *I'm* worried about getting banned for life."

"Okay. It's gonna be a long time before this guy comes back anyway, by the looks of it." Orlando began to close the window, then stopped, arrested by something he'd seen, and enlarged it again. He stared for a long while, long enough to make his friend start to shuffle nervously, then shut it and sent the information to his home system.

"What? What was it?"

"Nothing." Orlando looked down at the hole. "Beezle? You done?"

As if to be contrary, the agent appeared from the general area of the ceiling, dangling on a very cartoony-looking rope that Orlando knew was not part of the wizard's tower decor. "Depends what you mean by done, boss. How fine you want the information sifted? You got all the big stuff already."

Long years of interaction had taught Orlando to translate Beezle's seeming informality. He was probably now tracing the provenance of every piece of snap-on software in the place.

"The big stuff will do. Do a backgrounder on the gryphon, though. A good one."

Beezle spun at the end of his rope for a moment. "Done."

"Then let's get out of here. Hit that rope and start climbing down, Frederico."

"Climbing? Why don't we just *go?*"

"Because I'm not leaving the way you are. You go the long way.

Keep an eye open and make sure we didn't leave any obvious traces—
you know, club keys from the Thieves' Quarter Lounge, stuff like
that."

"Very funny. What are you going to do?"

"Trust me—you don't want to know."

Orlando gave Fredericks a decent head start. Then, when he felt
sure his friend should be shinnying down the rope—Fredericks had
spent lots of points on rope-shinnying ability, so Orlando figured he
wouldn't be at it too long—he summoned Beezle back.

"What now, boss? We goin' somewhere interesting?"

"Only home. But first I want you to do something. Can we leave a
little data bomb behind?"

A grinning mouth appeared in the inky mop of legs. "We *are* having
fun today. Whatcha wanna do, exactly?"

"I can't do anything to the central record, and I certainly can't make
a seamless edit like someone did to me, even in this guy's house
file—but I can make sure that whoever comes in here next won't
know who was here or what happened, not unless they've got Table
of Judgment authority."

"Your call, boss. But I can scorch it good, yeah. Complete scramble."

Orlando hesitated. He was taking a big risk—bigger even than Fredericks knew. This had become so important to him so quickly, and he
was basing it all on one look at Beezle's data. But he hadn't become
Thargor, scourge of the Middle Country, by being afraid to go for
broke.

"Scorch it."

"You did *what?*"

"Pulled it down. Not from the outside—no one will be able to tell
unless they actually get into the place."

Fredericks, back in one of his bodybuilder sims, leaped out of his
chair so quickly that he flew into the air and caromed off the cottage
wall. Orlando adjusted the gravity and his friend floated down and
bumped to rest beside the pyramid of display cases. "Are you scanned
utterly?" Fredericks shouted. "That's not just the Middle Country
death penalty, and maybe thrown off the whole net—that's criminal
prosecution, too! You destroyed someone's property!"

"Don't get your *fenfen* in an uproar. That's why I sent you out first.
You're in the clear."

Fredericks raised his chunky fists, his sim face (slightly less realistic
than Pithlit's, which probably indicated something profound, al-

though Orlando couldn't say what exactly) screwed up in fury. "I don't *care* about me! Well, that's not true—but what the hell is going on with you, Gardiner? Just because Thargor's dead, you're trying to get yourself thrown off the net. What are you, some kind of martyr?"

Orlando settled back into his virtual couch, smiling. "You sound like my mother."

His friend's cold anger was fierce and surprising. "Don't say that. Don't you dare say that."

"Sorry. Just . . . just spanking you. Look, I'll let you in on something. Beezle! Run that information out for me again, will you?"

The window appeared and hung gleaming in midair like an angelic visitation.

"Now, orb this." Orlando boxed and expanded a small section. "Go on, read it."

Fredericks squinted. "It's . . . it's a shutdown order." He straightened up, a little relief evident in his voice. "Senbar-Flay's tower is gonna be taken down? Then . . . but it still doesn't make sense, Gardiner, what you did. If they're going to drez it anyway. . . ."

"You didn't finish reading. Look at who told the Middle Country gaming board to shut it down."

"Some judge in . . . Palm Beach County, Florida?"

"And the date—six months ago. And it's only been used twice since that time."

Fredericks shook his head. "I don't get it."

"This guy Diller's dead! Or in jail, or something. Anyway, he ceased to be the operator, pretty much, six months ago. But for some reason it hasn't been drezzed. And, more importantly, someone's used it—used Diller's sim, even! Used it to hire me!"

"Wow. Barking. Are you sure?"

"I'm not sure of anything. But Beezle's checking for me. You got anything yet, Beezle?"

The agent popped out of a crack in the wall beside the picture window. "Got the Diller stuff. Still working on the watch-gryphon."

"Give me what you've got so far. Just tell me."

"Diller, Seth Emmanuel—you want dates and everything?"

"Just summarize. I'll stop you if I want more data."

"He's a coma case—date of shutdown coincides with the date of a trustee being named for his estate. Thirteen years old at last birthday. Parents dead, grandmother applied for legal aid—she's started a lawsuit against Middle Country, plus the hardware manufacturers, primarily Krittapong Electronic and subsidiaries."

Orlando pondered. "So he had enough money to have good equipment, but the grandmother doesn't have enough money to sue?"

Beezle waved his legs for a moment. "All the hardware and gear named in the lawsuit's at least four years old, some much older. You want me to get the grandmother's finances? Diller, Judith Ruskin."

"Nah." He turned to Fredericks, who was sitting forward, beginning to believe. "This guy's in a coma, as good as dead. His estate wants his online stuff shut down—probably to save money. And his grandma's suing the Middle Country, too. But it doesn't shut down. And someone else uses it, at least two times. His equipment was nice once, but it's old now and his grandmother doesn't have any money. But there's a top-of-the-line, utterly scorching red gryphon on the site to keep people out. How much you want to bet it was purchased *after* this Diller kid checked out?"

"I'm working on the gryphon, boss," said Beezle. "But it ain't easy."

"Keep trying." He put his feet up on nothing. "What do you think now, Frederico?"

His friend, who had seemed quite excited only a few moments ago, now grew strangely still, as though he had left his sim entirely. "I don't know," he said at last. "This is getting weird, Orlando. Really scanbark. How could someone keep a node open in the Middle Country when the people who run it wanted it shut down?"

"I'll bet that somebody fiddled the central records. We only know because the shutdown order was registered on the node itself when the judge made her decision. But if someone went in and adjusted the central records, the automatic drezz would never happen. You know the system's too big for anyone to notice, at least until the case comes to court and the whole thing gets dragged out again."

"But that's what I mean! You're talking about someone hacking the Middle Country central records!"

Orlando made a noise of annoyance. "Fredericks! We already *knew* they could do that. Look at what happened to me down in that tomb. They just took the whole sequence out and then sewed it back up again. Like they were surgeons."

"But why?"

"Don't know." Orlando turned to examine his MBC window. Watching the constructor robots patiently excavating the red Martian soil was soothing, like watching cows in a field. He needed to slow his excited thoughts. "I just know I'm right."

Fredericks got up, a little more carefully this time, and walked to the center of the room. "But, Orlando, this is . . . it isn't Morpher or

Dieter. This isn't just someone trying to get over on us. These people are, like . . . criminals. And why are they messing with things, taking all these risks—just to show you some *city*? It doesn't make sense."

"Not much."

Sifting, digging, then sifting some more, the constructor robots went on about their tasks. They were just on the other side of an imaginary window, and simultaneously millions of miles away. Orlando tried to remember the time lag of the transmission, but couldn't. Not that what they were doing at this exact moment probably looked any different from this delayed version he was looking at. And the mindless things would continue, working and working, dying off and being replaced from their own self-created factory. In another few years the project would end. A tiny blister of plastic would hug the Martian surface, a place where a few hundred humans could shelter against the harshness of an alien world.

"Orlando?" His friend's voice tugged him back to the equally alien world of his virtual house. Fredericks' broad-shouldered sim had crossed its arms as though to hold something inside its barrellike chest. "Gardino, old man? This scares me."

Orlando sat up, pillows bunched behind him, his blanket wrapped around his thin legs as tightly as a cold beggar's robe, and listened to Nothing.

He knew from books that houses had not always been like this. He suspected that most houses in other parts of the world, and even lots of them here in America, were not like this even now. He knew that in many places boards creaked, and upstairs neighbors thumped, and people talked on the other side of walls. He had visited a friend from the medical center once, a boy named Tim whose parents lived in a house on a street with nothing separating them from the rest of the city. Even during the day you could hear cars moaning past on the freeway half a mile distant.

On nights like this, when his father had stopped snoring for a bit, Orlando couldn't hear anything at all. His mother always slept like a dead person. The Gardiners had no pets except for a few dozen exotic fish, but fish were quiet animals and all the systems that supported life in their tank were noiselessly chemical. The building's human residents were cared for no less discreetly. Machinery in the house's walls adjusted temperatures, monitored air quality, random-tested the circuitry on lights and alarm systems, but all in silence. Outside, an army might be trooping past beyond the heavy walls and insulated windows of their house, but as long as no one stepped in front of a sensor beam, Orlando would never know.

There was something to be said for the kind of safety and security money could buy. Orlando's mother and father could go shopping, attend the theater, walk the dog—if they'd had one—all without leaving the vast security estate that was Crown Heights. His mother claimed they had only done it for Orlando's sake. A child like him should not be subjected to the dangers of city life, they had decided, but equally clearly should not be raised in some rural place, a long car- or helicopter-ride away from modern conveniences. But since most of his parents' friends also lived either in Crown Heights or in similar fortified mid-city security townships (they were called *exclusive communities* in the ads), and didn't have his parents' excuse for it, he wondered if she was telling him the truth. Sometimes he wondered if she even knew the truth herself.

The house was silent. Orlando was lonely and a little unsettled.

His fingers found the link cable by his beside. He thought for a moment about going to the net, but he knew what would happen if his mother got up to pee or something while he was oblivious and saw him plugged in. She was on an anti-net campaign as it was, although what else she expected him to do she'd never made clear. If she caught him, he might lose the "privilege," as she termed it, for weeks. He didn't dare risk it just now. Not with all the things that were happening.

"Beezle?" There was no response. He had spoken too softly, apparently. He crawled to the foot of the bed and leaned over. "Beezle?" Voice activation was a bitch when you were worried about waking up your parents.

A minute hum wafted out of the darkness. A small, dim light brightened, then seven more tiny red lights blinked on in circular sequence until he could see a small scarlet ring gleaming in the shadows near his closet door.

"Yes, boss?"

"Quieter. Like me."

Beezle matched his volume level. "Yes, boss?"

"Anything to tell me?"

"A few things. Some of them strange. I was going to wait until morning."

The conversation was still making Orlando nervous. His mother had been on a bulk scorch lately about not sleeping, and sometimes the woman had ears as sharp as a bat's, even in her sleep. He was sure it was some kind of mother thing, a latent genetic abnormality that only emerged after giving birth and lasted until you'd driven your children out of the house.

He briefly considered doing the whole thing silently onscreen, but at least if his mother woke up and heard him talking, he could pretend it had been in his sleep. If she caught him with a glowing screen, it would be harder to explain away. Besides, he was lonely, and having someone to talk to was still the best cure for that. *"Bug.* Come over here so we don't have to talk so loud."

A couple of near-silent clicks indicated that Beezle was detaching his robot body from the power outlet, where it had been quietly sucking nourishment like a flea on a dog's back. The ring of red lights slid down the wall and then came across the carpet at about shoetop height. Orlando scrambled back to his pillows and got under the blankets again so he could enjoy the ticklishly amusing sensation of Beezle clambering up the bedclothes. He enjoyed it mostly because he was not so grown-up as to have forgotten the slightly creepy way it had felt when he was a little boy.

Beezle approached the pillow, humming and clicking as faintly as a cricket wrapped in a yard of cotton. He crawled onto Orlando's shoulder and adjusted for stability, rubber-tipped feet scrabbling to get a satisfactory grip. Orlando wondered if someday Beezles, or things like Beezle, would be able to move as freely in RL as they did in the virtual world. He had already seen news stories about agents with robotic bodies going feral because of bad programming or aging software, escaping their owners to live like woodlice in the infrastructures of buildings. What would such things want out of life? Did they run away on purpose, or just lose the ability to follow their original programming and wander off into freedom? Did they retain vestiges of their original artificial personality?

Beezle had settled with his speaker beside Orlando's ear, and now spoke so quietly as to be barely audible. "Better?"

"That's fine. So tell me what you have."

"Which first?"

"The gryphon."

"Well, first off, we don't know for sure when it was purchased, but everything else lines up with your guess. It was first introduced into the node after the shutdown order."

"So Diller didn't buy it."

"Well, a call on the hospital databank says he's still there and still listed as comatose, so even if he bought it, he sure didn't install it."

"Where's it from?"

Beezle readjusted in response to Orlando's small change of position. His Brooklyn cabdriver accent continued to purr into his master's ear. "That's one of the strange things. It doesn't correspond exactly to anything. It's been customized from several different chunks of code—I think it did more than just perform its Middle Country duties, but it's too late now to go back and check those possibilities. Maybe if you go back in, boss."

"I doubt it. So you can't find out who bought it *or* who made it?"

"The chain of manufacture is messed up all to hell. I can't trace an unbroken line—companies have gone out of business, trademarks on some parts of it are held under what seem to be invented names—not in any indexes I can find anywhere." If an agent in a robot body could sigh, Beezle would have sighed. "It's been hell, I'm tellin' ya. But one thing keeps coming up."

"Which is?"

"TreeHouse."

At first Orlando thought he had misheard Beezle's whisper. "You mean . . . the place?"

"Most of the invented names are hacker tags, and a lot of them show up in TreeHouse-related material."

"Wow. Let me think."

Beezle sat patiently. Unlike his parents or Fredericks, you could tell Beezle to do something and he'd do it. He knew "Let me think" meant don't talk, and if Orlando didn't prompt him to speak again, the robot would crouch silently in place until he had to crawl back to his socket to recharge.

Orlando needed a few moments of quiet. He didn't quite know what to say. If this trail he seemed to be following led toward TreeHouse, that was both exciting and extremely daunting. Exciting because TreeHouse, often called "the last free place on the net," was supposed to be an anarchistic hacker's paradise, an outlaw node that floated through the system like an illegal streetcorner craps game. Net gossip said that it was supported not by massive corporate structures like the other big nodes, but by an ever-changing network of its residents' own small systems. It was supposed to be like a gypsy camp—the whole thing could be taken down in minutes, stored as small and widely-distributed individual chunks, then fitted back together again equally swiftly.

The daunting aspect was that nobody just *went* to TreeHouse. It was pretty much invitation only, and since it had no commercial purpose—and was in fact by its own governing principles opposed to being useful in any meaningful way—those who found it usually wanted only to enjoy and help preserve its exclusivity.

So you couldn't just go to TreeHouse like you could to some other node. Being told that the answers to his questions might be discovered there was like telling a medieval peasant that he could find something in Cathay or Samarkand. For a teenager with no connections, if it wasn't actually mythical, it was still so unreachable as to be in effect purely imaginary.

TreeHouse. Excitement moved inside him, but something else fought for room beside it, something he knew very well, although he had never before felt it about something on the net. Just like Fredericks, he was scared.

"Beezle," he said at last, "are you sure?"

"Boss, please." Beezle was old equipment, but he was an impressive piece of work. There was nothing artificial about his tone of scorn.

"Then get me everything you can on TreeHouse. No, not everything. At least at first you'd better just give me stuff with a reasonable believability weight—information with multiple sources. We can decide whether we want to start hunting through the really scanny stuff later."

"Even so, boss, it's gonna take a while."

"I'll take whatever you've got in the morning." He remembered that tomorrow was an appointment day. "No, after lunch. I'll look at it, then decide."

"If you want a really thorough search by tomorrow, I'd better lose this body and get to it. Crawling around wastes an awful lot of bandwidth, ya know."

Orlando made a face. One problem with hanging onto your childhood agent was that they tended to lecture you. "Tell me something new. Go on, get out of here."

The rubber-clad metal polyps riffled in sequence as Beezle backed away from his ear. "Good night, boss."

"'Night, Beezle."

The agent made its laborious way down the blankets to the floor. Like cats, Bugs found it easier to climb up than down. Orlando watched the faint gleam of red until it reached the wall outlet once more, socketed in, and turned off its display.

TreeHouse. It was so strange to think of that name in connection with something he, Orlando Gardiner, was going to do. It was like deciding you were *really* going to fly to Never-Never Land, or go down a rabbit hole to look for Alice's friends.

But it made sense, in a weird way. If people existed who could hack into a system as sophisticated as the Middle Country, excise an entire five minutes or whatever it had been, then leave no trace—not only of who had done it, but that anything had even been done!—they would be the kind of people who hung around in TreeHouse.

He sank down into the pillows, but he knew sleep would not come soon. There was so much to think about. Had he really found something unusual, something worth causing all this trouble over, something worth taking so many risks? Or was it only that the vision of the strange city made him think about things he'd stopped considering? Fredericks would tell him he was getting carried away. Certainly data bombing someone's node was not a normal kind of thing to do. His parents would be horrified.

A sudden thought made his neck go prickly. Orlando sat up; the idea was too uncomfortable to consider lying down.

He had figured that only someone with access to the Middle Country records would ever know he had been in Senbar-Flay's tower—he had even said so to Fredericks. But clearly whoever had snipped out the sequence in the tomb and managed to suppress a shutdown order for half a year could walk in and out of the Table of Judgment's master files at will, and do things to them that even their owners couldn't do.

If that was the case, then whoever had rigged the whole thing in the first place could find out about Thargor's visit any time he or she wanted to. And the mystery hacker could find out about Thargor's creator with even greater ease.

Sour bile rose to Orlando's mouth. With the kind of stupid self-confidence that would make any imaginary barbarian proud, he had as good as told this person of near-limitless skills and an obvious desire for secrecy that there was a fourteen-year-old kid looking for him. Surely the whole thing was just the work of some extremely talented, slightly childish prankster. But if the city and the records-fixing were indicative of something bigger, something far more illegal? He could only hope that his adversary had a really good sense of humor.

Yoo-hoo, Mister Big-League Computer Criminal, it's me, Orlando Gardiner. Drop by any time. I won't put up much of a fight.

Hell, all someone would have to do was fiddle his medical records. The wrong dermal patch and it would be Sayonara Irene.

TreeHouse. An image out of childhood, a place to escape the real world of grownups and rules. But who else liked to lurk beyond the edge of the playground, out of reach of authority? Bullies. Serious troublemakers. Bad guys.

Eyes wide open, Orlando sat in the dark and listened to Nothing.

CHAPTER 17

A Call From Jeremiah

NETFEED/SPORTS: Caribe Youth Signs "Guinea Pig" Contract
(visual: Bando playing dirt court basketball game)
VO: Solomon Bando, a twelve-year-old Dominican boy, will become the first
child to receive hormone treatments paid for and administered by a
professional sports franchise. Bando's family signed a contract with the
Ensenada ANVAC Clippers of the World Basketball Association that permits
their son, chosen as an optimum specimen from several hundred applicants,
to undergo a series of body-building hormone treatments and bone grafts
designed to help him reach an adult height of at least seven and a half feet.
(visual: Roland Krinzy, Clippers vice president)
KRINZY: "We're building for the future, not just taking the short view. Our
fans appreciate that."

Renie fumbled with her packages, trying to juggle them into some kind of manageable arrangement. The bus wheezed and rolled slowly away on underinflated tires, off to deposit a few more souls on a few more corners, like a strange animal marking the circuit of its territory.

The day had turned even hotter while she had been on the bus, although the sun was well down toward the horizon; she could feel sweat trickling down the back of her neck and along her spine. Before the fire, her stop had been only a few streets from her flat, although that had always seemed a terrible trudge at the end of a working day. Only two weeks later, she was beginning to look back on the old days with nostalgic fondness.

The streets of Lower Pinetown were full, as they usually were this time of the day. People of all ages lounged in doorways or on front steps, gossiping with neighbors next door or even across the street— shouting something scurrilous so everyone who could hear was part of the fun. In the middle of the road a group of young men were playing football, the contest watched closely by a pack of children who ran up and down the sidewalks as the progress of the match shifted from one end of the street to the other, and more casually by the audience on the stoops. Most of the players wore only shorts and battered *takkies*. As she watched their perspiration-slicked bodies move, listened to them laughing and shouting, Renie felt a deep, hollow craving for someone to hold her and love her.

Waste of time, girl. Too much to do.

One of the young men in the match, lean and shaven-headed, looked something like her old boyfriend Del Ray, even had a little of his insolent grace. For a moment he was there in the street in front of her, even though she knew the boy who had captured her attention was years younger. She wondered what the real Del Ray was doing, where he was at this very moment. She hadn't thought of him in a while, and wasn't sure she was happy to be reminded. Had he gone to Johannesburg, as he had always sworn he would? Surely nothing could have kept him from going into government and making his way up the ladder of respect—Del Ray had been very ambitious. Or was he still here in Durban, perhaps returning home from work to a waiting woman—to his wife, maybe. It had been at least five years since she'd seen him, time enough for anything to have happened. He might have children. For all she knew, he might be dead.

She shivered a little and realized she had stopped in the middle of the sidewalk. The young man, who now raced ahead of the entire pack dribbling the scuffed ball, flew past her. She saw a flash of gold in his grin of exertion. He didn't really look much like Del Ray.

A group of small children swept past her like an ocean wave, following the young man who wasn't her old boyfriend as he hurtled toward the goal. She had to cling to her packages as the shrieking troop swirled by, then she began walking again. A few hundred yards took her past the stoops and into the small and rather depressing shopping district.

A dress in a window caught her eye. She slowed. The pale fabric had a strange sheen, and the slanting sunlight seemed to move across it unevenly. It was odd but somehow striking, and she stopped to look more closely. It had been a long time since she'd bought herself any clothes that weren't practical.

She shook her head with a small sense of triumphant martyrdom. If there was ever a time when she needed to save her money, when she couldn't afford something just because it would make her feel nice, now was that time.

A movement in or behind the reflection caught her eye as she turned back to the sidewalk. For a moment she thought it was someone in the shop window, but when she moved to a different angle, she could see the window was empty but for mannequins. Something had moved quite close behind her. She whirled, but saw only a bit of dark clothing disappearing down a sidestreet a dozen yards away. Just the other side, walking away from Renie on the sidewalk, two young women were looking back over their shoulders with faintly puzzled expressions, as though watching whoever it might have been.

Renie readjusted her bag and walked a little more purposefully. It was not as if it were after dark, or she were the only person on the street. A small crowd stood in front of the corner market just a hundred steps ahead, and there were at least a half-dozen people closer to her than that. She might well be in some kind of trouble, but it was dangerous to start believing that people were following you.

As she waited to cross the street, she casually turned and looked back. A rangy man in a dark shirt and metal-framed sunglasses was staring fixedly into the dress shop window. He did not meet her eyes or show any sign that he even knew she existed, but she still felt a kind of attention emanating from him.

Perhaps she was jumping at shadows. Then again, that was what they called it when somebody followed somebody, wasn't it—shadowing?

It's dangerous to believe that people are following you, but maybe it's dangerous to disbelieve it, too.

She went into the market on the corner even though she'd already done her shopping near the Poly, where the better stores were. When she came out with a soft drink in her hand, there was no sign of the man in the dark shirt.

The shelter had been a truck depot, and it still retained its former sense of intimacy and warmth. The twelve-meter-high ceilings gaped in places where the cheap corrugated fibramic didn't quite meet. The floor was concrete, still blackened in places with ancient oil stains. The Greater Durban Social Welfare Department had done what it could, mostly with volunteer labor—the huge space had been hived with fiberboard partitions across which curtains could be hung, and a wide, carpeted common area in one corner held a wallscreen, a large gas fire, dartboards, and an old billiards table—but the building had been converted hastily in the wake of the flooding three years before and hadn't been modified since. At the time it had been meant only as temporary housing for those displaced from the lower townships, but after the overspill had receded, the local government had kept the building. They hired it out between the fairly infrequent emergencies for dances and political rallies, although it had a core population that had never found other homes.

Keeping the shelter had not meant being able to improve it, though. Renie wrinkled her nose as she walked across the open area near the front door. How could a place that was so drafty in cold weather hold in the heat and stink so effectively during the summer?

She dumped the packages in the four-by-three-meter booth which was their temporary home. Her father wasn't there, but she had not expected him to be. She pulled the tab on a cigarette, kicked off her shoes, then pulled the curtain closed so she could take off her work clothes and keep them relatively clean. When she had changed into shorts and a loose-fitting shirt, she put the groceries in the tiny refrigerator, set the kettle on the hot plate, stubbed her cigarette, and went off to search for Long Joseph.

He was over by the wallscreen with the usual bunch of men, some his age, some younger. They were watching a football match being played on green grass somewhere, a contest between well-paid professionals in one of the commercial sportsground Neverlands that only existed on broadcasts; she couldn't help thinking about the real game in the street only a short distance away. What brought the young men in out of the sunshine and turned them into the only slightly older ones here—slow of speech but quick to argue, shallow-swimming, content to sit and nurse a few beers through a long afternoon in a steamy warehouse? How could men start out so strong, so vital, and then turn so sour?

Her father looked up at her approach and, in guilty reflex, attempted to hide his beer. She ignored it. "I'm making some coffee, Papa, then we have to go see Stephen."

He sneaked a quick look down at the bottle held against his leg. It was almost empty. The other men were watching the screen intently. Renie had heard a colleague say that men were like dogs; if so, it was never more apparent than when they watched the movement of a ball. Long Joseph swallowed the last mouthful, then put it down on the concrete with a defiant flourish. "I'll come. Got to see the boy."

As they walked back across the broad expanse, Renie thought she saw the man in the dark shirt again, this time silhouetted in the front doorway, but it was hard to be certain with the light streaming in from behind him. She pushed down a surge of unease. Even if it were him, that didn't mean anything. There were almost five hundred people living in the shelter, and many more who just came in during the day to hang around. She knew only the few dozen other refugees from their burned flatblock.

She looked again when the light wasn't in her eyes, but couldn't see him anymore.

"It used to be good," her father said suddenly. "Every day. Good to do it."

"What?"

"When I was working. When I was an electrician. Finish up, put down the tools, stop with my friends to have a drink. Good to be finished. But then my back got hurt."

Renie said nothing. Her father's back injury had occurred, or at least he claimed it had occurred, in the year after the death of her Uma' Bongela, her grandmother, who had been the children's caretaker after their mother's death in the store fire. Long Joseph's injury had also coincided with his much greater interest in drinking, and in his coming back so late from his social evenings that Renie had usually taken her baby brother into bed with her to quiet his crying. She had always had her doubts about his back injury.

Unless he had been bowed down so long by hard work piled on hard work, and then by the added, almost impossible burden of losing wife and mother-in-law and being left as sole parent to two young children, that he had just reached a point where he could not straighten up anymore. That, too, could be called a back injury of sorts.

"You could still do it, you know."

"What?" He was distracted, staring out into the middle distance as he walked.

"Be an electrician. God knows, there're lots of people with problems around here. I bet they'd love to have you help them."

He gave her a quick, angry look before staring ahead again. "My back."

"Just don't do anything that will make it worse. I'm sure there're lots of other things you could do. Half the people in this building have their power outlets overloaded, old wires, bad appliances. You could go around and have a look . . . ."

"Goddamn, girl, if you want to get rid of me, just say it to me!" He was suddenly furious, his hands clenched into fists. "I'm not going 'round begging people for jobs. Trying to tell me my monthly payment isn't enough?"

"No, Papa." In his early fifties, he was becoming a querulous old man. She wanted to touch him but didn't dare. "No, Papa. It was just an idea. I'd just like to see you . . . "

"Make myself useful? I'm useful to me, girl. Now you mind your own business."

They walked in silence back to their space. Long Joseph sat down on the bed and conducted a long, critical examination of his slippers while Renie made two cups of instant coffee. When the tablets had finished effervescing, she passed one to her father.

"Can I ask you something else, or are you going to be in a bad mood all evening?"

He looked at her over the rim of his cup. "What?"

"What did the man look like in front of our flatblock? Remember? The one you saw waiting in the car that night when !Xabbu came over."

He shrugged and blew on his coffee. "How do I know? It was dark. He had a beard, a hat. Why do you want to know that?"

The man shadowing her had been beardless, but that proved nothing—anyone could shave.

"I'm . . . I'm worried, Papa. I think there might be someone following me."

He scowled. "What nonsense is this? Following you? Who?"

"I don't know. But . . . but I think I may have upset somebody. I've been looking into what happened to Stephen. Doing some research on my own."

Long Joseph shook his head, still frowning. "What kind of silliness you talking, girl? Who following you, a crazy doctor?"

"No." She wrapped her hands around her own cup, strangely glad of the warmth despite the hot day. "I think something happened to him because of the net. I can't explain, but that's what I think. That's why I went to see my old teacher."

"What good that old white witch do you?"

"Damn it, Papa. I'm trying to talk to you! You don't know anything about Doctor Van Bleeck, so just shut up!"

He made a motion as if to rise, sloshing his coffee.

"Don't you dare get up. I'm talking to you about something important. Now, are you going to listen to me? I'm not the only relative Stephen has, you know—he's your son, too."

"And I'm going to him tonight." Long Joseph was full of wounded dignity, despite the fact that it was only his fifth visit, and all of them at Renie's strenuous urging. But he had settled back now, pouting like a scolded child.

She told him as much as she could, leaving out the more arcane bits of speculation and avoiding entirely the story of her last hour in Mister J's. She was too old and far too independent to be forbidden to do what she was doing, but she could not ignore the possibility that he might decide to protect her from herself, perhaps by damaging her pad or other equipment after a few drinks reminded him he was partly descended from warrior Zulus. She could carry on with her investigation from work if she had to, but she had already involved the Poly more than she'd liked, and she was also far behind on work because of her illness.

Long Joseph was oddly quiet after she finished her explanations. "I'm not surprised you almost kill yourself, working all day and then running around with all that other mess," he said at last. "That sounds like a lot of craziness to me. Something in a computer made that boy sick? I never heard of that."

"I don't know. I'm just telling you what I've been thinking about and doing. I have no proof."

Except one very blurry picture of a city, she thought. *But only because I took my pad with me to Susan's. Only because I wasn't at home when that fire happened.*

As if hearing her thoughts, her father abruptly said: "You think somebody came and set our flat on fire?"

"I . . . I don't know. I don't want to think it's that serious. I've been assuming it was just a normal fire—you know, an accident."

" 'Cause if you been messing with the wrong people, they'll burn you out. I know about that, girl. I seen it happen." Long Joseph stretched out his legs, staring at his stockinged feet. Despite his height, he suddenly seemed very small and very old. He leaned down, grunting softly as he felt on the floor for his shoes. "And now you think someone following you?"

"Maybe. I don't know. I just don't know anything right now."

He looked up at her, sullen and a little frightened. "I don't know what to say either, Irene. I hate to be hoping that my daughter is crazy in the head, but I don't like that other idea very much." He straightened up, captured shoes in his hand. "Let me put these on, then we better go see that boy."

After the visit, she led her father to the changing room so he could take off his Ensuit, then carefully changed her own, folding it before dropping it into the chute marked for the purpose. When she had finished, she walked to the restroom, sat down on the toilet, and cried. It started modestly, but within a few moments she could barely catch her breath. Her nose was even running, but she didn't care.

He was there, somewhere. Her Stephen, the little baby boy with the surprised eyes who used to crawl into her bed, was there somewhere inside that body. The lights on the machines, the monitors on his skull, all the instrumentation of modern medicine—or as much of it as was available in the Durban Outskirt Medical Facility—declared that he was not brain-dead. Not yet. But his limbs were more contorted every day, and his fingers had curled into tight fists despite the physical therapy. What was that horrible, horrible phrase? "Persistent vegetative state." Like a shriveled root. Nothing left but something stuck in the ground, darkly motionless both inside and out.

She couldn't feel him—that was the most horrifying thing. !Xabbu had said his soul was somewhere else, and although it was the sort of spritualist homily that she usually nodded at while remaining privately scornful, she had to admit she felt the same way. The body was Stephen's, and it was still alive, but the real Stephen was not in it.

But what was the difference between *that* and a persistent vegetative state?

She was tired, so tired. The more she ran, the more she felt stuck in the same place, and she did not know where she would find the strength to keep running. At times like this, even a death as terrible as her mother's seemed a blessing by contrast—at least there was rest and peace for the victim and some kind of release for the mourning family.

Renie pulled down a hank of industrial-rough toilet paper and blew her nose, then took some more and wiped her eyes and cheeks. Her father would be getting restless. The kind of old magazines lying around the waiting room were not the kind of magazines that would keep his attention. Why was that? Were hospital magazines only ever provided by kindly little old ladies? The scarcity of sports news or semi-naked women showed that the reading material was never selected by men.

She dabbed at her face a little more as she stood in front of the mirror. The smell of disinfectant was so strong she thought her eyes would start watering all over again. That would be perfect, she thought sourly—work hard to look like you haven't been crying, then come out of the toilet with your eyes streaming anyway. She gave her lashes a last defiant blot.

Her father had indeed become restless, but he had found something to do. He was annoying a nicely-dressed woman only a little older than Renie who had slid all the way down to the end of the couch to avoid Long Joseph's attentions. As Renie approached, her father scooted a little way nearer.

". . . A terrible ruckus, you see. Fire trucks, helicopters, ambulances. . . " He was recounting the fire at their flatblock. Renie smiled a little, wondering if by showing up she'd spoiled the story of how he'd carried out all those women and children by himself.

"Come on, Papa," she began, then recognized the woman as Patricia Mwete, Soki's mother. They had not spoken since the disastrous conversation when Stephen's friend had fallen abruptly into seizure. "Oh, hello, Patricia," she said politely. "Papa, this is Soki's mother. Sorry, I didn't recognize you at first."

The other woman regarded her face—undoubtedly still tear-stained despite her best efforts—with a curious mixture of fear and uncomfortable sympathy. "Hello, Irene. Nice to meet you, Mister . . . " She nodded carefully toward Long Joseph, obviously not yet sure that he wasn't going to come sliding farther down the couch toward her.

Renie paused for a moment, uncertain of what to say. She wanted to ask why Patricia was here, but the curious, almost superstitious courtesy of hospital waiting rooms didn't permit it. "We've been visiting Stephen," she said instead.

"How is he?"

Renie shook her head. "Just the same."

"They make you wear a foolish damn suit," Long Joseph offered. "Like my boy had the fever or something."

"It's not for that . . . " Renie began, but Patricia interrupted her.

"Soki's in for tests. Three days, two nights. Just routine." She said that last defiantly, as if daring Renie to tell her otherwise. "But he gets so lonely, so I come see him after work." She lifted a package.

"I brought him some fruit. Some grapes." She seemed about to cry herself.

Renie knew that Soki's troubles had not been either as mild or temporary as Patricia had claimed during their last meeting. She wanted to ask more, but didn't think it was the right time. "Well, give him my best. We'd better be going. I've got a long day tomorrow."

As her father began the apparently complicated process of standing up, Patricia suddenly put her hand on Renie's arm. "Your Stephen," she said, then stopped. The look of controlled worry had slipped; a mask of terror peeped through.

"Yes?"

Patricia swallowed and wavered a little, like someone about to faint. Her formal business clothes seemed the only thing keeping her upright. "I just hope he gets better," she finished lamely. "I just hope they all get better."

Long Joseph was already heading for the exit. Renie watched him a little anxiously, as if he, too, were a troubled child. "Me, too, Patricia. Don't forget to say hello to Soki for me, okay?"

Patricia nodded her head and settled back on the couch, feeling for a magazine on the table without looking.

"She wanted to tell me something," Renie said as they waited for the bus. "Either that or she wanted to ask me something about Stephen."

"What are you talking about?" Her father prodded a discarded plastic bag with the toe of his shoe.

"Her boy Soki . . . something happened to him, too. While he was on the net. Like Stephen. I saw him having a fit afterward."

Long Joseph looked back toward the hospital entrance. "Her boy in a coma, too?"

"No. Whatever happened, it was different. But his brain was affected. I know it."

They sat side by side in silence until the bus pulled up. When her father was settled into his seat, he turned to her. "'Somebody should find those net people, make them answer. Somebody should do something."

I am doing something, Papa, she wanted to say, but Renie knew that she was not the kind of somebody he had in mind.

It was dark. Even the stars barely shone, faint as mica chips in black sand. The only light in all the universe, it seemed, was the small fire burning within the circle of stones.

She heard voices, and knew that she was listening to her own children, and yet in some way they were also a tribe of strangers, a band that traveled through unimaginable lands. !Xabbu was one of them, and although she could not see him, she knew he was sitting beside her, one of the thin murmur of invisible souls.

A greater darkness lay on the distant horizon, the space it occupied the only part of the sky that contained no stars. It was a vast triangular shape, like a pyramid, but it stretched up impossibly high, as though they sat close to its base. As she stared at the great shadow, the voices around her murmured and sang. She knew they were all aware of that tall dark mass. They feared it, but they also feared to leave it behind, this the only familiar thing in all the night.

"What is it?" she whispered. A voice that she thought was !Xabbu's answered her.

"It is the place where the Burned One lives. On this night, he comes."

"We have to run away!" She suddenly knew that something was moving out beyond the firelight, something that lived in darkness the way fish lived in water. They were being stalked by something vast and tenebrous, and in all the twilit universe the only uncorrupted light came from the flames of this small fire.

"But he will only take a few," the voice said. "The others will be safe. Only a few."

"No! We can't let him have any of them!" She reached out, but the arm she clutched turned insubstantial as smoke. The murmuring grew louder. Something was coming nearer, something huge that rattled the trees and stones, that hoarsely breathed. She tried to pull her friend back, but he seemed to come apart in her hands. "Don't! Don't go!"

Old Night itself was coming down on them, the jaws of darkness stretching wide. . . .

Renie sat up, panting. The murmuring still filled her ears, louder now, voices gasping and growling. Something was thumping in the darkness nearby. She did not know where she was.

"Quiet yourself in there!" someone shouted, and she remembered that they were in the shelter. But the sounds were not distant. Bodies were struggling on the floor only a meter away from her.

"Papa!" She fumbled for the torch, turned it on. By its light she could see limbs moving erratically, thrashing and rolling, banging up against the fiberboard partitions. She could see the pale striped length

of her father's pajamas, and nearby another torch lying on its side, spilling light like a tipped goblet. She rolled off the bed and grabbed Long Joseph's attacker around the neck, shouting: "Help! Someone, help us!"

There were more noises of complaint from other compartments, but some of the occupants seemed to be rousing themselves. She kept her grip on the stranger and curled her fingers in his hair, then pulled back hard. He let out a high-pitched shriek of pain and clawed at her hand.

Her father used the moment's respite to scramble free. The stranger had wriggled loose from Renie, but instead of fleeing, he crawled into a corner of the compartment and huddled there with his hands wrapped around his head to ward off further attacks. Renie kept the flashlight on him, then saw her father coming back with a long dull carving knife in his hand.

"Papa! Don't!"

"I kill the bastard." He was breathing painfully hard. She could smell the rank alcohol sweat coming off him. "Follow my daughter around!"

"We don't know! He could have got the wrong room. Just wait, damn you!" She crawled a little way toward the cowering stranger. "Who are you?"

"He knew what he doing. I hear him whisper your name."

Renie had a moment of horror—could it be !Xabbu, looking for her? But even in partial darkness, the stranger seemed far too large. She reached out carefully and touched his shoulder. "Who are you?" she repeated.

The man looked up, blinking in the torchlight. He had a cut across his hairline which was sheeting blood down his forehead. It took her a long moment to recognize him.

"Jeremiah?" she said. "From Doctor Van Bleeck's house?"

He stared for a moment, clearly unable to see her behind the torch. "Irene Sulaweyo?"

"Yes, it's me. For God's sake, what's happening here?" She stood. Already several people from the neighboring compartments were gathering outside the curtain, some with defensive weapons in hand. She went out and thanked them, telling them it had been a case of mistaken identity. They gradually dispersed, all relived, some muttering imprecations about her drunkard father.

She went back inside to find Jeremiah Dako sitting against the wall, watching her father with some distrust. Renie found the small electric lantern and turned it on, then gave Dako some paper toweling to wipe his bloodied face. Her father, who was still staring at the intruder as though he might sprout fur and fangs at any moment, allowed himself to be conducted to a folding chair.

"I know this man, Papa. He works for Doctor Van Bleeck."

"What's he doing this hour, coming round here? He your boyfriend?"

Dako snorted with indignation.

"No, he's not my boyfriend." She turned. "What *are* you doing here at . . . " she looked at her watch, ". . . one in the morning?"

"The doctor sent me. I couldn't find your number to call you."

She shook her head, puzzled. "She has my number—I know she does."

Jeremiah stared at the bloodsoaked paper in his hand for a moment, then looked up at Renie, eyes blinking rapidly.

Everybody's crying today, she thought. *What's going on?*

"Doctor Susan is in the hospital," he said abruptly, furious and miserable. "She's very bad . . . very bad."

"Oh, my God." Renie reflexively tore off several more sheets of paper towel and gave them to him. "What happened?"

"Some men beat her up. They broke into the house." Dako just held the towel. A rill of blood descended to his eyebrow. "She asked to see you." He closed his eyes. "I think . . . I think she might die."

Smugly ensconced in his role as defender of the household, Long Joseph at first insisted on accompanying them. Only after Renie pointed out that they might have to spend several hours in the hospital waiting room did he decide to remain at the shelter as a bulwark against other, less forgivable prowlers.

Jeremiah drove swiftly through the nearly empty streets. "I don't know how the bastards got in. I went to see my mother—it's the night I always go. She's very old now, and she likes me to come and do things for her." The piece of toweling gleamed on his dark forehead, rorschached by drying blood. "I don't know how the bastards got in," he repeated. It was obviously something he considered a personal failure, despite his absence. In such circumstances, Renie knew, the housekeeper or other employees were usually the first suspects, but it was hard to doubt Dako's misery.

"Was it a robbery?"

"They didn't take much—some jewelry. But they found Doctor

Susan in her lab downstairs, so they must have known about the elevator. I think they tried to make her tell where she kept the money. They broke everything—everything!" He sobbed, then clenched his lips tightly and for a few moments drove in silence.

"They destroyed things in her lab?"

He scowled. "They smashed things. They are like animals. We keep no money in the house! If they wanted to steal, why did they not steal the machines? They are worth more than the few rands we keep around to tip delivery boys."

"And how did you know the doctor wanted to see me?"

"She told me, while we were waiting for the ambulance. She could not talk much." Another sob shook him. "She was just an old woman! Who could do such a thing?"

Renie shook her head. "Terrible people." She could not cry. The streetlights sliding past had lulled her into a sort of dream state, as though she were a ghost haunting her own body. What was going on? Why did dreadful things keep happening to those around her? "Terrible, terrible people," she said.

Asleep, Susan Van Bleeck looked like an alien creature. She was festooned with sensors and tubes, and only the mummifying bandages seemed to be holding her discolored and broken body in something like human form. Her breath wheezed in and out of her parted lips. Jeremiah burst into tears once more and slumped to the floor beside her bed, hands clasped at the back of his neck as if to keep his head from flying off with the force of his grief.

As horrifying as it was to see her friend and teacher this way, Renie was still in a state of cold removal. This was the second time today she had been in a hospital, standing over the body of a silent loved one. At least the Westville University Medical Center did not have a Bukavu quarantine.

A young black doctor wearing a stained smock and glasses with a taped nosepiece looked in. "She needs rest," he said, frowning. "Concussion, lots of bones broken." He gestured loosely down the ward full of sleeping patients. "And it's not visiting time."

"She asked to see me," Renie explained. "She said it was important."

He frowned again, already distracted by some other thought, and wandered out.

Renie borrowed a chair from beside one of the other beds. The patient in the bed, a cadaverously thin young man, blinked awake to watch her with a caged beast's eyes, but did not speak or move. She returned to the bed and adjusted herself in a comfortable position to keep vigil, taking the less-bandaged of Susan's hands in hers.

She had sagged into a half-sleep when she felt a pressure on her fingers. She sat up. Doctor Van Bleeck's eyes were open and moving from side to side, as though she were surrounded by fast-moving shapes.

"It's me, Renie." She gently squeezed. "Irene. Jeremiah's here, too."

Susan stared at her for a moment, then relaxed. Her mouth was open, but nothing came out past the tube except a dry sound like an empty paper sack being blown along a street. Renie stood to go in search of water, but Dako, kneeling beside her, pointed to the "Nothing By Mouth" sign hung on the bedstand. "They put wire in her jaw."

"You don't need to talk anyway," Renie told her. "We'll just stay here with you."

"Oh, little grandmother." Jeremiah pressed his forehead to the tube-girded arm. "I should have been there. How could I let this happen?"

Susan pulled her hand free from Renie's grip and lifted it slowly until she could touch Dako's face. Tears from his cheeks ran into her bandages. Then she gradually and deliberately put her hand back into Renie's once more.

"Can you answer questions?"

A squeeze.

"Two squeezes for no, then?"

Another squeeze.

"Jeremiah said you wanted to see me."

Yes.

"About the thing we talked about? The city?"

Yes.

Renie suddenly wondered if she could be misinterpreting, since she hadn't received anything but single squeezes. Susan's face was so swollen it was hard even to be sure of her expression; only her eyes moved.

"Do you want me to go home now and let you sleep?"

Two squeezes, quite firm. *No.*

"Okay, let me think. Did you find the place in the picture?"

No.

"But you found out something about it."

The squeeze was gentle and prolonged.

"Maybe?"

Yes.

Renie hesitated. "Did the men who hurt you . . . did they have something to do with this? What we talked about?"

Another long, slow pressure. *Maybe.*

"I'm trying to think of yes or no questions. This is really difficult. Do you think you could write or type?"

A long pause, then two squeezes.

"Then is there someone I should talk to? Someone who gave you information and who could give me the same information."

No. Then, a moment later, an additional pressure. *Yes.*

Renie briskly named all of Susan's colleagues she could remember, but received a negative response to all of them. She worked her way through various police and network agencies, but had no better luck. As she despairingly considered the amount of time an elimination process carried out entirely in manual binary might take, Susan pushed her hand farther into Renie's and turned it so all her fingers were against Renie's palm. They moved fitfully, like the legs of a dying moth. Renie gripped the old woman's hand, trying to give comfort. Susan hissed at her.

"What?"

The doctor laboriously moved her fingers in Renie's palm again. Where the full-hand squeezes had been easy to interpret, these movements were so light and so cramped as to seem nothing more than wriggling. Renie was defeated. "This is terrible. There must be some better way—typing, writing notes."

"She can't type," Jeremiah said mournfully. "Even when she could still talk. I tried before. I gave her pad to her, when she said call you, but she couldn't push the squeezer keys hard enough."

Susan weakly bumped her hand against Renie's palm again, glaring from the purple and red mask. Renie stared.

"That's it. That's what she's doing! Typing!"

Susan opened her hand again and squeezed Renie's fingers.

"But only the right hand?"

Two squeezes. *No.* Susan bumped the heel of her hand against Renie's palm, then laboriously lifted her arm and moved it across her body. Renie gently caught it and brought it back.

"I get it. You push like that when it means you're switching typing hands. That's what you mean, isn't it?"

Yes.

It was still a laborious process. Susan had great difficulty making Renie understand what squeezer keys the fingers of her right hand would be touching if they belonged to her left. It took almost an hour, with frequent stops for yes-and-no editing and correction, before she had finished her message. Susan had grown weaker throughout, and during the last fifteen minutes had barely been able to move her fingers.

Renie stared at the letters she had jotted in the margin of the hospital diet sheet. "B-L-U-D-G-A-N-C-H-R-I-T-B-C-R-F-L. But it doesn't make sense. Some of it must be abbreviated."

A final, weary squeeze.

Renie stood and leaned over the bed to brush her lips against Susan's broken-veined cheek. "I'll figure it out, somehow. Now, we've kept you awake far too long. You need some sleep."

Jeremiah stood, too. "I'll give you a ride back." He leaned over the doctor. "Then I'll be right back, little grandmother. Don't you be scared."

Susan made a whistling noise that was almost a moan. He paused. She stared at him, clearly frustrated by her inability to speak, then at Renie. Her eyes blinked slowly, once, twice.

"Yes, you're tired. You sleep now." Dako also leaned and kissed her. Renie wondered if that was the first time he had ever done so.

On the way out to the car, she had a sudden feeling that she knew what those blinks had been meant to say. *Good-bye.*

By the time Dako dropped her off, it was past four in the morning. She was too full of furious, frustrated anger to sleep, so she spent the hours before dawn staring at her pad, trying every way she could to find some shape behind the sequence of letters Doctor Van Bleeck had given her. The databanks of the net dumped back hundreds of names from all over the world—a dozen came from Brazil alone, and almost as many from Thailand—that actually contained most of the letters in sequence, but none of them seemed particularly likely. But if she couldn't turn up any better information, she would have to contact every one of them.

She watched as a codebreaking algorithm she had downloaded from the Polytechnic library assembled thousands of combinations that fit smaller segments of the letters, a dizzying assortment that made her eyes ache and her head buzz.

Renie smoked and watched the screen, punching in additional queries as they occurred to her. The day's first light began to leak in through the cracks in the roof. Her father snored happily in his bed, still wearing his slippers. Somewhere else in the shelter, some other early riser was playing a radio, bringing in news in an Asian language she didn't recognize.

Renie was just about to call !Xabbu, who she knew got up with the dawn, and tell him the news about Susan, when she suddenly saw the obvious thing she had missed. The last five letters of the doctor's laborious message: B-C-R-F-L. Be Careful.

Her irritation at her own weary blindness was quickly pushed aside by a clench of fear. The doctor, in the hospital with critical injuries quite possibly given to her by the very people Renie had offended, had taken a great deal of effort to tell her old student something that should have gone without saying. Susan Van Bleeck was not someone who wasted effort at the best of times, let alone when struggling for every movement.

Renie set the code algorithm back to work minus the last five letters, then phoned !Xabbu. After some time his landlady answered, keeping the visual blacked out, and said crossly that he was not in his room.

"He said he sleeps outside sometime," Renie said. "Could he be out there?"

"That little man isn't anywhere here, I told you—not inside, not outside. Tell the truth, I don't think he came back last night at all." The line went dead.

Her fears rapidly multiplying, she checked her mail to see if !Xabbu had left her a message. He had not, but to her astonishment, there was a voicemail from Doctor Van Bleeck.

"Hello, Irene, I'm sorry it's taken me so long to get back to you." Susan's voice sounded strong and cheerful, and for a moment Renie was completely baffled. *"I'll try to get hold of you later tonight directly, but I'm in the middle of something right now and don't have time to talk much, so I thought I'd just dump this quickly."*

It had been recorded before the attack. It was a message from another world, another life.

"I haven't found anything definite yet, but I've got a few connections that may prove fruitful. Let me tell you, dear, this whole thing is very strange indeed. I can't find anything like an actual match with your picture anywhere, and I've had every single urban area on the globe under scrutiny. I know things about Reykjavik that even the Reykjaviktims, or whatever they call themselves, don't know. And, although I know you didn't agree, I've been running searches

on image banks as well, just in case it was something cobbled up for a simworld or a netflick. No luck there either.

"But I have had some success with statistical similarity searches—nothing definite, just some intriguing clusters of hits. Martine should be calling back soon, and she may have some ideas, too. In any case, I won't say more until some of the calls I've put out get answered—I'm too old to enjoy looking foolish—but I'll just say I'm going to be renewing some previous acquaintances. Very previous.

"Anyway, dear, that's it. Just wanted to let you know I was working on it. I haven't forgotten. And I hope you haven't become so wrapped up in this yourself that you're skipping meals or sleep. You used to have a very bad habit of trying to make up for initial laziness with last-moment diligence. Not a good plan, Irene.

"Take care. I'll talk to you in person, later."

The line clicked. Renie stared at her pad, wishing that she could make it say more, feeling that if she could just push the right button, her teacher would come back on and tell her all the things she'd been holding back. Susan *had* talked to her in person later, which made the whole thing an even crueler joke.

Previous acquaintances. What could that mean? She had already tried the names of all of the doctor's colleagues she could remember.

Renie sent the computer searching through various educational guild records, trying to match the letters of Susan's message with the names of anyone at any of the institutions that had employed her. Her eyes were blurry from staring at the padscreen, but there was nothing else to do until it was time to go to work. There wasn't a chance in hell she would be able to catch any sleep in her current frame of mind. Besides, work made it easier not to worry about !Xabbu.

She was on her seventh or eighth cigarette since dawn and watching a coffee tab dissolve in her cup when someone tapped lightly on the front of the partition, near the curtain that served as the front wall. Startled, she held her breath for a moment. She looked around for something to use as a weapon, but the torch had disappeared somewhere. She decided that the cup of boiling water in her hand would have to suffice. As she moved quietly toward the curtain, her father coughed in his sleep and rolled over.

She jerked back the heavy cloth. !Xabbu looked up at her, slightly startled.

"Did I wake you. . . ?" he began, but did not finish his sentence. Renie stepped forward and hugged him so incautiously that she spilled coffee on her own hand. She swore and dropped the cup, which shattered on the concrete.

"Damn! Ow! Sorry!" She waved her singed hand.

!Xabbu stepped forward. "Are you well?"

"Just burned myself." She sucked her fingers.

"No, I mean . . . " He stepped inside, pulling the curtain closed. "I . . . I had a fearful dream. I feared for you. So I came here."

She stared. He did look quite out of sorts, his clothes rumpled and clearly donned in haste. "You . . . but why didn't you call?"

He looked down at his feet. "I am ashamed to say that I did not think of it. I awakened and was afraid, and set out to come here." He squatted beside the wall, a simple, lithe movement. There was something about the way he did it that reminded Renie he was not entirely of her world, something that remained archaic despite his modern clothes. "I could not find a bus, so I walked."

"From Chesterville? Oh, !Xabbu, you must be exhausted. I'm fine—healthy, anyway—but bad things have happened."

She quickly told him about Doctor Van Bleeck, describing what she knew of the attack and its aftermath. Instead of growing wide with surprise at the news, !Xabbu's heavy lidded eyes narrowed, as though he were being forced to look at something painful.

"This is very sad." He shook his head. "Ay! I dreamed that she shot an arrow at you and that it pierced your heart. It was a very strong dream, very strong." He clapped his hands softly together, then pressed them tight. "I feared it meant that you had been injured in some way by something the two of you had done."

"She shot something to me, but I hope it will save people, not kill them." She curled her lip. "Or at least, I hope it will help us find out if I'm going mad or not."

When she had finished explaining the doctor's messages and her night's work, speaking swiftly but quietly so as not to bring her father into things any earlier than she had to, the little man remained squatting on the floor, his head down.

"There are crocodiles in this river," he said at last. In her weariness, it took her a moment to make sense of what he said. "We have pretended as long as we could that they were only rocks pushing above the surface, or floating logs. But we can ignore them no longer."

Renie sighed. She had sparked a bit in relief at seeing !Xabbu safe. Now she suddenly felt that she *could* sleep—sleep for a month, given the chance. "Too many things have happened," she agreed. "Stephen lost, Stephen's friend with some kind of brain damage, what happened to us in the club. Now our flatblock's been burned and Susan's been attacked and beaten. We'd be idiots not to believe something's very wrong here. But," she felt her anger turn sour and miserable, "*we can't prove anything.* Nothing! We'd have to bribe the police just to get them not to laugh out loud when we told them."

"Unless we find that city, and finding it teaches us something. Or unless we go back in again." His face was curiously blank. "To that place."

"I don't think I could ever go back in there," she said. She blinked, sleepiness pulling at her very hard. "No, I could—for Stephen. But I don't know what good it would do us. They'll just be waiting for us this time. Unless we could find some better, more secret way to hack in—" She stopped, thinking.

"Do you have an idea?" asked !Xabbu. "Surely a place like that would have very good . . . what is the word? Security."

"Yes, of course. No. That's not what I was thinking. I was just re-membering something Susan told me once. I had been involved in some stupid thing—messing with the college record systems, just for fun, something like that. Anyway, she was completely scorched, not because I'd done it, she said, but because I was risking my chance to make something of myself." Renie ran her fingers across her pad-screen, calling up options. "She told me the thing itself was no big deal—all the students did it. *She'd* done it, she said, and lots worse. She'd been quite a daredevil in the early days of the net."

Long Joseph Sulaweyo grunted and sat up in bed, stared at Renie and !Xabbu for a moment with no sign of recognition, then fell back into his thin mattress, snoring again within seconds.

"So you are thinking . . . "

"She said 'previous acquaintances, *very* previous.' What do you want to bet she's been talking to some of her ancient hacker buddies? What do you want to bet?" She stared at the screen. "Now, all I have to do is think up some kind of search criteria for retired online troublemakers, match it to what we've got in the way of letters, and just see if we don't come up with Doctor Susan's mystery source!"

It took fifteen minutes, but the hit, when it came, seemed conclu-sive.

"Murat Sagar Singh—and look at this guy's background! University of Natal, same time as Susan, then extended work with Telemorphix, S.A., and a bunch of smaller companies over the next twenty years or so. And there's a six-year gap just a few years after he got out of

school—what do you want to bet he was working for the government
or military intelligence?''

"But this Sagar Singh—those letters do not match . . . ''

She grinned. "Ah, but look at this—he had a handle! That's a code-
name that hackers used, so they could sign their work without using
their real names, which tends to get you prosecuted." She tilted the
pad so !Xabbu could see it better. "Blue Dog Anchorite. The world
must be full of Singhs, but she knew there wouldn't be many of
those!''

!Xabbu nodded. "It seems that you have solved the puzzle. Where
is this person? Does he still live in this country?''

"Well, that's a problem." Renie frowned. "The addresses kind of dry
up about twenty years ago. Maybe he got into some sort of trouble
and had to disappear. Of course, a gifted hacker can disappear in plain
sight." She ran a few more criteria through and sat back to wait for
an answer.

"Girl?" Long Joseph was sitting up again, this time eyeing !Xabbu
with obvious suspicion. "What the hell's going on here?''

"Nothing, Papa. I'll get you some coffee.''

As she poured water into a cup, guiltily remembering the shards of
her own mug which were still scattered in front of their compartment
where someone might step on them, !Xabbu stood over her pad.

"Renie," he said, eyeing a row of listings, "there is a word coming
up here several times. Perhaps it is a place or a person? I have not
heard of it.''

"What?''

"Something called 'TreeHouse.' ''

Before she could reply, the pad's phone light began to blink. Renie
set down the cup and the package of coffee tablets and hurried to
answer it.

It was Jeremiah Dako, and he was crying. Before he had even said
an intelligible word, Renie already knew what had happened.

CHAPTER 18

Red And White

Gally could barely stand. Paul stooped and lifted him in his arms and carried him out of the Oysterhouse. The boy was sobbing so convulsively it was difficult to hold him.

"No! I can't leave them ! Bay! Bay's in there!"

"You can't help. We have to get out. They'll be coming back—the ones who did that."

Gally struggled, but weakly. Paul pushed out through the door and plunged into the forest without even looking to see if they were observed. Surprise and speed were their best hopes. The light was dying, and they could be well into the thick forest before anyone followed them.

He staggered for a long time with the boy in his arms. When he could run no farther, he set the boy down as carefully as he could and then slumped to the ground, cushioned by a thick carpet of leaves. The sky had turned the dark gray of a wet rock. The branches over- head were only wiry silhouettes.

"Where do we go?" When he got no response, he rolled over. Gally was curled like a woodlouse, knees tucked, head in hands. The boy was still crying, but most of the force was gone. Paul leaned over and shook him. "Gally! Where do we go? We can't just stay here forever."

"They're gone." It was a kind of astonishment, as though it were only now becoming clear to him. "Gone."

"I know. There's nothing we can do. If we don't find our way out, the same will happen to us." In fact, Paul knew that he would face worse things if his two pursuers ever caught him—but how could he know that, and how could it be true, in any case? The strangers had . . . *cored* the Oysterhouse children, torn out their insides.

"We belonged together." Gally spoke slowly, as though reciting a lesson he wasn't entirely sure of. "I don't remember a time when it was different. We crossed the Black Ocean together."

Paul sat up. "What ocean? Where? When did this happen?"

"I don't know." Gally shook his head. "I only remember traveling— that's the first thing I remember. And we were together."

"All of you? That can't have been very long ago—some of . . . some of them were only a few years old."

"We found the littleuns along the way. Or they found us. We're twice as many now as when I first remember. Twice as many. . . . " His voice trailed off and he began to weep again, a thin hitching noise. Paul could only put an arm around the boy's shoulders and draw him to his chest.

Why did this child remember more of his short life than Paul did of his own? Why did *everyone* seem to know more of the world than he did?

The boy calmed. Paul rocked him against his chest, awkwardly, but he had no better idea. "You crossed the black ocean? Where is that?"

"Far away." Gally's voice was muffled in his chest. The day had almost failed now, and Paul could see only different forms of shadow. "I don't know—the big ones told me about it."

"Big ones?"

"They're gone now. Some stayed behind in places they liked, or they got stuck, but the rest of us moved on, 'cause we were looking for something. Sometimes the big ones just disappeared, like."

"What were you looking for?"

"The White Ocean. That's what we called it. But I don't know where it is. One day, the last one bigger than me was gone, and then it was my turn to lead. But I don't know where the White Ocean is. I don't know where it is at all, and now it doesn't matter."

He said this with a terrible, weary finality, and grew quiet in Paul's arms.

For a long time, Paul sat and held him, listening to the night noises, trying to forget—or at least to avoid reviewing—what he had seen in the Oysterhouse. Crickets ratcheted all around. The wind rustled the uppermost treetops. Everything was very calm, as if the universe had paused.

Paul realized there was no movement against his breast. Gally was not breathing. Paul sprang up in a panic, rolling the boy onto the ground.

"What? What are you doing?" Gally's voice was sluggish with sleep, but strong.

"'I'm sorry, I thought . . . " He gently laid his hand on the boy's chest. There was no movement. Equally gently, moving with an instinct or memory he could put no name to, he slid his hand up to the hollow beneath the narrow jaw. He could feel no pulse. He tested himself. His own heart was beating rapidly.

"Gally, where do you come from?"

The boy mumbled something. Paul leaned closer. "What?"

"You're the big one, now. . . ." Gally murmured, surrendering again to sleep.

"Bishop Humphrey, he said this was the best way." Despite his miserable, dark-ringed eyes, the boy spoke firmly.

It had been a bad night, full of bad dreams for both of them. Paul was so glad to see the daylight again that he found it hard even to argue, although he was not entirely sure he trusted the bishop's advice.

"He also said there was some kind of horrible something this way. Something dangerous."

Gally gave him a pained look which clearly said that Paul was now the oldest and tallest, and shouldn't burden his younger subordinates with such worries. Paul saw a certain justice in this. He fell silent and concentrated on following the boy through the thick forest tangle. Neither of them spoke, which made traveling a little easier. Paul was heavily distracted: the bright morning could not quite burn away his terrible memories, either of what had happened at the Oysterhouse or of the night's dreaming.

In the dream he had been a sort of herder, forcing animals onto a great ship. He did not recognize them, although there was something of sheep about them and something of cattle. Bleating, eyes rolling, the creatures had tried to resist, turning in the doorway as though to struggle for freedom, but Paul and the other silent workers had forced them up over the threshold and into the darkness. When all the animals were loaded, he had pushed the great door into place and locked it. Then, as he stepped away, he had seen that the place of imprisonment was not so much a ship as some kind of huge bowl or cup—no, a *cauldron,* that was the word, a thing for boiling and rendering. He could hear increasing noises of fear from within, and when he finally awakened, he was still full of shame over this betrayal.

The dream memories lingered. As he tracked along behind Gally, the huge cup-shaped thing shimmered in his mind's eye. He felt he had seen it before in another world, another life.

A head full of shadows. And all the sunlight in the world won't drive them away. He rubbed at his temples as if to squeeze out the bad thoughts and almost walked into a swinging branch.

Gally found a stream which ran past them all the way down to the great river beside the Oysterhouse, and they followed its course upward, through sloping lands where the grass grew thick in the clearings and the birds made shrill noises of warning at their approach, fluttering from branch to branch ahead of them until the invaders were safely distant from hidden nests. Some of the trees were laden with blossoms, powdery flares of white and pink and yellow, and for the first time Paul wondered what season it was.

Gally did not understand the question.

"It's not a place, it's a time," Paul said "When there are flowers, it should be spring."

The boy shook his head. He looked pale and incomplete, as though a part of him had been destroyed with his tribe of fellow children. "But there *are* flowers here, governor. None near the Bishop's. Stands to reason all places couldn't be the same, then everything would happen all in the same spot. Confusion, y'see. Everyone'd be running into each other—a terrible mess."

"Do you know what year it is, then?"

Gally looked at him again, this time with something almost like alarm. "Yee-ee-r?"

"Never mind." Paul closed his eyes for a moment to simplify matters. His mind seemed full of complicated strings, all knotted together, the whole an insoluble tangle. Why should Gally not knowing something like what year or season it was, things which he himself hadn't even thought of until just this moment, make him so uneasy?

I am Paul, he told himself. *I was a soldier. I ran away from a war. Two people . . . two things . . . are following me, and I know they must not find me. I had a dream about a big cup. I know something about a bird, and about a giant. And I know other things that I can't always put names to. And now I am in the Eight Squared, whatever the hell that is, looking for a way out.*

It was not a satisfying inventory, but it gave him something to cling to. He was real. He had a name, and he even had a destination—at least for the moment.

"Hard climbing now," said Gally. "We're near the edge of the square."

The slope had indeed changed, and now mounted upward steeply. The forest began to thin, replaced by low, scrubby bushes and moss-covered slabs of rock, bejeweled here and there with clusters of wild-flowers. Paul was growing tired, and was impressed by his companion's vigor: Gally had not slowed at all, even as Paul was forced to bend almost double against the rising angle of the ground.

The whole world suddenly seemed to shimmer and blur. Paul struggled to find his balance, but in that moment there was neither up nor down. His own body seemed to grow insubstantial, to drift into component fragments. He shouted, or thought he did, but a moment later things were ordinary again, and Gally seemed not even to have noticed. Paul shivered, wondering if his own weary body could have betrayed his mind.

When they reached the top of the hill, Paul turned to look back. The land behind them seemed nothing like the bishop's grid—trees and hills ran seamlessly together. He could see the bend of the river sparkling blue-white in the sun, and the now sinister bulk of the Oyster-house huddling beside it. He could see the spire of Bishop Humphrey's castle through the woods, and farther away other towers jutting up through the great blanket of trees.

"That's where we're going," Gally said. Paul turned. The boy was pointing to a spot some miles away, where a thickly forested ridge of hills descended almost to another curving stretch of the river.

"Why didn't we just take a boat?" Paul watched the light bounce up from the surface, covering the wide river with a mesh of diamond-shaped glints so that it almost seemed made from something other than water, like moving glass or frozen fire. "Wouldn't that be faster?"

Gally laughed, then looked at him uneasily. "You can't cross squares on the river. You know that, don't you? The river . . . the river's not like that."

"But we went on it."

"Just from the inn to the Oysterhouse. That's inside a square—permitted, like. Besides, there's other reasons to stay off it. That's why we went at night." The boy looked at him with a worried expression. "If you go on the river, *they* can find you."

"They? You mean those two. . . ?"

Gally shook his head. "Not just them. Anyone that's looking for you. The big ones taught me that. You can't hide on the river."

He could not explain any more clearly, and at last Paul let the subject drop. They crossed the hilltop and began to descend.

Paul could not immediately tell that they had entered into another square, as Gally called it. The land seemed much the same, gorse and bracken in the heights thickening to forested hillsides as they moved downward. The only immediate difference was that there seemed to be more animal life on this side of the hill. Paul heard rustling in the bushes and saw an occasional bright eye peering out from the foliage. Once a drift of tiny piglets the color of spring grass came trotting out into the open, but they quickly fled, squawking in alarm or annoyance, when they saw Paul and Gally.

Gally did not know anything about them or the other creatures. "I've never been here before, have I?"

"But you said you came here from somewhere else."

"We didn't come in this way, governor. All I know about is what everyone knows about. Like that." He pointed. Paul squinted, but could see nothing more unusual than the endlessly meshed branches of the forest. "No," the boy told him, "you have to get down here, lower."

Kneeling, Paul could see a single mountain peak between the trunks, so far away that it seemed painted with a thinner paint than the rest of the landscape. "What is it?"

"It's a mountain, you eejit." Gally laughed, for the first time all day. "But down at the bottom of it, they say, is where the Red King is sleeping. And if someone ever wakes him up, then the whole Eight Squared will just go away." He snapped his fingers. "Poof! Like that! That's the story they tell, anyway—I don't see how anyone would ever know that unless they actually woke him, and that would fairly spoil the point."

Paul stared. Except for its slenderness and height, it seemed a rather average mountain. "What about the White King? What if someone wakes *him* up? Same thing?"

Gally shrugged. "S'pose so. But no one knows where he's sleeping except Her White Ladyship, and she ain't telling."

By the time the sun had tilted past the topmost point of the sky they had reached the bottomlands once more, a rolling sea of meadows and low hills interspersed with wide swathes of forest. Paul was again feeling tired, and realized that he had eaten nothing for more than a day. He felt the absence of food, but nothing like as strongly as he felt he should, and he was just about to ask Gally when the boy suddenly grabbed his arm.

"Look! On the hill behind us."

Paul found that he was crouching almost before he understood what the boy had said; some reflex against danger from above, some old story his body still told, had driven him down. He peered along the length of Gally's pointing finger.

A shape had appeared on the hilltop. It was joined a few moments later by another, and Paul felt his heart go stone-cold in his chest. But then a half-dozen more shapes appeared beside the first two, one of them apparently on horseback.

"It's the redbreasts," Gally said. "I didn't know they had taken this square, too. Do you think they're looking for you?"

Paul shook his head. "I don't know." He was not as frightened of these pursuers as he was of the two who had called at the Oyster-house, but he did not trust anyone's soldiers. "How far is it to the edge of the square?"

"A ways. We'll be there before sundown."

"Then let's hurry."

It was hard going. The thick undergrowth tore at their clothes with branches like claws. Paul no longer thought of food, although he still felt weak. Gally took a snaking course, trying to keep them out of the densest forest for greater speed, but also away from the places where they would be most visible from the hillside. Paul knew the boy was doing a better job than he could, but they still seemed to be traveling at an agonizingly slow pace.

They had just leaped from the security of a copse and were pounding across an open slope when they heard a clatter from the undergrowth. A moment later a horse burst out and drummed across the open space in front of them, then turned, rearing. Paul dragged Gally back from beneath flailing hooves.

The rider wore armor of a deep blood-red. A helmet of the same color, in the perfect likeness of a snarling lion's head, hid his features. He stamped his long lance upon the ground. "You cross territory that has been claimed for Her Scarlet Majesty," he said, his self-important tones made louder and more hollow by his helmet. "You will surrender yourself to me."

Gally struggled beneath Paul's hand. He was small and dirty, and it was difficult to keep a grip on him. "We're free folk! What gives you the say-so to stop us going where we please?"

"There is no freedom but that of Her Majesty's vassals," the knight boomed. He tilted the lance so that its sharpened head wavered at the height of Paul's chest. "If you have committed no crimes, and bind yourself to her in honorable fealty, then you will have nothing to fear." He spurred his horse forward a few paces until the bobbing lance almost touched them.

"I'm a stranger." Paul was still struggling to catch his breath. "I am passing through. I care nothing about local troubles."

"The urchin is an outsider, too," the knight said through the lion's snarling muzzle. "And he and his starvelings have caused nothing but problems since they arrived—thieving, lying, spreading nonsensical tales. Her Majesty will have no more of it."

"That's a lie!" Gally was on the verge of tears. "Them are all lies!"

"Kneel, or I will treat you as harshly as one of your capons, spit boy."

Paul pulled Gally back; the knight spurred forward. There was nowhere for them to go—even if they could reach the trees behind them, it would only be a matter of time before he rode them down. Deadened, Paul slowly dropped to one knee.

"What, what, then? Who goes there?" Another knight now cantered into the clearing from the side nearest the river, this one dressed all in shining white, his helmet shaped like a horse's head with a single horn protruding from its brow—an animal whose name Paul felt he should remember, but couldn't. A wide array of weapons, flasks, and other objects dangled from the knight's saddle, so that his horse clattered like a tinker's wagon every time it moved. *"Avaunt!"* he shouted. "'Or is it 'aroint!'?"

The red knight could not keep a note of surprise from his voice. "What are *you* doing here?"

The figure in white armor paused as though the question were difficult. "Took a bit of a dodgy turn, I suppose. Unexpected. Suppose we'll have to have a battle now."

"These are the queen's prisoners," declared Lion-helm, "and I cannot waste my time with you. I will allow you to retreat, but if I see you again once I have finished with these . . . " he waggled his lance at Paul and the boy, "I will have to kill you."

"Retreat? Oh, hardly possible—no, can't do it. She's not my queen, you see." The white knight paused as if trying to remember something important. He reached up and pulled off his helmet, exposing a damp halo of pale hair, and scratched vigorously at his scalp.

Paul stared in astonishment. "Jack? Jack Woodling?"

The knight turned to stare at him, obviously puzzled. "Jack? I'm no Jack. See here," he turned to the red knight, "there's prisoners for you. I've had 'em myself. No respect, no understanding of the niceties."

"It's not him," Gally said in a loud whisper.

Paul shook his head. This was rapidly becoming farce. "But—but I've met you before! The other night, in the woods. Don't you remember?"

The man in white armor stared at Paul. "In the woods? Fellow that looked like me?" He turned again to the red knight. "I believe this chap's met my brother. Fancy. He's been missing for some time. Always was a rover." He swiveled again. "Did he seem well?"

Lion-helm was neither interested nor amused. "Turn and depart, you lackwit White, or it will go badly with you." He drew his horse back a few restive paces, then couched his lance and pointed it at the newcomer.

"No, that won't do." The white knight was growing perturbed. "Have to claim this square, do you see—Her Serene and Alabaster Highness' now, sort of thing." He pulled his helmet on again. "So I suppose it's a battle."

"Idiot!" screamed the red knight. "You prisoners—you will stay there until I have finished!"

The white knight had now lowered his lance and was cantering forward, banging and clanking as he went. "Prepare yourself!" he shouted, then undercut the effect by asking "Quite sure you're ready?"

"Run!" Gally sprinted past the red knight, who turned his head to bellow at the boy, only to receive his enemy's lance in the middle of his breastplate. He flailed as he lost his balance, tumbled off his horse and fell heavily to the ground.

As Paul dashed past, the lion knight was already clambering to his feet, pulling a huge and unpleasant looking mace from a strap on his saddle.

"A good one—oh, very good, you must admit!" said the white knight. He did not seem to be preparing any defense as the red knight approached.

"But he'll kill him!" Paul hesitated, then took a tentative step back into the clearing as the red knight swung his cudgel and smashed his opponent out of his saddle and onto the damp earth.

Gally grabbed his sleeve and yanked him hard, almost pulling him off his feet. "Leave them to go at it! Come on, governor!" He darted down the hill again, this time retaining his grip on Paul's sleeve. Paul had no choice but to follow stumblingly after him. Within moments the clearing was hidden in the trees behind them, but they could hear grunting, cursing, and a ponderous clang of metal on metal for some time.

"He rescued us!" Paul gasped, when they had stopped for a moment to rest. "We can't just leave him to die."

"The knight? Who gives a toss?" Gally tossed his damp hair out of his face. "He's not one of us—if he snuffs it, he'll be back again. In the next match."

"Back? Next match?"

But the boy was running again. Paul staggered after him.

The shadows were long and angular. Afternoon was fading quickly, the sun just resting on the spine of the hills. Paul grabbed at the boy for support when they stopped and almost dragged them both to the ground.

"Can't . . . " he panted. ". . . Rest. . . "

"Not for long." Gally seemed tired also, but far less so than Paul. "The river's just over the rise, but we've still got to follow it a ways before we reach the border."

Paul set his hands on his knees, but could not unbend his waist and stand straight. "If . . . if those two are fighting . . . why . . . we . . . running. . . ?"

"Because there were others—you saw them on the hill. Redbreasts. Foot soldiers. But they can move steady and quick when they want to, and they don't need to stop and wheeze their guts out." He slid to the ground. "Catch your breath, then we got to move fast-like."

"What did you mean before? About the knight dying?"

Gally rubbed his face, leaving streaks of dirt like primitive face paint. "Them all, they just go round and round. They fight and fight until one side wins, then it starts all over again. This is the third match since we came here, that I remember."

"But don't people get killed?"

" 'Course they do. But only till the end of the match, as they call it. Then everything starts up again. They don't even remember."

"But you do, because you're not from here?"

"Suppose." The boy frowned, then grew thoughtful. "Do you think maybe all the littleuns, Bay and the rest, will be back the next time? Do you think?"

"Has it ever happened before? Have you . . . lost any of your littleuns that way, then had them come back?"

Gally shook his head.

"I don't know," Paul said at last. But he thought he did know. He doubted that whatever magic protected the natives of the Eight Squared extended to outsiders.

When he could stand upright again, Gally led them on. After a short trek through thick forest they pushed through a spinney of twisted trees and found themselves looking down a long grassy slope to the river. Paul had no chance to savor the view. Gally led him down to within a few hundred yards of the water's edge, then turned them toward the ridge of hills. They walked as quickly as they could across the sparse, sandy meadows, the sun's orange glare in their eyes until they passed into the shadow of the hills.

Paul stared out at the river and the dim breakfront of trees that ran along its farther bank. Just beside them the shadowed water seemed full of blue-gleaming depths; behind them, outside the shadows in which they stood, it seemed to smolder in the sunset light like a long ribbon of molten gold. Somehow, the river seemed at once both more and less real than the landscape it transected, as if a feature from one famous painting had been inserted into another.

He slowed for a moment, suddenly aware of a cloud of partial memories that had gradually been making themselves more and more a part of his thoughts. Famous painting? What would that be? Where had he seen or heard of such a thing? He knew what it meant without quite being able to visualize anything that would correspond to the idea.

"Hurry yourself, governor. We want to be in the caves by dark or they'll find us."

"Why don't we just swim across the river to the other side?"

Gally turned to glare at him. "Are you barmy?"

"Or we could make a raft if it's too far—there's lots of wood."

"Why would we want to do that?"

Paul, as usual, had moved into conceptual territory where the bits of knowledge floating up did not seem to match the world around him. "To . . . to escape. To get out of the Eight Squared."

Gally stopped and planted his hands on his hips, scowling. "First off, I told you, you don't want to go on the river because you can be found. Second thing is, there ain't no other side."

"What do you mean?"

"Just what I said—there ain't no other side. Even an eejit knows that. You don't get *out* of the Eight Squared that way—the river just goes *past* it."

Paul could not understand the distinction. "But—but what's that?" He pointed at the distant bank.

"It's . . . I don't know. A mirror, sort of. A picture, maybe. But there's nothing there. That's how we lost one of the big ones. She thought she could cross, even though she'd been told."

"I don't understand. How can there be nothing out there when I can *see* something?"

Gally turned and resumed walking. "You don't have to believe me, governor. Get yourself killed if you want. But you and me, we won't pop up again next match, I'm thinking."

Paul stood staring at the far trees for some time, then hurried after him. When the boy saw he was following, he gave Paul a look of mixed relief and disgust, but then his eyes opened wide, staring at something even farther back. Paul turned.

An object was speeding across the meadow toward them, still a long distance back and moving too fast to be clearly seen. A trail of thin smoke hung in the air where the grass smoldered in its wake.

"Run!" shouted Gally.

Despite his weariness, Paul did not need encouraging. They pelted toward the looming purple hills, whose skirts were now only a thousand paces away. A nearer jut of stone, which Paul had at first taken to be another rock formation, revealed itself to be the work of human hands as they sped across it. The single triangular spike, taller than a man, stood at the center of a broad circle of flat stone tiles incised with strange patterns. Running across the smooth hard face of what Paul guessed was an enormous sundial actually sped their pace, and for a moment Paul thought they might reach the cave safely. Small animals with contorted, curving muzzles scuttled out of their path and into the surrounding scrub.

They were just stumbling across the sand and rocky scree that marked the hem of the hills when a red something rushed past them with the noise and force of a small freight train.

Freight train? wondered Paul, even in his disordered panic. *What. . . ?*

The thing pulled in front of them and skidded to a halt, throwing up a trailing barrage of hot gravel. Tiny stones pinged against Paul's chest and face.

She was at least a head taller than he was and bright red from head to foot. Every bit of her was the same glossy shade, even her haughty face and her upswept hair. Her vast, flared gown seemed made of something heavier and stiffer than cloth. A few wisps of smoke still drifted from beneath the hem.

"You! I am told you refused my offer of vassalage." Her voice was pump-engine loud, but chilly enough to freeze birds on the wing. "That is not the way to gain my favor."

Gally was slumped beside him. Paul sucked in just enough breath to talk without squeaking. "We meant no offense, Your Highness. We only sought to . . . "

"Silence. You will speak when spoken to, but only when I tell you that you *have* been spoken to. Now you have been spoken to. You may speak."

"We meant no offense, Your Highness."

"You said that already. I am not sure I wish to have you as vassals, in any case—you are frightfully stupid creatures." She lifted her hand in the air and snapped her fingers, a noise as loud as a gunshot. From the trees far away along the ridge, three armored foot soldiers appeared and began skidding and tumbling down the hillside, hurrying to their lady's summons. "I suppose we shall simply have your heads off. Not the most original punishment, but I find that the old ways are the best, don't you?" She paused and glared at Paul. "Well, have you nothing to say?"

"Let us go. We are leaving. We have no wish to interfere."

"Did I say you had been spoken to?" She frowned, honestly pondering. "Ah, well, if I remember and it turns out you have spoken out of turn, I shall simply cut your head off twice."

The soldiers had reached flat ground and were hurrying toward them. Paul considered trying to dodge past the queen and sprint for the beckoning darkness of a large cave in the rocks only a hundred paces away.

"I see you," said the queen. "I know what you are thinking." There was not an iota of levity or human feeling in her voice—it was like being trapped by some horrible machine. "You may not plot escape without permission either. Not that it would do you any good." She nodded; an instant later she was ten paces to one side. Paul had seen only a brief scarlet blur. "You are much too slow to outrun me," she pointed out. "Although you have moved a little more swiftly than I would have guessed. It is most infuriating when pieces come into the Eight Squared and move just as they choose. If I knew who was responsible, heads would roll, I promise you." She momentarily blurred again, ending up less than a yard from Paul and the boy, staring down at them with evident distaste. "Heads will roll in any case. It is only a question of *which* and *how many.*"

The first of the soldiers trotted up, closely followed by his two companions. Before Paul could shake off his surprise at the queen's astonishing speed of movement, strong and ungentle hands pulled his arms behind his back.

"It seems there was something else," the queen said abruptly. She raised one scarlet finger to her chin and tilted her head to the side, woodenly childlike. "Was I perhaps going to cut some other parts of you off instead of your heads?"

Paul struggled uselessly. The two soldiers who held him were as painfully solid as the queen appeared to be. Gally was not even trying to fight free of the man-at-arms who held him. "We have done no harm!" Paul cried. "We are strangers here!"

"Ah!" The queen smiled, pleased at her own cleverness. Even her teeth were the color of fresh blood. "You have reminded me— *strangers.*" She lifted her fingers to her mouth and whistled, an ear-jabbing blast of sound that echoed from the hillstones. "I promised I would hand you over to someone. Then I will have the heads off whatever is left."

Paul felt a sudden chill that moved through him like a damp wind from the night ocean. He swiveled, knowing what he would see.

Two figures had appeared on the meadow behind them, both wearing hats and cloaks, their faces shadowed. They moved forward deliberately, with no apparent haste. As the smaller of them spread its arms in a horrible mock-display of surprise and pleasure, something glinted in the shadow beneath its hat brim.

"There you are!" The voice made Paul want to scream and bite at his own flesh. *"We had wondered how long it would be until we found you again. . . ."*

Gally moaned. Paul threw himself forward, trying to break free, but the queen's soldiers had him gripped fast.

"We have such special things waiting for you, our dear old friend." The pair were closer now, but still not quite distinguishable, as though

they carried some deeper darkness wrapped around them in a cloud. *"Such special things. . . ."*

Even as Paul's knees gave way, and he sagged into the strong arms of his captors, he heard a strange sound. Either Gally's moaning had become almost as loud as the queen's whistle had been, or . . . .

The rumbling grew stronger. Paul dragged his eyes from the terrible yet fascinating spectacle of his pursuers and looked toward the hills. He wondered if an avalanche were beginning—surely only the friction of stone on stone could make such a deep, grating noise. But there was no avalanche, only a vast, winged thing that growled as it emerged from the cavern in the hillside. Paul stared. The queen's mouth hung open.

"Jabberwock!" choked one of the soldiers—a hopeless, terrified sound.

Once out of the confining cave the thing stood and spread its wings until the tips rose high enough to catch the sun's last rays in their veined membrane. The heavy-lidded eyes blinked. The head snaked forward on the end of an impossibly long neck, then the wings bellied and cracked as the creature took flight. Gally's captor toppled over onto his back, where he lay making a thin screeching noise.

The beast went straight up until it hung in the bright sky above the hilltops, a black silhouette like a bat stretched across a lantern, then dropped into a dive. The soldiers holding Paul both let loose at the same moment and turned to run. The queen raised her arms and bellowed at the thing as it descended. Paul was staggered and then toppled by the gale as the creature spread its vast wings and banked upward, one of the terrible cloaked figures kicking in its birdlike grip.

"Gally!" screamed Paul. There was dust everywhere, swirling funnels of it. Somewhere, through the grit and shadow and rush of wind, he could hear the outraged screams of the Red Queen. "Gally!"

He found the boy huddled on the ground and snatched him up, then turned and began running toward the river. As they stumbled across the uneven terrain, the boy glanced up and saw their destination.

"No! Don't!"

Paul splashed into the shallows with the struggling child in his arms. As he waded out into the current, he heard a voice calling from the chaos behind them.

"You are only making it worse! We will find you wherever you go, Paul Jonas!"

He let the boy go, then began swimming toward the far bank. Gally was floundering beside him, so Paul caught the boy's collar and kicked hard against the water and the tangling reeds. Something swooped past overhead, the wind of its passage beating the water into white-caps. A scarlet figure that shrieked like a boiling kettle dangled in its claws. The waves battered Paul and pushed him back toward the bank. He was growing weak and the other side of the river was still very far away.

"Swim, boy," he gasped, letting Gally go. Together they struggled a little farther, but the current was sweeping them apart and also pushing them at a right angle to the bank, which seemed to grow no closer.

A cramping pain shot through Paul's leg. He gasped and slid under, then thrashed in circles in the muddy water, trying to find his way upright again. Something was gleaming nearby, something distorted but bright, like a candle seen through wavy glass. Paul struggled to the surface. Gally was paddling desperately beside him, chin barely held above the water, panic on his straining face.

Paul stuck his head under the water again. It was there—something golden, shimmering in the depths. He broke the surface, grabbed Gally, and pushed the boy's mouth shut.

"Hold your breath!" he gasped, then dragged them both under.

The boy fought wildly. Paul kicked as hard as he could, trying to drive them both downward toward the distorted glow. Gally caught him with an elbow in the stomach and air leaked from him; Paul coughed and felt the river rush into his nose and mouth. The yellow gleam seemed nearer now, but so was the blackness and the blackness was closing in swiftly.

Paul reached out toward the bright spot. He saw black water, swirl-ing yet stone-solid, and bubbles, golden-lit, trapped as though in amber. He saw a frozen moment of Gally's face, eyes bulging, mouth wide in betrayed horror. Paul reached out. Then everything went away.

CHAPTER 19

Fragments

NETFEED/NEWS: Indoor Storm Kills Three
(visual: beach wreckage, torn dome overhead)
VO: Three people were killed and fourteen more hospitalized when an
artificial indoor beach attraction went out of control in Bournemouth,
England.
(visual: Bubble Beach Park during normal operation)
Malfunctioning wave machines and the collapse of the building's domed
ceiling caused what one witness called an "indoor tsunami" that resulted in
three drownings and numerous other injuries when sixteen-foot-high waves
swept up onto the artificial beach. Sabotage has not been ruled out. . . .

She had avoided it for two days, but she couldn't any longer. The doctor's death had raised the stakes. It was time to start looking for help, and this particular source couldn't be ignored, however much she might wish to. At least now she could do it at work, which wasn't quite so awful as having the squalor of the shelter all around her. She didn't dare black out the visual—it would be an admission of something, or it would be perceived that way, that she had gotten fat or that she couldn't face him.

Renie tilted the pad so that she would be posed in front of the least cluttered wall and the one potted plant which had survived the toxic office atmosphere. She knew the number—she had tracked it down the day after Susan's death. It had been something to do, something to keep her active; but she had realized even at the time that if she found it, she would have no choice but to use it.

She lit a cigarette, then looked around the office again, making sure that nothing in view of her pad's wide-angle lens looked too pathetic. She took a deep breath. Someone knocked at the door.

"Damn. Come in!"

!Xabbu poked his head inside. "Hello, Renie. Is this a bad time to visit you?"

For a moment, her mind leaped at the chance of a reprieve. "No, come in." It was disgusting, groveling after excuses this way. "Well, actually, it is a bad time. I have to make a phone call I don't really want to make. But I'd better do it. Will you be on campus for a while?"

He smiled. "I came to see you. I will wait."

For a moment she thought he meant he would wait in the office—a breathtakingly daunting prospect—but the small man merely bobbed his head and backed out, shutting the door behind him.

"Right." She took another drag on her cigarette. They were supposed to be relatively harmless, but if she smoked many more today, she would set herself on fire from the inside, a genuine case of spontaneous human combustion. She called the number.

The male receptionist left the screen blacked, which was fine with her. "I'd like to speak with Mister Chiume. Tell him it's Renie. Irene Sulaweyo." Much as she disliked her full name—she had been given it in honor of a hugely fat, hugely Christian great-aunt—it might establish a proper tone of detached adulthood.

He answered quickly enough to catch her off-balance, the visual flicking on as abruptly as if he had leaped out of a cupboard. "Renie! I am really surprised—but it's a good surprise! How are you? You look great!"

Del Ray looked good himself, which was probably why he'd brought the subject up—stylish if slightly conservative haircut, nice suit, shirt collar embroidered with metallic thread. But more had changed than just the shedding of his student guise—he looked different in some deeper, more profound way that she couldn't immediately categorize.

"I'm okay." She was pleased with how steady her voice sounded. "Things have been . . . interesting. But I'll tell you about that in a moment. How is your family? I talked to your mother for a minute or so, but she was just leaving."

He briskly filled her in. Everybody was doing well except for his younger brother, who had been in conflict with authority almost since his cradle days and continued to fall into and (usually) out of trouble. Renie felt a little dreamy watching Del Ray talk, listening to his voice. It was all very strange, but not as painful as she'd expected. He was a completely different person than the one who had left her, who had—as she'd felt sure at the time—broken her heart forever. Not that he'd changed so drastically; it was more that he no longer mattered much. He might as well have been a friend's ex-lover and not her own.

"So that's my story," he said. "I'm sure yours makes better listening and I'm ready to hear it. Somehow I'm sure you didn't call me just for the sake of old times."

Damn, thought Renie. Del Ray might be a bureaucrat now, he might be a suit of the very kind they used to make fun of, but he hadn't become stupid.

"I seem to be in some trouble," she said. "But I don't feel comfortable talking about it on the phone. Could we get together somewhere?"

Del Ray hesitated. *He's got a wife,* she realized. *Or a steady girlfriend. He doesn't know what exactly I'm asking for.*

"I'm sorry to hear you're having a problem. I hope it's nothing serious." He paused again. "I suppose . . . "

"I just need your advice. It's nothing that will get *you* in any trouble. Not even with the woman in your life."

His eyebrow went up. "Did Mama tell you?"

"I just guessed. What's her name?"

"Dolly. We got married last year." He looked a little embarrassed. "She's a solicitor."

Renie felt her stomach churn, but again it was not as bad as she'd anticipated. "Del Ray and Dolly? Please. I assume you don't go out much."

"Don't be nasty. You'd like her if you met her."

"I probably would." The idea, in fact the whole conversation, made her feel tired. "Look, you can bring her along if you want to—this isn't some desperate attempt by a jilted lover to lure you back."

"Renie!" He seemed honestly indignant. "That's foolish. I want to help you if I can. Tell me what to do. Where should we meet?"

"How about someplace on the Golden Mile, after work?" She would have a long bus ride back to the shelter, but at least she could do her groveling for favors in a pleasant atmosphere.

Del Ray named a bar, quickly enough that she guessed it was a

regular hangout of his, and asked her to give his best to her father
and Stephen. He seemed to be waiting for news about them, her half
of an informational hostage exchange, but there wasn't much she
could tell without opening the whole thing up. She ended the conversation as quickly as she decently could and disconnected.

He looks tame, she realized. It wasn't just the suit or the hair. Something that had been a little wild was gone, or at least very well hidden.
*Is that me, too? Did he look at me and think, well, there she is, turned into a
drab little teacher?*

She straightened up, stubbed out the cigarette, which had burned
down unsmoked, and lit another. *We'll see about that.* Perversely, she
felt almost proud of her strange and extensive problems. *When was the
last time he or his little Dolly-wife had their house burned down by an international conspiracy of fat men and Hindu deities?*

!Xabbu returned a few minutes later, but she didn't stop giggling
for some time. It was close to hysterical, she knew, but it beat the hell
out of crying.

Del Ray regarded !Xabbu carefully. It was almost worth the extreme
discomfort of having to meet him to watch him struggle to figure out
who the Bushman was and what his position was in Renie's life. "Nice
to meet you," he said, and shook the small man's hand with an admirably firm sincerity.

"Del Ray is an assistant minister with UNComm," she explained,
although she'd already told !Xabbu that on the ride over. She was
pleased she'd brought her friend along; it tipped the balance in a
subtle way, made her feel less like a discarded girlfriend begging a
favor. "He's a very important fellow."

Del Ray frowned, hedging his bets in case he was being teased. "Not
very important, actually. A career man, still in the early stages."

!Xabbu, who did not have the polite chitchat reflexes of the urban
middle class, simply nodded and then sat back against the thick cush-
ion of the booth to stare at the antique (or imitation, more likely)
swag chandeliers and heavy wooden paneling.

Renie watched Del Ray summon a waitress, impressed by his casually proprietorial attitude. During the previous century, the bar would
have been the preserve of white businessmen, a place where he and
Renie and !Xabbu would have been discussed under the general heading of "the Kaffirs" or "the black problem," but now Del Ray and
other black professionals sat enthroned amidst the trappings of colo-
nial empire. At least that much had changed, she thought. There were

more than a few suited white men in the room, white women, too, but they were only part of a clientele that also included blacks and Asians. Here a form of real equality prevailed at least, even if it was an equality of wealth and influence. The enemy now had no identifying color; its only recognizable attribute was discontented poverty.

!Xabbu ordered a beer. Renie asked for a glass of wine. "Just one drink," she said, "then I'd like to take a walk."

Del Ray raised his eyebrows at this. He continued to make casual conversation as the drinks came, but with a sort of wariness, as though he suspected that any moment Renie might spring some unpleasant surprise. She skirted the main issue, telling him of Stephen's condition and of the fire without a hint of what might connect the two.

"Renie, that's terrible! I'm so sorry!" He shook his head. "Do you need something—help finding a place, money?"

She shook her head, then swallowed the last of her wine. "No, thank you, but you're kind to ask. Can we take that walk now?"

He nodded, bemused, and paid the bill. !Xabbu, who had drunk his beer in silence, followed them out onto the promenade.

"Let's walk down the pier," Renie suggested.

She could tell that he was growing irritated, but Del Ray had indeed become a politician. If he had still been his student self, he would have been angrily demanding answers, wanting to know why she was wasting his time. Renie decided that she approved of at least some of the ways he had changed. When they reached the end of the pier and were alone except for a few fishermen and the purring of the breakers, she led them to a bench.

"You will think I'm crazy," she said, "but I don't feel comfortable talking inside. It's very unlikely anyone can eavesdrop on us out here."

He shrugged. "I don't think you're crazy." His voice sounded less certain than his words.

"Someday you may be glad I'm taking such trouble. I don't particularly want to meet your wife, Del Ray, but I don't want anything to happen to her either, and I seem to have gotten myself in trouble with people who aren't very selective."

His eyes narrowed. "Why don't you just talk to me."

She started from the beginning, staying as general as she could and skipping as lightly as possible over the several times she had misused her position at the Poly or subverted UNComm regulations. From time to time she asked !Xabbu to corroborate what she was saying and the small man did, although always with a somewhat distracted air. Renie could spare little attention, but she wondered briefly at his mood and what it might signify.

Del Ray was largely silent, breaking in only to ask specific questions. He seemed interested by the inner workings of Mister J's, but only shook his head, expressionless, when she told him of her speculations about the club.

When she had brought him up to the present, describing the fire in her flatblock and Susan's murder, he did not respond immediately, but sat watching a gull preen itself on a railing.

"I don't know what to say. The whole story is . . . astonishing."

"What does that mean?" A spark of anger flared. "Does that mean astonishingly crazy, or astonishing so you'll do whatever you can to help me?"

"I . . . I just don't know. It's a lot to absorb." He stared at her, perhaps trying to gauge how well he knew her after all these years without contact. "And I'm not quite sure what you want me to do either. I'm not part of UNComm security or law enforcement. I'm a business liaison, Renie. I help chain stores make sure their systems follow UN guidelines. I don't know anything about the stuff you're talking about."

"Damn it, Del Ray, you're part of the Politburo, as we used to call it—you're an insider! You must be able to do something, if only help me get information. Are these people under investigation at all? Has anyone beside me had weird experiences with this Happy Juggler Novelty Corporation? Who *are* they? I need answers from someone I can trust. I'm scared, Del Ray."

He frowned. "Of course, I'll do what I can. . . . "

"Also, I think I need to get into TreeHouse."

"TreeHouse? What in hell for?"

She briefly considered telling him of Susan's deathbed message, but decided against it. Susan's laborious last words were known only to her, !Xabbu, and Jeremiah Dako. She would keep them secret a while longer. "I just need to go there. Can you help me?"

"Renie, I never made it into TreeHouse when I was a hash-smoking, full-time student hacker." He smiled self-mockingly. "Do you think I could get within miles of it now that I'm part of the UNComm establishment? We're the enemy as far as they're concerned."

Now it was her turn to frown. "This isn't easy. You know I wouldn't ask if I didn't really really need help." She blinked hard. "Damn it, Del Ray, my baby brother . . . is . . ." She stopped, unwilling to go any farther in that dangerous direction. She would die before she would cry in front of him.

He stood, then reached down to take her hand. He was still very handsome. "I'll check around, Renie. Really, I will. I'll see what I can find."

"Be careful. Even if you think I'm crazy, just pretend I'm not and make your mistakes on the side of caution. Don't do anything stupid, and don't be obvious."

"I will call you by the end of the week." He extended his hand to !Xabbu. "Nice to have met you."

The little man accepted the handshake. "Everything Ms. Sulaweyo spoke of is true," he said gravely. "These are bad people. You must not take this lightly.

Del Ray nodded, a little flustered, then turned back to Renie. "I'm truly sorry about Stephen. Give my regards to your father." He leaned forward and kissed her on the cheek, squeezed her once, then turned and walked back up the pier.

Renie watched him go. "When we broke up," she said at last, "I couldn't imagine life without him."

"Always things change," said !Xabbu. "The wind blows everything."

"I am frightened, Renie."

She looked up. He had been silent for most of the bus ride, staring up at the buildings as they traveled through the windowed canyons of downtown Durban.

"Because of what happened to Susan?"

He shook his hand. "I mourn for her, yes, and I am angry at the people who did such a terrible thing. But I am frightened in a bigger way." He paused, looking down, his hands folded in his lap like a child threatened into good behavior. "It is my dreams."

"You said you dreamed of something bad happening to me the night Susan was attacked."

"It is more than that. Since we went into that place, that club, my dreams have been very strong. I do not know what I fear, exactly, but I feel that I am—no, that we are all—being stalked by something large and cruel."

Renie's heart sped. She had dreamed something like that herself, hadn't she? Or was she remembering some dream of !Xabbu's, described by him then absorbed as her own? "I'm not surprised," she said carefully. "We had a terrible experience."

He shook his head sternly. "I am not speaking of that kind of dreaming, Renie. Those are the dreams that trouble individuals, made up of the things in their own lives—the dreams of city-people, if you will not take offense at my saying it. But I am speaking of something different, a kind of ripple in the dream that is dreaming *us*. I know the difference. What has come to me in the past days is the kind of dream my people have when the rain will soon fall after a long drought, or when strangers are approaching across the desert. This is a dream of what *will be*, not of what has been."

"You mean seeing the future?"

"I do not know. It does not seem that way to me, any more than seeing the shadow of something and knowing that the thing itself will follow is seeing the future. When Grandfather Mantis knew that his time on this earth was ending, when he knew that the time had come at last to sit down at the campfire with the All-Devourer, he had such dreams. Even when the sun is high, we know that it will sink again and night will come. There is nothing magical about such knowledge."

She didn't know how to respond. Ideas like that irritated her sense of the rational, but she had never found it easy to dismiss !Xabbu's concerns and insights. "Let's say I believe you, just for the sake of discussion. Something is stalking us, you said. What does that mean? That we have made enemies? But we know that already."

Outside the bus window, the gleaming security towers of the business district were being supplanted by an increasingly shabby landscape of jerry-rigged flatblocks and storefront businesses, each with its own garish squirt of chemical neon on the front. The street crowds seemed purposeless from her perspective, eddying randomly like an inanimate, liquid thing.

"I am speaking of something greater. There is a poem that I was taught in school—an English poet, I think. It spoke of a beast slouching toward Bethlehem."

"I remember that, sort of. Blood-dimmed tides. Anarchy loose in the world."

He nodded. "An apocalyptic image, I was told. A vision of the end of things. I spoke a moment ago of Mantis and the All-Devourer. Grandfather Mantis was told in a vision that a great time of change was coming, and he prepared his people to leave the earth forever because their time upon it had finished." His small, fine-featured face was solemn, but she could see something in his eyes and the set of his mouth, a kind of feverish despair. He was terrified. "I feel that I am being granted such a vision, Renie. There is a great change coming, a . . . what were the words? A rough beast waiting to be born."

A chill ran across the surface of Renie's skin, as though the bus cabin's long-expired air-conditioning had suddenly sprung back to life. Was her friend going mad? He had said that city life had destroyed many of his people—was this obsession with dreams and the myths of his ancestors the beginnings of a religious mania that would eventually destroy him, too?

I've done this to him. Bad enough that he's had to adjust to a completely different kind of life. But now I've dragged him right in over his head, into the weirdest things our society has to offer. It's like dropping a young child onto a battlefield or into an S & M orgy.

"And what should we do?" she asked, struggling to remain at least outwardly calm. "Where is this threat coming from—do you know?"

He stared at her for a moment. "Yes. I could not say what are its causes or what the results might be, but I do not need those things to sense the place the problem comes from—even a blind man can find the campfire. I told you that the club, Mister J's, was a bad place. It is, but it is not the heart of the shadow. I think it is like a hole in some very large nest of hornets—do you see? If you put your ear to that hole, you will hear the sound of things that fly and seize and sting, but even if you seal it with mud, the hornets are still alive in the darkness inside and they will find their way out of other holes."

"I'm confused, !Xabbu. I don't really know what you're saying."

He gave her a tiny, sad smile. "I do not know exactly myself, Renie. Just because I can see the shadow does not mean I can recognize what casts it. But there is more involved in this thing than merely your brother—more perhaps than even the lives of many other children like him. I smell it like I smell the approach of a storm. I may not be able to understand any more clearly than that, but it is enough to frighten me very badly."

They continued in silence until !Xabbu got off at his stop in Chesterville a few minutes later. Renie waved to him from the window as the bus pulled away, but his words had upset her. She was torn. It was hard to know which was worse, to believe that her friend might be going mad, or to think that he might truly know something that others did not, something dreadful.

The sun was going down as her bus headed toward Pinetown. The square, drab buildings cast long shadows. Renie watched the orange streetlamps kindle and tried to imagine what kind of beasts might wait in the darkness beyond the circle of light.

* * *

Del Ray was smiling, but he did not seem entirely happy to receive her call. Renie moved the exam she'd been preparing to one side of the screen, then enlarged Del Ray's window.

"Have you found out anything?"

He shook his head. "This isn't a good time for me to talk."

"Then would you like me to meet you somewhere?"

"No. Look, I don't have much for you yet—it's a tricky situation. There's been a lot of interest in the corporation you asked about, but nothing obviously out of the ordinary. They own a bunch of clubs, some production companies, a couple of gear houses, mostly net-related stuff. There was one court case involving one of their other clubs that got as far as a lower court in China, filed by a woman named Quan."

"What do you mean, court case? What about?"

Again he shook his head. "A suit for negligence, something like that. It's probably nothing—the family dropped it before trial. Look, there's not much I can find out without getting access to sealed legal records. And it's not something I'm supposed to be doing, really." He hesitated. "How's Stephen? Any better?"

"No. Things have been pretty much the same for weeks now." She had dreamed of Stephen the night before, of him screaming for help at the bottom of a deep hole while she tried to explain the urgency to some kind of policemen or the petty official who was paying more attention to stroking a sleek dog. Just thinking about the dream made her angry. "So, is that all you're going to tell me—there's not much? What about the people who own that horrible place? There must be names on the licenses. Or is that too much trouble to find out?"

For a moment his professional composure slipped. "I don't have to do anything for you at all, you know."

"No." She stared at the screen, wondering what exactly she had once found so utterly engaging about him. He was just a nice-looking man in a suit. "No, you don't."

"I'm sorry. I didn't mean . . . I want to help, Renie. Things are just . . . " He hesitated. "Things are didfficult for me at the moment."

She wondered if he was referring to his domestic life, or ordinary work crises, or something more sinister. "Well, I meant what I said. Be careful. And I *do* apreciate your help."

"I'll get you everything I can. It's . . . well, it's just not as easy as it sounds. Take care."

"I will. Thank you."

When he had hung up, she lit a cigarette, too, unsettled to get back to work on the examination. It was hard to tell whether Del Ray's apparent agitation had to do with guilt over the way their relationship had ended, discomfort at having become embroiled in someone's bizarre conspiracy theory, or something else entirely. If it was the second thing, she couldn't really blame him. Six months ago, if someone had brought the same crazy story to her, she would have been doubtful, too. Even now a strong case could be made that she had merely hit a patch of bad luck and was finding a way to string it all together into a structure that made sense. Wasn't that the way someone said religions—and paranoid obsessions—got started? As an attempt to make sense of a universe too large and too random for human comprehension?

What did she have, really? Her brother had mysteriously fallen ill, but strange, inexplicable illnesses were the stuff of historical record since time out of mind, and continued right up until the present day. There had been more sudden outbreaks of previously unknown viruses in the past fifty years than there had been in the five centuries before.

She and !Xabbu had discovered a seeming correlation between the incidences of coma and net usage, but there were dozens of other possible explanations for that.

Her flatblock had burned, and although there had been no definitive report, there were certainly whispers of arson. But that, too, was remarkably unremarkable. She had no idea of the statistics, but she was quite sure there must be hundreds of arson fires in Durban every year, not to mention the thousands of accidental ones.

The only things that even halfway held up as evidence were the murderous attack on Susan, the truly peculiar events surrounding Mister J's, and the appearance of that astonishing golden city. But even these things could be odd but explicable happenstance. Only the strong links between these apparent coincidences separated her certainty that she was onto something from the most pathetic examples of persecution mania.

Renie sighed. *So, are !Xabbu and I legitimate whistle-blowers? Or are we turning into the kind of people you see on the tabnets claiming space aliens are beaming messages into their brains?*

Susan hadn't thought so, or at least she had discovered something she thought was significant, even if Renie hadn't found a way to follow it up yet. Doctor Van Bleeck had not been not the kind of person to indulge anything she judged unwarranted foolishness in even her closest of colleagues, let alone an ex-student she hadn't seen in years.

What did she find out? What if we can't locate this Murat Sagar Singh? Or what if we do, but he doesn't know what it was that Susan thought was significant?

It was terrible to think she might have brought that dreadful attack onto her mentor, but it was also frustrating to think of the doctor working in her lab that night before it happened, perhaps discovering all manner of important things, even taking time to leave a message for her, but not bothering to record any of it. Who ever expected the world to change that rapidly? But it did.

Renie had been unsealing another pack of cigarettes, but now she dropped them on the desk and asked her pad to call Susan's house, hoping to reach Jeremiah Dako. The doctor's voice came on with her voicemail, dry and brisk.

"This is Susan Van Bleeck. I'm doing something interesting right now. Yes, at my age. Leave a message, please."

Renie found it hard to speak for a moment, but when she regained her voice, she asked Jeremiah to call her as soon as he could.

She picked up her cigarettes again and moved the exam template back to the center of the screen.

Jeremiah Dako hung back at the door of the elevator. "I cannot look at that place today." His eyes were red and he looked ten years older than the first time Renie had seen him. "It makes me too angry, too sad."

"That's no problem." Renie let !Xabbu step out and patted Dako's arm. "Thank you for letting us have a look. I hope we find something. We'll come back upstairs if we need you."

"The police have been here and gone. I suppose it doesn't matter what you touch anymore." He helped Renie lift her bags out onto the floor and then pushed the button. The door shut, the elevator hummed upward, and Renie turned for her first look at the lab.

"Oh, my God." Sour liquid rose in her throat and she swallowed hard. She had not expected the damage to be so extensive. The people who had beaten Susan so viciously had done a savagely thorough job on her workplace as well. "They must have brought sledgehammers with them."

Every single one of the long tables had been smashed to the ground and its contents pulverized. Flindered housings and shattered components made a carpet of plastic mulch half a foot deep across nearly the entire lab floor, a jigsaw puzzle without a solution. The screens on every wall had been shattered, too, their inner workings wrenched out through the jagged holes, cables dangling like the innards of a medieval torture victim.

!Xabbu looked up from where he squatted, sifting jagged bits of debris through his fingers. "Surely these men were not merely robbers. No robber would spend so much time ruining expensive equipment, even if they were looking for money instead."

"I can't imagine it. God almighty, look at this." The thoroughness of the ruin exerted a horrifying fascination—universal entropy demonstrated for beginners.

Pay attention, the wreckage seemed to declare. *Some things cannot be undone, short of time pivoting in its groove and crawling back on itself.*

Renie tried to imagine such a thing, like a video clip running in reverse, every ruptured piece flying back to its original site, equipment reforming, tables rising again like animals startled awake. And if she could run it all back, Susan would return, too, the spark of life leaping back into her cold body, her bones reknitting, the spatters of dried blood hidden under this wreckage liquescing and flowing together like mercury to leap from the floor and back into the doctor's closing wounds. Death itself would turn coward and flee.

Renie shuddered. She suddenly felt weak and sick. It was all too terrible, too hopeless.

She looked at !Xabbu as he idly handled the broken pieces of the doctor's work, at his slender, childlike back, and the weight of her responsibility returned to her. At this moment, it was not an unpleasant sensation. People needed her. Susan was gone and this horrible thing could not be undone—better to think about real things, problems that could be solved. She took a breath, unsnapped one of the equipment bags she'd borrowed from the Poly, and lifted out a small station node. Her hands were shaking. She cleared a place on the floor next to a wallport and jacked it in. "We'll just hope this station box has enough power to run the domestic system," she said, pleased with the steadiness of her voice. Crisis passed. "Jeremiah said he's had to turn the lights and everything else on and off manually, so they've disabled it somehow."

"Could ordinary criminals do that?"

"There's a lot of bootleg house-busting gear to be had these days, some of it very cheap. But I wouldn't think Susan would be the kind of person to leave her home vulnerable to that kind of assault, which suggests they must have had a pretty good package. I'll be able to tell you more if I can get into the house system."

!Xabbu frowned. "Did the police not investigate this?"

"Of course they did. Murder of a rich and well-known professor? Jeremiah said they were down here for three days—the private guard people, too. And you and I certainly answered enough questions about our last afternoon here. But even if they found something, they won't share it with us civilians—I tried, Jeremiah tried. About six months from now we might find out something useful. We can't wait that long." She turned on the station node, which blinked instantly to life. It was a very nice piece of Asian hardware which, if she dropped it anywhere between here and the Poly's lab, would cost her about half a year's salary to replace. "Let's see what's left and what it can tell us."

Renie slumped into the chair. Dako poured tea for her.

"Will your friend want some?"

"I guess so." She stared at the steaming cup, too tired for the moment even to lift it.

Dako hesitated, then sat down across from her. "Did you find anything? Anything to catch those . . . murderers?" He held his own cup in trembling fingers. Renie wondered what it had been like for him to come back to this house the first time after the doctor's death.

"No. They put some kind of datakiller into the house system—I've tried every form of retrieval gear I could lay my hands on. It's a wonder anything still works here at all."

"The doctor made sure everything ran in parallel. That's what she called it. In case the system broke down." There was quiet pride in his voice.

"Well, those bastards did their work in parallel, too. Not only did they bomb the system, but they broke every piece of hardware they could get their hands on, too."

!Xabbu walked into the kitchen holding something in his hands. Renie looked up, heart quickening. "What's that?"

"I found this as I was leaving. Caught between a lab table and the wall. It means nothing that I can see."

Renie grabbed at the piece of paper and smoothed it. Her own name, *Irene*, headed the page. Below, in Susan's unmistakable shaky handwriting, were the words *Atasco* and *Early M.*

"It doesn't mean anything to me," she said after some moments. "It could have been there for months, I suppose—it may be some other Irene entirely. But we'll check it out. It's something, anyway."

Jeremiah could make no sense of it either. Renie's momentary excitement began to fade.

!Xabbu sat down, his face solemn. "I saw the picture in the living room again as I passed," he said. "The rock painting." He stared at the cup before him. For a moment they were all silent. Renie thought they must look like they were conducting a seance. "I am very sorry," he continued abruptly.

"About what?"

"I fear that I made Doctor Van Bleeck feel uncomfortable about the picture on her wall. She was a good person. She valued it for what it meant, I think, even though it was not the work of her own people."

"She was so good. . . ." Jeremiah sniffed angrily and dabbed his eyes with a napkin, then wiped his nose. "Too good. She didn't deserve this. They should find these men and hang them, just like they did in the old days."

"She told us something important, anyway," Renie said. "And she may have left us this note. We'll do our best to find out what she learned. And if it leads us to the people that did that—" She paused, remembering the brutally impersonal thoroughness of the destruction below. "Well, I'll do whatever I can do—*whatever* I can do—to see them brought to justice."

"Justice." Dako said the word like it tasted bad. "When has anyone ever gotten justice in this country?"

"Well, let's face the facts. She was rich and she was white, Jeremiah. If anyone's murder is going to be solved by the authorities, hers will."

He snorted, whether in disbelief or agreement, Renie couldn't tell.

They finished their tea while Jeremiah told them all the things that had to be done to prepare for the doctor's memorial service, and how much of the work had been left to him. A niece and nephew were flying in from America, and on past experience Jeremiah fully expected to be pushed aside without thanks. His bitterness was understandable but depressing. Renie ate a few biscuits, more from politeness than hunger, then she and !Xabbu stood up to go.

"Thank you for letting us look," she said. "I would have felt terrible if we hadn't at least tried."

Jeremiah shrugged. "No one will be punished for this. Not as they deserve. And no one will miss her as much as I will."

Something sparked in Renie's memory. "Hold on. Jeremiah, Susan mentioned a friend named Martine, a researcher. I can't remember the last name—Day-roo-something."

Dako shook his head. "I do not know the name."

"I know the house systems were purged, but might there be any-where you could look? Did she keep an old-fashioned diary, a note-book, anything on paper?"

Jeremiah began to shake his head again, then paused. "We have a household accounts book. The doctor always worried that there might be tax problems, so we kept duplicate records." He bustled out of the room, his body language showing his gratitude at having something to do.

Renie and !Xabbu sipped at cold tea, too tired to make conversation. After about a dozen minutes had passed, Jeremiah hurried back in carrying a leather-bound ledger. "There is one small payment from three years ago, credited as 'research,' to a 'Martine Desroubins.' " He pointed. "Could that be it?"

Renie nodded. "It certainly sounds right. Any net adddress or number?"

"No. Just the name and the amount paid."

"Ah, well. It's a start."

Renie fingered the piece of folded paper, which now had the re-searcher's name written on it as well.

Fragments, she thought. *Just bits of things—voices in the dark, confusing images, names half heard. That's all we have to go on.* She sighed as Jere-miah steered onto the dark hill road. Here and there a glow through the trees showed the location of another of Kloof's isolated for-tresses—the light, as always, a display of bravery against the huge and frightening darkness.

Bravery? Or was it ignorance?

Fragments. She let her head rest against the cool window. !Xabbu had closed his eyes. *I suppose that is all we ever have to go on.*

Renie sat down on the edge of the bed to dry her hair, glad of a quiet moment by herself. The evening line for the shelter's communal shower had been long, and she hadn't been in a gossipy mood, so the twenty-minute wait had made her yearn for a little solitude.

As she undid the turban she had made of her towel, she checked her messages. Someone from the Poly had called to tell her she was summoned to the chancellor's office the next day, which didn't sound like anything good. She set her search gear to work on the two names from Susan's scrap of paper. The more she thought about it, the more she wondered why Doctor Van Bleeck, who had spent her entire life working with information machinery, would make a written note instead of just recording a voice message on her home system. Perhaps there was more significance to !Xabbu's discovery than she had first thought.

The gear turned up a match between *Atasco* and *Early M.* fast enough, a twenty-year-old book in its third revision entitled *Early Mesoamerica*, written by a man named Bolivar Atasco. The first search through South African directories for Susan's reseracher friend's name was less successful, so Renie started a worldwide investigation through the online directories for net addresses matching or close to *Desroubins*, then returned to consider the Atasco book.

As long as she was spending money she couldn't really afford, she decided, she might as well download the book itself. It was a little more expensive than normal, since it was apparently heavy on illustrations, but if Susan had left her some kind of clue, then by God she was going to find it.

By the time she finished drying her hair, it was on her system.

If *Early Mesoamerica* contained some kind of message from Susan Van Bleeck, it did not immediately yield up the secret. It seemed to be nothing more than a work of popular anthropology about the ancient history of Central America and Mexico. She checked the index for anything that might be significant, but found nothing unusual. She scanned through the text. The color pictures of Aztec and Mayan ruins and artifacts were striking—she was particularly taken by a skull made entirely of jade, and by some of the more elaborate stone carvings portraying flower-faced and bird-clawed gods—but none of it seemed to have anything to do with her problem.

A blinking light brought her attention back to her other inquiry. Nothing had turned up about anyone named Martine Desroubins on any of the conventional international directories. Renie called the Poly and accessed the school's much more comprehensive search engines—if she was going to get in trouble, she might as well get the most out of it while she still could—and then returned to the Atasco book, hunting for anything that might connect the text or pictures to the mysterious city. She had no better luck this time, and began to doubt that the crumpled piece of paper had been anything other than some old research note of Susan's. She skimmed back to the introduction and was reading about the author, Bolivar Atasco, who had apparently done a lot of interesting things in a lot of interesting places, when her father returned from the store.

"Here, Papa, let me help you." She put her pad down on the bed and went to take the bags from him. "Did you get me some more painblockers?"

"Yes, yes." He said it as though shopping were an underappreciated lifelong specialty of his instead of something he had just done for only the second or third time in his adult life. "Got the painblockers, got the other things. Those people in that store, they crazy. Make you stand in a line even when you only got a few little things."

She smiled. "Have you eaten anything?"

"No." He frowned. "I forgot to cook."

"I'll make you something. You're going to have to get your own breakfast tomorrow because I'm going to work early."

"What for?"

"It was the only chance I could get for some uninterrupted lab time."

"You never home, girl." He slumped onto the edge of his bed, looking sullen. "Leave me here alone all the time."

"I'm trying to do something about Stephen, Papa. You know that." She suppressed a frown as she pulled out a six-pack of beer and put it under the table, then hitched up her bathrobe and got down on her knees on the rough sisal mat to look for the vacuum-sack of *mielie* flour. "I'm working hard."

"You doing something about Stephen at your work?"

"Trying to, yes."

While she fried griddle cakes on the two-ring halogen minirange, her father pulled her pad onto his lap and scanned a few pages of *Early Mesoamerica*.

"What's this about? This whole book about some kind of Mexicans. These the people that used to cut out people's hearts and eat them?"

"I guess so," she said, glancing up. "The Aztecs used to perform human sacrifices, yes. But I haven't had much chance to look at it yet. It's something that I think Susan might have left for me."

"Huh." He snorted and closed the book. "Rich white woman, big old house, and she leaves you a book?"

Renie rolled her eyes. "It isn't that kind . . . " She sighed and flipped the griddle cakes. "Papa, Susan had relatives of her own. They'll get her property."

Her father stared at the book, frowning. "You said they didn't come to the hospital. You better come to the hospital when I'm dying, girl. Otherwise . . . " he stopped and thought for a moment, then grinned and spread his arms, encompassing their tiny room and few salvaged possessions. "Otherwise, I give all this to somebody else."

She looked around, not realizing for a moment that he had made a joke. Her laugh was as much surprise as amusement. "I'll be there, Papa. I'd hate to think someone else might get that mat I love so much."

"You remember, then." He lay back on his bed, pleased with himself, and closed his eyes.

Renie was just beginning to fall asleep when the pad beeped. She fumbled for it, groggy but alarmed—there were very few good things anyone might be calling her about just before midnight. Her father grunted and rolled over on the far side of the compartment, mumbling in his sleep.

"Hello? Who is it?"

"I am Martine Desroubins." She pronounced it *day-roo-ban*. "Why are you trying to find me?" Her English was accented, her voice deep and assured—a late-night radio announcer's voice.

"I didn't . . . that is . . . " Renie sat up. She unblocked her visuals, but the screen remained black, the other party choosing to retain her privacy. Renie lowered the volume slightly so it wouldn't wake her father. "I'm sorry if it seems like . . . " She paused, struggling to collect her thoughts. She had no idea how well Susan had known this person, or how far she could be trusted. "I came across your name through a friend. I thought you might be able to help with—might even have been contacted about—some family business of mine." This woman had already tracked her back through her inquiries, so it wouldn't do any good to lie about her identity. "My name is Irene Sulaweyo. I'm not anything to do with a business or anything. I'm not trying to cause trouble for you, or interfere with your privacy." She reached out for her pack of cigarettes.

There was a long pause, made to seem even longer by the darkness. "What friend?"

"What. . . ?"

"What friend gave you my name?"

"Doctor Susan Van Bleeck."

"She told you to call me?" There was real surprise and anger in the woman's voice.

"Not exactly. Look, I'm sorry, but I don't feel very comfortable talking about this over the phone with a stranger. Is there somewhere we could meet, maybe? Someplace where we'd both feel safe?"

The woman abruptly laughed, a throaty, even slightly raspy

sound—another smoker, Renie guessed. "Where is halfway between Durban and Toulouse? I am in France, Ms. Sulaweyo."

"Oh . . ."

"But I can promise you that at this moment, outside of a few government and military offices, there is not a more secure phone line than this one in all of South Africa. Now, what do you mean, Doctor Van Bleeck told you to call me, but not exactly? Perhaps I should simply check with her first."

Renie was taken aback for a moment, then realized that this woman did not know, or was pretending not to know, what had happened. "Susan Van Bleeck is dead."

The silence stretched for long seconds. "Dead?" she asked softly. If she was pretending surprise, this Martine, she was a gifted actress.

Renie fished another cigarette from the package and explained what had happened without mentioning anything of her own involvement. It was very strange, sitting in the dark and telling the story to a stranger in France.

To someone who says *she's in France,* Renie corrected herself. *Who says she's a she, for that matter.* It was hard to get used to this cloak and dagger stuff, but you couldn't take anything for granted on the net.

"I am very, very sad to hear this," the woman said. "But it still does not explain what you expect from me."

"I don't feel very comfortable talking on the phone, as I said." Renie considered. If this woman was truly in Europe, she was going to have to resign herself to phone conversations. "I suppose I don't have any choice. Does the name Bolivar Atasco mean anything to you, or a book called. . . ?"

"Stop." There was a brief hum of static. "Before I can speak with you further, I must make certain inquiries."

Renie was startled by the sudden shift. "What does that mean?"

"It means I cannot afford to be too trusting either, *entendu*? But if you are who and what you seem to be, we will speak again."

"Who and what I *seem to be?* What the hell does that mean?"

The caller had noiselessly disengaged.

Renie put down her pad and leaned back, letting her tired eyes droop closed. Who was this woman? Was there a chance she could actually help, or would it be just a bizarre accidental connection, a sort of drawn-out wrong number?

A book, a mysterious stranger—more information, but no shape to any of it.

Round and around again. Weariness tugged at her like a cranky child.

It's all just bits of things, fragments. But I have to keep going. No one else will do it. I have to.

She could sleep for a while—she had to sleep for a while—but she knew she would not wake feeling rested.

CHAPTER 20

Lord Set

No sun marred the faultless blue of the sky, yet the sands sparkled with light and the great river gleamed. At a gesture from the god the barque slid out into deeper water and turned against the sluggish current. Along the banks, thousands of worshipers threw themselves onto their faces in supplication, a massive, ecstatically groaning ripple of humanity far more violent than the sleepy motion of the river itself. Others swam after the barque, shouting praise even as their mouths filled with water, happy to drown in the attempt to touch the side of their lord's painted boat.

The continuous and noisy worship, which usually provided a soothing background for his self-designed narrative, suddenly annoyed Osiris. It hindered his thinking, and he had chosen this method of transportation precisely for its slow and tranquil pace, to compose himself for his appointment. If he had not wanted an extended meditative interlude, he could have traveled to his destination instantly.

He gestured again and the crowds simply vanished, flicked into nonexistence more swiftly than a man could swat a fly. Nothing remained along the banks but a few tall palm trees. The swimmers, too, were gone, the shallows empty but for thickets of papyrus. Only the helmsman of the barque and the naked children who fanned the Lord of Life and Death with ostrich feathers remained. Osiris smiled and grew calmer. It was a pleasant thing to be a god.

His nerves calmed by the gentle water sounds, he turned his thoughts to the approaching encounter. He searched himself for signs of anxiety and, unsurprisingly, found several. Despite all the times he had done this, it never grew any easier.

He had tried in many different ways to restructure his encounters with the Other, struggling always to make the interaction more palatable. For the first formal meeting he had created an innocuous office simulation, more anodyne than anything he owned in the real world, and had filtered the Other through the persona of a callow young employee, one of the interchangeable nonentities whose careers and even lives he had crushed without hesitation countless times. He had hoped in this way to make the Other an object so devoid of menace that any discomfort of his own would be removed, but that early experiment had turned out very badly. The Other's alien qualities had been even more disturbing as they forced their expression through the simulation. Despite the fact that the meeting had taken place in a simworld belonging to and controlled by Osiris, the Other had warped and scrambled his avatar in a most frightening way. Despite his own vast experience, Osiris still had no idea how the Other managed to disrupt complex simulation machinery so completely, especially since he very seldom seemed even rational.

Other experiments had been no more successful. An attempt to hold a meeting in a nonvisual space had only succeeded in making Osiris feel that he was trapped in infinite blackness with a dangerous animal. Attempts to make the Other subtly ridiculous failed as well—a cartoonish simulation designed by programmers from the Uncle Jingle children's program had simply expanded until it blotted out the rest of the simulation and filled Osiris with such intensely terrifying claustrophobia that he had been forced offline.

No, he knew now that this was the only way he could handle the unpleasant task—a task that the other members of the Brotherhood would not even attempt. He had to filter the Other through his own and most familiar simulation, and construct as much of a framework of ritual and distance around the encounter as he possibly could. Even the slow journey up the river was necessary, a period in which he could find the state of meditative calm that made useful communication possible.

It was quite astonishing, really, to think that anyone could inspire fear in Osiris, the master of the Brotherhood. Even in the mundane world he was a figure of terror, a man of power and influence so great that many considered him a myth. Here in his own created microcosm he was a god, the greatest of gods, with all that such stature brought. If he chose, he could destroy entire universes with only the blink of an eye.

He had made this journey dozens of times now, yet the prospect of simple contact—you could not term such interactions "conversations"—with the Other left him as frightened as when he had huddled in his bedroom in the oh-so-distant days of his childhood, conscious of his guilt and coming punishment, waiting for his father's footsteps to come booming up the stairs.

What the Other was, how he thought, what gave him the ability to do what he could do—all of these were questions that might have no comprehensible answer. There might also be simple explanations, as straightforward as the bioluminescence by which a firefly lured its mate. But it did not matter, and in a perversely terrified way, Osiris was glad. Humanity reached out, farther and farther, and still the Universe pulled away. Mystery was not dead.

The barque of the Lord of Life and Death glided up the great river. The burning sands ran unbroken to the horizon on either side. In all the world, it seemed, nothing moved at that moment but the boat itself and the slow rise and fall of the feathered fans in the hands of the god's attendants. Osiris sat upright, bandaged hands crossed on his chest, gold mummy mask staring into the infinite south of the red desert.

Set, the Beast of Darkness, awaited.

* * *

From the air, this section of Oregon coastline looked little different than it had ten thousand years before, the pine and fir trees leaning in wind-bitten array along the headlands, the stony beaches accepting the ceaseless attentions of the restless Pacific. Only the helipad thrusting up from the trees, a halogen-studded circle of fibramicized concrete three hundred feet wide, betrayed any sign of what lay hidden beneath the hills.

The jumpjet bucked slightly as a strong gust sheared in off the ocean, but the pilot had made landings on pitching carrier decks in worse weather, and under enemy fire as well; a few slight corrections as the VTOL jets roared, then the plane settled down onto the pad as gently as a falling leaf. A group of figures dressed in orange coveralls raced out of the low, featureless building on one side of the pad, followed more leisurely by a man wearing a casual blue suit that seemed to change hues slightly with every step, so that he flickered like a badly colorized film.

The late arrival stood at the bottom of the plane's ramp and extended his hand in greeting to the stocky older man in uniform who emerged from the jet. "Good afternoon, General. Welcome to Telemorphix. My name is Owen Tanabe. Mister Wells is waiting for you."

"I know that. I just spoke to him." The uniformed man ignored Tanabe's outstretched hand and headed toward the elevator doors, forcing him to turn and hurry to catch up with him.

"You've been here before, I take it?" he asked the general.

"Been here when this was just a hole in the ground and a bunch of blueprints, and a couple of times since." He punched at the elevator buttons with a stubby finger. "What's the damn thing waiting for?"

"Authorization." Tanabe ran his fingers over the array of buttons, a smooth, practiced movement like someone reading braille. *"Down,"* he said. The elevator door closed and the car dropped noiselessly.

The young Japanese-American man's further attempts at sociability were ignored. When the elevator door opened again, Tanabe gestured to the deeply-carpeted room and its deeply-cushioned furniture. "Mister Wells asks that you go in and wait. He'll be with you in a moment. May I bring you anything?"

"No. Is he going to be long?"

"I very much doubt it."

"Then you might as well get on your horse."

Tanabe shrugged gracefully and smiled. *"Up."* The door closed.

*   *   *

General Yacoubian had lit a cigar, and was squinting with outraged suspicion at a piece of modern art—multicolored electrosensitive gases housed in a clear plastic shell made from a death-cast of an accident victim—when the door behind the desk hissed open.

"Those aren't very good for you, you know."

Yacoubian turned his look of disapproval from the sculpture to the speaker, a slender, white-haired man with a lined face. The newcomer wore a rumpled antique sweater and slacks. "Jesus Samuel Christ," the general said, "are you going to start that stop-smoking shit all over again? What the hell do you know about it?"

"I must know something," Wells said mildly. "After all, I'm a hundred and eleven years old next month." He smiled. "Actually, it makes me tired just considering it. I think I'll sit down."

"Don't get comfortable. We need to talk."

Wells raised an eyebrow. "So talk."

"Not here. No offense, but there are certain things I don't want to talk about within a half-mile of any kind of listening or recording devices, and the only place that's got more of them per square inch than this gear-farm of yours is the Washington embassy of whatever Third World Country we're deciding to blow the shit out of this week."

Wells smiled, but it was a little chilly. "Are you saying that you don't think I can talk securely in my own office? Do you really think anybody could penetrate Telemorphix? I've got gear that even the government can only dream about. Or are you trying to say that you don't trust me, Daniel?"

"I'm saying I don't trust anybody with this—you, me, or anyone who might ever work for us. I don't trust TMX and I don't trust the U.S. Government, the Air Force, or the Emporia, Kansas, chapter of the Boy Scouts of America. Got it? Don't take it too personally." He took the cigar from his mouth and regarded the wet, chewed end with distracted annoyance, then replaced it and sucked until the other end was glowing red. Wells frowned at the cloud of thick smoke generated but said nothing. "Now, here's my suggestion. We can be in Portland in half an hour. I don't trust a conversation on my plane either, if that makes you feel any better, so we'll talk about the weather until we're back on the ground. You pick the part of town, I'll pick a restaurant in it. That way, we know neither of us is running a setup."

Wells frowned. "Daniel, this is . . . very surprising. Are you sure all this is necessary?"

Yacoubian grimaced. He removed his cigar, then ground it out in an Art Deco ashtray that was being used for its original purpose for the first time in at least half a century. His host's flinch did not go unnoticed. "No, Bob, I flew all the way here just because I thought you weren't getting enough protein in your diet. Damn it, man, I'm telling you, we need to talk. Bring along a couple of your security boys. We'll send 'em in with mine to make sure wherever we pick is clean."

"We're just going to sit there? With . . . with the customers?"

The general laughed. "Jesus, that scares you, huh? No, we'll clear 'em out. We can pay the owners enough to make it worth their while. I'm not worried about publicity, although we can throw a little scare into them about that as well. I just want a couple of hours when I don't have to worry about who might be listening."

Wells still hesitated. "Daniel, I haven't been out to dinner in I don't know how long. I haven't been off this property since I went to Washington for that Medal of Freedom thing, and that was almost five years ago."

"Then it will do you good. You own about half the world, man—don't you ever want to see any of it?"

To an outsider—like the nervous young waitress who had arrived at work to discover she would only have two customers that night, and now stood peering out at them from the relative security of the kitchen door—the men at the table seemed to be of a similar age, old enough to be looking forward to their first grandchidren. Very few ordinary grandfathers, though, had their table and chairs sterilized by a security team, or their food prepared under the watchful eyes of a half-dozen bodyguards.

The general was, in fact, a young-looking seventy, small and solid-bodied, skin darkened to coffee-with-cream from his years in the Middle East. He had been a wrestler at the Air Force Academy and still moved with a compact swagger.

The taller man was also very tan, although his skin color came from melanin alteration, a shield against the aging effect of ultraviolet light. By his erect posture and firm flesh, the waitress—who was disappointed that she didn't recognize either one of such an obviously important pair of customers—guessed him to be the younger of the two. It was an understandable misjudgment. Only the slow brittleness of his movements and the yellow tint to the whites of his eyes gave any hint of the scores of operations and the painful daily regimen which kept him alive and allowed that life to resemble something like normality.

"I'm glad we did this." Wells sipped his wine carefully, then set the glass down and dabbed his lips, every motion performed with meticulous deliberation. He seemed made of delicate crystal, like a creature from a fairy tale. "It's good to be . . . somewhere else."

"Yeah, and if our guys are doing their jobs, we can have a safer conversation here than we could have even in that hardened Twilight of the Gods bunker under your office. And the food was okay, too. You just can't get salmon like that on the East Coast—actually, there probably isn't any such article as East Coast salmon anymore, since that infestation thing." Yacoubian pushed his plate of fine bones aside and unwrapped a cigar. "I'll get to the point. I don't trust the old man any more."

Wells' smile was thin and ghostly. "Careful with that word 'old.' "

"Don't waste time. You know who I mean, and you know what I mean."

The owner of the world's most powerful technology company stared at his dinner companion for a moment, then turned as the waitress approached. His vague, distracted expression suddenly changed to something altogether colder. The young woman, who had finally worked up her courage to leave the kitchen doorway and come clear the plates, saw the look on Wells face and froze a few feet from the table.

The general heard her startled intake of breath and looked up. "We'll let you know if we want you. Go sit in the kitchen or something. Get lost."

The waitress scurried away.

"It's no secret you don't like him," said Wells. "It's no secret I don't like him either, although I feel a certain grudging respect for what he's done. But, as I said, none of that's a secret. So why all this running around?"

"Because something's gone wrong. You're right, I don't like him, and frankly all that pissy Egyptian stuff gets under my skin. But if everything was going as planned, I wouldn't give a shit."

"What are you talking about, Daniel?" Wells had grown rigid. His strange eyes, bright blue set in old ivory, seemed even more intense in his expressionless face. "What's gone wrong?"

"The one who got away—'the subject,' as our Fearless Leader calls him. I've been having some of my own people run a few simulations— don't worry, I haven't given them any kind of specifics, just some very broad parameters. And they keep coming back with the same results. Namely that it couldn't happen by accident."

"There is no such thing as accident. That's what science is all about—I've explained that to you enough times, Daniel. There are only patterns we don't yet recognize."

Yacoubian crumpled his napkin. "Don't you goddamn patronize me, Wells. I'm telling you that it wasn't an accident, and I don't want a lecture. My information says that someone must have helped it to happen."

"Someone else in the . . . in the group? The old man himself? But why? And how, Daniel? They'd have to come in and do it right under my nose."

"Now do you see why I didn't want to talk in your office?"

Wells shook his head slowly. "That's circular reasoning, Daniel. An accident is still the most likely possibility. Even if your SitMap boys say it's ninety-nine-point-ninety-nine in favor of outside intervention—and I'm only assuming they've got the right figures for the sake of argument—that's still a one in ten thousand chance that it's a fluke. Nobody on my end doubts it was an accident, and it's my engineers who have to troubleshoot the thing. I have a much easier time believing we hit the jackpot on those odds, which aren't really that long, than believing someone from outside got into the Grail Project." Another chilly smile. "Or 'Ra,' as our fearless leader is pleased to call it. Pour me a little more wine, will you? Is it Chilean?"

Yacoubian filled the taller man's glass. "Haven't been out of your goddamn bunker for years and now you're going to get drunk on me. A century-old teenager."

"Hundred and eleven, Daniel. Nearly." His hand stopped, the glass halfway to his mouth. He set the glass down.

"Damn it, Bob, this is crucial! You know how much time and energy we've all put into this! You know the risks we've taken—that we're taking even as we speak!"

"I do, Daniel." Wells' smile appeared fixed now, like something carved onto the face of a wooden dummy.

"Then start taking me seriously. I know you don't think much of the military—nobody in your generation did, from what I gather—but if you think someone gets to where I am without having something on the ball . . . "

"I have a lot of respect for you, Daniel."

"Then why the hell are you staring at me with that stupid grin on your face when I'm trying to get you talk about something important?"

The taller man's mouth straightened into a thin line. "Because I'm thinking, Daniel. Now shut up for a few minutes."

*   *   *

The now-thoroughly-terrified waitress had been allowed to clear the plates. As she put down coffee for both men and a snifter of cognac for the general, Wells reached up and gently clasped her arm. She jumped and gave a little squeak of surprise.

"If you were lost somewhere, and you didn't know how you'd gotten there and you didn't recognize the place, what would you do?"

She stared at him, eyes wide. "I . . . beg your pardon, sir?"

"You heard me. What would you do?"

"If I was . . . lost, sir?"

"And it was an unfamiliar place, and you didn't know how you'd wound up there. Maybe you even had amnesia and didn't remember where you came from."

Irritated, Yacoubian started to say something, but Wells flicked a glance at him. The general made a face and dug in his pocket for his cigar case.

"I'm not sure." The young woman tried to straighten up, but Wells had her arm held tightly. He was stronger than his careful movements suggested. "I suppose I'd . . . wait somewhere. Stay in one place so that someone could find me. Like they teach you in Girl Guides."

"I see." Wells nodded. "You have a bit of an accent, my dear. Where are you from?"

"Scotland, sir."

"That's nice. You must have come over after the Breakdown, right? But tell me, what if you were in a land full of strangers and didn't know if anyone would ever come to look for you? What would you do then?"

The girl was beginning to panic. She put her other hand on the table for support and took a deep breath. "I would . . . I would try to find a road, try to find people who'd traveled a lot. And I'd ask people about places that were nearby until I recognized a name. Then, I suppose I'd just stay on the road and try to get to the place that sounded familiar."

Wells pursed his lips. "Hmmm. Very good. You're a very sensible girl."

"Sir?" Her tone was questioning. She tried again a little louder. "Sir?"

He wore that half-smile again. It took him a few moments to respond. "Yes?"

"You're hurting my arm, sir."

He let her go. She moved rapidly toward the kitchen without looking back.

"What the hell was that all about?"

"Just seeing how people think. Ordinary people." Wells lifted his coffee and carefuly sipped. "If it *were* possible to penetrate the Grail Project and free this particular subject—and I'm not saying it is, Daniel—then who could do it?"

The general bit down, making the glowing tip of his cigar rise dangerously near to the tip of his nose. "Not too damn many, obviously. One of your competititors?"

Wells bared his perfect teeth in a different sort of smile. "I don't think so."

"Well, what else is left? UNComm? One of the big metros or states?"

"Or someone from the Brotherhood, as we already mentioned. A possibility, because they would have an advantage." Wells nodded, considering. "They know what to look for. No one else even knows that such a thing exists."

"So you're taking this seriously."

"Of course I'm taking it seriously." Wells lifted his spoon from the coffee and watched it drip. "I was already concerned about it, but talking about percentages made me realize that it's a bad gamble to ignore it any longer." He dipped the spoon again, this time letting the coffee pool on the tablecloth. "I never understood why the old man wanted this . . . modification, and it sure as hell made me and TMX look bad when the guy fell off the radar. I've been letting the old man handle it so far, but I think you're right—we need to be a little more proactive."

"Now you're talking. Do you think this South American deal has anything to do with it? He got awful interested all of a sudden in having our old friend taken out of the picture. Bully's been retired from the Brotherhood for almost five years—why now?"

"I don't know. Obviously, we'll have a close look when he brings back the specifications for the job. But right now I'm more interested in finding out where the hole in my fence is . . . if there is one."

Yacoubian finished his cognac and licked his lips. "I didn't bring along that whole security squad just to clear a restaurant, y'know. I thought I might leave a few of them with you to help out. Two of these guys worked at Pine Gap, and another one's right out of Krittapong's industrial espionage finishing school—he knows all the latest tricks."

Wells lifted an eyebrow. "He just walked out of Krittapong USA to come work for you? At military pay?"

"Nah. We recruited him before he ever went to work there." The general laughed as he ran his finger around the rim of the snifter. "So you're going to concentrate on finding out how someone got into the Project and sprang the old man's guinea pig?"

"*If* someone got in—I'm not conceding it happened yet. Good God, think of what it could mean if someone has. But yes, that will be one of my lines of inquiry. I can also think of something else we need to do."

"Yeah? What's that?"

"Now who's had too much to drink? Surely if you weren't getting a little fuzzy, a top-flight military mind like yours would see it immediately, Daniel."

"I'll ignore that. Talk to me."

Wells folded his curiously unwrinkled hands on the tabletop. "We have reason to believe that a breach of security may have occurred, yes? And since my organization has ultimate responsibility for the safety of the Grail Project, I must not grant immunity from suspicion to anyone—not even to the Brotherhood. Not even to the old man himself. Am I right?"

"You're right. So?"

"So I think that it's up to me, now—with your help, of course, since Telemorphix has always had a very warm relationship with government—to see if I can locate not just the security breach, but the runaway himself. *Inside* the system. And if in locating the fugitive we also find out what it is that made him so special to the old man, and that knowledge proves to be harmful to our esteemed colleague's interests . . . well, that would be an unavoidable shame, wouldn't it, Daniel?"

"I love the way you think, Bob. You just get better and better."

"Thank you, Daniel."

The general rose. "Why don't we hop back? Those boys out there are itching to get to work on this."

The tall man stood, too, more slowly. "Thanks for the meal. I don't think I've had such a nice evening for a long while."

General Yacoubian swiped his card across the window on the counter, then waved cheerfully to the waitress, who stared out from the doorway like a cornered animal. The general turned and took Wells by the arm.

"It's always good to get together with old friends."

*A*nd the wolf ran and ran, trying to escape from the burning hot stones, but the woodsman had sewn them firmly into his belly. He ran to the river to *drink, and swallowed the river water until the stones inside him finally grew cold, but they were too heavy, and their weight pulled him down beneath the water where he drowned.*

"Little Red Riding Hood and her grandmother embraced in joy, then they thanked the woodsman for his good deed. And they all lived happily ever after. Excuse me. . . ." Mister Sellars coughed and reached out with his trembling hand for the water glass. Christabel handed it to him.

"But that's not how it goes in my Storybook Sunglasses." She felt slightly upset. Stories were not supposed to have more than one ending. "In the real story the wolf is sorry and promises he won't ever do it again."

Mister Sellars took a drink of water. "Well, things change, stories change. In the original version, I believe, even Red Riding Hood and her grandmother did not survive, let alone the wicked wolf."

"What's a 'norishinal virgin'?"

He showed her his crooked smile. "The very beginnings of a story. Or the true thing that someone weaves a story around."

Christabel frowned. "But they're *not* true. My mommy said so. They're just stories—that's how come you're not supposed to be frightened."

"But everything comes from somewhere, Christabel." He turned and looked out the window. You could only see a little sky through the thick, tangly leaves of the plants growing in front of it. "Every story is at least slenderly rooted in the truth."

Her wristband began to blink. She frowned, then stood up. "I have to go now. Daddy's got the day off tomorrow, so we're going to go away tonight and I have to pack up my toys and clothes." She remembered what she was supposed to say. "Thank you for the story, Mister Sellars."

"Oh." He sounded a little surprised. He didn't say anything more until she came back into the living room after changing into her regular clothes. "My young friend, I am going to have to ask you to do something. I haven't wanted to impose on you. I feel tremendously bad about it."

Christabel didn't know what he meant, but it sounded like something sad. She stood quietly, finger to her mouth, and waited.

"When you come back from this trip, I'm going to ask you to do some things for me. Some of them might be things you think are bad. You may feel frightened."

"Will they hurt?"

He shook his head. "No. I would not do anything that would cause you pain, little Christabel. You are a very important friend of mine. But they will be secret things, and this will be the most important secret anyone ever asked you to keep. Do you understand?"

She nodded, eyes wide. He looked very serious.

"Then go on now and have a nice weekend with your family. But please come see me as soon as you possibly can when you get back. I hadn't known you were going, and I'm afraid it . . . " He trailed off. "Will you come and see me as soon as you can? Will you be back on Monday?"

She nodded again. "We're flying back Sunday night. My mommy told me."

"Good. Well, you'd better go now. Have a good time."

Christabel started toward the door, then turned. He was looking at her. His funny, melted-looking face seemed very unhappy. She rushed back and leaned over the arm of his chair and kissed him. His skin felt cold, and smoother than her daddy's bristly cheek.

"Good-bye, Mister Sellars." She closed the door fast so his wet air wouldn't get out. He called something after her as she ran down the path, but she couldn't understand him through the thick glass.

She walked slowly out of Beekman Court, thinking very hard. Mister Sellars had always been nice to her, and he was her friend, even if her parents told her never to visit him. But now he said he was going to ask her to do bad things. She didn't know what the bad things were, but it made her stomach feel upset thinking about them.

Would they be little bad things, like when she took the soap? That was little because no one found out and she hadn't got in any trouble, and it wasn't like she stole it from a store or someone else's house, anyway. Or would they be a different kind of bad—the very, very, very bad thing of getting into a stranger's car, which always made her mommy so upset when she talked about it, or a confusing secret bad thing like Daddy's friend Captain Parkins once did that made Missus Parkins come over to their house crying? These were bad things that no one ever explained, they just made faces and said "you know," or talked about them after Christabel went to bed.

In fact, Mister Sellars himself was a bad thing that no one ever explained. Her mommy and daddy had told her he wasn't well, and that he shouldn't have visitors, especially little children, but Mister Sellars had said that wasn't really true. But then why would her parents tell her not to visit a nice, lonely old man? It was very confusing.

Worrying, she cut across the corner lawn and onto Redland. She heard a dog bark in the house and wished she had a dog, too, a pretty little white dog with floppy ears. Then she would have a friend she could talk to. Portia was her friend, but Portia only wanted to talk about toys and Uncle Jingle and what other girls at school said. Mister Sellars was her friend, too, but if he wanted her to do bad things, maybe he wasn't a very good friend.

"Christabel!"

She looked up, startled. A car had stopped next to her and the door was swinging open. She made a little screaming noise and jumped back—was this the bad thing Mister Sellars meant, coming for her now? The worst bad thing of all?

"Christabel, what are you doing? It's me."

She bent down so she could look in the car. "Daddy!"

"Hop in, I'll give you a ride."

She climbed into the car and gave him a hug. He still had a little shaving-smell on his cheek. He was wearing a suit, so she knew he was on his way back from work. She sat back while her seatbelt fitted itself.

"Didn't mean to startle you, baby. Where were you coming from?"

She opened her mouth, then had to stop for a moment. Portia lived in the other direction. "I was playing with Ophelia."

"Ophelia Weiner?"

"Uh-huh." She kicked her feet and watched the trees slide past above the windshield. The trees slowed down, then stopped. Christabel looked out the side window, but they were only on Stillwell, two blocks from home. "Why are we stopping here?"

Her father's hard hand touched her under her chin. He turned her face around to look at his. His forehead was wrinkled. "You were playing with Ophelia Weiner? Just now? At her house?"

Her daddy's voice was careful and scary. She nodded.

"Christabel, I gave Mister and Missus Weiner and Ophelia a ride to the airport at lunchtime. They've gone on vacation, just like we're going on vacation. Why did you lie to me? And where have you been?"

His face was scary now too, that quiet angry face she knew meant she'd done a bad thing. That was a spanking face. It went all blurry as she started to cry.

"I'm sorry, Daddy. I'm sorry."

"Just tell me the truth, Christabel."

She was really scared. She wasn't supposed to visit Mister Sellars, and if she told her daddy, she'd be in big trouble—she'd get a spanking for sure. And maybe Mister Sellars would get in trouble, too.

Would they give him a spanking? He was very small and weak and would probably get hurt. But Mister Sellars wanted her to do bad things, he said, and now her daddy was angry. It was hard to think. She couldn't stop crying.

"Christabel Sorensen, we're not going anywhere until you tell me the truth." She felt his hand on top of her hair. "Look, don't cry. I love you, but I want to know. It's much, much better to tell the truth."

She thought of funny-looking Mister Sellars and how unhappy he looked today. But her daddy was sitting right next to her, and her Sunday School teacher always said that telling lies was bad, and that people who told lies went to hell and burned. She took a deep breath and wiped her nose and her upper lip. Her face was all yucky and wet.

"I . . . went to see . . . "

"Yes?" He was so big the top of his head touched the car roof. He was as big as a monster.

"This . . . this lady."

"What lady? What's going on, Christabel?"

It was such a big lie—such a *bad* lie—that she could hardly say it. She had to take another breath. "She h–h–has a *dog*. And she lets me play with him. His name is M–M–Mister. And I know Mommy said I can't have a dog, but I really, really want one. And I was afraid you'd say I couldn't go over there any more."

It was so surprising to hear the terrible big lie come out of her own mouth that she started crying again, really loud. Her daddy looked at her so hard that she had to look away. He took her chin and gently pulled her back.

"Is that the truth?"

"I swear it is, Daddy." She sniffed and sniffed until she wasn't crying too hard, but her nose was still running. "It's the truth."

He sat up and made the car go again. "Well, I'm very angry with you, Christabel. You know that you're always supposed to let us know where you're going, even on the Base. And you are never, *never* to lie to me again. Got it?"

She wiped her nose again. Her sleeve was wet and sticky now. "Got it."

"A dog." He turned into Windicott. "Of all the damn fool things. What's this lady's name, anyway?'

"I . . . I don't know. She's just a grown-up lady. Old like mom."

Her daddy laughed. "Whoops. I don't think I'd better pass *that* along." He made his face grouchy again. "Well, I'm not going to give you a spanking, because you finally told me the truth and that's the most important thing. But you told a lie to begin with, and you went off without telling us where you were going. I think when we get back from Connecticut you're going to be grounded for a little while. A week or two. That means you'll stay in the house—no playing at Portia's, no trips to the PX, and no grown-up-old-lady with a dog named Mister. Is that fair?"

Christabel was full of different feelings, scary jump-off-the-high-board feelings and upset-stomach feelings and exciting-secret feelings. Her insides were all whirly and raw. She sniffed again and rubbed her eyes.

"That's fair, Daddy."

He felt his heart quicken. The sandstorm which had briefly swept across the red desert was failing, and through its dying flurries he could see the great, squat shape of the temple.

It was huge and curiously low, a great fence of columns, an immense grin set in the vast dead face of the desert. Osiris himself had designed it that way, and apparently it suited the Other. This was his tenth visit to the place, and the temple remained unchanged.

His great barque slowly drifted toward its mooring. Figures dressed all in billowing white, with masks of white muslin stretched over their features, caught the rope thrown by the captain and pulled the boat toward shore. A line of musicians, similarly faceless, blossomed into existence on either side of the road, plucking at harps, blowing on flutes.

Osiris waved his hand. A dozen muscular Nubian slaves appeared, naked but for loincloths and dark as grapeskin, already sweating in the desert heat. Silently, they bent and lifted the god's golden litter and carried it down the quay toward the temple road.

He closed his eyes and let the gentle swaying put him deeper into his contemplative mood. He had several questions, but he did not know how many he would get to ask, so he had to decide in advance which were the most important. The attending musicians played as he passed. They also sang, a quiet up-and-down murmuring that hymned the glories of the Ennead and especially its master.

He opened his eyes. The massive temple seemed to rise out of the desert as he approached, stretching on either side to the limits of the horizon. He could almost sense the nearness of its inhabitant . . . its prisoner. Was it only the force of anticipation and the familiarity of his habitual progress, or could the Other actually make himself felt through what should be the unbreachable walls of the new mechanism? Osiris did not like that idea.

The litter made its slow way up the ramp, climbing until even the great river seemed only a thread of murky brown. The Nubians bearing him groaned softly—a small detail, but Osiris was a master of the particular and took joy in these tiny bits of authenticity. They were only Puppets, of course, and were not actually lifting anything. In any case, they would no more groan of their own accord than they would ask to be moved into a different simulation.

The slaves carried him through the massive door and into the cool shadows of the antechamber, a hypostyle hall lined by tall columns. Everything was painted white and covered with the words of spells which would calm and restrain the temple's inhabitant. A figure lay prostrate on the floor before him, and did not look up even when the god's processional music reached a feverish pitch and then fell silent. Osiris smiled. This high priest was a real person—a Citizen, as it was so quaintly put. The god had chosen him very carefully, but not for his abilities as an actor, so Osiris was glad to see he remembered at least some proper comportment.

"Up," he said. "I am here." The bearers stood resolutely, holding the litter now without a tremble. It was one thing for his Nubians to simulate human frailty when he was on the move, but there were times when he did not wish to be pitched around like a saint's icon being carried down a steep Italian street, and facing a living underling was such a time. It was not conducive to dignity.

"O, Lord of Life and Death, by whose hand the seed is germinated and the fields are renewed, your servant bids you welcome." The priest stood and made several ritual obeisances.

"Thank you. How is he today?"

The priest folded his arms across his chest as if hugging himself for warmth. The god guessed it was a gesture of actual physical unease, not a response to the simulation: as carefully as with every other detail, Osiris had made sure that the temple sweltered in desert heat. "He is . . . active, sir," the priest said. "O Lord, I mean. He's driven the readings up as high as they've been for some time. I wanted to take the container temperature down a few more degrees, but I'm afraid that if we go any colder, we'll risk losing him altogether." The priest shrugged. "In any case, I thought it best to talk to you first."

Osiris frowned, but only at the anachronistic language. It was impossible to make technicians remember where they were for very long—or, rather, where they were supposed to be. Still, this one was

the best he'd found; allowances had to be made. "You did well. Do
not adjust the temperature. It is possible he knows that I am coming
and it has excited him. If he remains too active when I have finished—well, we shall see."

"Go ahead, then, sir. I've opened the connection." The priest backed
out of the way.

Osiris made a gesture and was carried forward to the stone doorway
on which the great cartouche of Lord Set had been carved, each hiero-
glyph as tall as one of the Nubian bearers. He gestured again and the
music fell silent. The door swung open. The god left his litter and
floated through the doorway into the darkened cavern beyond.

Osiris drifted toward the massive black marble sarcophagus, which
stood alone in the middle of the empty, rough-hewn chamber, its lid
carved to resemble a sleeping figure with the body of a man and the
head of an unrecognizable beast. He hovered before it for a moment,
composing his thoughts. A pulse of orange light leaked through the
crack between coffin and lid, as though in greeting.

"I am here, my brother," he said. "I am here, Lord Set."

There was a crackling hiss and a moment of grating noise that hurt
the god's ears. The words, when they came, were almost unrecognizable.

"*. . . Not. . . brother. . . .* " There was another rush of interference.
"*Tiyuh . . . t–time . . . too slow. Slowwww. Want . . . want . . .* "

As always, Osiris felt the distant distress signals from his real body,
far away and safe in its soothing fluids. It was fear, stark fear racing
through him, making his nerves flare and his limbs twitch. It was the
same every time he heard that inhuman croaking.

"I know what you want." He forced himself to keep his mind on
what he had come to do. "I am trying to help you. You must be patient."

"*. . . Hear . . . blood-sound. Sm–sm–smell voices . . . want light.*"

"I will give you what you want. But you must help me. Do you
remember? Our bargain?"

There was a deep, wet moaning. For a moment the sarcophagus
shimmered before the god's eyes, individual monads separating like
an exploded diagram. Within, in a shadow deeper than ordinary darkness, something smoldered with its own faint light, something
twisted that writhed like an animal. For a moment its outline shifted
again, and he thought he could see a single eye staring out of the
whirling chaos. Then the whole thing shivered and the sarcophagus

was back, as solid and black as simulation engineering could make it appear.

"*. . . Remember . . . trick . . .*" If the oozing, rattling voice could be said to have expression, the Other sounded almost sullen, but some far deeper fury seemed to be bubbling beneath, a thought that made Osiris suddenly wish he could swallow.

"There was no trick. You would not be alive without my help. And you will never be free without my help either. Now, I have some questions for you."

There was another burst of cacophony. When it had quieted, the voice came grinding and scraping again. "*. . . Bird . . . from . . . your cage. Primary . . . and the running . . .*" The sound became unintelligible.

"What? What does that mean?"

The sarcophagus shuddered. For a split second it had too many facets, too many angles. The voice lurched and slurred like a piece of equipment with dying batteries. "*. . . From other side . . . voices are . . . soon. Coming.*"

The god's fear was mixed with frustration. "Who's coming? From the other side? What does that mean?"

This time, it sounded almost human—as close as it ever came. "*Other . . . side . . . of . . . everything.*" It laughed—at least Osiris thought it was a laugh—a deep, soggy crunching that abruptly squealed up into an almost inaudible steady tone.

"I have questions!" the god shouted. "I have important decisions to make. I can make things go even slower if you don't cooperate." He searched his mind for a suitable threat. "I can keep you this way *forever!*"

At last it returned and spoke to him. In the end, it answered several of his questions, but not always in ways that he found useful. In between the few comprehensible phrases, it cried and hissed and sometimes bayed like a dog. Once it spoke to him in the voice of someone he had known who was now dead.

When the audience was finished, the god did not bother with his litter or his bearers or even the great river. He went directly and instantly to his hall in Abydos-That-Was, extinguished all the lights, banished all the priests, and sat for a very long while in darkness and silence.

CHAPTER 21

Up The Ladder

NETFEED/NEWS: Mars Funding Shaky
(visual: Martian skyline, Earth on horizon
VO: The ancient human dream of conquering Mars may be coming to an
end, brought down by funding problems.
(visual: MBC robots at work on Martian surface)
Now that its two largest corporate sponsors, ANVAC and Telemorphix, have
ended their involvement, the Mars Base Construction project, long a target of
both left-wing and right-wing pressure groups, seems likely to lose its funding
support in Congress as well. President Anford has promised to search for
other business sponsorship, but his funding request to the Assembly of
Governors—a presidential endorsement of the project which one UNSpace
official called "pretty damn lukewarm"—is not deemed likely to move the
governors, who are having trouble with their own state and city
infrastructures. . . .

Renie answered on the first flash. When the screen came up black, she felt sure she knew who it would be.

"Irene Sulaweyo?"

"So you know my work number, too." She was faintly nettled by this Martine woman's here-then-gone mystery. "Did you just make a lucky guess that I'd be here before school started?"

"Please remember, Ms. Sulaweyo, it was you who began this by searching for me." The French woman sounded amused. "I hope you are not going to be difficult because I have taken the initiative."

"It's not that. I just didn't expect . . . "

"That I would be able to find you so easily? Information is my business, if you will forgive an old cliché. And I know far more about you now than simply your work number and your whereabouts, Ms. Sulaweyo. I know your employment history, your grades in school, your salary. I know that your mother Miriam who died in the Shopper's Paradise fire was of Xhosa lineage, that your father Joseph is half-Zulu, and that he is currently listed disabled. I know about your brother Stephen in the Durban Outskirt hospital. I know what net services you subscribe to, what books you download, even what kind of beer your father drinks."

"Why are you telling me this?" she said tightly.

"Because I wanted you to know that I am thorough. And because I needed to find out these things for myself, to find out who you really were, before I could talk to you."

This time she could not keep the fury from her voice. "So I passed the test? Thank you. *Merci*."

There was a long pause. When the mystery woman spoke, her voice was gentler. "You came looking for me, Ms. Sulaweyo. I am sure you value your privacy. So do I."

"So where do we go from here?"

"Ah." Martine Desroubins was suddenly businesslike. "That is an excellent question. I think a controlled exchange of information is in order. You said that you got my name through Susan Van Bleeck. I had hoped to speak to her about a subject which interests me. Perhaps you and I, we share this interest?"

"What subject—what interest is that?"

"First things first." The invisible woman sounded as though she were settling in. "Tell me again what happened to Susan. And this time, tell me the whole truth, please."

It was a laborious process, but not an entirely unpleasant one. The woman on the other end was grudging with information, but there were hints of a dry wit and perhaps even a kind heart hiding behind the reserve.

According to Martine Desroubins, she *had* received a call from Susan after Renie's visit, but had not been able to talk at the time. The postponed conversation had never occurred. Renie did not divulge the doctor's deathbed message, but after she described her brother's illness, her attempts to discover its cause, and the strange city-virus left on her machine, the other woman was quiet for a long moment. Renie could sense a sort of turning point, as though a chess game played through its opening moves was finally beginning to take its real shape.

"Was Doctor Van Bleeck calling me because she thought *I* could help with the problem of your brother? Or just help identify this strange city?"

"I don't know. She never told me what she wanted to talk to you about. There was also a book—she left a note behind with the title."

"Ah, yes, I remember you began to tell me about the book. Could you tell me the title?"

"*Early Mesoamerica*. By someone named Bolivar Atasco."

This time the pause was shorter. "The name sounds somewhat familiar. Have you examined the book?"

"I downloaded it, but I can't see anything relevant. I haven't had much chance to really look, though."

"I am obtaining a copy for myself. Perhaps I will notice something you would not."

Renie felt an unexpected sense of relief. *Maybe she really can help. Maybe she can help me get into TreeHouse, find this man Singh.* Her brief moment of gratitude was followed by a pang of uncertainty. Why should she so quickly accept this mystery woman as a possible ally? *Because I'm desperate, of course.* Out loud, she said: "Now you know about me, but what about you? All I've heard is that you knew Susan and she tried to reach you."

The smooth voice sounded amused. "I have not been forthcoming, I know. I value my privacy, but there is nothing mysterious about me. I am what I told you—a researcher, and a fairly well-known one. That you can verify."

"I've put my life in your hands, you know. I don't feel very secure."

"That may change. In any case, let me examine the anthropology book, then I will call you back again at your lunch break. In the meantime, I will send you information on this Atasco. It will save you some time searching. And, Ms. Sulaweyo. . . ?" She made even Renie's own name sound like something Gallic.

"Yes?"

"Next time, perhaps we should call each other Martine and Irene, yes?"

"Renie, not Irene. But yes, I suppose we should."

"*Á bientot,* then." Just when Renie thought the woman had rung off, as silently as the first time, her voice came again. "One more thing. I will give you some other information for free, although it will not make you happy, I am afraid. The Durban Outskirt Medical Facility, where your brother stays, has gone to full Bukavu 4 quarantine this morning. I think there will be no more visitors allowed." She paused again. "I am very sorry."

Renie stared at the empty screen, mouth open. By the time she began to ask questions, the line was dead.

!Xabbu found her in her office during the first break.

"Look at this," she snarled, gesturing at the screen of her pad.

"*. . . all questions on our answer line, or contact the Durban Department of Public Health. We hope this will be a temporary measure. Daily updates will be posted . . .*" the tired doctor was saying for about the dozenth time.

"It's on a goddamn loop. They're not even answering their phones."

"I do not understand." !Xabbu stared at the screen, then at Renie. "What is this?"

Tired already at 9:45 in the morning, and yet jittery with furious tension, she told him about the expanded hospital quarantine. Halfway through, she realized he didn't know about Martine Desroubins yet, so she started the explanation over.

"And do you think this woman is trustworthy?" he asked when she had finished.

"I don't know. I think so. I hope so. I'm beginning to run out of ideas, not to mention strength. You can be here when she calls at lunch and tell me what you think."

He nodded slowly. "And the information she gave you so far?"

Renie had already muted the hospital-loop; now she broke the connection completely and brought up the Atasco files. "See for yourself. This Bolivar Atasco is an anthropologist *and* an archaeologist. Very famous. Rich as hell, too, from a wealthy family. He more or less retired a few years back, but he writes an occasional scientific article. He seems to have houses in about five different countries, but South Africa isn't one of them. I don't see what any of it has to do with Stephen."

"Perhaps it does not. Perhaps it is something in the book itself, some idea, that Doctor Van Bleeck meant you to see."

"Maybe. Martine's looking at it, too. She might come up with something."

"What about that other thing—the thing you discovered before the doctor died?"

Renie shook her head wearily. It was hard to think of anything besides Stephen, now even farther from her, sealed in that hospital like a fly locked in amber. "What thing are you talking about?"

"TreeHouse, you said. All the references to this Singh, this Blue Dog Anchorite man, pointed to TreeHouse. But you never told me what TreeHouse *is*."

"If you had spent more time gossiping with other students instead of studying so much, you'd have heard all about it." Renie closed the Atasco files. She had the beginnings of a bad headache and couldn't stand looking at the compact text any longer. "It's an urban legend in the VR world. Almost a myth. But it's real."

!Xabbu's smile was slightly pained. "Are all myths false, then?"

She winced inwardly. "I didn't mean to imply anything. Sorry. It's been a bad day already, and it's just started. Besides, I'm not good on religion, !Xabbu."

"You did not offend me, and I did not mean to cause you more upset." He patted her hand, a touch as light as the brush of a bird's wing. "But often I think that people believe things which can be measured are true things, and things which cannot be measured are untrue things. What I read of science makes it even more sad, for that is what people point to as a 'truth,' yet science itself seems to say that all we can hope to find are patterns in things. But if that is true, why is one way of explaining a pattern worse than others? Is English inferior to Xhosa or my native tongue because it cannot express all the things they can?"

Renie felt a vague sense of oppression, not because of her friend's words, but because of what seemed the increasing impossibility of understanding *anything*. Words and numbers and facts, the tools she had used to measure and manipulate her world, now seemed to have lost their sharp edges. "!Xabbu, my head's hurting and I'm worried about Stephen. I can't really have a decent discussion about science and religion right now."

"Of course." The little man nodded, watching as she pulled a pain-blocker from her bag and swallowed it. "You look very unhappy, Renie. Is is just the quarantine?"

"God, no, it's everything. We still don't have any answers or any way to bring my brother back, and the search just seems to get more complicated and more vague. If this were a detective story, you'd have a body and some bloodstains and footprints in the garden—it's definitely a murder, and you've definitely got clues. But all we have here are things that seem a little strange, bits of information that *might* mean something. The more I think, the less sense it makes." She pushed at her temples with her fingers. "It's like when you say a word too many times, and suddenly it doesn't mean anything anymore. It's just . . . a word. That's how I'm feeling."

!Xabbu pursed his lips. "That is something like what I meant when I said I could no longer hear the sun." He looked around Renie's office. "Perhaps you have been too long inside—that cannot help your mood. You came in early, you said."

She shrugged. "I wanted some privacy. I can't get that back in the shelter."

!Xabbu's expression became impish. "Not much different than my rooming house. My landlady was watching me eat this morning. Very closely, but pretending not to do so. I think since she has never seen anyone like me before, she is still not quite sure I am human. So I told her the food was good, but I preferred to eat people."

"!Xabbu! You didn't!"

He chortled. "Then I told her she need not worry, because my folk only ever eat the flesh of their enemies. After that, she offered me a second helping of rice, which she has never done before. Perhaps now she wishes to make sure my stomach will be full."

"I'm not entirely sure that city life is having a good effect on you."

!Xabbu grinned at her, pleased that he had cheered her a little. "Only when they have put great distance between themselves and their own histories can people convince themselves that those they consider 'primitive' people do not have a sense of humor. My father's family, living from meal to scant meal in the middle of the Kalahari, walking miles to find water, still loved jokes and funny stories. Our Grandfather Mantis loves to play tricks on others, and it is often by such tricks that he defeats his enemies when his strength is not sufficient."

Renie nodded. "Most of the white settlers here thought the same thing about *my* ancestors—that we were either noble savages or dirty animals. But not normal people who told each other jokes."

"All people laugh. If there is ever a race that comes after us, as we came after the Early Race, then I expect they will have a sense of humor, too."

"They'd better," Renie said sourly. The moment's diversion had not changed anything much; her head still throbbed. She pulled a second painblocker out of her desk and swallowed it. "Then maybe they'll forgive us for what a mess we've made of things."

Her friend examined her carefully. "Renie, will we not have just as much privacy if we take your pad outside and receive the call from this Martine woman there?"

"I suppose. Why?"

"Because I think you truly have been inside for too long. Whatever your cities might resemble, we are *not* termites. We need to see the sky."

She started to argue, then realized she did not want to. "Okay. Meet me back here at lunchtime. And I still haven't answered your question about TreeHouse."

The small hill was bare except for a thin mat of tangled grass and an acacia tree, in whose shade they were hiding from the high, strong sun. There was no wind. A yellowish murk hung over Durban.

"TreeHouse is a holdover from the early days of the net," she said. "An old-fashioned place where they make their own rules. Or at least that's what it's supposed to be—people who can go there don't talk about it much, so a lot of the information is inflated by rumors and wishful thinking."

"If they are old-fashioned, how can they keep this place hidden, as you say they do?" !Xabbu picked up a seedpod and rolled it in his fingers. He was squatting in his effortless manner, a pose that Renie found, as always, evocative of some dreamlike, distant past.

"Oh, their equipment and gear is up to date, believe me. More than up to date. These are people who have spent their entire lives on the net—some of them practically built the thing in the early days. Maybe that's why they're so militant. Because of guilt about how it's turned out." The tightness in her jaw and neck had loosened a little: either the painblocker or the open sky had done some good. "In any case, the old-fashioned part is that a lot of these people were engineers and hackers and early users of the net, and they had an idea back then that the communications network spreading across the world was going to be a free and open place, somewhere that money and power didn't matter. No one would censor anyone else, and no one would be forced into conforming with what some corporation wanted."

"What happened?"

"About what you'd expect. It was a naive idea, probably—money has a way of changing things. People started to make more and more rules, and the net began to look like the rest of the so-called civilized world."

Renie heard the lecturing rancor in her own voice and was surprised. Were !Xabbu's feelings about the city beginning to alter her? She looked out at the vast patchwork of buildings spread across Durban's hills and valleys like a colorful fungus. Suddenly it seemed almost sinister. She had always felt that industrial progress in Africa, a continent so exploited for the material gains of others and so long denied the benefits itself, was generally a good thing, but now she was not so sure.

"Anyway, the TreeHouse people took a kind of Noah's Ark approach, I guess you could say. Well, not exactly. They didn't have any *things* they wanted to save, but they did have some ideas they wanted to hang onto—anarchic stuff, mostly, complete freedom of expression and so on—and some other ideas they wanted to keep out. So they created TreeHouse, and constructed it in such a way that it wasn't dependent on corporate or government sponsors. It's distributed over the machinery of its users with a lot of redundancy built in, so any number of them could drop out and TreeHouse would still continue to exist."

"Why does it have that name?"

"I don't really know—you should ask Martine. Maybe from logic trees or something. A lot of these things from the early days of the net have funny names. 'Lambda Mall' comes from an early experiment in text-only VR."

"It sounds as though it would be a haven for criminals as well as those who wish freedom." !Xabbu didn't sound as if he particularly disapproved.

"It is, I'm sure. The more freedom you give people to do good, the more freedom they have to do bad as well."

Her pad beeped. Renie flipped it open.

"*Bon jour.*" The voice, as previously, issued from a blacked-out screen. "This is your friend from Toulouse. I am calling as we arranged."

"Hello." Renie had her own videolink operating, but it seemed politic to assume the other was not receiving either. "I'm not alone. My friend !Xabbu is here. He was at Susan's with me, and knows everything I know."

"Ah." Martine's pauses were becoming characteristic. "You are outside, somewhere, yes?"

So the French woman *did* have her own video on. It seemed obscurely unfair. "Outside the Polytechnic where I work."

"This line is secure, but you must be careful not to be observed." Martine spoke briskly, not chiding but stating facts. "People can read lips, and there are many ways of bringing distant things close enough to see."

Renie, a little embarrassed by having something that she had neglected pointed out to her, looked to !Xabbu, but he had his eyes closed, listening. "I'll try not to move my lips too much."

"Or you could shield your mouth with your hand so it is hard to see. This may sound extreme, Irene . . . Renie, but even if I did not understand your own problem to be serious, I have my own concerns."

"I've noticed." Her irritation escaped her control. "What are we really doing here, Martine? Are we supposed to trust each other? What am I supposed to think of someone who won't even show her face?"

"What good would that do you? I have my own reasons, Renie, and I do not owe you or anyone an explanation."

"But you trust me now?"

Martine's laugh was dourly amused. "I trust no one. But I think you are what you say you are, and I have no reason to doubt your story."

Renie looked at !Xabbu, who wore an odd, distracted expression. As if sensing her stare, he opened his eyes and gave a little shrug. Renie suppressed a sigh. Martine was right; there was nothing much at this point that either of them could do to prove good faith. She either needed to break off the connection, or close her eyes, hold her nose, and jump.

"I think I need to get into TreeHouse," she said.

The other woman was clearly caught off-balance. "What do you mean?"

"Are you certain this line is safe?"

"Certain. Any security risk would come from your end."

Renie looked around. There was not a person in sight, but she still leaned close to the screen. "I think I need to get into TreeHouse. Before she died, Susan gave me a message about an old hacker friend of hers—she seemed to think he had some information we could use. His name is Murat Sagar Singh, but he also goes by 'Blue Dog Anchorite.' I think I can find him through TreeHouse."

"And you wish me to help you get into there?"

"What else can I do?" A sudden upwelling of pain and anger forced her to measure her words. "I'm just going forward the best I can. I can't think of any other way. I think my brother is as good as dead if I don't get some answers. And now I can't even . . . even . . ." She took a shaky breath. "I can't even get in to visit him."

The mystery woman's voice was sympathetic. *"Entendu,* Renie. I think I can help you to get in."

"Thank you. Oh, God, thank you." A part of her stood aside, disgusted with such pathetic gratitude. She still had no idea who this faceless woman was, but she was trusting her in a way she had trusted few others. She reached for firmer conversational footing. "Did you find out anything about Atasco?"

"Not much, I am afraid. He has no involvement that I can discover with the people who own the club you spoke of, Mister J's, or anything else of significance on the net. He seems to keep a low profile."

Renie shook her head. "So we don't really know whether Atasco or his book have anything to do with anything." !Xabbu had pulled a piece of string from his pocket and constructed a sort of cat's cradle between his outstretched fingers. He was staring at it meditatively.

"No. We will hope that we can find out something useful from this man Singh. I will see what I can do about getting us into TreeHouse. If I can arrange it, will you be available after work today?"

Renie remembered the meeting in the Chancellor's office. "I have to do something after class, but I should be finished by 1700 hours, my time."

"I will call you. And perhaps next time your friend will speak to me." Martine rang off.

!Xabbu looked up from his string-design to the blank screen, then back down again.

"Well?" Renie asked. "What did you think?"

"Renie, you said once you would tell me what a 'ghost' is."

She closed her pad and turned to face him. "A ghost? You mean the VR kind?"

"Yes. You once spoke of it, but never explained."

"Well, it's a rumor—not even that. A myth." She smiled wearily. "Am I still allowed to say that?"

He nodded. "Of course."

"Some people have claimed that if you spend enough time on the net, or if you die while you're online . . . " She frowned. "This sounds very foolish. They say that sometimes people stay on the net. After they're dead."

"But that is not possible."

"No, it's not possible. Why do you ask?"

He moved his fingers, changing the string-shape. "This woman Martine. There is something unusual about her. I thought if a ghost was a kind of strange person on the net, and she was one, then I might understand better. But she is obviously not a dead person."

"Unusual? What do you mean? Lots of people don't want to show their faces, even if they're not quite as crazy about security as she is."

"There was . . . something in the sound of her."

"Her voice? But voices can be distorted—you can't base anything on that. You remember when we went to the club and I made both our voices sound deeper."

!Xabbu shook his head in mild frustration. "I know, Renie. But something in the way she talked was unusual. And also, the sound of the place where she was. She was in a room with very, very thick walls."

Renie shrugged. "She might be in some bombproof government building or something—I have no idea what she does besides spook around on the net. God, she had better be legitimate. She's my main hope right now. It might take months to get into TreeHouse on our own. But how can you tell about the walls?"

"Echoes, sounds. It is hard to explain." He squinted, looking more childlike than ever. "When I lived in the desert, I was taught to hear the sounds of birds flying, of game moving across sand many miles away. We listen closely."

"I don't know anything about her. Maybe she's . . . no, I can't even imagine." She stood up. Down below, she could see students returning to class. "I'll be back in the lab after my meeting. Let me know if you figure anything out."

Renie barely restrained the impulse to kick the office door off its hinges. As it was, the closing slam blew papers off her desk and almost knocked !Xabbu out of his chair.

"I can't believe this! They've suspended me!" She was tempted to open the door and thump it closed again, just for something to do with the rage that was running through her like lava.

"You have lost your job?"

She brushed past him and flung herself down in her chair, then scrabbled out a cigarette. "Not completely. I'm on salary until my disciplinary hearing. Damn, damn, damn!" She flung the broken ciga-

rette away and seized another. "I can't believe this! Shit! One thing
after another!"

!Xabbu reached out a hand as though to touch her, then pulled it
back again.

Afraid he might lose a finger, she thought. She did feel like biting
someone. If Chancellor Bundazi had yelled at her, it would have been
bearable, but the look of disappointment had been far more devastating.

"We've always thought a lot of you, Irene." That slow head-shake, the
small diplomatic frown. *"'I know things have been difficult for you at home,
but that's no excuse for this kind of bad judgment."*

"Shit." She'd broken another cigarette. She took a little more care
on the next. "It's the equipment I borrowed—I didn't really have permission. And they found out that I fiddled the chancellor's e-mail."
She got the cigarette lit and inhaled. Her fingers were still trembling.
"And some other things, too. I haven't been very smart, I guess." She
was dry-eyed, but she felt like crying. "I can't believe this!" She took
a deep breath and tried to calm herself. "Okay, come with me."

!Xabbu looked bewildered. "Where are we going?"

"In for a penny, in for a pound. This is my last chance to use the
Poly's equipment. We'll see if Martine comes up with anything."

Yono What-was-his-name was in the Harness Room, oblivious behind his headset as he swayed from side to side, waving his hands
and jabbing at invisible objects. Renie leaned hard on the *interrupt*
button. He jerked the helmet off like it had caught fire.

"Oh, Renie." There was a flicker of guilt in his eyes, evidence of
gossip heard and gossip passed. "How are you?"

"Get out, will you? I need the lab and it's urgent."

"But . . . " He smiled crookedly, as though she had made a joke in
poor taste. "But I have all this three-double-D work to do. . . . "

She resisted the urge to scream, but just barely. "Look, I've just
been suspended. After this, you won't need to deal with me anymore.
Now, be a nice man and *get the hell out,* will you?"

Yono picked up his belongings in a hurry. The door was closing
behind him as Martine's call came in.

The access path Martine gave them led to an area of the net Renie
had never visited, a small commercial node as unlike the mass-market
flash of Lambda Mall as a broom closet was to an amusement park.
The databank at the end of the French woman's coordinates was of a

very basic kind rented out to small businesses, the VR equivalent of the cheap modular storage centers in the real world of Durban Outskirt. The databank's visual representation was as unprepossessingly functional as the unit it represented—a cube whose half-toned walls were covered with buttons and windows which activated and displayed the various services.

Renie and !Xabbu hung in the center of the cube, their rudimentary sims made even more crude by the node's cut-rate rendering.

"This looks like the VR equivalent of a dark alley." Renie was in a foul mood. The day had already been hideously long, she had been suspended from her job, and her father had complained when she had phoned to say she'd be home late and he'd have to make his own supper—in fact, he had seemed more upset about that than the news about Stephen or her job. "I hope Martine knows what she's doing."

"Martine also hopes so."

"Ah. You're here." Renie turned, then stared. "Martine?"

A glossy blue sphere hung beside them. "It is me. Are you ready to begin?"

"Yes. But . . . but won't you find it difficult to . . . to work the interface?"

The blue sphere hung motionless. "It is not necessary to use the virtual interface to get into TreeHouse—it is perhaps easier not to, especially for someone like me who prefers other methods of manipulating data. But since you work with such environments, I thought you would be more comfortable entering it this way. It will certainly make the experience easier to handle when we reach TreeHouse itself, since the VR interface works a little more slowly than other versions. TreeHouse is *very* fast and confusing."

Which still doesn't explain why her own sim is so weird-looking, noted Renie. *But if she doesn't want to tell me, I suppose that's her business.*

Several of the buttons on the databank interface flared as though they had been pressed, and data began to blur through the windows.

She's not even using the VR interface, Renie realized. *This billiard-ball thing is just a marker, so we'll know she's here with us. She must be doing all this stuff directly from her keys, or offline voice controls, or something. . . .*

"Do you know why this place is called TreeHouse?" Martine asked.

"I told !Xabbu we should ask *you* that question. I don't know—logic trees was my guess."

"It is not so complicated." Martine's laugh was derisive. "It is very simple—they were boys."

"What? Who were?"

"The people who first made TreeHouse. Not all were male, of course, but most of them were, and they were making a place that was their very own. Like little boys who build a tree house and have a club and do not let anyone else in. Like the old story of Peter Pan. And do you know how you get into TreeHouse?"

Renie shook her head.

"You will appreciate the joke, perhaps. You have to find the Ladder." As she spoke, one of the windows suddenly expanded until it covered an entire wall of the cube. "The Ladder can always be lowered," Martine continued, "but the places where it will appear are always different. The people of TreeHouse do not want to encourage people to try to hack their way in. Only those who have climbed the Ladder before know how to find it."

!Xabbu suddenly broke his silence. "Then you have been to this TreeHouse?"

"I have, but as a guest. I will tell you more, but now please remember we are in a public place. This is a real databank, but with a connection to the Ladder, or at least that is true today—if you returned to this node tomorrow, I doubt the connection would still be here. But, in any case, someone could come here with legitimate business at any time. Step through."

"Step through that window?" asked Renie.

"*S'il-vous plait.* Please. There is no danger on the other side."

Renie moved her sim through the data window. !Xabbu followed her into a virtual space even less detailed than the one they had left, a larger cube of almost pure white. The window irised shut, leaving them alone in the featureless cube: the blue sphere had not accompanied them.

"Martine!"

"I am here," said the bodiless voice.

"But where is your sim?"

"I do not need any sim here—the bottom rung of the Ladder, like TreeHouse, is beyond the laws of the net. There is no requirement to be embodied."

Renie remembered her friend's question about ghosts, and although it was perfectly reasonable that Martine should want to escape one of the petty rules of net life, she still felt a moment of unease. "Do !Xabbu and I need to do anything?"

"No. I have . . . called in a favor, do you say? I have been allowed back in, and I am privileged to bring guests of my own."

The white walls abruptly fell away, or rather something different grew out of them. The empty space took on shape and depth. Trees, sky, and earth seemed to form themselves out of invisible atoms in a matter of seconds. Renie and !Xabbu stood before a leaf-scummed pond which was surrounded by a stand of oaks. Martine, if she was still present, was invisible. The sky stretching limitlessly above the branches was summer-blue, and everything was suffused with a warm, buttery light. Near them, reclining between two large roots, his back against a tree trunk and his bare feet dangling in the water, was a small Caucasian boy. He wore overalls, a battered straw hat with a bent brim, and a sleepy, gap-toothed smile.

"I have permission to visit TreeHouse," Martine said.

The boy did not seem in the least surprised by the bodiless voice. He squinted at Renie and !Xabbu for a moment, then raised one of his hands in the air, as lazily as if he were reaching to pluck an apple. A rope ladder tumbled down out of the branches above him. His grin widened.

"Go on," said Martine.

!Xabbu went first. Renie felt sure he would climb just as deftly in real life. She followed a little more slowly, overwhelmed by the day's experiences and half-fearing whatever might happen next. Within moments the pond and the woods were gone and shadows had pulled in close around her. She was still climbing, but there was nothing to grip beneath her hands, and no feeling that she might fall. She stopped and waited.

"We have reached TreeHouse," Martine announced. "I am putting us on a private line running parallel to the main soundline—otherwise it will be very difficult to hear."

Before Renie could ask what she meant, the darkness abruptly fell away on all sides and the universe seemed to leap into chaos. An earsplitting Babel filled her ears—music, snatches of speech in different languages, odd noises, as though she and her companions were trapped between channels on a short-wave radio. She lowered the overall volume on her system, reducing the noise to a cacophonous murmur.

!Xabbu's voice came to her clearly on the Frenchwoman's private band. "What sights you have brought to me, Renie. Look!"

She could not have done anything else. The visual environment that had blasted away the darkness was like nothing she had ever seen.

There was no up and down—that was the first and most disorienting thing. The virtual structures of TreeHouse connected with each other at every conceivable angle. Neither was there a horizon. The

ragged mesh of buildinglike shapes stretched away in all directions. It
was, Renie realized, like standing in the imaginary center of an Escher
print. She could see empty blue that might be sky peeping from between some of the odd structures, but the color was just as likely to
appear below the level of her feet as above her head. In other places,
gaps were filled with rain clouds, or swirls of snow. Many of the structures appeared to be virtual dwellings, formed in every conceivable
size and shape, towering multicolored skyscrapers crossed like dueling
swords, collections of pink bubbles, even a glowing orange mushroom
the size of an aircraft hangar, complete with doors and windows. A
few of these shifted and changed into something else even as she
watched.

There were people, too, or things that might have been people—it
was difficult to tell, since the embodiment codes of the net had apparently been abandoned here—but there were other moving things that
barely fit the definition of "object," ripples of color, streaks of interference, whirling galaxies of pulsing spots.

"It's . . . it's just crazy!" she said. "What is it all?"

"It is whatever the people who belong here want it to be." Martine's
voice, the source of irritation earlier, was now a sublimely familiar
thing in a mad place. "They have rejected rules."

!Xabbu made a startled noise and Renie turned. A floating tugboat
covered in leopardskin had suddenly popped into existence beside
him. A figure resembling a child's rag doll leaned out of the captain's
cabin, examined them for a moment, then shouted something in a
language Renie didn't understand. The tugboat vanished.

"What was that?" Renie asked.

"I do not know." Her invisible companion sounded dryly amused.
"Someone stopping to look at the new arrivals. It is possible to have
my system translate the languages spoken here, but it takes a great
deal of processing power."

A high-pitched screaming echoed above the muted babble on the
hearplugs, cresting, then dying off. Renie winced. "I . . . how are we
going to find anything here? This is insane!"

"There are ways to operate in TreeHouse, and it is not all like this,"
Martine assured her. "We will find one of the quieter places—this is
public, like a park. Go forward and I will direct you."

Renie and !Xabbu headed toward one of the gaps between the
buildings, rising above a troop of dancing paisley mice, then swerving
to avoid contact with something that looked like a huge tongue protruding from the sweating side of one of the structures. At Martine's

urging they sped up, and the bizarre tangle of shapes blurred. Despite their rapid progress, some things moved as fast as they did— TreeHouse residents, Renie guessed, coming to take a look at them. These curious folk appeared in such a strange and disturbing assortment of shapes and effects that after a while Renie could no long bear to look back at them. A burble of sound washed through the gaps between Martine's directions, some of them clearly greetings.

Renie looked to !Xabbu, worried, but the little man's sim was gazing from side to side like any tourist new to the big city. He did not seem too upset.

A giant red flower of a sort she did not recognize hung upside down before them, as big as a department store. They slowed at Martine's urging, then rose up into the petals from beneath. As the forest of crimson banners enfolded them, the babble in her hearplugs dropped away.

Writing flashed in the air before them as they drifted upward, a greeting in several languages. The English section read *"This is our property. All who enter remain here under our rules, which are whatever we decide they are at any given time. Most of them have to do with respecting other people. Permission to enter may be revoked without notice. Signed, The Ant Farm Collective."*

"How can you have private property if this is all anarchy?" Renie complained. "Some anarchists!"

Martine laughed. "You would fit in here very well, Renie. People sit and argue about such things for hours and hours."

The inside of the flower—or the simulation connected to the simulation that looked like a flower, Renie reminded herself—was a vast grotto honeycombed with passages and small open areas. The whole of it was covered floor to ceiling in velvety red, and the light came from no particular source; Renie thought it was rather like being in someone's intestine. Conventional sims and their much less humanoid counterparts sat, stood, or drifted, with no greater attention to up and down than those in what Martine had called the "park." The roar of sound was more muted here, but clearly there were a lot of conversations going on.

"Martine? Is that you? I was *so happy* to hear from you!"

!Xabbu and Renie turned at the stranger's faintly-accented voice, which came strong and clear across the private band. The Bushman burst out laughing, and Renie was hard-pressed not to join him. The new arrival was a breakfast—a plate full of eggs and sausage hovering in midair, with silverware, cereal bowl, and a glass of orange juice orbiting around it like satellites.

"Are you laughing at my new sim?" The breakfast bounced gently in mock-despair. "I'm *shattered.*"

Martine's disembodied voice was warm. "Ali. It is good to meet you again. These are my guests." She did not use names; Renie, despite finding it hard to feel threatened by a floating meal, did not volunteer them.

The breakfast quite visibly looked them up and down, examining their rudimentary sims for a long moment. For the first time ever in VR, Renie felt self-conscious about the quality of her appearance. "Somebody must do something about what you're wearing," was the final verdict.

"That's not why we're here, Ali, but if they ever come back, I'm sure my friends will come to see you. Prince Ali von Always-Laughing-Puppets was one of the first truly great designers of simulated bodies," Martine explained.

"*Was?*" Even his horror was arch. "Was? Good God, am I forgotten already? But I've gone back to just being Ali, dearest. Nobody's doing those long names at the moment—my idea, of course. Still, I'm ever so honored you remembered." The plate slowly rotated; the sausages gleamed. "Not that *you've* changed much, Martine dear. I suppose you've found the one way to avoid the entire fashion question entirely. Very minimal. And there is something to say for consistency." Ali could not entirely hide his disapproval. "Well, what brings you here again? It's been so long! And what shall we do? They're going to have some horrible ethics discussion here at Ant Farm tonight, and frankly I'd rather surrender to RL than endure that. But Sinyi Transitore is going to do a weather piece out of the conference center node. His things are always dreadfully interesting. Would your guests like to see that?"

"What is a weather piece?" asked !Xabbu. Renie was relieved to hear that he sounded quite calm. She had been wondering how he was holding up under all this strangeness.

"Oh, it's . . . weather. You know. You two must be African—*so* distinct, that accent. Do you know the Bingaru Brothers? Those clever fellows who shut down the Kampala Grid? They claim it was an accident, of course, but no one believes them. You must know them."

Renie and !Xabbu had to admit they did not.

"It sounds lovely, Ali," Martine cut in, "but we haven't come for entertainment. We need to find somebody, and I called you because you know *everybody*.''

Renie was glad her own sim didn't show much in the way of facial expressions—it would be difficult to keep a straight face. She had never seen a breakfast swell with pride before.

"I do. But of course I do. Who are you looking for?"

"One of the older TreeHouse folk. His handle is the Blue Dog Anchorite.''

The plate slowed its rotation. The fork and spoon drooped a little. ''The Dog? That old crust? My goodness, Martine, what would you want with him?''

Renie could not contain her eagerness. "You know where to find him?''

"I suppose. He's out in Cobweb Corner with the rest of his friends.''

"Cobweb Corner?" Martine sounded puzzled.

"That's just what we call it. Inside Founder's Hill. With the other old people.'' Ali's tone suggested that even to speak of it was to risk it. "My God, what is *that?*''

!Xabbu and Renie turned to follow what seemed to be the floating breakfast's line of sight. Two bulky Caucasian men were gliding past, surrounded by a cloud of tiny yellow monkeys. One of the men was dressed like something out of an extremely stupid netflick, sword and chain mail and long Mongol mustache.

"Thank you, Ali,'' said Martine. ''We must go. It was lovely to meet you again. Thank you for answering my call.''

Ali was still apparently riveted by the newcomers. "Heavens, I haven't seen anything like that in *years*. Someone should help them quickly." The assembly of flatware turned back to face them. "Sorry. The price we pay for freedom—some people will simply wear *anything*. So you're running off just like that? Martine, dearest, I am absolutely destroyed. Ah, well. Kiss.'' The fork and spoon did a complicated pirouette, then the breakfast began to drift leisurely after the two burly men and the cloud of monkeys. "Don't be strangers!'' he called back at them.

"Why did that man choose to look like food?'' !Xabbu asked a moment later.

Renie laughed. "Because he could, I suppose. Martine?''

"I am still here. I was checking the Founder's Hill directory for a listing, but I have no luck. We must go there.''

"Let's go then.'' Renie surveyed the duodenal interior one last time. ''Things can't get much stranger.''

* * *

Founder's Hill, whatever it had once been, now displayed itself as nothing more complicated than a door, although it was a suitably large and impressive door, carefully rendered to resemble ancient, worm-eaten wood, with a huge, corroded brass knocker in the shape of a lion's head. An oil lantern hung from a hook overhead, filling the porch with yellow light. The doorstep of Founder's Hill was also suitably quiet, like the forgotten place it resembled, although only moments before they had been in the full hurlyburly of TreeHouse life. Renie wondered if its appearance was the residents' sly joke at their own expense.

"Why do we not go in?" !Xabbu asked.

"Because I am doing the things that will enable us to go in." Martine sounded a little tense, as though she were trying to juggle and skip rope simultaneously. "Now you may knock."

Renie banged the knocker. A moment later the door swung open.

Before them stretched a long hallway, which was also lit by hanging lanterns. A succession of doors faced each other, continuing down both walls in file until the hallway dwindled into apparently infinite distance. Renie looked at the blank face of the nearest door, then put her hand on it. Writing appeared, as she had expected, but it was in a script she couldn't read that had the flowing look of Arabic. "Is there a directory?" she asked. "Or are we going to have to knock on every door."

"I am searching for a directory now," said Martine.

Renie and !Xabbu could only wait, although the small man seemed to bear it better than Renie did. She was cross again, not least at having to wonder what their invisble guide was doing.

What is her problem? Why is she so secretive? Is she damaged somehow? But that doesn't make sense. Her brain is obviously fine, and anything else wouldn't prevent her using a sim.

It was like traveling with a spirit or a guardian angel. So far, Martine seemed to be a good spirit, but Renie disliked having so great a reliance on someone about whom she knew so little.

"There is no directory," the guide announced. "Not of individual nodes. But there are common areas. Perhaps we can find some help in one of those."

With no sensation of movement, they moved abruptly to a spot farther down the seemingly endless corridor, out of sight of the front entrance but still standing in front of one of the identical doors. It opened, as though pushed by Martine's invisble hand, and Renie and !Xabbu floated in.

The room, not surprisingly, was far bigger on the inside than the distance between doors in the corridor. It stretched for what seemed hundreds of yards, and was dotted with small tables, like the reading room of an old-fashioned library. It had a vaguely clublike feel, with pictures hanging on the walls—when Renie looked more closely, she saw they were posters for ancient musical groups—and virtual plants everywhere, some of them claiming space quite aggressively. The windows on the far wall looked out over the American Grand Canyon as it would look if filled with water and inhabited by extremely alien-looking aquatic life; Renie wondered briefly if they had chosen the view by popular vote.

There were sims everywhere, huddled in groups around tables, floating lazily near the ceiling or hovering midway between the two in gesticulating, argumentative flocks. They seemed to lack the hubristic display of the other denizens of TreeHouse: many of the sims were only a little more complex than the ones Renie and !Xabbu were wearing. She guessed that if these were, as Ali had suggested, the colony's oldest residents, perhaps they were wearing the sims of their youth, as old people in RL still tended to sport the fashions of their young adulthood.

A fairly basic female sim drifted by. Renie raised a hand to catch her attention.

"Pardon me. We're looking for Blue Dog Anchorite."

The sim watched her with the expressionless eyes of a painted mannequin, but did not speak. Renie was puzzled. English was usually the common language in most international VR environments.

She moved herself farther into the room, heading for a table where a loud discussion was in progress. As she drifted up, she heard fragments of conversation.

". . . Most certainly didn't. I was opping En-BICS just before they went full-bore, so I ought to know."

Someone responded in what sounded like an Asian language, evidently with some heat.

"But that's just the point! It was *all* multinational by then!"

"Oh, McEnery, you are such a *cabron*!" said another voice. "*Chupa mi pedro!*"

"Pardon me," said Renie when the argument had quieted for a moment. "We're looking for Blue Dog Anchorite. We were told he lives on Founder's Hill."

All the sims swiveled to look at her. One, a teddy bear with incongruously masculine characteristics, guaffawed in the cracked voice of an old man. "They're looking for the Dog. The Dog's got fans."

One of the other sims cocked a vestigial thumb toward the far corner of the room. "Over there."

Renie looked, but could not make out any individuals at that distance. She beckoned for !Xabbu to follow her. He was staring at the teddy bear.

"Don't even ask me," Renie said.

There was indeed one sim sitting by itself in the corner, an odd one—a dark-skinned old man, with fierce eyes and a bristling gray beard who appeared strangely real in some ways and strangely unreal in others. He was dressed in the casual style of fifty years earlier, but with a turban and what Renie at first took to be some kind of ceremonial garment over the clothes. It was only after a few moments that she realized the outer wrap was an old bathrobe.

"Pardon me . . . " she began, but the old man cut her off.

"What do you three want?"

It took Renie a moment to remember Martine, who was being unusually silent. "Are you . . . are you Blue Dog Anchorite?" Not only his sim was puzzling: there was something odd about his virtual chair, too.

"Who wants to know?" He had an unmistakable South African accent. Renie felt a surge of hope.

"We're friends of Susan Van Bleeck. We have reason to believe she spoke with you fairly recently."

The turbaned head came forward. The old hacker looked like a vulture startled in its nest. "Friends of Susan's? Why the hell should I believe that? How did you find me?"

"You have no cause to fear us," Martine said.

Renie cut in. "We need your help. Did Susan contact you about a golden city, something she couldn't identify. . . ?"

"Ssshhh! Good God!" The old man, startled for a moment out of bad temper, waved violently to silence her. "Don't make such a goddamn fuss. No names, no pack drill. And no talk here. We'll go to my place."

He moved his fingers and his chair rose. "Follow me. No, never mind, I'll give you the location and you can meet me there. *Damn.*" He said this with some feeling. "I wish you and Susan had come to me sooner."

"Why?" Renie asked. "What do you mean?"

"Because it might have been early enough to do something then. But now it's too damn late."

He vanished.

CHAPTER 22

Gear

NETFEED/INTERACTIVES: GCN, Hr. 5.5 (Eu, NAm)—"HOW TO KILL
YOUR TEACHER"
(visual: Looshus and Kantee in tunnel)
VO: Looshus (Ufour Halloran) and Kantee (Brandywine Garcia) are on the
run, pursued by Jang (Avram Reiner), the assassin from the Educators'
Union. 10 supporting characters open, audition for long-term role of Mrs.
Torquemada. Flak to: GCN.HOW2KL.CAST

He was thinking hard, but not getting much of anywhere.
"Beezle," he whispered, "find me that weird little snippet on
'bandit nodes.' See if you can get an address on the author."

His mother looked into the rearview mirror. "What did you say?"

"Nothing." He slumped lower in the seat, watching the perimeter
fences move past the safety windows. He reached up to his neck, fond-
ling the new wireless connector, a birthday gift he had bought himself
through mail order. The telematic jack was light and almost unnotice-
able—all that showed was a rounded white plastic button fitted over
the top of his neurocannula. It seemed to work as well as the reviews
had suggested, and it was an incredible pleasure to be able to go online without being tied to a cable.

"I've got the address," Beezle rasped. *"Do you want to call it now?"*

"No. I'll deal with it later."

"Orlando, what are you doing? Who are you talking to back there?"

He brought his hand up to hide the t-jack. "Nobody, Vivien. I'm just . . . just singing to myself."

The matte-black cylinder of the guardhouse loomed up beyond the windshield, distracting her. She stopped at the inside checkpoint to beam in the security code, then, when the barrier dropped, drove forward to the guardhouse itself.

Orlando took his new wireless squeezers from his pocket. *Beezle—any messages?* he typed.

"Just one." Beezle was right beside his ear—or at least it sounded like it. In fact, Beezle was pumping data directly into his auditory nerves. *"From Elaine Strassman at Indigo Gear. She asked for an appointment."*

"Who?" Orlando said out loud, then looked up guiltily. His mom was busy talking to the security guard, a burly figure whose black Fibrox anti-impact suit matched the tiles on the guardhouse. *What's Indigo?* he fingered.

"Small, very new technology company. They did a presentation on SchoolNet last semester."

It rang a bell, but only vaguely. He had been putting out a lot of feelers about TreeHouse, but couldn't think of any that might have wound up at Indigo, a ferociously trendy company based in Southern California, if he remembered their presentation correctly.

Go ahead and set up a meeting. Tonight after I get home or tomorrow morning when Vivien goes to class.

"Gotcha, boss."

"We should be back no later than four," his mother was telling the guard.

"If you want to stop and do some shopping, ma'am, you just call us and let us know and we'll set back your ETR." The guard, a young, round-headed blond, had his thumbs tucked into his belt; his fingers absently fondled the sidearm sitting high in its holster. "Don't want to get an alarm situation going if we don't need to."

"Thank you, Holger. We'll be back on time, I'm sure." She thumbed the window button and waited for a gap to open in the large external barrier before sliding through to the street. "How are you doing, Orlando?" she called back.

"Fine, Vivien." In truth he was feeling a little achy, but it wouldn't help to mention it, and it would just make her feel she should do something. He straighted up in the seat as Crown Heights Community and its sheltering walls disappeared behind them.

Not long after they rolled down off the curving hill-roads and onto level ground, leaving the wire-fenced tree preserve behind, the car began to shudder. Even expensive shock absorbers could do little to compensate for potholes like moon craters. The State of California and local governments had been arguing for years about who had responsibility for the larger arterial roads. They hadn't resolved the disagreement yet.

"You're driving too fast, Vivien." He winced. He could feel each bounce in his bones.

"I'm fine. We're almost there." She spoke with clenched-teeth cheerfulness. She hated driving, and hated having to take Orlando down to the flats to see his doctor. He sometimes thought that one of the reasons she got mad at him was because he'd been stupid enough to have a disease that couldn't be treated remotely, or at the friendly and very secure Crown Heights Medical Center.

She also got mad because she was afraid for him. Vivien was very sensible, and so was his father, Conrad, but it was the kind of sensible that liked to throw reasonable arguments at things until they went away. If they didn't go away—well, Vivien and Conrad just sort of stopped talking about them.

It was strange to be out from under the trees and back into the flatlands. In Crown Heights, behind the green belt and its army of private guards, it was possible to believe that things hadn't changed much in the last couple of hundred years, that Northern California was still an essentially open place, a temperate paradise of redwoods and well-spaced, secure communities. Which, Orlando reflected, was probably why people like his parents lived in Crown Heights.

The San Francisco Bay Area metroplex had once been a discrete cluster of cities on the edge of the v-shaped bay, like fingertips delicately holding something of value. Now the cities had grown together into a single mass that clenched the bay and its connected waterways in a broad fist well over a hundred miles square. Only the fabulously valuable corporate farming land of the Central Valley had kept the metroplex and its southern rival, metastasizing around Los Angeles, from merging into a single uniform smear of dense urban growth.

As they passed under the cantilevered bulk of Highway 92, Orlando scrunched down in his seat so he could see the hammock city. He had long been fascinated by the multilevel shantytowns, sometimes called "honeycombs" by their residents—or "rats' nests" by the kind of people who lived in Crown Heights. When he had asked his parents about them, they had failed to tell him much more than the obvious, so he had searched the net for old news footage.

Long ago, he had discovered, during the first great housing crisis at the beginning of the century, squatters had begun to build shanty-towns beneath the elevated freeways, freeform agglomerations of cardboard crates, aluminum siding, and plastic sheets. As the ground beneath the concrete chutes filled up with an ever-thickening tide of the dispossessed, later arrivals began to move upward into the vault-ing itself, bolting cargo nets, canvas tarpaulins, and military surplus parachutes onto the pillars and undersides of the freeways. Rope walkways soon linked the makeshift dwellings, and ladders linked the shantytown below with the one growing above. Resident craftsmen and amateur engineers added intermediary levels, until a marrow of shabby multilevel housing ran beneath nearly every freeway and aqueduct.

With the sun near noon, the underside of Highway 92 was dark, but the webwork city was full of movement. Orlando lowered the win-dow to get a better view. A group of young children were chasing each other across a broad expanse of netting seventy feet above his head. They looked like squirrels, swift and confident, and he envied them. Then he reminded himself of their poverty, of the overcrowding and unsanitary conditions, and of the dangers that came purely from their environment. Besides the violence that always threatened urban poor, the residents of the hammock cities also had gravity to contend with: not a day went past without someone falling onto a freeway and being crushed, or drowning in a waterway. Just last year, the sheer weight of the Barrio Los Moches honeycomb had brought down a section of the San Diego Freeway, killing hundreds of residents and score of drivers.

"Orlando? Why is that window open?"

"I'm just looking."

"Close it. There's no reason to have it open."

Orlando ran the window back up, putting both the children's voices and most of the sunlight on the other side of the smoked glass.

They crept along the El Camino Real, the broad main strip of neo-neon and holographed advertising images that stretched fifty miles down the peninsula from San Francisco. The sidewalks were full of people, half of whom seemed to be living in the doorways of buildings or lounging in informal congregation outside the sealed, card-acti-vated bus stops. Orlando's mother was driving edgily, despite being hemmed in by shoals of smaller automotive fish, mopeds and minicars. Pedestrians walked past slowly at the intersections, studying the one-way windows of the Gardiners' car with the calculating faces of shoplifters observed on closed-circuit security video.

Drumming her fingers on the wheel, Vivien stopped the car at another traffic light. A group of young Hispanic men stood in a ragged circle on the near corner, the goggles pushed up on their foreheads making it seem they had extra sets of eyes. Even in the bright sun their faces seemed to pulse with light, although the implants—slender tubes of chemical neon beneath the skin, arranged in fetishistic tribal patterns—were far more impressive at night, under the dark concrete overhangs.

Orlando had heard his parents' friends talk about Goggleboys with a mixture of fear and mythmaking relish, claiming they wore the distinctive eyewear to protect themselves from chemical spray reprisal when they were mugging people, but Orlando recognized most of the lenses they wore as flashy but low-power VR rigs, little more use than old-fashioned walkie-talkies. It was a trend, just a way of looking like you might have to pop into a virtual meeting at any moment, or take an important call, but in the meantime you were just hanging around on the corner.

One of the young men broke off from the group and headed toward the crosswalk. His long coat of magenta 'chute flapped in the wind behind him like a flag. A tattoo of a chain began in the hairline beside his temple and ran down to his jaw, and jumped into darker relief every few seconds as the implants pulsed the skin. He was smiling as though remembering something funny. Before he reached their car— before it was clear he was even approaching the car—Vivien accelerated through the red light, narrowly missing one of the battle cruisers euphemistically called a "family wagon." The other car's proximity lights blazed out like the warning flash of a cobra's hood.

"Vivien, you ran that signal!"

"We're almost there."

Orlando turned to look out the rear window. The young man stood on the corner staring after them, coat flapping. He looked like he was waiting for the rest of the parade to show up.

"All things considered, I think you're doing pretty well. The new anti-inflammatories seem to be helping." Doctor Vanh stood up. "I don't like that cough, though. Have you had it long?"

"No. It's not too bad."

"Okay. But we'll keep an eye on it. Oh, and I'm afraid we're going to have to take some more blood."

Orlando tried to smile. "You've got most of it. I guess you might as well have the rest."

Doctor Vanh nodded approvingly. "That's the spirit." He reached out a slender hand, indicating that Orlando should stay on the table. "The nurse will be here in just a minute. Oh, let me check those patch-sites." He turned Orlando's arm over and examined it. "Are you still getting rashes?"

"Not too bad."

"Good. Glad to hear it." He nodded again. Orlando was always intrigued by the way such cheerful sayings came out of the doctor's thin sad face.

Whie Doctor Vanh checked something on the pad on the corner table—they knew better than to put things up on a wallscreen where the patient could see—a nurse named Desdemona came in and took some of Orlando's blood. She was pretty and very polite; they always used her, so he would be too embarrassed to make a fuss. They were right. Even though he was tired and hurting and sick of needles, he clenched his teeth and made it through. He even managed a weak return of Desdemona's cheerful farewell.

"How are you feeling, Orlando?" his mother asked. "Can you walk out to the waiting room by yourself? I want to talk to Doctor Vanh for a few minutes."

He made a face. "Yes, Vivien. I think I can drag myself down the corridor."

She gave him a nervous smile, trying to show she appreciated the joke, even though she didn't. The doctor helped him off the table. He fastened his own shirt on the way to the door, waving Vivien off despite the painful stiffness in his fingers.

He stopped by the drinking fountain to rest for a moment; when he looked back, he could see his mother's head through the tiny window in the examining room door. She was listening to something and frowning. He wanted to go back and tell her that all this whispering and secrecy was a waste, that he knew more about his own condition than she did. And, he was fairly certain, she knew that he did, too. Being a starhammer netboy meant more than being able to kill lots of monsters in the fantasy simworlds—he could avail himself of medical libraries from universities and hospitals all over the world, whenever he wanted to. His mother couldn't really believe that he would remain in ignorance about his own case, could she? Maybe that was one of the reasons she had a thing about him spending so much time on the net.

Of course, she might have a point. Maybe you could have too much information. For a while he had made a habit of reading his own medical records out of the hospital files, but had eventually given it up. VR death-trips were one thing, RL another—especially when it was his own RL.

"After all, they can't work miracles, Vivien," he murmured, then pushed himself away from the fountain and resumed his slow progress up the hall.

Beezle beeped him five minutes before the call was due. He sat up in bed, surprised and a little disoriented. The new t-jack was so comfortable he had forgotten it was still in, and had fallen asleep wearing it.

"Incoming," Beezle said in his ear.

"Right. Give me one of the standard sims, then connect."

He closed his eyes. The screen hung in the darkness behind his lids, routed directly through the telematic jack to his optical nerves. He opened his eyes again and the screen still hovered before him, but now he could also see the darkened walls of his room and the skeletal silhouette of his IV unit, as though in a photographic double exposure. He had spent hours getting the calibrations right, but it was worth it.

This is chizz! It works just as well as the fiber—no, better. I never have to be offline again.

Elaine Strassman popped onto the screen. She was young, probably mid-twenties, and wore lots of jewelry. Her dark hair was twisted up into a topknot and wrapped in something gleamingly metallic. Orlando closed his eyes to block out his room, so he could examine her more closely. He thought he recognized her, but wasn't quite sure.

"Uh . . . Orlando Gardiner?" she asked.

"That's me."

"Hi, I'm Elaine Strassman? From Indigo?" She hesitated, clearly a little confused, and squinted. "The . . . the Orlando Gardiner I'm looking for is fourteen years old."

Jesus, she worked in the gear trade and she couldn't recognize a sim? She was either utterly impacted or her vision was bad. Hadn't everybody in LA/SD had their eyes fixed by now? "That's me. This is a sim. I couldn't get to the regular phone, so no video picture."

She laughed. "I'm used to sims, but most kids . . . most people your age have . . . "

"Something flashier. Yeah, but this is what I use. Makes it easier to talk to grown-ups like you. It's supposed to, anyway." He wondered what sim Beezle had chosen for him. They ranged in apparent age from one just a little older than he actually was to a rather mature and avuncular persona particularly useful for dealing with institutions and authority in general. "What can I do for you?"

She took a breath, trying to find the breezy tone she had lost. It was good to keep people off balance, Orlando reflected. You found out more about them that way—and they found out less about you. "Well," she said, "our records show that you monitored a presentation I gave on SchoolNet, and you also queried us afterward about some of the things I had discussed. Proprioception loops?"

"I remember now. Yeah, that was pretty interesting. But one of your engineers already sent me some data."

"We were most impressed by your questions. And we thought some of them were particularly perceptive."

Orlando said nothing, but his mental antennae tingled. Could this be some roundabout method for the mystery hacker to get at him? It was hard to believe that Elaine Strassman, with her fashion hair and hummingbird-skull jewelry, could be the person who had hacked the Middle Country so effectively, but appearances could be deceiving. Or she might be working for someone else, perhaps unwittingly.

"I do okay," he said as evenly as he could. "I'm pretty interested in VR."

"We know that. I hope this doesn't sound awful, but we've been asking some questions about you. At SchoolNet, for instance."

"Questions."

"Nothing private," she said hurriedly. "Just about your grades and your special interests in the field. Talked to some of your instructors." She paused as though on the brink of revelation. Orlando realized by the ache in his fingers that he was clenching his fists. "Do you have any plans after graduation?" she asked.

"After *graduation?*" He opened his eyes and Elaine Strassman once more appeared to hover in midair above the foot of his bed.

"We have an apprenticeship program here at Indigo," she said. "We would be willing to sponsor you through college—we have a wide range of the best high-technology programs to choose from—pay all your expenses, even send you to special seminars in all kinds of utterly *detail* places." She used the expression with the faint overemphasis of someone who knew she would not be able to get away with using netgirl slang much longer. "It's a great deal."

He was relieved but faintly disappointed. He had been approached by recruiters before, although never quite so directly. "You want to sponsor me."

"It's a great deal," she repeated. "All you have to do is promise to come work for us for a certain amount of time after you graduate. It's not even that long—just three years! Indigo Gear is so certain that you'll like our environment that we're willing to bet you an education that you'll stay."

Or at least willing to bet that I come up with some useful patents for them during the first three years, he thought. *Not that it's such a bad deal, even so. But these people don't understand what kind of bet they'd really be making.*

"Sounds like a nice deal." It was almost painful to watch her smile widen. "Why don't you send me some information." If nothing else, it would give his mother a few moments of pleasure.

"I'll do that. And listen—you have my number now. If you have any questions, Orlando, you just phone me any time. Any time. I mean that."

She almost sounded like she was promising to sleep with him. He couldn't help smiling. Dream on, Gardiner!

"Okay. Send me the stuff and I'll definitely think about it."

After several more enthusiastic assurances, Elaine Strassman hung up. Orlando closed his eyes again. He selected the new *Pharaoh Had To Shout* album from his music library and set it playing quietly, then settled back to think.

Five minutes into the first track, he opened his eyes. "Beezle," he said. "*Bug.* Call Elaine Whatsername back at that number."

"Strassman."

"Yeah. Let's get her on the phone."

She had said to call if he had any questions. He'd just thought of a question.

"I understood you the first time—you don't have to say it again. I just don't believe you." Fredericks folded his arms in front of his chest like an aggrieved child.

"What don't you believe? That the people who made the gryphon have connections to TreeHouse?" Orlando was trying to curb his temper. Being impatient with Fredericks never made anything happen any faster—he had a stubborn streak as wide as his simulated shoulders.

"I believe that okay. But I can't believe that you actually think you can get in there. That's utter *fenfen*, Gardiner."

"Oh, man." Orlando moved himself into Fredericks' line of sight, blocking off the Cretaceous-swamp window at which his friend had been sullenly staring. "Look, I don't think, I know! I've been trying to explain. This engineer at Indigo Gear is going to get me in—get *us* in, if you want to come along."

"Into TreeHouse? Some guy you've never met is going to slip a couple of kids into TreeHouse? Just for fun? Shoot me again, Gardiner, I'm still breathing."

"Okay, not just for fun. I told them that I'd sign their sponsorship agreement if someone could get me into TreeHouse for a day."

Fredericks sat up. "You what? Orlando, this is too far scanny! You signed up to go work for some gear company for half your life just to find out who made that stupid gryphon?"

"It's not half my life. It's three years. And it's a pretty good deal, anyway." He didn't tell Fredericks about his private disbelief that he would ever serve that sentence. "Come on, Frederico. Even if I have lost my mind—it's TreeHouse! You're not going to turn down the chance to go there, are you? To see it? *You* don't have work for Indigo."

His friend looked at him carefully, as though hoping to see through the sim to the real person beneath—a futile hope. Orlando wondered briefly if there was something bad for your brain about having years-long friendships with people you'd never met in the real world.

"I'm worried about you, Gardiner. You're taking this much too seriously. First you get Thargor killed, then you blow your chances with the Table of Judgment, now you've . . . I don't know, sold your soul to some corporation—and it's all because of this city you saw for about five seconds. Are you going mental or something?"

Orlando paused on the verge of saying something sarcastic. Instead, he found himself wondering if Fredericks might be right, and the mere fact of wondering, the momentary loss of certainty, brought a stab of cold fear. The word was "dementia," and he had seen it in more than a few medical articles.

"Gardiner?"

"Shut up for a second, Fredericks." He tested the fear, felt its clammy extent. Could his friend be right?

Then again, did it matter? If he *was* losing his mind, did it matter if he made a fool of himself? All he knew was that when he had seen the city, it had made him feel that there was something left to wonder about, in a life that was otherwise full of dreadful certainties. And in his dreams, the city had taken on an even greater significance. It was the exact size, shape, and color of hope itself . . . something he had never thought he would see again. And that was more important than anything.

"I guess you'll just have to trust me, Fredericks old chum."

His friend sat silently for some time. "Okay," he said at last. "But I'm not going to break any laws."

"No one's asking you to break the law. TreeHouse isn't illegal, really. Well, maybe it is, I'm not sure. But remember, we're both minors. The guy who's taking us is an adult. If anyone gets in trouble, it'll be him."

Fredericks shook his head. "You're so stupid, Gardino."

"Why?"

"Because if this guy is willing to break the law to get you to sign up for Indigo, they must really want you. Jeez, you probably could have gotten them to give you a private jet or something."

Orlando laughed. "Frederico, you are one of a kind."

"Yeah? All the more reason not to get wiped out on one of your stupid excursions, Gardiner."

"You're not going to wear *that* sim, are you?"

"Detox, Fredericks. Of course I'm going to wear it." He flexed Thargor's leather-vambraced arm. "I know it better than my own body."

Oh, yeah, he thought. *I wish.*

"But it's . . . it's TreeHouse! Shouldn't you wear something . . . I don't know . . . more interesting?"

Orlando glowered, something the Thargor sim did very well. "It's not a costume party. And if the people in TreeHouse have been hacking forever, they probably wouldn't be very impressed by some fancy sim. I just want to get the job done."

Fredericks shrugged. "I'm certainly not going to wear anything that someone might recognize. We might get in trouble—this is illegal, Orlando."

"Sure. Like there are a bunch of people hanging around in Tree-House who are going to say, "Look, isn't that Pithlit, the famous slightly nervous person from the Middle Country simworld?"

"Get locked. I'm just not taking any chances." Fredericks paused for a moment. Orlando felt sure he was doing the online equivalent of looking at himself in the mirror—studying his specs. "I mean, this is just an ordinary body."

"Still pretty musclebound, as usual." Fredericks didn't respond, and Orlando wondered for a moment if he'd hurt his friend's feelings.

Fredericks could turn sensitive pretty quickly. "So, you ready?" he asked.

"I still don't get it. This guy's just going to send us there? We don't have to do anything?"

"Basically, he wants to stay in the background, I think. Elaine Strassman—this recruiter—wouldn't tell me his name or anything. Just said 'you will be contacted,' all spyflick. And then he rang me up, calling himself 'Scottie.' Blacked-out visual, distorted voice. Said he'd go up the ladder, whatever that means, and then when he was in, bring us aboard as guests. He doesn't want us to know anything about him."

Fredericks frowned. "That doesn't sound good. How do we know he'll really do it?"

"Oh, and instead what? He'll just whip up some little simulation that will fool us into thinking we're in the most chizz major bandit outpost in the history of the net? Come on, Frederico."

"Okay. I just wish he'd hurry up and do it." Fredericks floated to the MBC display and stared balefully at the Martian diggers.

Orlando opened a data window and checked to make sure that he had all the information straight on the various handles and company names linked with the watch-gryphon, but he was just killing time. There wasn't really any need to memorize. Even if TreeHouse's security gear prevented him from connecting directly to his own database, there were other methods he could use to move information back and forth. He had been planning all evening. Now, if his mother and father would just leave him alone. . . .

He had gone up to his room early on the pretext of feeling tired after the appointment with Doctor Vanh. His parents hadn't resisted much—it was pretty obvious that Vivien wanted a little private time with Conrad to discuss what the doctor had said. It was ten o'clock now. Vivien might come in to check on him before she went to bed, but he didn't think he'd have too much trouble pretending to be asleep, and he should be able to hide the new t-jack with his pillow. Then he should have at least another seven hours, which should be plenty of time.

He looked up at Fredericks, who was still peering worriedly at the MBC window, as though he were a mother hen and the little digger robots were straying chicks. Orlando smiled.

"Hey, Frederico. This could take us hours. Are you going to have any problem with that? I mean, at home?

Fredericks shook his head. "Nah. They're coming back late from some party on the other side of the complex." Fredericks' family lived in the West Virginia hills. Both parents worked for the government, something to do with Urban Planning. Fredericks didn't talk about them much.

"You know, I never asked you where the name 'Pithlit' came from."

His friend gave him a sour look. "No, you didn't. Where does 'Thargor' come from?"

"A book. This kid I used to go to school with, his father had all these old books—y'know, paper. One had a picture on the cover of this *ho ying* guy with a sword. It was called 'Thangor' or something like that. I just changed it a little bit when I first started out in the Middle Country. Now, how about 'Pithlit'?"

"I don't remember." He didn't say it like it was the truth.

Orlando shrugged. You couldn't drag something out of Fredericks with a tractor by arguing with him, but if you let it alone, it would come out all by itself eventually. It was one of the things Orlando had learned about him. It was strange to think how long he'd known him. For a pure net friendship, it had lasted a long time.

The doorway of Orlando's electronic hideaway blinked. "Who's there?" he asked.

"*Scottie.*" The distorted voice certainly sounded the same, and it was no easier to copy a distortion pattern than an actual voice.

"*Enter.*"

The naked sim that appeared in the middle of the room was very basic, the face only dots for eyes and a slit for a mouth. The eggshell-white body was covered head to foot with tattoolike calibration marks. Apparently a typical engineer, "Scottie" hadn't bothered to change out of whatever he was wearing before going out. "You kids ready?" he asked, slurring and crackling like an ancient recording. "Give me your handles—you don't need indexes, but you need designations."

Fredericks was staring at the test-sim with a mixture of distrust and fascination. "Are you really going to take us to TreeHouse?"

"I don't know what you're talking about."

"But. . . !"

"Shut up, scanmaster." Orlando shook his head. Fredericks ought to know better than to expect this guy to admit to something illegal while visiting a stranger's node. "I'm Thargor."

"I'll bet you are." Scottie turned to Fredericks. "You?"

"Uh . . . I don't know. James, I guess."

"Beautiful. You set up a blind link, so you can follow me, like I told you? Beau-ti-*ful.* Here we go."

There was an instant of darkness, then the world went mad.

"Oh, my God," said Fredericks. "*Dzang!* This is unbelievable!"

"It's the net, Jim," said Scottie, "but not as we know it." His laugh was a strange thing, full of wow and flutter. "Never mind. Old, old joke."

Orlando was silent, trying to make sense of TreeHouse. Unlike the commercial spaces of the net, which had carefully enforced certain real-world rules such as horizon and perspective, TreeHouse seemed to have turned its collective back on petty Newtonian conventions.

"You're on your own, kids." Scottie raised an index finger that was ticked with red markings. "The system will spit you out at 16:00 GMT—about ten hours from now. If you want to go before then, you shouldn't have any problem, but if you drop offline and then change your mind, I won't be around to get you back."

"Got it." In ordinary circumstances Orlando would have chafed at the engineer's patronizing older-brother tone, but at the moment he was too busy watching a wave of distortion ripple across the structures just in front of him, leaving changed colors and malformed designs in its wake.

"And if you get in trouble and want to mention my name, go ahead. It won't do you any good, though, since that's not the handle I use here."

Jeez, this guy thought he was real funny. "So are we not supposed to be here or something?"

"No, you're guests. You have as many rights as any other guest. If you want to know what those are, you can check the central index, but this place is caca for organization—you might still be looking for the rules when your time runs out. See ya." He curled the upraised finger and vanished.

As Orlando watched, a blue diesel truck made of what appeared to be twigs and branches sped out from between two structures and rumbled through the area Scottie had just vacated. Its blatting horn was loud even by TreeHouse standards, and made them both jump, but though it passed within inches of them there was no wind, no vibration. It turned a corner and headed uphill at an angle, climbing across open air toward another cluster of buildingish things hanging overhead.

"Well, Frederico," said Orlando, "here we are."

Within the first few hours they had received several invitations to join discussion groups, several more to attend demonstrations of new gear—which, under ordinary circumstances, Orlando would have been happy to accept—and two proposals of group marriage. What they did not get was any closer to having their questions about gryphon-manufacture answered.

"This index is impacted utterly!" said Fredericks. They had found a comparatively quiet backwater, and were staring at a data window which resolutely refused to give them useful information. "You can't find anything!"

"No, it's perfectly good gear—great gear, even. The problem is, no one updates it. Or rather, they do, but it's all haphazard. There's tons of data here, terrabytes of it, but it's like someone tore the pages out of a million paper books and dumped them in a pile. There's no way of knowing where anything is. We need an agent."

Fredericks loosed a theatrical groan. "Not Beezle Bug! Anything but that!"

"Get locked. I can't use him, anyway—TreeHouse is sealed off from the rest of the net, and Scottie kept us from seeing how we got here. Beezle's in *my* system—I could talk to him if I wanted to, or send him out to check other net databases—but I can't get him into this system."

"So we're scorched."

"I don't know. I think we may just have to ask around. One of the natives might be able to help."

"That's perfect, Gardino. What are we gonna do, offer to marry them if they do us a favor?"

"Could be. I thought that turtle-woman was kind of your style."

"Get locked."

A sequence of musical tones intruded above the muffled clamor. Orlando turned to see a whirling yellow tornado hanging in the air behind them. The tones repeated in ascending scale, a questioning sound.

Orlando wasn't quite sure of TreeHouse etiquette. "Um . . . can we help you?"

"English," said a voice. It was high-pitched and slightly metallic. "No. We help you?"

"What is it?" asked Fredericks worriedly.

Orlando waved at him to detox. "That would be nice. We're new here—guests. We're trying to get some information, find some people."

The yellow tornado slowed its spin, resolving itself into a cloud of yellow monkeys, each no longer than a finger. "We try. Like to help.

We are Wicked Tribe." One of the monkeys floated closer, pointing at itself with a tiny hand. "Me Zunni. Other Wicked Tribe—Kaspar, Ngogo, Masa, 'Suela . . ." Zunni went on to name a dozen more. Each monkey waved and pointed to itself in turn, then returned to spinning, midair shenanigans.

"Who are you?" asked Orlando, laughing. "You're kids, aren't you? Little kids?"

"No, not little kids," said Zunni seriously. "We are Wicked Tribe. Culture club number one."

"Zunni says that because she is youngest," said one of the other monkeys—Orlando thought it might have been the one named Kaspar, but they were all identical, so it was hard to tell. His English, though accented, was very good. "We *are* culture club," Kaspar went on. "When you are ten years, we kick you out."

"No Wrinkles in Wicked Tribe!" shouted one of the other monkeys, and they began to spin in a circle, around Orlando and Fredericks, laughing. "Wicked Tribe! *Mejor* club! Ruling, ruling tribe!" they sang.

Orlando lifted his hands slowly for fear of hitting one. He knew the tiny bodies were only sims, but he didn't want to offend them. "Could you help us find some people? We're strangers here and we're having trouble."

Zunni peeled off from the group and hovered before his nose. "We help you. Tribe know all things, all places."

Even Fredericks had to grin. "Saved by the flying monkeys," he said.

In fact, the Wicked Tribe did indeed prove helpful. Children seemed to be indulged in TreeHouse, allowed to go more or less wherever they wanted. Orlando guessed it was because privacy was so easily attainable here that if someone remained visible to other folk then he, she, or it truly wanted to be part of the community. The tribe seemed to know most of the hundreds of TreeHouse residents who crossed their path in the first couple of hours. Orlando was enjoying the experience, and repeatedly found himself wishing he had the leisure for a real conversation, even if none of his new acquaintances could provide the information he sought.

I could hang out here all the time, he thought. *How come I've never been here before? Why didn't anybody ever bring me?*

He balanced this sliver of resentment against the knowledge that one of the things that seemed to make the TreeHouse community work was that it was only a pool at the edge of the great ocean of the net: the anarchic lack of structure only worked because it kept itself exclusive. So what did that mean? That you couldn't trust most people not to ruin something? He wasn't sure.

Led on by the Wicked Tribe, they were introduced to the variety of TreeHouse in greater detail. For longer than they had intended to, they watched a group of candy soldiers fighting a massive battle on a plain of marzipan. Cannons fired marshmallows against the battlements of a taffy castle. Sticky little men flailed and fought across fudge swamps and barbed wire made from cotton candy. In the exertion of battle, chocolate pikes and bayonets melted and drooped. The monkeys themselves participated gleefully, flying over the battlefield and dropping Lifesavers to soldiers drowning in the fudge pits. Zunni told the visitors that the battle had been going on for a week. Orlando reluctantly dragged Fredericks away.

The monkeys took them to many corners of TreeHouse. Most of the inhabitants were friendly, but few seemed interested in answering their particular questions, although they continued to receive other sorts of suggestions. A living breakfast even offered to help them "re-think their entire approach, sim-wise"—and urged them to accept its help toward a complete makeover of what the breakfast called their "rather unfortunate presentation." It seemed surprised when Orlando politely declined.

"I think you'll want to sit in on one of the programming discussion groups."

The speaker was a European-accented woman in a more than usually understated sim. In fact, except for a few giveaway indications, such as overly-smooth rendering and a certain indefinable stiffness of movement, she looked very much like a person you might meet in RL, perhaps at one of his parents' parties. The Wicked Tribe called her "Starlight" (although Orlando also heard one of them refer to her as "Auntie Frida"). She was making weather over a large stretch of virtual landscape, moving clouds, adjusting wind velocity. Orlando couldn't decide if it was art or an experiment. "That would give you a chance to ask around," she continued. "You could comb through the accounts of previous discussions, but there must be thousands of hours of that stuff, and to tell you the truth, the search engine is kind of slow."

"Discussion?" said one of the monkeys, buzzing beside Orlando's ear like a mosquito. "Boring!"

"Talk, talk, talk! Boring, boring, boring!" The Wicked Tribe whirled into another spontaneous dance.

"Actually, that sounds like a good idea," Orlando told her. "Thanks."

"Will anyone mind?" Fredericks asked. "I mean, if we ask questions?"

"Mind? No, I shouldn't think so." The woman seemed surprised by the idea. "It might be a good idea to wait until they've finished with the other business. Or, if you're in a hurry, I suppose you could ask the discussion leader to let you put your questions before they get started."

"That would be great."

"Just don't get into any arguments with the real crazies. At best, it's a waste of time. And don't believe about ninety percent of what you hear. They were *never* as dangerous and cool as they'll tell you they were."

"Don't go!" Zunni's tinny voice swooped past. "We find fun game instead!"

"But this is what we came for," Orlando explained.

After a few moments of midair colloquy, the Wicked Tribe formed themselves into hovering monkey-letters, clutching each other to spell out the word "B-O-R-R-I-N-G".

"We're sorry. We'll need some help afterward, probably."

"We come find then," said Zunni. "Now—fly and make noise!"

The Tribe contracted into a small yellow cumulonimbus.

"Ruling tribe! *Yeeeee! Mejor* prime monkeys! Wicked, wicked, wicked!"

Like a swarm of bees, they circled Orlando and the others, then vanished through a gap in TreeHouse's higgle-piggle geometry.

"The clubkids are a lot of fun if you're not trying to concentrate," Starlight said, smiling. "I'll tell you where to go."

"Thank you." Orlando did his best to make his Thargor-face return the smile. "You've been a lot of help."

"I just remember, that's all," she said.

"Do you understand any of this?" Fredericks' sim was frowning, a not particularly subtle creasing like a lump of bread dough being folded in half.

"A little. Proprioception—I've done some work with that stuff in school. That's where all the input—tactors, visual, audio—works together to make you feel like you're really *in* the place you're supposed to be in. There's a lot of brain science in it."

They were sitting in the highest row of seats, far away from the center of the discussion, although every voice was still perfectly audible. The amphitheater, Orlando guessed, was supposed to be like something from ancient Greece or Rome, all pale stone, attractively weathered. The greater chaos of TreeHouse was not visible here: the amphitheater sat beneath its own bowl of blue sky. A dim reddish sun crouched low on the horizon, casting long shadows across the benches.

The shadows of the discussion's participants were more or less humanoid. The four or five dozen engineers and programmers, like the mystery man who had brought Orlando and Fredericks to TreeHouse in the first place, didn't seem quite as interested in personal adornment as the rest of the place's inhabitants. Most wore very basic sims, no more lifelike than test dummies. Others did not bother to wear sims at all, and were only distinguishable as physically present by small points of light or simple iconic objects indicating their position.

Not all were so boringly functional. A giant gleaming bird made of golden wire, a plaid Eiffel Tower, and three small dogs dressed in Santa Claus suits were among the most vociferous debaters.

Orlando was fascinated by the conversations, although he found them difficult to understand. This was high-level programming as discussed by a highly unorthodox group of hackers, mixed up with Tree-House security issues and general systems operation for the whole renegade node. It was a little like listening to someone argue existential philosophy in a language you'd only studied in junior high school.

But this is where I belong, he thought. *This is what I want to do.* He felt a swift stab of mourning that his apprenticeship with Indigo Gear and return visits to TreeHouse were both so unlikely to happen.

"God," Fredericks groaned. "This is like a Student Government meeting. Can't we just ask them some questions and get out of here? Even the flying monkey-midgets were more interesting than this."

"I'm learning things. . . ."

"Yeah, but not about what we need to know. Come on, Gardiner, we only have a couple of hours left and I'm going crazy." Fredericks abruptly stood up and waved one of his sim's stocky arms, as though hailing a cab. "Excuse me! Excuse me!"

The discussion group turned toward the source of the disruption with the uniformity of a flock of swallows banking against the wind. The Eiffel Tower, which had been explaining something controversial about visual information protocols, stopped and glared—inasmuch as a large plaid building could glare. In any case, it did not look like a happy building.

"Okay," Fredericks said. "I got their attention. Go ahead and ask 'em."

Orlando's well-honed Thargor reflexes urged him to brain Fredericks with a heavy object. Instead he rose to his feet, conscious for the first time of how . . . *teenage* the Thargor body looked. "Ummm . . . I'm sorry my friend interrupted," he said. "We're guests, and our time is running out, and we had some questions we need answered, and . . . and someone sent us to this meeting."

One of the points of light glittered angrily. "Who the hell are you?"

"Just . . . just a couple of guys."

"You're doing great, Gardino," Fredericks offered helpfully.

"Shut up." He took a breath and began again. "We just wanted to find out about some gear—some software. We heard that the people who worked on it hung out here."

There was a low hum of irritation from the group of programmers. "We do not wish to be interrupted," said someone with a distinctly Germanic accent.

One of the more rudimentary sims stood up, extending its hands as though to quiet the crowd. "Just tell us what you want," it said. The voice might have been female.

"Um, well, some gear that eventually wound up in a creature in the Middle Country simworld—the creature was a Red Gryphon, to be specific—is listed on all the InPro databases as being authored by someone called Melchior." There was a brief, but muted reaction, as though the name were familiar. Orlando went on, heartened. "From what we could learn, he or she hangs out here. So we'd like some help finding Melchior."

The basic sim that had quieted the crowd stood motionless for a moment, then lifted a hand and made a gesture. The world suddenly went black.

Orlando could see nothing, hear nothing, as though he had been abruptly flung into the vacuum of starless space. He tried to reach up to see what had blocked his vision, but his sim would not respond to his thoughts.

"You may be a guest here longer than you meant to be," a voice murmured in Orlando's ear—a distinctly menacing voice. "You and your friend have just made a really, really stupid mistake."

Sealed in darkness, Orlando raged. *We were so close—so close!* With a growing sense of having lost more than an opportunity, he pulled the ripcord and dumped them out of TreeHouse.

CHAPTER 23

Blue Dog Anchorite

NETFEED/BUSINESS: ANVAC Posts Record Profits
(visual: ANVAC corporate headquarters—featureless wall)
VO: ANVAC Security Corporation declared the highest business profit margin
in fifty years. Zurich Exchange observers cite the ever-growing worldwide
need for individual and corporate security, as well as ANVAC's ground-
breaking line of "smart" biological weaponry, as reasons for the soaring
profits.
(visual: ANVAC vice-president, face and voice disguised)
VP: "We fill a need. The world is a dangerous place. Overkill? That's
easy—would you rather be morally right or alive?"

The Anchorite's 'cot—hacker slang for a virtual home-away-from-home—was the least impressive Renie had ever seen. With all of virtuality's prizes to choose from, he had created a decidedly uninspiring setting: with its tiny bed, poor-resolution wallscreen, and miserable flowers in a plastic jug on an institutional table, it looked very much like an old man's room in a nursing home. It also had the same curious real/unreal quality as the Anchorite's own sim. Renie, tired and frustrated, wondered if this old man could be any help to them at all.

"Do you want to sit down?" Singh asked. "I'll make chairs if you

want some. Goddamn, I haven't had anybody in here for a long time."
He lowered his sim onto the bed, which creaked convincingly, and
Renie suddenly realized why both the old hacker and his room seemed
so oddly lifelike. It was all *real*. He was using an actual real-time video
of himself as a sim; the bed he was sitting on, the entire room, was
probably real as well, a projection turned into a functional VR environment. She was looking at the Anchorite's actual face and body as they
looked at this very moment.

He stared back at her, sneering. "Yeah, you guessed it. I used to
have the whole fancy kit—good looking sim, forty-thousand-gallon
aquarium for an office, full of sharks and mermaids—but I got tired
of it. The only friends I had all knew I was a useless old bastard, so
who was I fooling?"

Renie was not particularly interested in Singh's philosophy. "Did
Susan Van Bleeck ask you about a golden city? And what did you
mean when you told us it was 'too late'?"

"Don't hurry me, girl," the Anchorite said crossly.

"Don't 'girl' me. I need some answers, and soon. This isn't a locked-
room murder mystery, this is my life we're talking about—more importantly, my little brother's life."

"I think Mister Singh is willing to speak to us, Renie." Martine's
voice, simultaneously coming from everywhere and nowhere, might
have been that of some offstage director. Renie did not like being
directed.

"Martine, I'm tired of talking to the air. I'm sure this is terribly
impolite, but would you put on a damn body so we at least know
where you are?"

After a long silent moment, a large flat rectangle appeared in the
corner of the room. The painted face wore a famously mysterious half-
smile. "Is this acceptable?" asked the Mona Lisa.

Renie nodded. There might be an element of mockery to Martine's
choice, but at least now they all had something to look at. She turned
back to the old man in the turban. "You said 'too late.' Too late for
what?"

The old man cackled. "You're a regular little Napoleon, aren't you?
Or perhaps I should say 'a regular little Shaka Zulu'?"

"I'm three-quarters Xhosa. Get on with it. Or are you afraid to talk
to us?"

Singh laughed again. "Afraid? I'm too bloody old to be afraid. My
kids don't talk to me, and my wife's dead. So what could they do to
me except shove me off the mortal coil?"

"They," said Renie. "Who are 'they'?"

"The bastards who killed all my friends." The old man's smile vanished. "And Susan's only the most recent. That's why it's too late—because my friends are all gone. There's only me." He raised his hand and gestured at the unprepossessing room as if it were the last place on earth, and he the world's only survivor.

Perhaps for Singh it *was* the last place on earth, Renie thought. She felt herself thawing a little, but she still wasn't sure whether she liked the old man or not. "Look, we desperately need information. Was Susan right? Do you know anything about the city?"

"One thing at a time, girl. I'll tell it in my own way." He spread his crooked fingers on the lap of his bathrobe. "It started happening about a year ago. There were only a half-dozen of us left—-Melani, Dierstroop, some others—you don't care about names of old hackers, do you? Anyway, there were a half-dozen of us left. We'd all known each other for years—Komo Melani and I both worked on some of the early revisions of TreeHouse, and Fanie Dierstroop and I had been in school together. Felton, Misra, and Sakata all worked at Telemorphix with me. Several of them were TreeHouse regulars, but Dierstroop never joined—he thought we were a bunch of left-wing, New Age idiots—and Sakata gave up her membership over a rules committee disagreement. We all stayed in touch, sort of. We had all lost friends—when you get to be my age, that's a fairly familiar pain—so we were probably a little closer than any of us had been in a while, just because the circle was getting smaller."

"Please," said the Mona Lisa. "A question. You knew these people from different places, *non*? So, when you say, 'a half-dozen of us,' it is a half-dozen of . . . what?"

Renie nodded. She had been looking for the connecting thread herself.

"Damn it, just hold your water." Singh scowled, but actually seemed to be enjoying the attention. "I'm getting there. See, I didn't *realize* at the time that there were just six of us, because I didn't see the link. I had other friends, too, you know—I wasn't such a miserable bastard as all that. No, I didn't see or think about the connection. Until they started to die.

"Dierstroop went first. A stroke, as far as anyone knew. I was sad, but I didn't think anything of it. Fanie always drank a lot, and I'd heard he got fat. I figured he'd had a pretty good innings.

"Next Komo Melani died, also a stroke. Then Sakata went—fell down the stairs of her house outside Niigata. It felt a little like a curse, losing three old comrades in a matter of months, but I had no reason to be suspicious. But Sakata had a gardener who took care of her property, and he swore that he saw two men dressed in dark clothes drive out of her front gate somewhere around the time she must have died, so all of a sudden it didn't look quite so much like an old gear consultant having a simple accident. As far as I know, the Japanese authorities still haven't closed her case.

"Felton died a month later. Keeled over in the London Underground. Heart failure. They had a memorial for him here at Founder's Hill. But I was beginning to wonder. Vijay Misra called me—he'd been wondering too, but unlike me, he'd put two and two together and come up with a nice round number. See, some of the people like Dierstroop I'd known for so long, I'd forgotten that there was only one time when all of us—me and Misra and the four people who'd just died—had worked together. There'd been others working there, too, but we six had been the last ones alive. And as Misra and I talked, we realized that we were the only two left. It wasn't a good feeling."

Renie was leaning forward. "Left from what?"

"I'm *getting* there, girl!"

"Don't shout at me!" Renie was in danger of losing her composure. "Look, I've been kicked out of my job, but I'm still using the school's equipment. Someone could call the police on me at any moment, for God's sake. Everywhere I go for information, I get a song and dance and a lot of mystery."

Through the machineries of virtuality, she felt !Xabbu touch her arm, a homely reminder to say calm.

"Well," Singh said, cheerful again, "beggars can't be choosers, girlie."

"Is this place secure?" Martine asked suddenly.

"Like a soundproof bunker in the middle of the Sahara." Singh laughed, revealing a gap in his teeth. "I should know—I *wrote* the security gear for this whole place. Even if there was a data-tap on one of your lines, I'd know it." He laughed again, a quiet, self-satisfied wheeze. "Now, you asked me to get on with it—let me get on with it. Misra was a security specialist, too . . . but it didn't do him any good. They got him as well. Suicide—a massive overdose of his anti-epilepsy medication. But I had just talked to him two nights before and he wasn't depressed, wasn't in the least suicidal. Frightened, yes—we had realized that the odds against us were getting worse and worse. So when he died, I knew for sure. They were killing off everyone that knew anything about Otherland."

"Otherland?" For the first time since Renie had met her—if that was the proper word—Martine sounded truly startled. "What does this have to do with the Otherland?"

A squirming chill traveled Renie's spine. "Why? What is it?"

The old man bobbed his head, pleased. "Ah, now you're interested! Now you want to listen!"

"We have been listening, Mister Singh—listening very carefully." !Xabbu spoke quietly, but with unusual force.

"Slow down," Renie demanded. "What is this Otherland thing? It sounds like an amusement park."

The painting rotated, the Mona Lisa's pale face swiveling toward her. "It is, of a sort—or so the rumors say. Otherland is even less known than TreeHouse. It seems to be some kind of playground for the rich, a large-scale simulation. That is all I have heard. It is privately owned and kept very quiet, so there is little information available." She leaned back toward Singh. "Please continue."

He nodded as though receiving his due. "We were contracted through Telemorphix South Africa. I was working for them then—this was nearly thirty years ago. Dierstroop actually managed the project, but he let me choose the people, which is why Melani and the others were involved. We put together a security installation for what I thought was some kind of business network—hush-hush, all very top secret, money no obstacle. Some huge corporate customer, that's all we knew. It was only as we worked at it that we found out it was actually a VR node, or rather a string of VR nodes on parallel supercomputers, the biggest, most high-speed VR net anyone had ever seen. The consortium that owned it was called TGB. That's all we knew about them. They were TGB, we were TMX." He barked a laugh. "Never trust people that like to call things by initials, that's my philosophy. It is now, anyway. I wish it had been then.

"Anyway, the TGB people—or at least some of their engineers—occasionally referred to this new network as the 'Otherland.' Like 'motherland' without an 'm.' I think it was a joke, but I never saw the point. Melani and I and some of the others used to try to guess what it was going to be used for—we figured it was meant to be some kind of huge VR theme park, an online version of that Disney monstrosity getting bigger every day over in Baja California, but it seemed pretty high-powered even for that. Dierstroop kept telling us we were wasting our time, that we should just shut up and collect our—admittedly—substantial paychecks. But there was something really weird about the whole project, and when a decade or so had gone by after we'd finished and there *still* hadn't been any announcement about it, we all pretty much admitted to ourselves that it wasn't a commercial property. I figured it was some kind of government thing—Telemorphix has always been really friendly with governments, especially the American one, of course. Wells has always known which side of his bread was buttered."

"So what *was* it, then?" Renie asked. "And why would someone kill your friends to keep it secret? And, more importantly to me, what does this have to do with my little brother? Susan Van Bleeck talked to you, Mister Singh—what did she say?"

"I'm almost there. Hang on for a moment." The old man reached out for nothing visible. A moment later a cup appeared in his hand. He took a long, shaky drink. "The whole room's not live," he explained, "just me. That's better." He smacked his lips. "Okay, now we come to your part of things.

"Susan had some luck researching that weird city of yours. The buidings had some odd little Aztec-type elements, according to this architecture gear she used on it—tiny details, things only an expert system would notice. So she started running searches on people who knew about such things, hoping to find someone who could maybe help her place your city."

"So why did she contact you?"

"She didn't, not until she'd run across a name in her list of experts that she remembered me mentioning to her. So she called me up. Startled the hell out of me. I recognized the bastard's name that she'd turned up, all right. He was one of the TGB muckamucks. We had to answer to him when we were doing the security for this Otherland thing of ours. Bolivar Atasco."

"Atasco?" Renie shook her head in befuddlement. "I thought he was an archaeologist."

"Whatever else he does, he was top man on the Otherland project," Singh growled. "I flipped out, of course. Because by now, I was the last one left, and I knew something was going on. I told Susan to get the hell away from it. I wish . . . I wish she'd called me sooner." For a moment, his stiff facade threatened to fall away. He fought for composure. "Those shits got her the same night. Probably within a few hours of her being on the phone with me."

"Oh, God. That's why she made that note and hid it," Renie said. "But why the book? Why not just his name?"

"What book?" asked Singh, nettled at losing the spotlight.

"A book on . . . Central American cultures. Something like that.

Written by this Atasco. Martine and I both looked it over, and we couldn't make anything of it."

A window flashed open next to Martine. "This is it. But as Renie said, we have examined it carefully."

The old man squinted at the window. *"Early Mesoamerica.* Yeah, I remember he'd written some famous textbook. But that was a long time ago—maybe you have the wrong edition." He scrolled the book. "There's no author picture in this version, for one thing. If you want to get a look at this bastard, you ought to find an older printing of the book."

The window closed. "I will see what I can discover," Martine said.

"So, what do we know, exactly?" Renie closed her eyes for a moment, trying to shut out the dingy room and pull together the tangled threads of information. "Atasco headed up this Otherland project, and you think that the people who worked on it with you have been murdered?"

Singh grinned acidly. "I don't think, girlie, I know."

"But what does that . . . that *city* have to do with anything—the image someone planted in my computer? And why would these people have anything to do with my brother? I don't get it!"

Another window popped open in the middle of the room.

"You are right, Mister Singh," Martine said. "The earlier edition does have a photo of the author."

The entire contents of the book scrolled past in a waterfall of gray, then Renie was staring at a picture of Bolivar Atasco, a handsome, narrow-faced man on the far side of middle-age. He was sitting in a room full of leafy plants and old statues. Behind him, in a frame on the wall, was . . .

"Oh, my God." Renie reached out a sim hand as though she could touch it. The picture behind him had none of the vibrancy of the original—it was only a sketch, a watercolor like an architect's rendering—but it was beyond any doubt the city, the impossible, surrealistic golden city. Beside her, !Xabbu made a clicking noise of surprise. "Oh, my God," she said again.

"I'm fine, !Xabbu. I just felt a little faint. This is a lot to take in." She waved her friend away. He retreated with a cartoonish worried look on his sim face.

"After your recent illness, I am concerned for you," he said.

"I'm not having a heart problem. More of a comprehension problem." She turned wearily to the old man and the Mona Lisa. "So what do we have here? I mean, let me get this straight. Some crazy archaeologist, maybe working for the CIA or something, builds a huge, superfast VR network. Then he starts killing off all the people who worked on it. At the same time, he puts my brother—and maybe a few thousand other kids—into a coma. Meanwhile, he's beaming *me* some kind of Aztec-influenced building designs. It all makes perfect sense."

"It is indeed very strange," Martine said. "But there must be a pattern."

"Tell me when you figure it out," Renie replied. "Why is this man sending me pictures of an imaginary city? Is this supposed to be a warning to back off? If so, it's the most damned obscure warning I can imagine. And I can believe—just barely—that there could be some project this TGB group, or whatever their name is, wants to keep hidden, even to the point of killing off a bunch of old programmers. But what does that have to do with my brother Stephen? He's lying unconscious in a hospital bed. I almost wound up the same, thanks to some bizarre horror movie with too many arms, but I'll just leave that out for now, to keep things simple." She snorted in disgust, the giddiness of fatigue threatening to overwhelm her. "What in the name of heaven does my Stephen have to do with an international plot?" She turned on Martine, who had been silent for some time. "And what do *you* know about all this? You've heard of Otherland before. What do you know about these people?"

"I know almost nothing," the French woman said. "But Mister Singh's story, combined with yours, makes me feel certain that there are larger concerns here, shapes that we have not fully understood."

Renie remembered !Xabbu's borrowed phrase. *A rough beast.* The little man met her eye, but the cut-rate sim kept his expression inscrutable. "Which means?" she asked Martine.

The Mona Lisa sighed, a fluting of breath out of keeping with the painted expression. "I have no answers to your questions, Renie, only information that raises perhaps more questions. The 'TGB' Mister Singh mentions is known to me, although I did not know before they were involved with Otherland. They call themselves The Grail Brotherhood, or sometimes simply The Brotherhood, although the group is reputed to have female members. There is no positive proof that the group even exists, but I have heard of it too many times from sources I trust. They are a very disparate collection, academics like Atasco, financiers, politicians. They are rumored to have other members of an even more unsavory nature. I know nothing else about them for certain, except that they are a magnet for . . . how do you say it? Theories of conspiracy. They are like the Bilderbergers or the Illuminati or the Masons. There are people who blame them every time the Chinese dollar drops, or a hurricane disrupts line service in the Caribbean. But what could they want with children? I have no idea."

This was the longest speech Renie had ever heard Martine make. "Could they be . . . pedophiles or something?"

"They seem to be going to a great deal of trouble without actually laying their hands on any children," Martine pointed out. "Surely rich and powerful people would not expend so much energy when they could procure victims much more simply. More likely, it seems to me that they are trying to frighten these children away from something important, and the illness is an accident, a . . . by-product."

"Organs," said Singh.

"What does that mean?" Renie stared at him.

"Rich people can have lousy health, too," the old man said. "Believe me, when you get to my age, you think a lot about what you could do with a couple of new lungs or kidneys. Maybe it's some kind of organ-harvesting thing. That would explain why they don't want to hurt them, just put them in comas."

Renie felt a cold pang, then a sense of helpless, scalded outrage. Could it be? Her brother, her almost-baby? "But that doesn't make any sense! Even if these children eventually die, the families still have to say the organs can be used. And hospitals don't just sell them to the highest bidder."

The old man's laugh was unpleasant. "You have a young person's faith in the medical establishment, girl."

She shook her head, giving up. "Maybe. Maybe they can bribe the doctors, get the organs. But what does that have to do with your friends and what they worked on, this . . . Otherland?" She turned and pointed to *Early Mesoamerica*, still hanging in the middle of Singh's room. "And why would Atasco the organ-robber send me a picture of this place? It just doesn't make sense."

"It makes sense to *somebody*," the old man said bitterly. "Otherwise, I wouldn't be the last security programmer on that project left alive." He sat up suddenly, as though he had been jolted with electrical current. "Just a minute." He remained silent for long moments as the others watched him, wondering. "Yeah," he said at last, speaking to someone not present. "Well, that's interesting, all right. Send me the information."

"Who are you talking to?" Renie asked.

"Some of my fellow TreeHouse residents—the Security Committee. Hold on." He went silent again, listening, then with a few terse sentences ended the conversation. "Apparently someone's been snooping around, asking about 'Melchior,' " he explained. "That was a handle for me and Felton—the one who had the so-called heart attack in the Underground. We used it for some gear contracts, stuff like that. These people came into the programming meeting and started asking for Melchior. Pretty arrogant of them, walking right into TreeHouse that way. Anyway, the programmers jumped on them."

Renie felt her skin bump into gooseflesh at the thought of their faceless enemies so close. "Them?"

"There were two. I'm getting a snapshot of them now. See, I'd posted a general message that anyone asking about any of my colleagues on the Otherland project should be viewed with extreme suspicion, and interrogated if possible."

!Xabbu put his hands on his thighs and stood. "But they have escaped?"

"Yes, but we'll have lots to work with—how they got in, their aliases, things like that."

"You seem pretty calm," Renie told him. "These are the people who killed your friends, killed Susan. They're *dangerous.*"

Singh raised a tufted eyebrow and grinned. "Back in RL they may be dangerous as hell, but TreeHouse is *ours.* When you come here, you play by our rules. Here comes the picture."

Two hefty figures popped into view in the middle of Singh's 'cot, the single-moment snapshot magnified until it took up most of the space in the room. The two sims hovered side by side in midair, one of them apparently frozen in the act of talking. One was fairly nondescript, but the speaker was dressed in furs and skins as though he had stepped out of some low-budget netflick.

"We have seen these people before," said !Xabbu.

Renie stared, appalled and fascinated, at the broad-muscled bodies. "Yes, we have. It was in the first place you brought us," she told Martine. "Your friend thought they needed fashion help, remember?" She frowned. "I suppose it's impossible to be conspicuous in a place like this, but he . . . " she fought back a smirk, indicating the mustachioed barbarian—". . . still has been pushing his luck. I mean, it looks like the kind of sim one of my little brother's friends would wear for some online game." The thought of Stephen sobered her, obliterating her small moment of amusement.

"We'll know more about them soon," Singh said. "I wish that lot at the meeting had been a little more low-key though—it would have been nice to find out more about what they wanted before letting them know we were on to them. But that's engineering types for you. Subtle as a flying mallet."

"So we add this in to the mix," Renie said. "All this other crazy stuff, then they send in a couple of spies who look like something out of one of those kiddie interactives—*Borak, Master of the Stone Age* or whatever."

"Makes sense for spies coming to TreeHouse," Singh said blithely. "Everybody's a freak here. I'm telling you, I worked for that Atasco guy and he was no fool. Slick as snail snot." He held up his hand, listening again to an inaudible voice. "That's something," he said. "Yeah, round them up. I'll come and talk to them when I'm finished here." He turned his attention back to the room. "Apparently, these guys were hanging around with some of the culture club kids, so we might get some information from them. Talking to those kids is like talking to static, though. . . ."

!Xabbu, who had been examining the flash-frozen intruders, floated back toward Renie. "What should we do now?"

"We can try to find out more about Otherland," Martine offered. "I fear that they have been as careful with information as they were with other forms of security, but we may be able to . . . "

"You can do whatever you want," Singh said, interrupting her. "But I'll tell you what I'm going to do. I'm going to go and find the bastards."

Renie stared at him. "What do you mean?"

"Just what I said. These people think they can hide behind their money and their fortress houses and their corporations. Most of all, they think they can hide in their expensive network. But I helped *build* that damn network, and I'm betting I can get back into it. Nothing like a little old-fashioned *akisu* to get things done. You want to take them to court or something? Go ahead. By the time you're finished getting the runaround, I'd be long dead. I'm not going to wait."

Renie was having trouble following him. "You mean you're going into this Otherland place? Is that right? Just going to bust in and have a look around, ask the people using it, 'Hey, did any of you people put a bunch of kids in comas or kill my friends?' Great plan."

Singh was unconcerned. "You can do what you like, girlie—this isn't the military or anything. I'm just tipping you what *I'm* going to do." He paused, chewing his lip. "But I'll tell you something for free. You want to know where that city of yours is? Why it looks so real,

but you can't find it anywhere in the known world? Because it's on
Atasco's net."

Renie was silenced. The old man's words had the feel of truth.

"The mystery centers around this Otherland," Martine said slowly,
the da Vinci eyes focused on nothing present. "All roads seem to lead
there. It is a thing, it is a place. Incredible amounts of money have
been lavished on it. The best minds of two generations labored to
build it. And it is surrounded in secrecy. What could this Grail Brotherhood want? Is it simply to harvest and sell organs? That would be
dreadful enough. Or is it something larger, harder to understand?"

"What, like they want to rule the world?" Singh laughed harshly.
"Come on, that's the oldest and worst cliché in the books. Besides, if
these people are what they seem to be, they already *own* half the
world. But they're up to something, that's for damn sure."

"Is there a mountain in this place?" !Xabbu asked suddenly. "A
great black mountain that reaches into the clouds?"

No one said anything, and Singh looked mildly annoyed, but Renie
suddenly felt a memory, a tattered scrap of dream, blow through her
mind on a chill wind. A black mountain. Her dream, too. Maybe Martine was right. Maybe all roads did lead to this Otherland. And if
Singh was the only person who could get her inside. . . .

"If you did hack in," she said out loud, "could you take other people
in with you?"

The old man raised an eyebrow. "You talking about yourself? You
want to come with me? I said this wasn't the military, but if I'm doing
the work, then I am definitely the general. Could you live with that,
Shaka Zulu?"

"I think so." She suddenly and inexplicably found herself liking the
cranky old bastard just a little. "But I've got no decent equipment—I
won't even be able to use this stuff anymore." She gestured at her
sim. "I've just been suspended from my job over all this."

"You have your pad and your goggles, Renie," !Xabbu reminded her.

"Never work." Singh waved his hand imperiously. "A home system? One of those little Krittapong station boxes or something? This
may take hours, days even, and that's just to get inside. Even twenty-
five years ago this would have been an almost impossible system to
hack—God knows how they've upgraded the defenses since then. If
any of you go in with me, you'll need to be ready to stay online for
hours. Then, if we get through, we're going to need the best input-
output equipment we can get. That city you're so impressed by is an

example of the processing power they have. There'll be an incredible amount of information, and any and all of it might be important."

"I would offer to bring you in on one of my links, Renie," Martine said. "But I doubt your pad could handle that much bandwidth. In any case, that would not solve your problem as far as being online for an extended period."

"Can you think of anything, Martine? I'm desperate. I can't just sit back and wait to see if Singh finds anything." Nor could she imagine putting much trust in Singh's capacity for subtlety once the security was breached. Better if she were there with him.

"I . . . I will consider the problem. There may be something I can do."

In her hopeful gratitude, it took Renie a moment to realize that Martine seemed to be planning to join the expedition, too. But before she could consider this, a swarm of tiny yellow monkeys abruptly popped into existence in the middle of the room, spinning like a cartoon tornado.

"Whee!" one of them shouted. "Wicked Tribe *ruling* tribe!" Whooping, they swirled like autumn leaves.

"Good God, get out of here, you kids!" shouted Singh.

"You want to see us, *Apa* Dog! Want to see! Here are we!" They swirled toward the snapshot of the two intruders, who still floated like parade blimps at the center of the elcot; one of the monkeys looped out of the banana-colored cloud to hover before them. "Knew it!" the tiny voice shrieked. "Our friends! Knew it!"

"Why you send them away?" another demanded. "Now boring boring boring!"

Singh shook his head in disgust. "I didn't want you here, I told them I'd talk to you later. How did you little monsters get in? What, do you eat code or something?"

"*Mejor* hacker tribe! Too small, too fast, too scientific!"

"Been snooping where you shouldn't. Christ, what else is new?"

The image of the intruders was now surrounded by tiny yellow creatures. Renie found herself staring. On the outskirts of the whirling crowd, several of them were playing catch with a small, shiny, faceted object. "What's that?" she said sharply. "What have you got there?"

"Ours! Found it!" A handful of microsimians bunched protectively around the golden nugget.

"Found it where?" Renie asked. "That's just like the thing that was left on my system!"

"Found it where our friends were," one of the monkeys said defensively. "They didn't see it, but we did! Wicked Tribe, *ojos mejores*!"

"Give that here," growled Singh. He skimmed toward them and plucked it from their midst.

"Not yours! Not yours!" they wailed.

"Be careful," Renie warned him. "It was something just like that which put the image of the city onto my system."

"What did you do to get it to display?" asked Singh, but before she could answer him, the gemlike object pulsed light, then vanished in a sudden whiteflare. For an instant, Renie could not see at all; moments later, as she contemplated the now familiar vista of the golden city, there were still afterimages of the flash on her eyes.

"That's not possible." Singh sounded furious. "Nobody could have walked that much information into TreeHouse under our noses—we *built* this place!"

The image abruptly shivered, then dissolved into a single blinking point of light. A moment later, it expanded outward again, taking on a new form.

"Look!" Renie dared not move, for fear she would disrupt the information. "Look at that! Martine, what is that?"

Martine remained silent.

"Don't you even recognize it?" asked Singh. "Jesus, I feel ancient. It's what they used in the old days, before they had clocks. It's an hourglass."

Everyone watched as the sand flowed swiftly through the narrow neck. Even the Wicked Tribe hung motionless and rapt. Just before the final grains had run out, the image vanished. Another object popped into view, this one more abstract.

"It's some kind of grid," Renie said. "No, I think it's supposed to be . . . a calendar."

"But there aren't any dates on it—no month." Singh was squinting.

Renie was counting. As she finished, the grid winked out, leaving nothing behind. "The first three weeks were x'd out—only the last ten days were blank."

"What in hell is going on here?" Singh rasped. "Who did this, and what the hell are they trying to say?"

" I believe I can answer the second question," !Xabbu said. "Whoever has tried to tell us about this city is now trying to tell us something else."

"!Xabbu's right." Something had seized her, an unshakable certainty like a vast cold hand. She had no choice anymore—that freedom had been taken from her. She could only go forward, dragged into the unknown. "I don't know why, and I don't know whether we're being taunted or warned, but we've just been told that our time is running out. Ten days left. That's all we have."

"Left before what?" demanded Singh. Renie could only shake her head.

One of the monkeys fluttered up and hung before her, yellow pinions beating as swiftly as a hummingbird's.

"Now Wicked Tribe *really* angry," it said, screwing up its tiny face. "What you do with our shiny thing?"

Third:

ANOTHER COUNTRY

The dews drop slowly and dreams gather: unknown spears
Suddenly hurtle before my dream-awakened eyes,
And then the clash of fallen horsemen and the cries
Of unknown perishing armies beat about my ears,
We who still labour by the cromlech on the shore,
The grey cairn on the hill, when day sinks drowned in dew,
Being weary of the world's empires, bow down to you,
Master of the still stars and of the flaming door.

–William Butler Yeats

CHAPTER 24

Beneath Two Moons

NETFEED/HEALTH: Charge Damage May Be Reversible
(visual: charge users on Marseille street corner)
VO: The Clinsor Group, one of the world's largest medical equipment companies, announced that they will soon be marketing a therapy for the damage caused by the addictive use of deep-hypnosis software, called "charge" by its users.
(visual: Clinsor laboratories, testing on human volunteers)
VO: The new method, which the inventors call NRP or "neural reprogramming," induces the brain to find new synaptic pathways to replace those damaged by excessive charge use . . . .

The golden light became blackness and noise.

Something was crushing him. He kicked, but there was nothing to kick against. For endless moments he thrashed helplessly. Then the world peeled back around his head and he was sucking air into his stinging lungs and struggling to keep his head above the water, straining to hold onto the beautiful, marvelous, silversweet night air.

The boy Gally, clutched in his arms, sputtered out water and rasped in breath. Paul loosened his hold and let the boy out to arm's length so he could use his other arm to help keep them both afloat. The water was gentler here than the place in the river where they had dived. Perhaps they had drifted away from the scarlet woman and that terrible creature.

But how could they have been underwater long enough for it to become night? It had been only late afternoon a moment ago, and now, except for a salting of stars, the sky was as dark as the inside of a coat pocket.

It was no good trying to understand. Paul could see a faint light from what must be the shore. He pulled Gally close and spoke to him in a low voice, worried in case their dreadful pursuers might be somewhere near. "Do you have your breath back? Can you swim a little?" When the boy nodded, Paul patted his sopping head. "Good. Swim ahead of me toward that light. If you get too tired, or begin to cramp, don't be frightened—I'll be right behind you."

Gally gave him a wide-eyed, inscrutable look, then began to dog-paddle toward the distant glow. Paul struck out after him with a slow stroke that felt strangely natural, as though there had been a time when he had done this frequently.

The waves were low and gentle, the current minimal. Paul felt himself relax slightly as he fell into the rhythm of his own movements. The river's character had become entirely different since they had first entered it: the water was almost pleasurably warm, and had a sweetish, spicy smell. He wondered briefly what it might be like to drink some, but decided that was an adventure better attempted when they had reached the safety of landfall. Who knew how different things might be here?

As they drew nearer to the light, Paul saw that it was a high flame like a bonfire or signal beacon. It burned, not on the shore, but atop a pyramidal shape on a stone island. The island itself was only a few dozen yards long, with stone steps leading down from the pyramid's base to the very edge of the water. Beyond the pyramid, at the island's farther end, another stone structure stood surrounded by a small grove of trees.

As they drew closer, Gally pulled up, thrashing. Paul stroked forward swiftly and put one of his arms around the boy's thin chest.

"Do you have a cramp?"

"There's something in the water!"

Paul looked around, but the surface, painted with jagged splashes of reflected flame, seemed unbroken. "I don't see anything. Come on, we're almost there."

He kicked hard, pushing them both forward, and as he did so, something heavy bumped along his shins. Paul made a startled noise and swallowed water. Coughing, he swam hard for the stone steps.

Something huge was moving just beneath them. It rose and dumped them sideways in a sluice of river water; Paul saw first one, then a half-dozen snakelike shapes break the surface only a few yards away, twining aimlessly. Gally was struggling, and Paul found himself floundering only a few strokes short of the steps.

"Stop it!" he shouted into Gally's ear, but the boy was still thrashing weakly. Paul lifted him as far out of the water as he could, swung him back while kicking hard for leverage, and threw him up onto the broad step. The effort pushed Paul back under the water. His eyes popped open. Something huge and dark and faceless, with a mouth like a puckered hole full of curving spikes and a corona of ropy arms, was reaching for him. It was too late to reach the steps. He flung himself downward as hard as he could, churning his legs to force himself deeper. The arms snaked past over his head. He felt a rubbery something scrape along his side, then he was snagged briefly and tossed end over end. He popped to the surface like a fishing float, not sure which end was up or down and not entirely certain that he cared anymore. A thin hand closed on his arm, a human hand.

"It's coming back!" Gally shrilled.

Paul struggled onto the step beneath the water; with the boy's help, he clambered up the slippery stone onto the island itself. As his feet left the water a shiny black shape lashed out at him, slapping on the stone a yard away. It slid back into the river, pushing waves a yard high onto the stairs.

Paul clambered up the steps onto the platform at the base of the small pyramid. He put his back against the lowest layer of square stones and sat clutching his knees until his shivering slowed.

"I'm cold," Gally said at last.

Paul stood on shaky legs, then reached down to help the boy. "Let's go look there, where the trees are."

A tiled path led from the pyramid to the grove. Paul absently noted the design passing beneath their feet, an intricate, braided swirl that seemed somehow familiar. He grimaced. There were so few things he could remember clearly. And where was he now?

The trees that ringed the clearing had long silver leaves which hissed softly as the wind rubbed them together. At the center, on a small grassy mound, stood a small stone building open on one side. Only a little light from the beacon atop the pyramid leaked through the silver trees, but it was enough for Paul to see that the building, like the rest of the island, was empty of inhabitants. They moved closer and found a stone table inside the building, piled high with fruits and conical loaves of bread. The bread was soft and fresh. Before Paul could stop him, Gally had torn off a piece and stuffed it in his mouth. Paul hesitated only a moment before joining him.

They ate several of the fruits as well, tearing open the tough skins to get to the sweet pulp inside. With juice on their fingers and chins, they sat down against the cool tiles of the building's interior wall and enjoyed a satiated silence.

"I'm very tired," Paul said at last, but the boy was not listening. Gally had already fallen into one of his deep, deathlike sleeps, curled up like a rabbit near Paul's leg. Paul struggled to stay awake as long as he could, feeling that the boy deserved protection, but weariness overcame him at last.

The first thing Paul saw when he started awake was the reassuring shape of the moon high in the sky. When he noted its strangely uneven silhouette, it lost some of its power to reassure. Then he saw the second moon.

The noise that had awakened him was growing louder. It was music, clear and unquestionable, a melodic chanting in a language he didn't recognize. He put his hand over Gally's mouth and gently shook him awake.

When the boy understood what was going on, Paul released him. They peered out of the building and saw a long flat boat sliding past the island, ablaze with torches. There were figures at the railing, but Paul could not make them out through the trees. He led Gally out of the sheltering stone and into the grove itself, which seemed a better place to hide.

Crouching behind one of the silver-leafed trees, they watched the front end of the boat drift to a halt at the pyramid end of the island. A squat but agile figure leaped off and made the boat fast, then turned from side to side, face held high as though sniffing the wind. For a moment Paul could see it clearly by the beacon's flame, and what he saw made him flinch. The creature's shiny skin and long-snouted face were more beastlike than human.

Other shapes clambered off the boat onto the pyramid's base, blades glinting in their hands. Paul took advantage of the confusion to lift Gally up to the lowest limb of the tree, then followed the boy into the branches where they would be less likely to be seen.

From this improved viewpoint, he saw that the boat itself was a barge a third as long as their entire island, elaborately carved and painted, with a sweeping fantail, a pillared cabin, and torches all along the rail. To his relief, not all its occupants were as bestial as the first. The snouted one and his fellows seemed to be the crew; the others, now stepping onto the island, though very tall, seemed otherwise manlike. They wore armor and carried long pikes or curved swords.

After a brief look around—they seemed unusually alert for such a large armed group on such a small island, he thought—those who had debarked turned and signaled to their companions on board. Paul leaned forward for a better view through the leaves. When the occupant of the cabin stepped out, he almost fell from his perch.

She was almost as tall as the soldiers and stunningly beautiful, despite what even by moonlight seemed an odd, azure cast to her skin. She kept her large eyes downcast, but showed a hint of defiance in the set of her shoulders and neck. Her mass of dark hair was swept up and held by a crown of glinting jewels. Most astonishingly of all, translucent wings trailed from her shoulders, paper-thin but colored like stained glass, flaring in the moonlight as she stepped from the confining cabin.

But it was something else that had startled him. He knew her.

Paul could not say where or when he had seen her before, but he knew this woman, the recognition as swift and complete as if he had seen his own face reflected in a looking glass. He did not know her name or anything about her, but he knew *her*, and knew that somehow she was dear to him.

Gally's small hand reached out to steady him. He took a deep breath and felt that he might weep.

She stepped down from the barge's high platform onto the gangplank that the bestial sailors had put in place, then walked slowly down onto the island itself. Her dress was constructed of countless filmy strands which surrounded her like fog, leaving her long legs and slender torso no more than shadows. The soldiers followed her closely, as though to protect her, but Paul thought he saw a reluctance in her movements that suggested the sharp blades were meant to spur her rather than protect her.

She stopped and knelt before the pyramid for a long moment, then got up slowly and started along the tiled path toward the building in which Paul and Gally had slept. A thin man in a robe had followed her down from the boat, and now walked a few paces behind her. Paul was so fascinated by the grace of her movements, by the strange familiarity of her face, that she was directly beneath them before he realized that these visitors would see that he and Gally had eaten the offerings in the little temple. What would happen when they discovered it? There was nowhere to hide effectively on an island this small.

He may have breathed a little louder at this sudden fear, or it might have been some sense other than hearing that drew her glance, but as the dark-haired woman passed beneath she looked up into the leaves and saw him. Their eyes met only for an instant, but Paul felt himself touched and recognized. Then she cast her eyes down again, giving no indication that she had been doing anything but gazing up at the night sky. Paul held his breath as the man in the robe and more soldiers passed beneath, but none of them looked up. As the company reached the grassy mound, Paul clambered down the tree as quietly as he could, then caught Gally as he jumped down. He was leading the boy through the trees toward the water's edge when a sudden shout of anger rose from the temple; the soldiers and the robed man knew there had been thieves on their sacred island.

Already Paul could hear the rattle of footsteps in the grove. He lifted Gally and eased him down into the water, then slid in beside him. The soldiers were calling to each other, and some still remaining on the boat were hurrying down the gangplank to aid in the search.

Gally clung to the island's rocky verge. Paul moved close to whisper in his ear. The boy nodded and struck out swimming toward the barge. Paul followed, trying to stay low in the water and make as little noise as possible. Two soldiers were loitering in the stern, leaning on their spears as they watched their fellows search the island. Gally and Paul silently eased past them toward the barge's far side, where they would be shielded from view by the boat's own bulk. Paul found a handhold in the intricate carvings near the waterline. Gally clung to his shirt. Together they bobbed in the shadows, bumping gently against the hull, and waited.

The searchers at last began to return. Paul wondered whether they should try to regain the island, but the sound of the woman's voice as she reboarded decided him. He tightened his hold on the carvings and on Gally as the barge was pushed away from the island. For a moment he wondered at his own blitheness, that he should commit himself and the boy to waters where only hours before they had been attacked by some unknown monster. Had seeing the woman clouded his judgment? He only knew he could not simply let her float away. Gally seemed calmly trusting, but that did not make Paul feel any less of a betrayer.

*   *   *

The night was berry-dark, and the disconcerting pair of moons were still the brightest things in the sky. The barge moved slowly but steadily against the weak current. It was not difficult for Paul to maintain his grip, but it was a tiring position. He reached down to unfasten his belt and realized for the first time that he was wearing something different than when he had first gone into the river. His memories were disturbingly vague. He and the boy had escaped from the Eight Squared, fleeing both a woman in red and some other, even more frightening threat, but he could remember little more. Surely he had been in some terrible war—but hadn't that been somewhere else? And what had he been wearing before, that he should be so certain now that this was different?

He was wearing baggy pants and a sort of leather waistcoat, with no shirt beneath it. He could not remember having anything on his feet when he had first reached the island, and he was certainly barefooted now. He did have a long belt, though, which wrapped twice around his waist. He dismissed all the other questions as unanswerable, removed the belt and looped it through a piece of filigree just above the barge's waterline. When it was secured, he dropped it over Gally's head and beneath the boy's arms, then stretched the loop wide and slid himself in behind the boy, his back pressed against the hull. Now they were both held securely and Paul could at last let his tired muscles go limp.

The barge pushed on, surging minutely as the oars pulled. Paul felt like a strand of kelp, tugged back and forth by the warm waters with Gally's head bumping gently against his throat. The gentle pressure of the waves nudged him into sleep.

He was startled awake by a tingling that seemed to sweep through his entire body. As he floundered in his makeshift harness, trying to sweep away whatever stinging things had attacked him, the purple sky abruptly blazed a harsh green and the water went a flat, coppery orange. The air crackled with static electricity. Half the watercourse suddenly rose, as though some huge thing had surged up from the bottom, but the other half did not, even as the displacement lasted into its third and fourth second. There was even a firm and delineated edge between the two halves, as though the water were something as solid as stone. A moment later, the tingling ran through Paul even more sharply and he cried out. Gally, newly awakened and frightened, shouted also. The sky twisted again, glowing ghastly white for a single instant, then the painful tingling stopped, the sky flickered back to normal, and the water was all of a piece again, with no waves, or even ripples, to mark the change.

Paul gaped at nothing, staring into the near-darkness. He had trouble remembering things, but he felt quite certain he had never seen a body of water behave in that way before. In fact, he realized, it had been more than just the watercourse. The entire world had seemed to twist for a moment, to distort grossly, as though it were all painted on a single piece of paper, and that piece of paper had been violently crumpled.

"What . . . what was that?" Gally struggled for breath. "What happened?"

"I don't know. I . . . I think . . . "

Even as he struggled for an explanation, the entire section of carving from which he and the boy hung ripped free from the side of the boat and they were suddenly floundering in open water. Paul grabbed for Gally, and when he had him safe, he helped him to the piece of carved trim, which was spinning slowly in the water a few yards away. The section that had broken off was longer than Paul was tall, and buoyant enough to give them something to cling to, which was just as well: the barge, ignorant of its lost stowaways, was swiftly pulling away down the watercourse. Within a few score of heartbeats it had disappeared into the mist and early morning darkness. They were alone again.

"Ssshhh," Paul told Gally, who was crying between watery coughs. The boy looked up at him with reddened eyes. "We'll be all right. See, we're just going to float here."

"No. I'm not . . . I . . . I was dreaming. I dreamed Bay was under the water, down on the sand at the bottom. He was lonely, see, and he wanted me to come down and play with him."

Paul squinted, trying to locate the shore: if it were close enough, they could swim, despite the quiet but steady drag of the current. But if the land was close enough to reach, it was hidden by mist and dim light. "Who did?" he asked, distracted.

"Bay. I dreamed about Bay."

"And who is that?"

Gally stared, wide-eyed. "My brother. You met him. Don't you remember?"

Paul could think of nothing to say.

They had clung to the bit of wreckage for some time. The sky had begun to lighten, but Paul was growing steadily more weary and feared he would not be able to hold onto the carving and Gally both for much longer. He was contemplating which direction he should choose for an all-or-nothing swim when a long shadow came slipping toward them through the mist.

It was a boat, not a large one like the ceremonial barge, but a modest fishing skiff. A single shape stood in the bow. As the boat drew closer, Paul saw that its occupant was one of the snouted creatures.

The creature backed water with its single long paddle so that the skiff stopped a few yards away from them. It crouched down in the bow and tipped its head to one side, examining them. Crooked fangs protruded from the long muzzle, but an undeniable intelligence gleamed in its yellow eyes. The sunlight showed Paul for the first time that the shiny skin was faintly greenish. After a moment, it stood and raised the paddle as though to strike them.

"Leave us alone!" Paul splashed frantically until he could put the bulk of the floating carving between them and the snouted thing.

The creature did not swing the paddle, but stood looking at them for a moment. Then it lowered the flat blade until it touched the water a few inches from Paul's hand. It lifted one of its own clawed, faintly froglike paws from the handle and made an unmistakable gesture— *take it, take it.*

Paul did not feel very trusting, but he also realized that holding one end of the paddle improved his defensive position enormously. He reached out and grabbed it. The creature began to draw the paddle back through the water, bracing itself in the bow so their weight would not overbalance it. When they were close enough, Paul lifted Gally into the small boat, then dragged himself over the side, keeping a close eye on their rescuer as he did so.

The creature said something in a voice that sounded more like duck-gabble than anything else. Paul stared, then shook his head. "We do not speak your language."

"What is he?" asked Gally. Paul shook his head again.

The stranger abruptly bent over and delved into a wide leather sack that lay in the bottom of the boat. Paul tensed and drew himself upright. The creature stood, its bright eyes and long face suggesting satisfaction, and held out its hands. In each was a length of leather thong with a large polished bead hung on it. The beads were creamily reflective, like silvery pearls. When Paul and Gally only stared, the creature bent and picked up a third beaded thong and tied it around its own neck, allowing the bead to rest in the hollow of its throat. Paul thought he saw the bead shimmer for a moment, then change color, taking on something of the yellowy jade tinge of the creature's skin.

"Now you do it," the creature said. There was still a slight quack to its voice, but it was otherwise perfectly comprehensible. "Hurry, now—the sun will be up soon. We must not be caught on the Great Canal outside our appointed time."

Paul and Gally donned their thongs. The bead grew warm against Paul's throat. After a moment, it began to feel like a part of him.

"What are you called?" the creature asked them. "I am Klooroo of the Fisher People."

"I'm . . . I'm Paul. And this is Gally."

"And you are both of the Tellari."

"Tellari?"

"Certainly." Klooroo seemed very certain. "You are Tellari, just as I am Ullamari. Look at you! Look at me!"

Paul shrugged. There was no question that their rescuer was of a different sort than they were. "You said we are on . . . the Great Canal?"

Klooroo wrinkled his low, doglike brow. "Of course. Even Tellari should know that."

"We're . . . we have been in the water a long time."

"Ah. And you are not right in your heads." He nodded, satisfied. "Of course. Then you must come and be my guest until you can think properly again."

"Thank you. But . . . where are we?"

"What a strange question, Tellari. You are just outside the mighty city of Tuktubim, Shining Star of the Desert."

"But where is that? What country? Why are there two moons?"

Klooroo laughed. "When have there ever not been two moons? Even the humblest *nimbor* knows that is the difference between your world and mine."

"My . . . world?"

"You must have been badly injured, to be so foolish." He shook his head sadly. "You are on Ullamar, the fourth world from the sun. I think your people, in their ignorance, call it 'Mars.' "

"Why must we be off the canal before the sun comes up?"

Klooroo kept paddling as he answered, dipping and pulling on first one side of the skiff, then the other. "Because it is Festival Season, and during the dark hours the canal is forbidden to all except the barges of the priests. But a poor *nimbor* like me, if he has been unlucky in his fishing during the daylight, must sometimes take the risk if he does not wish to starve."

Paul sat up straight; Gally, who was slumped against his knee, protested sleepily. "So it *was* some kind of religious ritual. We climbed ashore onto an island and then later a boat landed there. They had a woman with them, a dark-haired woman with . . . with wings, as strange as that sounds. Is there any way to find out who she is?"

The bank of the canal was at last coming into view. Paul stared at the ghostly collection of huts slowly appearing through the mist, waiting, but Klooroo did not answer. When he looked up, the self-named *nimbor* was staring at him in horror.

"What? Have I said something wrong?"

"You . . . you have looked on the Summer Princess? And the *taltors* did not slay you?"

Paul shook his head. "If you mean the soldiers, we hid from them." Bemused by the creature's reaction, he told Klooroo how they had stolen a ride on the barge. ". . . And that is why we were floating in the water where you found us. What have we done that is so terrible?"

Klooroo made several hand gestures which seemed meant to ward off evil. "Only a Tellari, and a mad one at that, would ask such a question. Why do you think the canal is forbidden to anyone below the *taltor* class during Festival Season? So lowly ones do not look on the Summer Princess and bring bad luck on the Festival's rituals. If the rituals fail, the canals will not flood next season and all the land will remain a desert!"

A faint memory, really a reflex, suggested to Paul that once he would have found such a belief ridiculous, but recalling as little as he did of his own past and immersed in such a strange present, he found it difficult to say that *anything* was ridiculous. He shrugged. "I'm sorry. We didn't know anything. I was only trying to save the boy and myself."

Klooroo looked down at slumbering Gally and the grim set of his long muzzle softened a bit. "Yes, but . . . " He blinked, then looked up at Paul. "I suppose you could not know. Perhaps since you are offworlders, it will not disturb the ritual."

Paul decided not to mention their gleeful consumption of the temple offerings. "Who is she, this Summer Princess? And why do you know so much about . . . Tellari? Are people like us common here?"

"Not here—not in the *nimbor* towns. But there are more than a few in Tuktubim, although mostly they stay in the Soombar's palace, and a few mad ones roam in the outer deserts, looking for only the gods know what. There are occasionally visitors from Vonar as well—the second planet. But they almost never come outside the rainy season."

Klooroo was nosing his skiff through an array of small docks that formed a set of channels along the canal's bank. Many of the huts were built directly on the docks; others, grouped together between the canal and a rising cliff wall, rose in high, ramshackle agglomerations. Most of Klooroo's neighbors seemed to be awake and moving, some preparing their boats to go out onto the canal, but others just as clearly bringing theirs back in from a night of forbidden foraging.

"But how about the woman?" Paul asked. "You called her a princess?"

"*The* princess. The Summer Princess." He turned down one of the waterways, and Paul's wide view was suddenly blocked by looming walls. "She is one of the Vonari, the Blue People with Wings. Long ago, we conquered them, and every year they send one of their noblewomen as tribute."

"Tribute? What does that mean? She has to marry the . . . what did you call him? The Soombar?"

"After a fashion." Klooroo used the long paddle to turn them again, this time through a small watergate into a small enclosed pool surrounded by flimsy wooden walls. He brought the skiff alongside an open doorway, then reached out his long, clawed hand and pulled out a rope, which he tied to a loop in the skiff's bow. "After a fashion," he repeated, "since the Soombar is the descendant of gods. What she does is marry the gods themselves. At the end of the Festival she is killed and her body is given to the waters so that the rains will come back."

Klooroo stepped out of the boat into the doorway, then turned back and reached his hand to Paul.

"Your face looks very strange—is your head hurting? All the more reason, then, that you and the child should come and guest with me."

The sun was strong in the middle of the day. At this moment, Klooroo was perhaps the only adult resident of Nimbortown not hidden indoors and protected from its rays. He stayed as much in shade as he could, huddling beneath the overhang of the neighboring building while his Tellari guest sat in the middle of the fish-skin roof reveling in the heat, doing his best to drive away the bone-deep chill of his long immersion. Below, Gally was working off his meal of soup and flatbread in an exuberant game of tag with some of the local children.

"In this way you are mad, too," Klooroo complained. "Can we not go inside? Much more of this bitter sun and I will be as unbalanced as you."

"Of course." Paul stood and followed his host back down the ladder into the shack. "I wasn't . . . I was thinking." He sat himself in the corner of the unfurnished room. "Is there nothing that can be done? You said there are others of her people here. Won't they do anything?

"Pfaugh." Klooroo shook his long-muzzled head in disgust. "You are still thinking about her? Have you not blasphemed enough by looking at that which should not be seen? As for the Vonari, they honor their ancient treaty. Three hundred Summer Princesses at least have been offered before her—why should they balk at one more?"

"But she's . . . " Paul rubbed his face, as though the pressure could drive the haunting memories from his head. "I know her. I know her, damn it! But I don't remember how."

"You do not know her." The nimbor was firm. "Only the taltors are allowed to see her. Off-worlders and humble folk like me—never."

"Well, I managed to see her last night, even if it was by accident. Maybe I saw her somewhere else as well, and just can't remember where." He looked up quickly as Gally shrieked outside, but it was a shout of pleasure, not fear. The boy seemed quite at ease with his new nimbor friends; if he was still grieving for the murdered Oysterhouse children, he did not show it. "My memory—there's something wrong with it, but I don't think it's recent," Paul said suddenly. "I think there's been a problem for some time."

"Perhaps you *did* spy on the Summer Princess before, and the gods have punished you. Or perhaps you have some illness or are under some curse. I do not know enough about Tellari to say." Klooroo frowned. "You should speak to some of your own people."

Paul turned. "Do you know some?"

"Have I friends among the Tellari? No." Klooroo stood, his knobby joints crackling. "But there will doubtless be off-worlders at the market in Tuktubim during this Festival Season. If you like, I will take you there. First I must find you some shoes—the boy, too. You will burn your feet like a badly-cooked meal, otherwise.

"I would like to go the market, and to see Tuktubim. You said that is where the Summer Princess is kept, too?

Klooroo lowered his head and snarled. For a moment he looked quite canine. "Gods! Is there no end to your madness? Forget her!"

Paul frowned. "I can't. But I will try not to speak of it in front of you."

"Or behind me. Or on my left side or on my right. Call the boy, Tellar-man. I have no family, so there is nothing to prevent us going now—ha! Such freedom is one of the small benefits of being nestless." He said it with a certain sadness, and Paul realized with a little shame that despite all Klooroo's kindness and hospitality, they had not shown much interest in *his* life. Born into the Martian underclass, kept in serflike conditions by the taltor nobility, Klooroo could not have had a very happy time of it.

"Paul, look!" Gally shouted from outside, splashing gleefully. "Raurau threw me in the water, but I'm swimming!"

The great city Tuktubim stood out of sight on the cliffs above, yet though it was only a mile or so away, there was no direct route up the hills. Instead, Klooroo herded them back into his skiff and they set out once more along the canal. Paul wondered if the impossibility of a direct approach was meant to reduce the chances of success for a violent uprising among the serfs.

As they pulled away from Nimbortown, Paul could finally see the full sweep of the cliffs, which were a deep brownish red in the midday sun. At the top, almost invisible, jutted the prickly tops of a dozen pointed towers, all that was visible of the city. As the cliffs fell away and the skiff circled wide around the perimeter of the hills, the vastness of the red desert became apparent. On either side of the Great Canal, broken only by distant mountains on one side and the cross-hatching of lesser canals, the sands stretched away as far as he could see, a shifting, softly hissing scarlet ocean.

"Are there other cities out there?" Paul asked.

"Oh, aye, although it's leagues to the nearest in any direction." Klooroo squinted ahead down the watercourse. "You wouldn't want to go off searching for them, even on the canals, without a great deal of preparation. Dangerous lands. Fierce animals."

Gally's eyes widened a little. "Like that thing in the water. . . !" he began, then something buzzed loudly in the sky above them. As he and Paul looked up, the light changed. For a moment, the bright, yellowish sky turned a sickly bruised green and the air itself became almost solid around them.

Paul blinked. For just a moment, the canal and sky had appeared to flow together into one sparkling, granulated whole. Now, everything was as it had been.

"What was that? It happened when we were on the river last night, too."

Klooroo was again making vigorous signs against evil. "I do not know. Strange storms. There have been several of them recently. The gods are angry, I suppose—fighting among themselves. If it had not begun some months ago, I would say it was because you broke the Festival taboo." He glowered. "I am certain, however, that you have not improved the gods' mood."

The Great Canal looped broadly around the hills on which Tuktubim sat. As the skiff made its way around the loop toward the peripheral canal which led to the city, Paul stared across the great expanses of cracked, muddy fields on either side. He could understand why the Ullamari held the rain in such reverence. It was hard to believe that anything could make those flat, baked expanses fertile, but Klooroo had said that every stalk of grain on Mars was grown, and every herd animal grazed, within a few miles of the Great Canal's banks. It was a tiny thread of life running through the vastness of the desert. A year without rain and half the population might die.

Th canal was not as busy now as it was just after sunrise and just before sunset, Klooroo had assured them—the heat kept most people indoors—but to Paul it still seemed almost choked with boats, large and small. Most were crewed by one or more nimbors like Klooroo, but some carried taltor soldiers as well, or others in less militaristic dress that Paul guessed were merchants or government officials. Some of these boats were even larger and more spectacular than the priestly barge that had docked at the island, so top-heavy with gilt and ornament, so draped with billowing fabrics and crammed with heavily bejeweled nobles that it was a wonder they didn't simply sink to the bottom of the canal. He thought the same could be said of some of the grotesquely overdressed taltor nobles as well.

Klooroo swung the boat into a smaller canal that doubled back beneath the hills. From this side they could see the city itself, nestled just beneath the crest and looking down on the fanlike array of farms spreading out from the loop of the Great Canal and fed by an intricate system of smaller waterways. Tuktubim stood over them like a crowned emperor, its towers of silver and gold glinting in the midsummer sun.

"But how can we get up there in a boat?" asked Gally, staring at the corona of towers.

"You'll see." Klooroo was amused. "Just keep your eyes rolled up, little sand-toad."

The secret was revealed as they reached the first of a series of locks; dozens more were ranged in tiers above them, each fitted with huge pumping-wheels. Even now Paul could see a ship with white sails being lifted up to the highest lock. It looked like a toy, but he knew it must be one of the large flat-bottomed merchant ships like those whose wakes had set their tiny skiff bobbing on the Great Canal.

It took the larger part of the afternoon for the skiff to be lifted up halfway. Nimbors were allowed to bring their boats no higher, and so they left it in a small marina built, paradoxically, on the side of a hill. Klooroo led them to the public path and they began the rest of the ascent. The walk was long, but not arduous: the fish-skin sandals Klooroo had found for them turned out to be surprisingly comfortable. They stopped occasionally to drink from the standpipes that dripped into basins by the side of the path, or to rest in the shade of tall stones, great red boulders shot through with streaks of gold and black.

Soldiers were waiting at the huge city gates, but they seemed more interested in observing the show than in asking questions of a nimbor and a pair of off-worlders. It was a parade worth watching—nobles in covered golden litters carried by sweating nimbors, others riding creatures that seemed part horse, part reptile, and almost all of them the same jade-green as Klooroo. Here and there Paul saw a glimpse of blue flesh or a shimmer of pale feathers in the jostling crowd, and each time he caught his breath, even though he knew it was false hope; there was little chance the woman he sought would be allowed to walk the noonday streets of Tuktubim. She would be kept somewhere, carefully watched, perhaps in the cluster of towers at the center of the city.

Klooroo led Paul and Gally through the tall gate-pillars of ivory and gold and into a street that seemed almost as wide as the Great Canal itself. On either side, sheltered from the fierce sun by vast striped awnings, all of Tuktubim's population seemed involved in either arguing or bargaining; most of the activity seemed to consist of a combination of the two.

"This is *all* the market?" asked Paul after they had walked for many minutes.

Klooroo shook his head. "This? No, these are just the street vendors. I am taking you to the bazaar—the greatest marketplace on all of Ullamar, or so I am told by those better-traveled than I."

He was about to say more, but Paul was suddenly distracted by a voice somewhere behind them shouting in his native language. Klooroo's translating necklaces made the nimbor and other Ullamari *seem* to be speaking his tongue, but there was a sense of both the original speech and the translation happening at the same time. This new voice, growing louder by the second, was clearly and unequivocally something he could understand without any necklace.

"I say! Hold on there, will you?"

Paul turned. A startled Gally turned, too, suddenly feral as an alley cat, his little fingers extended like claws. A man was running toward them with the easy grace of an athlete. He seemed unquestionably human and an Earthling.

"Ah, thank you," he said as he reached them. "I was afraid I'd have to chase after you all the way to the bazaar. Not much joy in this heat, what?"

Paul was a little uncertain. He had a reflexive feeling that he should fear recognition or pursuit of any kind, but it was difficult to reconcile that with the stranger's apppearance. The smiling newcomer was a tall and handsome young man, blond-bearded and lithely muscular. He wore an outfit similar to Paul's, except that he had a loose white shirt beneath his waistcoat, and instead of sandals made from canal-fish hide, he wore high leather boots.

"Say, dashed rude of me just to come belting up to you this way and not introduce myself," the blond man said. "Brummond—Hurley Brummond. Used to be Captain Brummond of Her Majesty's Life Guard, but that was long ago and far away, I suppose. Ah, and here's my friend, Professor Bagwalter, caught up at last. Say hello, Bags!" He gestured to an older man, also bearded, but more formally dressed, who was limping toward them, a frock coat draped over his arm. The new arrival paused before them, panting, removed spectacles which had been steamed opaque, then took out his handkerchief and wiped at his streaming brow.

"Good Lord, Brummond, you have led me a chase." He waited for a few more breaths before continuing. "Pleasure to meet you folks. We saw you go in at the gate."

"That's right," said the blond man. "We don't see many of our folk here, and we know pretty near all of them. Still, we didn't chase you just because you were new faces." He laughed. "It's not *that* boring at the Ares Club."

The professor coughed. "*I* didn't chase them at all. I was trying to keep up with you."

"And a damn foolish idea, too, in this swelter." Brummond turned back to Paul. "Truth is, for a moment I thought you were an old mate of mine—Billy Kirk, his name was. 'Kedgeree' Kirk, we used to call him, on account of he was so particular about breakfast. He and I fought together in Crimea, at Sevastopol, and Balaklava. Fine gunnery

man, one of the best. But I saw as soon as I caught up that it wasn't
so. Damned remarkable likeness, though."

Paul was having trouble keeping up with Brummond's swift,
clipped speech. "No, my name is Paul. Paul . . . " he hesitated as for a
moment he felt even his name grow slippery and dubious. "Paul
Jonas. This is Gally. And Klooroo here, who pulled us out of the Great
Canal."

"Fine boy," said Brummond, ruffling Gally's hair. The boy scowled.
Klooroo, who had fallen silent at the man's initial approach, seemed
just as happy to be ignored.

Professor Bagwalter was looking at Paul speculatively, as though he
were an interesting example of some rather arcane scientific effect.
"You have a strange accent, Mister Jonas. Are you Canadian?"

Paul stared, caught off-balance. "I . . . I don't think I am."

Bagwalter raised a bushy eyebrow at Paul's answer, but Brummond
reached out and clasped Paul by the shoulder. His grip was very
strong. "Good Lord, Bags, we aren't going to stand here in the blazing
sun while you riddle away some linguistic nonsense of yours, are we?
Pay no attention, Jonas—the professor can't listen to the first bluebird
of spring without wanting to dissect it. But as long as we've interrupted your day, let us buy you a drink, what? There's a fair-to-mid-
dling *soz*-house just down that little sidestreet, there. We'll get the boy
something weaker, eh?" He laughed and squeezed Paul's shoulder
companionably; for a moment, Paul was afraid something might be
pulled loose. "No, better still," Brummond said, "we'll take you to the
Ares Club. Do you good—give you a taste of home. Come, then, what
do you say?"

"That's . . . that's fine," Paul replied.

Paul was dismayed to discover that the Ares Club doorman—a
rather ill-favored taltor—would not allow Klooroo to enter. "No dog-
faces," he pronounced, and would not entertain further discussion.
A potentially embarrassing situation was avoided when the nimbor
volunteered to show Gally around the bazaar. Paul accepted the offer
gratefully, but Brummond did not seem to approve.

"Listen, old man," he said as Gally and Klooroo walked away, "love
thy neighbor, all well and good sort of thing, but you won't get far
putting too much faith in greenskins."

"What do you mean?"

"Well, they can be all right in their way, and this one seems fond of you and the boy, but just don't expect him to cover your back. They're not trustworthy. Not like an Earthman, if you see what I mean."

The inside of the club seemed strangely familiar. A word, *Victorian*, drifted through Paul's head, but he did not know what it meant. The furniture was heavy and overstuffed, the walls paneled in dark wood. Dozens of strange creatures' heads on plaques—or unplaqued, but companioned by the rest of their stuffed bodies—stared down at the visitors. Except for Paul and his two companions, the club seemed empty, which gave the ranked glassy stares an even more intimidating effect.

Brummond saw Paul staring at a huge shaggy head, vaguely feline, but with the mandibles of an insect. "Nasty-looking customer, eh? That's a yellow stonecat. Live in the foothills, eat anything they can get, including you and me and Auntie Maude. Almost as unpleasant as a blue squanch."

"What Hurley's not mentioning is that he's the one who dragged in that particular trophy," said Professor Bagwalter dryly. "Killed it with a cavalry saber."

Brummond shrugged. "Got a bit lucky, you know the sort of thing."

With a wide choice of tables, they selected one at a small window overlooking what Paul assumed was the bazaar, a massive public square almost completely covered with small awnings. A vast crowd, primarily Martian, swirled in and out beneath them. Paul watched it, amazed by the vitality and activity. He almost thought he could see patterns in the ebb and flow of the marketers, repeating designs, spontaneous shared movements like a flock of birds on the wing.

"Jonas?" Brummond nudged him. "What's your poison, old man?"

Paul looked up. An aged nimbor wearing an incongruous-looking white dinner jacket was waiting patiently for his order. Without knowing where the idea came from, he asked for a brandy. The nimbor inclined his head and disappeared on soundless feet.

"You know, of course, that the local brandy is barely fit to hold the name," said Professor Bagwalter. "Still, it's a damn sight better than the local beer." He fixed Paul with his sharp brown eyes. "So, what brings you to Tuktubim, Mister Jonas? I asked you if you were Canadian because I thought you might have come in with Loubert on *L'Age D'Or*—they say he's got a lot of Canucks in his crew."

"Blood and thunder, Bags, you're interrogating the poor fellow again," laughed Brummond. He leaned back in his chair as if to leave the field to two well-matched adversaries.

Paul hesitated. He didn't feel well-matched at all, and there was

something about Professor Bagwalter that made him decidedly uncomfortable, although it was hard to define just what it was. Where
Brummond, like Klooroo and others he'd met here, seemed as comfortable with life on Mars as a fish in a stream, the professor had a
strange edge, a questioning intelligence that seemed out of place. Still,
just a few moments of listening to them talk about someone named
Loubert and someplace called Canada made it clear he would never be
able to bluff his way through.

"I'm . . . I'm not sure how I got here," he said. "I've had a head
injury, I think. I found the boy . . . actually, I don't remember very
well. You'll have to ask him. In any case, there was some trouble,
I remember that, and we escaped. First thing I really remember is
floundering in the Great Canal."

"Well, doesn't that trump all," said Brummond, but he sounded
less than astonished, as though this kind of thing happened rather
frequently in his vicinity.

Bagwalter, on the other hand, seemed quite pleased to have something around which to base an inquiry, and to Paul's discomfort and
Hurley Brummond's great disgust, spent the next half hour questioning him closely.

Paul was finishing his second throat-burning brandy and feeling a
little more relaxed when the professor returned to the subject that
seemed to interest him most. "And you say you've seen this Vonari
woman before, but you don't remember where or when."

Paul nodded. "I just . . . know."

"Maybe she was your fiancée," offered Brummond. "Yes, I'll bet
that's it!" After sitting in bored silence for some time, he had suddenly
warmed to the subject matter. "Maybe you were injured trying to protect her from the Soombar's guards. They're heavy-handed fellows,
you know, and pretty nimble with those scimitarish noggin-loppers of
theirs. That time they were going to pop Joanna into the Soombar's
seraglio—well, I had my hands full and then some."

"Hurley, I wish . . . " the professor began, but Brummond was not
to be held back. His blue eyes sparkled, and his golden hair and beard
seemed almost to crackle with static electricity.

"Joanna—she's my fiancée, the professor's daughter. I know, I
know, damn presumptuous to call one's fiancée's father 'Bags,' but
the professor and I had been through a great deal before I ever met
Joanna." He waved his hand. "She's back at camp with *The Temperance*
right now, laying in supplies for an expeditionary voyage we're going
to make to the interior. That's why I chased after you, to tell the truth.

If you'd been good old Kedgeree Kirk, I was going to offer you a place in the crew."

"Hurley . . . " said the professor with some irritation.

"In any case, it seems like every time I turn around, one of these green-skinned *wallahs* is trying to abduct Joanna. She's a sturdy gal, and admirable as all get out, but it's really a bit much. And monsters—I can't tell you how many times I've had to pull her out of some squanch-hole or other. . . ."

"For goodness sakes, Hurley, I'm trying to ask Mister Jonas some questions."

"Look here, Bags, just for once you've got to let go of all this science twaddle. This poor fellow's fiancée has been kidnapped by the priests and they're going to sacrifice the girl! They've beaten him so badly that he can hardly remember his own name! And you'd just as soon poke and prod him as offer him any help, wouldn't you?"

"Here now," said the professor, taken aback.

"I'm not sure . . . " Paul began, but Hurley Brummond stood up, unfolding to the full extent of his impressive height.

"Don't you worry, lad," he said, and almost knocked Paul across the table with a comradely crack on the back. "I'll ask around—there's more than a few, both green and white, who owe a favor to Brummond of Mars. Yes, that's just what I'll do. Bags, I'll meet you both in back of the club at sundown."

He was gone from the room in three strides, leaving Paul and the professor almost breathless.

"He's a good lad," Bagwalter said at last. "Tough as nails and bighearted. And my Joanna loves him dearly." He took a sip of his sherry. "But I do wish sometimes he weren't so damned stupid."

Far across the desert, the sun had almost disappeared behind the distant mountains, going to its rest contented after a long day scorching the upturned face of Mars. The last rays struck crimson glints from all of Tuktubim's windows and translucent spires.

From the balcony at the back of the Ares Club, Paul stared down the hillside on what seemed to be a vast scatter of rubies and diamonds. For a moment, he wondered if this place could be the home he had sought. It was strange, but somehow quite familiar as well. He could not remember where he had been last, but he knew it had been somewhere different—there had been *several* somewheres in his past, he felt sure—and even without the specific memories, he felt rootless weariness in his bones and thoughts.

"Look at that!" said Gally, pointing. Not far away a huge flying ship, similar in shape to the ceremonial barges they had seen on the Great Canal, was slowly rising past the towertops into the evening sky, guide ropes dangling. Hundred of dark shapes moved on its decks and in the complicated rigging. Lanterns glowed along its length, dozens of bright-burning points. The barge almost seemed to be a living constellation sprung from the vaults of the night.

"It's beautiful." Paul looked down. Gally was rapt, wide-eyed, and Paul felt something like pride that he had protected this boy, had brought him safely out of . . . out of. . . ? It was useless—the memory would not come. "It's too bad Klooroo didn't stay to see this," he continued. "But I suppose it's all very familiar to him." Klooroo of the Fisher People, perhaps feeling he had fulfilled his promise once Paul had discovered other Earthmen, had brought Gally back from the bazaar and then headed off to his shantytown beside the canal. "Still, he was kind to us, and I was sad to see him go."

"He was only a nimbor," said Gally dismissively.

Paul stared at the boy, who was still raptly watching the airship. The remark seemed oddly out of character, as though Gally had absorbed some of the attitudes of those around him.

"Wind from the desert tonight." Professor Bagwalter released a thin stream of smoke from his lips, then screwed his cigar back into the corner of his mouth. "It will be hotter tomorrow."

Paul found that hard to imagine. "I don't want to keep the boy up too late. Do you think Mister Brummond is going to be here soon. . . ?"

The professor shrugged. "You never can tell with Hurley." He produced and examined his pocketwatch. "He's only a quarter of an hour late. I shouldn't worry."

"It's flying away!" said Gally. The large airship was disappearing into the growing darkness. Only the lights were visible now, bright pinpoints growing ever smaller.

Bagwalter smiled at the boy, then turned to Paul. "The little fellow tells me you rescued him from a place called the Eight Squares or something. Was that back on Earth?"

"I don't know. I told you, my memory is bad."

"The boy says it's just down the Great Canal, but I haven't heard of any such place here and I've done a lot of traveling." His voice was light, but the shrewd eyes were again watching Paul closely. "He also said something about the Black Ocean, and I can *promise* you there's nothing like that here."

"I don't know." Paul felt his voice rising, but could not make it sound normal. Gally turned from the balcony railing to look at him, eyes wide. "I just don't remember! Anything!"

Bagwalter removed his cigar and stared at the smoldering tip, then lifted his eyes to Paul's once more. "No need to get worked up, old man. I'm being a bit of a bore, I know. It's just that there were some rather odd fellows asking questions at the club a few days ago. . . ."

"Look out below!"

Something whizzed between them and hit the balcony floor with a loud slap. It was a rope ladder, and it seemed to have dropped onto them from nowhere. Stunned, Paul looked up. A shape hovered overhead, like a dark cloud in the otherwise clear sky. A head poked out, peering down at them.

"Hope I didn't hit anyone! Damnably hard to keep this thing steady."

"It's Mister Brummond!" said Gally, delighted. "And he has a flying ship, too!"

"Climb up!" shouted Brummond. "Hurry—no time to waste!"

Gally went up the ladder, shinnying as quickly as a spider. Paul hesitated, still not quite sure what was happening.

"Go on," said the professor kindly. "It does no good—once Hurley's got a bee in his bonnet, there's no stopping him."

Paul grabbed the swaying ladder and began to climb. Halfway to the waiting airship he paused, beset by a kind of spiritual vertigo. There was something tragically familiar in this situation, leaving one barely-understood place to scramble toward another, even less comprehensible refuge.

"Would you mind moving on," Bagwalter said gently from below. "I'm not getting any younger, and I'd just as soon be off this ladder as quickly as possible."

Paul shook his head and resumed his climb. Brummond was waiting at the top, and pulled him over the railing with a single tug.

"What do you think of this little beauty, eh, Jonas?" he asked. "I told you there were a few favors I could call in. Let me show you around—she's a lovely piece of work, fast as a bird, quiet as grass growing. She'll do the job for us, you'll see."

"What job?" Paul was getting tired of asking questions.

"What job?" Brummond seemed dumbfounded. "Why, we're going to rescue your fiancée! At dawn she goes to a special cell underneath

the Soombar's palace, and then it'll be too late, so we're taking her
out tonight! Only a dozen guards, and we probably won't have to kill
more than half of them."

Before Paul could do more than open his mouth and close it again,
Brummond had sprung away to the airship's oddly-shaped, ornately-
carved wheel. He pulled on it, and the ship rose so swiftly that Paul
almost fell from his seat. The city dwindled below them.

"For the honor of your lady, Jonas!" Brummond shouted. His
golden hair fluttered in the strong wind of their ascent; his grin was
a glinting spot in the gloom. "For the honor of our dear old Earth!"

With mounting discomfort, Paul realized that they were in the
hands of a madman.

CHAPTER 25

Hunger

NETFEED/NEWS: DA Cries Foul As "Snipe" Case Dropped·
(visual: Azanuelo holding press conference
VO: Dallas County District Attorney Carmen Azanuelo said that the defection
and disappearance of witnesses from her landmark murder prosecution is
"the clearest example of subversion of justice since the Crack Baron trial."
(visual: Defendants at arraignment)
The prosecution of six men, including two ex-police officers, for the murder
of hundreds of street children, often called "snipes," excited tremendous
controversey because of the allegations that local merchants hired the men as
a "death squad" to keep the upscale areas of Dallas-Forth Worth free of street
children.
(visual: children panhandling in Marsalis Park)
Prosecutions for "snipe-hunting" in other American cities have also had
trouble obtaining convictions.
AZANUELO: "They have intimidated, kidnapped, or killed our witnesses,
often with help from elements inside the police department. They are
murdering children on the streets of America, and they're getting away with
it. It's as simple as that. . . ."

Good heavens, Papa, will you quit complaining?"
"I'm not complaining, girl. I'm just asking."

"Over and over again." Renie took a breath, then bent to try to pull the strap tight on the suitcase again. Few of their possessions had survived the fire, and the confusion of recent events had left Renie no time for shopping, but they still seemed to have more things than they did storage. "We're not safe here in this shelter. Anyone can find us. I've told you a hundred times, Papa, we're in danger."

"That's the damned silliest thing I ever heard." He crossed his arms over his chest and shook his head as if to banish the whole concept into the oblivion it deserved.

Renie fought a powerful urge to give up, to stop fighting. Maybe she should just sit down beside her father and join him in wishing the real world away. There was a freedom in being obstinate, the freedom of ignoring unpleasant truths. But someone finally had to acknowledge those truths—and that someone was usually her.

She sighed. "Get up, you old troublemaker. Jeremiah's going to be here any moment."

"I'm not going nowhere with no girly-man."

"Oh, for God's sake." She bent over, pulled the strap tight across the straining suitcase, and secured it on the magnetic tab. "If you say one stupid thing to Jeremiah, just one stupid thing, I'm going to leave you and your bloody suitcase by the side of the road."

"What kind of way is that to talk to your father?" He glowered at her from under his brows. "That man attacked me. He tried to strangle my throat."

"He came looking for me in the middle of the night and you two had a fight. You were the one who went and got a knife."

"That's right." Long Joseph's face brightened. "Hoo-hoo, that's right. And I was going to cut him up for damn good, too. Teach him to come sneaking round my place."

Renie sighed again. "Just remember, he's doing us a big favor. I'm on half-pay while I'm suspended, Papa, remember? So we're lucky to find somewhere to go at all. There isn't supposed to be anyone living in that house until they sell it. Do you understand that? Jeremiah could get in trouble, but he wants to help me track down the people who did this to Susan, so he's helping us."

"Okay, okay." Long Joseph waved his hand, indicating that as usual, she was underestimating his social graces. "But if he comes sneaking in my room at night and try to get mannish with *me*, I knock off his head."

*   *   *

"It's all new." Jeremiah pointed to the mesh fence that now surrounded the house. "The doctor's nephew decided to improve the security. He thinks it will make it easier to sell the place." His pursed lips made it clear what he thought of these absentee landlords. "So you should be safe. Very high-tech thing, this security system. Top of the line."

Renie privately had doubts that the kind of people they seemed to be up against would have any problems getting through even top-of-the-line domestic security, but she kept them to herself. It was certainly an improvement over the shelter.

"Thank you, Jeremiah. I can't tell you how grateful we are. We really had no friends or family to go to. Papa's older sister died two years ago, and his other sister lives in England."

"Wouldn't give you a stick to scratch your back, that one," grumbled Long Joseph. "I wouldn't take nothing from her, anyway."

The security gate hissed shut behind the car as they entered the semicircular drive. Renie's father looked up at the house with sullen amazement. "God Almighty, look at that. That's not a house, it's a hotel. Only white people have a house like that—you have to stand on the back of the black man to own a place so big."

Jeremiah hit the brakes, skidding more than a few inches along the gravel drive. He turned in the seat and stared back at Long Joseph, his long features pinched in a scowl. "You are talking like an idiot, man. You don't know anything about it."

"I know an Afrikaaner mansion when I see one."

"Doctor Van Bleeck never did anything but good for anyone." Tears were welling in Jeremiah Dako's eyes. "If you're going to say things like that, you can find somewhere else to stay."

Renie winced, embarrassed and angry. "Papa, he's right. You're talking like an idiot. You didn't know Susan and you don't know anything about her. We're coming to her house because she was my friend and because Jeremiah is doing us a kindness."

Long Joseph raised his hands in martyred innocence. "My God, you people get touchy. I didn't say nothing against your doctor lady, I just said that's a white people's house. You a black man—don't tell me you think white people have to work hard as a black man."

Jeremiah stared at him for a moment, then swung around again and inched the car forward to the front of the *stoep*. "I'll get your bags out of the boot," he said.

Renie glared at her father for a moment, then got out to help.

Jeremiah took them upstairs, showed them to a pair of bedrooms and pointed out the bathroom. Renie thought that her room, its walls papered in a faded design of cavorting rag dolls, must have been intended for a child, although the Van Bleecks had never had one. She had never thought much about Susan's childlessness, but now she wondered if it had been a greater sorrow than the doctor had let on.

She poked her head into her father's room. He was sitting on the bed, examining the antique furniture with suspicion. "Maybe you should lie down and have a nap, Papa." She deliberately made it more of an order than a request. "I'll make some lunch. I'll call you when it's ready."

"I don't know if I can get comfortable. Big old empty house like this. I can try, I guess."

"You do that." She shut the door and stood for a moment, letting her irritation subside. She let her gaze slide along the walls, the wide, high-ceilinged hall.

Stephen would love this, she thought. The thought of him bouncing excitedly down the hallway, exploring this new place, suddenly made her almost dizzy with loss. She swayed, her eyes stinging with tears, and had to clutch the banister. Minutes passed before she felt composed enough to descend to the kitchen and apologize for her father's behavior.

Jeremiah, who was polishing an already gleaming pan, waved her explanations away. "I understand. He's just like my father. That man never had a good thing to say about anyone."

"He's not that bad," Renie said, wondering if that were in fact true. "He's just had a hard time of it since my mother died."

Dako nodded, but did not seem convinced. "I'm picking up your friend later tonight. I'll be happy to make dinner for you all."

"Thank you, Jeremiah, but you don't need to do that." She hesitated, wondering at the look of disappointment on his face. Perhaps he, too, was lonely. She knew of no other people in his life besides Susan Van Bleeck and his mother, and Susan was gone. "You've done us so many favors, I feel like I should cook for you tonight."

"You're going to mess around in my kitchen?" he asked sourly, only half-joking.

"With your permission. And with any advice you want to give gladly taken."

"Hmmm. We'll see."

It was a long walk between the kitchen and the living room, and Renie did not know where the light switches were. She made her way with great care down halls lit only by the thin orange light leaking in through the high windows from outside, trying to keep the ceramic lid on the casserole dish despite hands made clumsy by potholders. The darkness seemed a tangible, powerful thing, an old thing, the security lights an inadequate human response.

She swore as she banged her knee against an almost invisible table, but the reassuring noise of the others came drifting down the hallway. There was always something on the other end of darkness, wasn't there?

Jeremiah and her father were making brittle conversation about the rich neighborhood of Kloof that surrounded them. !Xabbu, who had arrived with all of his wordly possessions in one small, cheap suitcase, looked up from his study of Susan's cave-painting photograph.

"Renie, I heard you strike against something. Are you hurt?"

She shook her head. "Just a bump. I hope you all have your appetites."

"Did you find what you needed in the kitchen?" Jeremiah cocked an eyebrow. "Break anything?"

Renie laughed. "Nothing but my pride. I've never seen so many cooking things in my life. I feel inadequate. I only used one dish and a couple of pans."

"Don't talk yourself down, girl," said her father sternly. "You a real good cook."

"I used to think so, until I saw Jeremiah's kitchen. Making my little chicken casserole there was kind of like hiking into the middle of the Kalahari just to dry your clothes."

!Xabbu laughed at this, a delighted gurgle that even made Jeremiah grin.

"Ah, well," she said, "everybody, hand me your plates."

Jeremiah and Renie were finishing the bottle of wine. Her father and !Xabbu had been sampling beers out of the cold pantry, although Long Joseph seemed to be getting a disproportionate share. Jeremiah had built a fire in the wide stone fireplace, and they had turned most of the other lights out, so that the light in the wide living room wavered and danced. But for the murmuring of the fire, the last minute had passed in silence.

Renie sighed. "This has been such a nice evening. It would be so easy to forget all the things that have happened and just relax . . . let go. . . ."

"You see, girl, that's your problem," her father said. "Relax, yes.

That's exactly what you must do. You always worrying, worrying." Surprisingly, he turned to Jeremiah as though for support. "She work herself too hard."

"It's not that easy, Papa. Remember, we're not here because we want to be. Somebody burned down our flatblock. Some other people . . . attacked Susan. No, let's be honest. They murdered her." She cut a quick glance toward Jeremiah, who was staring at the fire, his long face somber. "We know a little about the people who seem to be responsible, but we can't get to them—not in real life, because they're too rich and too powerful, and probably not by stealth either. Even if Mister Singh—that's the old man, Papa, the programmer—knows what he's talking about, and we need to investigate this big network they've built, I don't see where I fit in anyway. I don't have the equipment to stay online long enough to get through the kind of security they must have for this . . . Otherland." She shrugged. "I'm feeling pretty hopeless about where to go from here."

"Did they smash up everything of the doctor's you could use?" Jeremiah asked. "I'm still not sure I understand everything you've told me, but I know that Doctor Van Bleeck would say you were welcome to anything that would help you."

Renie smiled sadly. "You saw what they did to her lab. Those bastards made sure there wouldn't be anything left *anyone* could use."

Her father snorted angrily. "That is the way. That is always the way. We throw the Afrikaaner bastards out of the government and the black man still can't get no justice. Nobody will help my boy! My . . . Stephen!" His voice abruptly cracked, and he brought one of his large callused hands to his face before turning away from the fire.

"If anyone can find a way to help him, then your daughter can," !Xabbu said firmly. "She has a strong spirit, Mister Sulaweyo."

Renie was surprised by the certainty of his words, but the small man would not meet her gaze. Her father made no reply.

Jeremiah opened a second bottle of wine, and the talk slowly and somewhat awkwardly turned to other things. Then Long Joseph began quietly to sing. Renie was at first only conscious of it as a low tone on the edge of her attention, but gradually it became louder.

> *"Imithi goba kahle, ithi, ithi*
> *Kunyakazu ma hlamvu*
> *Kanje, kanje*
> *Kanje, kanje"*

It was an old Zulu nursery song, something Long Joseph had learned from his grandmother, a lilting, repetitive melody as gentle as the wind it described. Renie had heard it before, but not for a long time.

> *"All the trees are bending,*
> *This way, now that way,*
> *All the leaves are shaking*
> *This way and that*
> *This way and that."*

A memory from her childhood surged up, from a time before Stephen had been born, when she and her mother and father had taken the bus to visit her aunt in Ladysmith. She had felt sick to her stomach, and had huddled against her mother while her father had sung to her, and not just the *Kanje Kanje* song. She remembered pretending to be sick even after she felt better, just to keep him singing.

Long Joseph was swaying gently from side to side as his fingers tapped out a spidery rhythm against his thighs.

> *"Ziphumula kanjani na*
> *Izinyone sidle keni"*

> *"See them resting*
> *On this sunny day*
> *Those lovely birds*
> *In their happy homes . . . "*

From the corner of her eye, Renie saw something moving. !Xabbu had begun to dance before the fire, bending and straightening in time to Long Joseph's song, his arms held out, stiff and angled, then brought back to his sides. The dance had a curious rhythm that was at once strange and soothing.

> *"Imithi goba kahle, ithi, ithi*
> *Kunyakazu ma hlamvu*
> *Kanje, kanje*
> *Kanje, kanje"*

> *"Children, children, children come home*
> *Children, children, children come home*
> *Children, children, children come home . . . "*

The song went on for a long time. At last her father trailed off, then looked around the firelit room, shaking his head as though he surfaced from a waking dream.

"That was very, very nice, Papa." She spoke slowly, fighting the wine-and-dinner thickness in her head: she didn't want to say the wrong thing. "It's good to hear you sing. I haven't heard you do that in a long time."

He shrugged, a little embarrassed, then laughed sharply. "Well, this man here has brought us to this big house, and my daughter cooked the supper. I figured it was my turn to pay for my keep."

Jeremiah, who had turned from the fire to listen, nodded soberly, as though approving the transaction.

"It reminded me of that time we went to Aunt Tema's. Do you remember?"

He grunted. "Woman had a face like a bad road. Your mama got all the looks in that family." He stood. "Going to get another beer."

"And your dancing was wonderful as well," Renie told !Xabbu. She wanted to ask a question, but hesitated, afraid she might sound patronizing. *God*, she thought, *I have to be an anthropologist just to talk to my father and my friend. No, that's not true—!Xabbu is a lot harder to insult.* "Was that a particular dance?" she finally asked. "I mean, does it have a name? Or were you just dancing?"

The small man smiled, his eyes crinkling almost shut. "I danced some of the steps of the Dance of the Greater Hunger."

Long Joseph returned with two bottles and offered the second one to !Xabbu, who shook his head. Long Joseph sat down, a bottle in each hand, satisfied with the way his good manners had been rewarded. The small man stood up and walked to the photograph on the wall and traced one of the bright-painted figures with his finger, then turned. "We have two hunger dances. One is the Dance of the Little Hunger. That is the hunger of the body, and we dance it to ask for patience when our stomachs are empty. But when we are full, we do not need that dance—in fact, it would be discourteous after such good food as we had tonight." He smiled at Renie. "But there is a hunger that is not solved by filling your belly. Not the meat of the fattest eland, not the juiciest ant eggs can cure it."

"*Ant eggs?*" said Long Joseph in exaggerated tones of outrage. "You eat eggs from a bug?"

"I have eaten them many times." !Xabbu wore a slight smile. "They are soft and sweet."

"Don't even say it." Long Joseph scowled. "Make me sick just to think about it."

Jeremiah stood and stretched. "But it's not crazy to eat bird eggs? Fish eggs?"

"Speak for yourself. I don't eat no fish eggs. As for bird eggs, just from chickens, and that is a natural thing."

"When you live in the desert, you cannot avoid anything that can be safely eaten, Mister Sulaweyo." !Xabbu's sly smile grew. "But there are some things we like better than others, of course. And ant eggs are one of our favorites."

"Papa's just a snob," Renie explained. "And for all the wrong reasons. Tell me more about the dance, please. About the . . . Greater Hunger."

"Call me what you want, girl," her father said with an air of magisterial finality. "Just don't put none of them on *my* plate."

"All people know the Greater Hunger." !Xabbu pointed to the figures in the rock-painting. "Not only the people dancing here, but the person who painted the dancers and all who have looked at the painting. It is the hunger for warmth, for family, for connection to the stars and the earth and other living things. . . ."

"For love?" Renie asked.

"Yes, I suppose that could be true." !Xabbu was thoughtful. "My people would not say it that way. But if you use the word to mean the thing that makes us glad of other people, which makes being together better than being alone, then yes. It is a hunger for the part of a person which cannot be filled by meat or drink."

Renie wanted to ask him why he had chosen that dance to perform, but felt it might be rude. Despite his robustness of body and spirit, there was something about the small man that made Renie feel clumsily protective. "It was a very nice dance," she said at last. "A fine thing."

"Thank you. It is good to dance among friends."

A not uncomfortable silence settled over the room. Renie decided it would be all right if she left the dishes until the next day and got up to go to bed. "Thank you, Jeremiah, for taking us in."

Jeremiah Dako nodded, not looking up. "It's fine. You are welcome."

"And Papa, thank you for the song."

He looked up at her, a strange, half-yearning look on his face, then laughed. "I'm just trying to pull my weight, girl."

* * *

She floated in and out of a half-doze, fretful and restless, knowing that there were too many problems without solutions to waste precious rest, but unable to do anything about it: sleep and its welcome oblivion stayed exasperatingly beyond reach. At last she surrendered and sat up. She switched on the lights, then switched them off again, preferring darkness. Something that !Xabbu had said kept coming back to her, running through her disordered thoughts like the chorus of a popular song: . . . *the thing that makes us glad of other people, which makes being together better than being alone.*

But what could she and a few others hope to do in a situation like this? And why did it have to be her in the first place—why didn't anyone else ever take responsibility?

She thought of her father, just two doors away, and only the pleasant evening they had just spent allowed her to fight down a hot surge of resentment. No matter how hard she had been working and how little sleep she got tonight, he would be quick to complain if there was no breakfast waiting for him when he got up. He was used to being waited on. That was her mother's fault, capitulating to—no, collaborating with—some old-fashioned idea of the Role of the African Male. It must have been like that in the old days, the men sitting around the fire bragging about some gazelle they'd speared three weeks ago while the women gathered food, made clothes, cooked, took care of the chidren. Yes, and took care of the men, who were children themselves, really, with their feelings so easily hurt if they weren't the center of the universe. . . . She was full of anger, she realized. Anger at her father, and at Stephen for . . . for running away from her, although it felt terrible to be angry at him. But she *was*—furious that he should go away, that he should lie in that hospital, silent and unresponsive, rejecting all her love, all her pain.

If her mother hadn't died, would things have been different? Renie tried to imagine a life in which there had been someone else to shoulder the burden, but couldn't quite make the thought feel real—a normal adolescence, or at least what would be normal in other places, nothing to think about except studies and friends? A summer job if she wanted one, instead of a full-time job on top of her school work? But it was a purely intellectual exercise, trying to imagine such a life, because the person who had grown up that way, who had spent the last ten years in that life, wouldn't be her. Another Renie, one from beyond Alice's Looking Glass.

Her mother Miriam, long-limbed and fragile. She shouldn't have gone away. If she had never gone to the department store, everything would be better today. Just her wide smile, which used to blaze suddenly and surprisingly across her dark face, like a hand opened to reveal a splendid gift, would have made Renie feel less alone. But Mama and her smile were only memories now, getting fainter every year.

. . . *Better than being alone*, !Xabbu had said. But wasn't that part of her problem? That she was never alone, that instead the people around were always expecting her to do something they could not do themselves?

She herself didn't ask for things, though. It was easier just to be strong—in fact, it helped her stay strong. To admit she needed help might lead to losing her ability to cope.

But I do need help. I can't manage this by myself. I've run out of ideas.

"I am doing my best to find a solution, Renie." Martine did not sound very hopeful. "The kind of equipment Singh was talking about costs very much money. I would lend you my own money, but it would not be enough nearly for what you need. I live a very simple life. Everything has gone into my own equipment."

Renie stared at the blank screen, wishing that she at least had Martine's Mona Lisa sim to look at. Human beings were hard-wired to look at faces for information, for clues, just for the confirmation that another human was out there. Renie was quite accustomed to malfunctioning video on public uplinks, but at least when the screen was out of order, you were usually talking to someone whose features you already knew. She was touched by Martine's generosity, but it was still hard to feel the connection. Who was this woman? What was she hiding from? And, strangest of all in a woman who worshiped privacy, why had she become so involved with this Otherland madness?

"I know it won't be easy, Martine, and I do appreciate your help. I just can't let Stephen go without a fight. I have to find out what happened. Find out who did this and why."

"And how are *you*, Renie?" Martine asked suddenly.

"What? Oh, fine. Confused. Tired."

"But in yourself. How are you?"

Renie abruptly saw the blankness of the screen as something else—the dark window of the confessional. She was tempted to tell the French woman everything, her obsessive fears about Stephen, her ridiculous mothering relationship with her own father, her actual terror of the forces they seemed to have engaged. All these things pressed down on her like a collapsing roof, and it would be good to have someone to complain to. There were moments when she felt the other woman, despite the self-created mystery surrounding her, could be a real friend.

But Renie was not ready to trust that deeply, however much she might already have put her life in Martine's hands. There was a fine line between ordinary desperation and the complete loss of self-control.

"I'm fine. Like I said, tired. Call me if you find out anything. Or if you hear from our friend the Anchorite."

"Very well. Good night, Renie."

"Thanks again."

She lay back again, feeling that she had at least done something.

When she checked her account at the Poly in the morning, there were several messages relating to her suspension—a warning about cessation of mail privileges, a date for a preliminary hearing, a request for various system codes and files to be handed over—and one flagged "personal."

"Renie, give me a call, please." Del Ray's face had been freshly shaved when he left the message, as though he were on his way to an important meeting. His beard grew faster than that of any other man she'd ever met. "I'm worried about you."

She had to fight the reflexive little kick in her stomach. What did "worried" mean, anyway? No more than what you'd say to any old friend who'd lost her job. He had a wife now—what was her name, Blossom, Daisy, something stupid like that—why should she care anyway? She'd dealt with her feelings for Del Ray a long time ago. She didn't need him back in her life. Besides, with all the other things crowding for attention, where would she put him?

She had a brief vision of a Del Ray shelf in the closet of her new ragdoll bedroom, and let herself laugh, just to feel and hear it.

Renie lit another cigarette, took a sip from her glass of wine—an afternoon luxury available to the recently unemployed—and stared out past the security fence at the surrounding hills of Kloof. Should she call him back? He hadn't delivered anything to speak of so far, and his message didn't sound like he was promising new information. On the other hand, he might know something about this Otherland place and, more importantly, somewhere she could get access to professional VR equipment. She had to do *something* soon. If she were forced to give up, there would be nothing at all to tell the board of the

Poly, except crazy-sounding allegations. Not to mention the fact that Singh, an old man seemingly marked for elimination, would be going it alone.

And Stephen. To give up now would also be to give up on Stephen, to leave him forever sleeping, like some princess in a fairy tale, but with no hope of any prince making his way through the thorns to deliver the life-giving kiss.

Renie put down the wine, which suddenly made her stomach feel sour. The whole mess seemed hopeless. She stubbed out her cigarette and then, since she had decided to call Del Ray back, lit another one. At the last moment, as her pad connected to the UNComm main number, she heeded a cautionary thought and turned off her visuals.

His assistant had only just gone off the line when Del Ray clicked on. "Renie, I'm glad you called! Are you all right? There's no picture."

She could see him very well. He looked a little harried. "I'm fine. I'm . . . having a problem with my pad, that's all."

He hesitated for a moment. "Oh. Well, never mind. Tell me where you are. I've been worrying about you."

"Where I am?"

"You and your father left the shelter. I tried to call you at the Poly, but they said you're on a leave of absence."

"Yes. Listen, I need to ask you about something." She paused on the brink of mentioning Otherland. "How did you know we left the shelter?"

"I . . . I went there. I was worried about you."

She fought against the stupid, schoolgirl flutter. Something about the conversation was bothering her. "Del Ray, are you telling me the truth? You came all the way across town to look for us at the shelter, just because I was on leave of absence?"

"You didn't return my call." It was a simple enough answer, but he looked tense and unhappy. "Just tell me where you are, Renie. Maybe I can be of some help. I have friends—maybe I can find you somewhere safer to stay."

"We're safe, Del Ray. No need for you to put yourself to trouble."

"Damn it, Renie, this isn't a joke." There was an edge beyond anger to his voice. "Just tell me where you are. Tell me right now. I don't believe that pad of yours is broken either."

Renie took a breath, startled. She ran her fingers across the touchscreen. The security gear Martine had sent her flashed its readings across Del Ray's face. One set of characters shone brighter than the others, blinking road-hazard yellow.

"You . . . you bastard," she breathed. "You're trying to trace my call!"

"What? What are you talking about?" But his expression suddenly twisted with shame. "Renie, you are acting very strangely. Why won't you let me help you. . . ?"

His face abruptly vanished as she cut off contact. Renie stubbed out her cigarette with shaking fingers and stared unhappily at the cable running out of her pad, through the window and into the house jack. Her heart was beating very swiftly.

Del Ray sold me out. The thought was almost surreal. That anyone could want her whereabouts enough to bend a government official was bizarre enough, but that Del Ray Chiume would do that to her! Their parting had been difficult, but never vindictive. *What did they do to him? Threaten him?* He had seemed frightened.

She picked up her glass of wine and drained it. If she hadn't gone completely mad—if what she thought had just happened had really happened—then even Susan's security-fenced, suburban-respectable house was no refuge. Even if Del Ray's trace had failed, how long would it take before the people looking for them made their way down the short list of Renie's acquaintances and paid another visit?

Renie unplugged her pad; then, as if to hide her tracks, she snatched up ashtray and wineglass before hurrying inside. The back of her neck was prickling and her heart had not slowed since she disconnected from Del Ray.

It was, she realized, the ancient fear of a hunted animal.

CHAPTER 26

Hunters and Prey

NETFEED/MUSIC: Horrible Animals Bring Back "Classic" Sound
(visual: clip from "1Way4U2B")
VO: Saskia and Martinus Benchlow, founding members of My Family and
Other Horrible Horrible Animals, say they are taking their onetime
diamond-selling flurry group in a new and "classical" direction.
(visual: Benchlows at home with guns and peacocks)
S. BENCHLOW: "We're going for the classic guitar sound of the twentieth
century. People who say it's just a gimmick . . . "
M. BENCHLOW: "They gracelessly squat."
S. BENCHLOW: "Gracelessly. They're utterly tchi seen. We're bringing
something back, follow? But we're making it our own. Segovia, Hendrix,
Roy Clark—that far classic sound."

"I think I better go now," she said. She didn't want to look at him because it made her feel funny.

"But you just arrived. Ah, but of course, you're still grounded, aren't you? So you can't take too long returning from school." He frowned a little. He looked sad. "Is it also because you're afraid I'm going to ask you to do something bad?"

Christabel didn't say anything, then she nodded her head. Mister Sellars smiled, but he still looked sad.

"You know I'd never do anything to hurt you, little Christabel. But I am going to ask you to do some things, and I want you to keep them secret." He leaned forward, his funny melted face very close to hers. "Listen to me. I'm running out of time, Christabel. I'm ashamed at having to ask you to break your parents' rules, but I'm truly desperate."

She wasn't quite sure what "desperate" meant, but she thought it meant in a hurry. Mister Sellers had sent her a secret message on her desk screen at school asking her to come over today. Christabel had been so surprised to see it where her subtraction problems had been a second before that she almost hadn't noticed that her teacher was coming over. She had just managed to turn it off before Miss Karman reached her, then had to sit quietly while her teacher scolded her for not working.

"If you don't want to do them," the old man continued, "then you don't have to. I'll still be your friend, I promise. But even if you won't do these things for me, please, *please* don't tell anyone I asked you. That's *very* important."

She stared. She had never heard Mister Sellars talk like that. He sounded scared and worried, like her mother when Christabel fell down the front steps in their old house. She looked at his yellowy eyes, trying to understand.

"What do you want me to do?"

"I'll tell you. It's just three things—like in a fairy tale, Christabel. Three tasks that only you can do. But first I want to show you something." Mister Sellars turned in his chair and reached for the table. He had to push the thick leaves of one of his plants out of the way so he could find what he was looking for. He held it out to her. "Now, what's that?"

"Soap." She wondered if he was going to eat some. She'd already seem him do that.

"Ah, yes. In fact, it's one of the bars that you brought me. But it's more than that. Here, see this?" He tilted the bar and pointed to a hole in one end. "Now, look." He took the bar in both of his shaky hands and pulled it into two pieces as though he were taking apart a sandwich. Nestled in the middle of the soap bar was a gray metal key. "Pretty good trick, isn't it? I learned it from watching a prison movie on the net."

"How did it get inside the soap?" she asked. "And what's it for?"

"I split the soap in half and made a carving of what I wanted," Mister Sellars explained. "Then I made this hole, see? And put the two halves together, then poured in some hot metal. When it cooled, it made a key. And I'm about to tell you what it's for. That's one of the three tasks I have for you, Christabel. Well? Are you ready to hear them?"

Christabel looked at the key lying on the soap like it was a mattress, like the key was sleeping until she woke it up, like Prince Charming. She nodded.

She had to take her bike because it was a long way. Also, because she had heavy things to carry in the bike basket.

She had waited until Saturday, when her mother and father went to the football game—Christabel had gone with them once, but she had asked so many questions about what the little tiny men down on the green field were doing that her daddy had decided she'd be more comfortable staying home.

On football game days Mommy and Daddy left her with Missus Gullison. On this Saturday, Christabel told Missus Gullison that she was supposed to go over and feed her friend's dog and take it for a walk. Missus Gullison, who was watching golf on television, told her to go ahead, but to come right back and not to look in any of her friend's parents' drawers. That was such a funny thing to say that Christabel had to stop herself from laughing.

It was starting to get cold. She wrapped her scarf tight around her neck and tucked the fluttery ends into her coat so they wouldn't get caught in her bike wheels. That had happened once and she had fallen off and skinned her knee. She pedaled hard down Stillwell, then turned across the little bridge and headed past the school. Mister Diaz the nice janitor was dumping a bag of leaves into a trash bin, and she almost shouted and waved until she remembered that Mister Sellars didn't want her to talk to anyone.

She went down the streets just the way the old man had told her, lots of streets. After a while she came to a part of the Base she'd never been to, a group of low huts made of wiggly curvy metal surrounding a field of grass that hadn't been mowed in a long time. In a line behind the farthest row of huts stood another group of boxy shapes that were a little like the huts, but lower and made of cement. They seemed to have been buried partway in the ground. Christabel couldn't figure out what they were for. If they were houses, they were very small ones. She was glad she didn't live in something like that.

Starting from the side she'd come in, she counted just like Mister Sellars had told her, *one, two, three,* until she reached the eighth cement

box. It had a door in it, and there was a padlock on the door just like
he'd said there would be. Christabel looked around, worried that people might be watching her, just waiting for her to do something bad
before they came running out at her, like in a police show she'd seen
the other night, but she couldn't see anyone at all. She took out the
funny rough key that Mister Sellars had made in the soap bar and put
it in the lock. At first it didn't quite fit, but she jiggled it a few times
and it slipped all the way in. She tried to turn it, but couldn't make it
move. Then she remembered the little tube Mister Sellars had given
her. She took the key back out and squeezed some goo from the tube
into the hole in the lock. She counted slowly to five, then tried again.
The lock snapped open. The sound and the sudden aliveness of it in
her hand made Christabel jump.

When no policemen with guns and armor ran out from behind the
metal huts, she pulled the door open. Inside was a hole in the cement
floor and a ladder leading down, just like Mister Sellars had said. The
ladder was rough beneath her fingers, and Christabel made a face, but
she had promised, so she climbed down. Even though she had seen
nothing down in the hole, she still didn't like going into it—Mister
Sellars had said there wouldn't be any snakes, but he might be wrong.
Luckily it was only a short ladder, and before she had a chance to get
too scared, she was on the floor again. When she looked down beneath her foot, the little room underneath the ground was empty of
everything, snakes included, except for the thing she was looking for,
a square metal door set into the wall.

Christabel squatted beside the door, which was wider than she was
and half as big as the entire wall. On one side of it was the bar of
metal that Mister Sellars had called the "bolt." She tried to wiggle it,
but it wouldn't move. She took out her tube and squeezed some more
goo. She couldn't remember exactly where Mister Sellars had said to
put it, so she kept squeezing all over the bolt until the tube was empty.
She counted five again, then tried to wiggle it once more. At first it
didn't seem like it was moving. After a while she thought she felt it
quiver just a little, but it was still stuck.

She sat and thought for a while, then climbed back up the ladder.
She peeked out the door to make sure there was still no one watching,
then climbed out of the cement box. It only took her a few moments
to find a big enough rock.

Christabel only had to hit it a few times, then the little sticking-
out-piece on the bolt suddenly tipped down and she could slide the
whole thing back and forth. She pulled it as far back in its slot as it

would go, like Mister Sellars had told her, then clambered back up the ladder toward the afternoon sunlight.

Pleased with herself for being brave, and for successfully doing the first thing the funny old man had asked, she stood beside her bike and stared at the cement box. It was locked again and the key was back in her pocket. It was a secret thing that only she and Mister Sellars knew about. It gave her a tickly, excited feeling. Now there were only two more jobs left to do.

She put on her Storybook Sunglasses for a moment to read Mister Sellars' list again. She looked at her Otterworld watch—Pikapik the Otter Prince was holding the numbers 14:00 between his paws, which meant she had fifteen minutes to get to the next place. She checked the grocery bag in her bike basket to make sure the bolt cutters were still there, then climbed onto the seat and pedaled away.

Except for the tip of his nose and the tops of his cheekbones, Yacoubian's face had gone pale with fury, a full shade lighter than his normal olive complexion.

"Say that again. Slowly. So I can tell your next-of-kin what you looked like just before I tore your face off and ruined any chance for an open-casket funeral."

Young Tanabe showed him a cool smile. "I'll be happy to say it again, General. All non-Telemorphix personnel going into the lab— *all*—will be searched. Period. By orders of Mister Wells. If you have a complaint, sir, you should take it up with Mister Wells. But you aren't going into this lab complex any other way. Sorry, General."

"And if I don't consent to a search?"

"Then you either wait here, or if you become too disruptive, we have you escorted out . . . sir. With respect, I don't think you want to mess with our security people." Tanabe casually indicated two very large men standing beside the doorway, who were listening to the conversation with a certain professional interest. That part of their bulk was due to the rubberized electro-catalytic body armor under their casual suits did not lessen the effect. "In fact, General, here at TMX we've got at least a half-dozen security men who are veterans of your command. You would recognize the quality of their work."

Yacoubian glowered, then seemed to make a visible effort to disengage. "I hope you enjoy this. Go ahead."

Tanabe summoned the guards with a flick of his head. While they made a quick and thorough investigation of the general's person,

Wells' assistant stood back, arms folded. "Enjoyment has nothing to do with it, sir. I have my job, just like your men have theirs."

"Yeah, but I can have my men shot."

Tanabe smiled again. "Maybe my boss will give you an unexpected Christmas present this year, General."

One of the guards pulled Yacoubian's gold cigar case from his pocket. "Not this, sir. Unless you want to wait half an hour while we have it and its contents checked out."

"My God, is the crazy old bastard even afraid to have an unlit cigar in the same room with him?"

Tanabe took the cigar case. "Your choice, General."

Yacoubian shrugged. "Jesus. Okay, little man, you win. Take me in."

Wells waited with some amusement until Yacoubian had finished swearing. "I'm sorry, Daniel. If I had known you'd be so upset, I would have come out and searched you myself"

"Very funny. After all this bullshit, it'd better be worth it." The general's hand strayed to his pocket, but finding no cigar case, retreated like a hibernating animal wakened too early. His scowl deepened. "What could you possibly have ready after only a couple of weeks? I mean, come on, Bob. Even your brainboys can't be that quick."

"Boys *and* girls, Daniel. Don't be so antediluvian. And, no, we haven't done it in two weeks. More like two years—but we've put in thousands of work-hours altogether during these last two weeks to finish it." Something chimed softly inside the wall. Wells touched the top of his desk and a drawer slid open before him. He withdrew a dermal patch and placed it carefully in the crook of his elbow. "Just my medication," he apologized. "So if you've calmed down, I'll show you what we've come up with."

Yacoubian stood. He was quieter now, but there was a tightness to his posture that had not been there before. "This whole thing was your idea of a joke, wasn't it? Keeping me waiting, then that search thing you knew would piss me off."

Wells spread his hands. Despite the ropy muscles and prominent bones, they did not tremble. "Daniel. That's a little wild."

Yacoubian was across the office and into his host's bodyspace in a moment. He pushed his face to within an inch of Wells' own, then reached down and lightly finger-touched Wells' hand as it trailed toward the desktop security alarm, arresting its progress. "Just don't ever dick me around . . . Bob. Remember that. Our relationship goes back a long way. We've been friends, even. But you don't *ever* want to find out what kind of enemy I can be."

Yacoubian stepped back, suddenly smiling, leaving Wells groping for the support of a chair arm. "Now. Let's go see this little toy of yours."

The general stood in the middle of the darkened room. "Well? Where is it?"

Wells gestured. The four wallscreens blazed with light. "This is a lab, Daniel, but it's not the Frankenstein kind. We work with information here. The 'toy,' as you called it, isn't the kind of thing I can put on a table and point at."

"Then don't be so damn theatrical."

Wells shook his head with mock-regret. "My people have put a lot of time into something we can't show anyone outside the company. Surely you won't begrudge me a little bit of showmanship." He waved his hand and all four screens darkened. A hologrammatic display of small white dots formed in midair in the center of the room. They seemed to move randomly, like fast-motion bacteria or superheated molecules. "I'll feel more comfortable if I can give you the context, Daniel, so I'm going to explain a little bit of the history of this project. Feel free to stop me if I tell you too many things you already know."

Yacoubian snorted. "Stop you? How? Your security boys took my gun away."

Wells favored him with a wintry smile. "The problem seems straightforward on the surface. The Grail Project is at bottom a simulation environment, although wildly more ambitious than any other thus far. As part of the experimental procedure, a subject chosen by our chairman—we'll call the subject '*X*' for convenience's sake, since we still haven't been told his real name—was placed into the simulation." Wells gestured. An image of a coffinlike metal cylinder festooned with cables appeared, momentarily displacing the dots. "It hasn't been easy getting *any* information about the subject, by the way—the old man is playing everything close to the vest—but apparently *X* was subjected to various conditioning techniques to alter or efface his memory before they delivered him to us."

"Conditioning techniques!" Yacoubian's laugh was short and harsh. "And you civilians make jokes about military euphemisms! What did they do, give him a bad haircut and an excessive shampoo? They pithed his mind, Wells. They goddamn well brainwashed him."

"Whatever. In any case, about a month or so back there was a disruption of the monitoring equipment and a triggering of the splitting sequence—we still haven't been able to say decisively whether this was accident or sabotage—and contact with X was lost. Contact with his mind, that is. His body is still here on the premises, of course. About fifty feet beneath where you're standing, to be precise. But that means his submersion in the simulation network is ongoing, and we have no idea where in the matrix he is."

"Okay, now you've finally gotten to something I don't know," Yacoubian said. "*Why* can't we find him? How hard can it be?"

"Let me show you something." Wells gestured again. The glowing white dots reappeared, then froze into something resembling a three-dimensional star map. Wells pointed; one of them turned red and began to blink. "The old-line simulations were very simple—everything was reactive. When the subject looked at something, or touched it, or moved in a direction, the simulation responded."

The red dot began slowly to move. The white dots clustered most nearly around it resumed their earlier motion, but all the other dots remained frozen.

"Everything occurred in relation to the subject. When there was no subject, nothing happened. Even with a subject involved, nothing happened beyond the edge of that subject's perceived experience. But this kind of simulation, like the early experiments in artificial intelligence it resembled, made for a very poor version of what it tried to simulate—real human beings don't think in a linear series of 'if-then' statements, and real environments don't stop changing if there's no human observer. So, artificial intelligence experimentation shifted toward 'artificial life' instead around the end of the last century. People started to create environments that evolved. The artificial organisms in these new environments—although very simple at first—evolved as well. An 'A-life' experiment continued all the time, with the various artificial organisms living, feeding, reproducing, dying, whether any scientist was watching them or not.

"And that's what the new generations of simulations do, too . . . at least the high-end ones." Wells finger-flicked again. The red dot disappeared, but all the white dots leaped into frenetic motion again, some moving slowly, others fast as bullets; some traveled in groups, other lone dots roved on what seemed purposeful paths. "Whether there is a human participant or not, the various components of the simulation—artificial living things, artificial weather, even artificial entropy—continue. They interact, combine and recombine, and through this interaction their individual simplicity begins to approach, and

perhaps in some situations even surpass, the complexity of real life."
He chuckled. "Or 'RL,' as we used to call it."

Yacoubian watched the sparkle of apparently random movement in
the middle of the room. "That still doesn't tell me why we can't find
this *X* bastard."

Wells summoned the red dot again. He froze the throng of dots,
then turned to the general, eyes mild but intent. "Okay, Daniel, I'll
show you the old-fashioned simulation first, the kind that only reacts
to the human participant. Let me just hide the subject." The red dot
turned a steadily-glowing white. "Now I'll turn the whole thing on."
The dots sprang to life again, or at least a few of them did, a pulsing
swarm that seemed to travel slowly through the mock-constellation
like a funnel cloud while the dots on either side remained static.
"Which one is the subject?"

Yacoubian leaned forward. "Got to be one of those in the middle
there. That one. No, that one."

The cloud froze and a single dot turned red. "Close, Daniel. I'm sure
you would have gotten it with just a little more observation. Now we'll
try it with a simulation model that's more like the Grail network."
The red dot turned white again, then all the dots began to move at
once.

"I . . . I've lost it."

"Exactly." Wells pointed and the hologram faded. The wallscreens
lit up in a muted gray etched with an almost invisible shadow of the
TMX logo. "When simulations behave as much like real life as ours
do, there's no easy way to discern which seemingly living object is a
human participant and which is just part of the pseudo-life."

Yacoubian looked around. Wells, anticipating, clapped his hands
gently; two chairs rose from recessed slots beneath the floor. "But it's
our goddamn simulation network!" The general dropped heavily into
one of the chairs. "Why don't we just turn it off? You can't tell me
he'd still be running around in there somewhere if we jerked out the
cord!"

Telemorphix's founder sighed. "It's not that easy, Daniel. If we simply freeze all the simulations on the network, we don't change anything. *X* is going to look just like an artifact in whatever simulation
he's in, and artifacts don't have individual histories that can be
checked. They just . . . exist. We don't have enough processors on this
planet to keep records of everything that's happened in the Grail Project since we went gold with it. And as for actually pulling the plug—
Christ, Daniel, do you realize how much time and money the people in

the Brotherhood have put into growing these environments? Because that's what they are, grown, self-created by evolution, just like a real environment. Trillions! They've spent trillions, and invested almost two decades' worth of high-speed processing as well. The complexity of this whole thing is almost incomprehensible . . . and you want to just pull the plug? That would be like going to the richest neighborhood in the world and saying, 'There's a cockroach loose around here. Do you mind if we burn down all your houses to drive it out?' It's just not going to happen, Daniel."

The general patted his pocket again, then scowled. "But you've got a solution, huh?"

"I think so. We've built an agent." He gestured and the wallscreens began to fill with text.

"Agent? I though there were already agents to do this kind of thing! King Tut or God Almighty or whatever he's calling himself these days said he already had state-of-the-art agents involved."

"Ah, but there's the rub, you see. Not that we know much about those either—his people have pretty much controlled that part of the project, and up till now I've stayed out of their way. But chances are that any agents he has in there, whether human or artificial, are going about their search in the old-fashioned way."

"Meaning?"

"Hunting for similarities. My people have found out what they could—it's hard to keep anything completely secret in a shared scientific environment—and as far as we can tell, the old man's team have been tracking X since he was put into the network. Which means that they've developed something like a behavioral profile—a map of how X has acted in several different simulations. So, whatever agents or tracking gear they're using now probably compare that map against the behavior profiles of all the units within the network."

"Yeah? Sounds like the right way to go about it." For a third time, Yacoubian patted his pocket.

"It would be on a less complex system. But as I've been trying to tell you for a long time, ours isn't like any other simulation network. For one thing, because there's no tracking of individal units, map comparisons have to be made one at a time, case by case." Wells frowned. "You know, you really should try to stay abreast of all this, Daniel—it's just as important to you as to any of the rest of us."

"Yeah? And how much do you know about my end of things, brainboy? How informed are you on the global security situation? Our use of military infrastructure?"

"Touché." Wells at last sat down. "All right, let me continue. The problem with trying to make a behavioral match in this old-fashioned way is not just the compexity of the network either. More importantly, the behavioral signature of any free agent will change from one simulation to another—not much, maybe, but it will still change. You see, almost all these simulations are designed to be immediately functional for a user. That is, if you don't choose characteristics for yourself before entering, the simulation will assign them to you based on its own logic. Therefore, if *X* is moving from simulation to simulation, he's probably being changed at least slightly each time by the simulations themselves. In this case, the brainwashing—as you so crudely but accurately put it—is working against us. If he has no memory, his sim is probably being shaped by the simulations rather than the other way around. And there's one last problem. Any old-fashioned agents that can move freely through the network will probaby have a certain amount of integrity to them—that is, *they* won't change much. They'll tend to be easy to spot after a while, and since they need a certain amount of time and proximity to the suspected unit before they can make a match and proceed to the capture, *X* may be able to stay ahead of them almost indefinitely."

"Shit. So what have you got that's better?"

"We think we have the *new* 'state-of-the-art.' " Wells quirked his lips. "Am I going to be accused of being overly dramatic again? No? Then here." He snapped his fingers and a cable was extruded from the arm of each chair. "Plug yourself in."

The general pulled out the cable and slotted it into an implant behind his left ear. Wells did the same.

"I don't see anything. Just a bunch of trees and a lake."

"That tree there? That's our agent."

"What the hell are you talking about? An agent that's a tree? Have you completely lost your mind?"

"Now see this scene? See the woman at the front table? That's our agent. Next one—and that's our agent, the soldier carrying the flamethrower."

Yacoubian squinted at nothing visible from the outside. "So the thing changes?"

"Blends into any environment. The reason I didn't bring you in and show you some model or drawing or something is because there isn't anything to *show*. It's the perfect mimic, and thus the perfect tracking device—it can fit into any environment."

"So it's going to blend in—what good is that?"

Wells sighed. "Even if he escapes it once or twice, it still won't be recognized by *X*, because it will never have the same form or figure. And it will learn as it goes, find more sophisticated ways to adapt and gather information. But more importantly, it's going to sift data at a higher level than the old-style agents, because it's not looking to find matches for a single map. In fact, it's doing the opposite—looking for anomalies."

"So if it finds an anomaly—boom! We got him."

"I should digitize you and make you part of my new-employee curriculum—'Explaining to the Non-Technical'. No, Daniel, it's not that easy. Remember, we started this network with less than a hundred different simulations, but there must be at least a few thousand by now—I mean, I've got about forty or so myself. Add to that the fact that at any given time there must be more than ten thousand real live humans using the simulations—a lot of our junior members are paying for their place on the Grail Project waiting list by letting their friends and business associates rent time on the network. So with constant change in the simulations, living users who are almost impossible to distinguish from artifacts, and . . . well, suffice it to say a few other bits of emergent weirdness that we're still studying, what I'm calling 'anomalies' are happening in the tens of millions. But still, our new agent will sift and track faster than anything else, and speed is important. Like it or not, we are in a bit of a race with our chairman. But this baby will be the one to find *X*, and anyone else we ever want to locate, that I promise." He chuckled. "You know what we code-named the agent? *Nemesis*."

The general thumbed the cable out of his neck. "I never thought much of those foreign cars." He watched as Wells popped loose his own cable. "Oh, for Christ's sake, I'm joking, you pissant. I know about Greek mythology. So, when are you going to launch your little monster? Going to break a bottle of champagne over the wallscreen?"

Wells looked a little put out. "I launched it already. Even as we speak, it's making its way through the system, learning, changing, going about its business. Never has to be fed, never needs a day off. The perfect employee."

Yacoubian nodded and stood. "I'm in favor. Speaking of perfect employees, when you're done with your man Tanabe, let me know. I'm either going to hire him or kill him."

"Doubt you'll get the chance for either, Daniel. TMX has even less turnover than the military. Our benefits package is very fine."

"Well, I can dream. Which way out of here?"

"I'll show you."

As they walked down a deeply carpeted hallway, the general turned and gently took the founder of Telemorphix by the arm. "Bob, we never really went into the lab at all, did we? Not the super-clean part where security matters. I mean, I didn't have to be searched just to go into that conference room, did I?"

Wells took a moment to answer. "You're right, Daniel. I did it just to piss you off."

Yacoubian nodded, but did not look at Wells. His voice was very, very steady. "Thought so. One to you, Bob."

He had never much liked flying. He did it with some frequency, and was aware that even with the modern age's traffic-choked skies, it was perhaps the safest way to travel. But this did not soothe the more primitive part of his spirit, the part that did not trust any experience he could not control with his own hands and mind.

That was the thing of it: he had no control. If lightning struck the Skywalker on takeoff or descent—storms of any kind were not a problem at the plane's cruising altitude of 105,000 feet—there was really nothing he could do about it. He could kill as many people as he wanted, disrupt the electronic equipment with the strange *twist* he had inherited from one of his long-dead parents, but that still would not bend an out-of-control suborbital Chinese-made passenger jet to his will.

Dread was gnawing at this sour thought and others like it because the descent into Cartagena was rough. The big plane had been bucking and slaloming for the last quarter of an hour. A tropical storm, the Qantas captain had informed them with studied Ocker nonchalance, was kicking up a bit of a fuss in the whole Caribbean basin, and the ride down would be a bit bumpy. Still, he reminded them, they should all be sure to look at the lights of Bogotá, which would be sliding past on the left side of the plane any moment now.

As the captain finished his sightseeing suggestions and winked off the seat screen, the plane heaved again, a thrash like a wounded animal. Nervous laughter rose above the hum of the engines. Dread lowered himself farther into his seat and clasped the armrests. He had turned off his inner music, since playing his soundtrack would only emphasize that he was helpless, that for the moment he wasn't writing the script for his own netflick at all. In fact, there was really nothing he could do to make himself feel any better. He would just have to hang on and hope for the best. It was like working for that old bastard, really.

Another roller-coaster swoop. Dread clenched his jaw, tasting bile at the back of his throat. To add insult to injury, the old man, the would-be-god, who was undoubtedly rich beyond Dread's comprehension, still made his employee fly commercial.

"Está usted enfermo, señor?" someone asked.

He opened his eyes. A pretty young woman with a round face and golden hair was leaning over him, her face expressing professional but still genuine concern. Her name tag read *Gloriana*. Something about her was strangely familiar, but it wasn't her name. It wasn't the unpleasantly spartan jumpsuit she wore either, a fashion for cabin assistants that he hoped would pass quickly.

"I'm fine," he said. "'Just not a very good flyer."

"Oh." She was a bit surprised. "You're an Aussie, too!"

"Born and bred." With his unusual genetic heritage, he was frequently taken for Latin American or Central Asian. He smiled at her, still trying to figure out why her appearance plucked at his memory. The plane shuddered again. "God, I hate this," he said, laughing. "I'm never happy until I've landed."

"We'll be down in just a few minutes." She smiled and patted his hand. "Never fear."

The way she said it, and the reemergence of the smile, suddenly popped the memory loose. She looked like the young kindergarten teacher at his first school, one of the only people who had ever been kind to him. The realization brought with it a kind of sweet pain, an unfamiliar and somewhat disconcerting sensation.

"Thank you." He put some energy into a return smile. He knew from experience that his smiles were impressive. One of the first things the Old Man had done was send him to the best cosmetic dentist in Sydney. "It's nice of you to be concerned."

The captain announced final descent.

"It's my job, isn't it?" She made a deliberately exaggerated cheerful face and they shared a chuckle.

Customs was easy, as always. Dread knew better than to carry anything unusual, leaving even his own perfectly legal hardware at home—you could never tell when you might bump into a border agent who was a closet hobbyist and might recognize and remember serious top-of-the-line ware. That was what carefully nurtured local contacts were for, after all—to supply you the things you didn't want to bring in. As usual, Dread carried nothing more controversial than a mid-level Krittapong pad and a few suits in an insulex garment bag.

After a short cab ride, he caught the elevated train across the causeway to the Getsemaní section of the old town, which looked back across the bay from behind the *Murallas*, the centuries-old military walls the Spanish had built to protect their port city. He checked into his hotel under the name "Deeds," unfolded his garment bag and hung it in the closet, set his pad on the polished desk, then went back downstairs to run some errands. He returned to the hotel in less than an hour, put away what he had acquired, then went out again.

It was a warm night. Dread walked down the cobbled streets, unnoticed by either tourists or locals. The smell of the Caribbean and heavy feel of the tropical air were not that different from home, although the humidity was more like Brisbane than Sydney. Still, he thought, it was strange to come so far and have only the aftereffects of an eight-hour flight to prove you were somewhere different.

He picked a public phone at random and gave it the number he'd memorized. When the call was answered—voice only, no picture—he reeled off another number and was immediately given an address, then the other party hung up.

The hovercab dropped him off in front of the club and grunted away, skirts fluttering over the uneven surface. A crowd of young people in scarlet moddy bands and imitation body armor, the Colombian version of Goggleboys and Gogglegirls, stood in front waiting to be admitted. He had only been in line for a few moments when a street urchin tugged at his sleeve. Many of the visible areas of the child's skin had been burned red-raw by the use of scavenged skin patches. The boy turned and walked off down the street, limping slightly. Dread waited a few moments before following him.

They were in the darkened stairwell of an old building near the waterfront when the urchin vanished, slipping away through some unseen exit so quickly and expertly that the man he had been guiding did not immediately notice his absence. Dread, who had been alert since entering the building for the slight but worrisome possibility of an ambush, was impressed by the child's skill: the sisters chose their minions well, even at the lowest level.

At the top of the stairs a half-dozen old wooden doors ran down each side of the hallway, standing guard over a solitary and rather unfortunate-looking rubber plant. Dread walked noiselessly along the hall scanning each door in turn until he found one with a handpad. He touched it and the door opened, revealing itself to be both thicker than its appearance suggested and hung on strong hinges in a fibramic box frame.

The room spanned the length of the entire floor—the other doors were false, at least on this side of the hallway. The exterior windows, however, had been left in place: from the doorway, Dread had six separate views of the seaport and the choppy Caribbean. Except for these Monet-like ocean vistas, the room's white walls, black marble table, and Yixing tea service were an almost perfect copy of his simulated office. Dread smiled at the sisters' little joke.

A light was blinking on the only object of modern furniture in the room, a huge sleek desk. He sat down, quickly found the retracting panel that contained the connection hardware, and plugged himself in.

The room stayed in place, but the Beinha Sisters abruptly appeared on the far side of the table, side by side, their sims as featureless as two parcels wrapped in brown paper. For a brief moment Dread was startled, until he realized that he was in a simulation which duplicated the room even more exactly than the room mirrored his own online office.

"Very nice," he said. "Thank you for preparing this welcome."

"Some people find their environment crucial to their ability to work," said one of the Beinhas, her tone implying that neither she nor her sister were such people. "Our program is ambitious. You will need to be at your best."

"We await the second third of our payment," said the other lumpy shape.

"You received the coded list?"

Both sisters nodded in synchrony.

"Then I'll download one of the two keys now." He felt around on the unfamiliar desk for the touchscreen, then opened the account the Old Man had created and dispatched the sisters one of the pair of encryption keys necessary to access the list. "You'll get the other when the operation launches, as we agreed."

When the Beinhas—or their expert system—had examined the goods, they nodded again, this time indicating satisfaction. "We have much work to do," one of them said.

"I've got time now, although I have something I really must do before too late tonight. Tomorrow I'm all yours."

There was a moment of silence from the twin shapes, as though they were considering this as a literal possibility.

"To begin with," said one, "the target has changed security companies since we last briefed you. The new company has come in and altered several aspects of the compound's defenses, not all of which we have discovered. We know little about the new company, whereas we had several informants at the previous firm."

"Which may be why they've changed their security people." Dread called up the report. The information hung in the air before him. He began to bring up the rest of his array, charts, lists, topographical maps, blueprints. Color-coded and gleaming, they turned the virtual office into a neon fairyland. "How does this change of security affect your program?"

"It means more danger to you and the rest of the ground team, of course," said one of the sister-shapes. "And it means we will undoubtedly have to kill more people than we planned."

"Ah." He smiled. "What a shame."

Even a cursory discussion of the new twists in the operation took several hours. When he had terminated the contact and left his new office, he was feeling stretched thin by work and the flight in. He walked back along the waterfront, letting the soothing sound of the ocean wash over him. As he passed large and imposing office buildings, a small formation of camera-drones, activated by motion or his body heat, came swarming out. They overflew him once, then retreated to the shadows, scanning him all the while. Tired and irritated, he resisted the impulse to lash out at this surveillance, to damage or confuse them. It would be a waste of time, as well as foolish. They were only doing their job, monitoring someone who was close to their building after hours; the pictures would be viewed briefly in the morning by a bored guard, then the information would be erased. As long as he didn't do anything rash, that was.

Confident, cocky, lazy, dead, he reminded himself, walking on without a backward glance. The Old Man would be proud of him.

He walked into his room and undressed, then hung his suit in the closet. He examined his naked form in the mirror for a few moments, then sat on the bed and turned on the wallscreen. He brought up his own inner music, a burst of deep-sonic *mono loco* dance dirge, in honor of his visit to Colombia. He found something on the wallscreen with abstract but fast-changing visuals, and turned up the sound in his head until he could feel the bass pulsing in his jawbone. He watched the images flicker by for a few moments, then checked himself in the mirror again. There was something predatory in his long, muscled limbs, in the flatness of his own expression, that excited him. He'd seen that face before. He'd seen that movie. He knew what was going to happen now.

As he walked to the bathroom, he threw a few dissonant horn-blasts into the music, sharp edges of sound that suggested mounting tension. He brought the volume down as he opened the door.

Camera zooms in . . . .

Her wrists were still bound to the shower-head with tape, but she was no longer standing upright. Instead, she hung with knees bent and her weight on her extended arms in a way that he knew must be painful. When she saw him, she screamed and began to struggle again, but the tape on her mouth reduced the cry to a muted bleat.

"I followed you," he said as he sat down on the edge of the bath-tub. In his head, with the music underneath it, his voice had a deep, leading-man resonance. "I followed your cab until it dropped you at your hotel. After that, it wasn't very difficult to find your room . . . Gloriana." He reached out to touch her name tag and she jerked away. He smiled, wondering if she noticed that it was the same smile he'd used on the plane. "Normally, I'd want a more extended hunt, a little more sport. I mean, that is what you're here for, isn't it— soothing the cares of the weary business traveler? But taking you out of there and bringing you up here, all in your own suitcase . . . well, I'd say that was pretty good for spur-of-the-moment, wouldn't you?"

Her eyes widened and she tried to say something, but the tape choked it off. Writhing on the shower-head, she swayed from side to side. Her blonde hair, so immaculately styled six hours ago, hung in lank, sweaty curls.

He reached out and plucked her name tag free. It was the electro-static kind with no interesting sharp bits, so he tossed it aside. "You know," he said, "I know your name, sweetness, but you never asked mine." He stood and walked out of the bathroom, slowing the music inside him until it was something like an underwater funeral march, deep and heavy and resonant. He came back in with the hardware store bag.

"It's Dread." He opened the bag and produced a pair of pliers and a file. "Now, let's get you out of that ugly uniform."

Christabel was worried. It was taking her a long time to ride to the place Mister Sellars had said. What if Missus Gullison went to her friend's house looking for her? What if her friend's parents were home? She would be in real trouble, and it would be even worse when Daddy found out.

Thinking about how angry her father would be made her close her eyes. She accidentally rode down off the curb and almost fell when her bike thumped down onto the road and her front wheel went all wobbly. She pedaled hard until the bike was going straight again. She had promised Mister Sellars that she'd help him, so she had to do it.

The place he'd told her to go was along the outside edge of the Base, another part she'd never seen before. It was way behind the athletic field—she could see men in white shorts and shirts doing some exercises on the grass. Music and a voice she couldn't understand because it was too far away were coming from speakers on poles by the field. The place Mister Sellars had sent her had lots of trees and bushes on this side of the fence, and trees and bushes on the other side of the far fence, but none in between. The empty space between the two fences looked like when she took her eraser and rubbed it across a drawing she'd done.

Mister Sellars had told her to pick a spot where there were some trees behind her so no one would see what she was doing. After a little hunting, she found one. When she looked back, she couldn't see the field or any of the houses or other buildings, although she could still hear the music coming from the field. She took her school bag out of her bike basket, took out the bolt cutters and put them on the ground, then took out the little scissor-things and the roll of screen. She took the scissors and went to the fence, which was made of something almost like cloth, with little boxes along the top that made a quiet clicking noise. Beyond the outer fence, far away, smoke from campfires floated up into the air. Some people lived underneath the trees outside—she saw them when she and her parents drove off the Base—and even more of them lived down in the valley near the freeway. They made their own homes, funny places built from old boxes and pieces of cloth, and her Daddy said some of them even tried to sneak into the Base by hiding in garbage trucks. She could see some of the box-people through the fence, far away and tinier than the men on the exercise field behind her, but the fence was funny to look through. Everything on the other side was a little cloudy, like when you could write your name on the inside of the car window.

She touched the scissors to the fence-cloth, then remembered that Mister Sellars had said not to cut it yet. She went back to the bike basket and got out her Storybook Sunglasses.

"CHRISTABEL" the message in them said, "IF YOU ARE AT THE FENCE, TURN YOUR SUNGLASSES OFF AND ON TWO TIMES FAST."

She thought about this for a moment to make sure she was going to do it right, then pushed the button on the side of her glasses four times, *off, on, off, on.* When the pictures had come back inside them again, there was a new message.

"COUNT TO TEN AND THEN CUT. WHEN YOU ARE AT THE SECOND FENCE, TURN THE SUNGLASSES OFF AND ON TWO MORE TIMES."

Christabel had gotten to six when the music from the field suddenly went quiet and the boxes stopped clicking. She was frightened, but no one came or shouted at her, so she kneeled down and pushed the scissors into the fence. At first it was hard, but after the point suddenly went through, everything else was easy. She slid the scissors up as far above her head as she could reach, then picked up the big cutters and ran to the second fence. There was still no music, and the sound of her footsteps on the dirt sounded very loud.

This fence was made all of diamond shapes of thick wire covered in plastic. She turned her glasses off and on twice.

"CUT THE SECOND FENCE ONE WIRE AT A TIME, THEN COME BACK. WHEN YOUR WATCH SAYS 14:38, COME BACK RIGHT AWAY, NO MATTER WHAT. DON'T FORGET THE LITTLE SCREEN."

Christabel squinted. Prince Pikapik was already holding 14:28 between his paws, so she knew that wasn't very much time. She put the cutters on one of the pieces of fence-wire and squeezed them with both hands. She squeezed and squeezed until her arms really hurt, and at last the biting part of the clippers snapped together. She looked at her watch and the numbers said 14:31. There were still a lot of wires left to cut to make a hole as big as Mister Sellars said to make. She began to cut the second wire, but it seemed even stronger than the first, and she couldn't make the big cutters bite through. She began to cry.

"What a hell you do, weenit? *Que haces?*"

Christabel jumped and made a squeaking sound. Someone was watching her from a tree on the far side of the fence.

"N–n–nothing," she said.

The person jumped down from the tree branch. It was a boy, his hair cut funny, his face dark and dirty. He looked like he was a few grades older than her. Two more faces poked out of the leaves along the branch where he had been, a little boy and girl even dirtier than he was. They stared at Christabel like monkeys with their big eyes.

"Don't look like nothing, weenit," the older boy said. "Look like cutting that fence. 'Come?'"

"It's . . . it's a secret." She stared at him, uncertain of whether to run. He was on the far side of the fence, so he couldn't hurt her, could he? She looked at her Otterworld watch. It read 14:33.

"*Mu'chita loca*, you never cut that. Too small, you. Throw those here." He gestured at the bolt cutters.

Christabel stared at him. He didn't have one of his front teeth, and he had funny pink patches on his brown arms. "You can't steal them."

"Just throw them over."

She looked at him, then grabbed the cutters by both handles. She swung them, then threw them as high as she could. They clattered against the fence and almost hit her as they fell back down.

The boy laughed. "You too close, weenit. Get back."

She tried again. This time the cutters skittered over the top, between the coils of sharp sticker-wire, and fell down on the other side. The boy picked them up and looked at them.

"I cut for you, I keep these?"

She thought for a moment, then nodded, not sure if Mister Sellars would be mad or not. The boy bent to the next wire up from the one she'd already cut and squeezed the cutters. It was hard for him, too, and he said some words she'd never heard, but after a little while the wire snapped. He moved on to the next.

Chrisabel's watch read 14:37 as he finished.

"I have to go home," she said. She turned around and ran across the bare ground toward the first fence.

"Hold on, weenit!" he called after her. "Thought you running away from Mamapapa Army Base. What you do this for?"

She ducked through the hole in the first fence and was just about to jump on her bicycle before she remembered. She turned back and unrolled the little screen Mister Sellars had given her. This kind of fence, he had said, the first fence, it talked to itself, and so it needed this little piece of screen so it could talk across the places she'd cut. She didn't know what that meant, but she knew it was very important. She spread the piece of screen until it covered all the part that was cut. It stuck where she pressed it.

"Hey, weenit, come back!" the boy shouted.

But Christabel was already throwing all of her things back in her school bag, and she didn't look back. As she jumped on her bike, the boxes on the fence started clicking again. A few seconds later, as she began to pedal toward home, she heard the music come back on again by the athletic field, strange and smeary in the distance.

CHAPTER 27

Bride of the Morning Star

NETFEED/NEWS: *Krellor Declares Bankruptcy Again*
(visual: Krellor on Tasmanian beach with Hagen)
VO: Colorful and controversial financier Uberto Krellor has declared
bankruptcy for the second time in ten years. Krellor, known as much for his
famously stormy marriage to net star Vila Hagen and his month-long parties
as his business interests, is reported to have lost Cr.S. 3.5 billion in the crash
of his Black Shield technology empire.
(visual: Black Shield employees leaving Madagascar factory)
Black Shield, which was an early and heavily-bankrolled entrant into
nanotechnology, suffered huge losses when the financial community lost faith
in the new industry after a series of disappointing technical failures . . . .

"**M**artine, please, we really need this." Renie was trying to keep her voice calm, but not succeeding. "Forget the equipment—we have to find somewhere to hide. We have nowhere to go!"

"I've never seen no craziness like this," her father said from the back seat. "Driving around and around."

The blank screen remained maddeningly silent for long moments as Jeremiah turned the car onto the motorway and headed back toward midtown Durban again. The pad was plugged into Doctor Van Bleeck's skyphone and the transmission was being scrambled, but although the Frenchwoman seemed content with the security of the line, Renie was on edge. The shock of Del Ray's betrayal had left her jumpy and unsettled.

"I am doing the best I can do," Martine said at last. "That is why I am being quiet—I have several lines going. I have been doing some other checking as well. There is no police bulletin mentioning you, at least."

"That doesn't surprise me." Renie struggled for calm. "I mean, I'm sure it's a lot more subtle, whatever they're up to. We haven't *done* anything, so they'll find some other excuse. One of Doctor Van Bleeck's neighbors will report people living in what's supposed to be an empty house, then we'll be arrested for squatting or something. But it won't be anything we can fight. We'll just disappear into the system somewhere."

"Or it may be something more direct that does not use the law at all," !Xabbu added somberly. "Do not forget what happened to your flatblock."

I wonder if Atasco and those Grail people had something to do with my suspension? Only the confusion of fleeing Susan's house had kept her from thinking of it earlier. The world outside the car seemed full of terrible but unforeseeable dangers, as though some poisonous gas were replacing the atmosphere. *Or am I becoming completely paranoid? Why would anyone go to so much trouble over people like us?*

"I think this is becoming a lot of foolishness," said her father. "We just move in, then we go running out the door again."

"With respect, Mister Sulaweyo, I think I must agree with Renie," Martine said. "You are all in danger, and should not go back to the doctor's house or anywhere else you are known. *Pour moi*, I will keep trying to find some solution for these problems. I have a possibility that may solve both, but I am following a very faint trail that is twenty years old, and I am also trying not to make too much attention, if you understand. I will keep a line open for you. Call me if anything else happens." She clicked off.

They drove on along the motorway for some minutes in a tense silence. Jeremiah was the first to break it. "That police car. I think it is following us."

Renie craned her head. The cruiser, with its protruding lightbar and bulging armor and crash bumpers looked like some kind of predatory insect. "Remember, Martine said there's no general alert out for us. Just drive normally."

"They probably wondering what four *kaffir* people doing in a big car like this," her father growled. "Afrikaaner bastards."

The police car pulled out from behind them and into the next lane, then gradually accelerated until it was skimming along beside them. The officer turned to stare at them from behind mirrored goggles with the calm confidence of a larger and more powerful animal. She was black.

"Just keep driving, Jeremiah," Renie whispered. "Don't look."

The police car paced them for almost a mile, then pulled ahead and darted down an offramp.

"What is a black woman doing riding around in one of *those?*"

"Shut up, Papa."

They were parked in the outermost marches of a vast parking lot outside a warehouse mall in Westville when the call came in.

Long Joseph was sleeping in the back seat, his feet sticking out of the open car door, six inches of bare skin showing between pants-cuff and socks. Renie was sitting on the hood with !Xabbu, drumming her fingers and smoking her dozenth cigarette of the young day, when the buzz sent her scrambling to the ground. She snatched the pad from the car seat and saw that it was displaying Martine's code.

"Yes? Any news?"

"Renie, you make me breathless. I hope so. Are you still in Durban?"

"Close."

"Good. Could you please switch the frequency again?"

She pressed a button and the doctor's skyphone cycled through to another channel. Martine was already there, waiting. Renie was again impressed by the mystery woman's expertise.

"I am dizzy and tired, Renie. I have examined so much information that I will be dreaming about it for days, I think. But I have found, perhaps, a thing that may help some of your problems."

"Really? You found some equipment?"

"A place also, I hope. I have come across a South African government program—a military project—closed because of budget problems some years ago. It was called 'Wasps' Nest,' and was an early experiment in unpiloted fighting aircraft. There is no official record of it, but it existed. I have found certain, how do you say, first-hand accounts of people who worked there, if that makes sense."

"No, it doesn't really, but I just need to know if the thing will do us

any good. Is there some way we can get access to the actual machinery?"

"I hope so. The closing was temporary, but it never reopened, so it
is possible that some of the equipment still remains on the site. But
the records are very . . . what is the word? Imprecise. You will have to
investigate it for yourself."

Renie could hardly bear the slight stirring of hope. "I'll take the
directions. Jeremiah's not back yet—he's getting us some food." She
fumbled open the panel on the back of the pad. "I'll just jack this
thing into the car so you can download the map coordinates."

"No!" Martine was surprisingly sharp. "That cannot be. I will tell
your friend Mister Dako how to get there, and he will follow my instructions. What if you are arrested while you are traveling, Renie?
Then not only would there be that trouble, but the authorities would
clear the car's memory as well, and this place, whatever hope it may
bring, would be known to them."

Renie nodded. "Okay. Okay, you're right." She looked across the
parking lot, hoping to see Jeremiah already returning.

!Xabbu leaned forward. "May I ask a question?"

"Certainly."

"Is there nowhere else we could go besides this place which may be
surrounded by soldiers? Are there not many businesses that have VR
connections, or who would sell or rent us the necessary equipment?"

"Not for what we are speaking of," Martine replied. "I am not sure
even the best equipment at your Polytechnic would have given you
the level of response you need, and it certainly would not permit you
to experience VR as long as may be necessary. . . ."

"Look, that's Jeremiah," Renie said suddenly, squinting at a distant
figure. "And he's running!" She set the pad on the car floor. "Come
on!" She hurried around to the driver's side. As she sat staring at the
dashboard, trying to remember her driving lessons from years before,
!Xabbu forced his way into the back seat, waking a protesting and
grouchy Long Joseph.

"What are you doing?" Martine's voice was muffled by the pad
cover, which had fallen closed.

"We'll tell you in a minute. Stay connected."

Renie got the car started and seesawed out of the parking space,
then headed toward Jeremiah. Forced to travel up and down rows of
stationary cars, she had only moved them a hundred feet closer when
she pulled up alongside him. He clambered into the passenger seat,
short of breath, and almost stepped on Renie's pad.

"What happened?"

"They took the credit card!" Jeremiah seemed stunned, as though this were the strangest thing that had happened so far. "They were going to arrest me!"

"Good God, you didn't use one of Susan's cards, did you?" asked Renie, horrified.

"No, no! My card! *Mine!* They took it and waved it over the machine, then they told me the manager needed to speak to me. He didn't come for a moment, so I just ran out. My card! How do they know *my* name?"

"I don't know. Maybe it was just a coincidence. This has all happened so fast." Renie closed her eyes, trying to concentrate. "You'd better drive."

They exchanged places. Jeremiah headed as rapidly as he could toward the parking lot exit. As they joined a line of cars funneling out past the front of the mall, two uniformed guards emerged, talking into their headset microphones.

"Don't look," said Renie. "Just drive."

As they pulled out onto the main thoroughfare, Jeremiah suddenly sat up straight. "If they have my name, what if they go after my mother?" He seemed on the verge of tears. "That's not right! She's just an old woman. She hasn't done anything to anyone!"

Renie put a calming hand on his shoulder. "Neither have we. But don't upset yourself. I don't think anyone would do anything to her— they can't know for sure you're even involved with us."

"I have to go get her." He pulled into a turn lane.

"Jeremiah, no!" Renie reached for an authority she did not feel. "Don't do it. If they're really looking for us that seriously, they'll be waiting for you to do just that. You won't do her any good at all, and we'll all be stuck, then." She forced herself to think. "Look, Martine says she thinks she's found something—a place we can go. We need you to get us there. I'm sure you can make some arrangement for your mother."

"Arrangement?" Jeremiah was still wild-eyed.

"Call one of your relatives. Tell them you've had to go out of town on some emergency. Ask them to keep an eye on her. If you stay away, whoever is after us won't have any reason to bother her." She wasn't sure that was true, and she felt like a traitor for saying it, but she could think of nothing else. Without Jeremiah and the mobility of the car, she and !Xabbu and her father stood no chance.

"But what if I want to see my mother? She's an old woman—she'll be lonely and frightened!"

"What about Stephen?" Long Joseph said suddenly from the back seat. "If they chase us and we hide, we can't go see my boy when that quarantine's done."

"For God's sake, I can't think of everything right now!" shouted Renie. "Everyone, just shut up!"

!Xabbu's slender fingers reached over the seat and came to rest on her shoulder. "You are thinking very well," he said. "We must do what we are doing, what you have said."

"I am sorry to interrupt," Martine said from the pad beneath Renie's feet, making her jump, "but do you wish me to give you some directions?"

Renie rolled down the window and took a deep breath. The air was warm and heavy with the threat of rain, but at the moment it smelled like escape.

The Ihlosi was speeding northwest along the N3, for the moment only another anonymous unit in the early thickening of the rush hour. Jeremiah had been able to reach an elderly relative and make arrangements for his mother's well-being, and Renie had dispatched businesslike messages to Stephen's hospital and the Poly that would cover for her with both institutions for a few days. They had sprung themselves free and seemed, at least temporarily, to have eluded their pursuers. The mood in the car was improving.

Martine had set them a destination high in the Drakensberg Range along the Lesotho border, in an area too wild and with roads too primitive to be usefully explored in darkness. As the afternoon came on, Renie began to worry they would not be able to reach the area in time. She was not happy when Jeremiah decided to stop at a highwayside chain restaurant for lunch. Reminding the others that they made an odd-looking party, and that !Xabbu in particular was bound to be remembered, she convinced Jeremiah to go in and order four meals to take away. He came back complaining about having to eat while driving, but they had only lost a quarter of an hour.

Traffic became more sparse as they ascended from the plain and into the foothills. The road grew smaller and the vehicles grew larger as little commuter runabouts were replaced by huge trucks, silver-skinned dinosaurs making their way to Ladysmith or beginning the long haul to Johannesburg. The silent Ihlosi slipped in and out between the bigger vehicles, some of whose wheels were twice as high as the car itself; Renie could not help but feel it was an all-too-accurate analogy for their own situation, the vast difference in scale between themselves and the people they had offended.

Except it would be even more like what's going on, she noted unhappily, *if these trucks were trying to run over us.*

Luckily, the analogy instead remained loose. They reached the Estcourt sprawl and turned west onto a smaller motorway, then left that after a short while for an even smaller road. As they climbed higher on the tightly-winding mountain roads, the sun passed the noon midpoint and then seemed to spiral down the sky, heading for the mantle of black thunderheads that shrouded the distant peaks. Signs of civilization were dwindling, replaced by grassy hillsides and swaying aspens and, increasingly, dark stands of evergreens. Long stretches of these smaller roads seemed deserted, except for occasional signs promising that somewhere in the trees was hidden this lodge or that camp. It seemed that they were not only leaving Durban, but the very world as they had known it.

The passengers had been silent for some time, caught up in the scenery, when !Xabbu spoke. "Do you see that?" He pointed to a high, square section of the looming mountains. "That is Giant's Castle. The picture, the cave-painting in Doctor Van Bleeck's house came from there." The small man's voice was strangely tight. "Many thousands of my people were driven there, trapped between the white man and the black man. This was less than two hundred years ago. They were hunted, shot on sight. A few of their enemies they killed with their spears, but they could not win against guns. They were driven into caves and murdered—men, women, children. That is why there are no more of my people in this part of the world."

No one could think of anything to say. !Xabbu fell into silence again.

The sun was just beginning to pass behind one particularly sharp mountaintop, impaled like an orange on a squeezer, when Martine made contact again.

"That must be Cathkin Peak you are seeing," she said. "You are nearly to the turning place. Tell me the names of the towns around you." Jeremiah named the last few they had passed through, unhappy little aggregations of second-hand neon and industrial refit. "Good," Martine said. "In perhaps a dozen kilometers you will reach a town named Pietercouttsburg. Turn on the exit there, then take the first cross-street to the right."

"How do you know this, all the way from France?" asked Jeremiah.

"Survey maps, I think they are called." She sounded amused. "Once

I discovered the location of this Wasps' Nest, it was not hard to find a route for you. Really, Mister Dako, you act as though I were a sorceress."

Within minutes, as she had predicted, a sign appeared proclaiming the imminence of Pietercouttsburg. Jeremiah turned off, then turned again at the cross-street. Within moments they were winding up a very narrow road. Cathkin Peak, shrouded in dark clouds and silhouetted by the vanishing sun, loomed high on Renie's left. She remembered the Zulu name for the mountains, Barrier of Spears, but at this moment the Drakensbergs looked more like teeth, a vast, jagged-tusked jaw. She remembered Mister J's and shivered.

Perhaps Long Joseph had also been reminded of mouths. "How we going to eat out here?" he asked suddenly. "I mean, this is nowhere, big nowhere."

"We picked up plenty of food from the store at lunch," Renie reminded him.

"Couple day's worth, maybe. But you said we running away, girl. We going to run away for two days? Then what?"

Renie bit back a snappish reply. For once her father was right. They could certainly buy food in small towns like Pietercouttsburg, but there was a real risk that strangers would draw attention, and certainly strangers who kept coming back again and again would be remarked. And what would they use for money? If Jeremiah's account was frozen, she and her father could expect nothing but the same. They would go through the cash they had with them in days.

"You will not starve," !Xabbu said. He was talking to her father, but she sensed that he was speaking to her and Jeremiah as well. "I have been little use so far, and that has made me unhappy, but there are no people better at finding food than my people."

Long Joseph raised his eyebrows in horror. "I remember you talking about the kind of things you eat. You a crazy little man, you think that I'm going to put any of that stuff in my mouth."

"Papa!"

"Have you reached the next road yet?" Martine asked. "When you do, go past it and look for a track leading from the left side of the road, like a driveway to a house."

The food controversy momentarily in abeyance, Jeremiah followed her instructions. A light mist had begun to dot the car windows. Renie heard thunder grumbling in the distance.

The track looked narrow, but that was because it had become overgrown near the road. Once they were past the encroaching thorn-bushes—and had thoroughly scratched the Ihlosi's finish, almost bringing Jeremiah to tears again—they found themselves on a wide and surprisingly firm road that zigzagged steeply up into the mountains.

Renie watched the deep woods roll by. Bottlebrush plants known as red-hot pokers stood out against the grayness, bright as fireworks. "This looks like a wilderness area. But there weren't any signs. Not to mention fences."

"It is government property," Martine said. "But perhaps they did not want to draw attention with signs and barriers. In any case, I have called Mister Singh on the other line. He will be able to help us through any perimeter security."

"Sure." Singh's lined face appeared on the screen, glowering. "I don't have anything better to do this week, other than about a hundred hours of cracking on this damned Otherland system."

A bend in the road abruptly revealed a gated chain-link fence blocking their way. Jeremiah braked the car, cursing under his breath.

"What you got there?" Singh asked. "Hold up the pad so I can see."

"It's . . . it's just a fence," said Renie. "With a lock on it."

"Oh, I'll be a lot of help with that," he cackled. "Yeah, just turn me loose."

Renie frowned and got out of the car, pulling up her collar against the light patter of rain. There wasn't a person in sight, and she could hear nothing but the wind in the trees. The fence sagged in places, and rust powdered the hinges of the gate, but it still made an effective barrier. A metal sign, all but scrubbed clean, still showed faint traces of the words "Keep Out." Whatever explanatory prose had accompanied the warning was long gone.

"It looks old," she said as she got back into the car. "I don't see anyone around."

"Big secret government place, huh? Doesn't look like nothing to me." Long Joseph opened the door and began to shoulder his way out of the back seat. "I'm going to have a piss."

"Maybe the fence is electrified," suggested Jeremiah hopefully. "You go pee on it, then let us know, old man."

Thunder cracked loud, closer now. "Get back in the car, Papa," Renie said.

"What for?"

"Just get in." She turned to Jeremiah. "Drive through it."

Dako stared at her as though she had suggested he sprout wings. "What are you talking about, woman?"

"Just drive through it. Nobody's opened that thing in years. We can sit here all day while it gets dark, or we can get on with this. Drive through it."

"Oh, no. Not in my car. It will scratch . . . "

Renie reached over and pushed her foot down on top of Dako's, forcing the accelerator to the floor. The Ihlosi spat dirt from beneath the tires, caught traction, then leaped forward and slammed against the gate, which gave a little.

"What are you doing?" Jeremiah shrieked.

"Do you want to wait until they track us down?" Renie shouted back. "We don't have time for this. What good will a paint-job do you in prison?"

He stared at her for a moment. The front bumper was still pushed against the gate, which had sagged back half a meter but still held. Dako swore and thumped his foot on the pedal. For a moment nothing changed except the noise of the engine, which rose to a shrill whine. Then something broke with an audible *clank*, the windshield spiderwebbed, and the gate burst open before them. Jeremiah had to stomp on the brake to keep the car from rolling into a tree.

"Look at this!" he screeched. He leaped out of the driver's seat and began a dance of rage in front of the car's hood. "Look at my windscreen!"

Renie got out, but walked instead to the gate, which she pushed shut. She found the chain where it had fallen, removed the wreckage of the padlock, and draped it back in place so it would still appear locked to a passing inspection. She looked at the front of the car before getting back in.

"I'm sorry," she said. "I'll find a way to make it up to you. Can we please just keep going now?"

"It is getting dark," said !Xabbu. "I think Renie is right, Mister Dako."

"Damn!" chortled Singh from the pad's speaker. "I hope you'll tell me what just happened. It sounded pretty entertaining from here."

The road beyond the gate was still unpaved and narrow. "This doesn't look like much," said Long Joseph. Jeremiah, scowling and silent, drove forward.

As they wound on through the evergreens, Renie felt her adrenal surge draining away. What had Singh called her—Shaka Zulu? Perhaps he had been right. It *was* only a paint-job, but what right did she have to push Jeremiah, anyway? And for what? As of now, they seemed to be going nowhere.

"I smell something odd," !Xabbu began, but before he could complete his sentence, they had negotiated a bend, passing into the shadow of a mountain, and Jeremiah was treading hard on the brake. The road before them had disappeared. They skidded to a stop a few meters away from a featureless cement wall that stood like a vast door in the mountainside.

"Good God." Jeremiah stared, goggle-eyed. "What is that?"

"Tell me what you see," urged Martine.

"It's a gate of some kind, about ten meters square, and looks like a single slab of concrete. But I don't see any way to open it." Renie got out of the car and laid her hand against the cold gray stone. "No handle, no nothing." A sudden thought filled her with gloom. "What if it's not a gate at all? What if they closed this facility and just sealed it up?"

"Look around. For God's sake, do you always give up so easily?" Singh's raspy voice made Renie stiffen. "See if there's a box or a recessed panel or something. Remember, it doesn't have to be right there on the gate."

The others climbed out of the car and joined Renie in her search. The twilight was thickening fast and the rain made it even more difficult to see. Jeremiah backed the car away and turned on the lights, but they were not much help.

"I believe I have found something." !Xabbu was ten paces to the left side of the gate. "This is not true stone."

Renie joined him. Holding her cigarette lighter's flame close to it, she could see hair-thin lines describing a square in the rock face. There was a small crevice in one seam that, although it appeared natural, might serve as a handle. Renie stuck her hand in and pulled with no result.

"Let me try, girl." Her father slid his large hand into the space and tugged. There was a heartening creak, but it still held fast. As if in answer, lightning flashed overhead, then thunder and its echoes came caroming down the mountainside. The rain grew heavier.

"I will get the jack from the car boot," said Jeremiah. "We might as well ruin that, too."

It took both Jeremiah and Long Joseph leaning on the jack, but the panel door finally popped open, long-unused hinges grating. Inside was a small panel crisscrossed with an array of tiny blank squares. "It takes a code," Renie announced, loud enough for Martine and Singh to hear her.

"Do you have a hizzy cable?" Singh asked. "HSSI?" When Renie said she did, the old hacker nodded. "Good. Pull the front of the panel off and hold the pad over where I can see. I'll tell you how to hook me up. Then I'm going to get funky."

Whatever Singh was doing did not pay immediate dividends. Once Renie had wired her pad into the control panel to his instructions, she propped it with a rock and returned to the car. The sun sank. A chill wind pushed the rain into a raking horizontal. Time seemed to pass very slowly, broken only by an occasional—and uncomfortably close— blaze of lightning above them. Jeremiah, despite Renie's cautions about conserving battery power, turned on some music, featherweight but piercing pop fluff that did nothing to soothe her ragged nerves.

"Why they put this here?" her father asked, staring at the gray slab.

"It looks like it's supposed to be bombproof or something." She looked up at the steep pitch of the mountain face above it. "And they've got it recessed a little. Hidden from anyone flying overhead."

Long Joseph shook his head. "Who they trying to protect this place from?"

Renie shrugged. "Martine says it was a government military base. I guess the answer is 'everyone.' "

!Xabbu returned with an armful of wood, dripping wet but apparently unmindful of the downpour. "If we do not get in, we will need a fire," he explained. Stuck into his pants pocket and looking somewhat incongruous beside his old-fashioned coat and antique necktie, was a large sheath knife.

"If we don't get in, we're going to find us somewhere decent to sleep." Jeremiah was sitting on the hood of the car, arms crossed on his chest, looking thoroughy unhappy. "There isn't room in this car, and I'm certainly not going to sleep in the rain. Besides, there are probably jackals up here, and who knows what else."

"Where are we going to go with no money. . . ?" Renie began when a grinding noise even louder than the thunder made her start in alarm. The cement slab was sliding to one side, revealing a black emptiness inside the moutain. Singh's triumphant cry rang out above the noise of the gate's passage.

"*Ichiban!* Got it!"

Renie shut off the music and stared at the opening. Nothing stirred within. She walked forward through the streaming rain and leaned in to have a look, wary of booby traps or some other spyflick danger, but saw nothing except a concrete floor disappearing into the darkness.

"Actually, that was a bitch." The old hacker's voice crackled in the sudden silence. "I had to work hard on that—pretty much of a brute-force job. One of the old government key-codes, and they were always a bastard to crack."

"!Xabbu," Renie called, "you said you were ready to make a fire? Well, why don't you make one. We're going inside, and we'll need torches."

"Are you crazy, girl?" Her father eased his way out of the back seat and stood. "We got this car, and this car got headlights. What you want torches for?"

Renie felt a moment of irritation, but quelled it. "Because it's easier for a person with a torch to see, so we'll lead the car in. That way, if they've pulled out the floor or something, we've got a better chance of noticing before we drive Jeremiah's expensive motor into a fifty-foot pit."

Her father looked at her for a moment, frowned, then nodded his head. "Pretty smart, girl."

". . . Just do not attempt to turn anything on," said Martine. "If there is still equipment here, even lights, electricity may still be connected also."

"But that's what we want, isn't it?" Renie was waiting impatiently for !Xabbu, who was kneeling beneath the overhang using her lighter to set fire to a long stick with its tip wrapped in dry brush. "I mean, we're looking for equipment, aren't we? We have to use the stuff, and I doubt any of it runs on good thoughts."

"We will solve that problem as soon as we can," Martine replied, a measure of strained tension in her voice. "But think. If this is a decommissioned base, as my research tells me, then will it not attract attention if it begins to draw power? Is that a risk you wish to take?"

Renie shook her head. "You're right. We won't touch anything yet." She was ashamed of herself for not having thought of it. Shaka Zulu, indeed!

"I will lead." !Xabbu waved his makeshift torch. "The rest follow in the car."

"But, !Xabbu . . ."

"Please, Renie." He kicked off his shoes and set them down in a dry spot on one side of the doorway, then rolled up his pants legs. "There is little I have done so far to help. This is one thing I can do better than anyone here. Also I am smallest, and will be best at getting through tight spots."

"Of course. You're right." She sighed. It seemed everyone was having better ideas than she was. "Just be very, very careful, !Xabbu. Don't go out of our sight. I mean that."

He smiled. "Of course."

As she watched !Xabbu move forward through the gaping emptiness of the doorway, a tremor of unease ran up Renie's spine. He looked like some ancient warrior going down into the dragon's den. Where were they going? What were they doing? Just a few short months ago, this flight and break-in would have seemed incomprehensible madness.

Jeremiah started the car and drove forward behind him, easing through the entrance. The headlights met nothing but murky emptiness; if !Xabbu had not been standing a few meters ahead of them, torch held high, Renie would have feared they were about to drive over the edge of some bottomless pit.

!Xabbu raised his hand, signaling them to stop. He walked forward a little way, torch swinging as he looked from side to side, up and down, then he turned and jogged back. Renie leaned out of the window.

"What is it?"

The little man smiled. "I think you can drive forward safely. Look." He held his torch near the ground. Renie stretched so she could look down. By the flickering light she could see a broad white arrow and the upside down word "STOP." "It is a parking lot," !Xabbu said. He lifted the torch high. "See? There are more levels going up."

Renie sat back in her seat. Beyond the headlights, the ramps led up into greater darkness. The lot was vast and absolutely empty.

"I suppose we won't have to worry much about finding a space," she said.

A fter hauling in a sufficient amount of firewood, and much against both Jeremiah's and Long Joseph's wishes, Renie connected Sagar Singh through her pad to the control panel on the inside of the lot so that he could close the great door. If someone should happen to discover them, she wanted every bit of protection the government's bomb-proof defenses could provide.

"I'm going to download the instructions for opening it again to your pad's memory right now," Singh said. "Because as soon as that door closes, you're going to lose me. If that's a hardened military site, an ordinary carphone connection isn't going to pass even a whisper out of there."

"There's a locked elevator with a different kind of code box on it," she told the old hacker. "I think it goes down to the rest of the installation. Can you get that open, too?"

"Not tonight. Jesus, let me get some rest, will you? It's not like I don't have anything else to do but play electronic butler for you lot."

She thanked him, then said good-bye to Martine as well, promising to open the door to make contact in twelve hours. Singh lowered the great slab. As it ground down, his beaky face on the screen dissolved into a flurry of electronic snow. Renie and her friends were cut off.

!Xabbu had a large fire burning, and he and Jeremiah were preparing some of the food they had picked up in the morning, making a stew of inexpensive vat-grown beef and vegetables. Torch in hand, Long Joseph was wandering around the more distant parts of the huge underground lot, which made Renie nervous.

"Just watch out for loose concrete or unmarked stairwells, or things like that," she called to him. He turned and gave her a look she could not quite make out by firelight, but which she assumed was disgusted. The shadowed ceiling was so high and the lot so broad that he seemed to stand far away across a flat desert; for a moment her perspective flipped and instead of inside they were outside, so completely outside that there were no walls anywhere. The sensation was dizzying; she had to put her hands down on the cool concrete to steady herself.

"This is a good fire," !Xabbu declared. The others, used to a larger selection of amenities, stared at him glumly. The meal had been satisfactory, and for a while Renie had been able to ignore their situation and almost enjoy herself, as if they were simply camping, but that had not lasted long.

!Xabbu studied his companions' expressions. "I think it would be a good time to tell a story," he said suddenly. "I know one that seems appropriate."

Renie broke the subsequent silence. "Please, tell it."

"It is a story of despair and what overcomes it. I think it is a good story to tell on this night, when friends are together around a fire." He flashed his eye-wrinkling smile. "First, though, you must know a little bit about my people. I have told Renie stories already, about Old Grandfather Mantis and others of the Early Race. The stories are of long ago, of a time when all animals were people, and Grandfather Mantis himself still walked the earth. But this is one story that is not about him.

"The men of my people are hunters—or were, since there are almost none left who live in the old way. My father himself was a hunter, a desert Bushman, and it was his pursuit of an eland that led him out of the land he knew to my mother. I have told Renie that story, and I will not tell it again tonight. But when the men of my people went out to hunt, often they had to travel far from their women and children to find game.

"The greatest hunters of all, though, are the stars up in the sky. My people watched them crossing the sky at night, and knew that the Bushmen were not the only ones who must travel long and far through difficult places. And the mightiest of all those great hunters is the one that you call the Morning Star, but we call the Heart of Dawn. He is the most tireless tracker in all the world, and his spear flies farther and more swiftly than any other.

"Back in the ancient days, the Heart of Dawn wished to take a wife. All the people of the Early Race brought their daughers in hopes that the greatest hunter of all would pick one for his bride. Elephant and python, springbuck and long-nosed mouse, all danced before him, but none spoke to his heart. Of the cats, the lioness was too large, the she-leopard covered with blotches. He solemnly dismissed them all, one at a time, until his eyes fell upon the lynx. She was like a flame to him, with her bright coat and her ears like the glimmering tongues of fire. He felt that she, of all those who had passed before him, was the one that he should marry.

"When her father agreed to Heart of Dawn's request—as of course he did—there was a feast and dancing and singing. All the people of the Early Race came. There was some jealousy among those whose daughters were not chosen, but food and music helped to ease that evil in most hearts. The only one who did not join in the celebration was Hyena, from whose daughter the Heart of Dawn had turned away. Hyena was proud, and so was his daughter. They felt themselves to be insulted.

"Once they were married, Heart of Dawn came to love his Lynx more and more. She conceived a child and soon a son was born to them. In his joy with his new wife the great hunter brought her back fine things from his journeys in the sky—earrings, bracelets for her arms and ankles, and a beautiful cape made of hide—and she wore them with happiness. Since she was a proper married woman, and so did not leave her fire at night while her husband was away hunting across the sky, her young sister came to visit with her. Together they spoke and laughed and played with Lynx's baby son while they awaited Heart of Dawn's return.

"But Hyena and his daughter still felt anger sour in their stomachs, and so old Hyena who was cunning beyond almost any other, sent his daughter in secret to the camp of Lynx and Heart of Dawn. There was a food, ant eggs, that Lynx enjoyed more than any other. If she had any fault, it was that she was a little greedy, since before she had married Heart of Dawn she had often been hungry, and always when she found the sweet white eggs, which look like grains of rice, she would eat them all. Knowing this, Hyena's Daughter gathered a pile of ant eggs to leave where Lynx would find them, but first she took her own musk, the perspiration from her armpit, and mixed it with them. Then Hyena's Daughter left the eggs and hid herself.

"Lynx and her sister were foraging for food when Lynx came upon the pile of ant eggs. 'Oh,' she cried, 'here is a good thing! Here is a good thing!' But her sister was suspicious, and said: 'There is something foul-smelling about this food. I do not think it is good to eat.' But Lynx was too excited. 'I must eat them,' she said, picking up all the ant eggs, 'because the time might be long until I find such a thing again.'

"Lynx's sister, though, would not eat any of the eggs, because the smell of Hyena's Daughter's musk was troubling to her.

"When they arrived back at camp, Lynx began to feel a pain in her belly and her head grew hot as though she leaned too near a fire. She could not sleep that night or the next. Her sister scolded her for being greedy, and brought their mother to help, but the old woman could do nothing and Lynx became sicker and sicker. She pushed away her young son. She cried and vomited and her eyes rolled up in her head. One by one her beautiful ornaments began to fall away and drop to the ground, first her earrings, then her arm bracelets and her ankle bracelets, her cape of hide, even the leather thongs of her sandals, until she lay naked and weeping. At that moment Lynx stood up and ran away into the darkness.

"Lynx's mother was so terrified that she ran back to her own camp to tell her husband that their daughter was dying, but her sister followed Lynx where she fled.

"When the camp was empty, Hyena's Daughter entered into it from the dark night beyond the firelight. First she put on Lynx's fallen earrings, then she picked up and donned her ostrich-shell bracelets and her cape of hide, even her sandals. When she had done this, Hyena's Daughter sat down beside the fire and laughed, saying: 'Now I am Heart of Dawn's wife, as I should have been.'

"Lynx fled into the bush and her sister followed her. In her unhappiness, Lynx ran until she came to a place of reeds and water, and there she sat, weeping and crying out. Her sister came to her and called: 'Why do you not come back to your home? What if your husband returns and you are not beside the fire? Will he not fear for you?' But Lynx only went farther back into the reeds, until she was standing knee-deep in the water, and said: 'I feel the spirit of the Hyena in me. I am lonely and afraid and the darkness has fallen on me.'

"Because of what happened to Lynx, my people still say 'the time of the Hyena' is upon someone when that person's spirit is ill.

"Lynx's sister held forth Lynx's son and said: 'Your baby wants to suckle—look, he is hungry! You must give him your breast.' And for a little while Lynx was persuaded to come and suckle her baby, but then she put him down and fled back into the water again, deeper this time, so that it reached her waist. Each time her sister persuaded her to come out and nurse her baby, Lynx held her son for a shorter time, and each time she retreated to the waters she went in deeper, until the water was almost to her mouth.

"At last Lynx's sister went away in sorrow, taking the baby boy back to the fireside to be warmed, for it was cold beneath the night sky and colder where the reeds grew. But when she approached the camp, she saw a person with glowing eyes sitting at the fire, dressed in all of Lynx's clothes and ornaments. 'Ah!' said this person, 'there is my baby son! Why have you stolen him? Give him to me now.' For a moment Lynx's sister was amazed, thinking that it was her sister returned from the reeds and the water, but then she smelled the stink of hyena and was fearful. She held the boy tightly in her arms and ran away from the fire while Hyena's Daughter howled after her, 'Bring back my child! I am the wife of Heart of Dawn!'

"Lynx's sister knew then what had happened, and knew that by the time her brother-in-law returned from his long journey across the sky, it would be too late to save her sister. She went to a high place and lifted her head to the dark night, and began to sing:

> Heart of Dawn, hear me, hear me!
> Heart of Dawn, come back from your hunt!
> Your wife is ill, your child is hungry!
> Heart of Dawn, this is a bad time!

"She sang this over and over, louder and louder, until at last the great hunter heard her. He came rushing back across the sky, eyes flashing, until he stood before Lynx's sister. She told him everything that had happpened and he grew furiously angry. He ran to his camp. When he got there, Hyena's Daughter stood up, her stolen earrings and bracelets tinkling. She tried to make her deep, growling voice sweet like Lynx's as she said to him: 'Husband, you have returned! And what have you brought back for your wife? Have you brought game? Have you brought gifts?'

" 'Only one gift have I brought you, and this is it!' said Heart of Dawn, flinging his spear. The she-hyena shrieked and sprang away, and the spear missed her—the only time Heart of Dawn ever missed his cast, for the Hyena magic is old and very strong—but as she dodged it, she stepped into the fire and the coals burnt her legs, which made her shriek even louder. She cast aside Lynx's stolen belongings and ran away as swiftly as she could, limping from the pain of her burns. And if you seee a hyena today, you will see that he walks as though his feet are tender, as do all the offspring of Hyena's Daughter, and that his legs are still blackened from Heart of Dawn's fire.

"And so when the hunter had driven the interloper away, he went to the place of waters and brought his wife out again, and gave her back her ornaments and clothing, and placed her young son in her arms once more. Then, with Lynx's sister beside them, they returned to their camp. And now, when the morning star we call Heart of Dawn returns from his hunting, he always comes swiftly, and even the dark night runs from him. When he appears, you can see night flee along the horizon, the red dust rising up from its heels. And that is the end of my story."

All was silent after the small man had finished. Jeremiah slowly nodded his head, as though he had heard something confirmed that he had long believed. Long Joseph was nodding, too, but for a different reason; he had dozed off.

"That was . . . wonderful," Renie said at last. !Xabbu's tale had seemed oddly vivid, yet familiar, too, as though she had heard parts of it before, although she knew she had not. "That was—it reminded me of so many things."

"I am glad you heard it. I hope you will remember it when you are unhappy. We all must pray for the kindness of others to give us strength."

For a moment, the glow of the fire seemed to fill the room, pushing the shadows back. Renie allowed herself the luxury of a little hope.

She stared down over a broad, night-blotted desert from above. Whether she sat in the branches of a tree or on the steps of a hillside, she could not tell. People perched on every side of her, although she could barely see them.

"I'm glad you've come to stay in my house," said Susan Van Bleeck from the darkness beside her. "It's too high in the air, of course— sometimes I worry that everyone will fall off."

"But I can't stay." Renie was afraid of hurting Susan's feelings, but she knew it had to be said. "I have to go and take Stephen his school things. Papa will be angry if I don't."

She felt a dry, bony hand close on her wrist. "Oh, but you can't leave. *He* is out there, you know."

"He is?" Renie felt a mounting agitation. "But I have to go across! I have to take Stephen his books for school!" The idea of her brother waiting for her, alone and crying, vied with the dreadful import of the doctor's words. She only vaguely knew what or who Susan meant, but she knew what it signified was bad.

"Of course he is! He smells us!" the grip on Renie's arm tightened. "He hates us because we're up here and because we're warm when he's so cold."

Even as the doctor spoke, Renie felt something—a spike of chill wind coming in off the desert. The other near-invisible shapes felt it, too, and there was a rush of frightened whispering.

"But I can't stay here. Stephen is out there, on the other side."

"But you can't go down there either." The doctor's voice seemed different now and so did her smell. "*He* is waiting—I told you! He's always waiting, because he's always on the outside."

It was not the doctor, sitting beside her in the darkness, it was her mother. Renie recognized her voice and the scent of the lemony perfume she had liked to wear.

"Mama?" There was no reply, but she could feel her mother's warmth only a few inches away. As Renie began to speak again, she sensed something new, something that froze her with fear. Something *was* out there, prowling in the darkness beneath them, snuffling for something to devour.

"Silence!" her mother hissed. "He's very close, child!"

A stink rose toward them, a strange chilly smell of dead things and old, once-burnt things and musty, deserted places. With the smell came a feeling, as strong and clear to Renie's senses as the stench—a tangible wave of wretched evil, of jealousy and gnawing hatred and misery and utter, utter loneliness, the emanation from something that had been consigned to darkness since before time itself began, and which knew nothing of the light except that it hated it.

Renie suddenly did not ever want to leave that high place.

"Mama," she began, "I need to . . . "

Suddenly her feet slipped out from beneath her, and she was plummeting helplessly into blackness, falling, falling, and the wretched, hateful, powerful thing below was opening its great foul jaws to catch her. . . .

Renie sat up gasping, her blood pounding in her ears. For a long moment she did not know where she was. When she remembered, it was not much better.

Exiled. Fugitive. Driven into a strange and unknown land.

The last sensation of the dream, of falling toward a waiting evil, had not entirely left her. She felt sickened, and her skin was stippled with gooseflesh. *The time of the Hyena,* she thought, tempted toward despair. *Like !Xabbu said. And it's really here.*

It was hard even to lie back down, but she forced herself. The regular breathing of the others, which floated and echoed in the great darkness above her, was her only link to the light.

"You mean we could have had the electricity on last night?" Long Joseph thrust his hands in his pockets and leaned forward. "Instead of sitting around some fire?"

"The power is on, yes." Renie was frustrated at having to explain again. "It's power for the building to do self-maintenance, and for the security systems. But that doesn't mean we should use it any more than we have to."

"I hurt my foot trying to find a toilet in the dark. I could have fallen down some hole and broke my neck. . . ."

"Look, Papa," she began, then stopped. Why did she keep fighting the same battles? She turned and walked across the wide cement floor toward the elevators.

"How is it going?" she asked.

!Xabbu looked up. "Mister Singh is still working."

"Six hours," said Jeremiah. "We aren't ever going to get this thing open. I didn't expect to spend the rest of my life in a bloody parking garage."

Singh's voice buzzed from the pad, compressed to a fraction of the usual bandwidth. "Jesus, all you lot do is complain! Just be grateful that this place has been shut down, or decommissioned, or whatever the hell you call it. It could have been a damn sight harder to get in than it was—not to mention the lack of armed guards, which certainly would have added to the difficulty." He sounded more hurt than angry, perhaps at having his abilities questioned. "I'll get it eventually, but these are the original palm-print readers. Those are quite a bit tougher to crack than a simple code system!"

"I know," Renie said."And we're grateful. It's been difficult, that's all. The last few days have been stressful."

"Stressful?" The old man's voice took on an offended tone. "You should try to break into the world's most carefully guarded network with the nurse coming in every few minutes to check your bedpan or insist you finish your rice pudding. And there aren't any locks on the doors in the goddamn place, so I've got senile old bastards pushing in on me all the time because they think it's their own room. Not to mention I have gastric pains like you wouldn't believe from the medi-cation I'm on. And meanwhile I'm just trying to get you past the security system of a top-secret military base. I'll tell *you* about stressful."

Thoroughly rebuked, Renie walked away. Her head hurt and she was out of painblockers. She lit a cigarette, although she didn't really want one.

"No one is happy today," !Xabbu said quietly. Renie jumped. She hadn't heard him approach.

"What about you? You seem happy enough."

!Xabbu's look was tinged with sad amusement. Renie felt a tug of guilt at the sharpness of her response. "Of course I am not happy, Renie. I am unhappy because of what has happened to you and your family. I am unhappy because I cannot go forward with the thing I wish to do most in all the world. And I am fearful that we have discov-ered something truly dangerous, as I have told you, and that it is beyond our powers to do anything about it. But being angry will not help us, at least not now." He smiled a little and his eyes crinkled at the corners. "Perhaps later, when things are better, I will be angry."

She was again grateful for his calm good nature, but with that grati-tude came a small mote of resentment. His even disposition made her feel she was being forgiven, time after time, and she did not like being forgiven for anything.

"*When* things are better? Are you that sure that things will be better?"

He shrugged. "It is a matter of words. In my birth language there are more *ifs* than *whens*, but I must make a choice every time I speak a sentence in English. I try to choose the happier way of saying things, so that my own words will not weigh me down like stones. Does that make sense?"

"I think so."

"Renie!" Jeremiah sounded alarmed. She turned in time to see the light flash above one of the elevators. A moment later, the door slid open.

It's like being that explorer, Renie thought as the elevator stopped noiselessly on the first level down, *the one who discovered the Pharaoh's Lost Tomb.* Her next thought, a disconcerting memory of a curse that had supposedly killed the discoverer, was interrupted but not banished by the hiss of the opening door.

It had been only a suite of offices, and was now empty of furniture except for a large conference table and some big file cabinets whose drawers gaped, fileless. Renie's heart sank. The place's bareboned condition did not bode well. She and the others walked through all the rooms on the floor, making certain there was nothing more useful in any of them, then got back into the elevator.

Three more levels of similarly stripped offices did not improve her state of mind. There were enough large pieces of furniture to suggest that the decommissioning had ground to a halt at some point, but the empty warrens contained nothing of real value. There were a few eerie reminders that this place had once been a living environment—a couple of calendars almost two decades old still hanging on walls, antique announcements about this or that function or rules change yellowed on bulletin boards, even a photo taped to an office window of a woman and children, all dressed in tribal costumes as though for some ceremony—but they only made the place seem more deserted, more dead.

The floor below was full of stainless-steel counters that made Renie think uncomfortably of a pathologist's examining room until she realized that this had been the kitchen. A large empty room stacked high with folding tables confirmed the guess. The next two floors contained cubicles she guessed had been dormitories, empty now like the cells of a long-unused beehive.

"People lived here?" Jeremiah asked.

"Some probably did." Renie picked up her pad and sent the elevator down again. "Or they may have just had the facilities ready in case of war, but never used them. Martine said this place was some kind of special Air Force installation."

"This is the last floor," her father observed, somewhat needlessly, since the buttons on the elevator wall were easy to count. "And there isn't anything above where we came in but two more floors of parking lot, like I told you. I looked." He sounded almost cheerful.

Renie caught !Xabbu's eye. The little man's expression did not change, but he held her gaze as if to send her strength. *He doesn't think there's anything here either.* She felt a sense of unreality wash over her. Or maybe it was reality—what had they expected, after all? A complete, functioning high-tech military base left for them like some magical castle under a spell?

The elevator door pulled back. Renie didn't even need to look, and her father's words held no surprises.

"Just some more offices. Looks like some kind of big meeting room over there."

She took a breath. "Let's walk through them anyway. It can't hurt."

Feeling more and more as if she were caught in a particularly tiresome and depressing dream, she led them out into the sectioned space. She stood staring as the others wandered off in separate directions. This first room had been stripped to the walls, everything taken except the ugly institutional-beige carpet. In her miserable state of mind, she could not help thinking about how hellish it must have been to work in this windowless place, breathing canned air, knowing you were sunk beneath a million tons of stone. She turned in disgust to head back to the elevator, too flatly miserable even to think about what they might do next.

"There is another elevator," !Xabbu called.

It took a moment to sink in. "What?"

"Another elevator. Here, in the far corner."

Renie and the others made their way through the labyrinth, then stood and gaped at the very ordinary-looking elevator as though it were a landed UFO.

"Is it another one down from the entrance?" Renie asked, not willing to reach out for hope again.

"There weren't any on this wall, girl," said Long Joseph.

"He's right." Jeremiah reached out and carefuly touched the door.

Renie ran back to unhook her pad from the other elevator.

There were no buttons inside the matte-gray box, and at first the door would not even close again. She rehooked the pad to the inside hand-reader and keyed in Singh's code sequence; a moment later, the doors shut. The car traveled down for a surprisingly long time, then the doors pinged open.

"Oh, my Lord," said Jeremiah. "Look at this place."

Renie blinked. It *was* the Pharaoh's Tomb.

Long Joseph suddenly laughed. "I see it! They built this damn place first, then they built the rest of the damn thing on top of it! They couldn't get this stuff outta here without blowing up the damned mountain!"

!Xabbu had already stepped forward. Renie followed him.

The ceiling was five times as high as that of the garage, a great vault of natural stone hung with scores of boxy light fixtures, each the size of a double bed. These were slowly smoldering into a yellowish half-light, as though someone had turned them on to honor the visitors. The walls were ringed with several tiers of offices which appeared to have been cut into the living rock, fenced with catwalks. Renie and the others stood on the third up from the bottom of the cavern, looking down to the floor at least a dozen meters below.

Banks of equipment, many covered with plastic sheets, were arrayed all around the floor, although there were gaps where things were obviously missing. Cables hung like titan cobwebs from a grid of troughs. And at the center of the room, massive and strange as the sarcophagi of dead god-kings, lay twelve huge ceramic coffins.

CHAPTER 28

A Visit to Uncle

NETFEED/NEWS: UN Fears New Bukavu Strain
(visual: Ghanaian Bukavu victims stacked outside Accra hospital)
VO: UNMed field workers are reporting a possible new variant of the Bukavu
virus. The new strain, already unofficially called "Bukavu 5," has a longer
dormancy period, which enables carriers to spread the disease more widely
than those infected with Bukavu 4, which kills in two to three days. . . .
(visual: UNMed Chief officer Injinye at news conference)
INJINYE: "These viruses are mutating very swiftly. We are fighting a series
of epidemiological brushfires across Africa and the Indian subcontinent. So
far, we have managed to keep these conflagrations under control, but without
better resources, a larger break-out seems inevitable."

A man was being buried alive out in the courtyard, thumping frantically on the inside of his casket as dirt rained down on the lid. In the upper reaches of the vaulted ceiling a huge, shaggy, spiderlike creature was wrapping another customer in webbing that, judging by the shrieks of the victim, burned like acid. It was all very, very boring.

Orlando thought even the house skeletons looked a little slow and tired. As he watched, the small squadron performing maneuvers on his tabletop failed in their attempt to shift the virtual sugar-bowl. It rolled over, crushing a dozen of them into tiny, simulated bone fragments. Orlando didn't even smile.

Fredericks wasn't here. None of the other Last Chance Saloon regulars could remember seeing him since the last time the two of them had been in together.

Orlando moved on.

His friend wasn't in any of the other Terminal Row establishments either, although someone in The Living End said she thought she'd seen him recently, but since this particular witness was nicknamed Vaporhead, Orlando didn't put much store in the sighting. He was more than a little worried. He had left several messages over the last week, directly to Fredericks' account and with mutual friends, but Fredericks hadn't responded to any of them, or even picked any of them up. Orlando had assumed that Fredericks, like himself, had been tumbled out of TreeHouse at the end of their sojourn there and back into his normal life, that his friend was just being quiet because he was mad at Orlando for dragging him into this latest obsession. Now he was beginning to wonder if something more serious might be going on.

Orlando shifted again, this time to the Middle Country, but instead of The Garrote and Dirk in ancient Madrikhor's Thieves' Quarter, his usual entry point for new adventures, he found himself on a vast stone staircase facing a massive pair of wooden doors decorated with a pair of titan scales.

Temple of the Table of Judgment, he thought. *Wow. That was a quick deliberation.*

The doors opened and the torch-flames leaped in the wall sconces. Orlando, now wearing his familiar Thargor sim, walked forward. Despite his current disaffection, it was hard not to respond to the gravity of the occasion. The high-ceilinged room was all in shadow but for a single column of light that angled down from the stained glass window. The window was also decorated with the Table of Judgment crest, and the light spilling through it perfectly illuminated the masked and robed figures sitting in a circle below. Even the stone walls looked convincingly old and impressive, smoothed by the passage of centuries. Despite having seen it all before, Orlando found himself admiring all the work that had gone into it. That was the reason he had always played the Middle Country exclusively: the people who built and owned it were gamers and artists, not slave-labor hired by a corporation. They wanted it right because they wanted to hang out in it themselves.

One of the figures rose and spoke in a firm, clear voice. "Thargor, your appeal has been considered. We are all aware of your history, and have admired your feats of daring. We also know you to be a competitor who does not lightly ask for the Table's intervention." There was a pause; all of the faces were turned toward him, unreadable beneath the cloth masks. "However, we cannot find merit in your appeal. Thargor, your death is ruled lawful."

"Can I get access to the records you used in your deliberation?" Orlando asked, but the masked figure did not even pause. After a moment, Orlando realized that the entire judgment was recorded.

". . . We are sure that with your skills, you will return to the Middle Country in another guise, and make a new name famous throughout the land. But those who revere the history of the Middle Country will never forget Thargor. Good luck.

"You have heard the decision of the Table of Judgment."

The Temple vanished before Orlando could say anything; an instant later he was in the Fitting Room, the place where new characters purchased attributes and, literally, built themselves before entering the Middle Country. He stood, staring around him, but not really seeing. He felt some pain, but surprisingly little. Thargor was definitely dead. After all the time he had spent *being* Thargor, it should have meant more than it did.

"Oh, it's you, Gardiner," said the attendant priest. "Heard about Thargor getting toasted. Really sorry, but we all gotta go sometime, I guess. What are you going to do now, another warrior-type or maybe something different? A wizard?"

Orlando snorted in disgust. "Listen, can you find out if Pithlit the thief has been in lately?"

The priest shook his head. "I'm not allowed to do that. Can't you leave him a message?"

"I've tried." Orlando sighed. "Doesn't matter. See you around."

"Huh? Aren't you going to refit yourself? Man, people are out there jockeying for your spot at the top, Gardiner. Dieter Cabo's already put out an open challenge to all comers. He just needs a few points to jump into your old place."

With only the smallest twinge of remorse, Orlando left the Middle Country.

He looked around his 'cot with disaffection. It was fine in its way, but it was so . . . young. The trophies in particular, which had meant so much when he acquired them, now seemed faintly embarrassing. And a simworld-window full of dinosaurs—dinosaurs! They were such a kid thing. Even the MBC window now seemed pathetic, souvenir of an obsession with an idea that only nostalgics and a few ware-heads even cared about any more. Human beings weren't ever going out into space—it was too expensive and too complicated. Taxpayers in a country that had to turn its sports coliseums into tent cities and house its excess prison population on barges weren't going to pay billions of dollars to send a few people to another star system, and the idea of making a nearer planet like Mars habitable was already beginning to fade. And even if everything changed, and humans sud-denly decided once more that space was the place, Orlando Gardiner would certainly never get there.

"Beezle," he said. "Come here."

His agent squeezed through a crack in the wall, legs flailing, and skittered toward him. "I'm all ears, boss."

"Anything on Fredericks?"

"Not a whisper. I'm monitoring, but there hasn't been any sign of activity."

Orlando stared at the pyramid of trophy cases and wondered what it would feel like simply to throw them away—to have them cleared right out of his system memory. Experimentally, he hid them. The corner of the virtual room suddenly looked naked.

"Find me his parents' home number. Fredericks, in West Virginia. Somewhere in the hills."

Beezle beetled a wobbly single eyebrow. "Ya can't narrow it down any? Preliminary says there's more than two hundred listings under the name Fredericks in West Virginia."

Orlando sighed. "I don't know. We never talk about stuff like that. I don't think he has any brothers or sisters. Parents work for the gov-ernment. I think they have a dog." He thought hard. "He must have registered some of this information in the Middle Country when he first signed up."

"Doesn't mean it's available to the public," said Beezle darkly. "I'll see what I can find." He disappeared through a hole in the floor.

"Hey, Beezle!" Orlando shouted. *"Bug!* Come back!"

The agent crawled out from beneath the virtual couch, dragging his legs in a self-pitying way. "Yes, boss. I live to serve you, boss. What is it now, boss?"

"Do you think this room is stupid?"

Beezle sat motionless, looking for all the world like the discarded head of a mop. For a moment Orlando thought he had gone past the bounds of the agent's gear. "Do *you* think it's stupid?" Beezle asked at last.

"Don't mirror back what I say." Orlando was exasperated. That was the cheapest kind of artificial-life programming trick—when in doubt, answer a question with the same question. "Just tell me—in your opinion, is it stupid or not?"

Beezle froze again. Orlando had a sudden pang of worry. What if he had pushed it too hard? It was only software, after all. And why was he asking a piece of gear something like this, anyway? If Fredericks were around he would be telling Orlando just how utterly he scanned.

"I don't know what 'stupid' means in this context, boss," said Beezle finally.

Orlando was embarrassed. It was like forcing someone to admit in public that they were illiterate. "Yeah, you're right. Go see if you can find that phone number."

Beezle obligingly dropped out of sight once more.

Orlando settled back to think of something to do to occupy the time while Beezle did his work. It was about four in the afternoon, which meant he only had a little while until Vivien and Conrad came home and he had to surface, so he couldn't afford to get into anything too complicated, like gaming. Not that he had any particular urge to get involved in any games at present. The golden city, and the several layers of mystery that surrounded it, had made chasing monsters in the Middle Country seem a bit of a waste of time.

He created a screen in the middle of his room and began flicking through net nodes. He browsed for a while in Lambda Mall, but the idea of actually buying anything made him feel depressed, and nothing looked very interesting anyway. He jumped through the entertainment channels, watching a few minutes here and there of various shows and flicks and straight commercial presentations, letting the noises and effects wash over him like water. He scanned some news headlines, but nothing sounded worth watching. At last he vanished the elcot, went full surround, and wandered into the interactive sections. After specifying view-only, he watched almost half-an-hour's worth of a program on living at the bottom of the sea until he got bored with floating around like a fish while people demonstrated underwater farming, then began to flick through some of the specialized children's entertainment.

As the nodes flipped by, a familiar, exaggerated smile caught his attention.

"I don't know why they stole my handkerchief," said Uncle Jingle. "All I know is . . . *snot fair!*"

All the children on the show—the Jingle Jungle Krew—laughed and clapped their hands.

Uncle Jingle! Orlando, just about to shift again, paused. He dismissed the Who Are You? query that popped up at the ten-second mark—he was way too old to sign on, and anyway, he didn't particularly want any attention at the present. Still, Orlando continued to watch, fascinated. He hadn't seen Uncle Jingle for years.

"Snot fair"—man, the scanny things you watch when you're a little kid.

"Well," continued Uncle, bobbing his tiny head, "whatever the reason, I'm going to track that handkerchief down, and when I find it, I think I'm going to teach Pantalona and old Mister Daddywhiner a lesson. Who wants to help me?" Several of the participating kids, promoted out of the daily audience of millions by some arcane selection process, jumped up and down and shouted.

Orlando stared, fascinated. He had forgotten how weird Uncle Jingle was, with his huge toothy smile and tiny black button eyes. He looked like a two-legged shark or something.

"Let's sing a song, okay?" said the host. "That'll make the trip go faster. If you don't know the words, touch my hand!"

Orlando did not touch Uncle's hand, and was thus spared the additional indignity of local-language subtitles, but was still forced to listen to dozens of happy childish voices singing about the sins of Jingle's arch-nemesis, Pantalona

> *". . . She simply loves to be unfair*
> *That vixen with the corkscrew hair,*
> *She doesn't wash her underwear!*
> *Pantalona Peachpit.*

> *"She tosses stones at little birds*
> *She loves to shout out naughty words*
> *She even eats the doggy's . . . food*
> *Pantalona Peachpit . . . !"*

Orlando grimaced. He decided that, after a childhood spent in the opposite camp, his sympathies were beginning to shift to Pantalona, the Red-Headed Renegade.

Uncle Jingle and his entourage were now dancing and singing down the street past The Graffiti Wall, headed for a rendezvous with the lost handkerchief and vengeance against Uncle's enemies. Orlando, nostalgia more than satisfied, was just about to shift to something else when a slogan on the simulated wall caught his attention—painted letters that read *Wicked Tribe—zRooling Tribe.* Orlando leaned forward. He had thought that with his one Indigo favor called in, he was out of connections to TreeHouse, and through Tree-House to the mystery of the gryphon and whatever light that might shed on the radiant, magical city. But here, here of all places, was a familiar name—a name that, properly followed, might get him back into TreeHouse.

It had been a long time since he had been a regular fan of *Uncle Jingle's Jungle,* and he had forgotten more than simply why he had liked it in the first place. There was some routine for posting a message, but he was damned if he could remember it. Instead, he pointed at Bob the Ball, the chuckling sphere that always bounced along through the air just behind Uncle Jingle. After he had pointed long enough for it to register as more than a casual gesture, Bob the Ball appeared to burst open (although none of the other viewers would see that, unless they, too, were requesting help), disgorging a number of pictographs designed to help Ungle Jingle's young audience make choices. Orlando found the one that concerned Making New Friends, and entered his message: *"Looking for Wicked Tribe."* He hesitated for a moment, then left a dead drop address for contacts. There was no immediate answer, but he decided to stay connected for a while, just in case.

"Oh, look!" Uncle Jingle did a little dance of pleasure, his long tuxedo coat flapping. "Look who's been waiting for us at the Bridge of Size! It's the Minglepig! But, oh, look! The Minglepig is big, big, big!"

The entire company of the Jingle Jungle Krew, along with an invisible worldwide audience, turned to look. Already as large as a house and growing larger by the second was the Uncle's friend and erstwhile pet, the Minglepig, an amorphous aggregation of dozens of porcine legs, trotters, snouts, eyes, and curly pink tails. Orlando felt a moment of recognition as he saw for the first time in its wriggling outline the roots of his own Beezle Bug design, but where he had once found the Minglepig thrillingly funny, he now found its centerless squirming unpleasant.

"Never spend too long on the Bridge of Size!" declared Uncle Jingle as seriously as if he were explaining the Second Law of Thermodynamics. "You'll get real big or you'll get real small! And what's happened to Minglepig?"

"He's *big!*" shouted the Jingle Jungle Krew, seemingly unfazed by the anemone-like mass that now loomed over them like a mountain.

"We have to help him get small again." Uncle looked around, his licorice-drop eyes wide. "Who can think of something to help him?"

"Stick a pin in him!"

"Call Zoomer Zizz!"

"Tell him to stop it!"

"Make him go to the other end of the bridge," suggested one of the children at last, a little girl by the sound of her, whose sim was a toy panda.

Uncle nodded happily. "I think that's a *very* good idea . . ." Uncle needed a split-second to call up the name, ". . . Michiko. Come on! If we all shout it at once, maybe he'll hear us—but we have to shout loud because his ears are very high up now!"

All the children began to screech. The Minglepig, like a particularly grotesque parade float losing its air, flattened itself toward the ground, listening. At the childrens' direction it moved a little way back along the bridge, but then stopped, confused. The Krew began to scream even more shrilly; the din became excruciatingly painful. Wicked Tribe or not, Orlando had reached his limit. He entered his message so that it would continue to appear on the Making New Friends band, then exited Uncle Jingle's Jungle.

"Orlando!" Someone was shaking him. "Orlando!"

He opened his eyes. Vivien's face was very close, full of concern and irritation, a combination Orlando was used to seeing. "I'm okay. I was just watching a show."

"How can you not hear me? I don't like that at all."

He shrugged. "I was just concentrating and I had it up pretty loud. It was this really interesting thing about farming in the ocean." That ought to hold her, he figured. Vivien approved of educational programs. He didn't want to tell her that, since he hadn't set the t-jack to keep a line open for normal external input—that is, stuff going from his actual ear to his auditory nerve—he *hadn't* heard her, any more than he would have if she'd been shouting his name in Hawaii.

She stared, dissatisfied, although she was clearly not sure why. "How are you feeling?"

"Sore." It was true. His joints had already been aching, and Vivien's energetic wake-up hadn't helped any. The painblocker must have worn off.

Vivien pulled a pair of dermals from the drawer beside the bed, one for pain, the other his evening anti-inflammatory fix. He tried to put them on, but his fingers ached and he fumbled them. Vivien frowned and took them from him, applying them with practiced skill to his bony arms. "What were you doing, plowing the bottom of the sea yourself? No wonder you're hurting, thrashing around on that stupid net."

He shook his head. "You know I can turn off my own muscle reactions when I'm online, Vivien. That's the great thing about the plug-in interfaces."

"For the fortune they cost, they'd better do something." She paused. Their conversation seemed to have moved through its usual arc, and now Orlando expected her either to shake her head and leave, or seize the chance to offer a few more dire predictions. Instead, she sat herself on the edge of the bed, careful not to put weight on his legs or feet. "Orlando, are you scared?"

"Do you mean right now? Or ever?"

"Either. I mean . . ." She looked away, then determinedly returned her gaze to him. He was struck for the first time in a while by how pretty she was. There were lines on her forehead and at the corners of her eyes and mouth, but she still had a firm jaw and her very clear blue eyes. In the dim afternoon light, with day fast fading, she looked no different from the woman who had held him when he was still young enough to be held. "I mean . . . it *isn't* fair, Orlando. It's not. Your illness shouldn't happen to the worst person in the world. And you're not that at all. You may drive me crazy sometimes, but you're smart, and sweet, and very brave. Your father and I love you a lot."

He opened his mouth, but no sounds came.

"I wish there was something else I could tell you, besides 'be brave.' I wish I could be brave for you. Oh, God, I wish I could." She blinked, then kept her eyes closed for a long moment. One hand stretched out to rest lightly on his chest. "You know that, don't you?"

He swallowed and nodded. This was embarrassing and painful, but in a way it also felt good. Orlando didn't know which was worse. "I love you, too, Vivien," he said at last. "Conrad, too."

She looked at him. Her smile was crooked. "We know that being on the net means a lot to you, that you have friends there, and . . . and . . ."

"And something like a real life."

"Yes. But we *miss* you, honey. We want to see as much of you as we can . . . ."

"While I'm still around," he finished for her.

She flinched as though he had shouted. "That's part of it," she said finally.

Orlando felt her then in a way he hadn't for some time, saw the strain she was under, the fears that his condition brought. In a way, he *was* being cruel, spending so much time in a world that to her was invisible and unreachable. But now, more than ever, he had to be there. He considered telling her about the city, but could not imagine a way he could say it that wouldn't make it sound stupid, like a sick kid's impossible daydream—after all, he couldn't really convince himself it was anything other than that. He and Vivien and Conrad already walked a very difficult line with pity; he didn't want to do anything that would make things more difficult for everyone.

"I know, Vivien."

"Maybe . . . maybe we could put aside some time every day to talk. Just like we're talking now." Her face was so full of poorly-hidden hope that he could barely watch. "A little time. You can tell me about the net, all the things you've seen."

He sighed, but kept it nearly silent. He was still waiting for the painblocker to take effect, and it was hard to be patient even with a person you loved.

Loved. That was a strange thought. He did love Vivien, though, and even Conrad, although sightings of his father sometimes seemed as rare as those of other fabled monsters like Nessie or Sasquatch.

"Hey, boss," said Beezle into his ear. *"I think I got something for you."*

Orlando pushed himself a little more upright, ignoring the throbbing of his joints, and put on a tired smile. "Okay, Vivien. It's a deal. But not right now, okay? I'm feeling kind of sleepy." He disliked himself more than he usually did for lying, but in a funny way it was her own fault. She had reminded him how little time he truly had.

"Fine, honey. You just lie down again, then. Do you want something to drink?"

"No, thanks." He slid back down and closed his eyes, then listened to her close the door.

"What do you have?"

"I got a phone number, for one thing." Beezle made the clicking noise he used to indicate self-satisfaction. "But first I think you got a call coming in. Something named 'Lolo.' "

Orlando shut his eyes, but this time left his external auditory channels open. He flicked to his 'cot and opened a screen. His caller was a lizard with a mouth full of fangs and an exaggerated, artifact-strewn topknot of Goggleboy hair. At the last moment, Orlando remembered to turn up his own volume so he could whisper. He didn't want to bring Vivien back into the room to check on him.

"You're Lolo?"

"Maybe," the lizard said. The voice was altered with all kinds of irritating noise, hums and scrapes and trendy distortion. "Why you beeped Wicked Tribe?"

Orlando's heart quickened. He hadn't expected to hear anything back on his query so soon. "Are you one of them?" He didn't remember a Lolo, but there had been quite a few monkeys.

The lizard stared at him balefully. "Flyin' now," it said.

"Wait! Don't go. I met the Wicked Tribe in TreeHouse. I looked like this." He flashed an image of his Thargor sim across. "If you weren't there, you can ask the rest of them. Ask . . ." He racked his brain, struggling to remember. "Ask . . . Zunni! Yeah. And I think there was someone named Casper, too."

"Kaspar?" The lizard tilted his head. "Kasper, he zizz near me. Zunni, chop it, she far, far crash. But still no gimme—why you beep Wickedness?"

It was hard to tell whether English was Lolo's second language or the reptile-wearing Tribesperson was simply so sunk in kidspeak as to be almost unintelligible, even to Orlando. He guessed it might be some of both, and guessed also that Lolo was younger than it wanted people to think. "Look, I need to talk to the Wicked Tribe. I'm involved in a special operation and I need their help."

"Help? Cred-time, maybe? Candy! Whassa charge?"

"It's a secret, I told you. I can only talk about it at a meeting of the Wicked Tribe, with everyone sworn to secrecy."

Lolo considered this. "You funny-funny man?" it asked at last. "Baby-bouncer? Skinstim? Sinsim?"

"No, no. It's a secret mission. You understand that? Very important. Very secret."

The tiny eyes got even tinier as Lolo thought some more. " 'Zoon. 'L'askem. Flyin' now." The contact was ended.

Yeah. Dzang. *That's something gone right, for once.* He summoned Beezle. "You said you found a phone number for Fredericks?"

"Only one that makes sense. These government people, they don't want anyone finding out where they live, ya know. They buy those data-eaters, send 'em out to chew up anything tagged to their names that's floatin' around the net."

"So how did you find it?"

"Well, I'm not sure I did. But I think it's right—minor child named 'Sam,' couple other hits as well. Thing about data-eaters, they leave holes, and sometimes the holes tell you as much as the things that used to be there."

Orlando laughed. "You're pretty smart for an imaginary friend."

"I'm good gear, boss."

"Call it for me."

The number beeped several times, then the house system on the other end, having decided that Orlando's account number didn't fit the first-level profile for a nuisance call, passed him through to the message center. Orlando indicated his desire to talk with a living human being.

"Hello?" It was a woman's voice, tinged with a slight Southern accent.

"Hello, is this the Fredericks residence?"

"Yes, it is. Can I help you?"

"I'd like to speak to Sam, please."

"Oh, Sam's not here right now. Who's calling?"

"Orlando Gardiner. I'm a friend."

"I haven't met you, have I? Or at least your name isn't familiar, but then . . ." The woman paused; for a moment she went away. "Sorry, it's a bit confusing here," she said when she came back. "The maid has just dropped something. What did you say your name was—Rolando? I'll tell Sam you called when she gets back from soccer."

"Chizz—I mean, thanks . . ." It took an instant to register. ". . . *She?* Just a second, Ma'am, I think . . ." But the woman had clicked off.

"Beezle, was that the only number you had that matched? Because that's not the one."

"Sorry, boss, go ahead and kick me. Closest to fitting the profile. I'll try again, but I can't promise anything."

Two hours later, Orlando started up from a half-sleep. The lights in his room were on dim, his IV throwing a gallows-shadow onto the wall beside him. He turned down the Medea's Kids record that was playing softly on his auditory shunt. A troubling thought had lodged itself in his mind and he could not make it go away.

"Beezle. Get me that number again."

He made his way back through the screening system. After a short delay, the same woman's voice came on.

"This is the person who called before. Is Sam back yet?"

"Oh, yes. I forgot to tell her you called. I'll just see."

There was another wait, but this one seemed painfully long, because Orlando didn't know what he was waiting for.

"Yes?"

Just from that one word, he knew. Because it wasn't processed to sound masculine, it was higher than he was used to, but he knew that voice.

"Fredericks?"

The silence was complete. Orlando waited it out.

"Gardiner? Is that you?"

Orlando felt something like rage, but it was an emotion as confusing as it was painful. "You bastard," he said at last. "Why didn't you tell me?"

"I'm sorry." Fredericks' new voice was faint. "But it's not like you think. . . ."

"What's to think? I thought you were my friend. I thought you were my *male* friend. Was it funny, listening to me talk about girls? Letting me make a total scanbox out of myself?" He suddenly remembered one now cringeworthy occasion where he had talked about how he would put together his ideal female from the different body parts of famous net stars. "I . . . I just . . ." He was suddenly unable to say more.

"But it's not like you think. Not exactly. I mean, it wasn't supposed to . . ." Fredericks didn't say anything for a moment. When the familiar-but-unfamiliar girl's voice spoke again, it was flat and sorrowful. "How did you get this number?"

"Tracked it down. I was looking for you because I was *worried* about you, Fredericks. Or should I call you Samantha?" He put as much scorn into it as he could summon.

"It's . . . it's Salome, actually. 'Sam' was a joke of my dad's when I was little. But . . ."

"Why didn't you *tell* me? I mean, it's one thing when you're just messing around on the net, but we were friends, man!" He laughed bitterly. *"Man."*

"That was it! See, by the time we were friends, I didn't know how to just tell you. I was afraid you wouldn't want to string with me anymore."

"That's your excuse?"

Fredericks sounded on the verge of tears. "I . . . I didn't know what to do."

"Fine." Orlando felt as though he had left his body, like he was just a cloud of anger floating free. "Fine. I guess you're not dead or anything. That's what I called to find out in the first place."

"Orlando!"

But this time he was the one who hung up.

They're out there, so close you can almost smell them.

*No, you **can** smell them, in a way. The suits pick up all manner of subtle clues, extending the human sensory range so that you can feel nearly a score of them moving toward you through the fog just the way a mastiff can scent a cat walking on the back fence.*

You look around, but Olekov and Pun-yi still haven't returned. They picked a bad moment to check the signaling equipment at the landing site. Of course, there aren't many good moments on this hellhole of a planet.

Something moves out on the perimeter. You focus the filter-lenses in your helmet; it's not a human silhouette. Your hand is already extended, your gauntlet beam primed, and it takes only a flick of thought to send a horizontal thread of fire razoring toward the intruder. The thing is fast, though—horribly fast. The laser tears another piece off the wreckage of the first expedition ship, but the thing that had crouched in front of it is gone, vanished back into the mist like a bad dream.

Your suit sensors suddenly blast into alarm mode. Behind you—half-a-dozen loping shapes. Idiot! You curse yourself for being distracted, even as you turn and throw out a coruscating tangle of fire. The oldest trick in the book! These things hunt in packs, after all. For all their resemblance to earth crustaceans, the creatures are terrifyingly smart.

Two of the creatures go down, but one of them gets back up and drags itself to shelter on one fewer jointed leg than usual. Illuminated by the residual fires from your assault, it darts a look at you as it goes, and you imagine you can see an active malice in the strange wet eyes. . . .

Malicious giant bugs! Orlando's finer sentiments went into revolt. This was the last time he'd ever trust a review from the bartender at The Living End. This kind of crap was years out of date!

Still, he'd paid for it—or rather his parents were going to when the monthly net bill was deducted. He might as well see if it got better. So far, it was a pretty standard-grade shoot-em-up, with nothing that appealed to his own fairly particular interests. . . .

There's a fireworks-burst of light along the perimeter. Your heart leaps— that's a human weapon. Olekov and Pun-yi! You rake a distant section of the perimeter to provide cover for your comrades, but also to let them know where you are. Another burst of fire, then a dark figure breaks into the clearing and sprints toward you, pursued by three shambling, hopping shapes. You don't have a very good angle, but you manage to knock one of them down. The pursued figure flings itself forward and rolls over the edge of the trench, leaving you an unencumbered shot at the things following it. You widen the angle, sacrificing killpower for coverage; they are caught, jigging helplessly in the beam as the air around them superheats. You keep it on them for almost a minute, despite the drain of battery power, until they burst into a swirl of carbon particles and are carried away on the wind. There is something about these creatures that makes you want to kill them deader than dead.

Something like what? Do they try to sell you memberships to religious nodes? How bad could they be?

Orlando was having trouble keeping his mind on the simulation. He kept thinking of Fredericks—no, he realized, not about Fredericks so much as the gap where Fredericks used to be. He had thought once that it was strange to have a friend you'd never met. Now it was even stranger, losing a friend you'd never really had.

Olekov crawls toward you down the length of the trench. Her right arm is mostly gone; there is a raw-looking blister of heavy plastic just above her elbow where the suit has sealed off at the wound site. Through the viewplate, Olekov's face is shockingly white. You cannot help remembering that planetfall on Dekkamer One. That had been a good time, you and Olekov and ten days' leave.

The memory rises up before you, Olekov as she emerged from a mountain lake, dripping, naked, her pale breasts like snowdrifts. You made love for hours with only the trees as witnesses, urging each other on, knowing that your time was short, that there might never be a day like this again. . . .

"Pun-yi . . . they got him," she moans. The terror in her voice snaps you back to the present. The atmosphere distortion is so great that even this close, you can barely hear her voice for the noise on the channel. "Horrible. . . !"

Dekkamer One is light-years away, forever lost. There is no time to help her, or even to humor her. "Can you shoot? Do you have any charge left in your gauntlet?"

"They took him!" she screams, furious at your seeming indifference. There is something irreparably broken in her voice. "They captured him—they've taken him down into their nest! They were . . . they were putting something through his . . . his eyes . . . as they dragged him away. . . ."

You shudder. At the end, you'll save the last charge of the gauntlet for yourself. You've heard rumors of what these creatures do to their prey. You will not allow that to happen to you.

Olekov has slumped to the ground, her shivers rapidly becoming convulsive. Blood is dripping back from her injured arm into her helmet—the seals are not working properly. You pause, unsure of what to do, then your suit sensors begin to shrill again. You look up to see a dozen many-jointed shapes, each the size of a small horse, skittering toward you across the smoking, debris-strewn planetary surface. Olekov's sobbing has become a dying person's hitch and wheeze. . . .

"Boss! Hey, boss! Let those poor imitations alone. I gotta talk to you."

"Damn it, Beezle, I hate it when you do that. It was just starting to get good." And God knew, distraction had been hard enough to come by during the last week. He looked around at his 'cot with irritation. Even without the trophies it still looked pretty dismal. The decor definitely needed to be changed.

"Sorry, but you told me you wanted to know if you had a contact from that Wicked Tribe group."

"They're on the line?"

"No. But they just sent you a message. You want to see?"

Orlando suppressed his irritation. "Yes, damn it. Play it."

A congregation of yellow squiggles appeared in the middle of the room. Orlando frowned and brought up the magnification. At the point where he could see the figures clearly, they had very poor resolution; either way, squinting at the fuzzy forms made his eyes hurt.

The monkeys hovered in a small orbital cloud. As one of them spoke, the others went on smacking each other and flying in tight circles. "Wicked Tribe . . . will meet you," said the foreground simian, melodramatic presentation belied by the pushing and shoving in the background. The spokesmonkey wore the same cartoonish grin as all the others, and Orlando could not tell whether the voice was one he'd heard before or not. "Wicked Tribe will meet you in Special Secret Tribe Club Bunker in TreeHouse." A time and node address flashed up, full of childish misprintings. The message ended.

Orlando frowned. "Send a return message, Beezle. Tell them I can't get into TreeHouse, so they either have to get me in or else meet me here in the Inner District."

"Got it, boss."

Orlando sat himself in midair and looked at the MBC window. The little digging-drones were still hard at work, pursuing their goals with mindless application. Orlando felt strange. He should have been excited, or at least satisfied: he had opened up a connection back into TreeHouse. But instead he felt depressed.

They're little kids, he thought. *Just micros. And I'm going to trick them into doing . . . what? Breaking the law? Helping me hack into something? And what if I'm right, and there are big-time people involved in this? Then what am I getting them into? And for what?*

For a picture—an image. For something he had seen for just a few moments and which might mean anything . . . or absolutely nothing.

But it's all I've got left.

It was a closet. He could tell that by the slightly musty scent of clothing, and the faint, skeletal lines of coat hangers revealed by the light seeping in from the crack beneath the door. He was in a closet, and someone outside was looking for him.

Long ago, when his parents still had visitors, his cousins had once come for Christmas. His problem had been less obvious then, and although they asked him more questions about his illness than he would have liked, in a strange way he had been pleased to be the center of attention, and had enjoyed their visit. They had taught him lots of games, the sort that solitary children like himself usually only played in VR. One of them was hide-and-go-seek.

It had made an incalculable impresson on him, the feverish excitement of hiding, the waiting in the dark, breathless, while "it" hunted for him. On the third or fourth game he had found a place in the closet off his parent's bathroom—cleverly deceptive, because he had to remove and hide one of the shelves to fit into it—and had remained there, undiscovered, until the "Olly Olly Oxen Free" had been called. That triumphant moment, hearing the surrender of his distant enemy, was one of the few purely happy memories of his life.

So why then, as he crouched in the darkness while something fumblingly investigated the room outside, was he now so terrified? Why was his heart pattering like a jacklighted deer's? Why did his skin feel like it was trying to slide all the way around to the back of his body? The thing outside, whatever it was—for some reason he could not imagine it as a person, but only as a faceless, shapeless presence—surely did not know where he was. Otherwise, why would it not simply pull open the closet door? Unless it *did* know, and was enjoying the game, reveling in its power and his helplessness.

It *was* a thing, he realized. That was what terrified him so. It wasn't one of his cousins, or his father, or even some baroque monster from the Middle Country. It was a thing. An it.

His lungs hurt. He had been holding his breath without realizing it. Now he wanted nothing more than to gasp in a great swallow of fresh air, but he did not dare make a noise. There was a scraping outside, then silence. Where was it now? Standing just on the other side of the closet door, listening? Waiting for that one telltale noise?

And most frightening of all, he realized, was that other than the thing outside, there was no one else in the house. He was alone with the thing that was just now pulling the closet door open. Alone.

In the dark, holding a scream clenched tight in his throat, he closed his eyes and prayed for the game to end. . . .

"I brought you some painkillers, boss. You were jerking around a lot in your sleep."

Orlando was having trouble getting his breath. His lungs seemed too shallow, and when he did manage at last to draw deeply, a wet cough rattled his bones. He sat up, accidentally dislodging Beezle's robot body which rolled helplessly down onto the bedcovers, then struggled to right itself.

"I'm . . . it was just a bad dream." He sat up and looked around, but his bedroom didn't even have a closet, not that old-fashioned kind anyway. It had been a dream, just the kind of stupid nightmare he had on bad nights. But there had been something important about it, something more important even than the fear.

Beezle, now set on rubber-tipped legs once more, began to crawl away down the quilt, back toward its nourishing wall socket.

"Wait." Orlando lowered his voice to a whisper. "I . . . I think I need to make a call."

"Just let me lose the legs, boss." Beezle clambered awkwardly down the bed frame, heading for the floor. "I'll meet you online."

The doors of the Last Chance Saloon swung open. An ax-murderer politely dragged his victim to one side before returning to active dismemberment. The figure that stepped over the spreading puddle of blood had the familiar broad shoulders and thick, weight-lifter's neck. Fredericks also had what seemed to be a certain wariness on his sim face as he sat down.

He? Orlando felt a kind of despair. *She?*

"I got your message."

Orlando shook his head. "I . . . I just didn't want to . . ." He took a breath and started again. "I don't know. I'm pretty scorched, but mostly in a weird way. Know what I mean?"

Fredericks nodded slowly. "Yeah. I guess."

"So—so what do I call you?"

"Fredericks. That was a tough one, huh?" A smile briefly touched the broad face.

"Yeah, but I mean . . . you're a girl. But I think of you as a guy."

"That's okay. I think of myself as a guy, too. When I'm stringing around with you."

Orlando sat quiet for a moment, sensing that this particular unexplored country might be treacherous. "You mean you're a transsexual?"

"No." His friend shrugged. "I just . . . well, sometimes I get bored being a girl. So when I first started going on the net, sometimes I was a boy, that's all. Nothing unusual, really." Fredericks did not sound quite as certain as he or she might have liked. "But it's kind of awkward when you get to be friends with someone."

"I noticed." He said it with his best Johnny Icepick sneer. "So do you like boys, or are you gay, or what?"

Fredericks made a noise of disgust. "I like boys fine. I have lots of friends who are boys. I have lots of friends who are girls, too. Shit, Gardiner, you're as bad as my parents. They think I have to make all these life decisions just because I'm growing breasts."

For a moment Orlando felt the world totter. The concept of Fredericks with breasts was more than he was able to deal with at the moment.

"So . . . so that's it? You're just going to be a guy? I mean, when you're online?"

Fredericks nodded again. "I guess. It wasn't a total lie, Orlando. When I'm hanging around with you . . . well, I *feel* like a guy."

Orlando snorted. "How would you know?"

Fredericks looked hurt, then angry. "I get stupid and I act like the whole world revolves around me. That's how."

Against his better judgment, Orlando laughed. "So what are we supposed to do? Just keep on being guys together?"

"I guess so." Fredericks shrugged. "If you can handle it."

Orlando felt his anger soften a little. There were certainly important things he hadn't told Fredericks, so it was hard to sustain much self-righteousness. But it was still difficult to wrap his mind around the idea.

"Well," he said at last, "I guess . . . " He couldn't think of any way
to end the sentence that wouldn't sound like a bad netflick. He settled
for: "I guess it's okay, then." It was an incredibly stupid thing to say,
and he wasn't sure it *was* okay, but he left it at that for now. "Anyway,
this all started because I was trying to find you. Where have you been?
Why didn't you answer my messages?"

Fredericks eyed him, perhaps trying to decide if they had found a
kind of equilibrium again. "I . . . I was scared, Gardiner. And if you
think it's because I'm really a girl or some *fenfen* like that, I'm gonna
kill you."

"Scared of what happened in TreeHouse?"

"Of everything. You've been weird ever since you saw that city, and
it just keeps getting more and more scanny. What's next, we try to
overthrow the government or something? We wind up in the Execution Chamber for the cause of Orlando Gardinerism? I just don't want
to get into any more trouble."

"Trouble? What trouble? We got chased out of TreeHouse by a
bunch of old *akisushi.*"

Fredericks shook his head. "It's more than that and you know it.
What's going on, Gardiner? What is it about this city that's got you so
. . . so obsessed?"

Orlando weighed the choices. Did he owe something to Fredericks,
some kind of honesty? But his friend had not told him anything of his
own secret voluntarily—it had been Orlando who had ferreted out the
truth.

"I can't explain. Not now. But it's important—I just know it is. And
I think I've found a way to get us back into TreeHouse."

"What?" Fredericks shouted. The other patrons of the Last Chance
Saloon, used to death rattles and agonized shrieks, did not even turn
to look. "Go *back?* Are you *scanning to the uttermost degree?*"

"Maybe." He was finding it hard to get his breath again. He turned
down the volume for another body-shaking cough. "Maybe," he repeated when he could speak again. "But I need you to come with me.
You're my friend, Fredericks, whatever you are. In fact, I'll tell you
one secret, anyway—you're not just my best friend, you're my only
friend."

Fredericks brought hands to face, as though to block out the sight
of a world in pain. When he spoke, it was with doomful resignation.
"Oh, Gardiner, you bastard. That's really unfair."

CHAPTER 29

Tomb of Glass

NETFEED/ENTERTAINMENT: *Blackness Wins Palme D'Or*
(visual: Ostrand accepting prize)
VO: *Pikke Ostrand seemed unsurprised at winning the grand prize at this year's Nîmes Film Festival, although most of the other insiders on the beaches and in the bars were stunned. Ms. Ostrand's four-hour film, Blackness, which except for low-light effects and subliminal sonics contains nothing but the blackness of the title, was considered too miserabilist to please the usually conservative judges.*
(visual: Ostrand at press conference)
OSTRAND: *"It is what it is. If you tell some people about smoke, they want to see the fire, too."*

One moment there was only the light of the fire !Xabbu had built, a soft red glow which left the corners and high places of the lab their mysteries. Then, following a series of clicks, the overhead fixtures sprang back on, washing white brilliance into every cranny.

"You did it, Martine!" Renie clapped her hands. "Every Pinetown resident's dream—free electricity!"

"I can't take all the credit." The humble deity's voice now echoed from the built-in wallspeakers, filling the room. "I could not have done it without Mister Singh. I had to get past some very formidable power company security before I could redistribute the electricity usage information to hide the trail."

"That's all very nice, but can I go now and do some goddamn *work?*" Singh sounded genuinely irritated. "This entire folly presupposes me being able to get through Otherland's defenses in the next few days, so if I don't manage to crack that, all this means is that you've found yourselves some really ugly-looking bathtubs."

"Of course," said Renie quickly. She definitely wanted and needed to stay on the old man's good side. She thanked him and Martine again, then let them disconnect.

"You can close the outside door and take the jack out of the car-phone," she announced to Jeremiah, who had been waiting on the now-functional phone at the entrance. "We have electricity *and* data-lines now, and they should both be untraceable."

"I'm doing it, Renie." Even through the small pad speaker, she could hear the outside door beginning to grind down. A moment later he came back on. "I don't like seeing that door close. I feel like I'm being locked in the tomb."

"Not a tomb at all," she said, ignoring her own quite similar impressions. "Unless it's Lazarus' tomb you're talking about. Because this is where we're finally going to start fighting back. Come downstairs. We've still got a lot of work to do." She looked up to see her father watching her. She thought he looked scornful. "Well, we *are* going to fight back. And we're going to see Stephen back among the living again, Papa. So don't give me that look."

"What look? God help me, girl, I don't know what you talking about sometimes."

As soon as the lights had come back on, !Xabbu had put out the fire. Now, as he stirred the last few embers with a stick, he turned to Renie. "There have been many things happening," he said. "Happening very fast. Perhaps we should sit and talk, all of us, about what we will do next."

Renie considered, then nodded. "But not now. I'm really anxious to get these V-tanks checked out. Can we do it this evening, before bed?"

!Xabbu smiled. "If anyone is the elder upon whose wisdom we rely, Renie, here in this place it is you. This evening would be a good time, I think."

The preliminary news seemed to be better even than Renie had hoped. The V-tanks, although cumbersome compared to more recent interface devices, seemed to have the potential to do what she needed—allow her long-term access and much more sophisticated sensory input and output than anything she had used at the Poly. Only an actual implant would have been better in terms of responsiveness, but there were some advantages to the V-tanks that even an implant couldn't match: because they seemed to have been expressly developed for long-term use, the tanks were fitted out with feeding, hydration, and waste processing equipment, so that with only occasional assistance, the user could be almost completely independent.

"But what *is* that stuff?" Her father stared into the opened casket, his mouth twisted in distaste. "Smell like something foul."

"It's gel." She reached her hand down and touched it with her finger. "At least, it will be."

Long Joseph cautiously extended one of his own callused digits and tapped on the translucent material. "This is no jelly, or if it is, it's all dried up and nasty. This some kind of plastic."

Renie shook her head. "It needs to be hooked up properly. You'll see. When you run a very mild current through it, it gets harder or softer, colder or warmer, in any part of the gel you want. Then there's the micropumps," she pointed to the array of pinprick holes on the inside wall of the tank, "to adjust the pressure. And the processors, the computer brains of the thing, will sense whenever you push back against the gel—that's the output part. That's why it makes such a good interface—it can mimic almost anything in a simulation, wind on your skin, rock under your feet, humidity, you name it."

He looked at her with a mixture of suspicion and pride. "You learn about all this stuff at that school you went to?"

"Some of it. I read a lot about this plasmodal process, because for a while it was going to be the next big thing. They still use it for other industrial stuff, I think, but most of the high-end computer interfaces now are direct neural connections."

Long Joseph stood up and regarded the ten-foot-long tank. "And you say that you put electricity in here? Right in this thing? In the jelly?"

"That's what makes it work."

He shook his head. "Well, girl, I don't care what you say. Only a fool climbs into a bathtub full of electricity. I won't get into something like that, ever."

Renie's smile was a little sour. "That's right, Papa. You won't."

It had been a very successful afternoon, Renie thought. With help from Martine, who had maintained her connection to whatever (no doubt quite illicit) source of information had brought them here in the first place, they had begun to understand how the V-tanks could be made ready. It would not be easy—Renie figured it would be several days' worth of hard going at least—but in the end, they should be able to make the things work.

The military had done more to help them than simply leave much of the equipment in place. The automated systems that had kept the underground location safe from intrusion—until now, anyway—had also kept the air dry and the gross machinery of the place in working order. Several of the tanks had still suffered damage from neglect, but Renie had no doubt that if they cannibalized a few parts, they could get at least one and perhaps more online. The computers themselves, which would supply the processing power, were hopelessly old-fashioned, but they were the biggest and best of their day. Renie thought that by a similar process of robbing Peter to pay Paul, they could get enouch CPUs working that a software alteration or two—something else they would need the old hacker Singh to accomplish—would enable them to get the power and speed necessary to make the V-tanks perform.

She scraped her spoon in the bottom of the bowl, finishing off the casserole Jeremiah had made, and risked a small sigh of content. Prospects were still bleak, but they were far less hopeless than they had seemed a few days ago.

"Renie, we said tonight we would talk." Even !Xabbu's quiet voice echoed in the huge, empty dining room.

"We're just about out of food, for one thing," Jeremiah reminded her.

"There must be emergency rations here somewhere," Renie said. "This place was built during the first Antarctica war scare, I think. They probably made this place capable of being self-sufficient for years."

Jeremiah gave her a look of undisguised horror. "Emergency rations? Do you mean meat cubes and powdered milk? Horrid things like that?"

"Do you remember what happened to you the last time you tried to use your card? You can only use cash so many times before someone notices, especially outside the inner city. Not that we have much cash left, anyway."

"So what does that mean?" He pointed to the casserole dish. "No more fresh food?"

Renie took a breath, struggling to be patient. "Jeremiah, this is not a holiday. This is serious business. The people we're after killed Doctor Van Bleeck!"

He gave her an angry, pained look. "I know that."

"Then help me! The whole point of being here is to give us a chance to get into this Otherland."

"I still think it's crazy," her father said. "Come all this way, all this work, just to play some computer trick. How all this going to help Stephen?"

"Do I need to explain it again? This Otherland thing is a network, an incredibly big and fast VR network like no other, and it's also a secret—a secret people will kill for. It belongs to the people who hurt Stephen and a lot of other children, the people who murdered Doctor Van Bleeck and probably firebombed our flat and got me fired from the Poly. Not to mention all of Mister Singh's friends who worked on it with him, and are now dead.

"These are rich people—powerful people. No one can get to them. No one can take them to court. And what would we say even if we got them there? All we have are suspicions, and pretty crazy-sounding suspicions they are, too.

"So we need to get inside this Otherland. If something about that network is the reason for what's happened to Stephen and other children—if they are using it to run black-market organ farms, or as the centerpiece of some kind of child pornography cult, or something we can't even imagine yet, some kind of political power play, or cornering the world market in something—then we need to get proof."

She looked around the table. At last, even her father was being attentive. Renie felt a rare moment of confidence and control. "If we can get a V-tank up and running, and if Singh can crack Otherland's network security, I'm going in with him. The tanks are meant to work long-term, with very little maintenance. That means there won't be much for the three of you to do once I've got my IVs and oxygen going, maybe just check on things every now and then. I think that !Xabbu alone should be able to do that."

"So what about us?" asked her father. "Just sit around while you playing in your jelly bath?"

"I don't know. I guess that's why we need to talk. To plan."

"What about Stephen? I'm supposed to sit here while that boy still sick in the hospital? That quarantine thing not gonna last forever."

"I don't know, Papa. Jeremiah's worried about his mother, too. But remember, these people don't hesitate to kill when they need to. At the very least, if you got caught outside you'd both get picked up and detained." She shrugged. "I don't know anything else you can do except stay here."

During the long silence that followed, Renie looked up to see !Xabbu watching her. He had a strangely abstracted expression. Before she could ask him what he thought, a beep from the wall speaker made them all jump.

"I have found some more information about the tanks," Martine announced, "and have downloaded it to the laboratory memory. Also, Sagar Singh called me to say that he has hit a 'rough patch,' as he calls it, and says that you should not get up your hopes he will be able to help you with the tank software."

"What does that mean?"

"I am not sure. The security system is very complicated for this Otherland network, and it is not very much used, so he finds it hard to work without attracting attention. He says it is only a chance of fifty-fifty he will be able to break in."

Renie felt her insides sink. "I suppose we've never had odds much better than that with any of this. From the start."

"But he also said that if he can do it, you must be ready to go very quickly."

"Wonderful. So he won't be able to help us, but we have to get the tanks ready right away."

Martine's laugh was rueful. "Something like that, yes. But I will help as much as I can, Renie."

"You've already been more help than I can say." Renie sighed. Her buoyant spirits had collapsed, punctured by reality. "We all will do what we have to do."

"Martine, I have a question," !Xabbu said. "Is it true that the data lines from this place are shielded? That they will not give us away if we use them?"

" 'Shielded' is not what I would say. I have routed them through various nodes which feed them through randomly chosen outgoing lines. That way, a trace will only follow them as far back as the last node, and there is no obvious connection from that node to the original source. It is a common practice."

"What does all *that* mean?" asked Long Joseph.

"So we can use the lines going in and out of here, even to ship data?" !Xabbu seemed to want something clarified.

"Yes. You should still use them responsibly. I would not call Telemorphix or UNComm and taunt them."

"God, no," Renie said in horror. "Nobody around here is going to ask for trouble, Martine. We already have enough."

"Good. Does that answer your question?"

"It does." !Xabbu nodded.

"Why did you want to know that?" Renie asked the small man after Martine had ended her call.

For one of the first times since she had known him, !Xabbu looked uncomfortable. "I would prefer not to say at this moment, Renie. But I promise you I will not do anything irresponsible, as Martine warned."

She was tempted to push him for an answer, but felt that after what they had been through, he deserved her trust. "I didn't think you would, !Xabbu."

"If the phone lines are safe, I could call my mother," Jeremiah said eagerly.

Renie felt a heavy weariness. "I think that falls under the heading of 'asking for touble,' Jeremiah. If they've managed to put a hold on your cards, then they've also probably managed to get a tap on your mother's phone line."

"But that Martine said the calls couldn't be traced!"

"Probably." Renie sighed again. "Probably. But she also said don't ask for trouble, and calling a number that's almost certainly tapped is asking for trouble."

Jeremiah's face darkened in anger. "You're not my master, young lady. You don't tell me what to do."

Before she could reply—and it would have been with some heat— !Xabbu spoke up. "Renie is doing her best for all of us. None of us is happy, Mister Dako. Instead of being angry, perhaps there is some other solution."

Grateful for his intervention, Renie followed his lead. "That's a good idea, !Xabbu. Jeremiah, are there any of your relatives we could reach through a public kiosk?" She knew that in Pinetown, among those who couldn't afford a regular dataline service, many people used the communal kiosks, and would fetch whichever neighbors were being called. "I doubt they'd tap every single kiosk near every one of your relatives. We haven't been declared public enemies, so this stuff has to be done fairly quietly."

As Jeremiah paused to think, his anger diffused, Renie smiled at !Xabbu, letting him know she appreciated his help. The little man still looked troubled.

"**W**e have two tanks that are complete," said !Xabbu.

Renie turned from her inspection of one of the objects in question.

She had been testing a handful of rubber-sheathed fiberlinks which hung from the tank's lid like the tentacles of an octopus dangling from a rock crevice. "I know. That way we have a backup if something goes wrong with the first one."

!Xabbu shook his head. "That is not what I mean, Renie. We have two. You are thinking that you will go by yourself, but that is not right. I have accompanied you before. We are friends."

"You want to break into this Otherland system with me? For Heaven's sake, !Xabbu, haven't I got you into enough trouble already? In any case, I'm not going in by myself—Singh's going, and maybe Martine as well."

"There is more to it than that. You are exposing yourself to more danger. Do you not remember the Kali? We have stood by each other, and should do so again."

Renie saw by his stubborn look that this would not end quickly. She let go of the snaky fibers. "But . . ." She suddenly could not think of an argument. More, she realized how much better she would feel if !Xabbu did accompany her. She still felt compelled to make a token protest. "But who will take care of things out here if we're both online? I told you, this could last days . . . maybe weeks."

"Jeremiah is intelligent and responsible. Your father is also capable, if he understands the importance. And as you said yourself, there is not much that needs to be done except to monitor us."

"So it's 'us' already?" She couldn't help but smile. "I don't know. I suppose you have as much right as I do."

"My life, too, has been caught up in this." The small man remained serious. "I have made the journey with you willingly. I could not turn back at this point."

She felt suddenly as though she might cry. He was so stern, so grave, and yet no larger than a boy. He had taken on her responsibilities as though they were his own, seemingly without a second thought. That kind of loyalty was so strange as to be a little frightening.

How did this man become so dear to me so quickly? The thought bloomed with surprising force. *He's like a brother—a brother my own age, not a child like Stephen who needs to be looked after.*

Or was there more to it than that? Her feelings were confused.

"Okay, then." She turned back to the fiberlinks, afraid that the warmth in her cheeks might show, might send him some sign she did not wish sent. "You asked for it. If Jeremiah and my father say yes, then you and I go together."

* * *

"I still say you crazy, girl," her father said.

"It's not as dangerous as you think, Papa." She lifted the thin, flexible mask. "This fits over your face. It's not that different from what a diver wears. See, there's a place where it locks down over your eyes—that's so the retinal projection stays focused. 'Retinal projection' just means it shoots a picture onto the back of your eye. That's pretty much how you normally see, so it makes the visual input feel very real. And here's how you breathe." She pointed to three valves, two small, one large, that made a triangle. "This fits over your nose and mouth, a very tight seal, and the air is pumped in and out through these tubes. Simple. As long as you and Jeremiah keep an eye on the air mixture, we'll be fine."

Long Joseph shook his head. "I can't stop you, so I won't even try. But if something goes all wrong, don't you come blame it on me."

"Thanks for that vote of confidence." She turned to Jeremiah. "I hope *you've* been paying attention, anyway."

"I'll keep a close eye on everything." He looked at the wallscreen a little nervously. "You're just testing it now, right? You're only going in for a short while?"

"Maybe as little as ten minutes, maybe a bit longer. Just to make sure we've got everything hooked up properly." She stared at the taped bundles of fiberlinks stretching between the two tanks and the old-fashioned processors. "Keep a close eye on the vital function readings, okay? I've tested everything as well as I can, but even with Martine and her schematics, there are so many damned hookups I'm not certain about anything." She turned to !Xabbu, who was rechecking his own tank, connection by connection, just as he had seen her do. "Are you ready?"

"If you are, Renie."

"Okay. What should we do? Some simple 3D manipulations, like the ones I used to teach you back at the Poly? Those should be comfortably familiar."

"Certainly. And then perhaps something else."

"Like what?"

"Let us wait and see." He turned away to unkink mask connectors which had surely been unkinked long before.

Renie shrugged. "Jeremiah? Can you turn on the tanks now? The main power switches?"

There was a click and then a quiet hum. For a brief instant the overhead lights flickered. Renie leaned forward to stare into the tank.

What appeared to be hard translucent plastic filling three-fourths of the tank turned foggily opaque. A few moments later the substance went clear again, but now seemed to be a liquid. Tiny ripples appeared in its surface, thousands of them in concentric whorls like finger-prints, but before she could make out the larger pattern, the ripples subsided.

"How are the readings?" she asked.

Jeremiah opened a series of windows on the wallscreen. "Everything is right where you wanted it." He sounded nervous.

"Okay. Here we go." Now that the moment had come she was suddenly apprehensive, as though poised at the end of a high diving board. She pulled her shirt over her head and stood for a moment in bra and knickers, looking down from the edge of the tank. Despite the warmth of the room, she felt her skin go pebbly.

It's just an interface, she told herself. *Just input-output, like a touchscreen. You let your father and his electricity-in-the-bathtub get to you, girl.* Besides, this was going to be a lot easier than when they did it for real—no catheters, no IV lines, and only down for a short time.

She pulled the mask over her face, inserting the plugs into her nostrils and positioning the flexible bubble with its built-in microphone over her mouth. Jeremiah had already started the pumps: except for a faint metallic coldness, the air tasted and felt quite unexceptional. The hearplugs were easy, but it was a little more difficult to get the eyepieces centered properly. When she finally got them locked down, she lowered herself into the tank by touch.

The gel had reached stasis—skin temperature and the same density as her body, so that she floated, weightless. She slowly stretched out her arms to make sure she was centered. The edge of the tank was beyond the reach of both hands; she was hanging in the center of nothing, a small, collapsed star. The darkness and silence were absolute. Renie waited in emptiness for Jeremiah to trigger the initial sequence. It seemed a long wait.

Light leaped into her eyes. The universe suddenly had depth again, although it was an unmeasurable gray depth. She could feel a subtle pressure shift as the hydraulics tilted the V-tank upright to its working angle of ninety degrees. She settled slightly. She had weight, although not much: the floating sensation was replaced by a gentle sensation of gravity, although the gel could adjust that back to weightlessness or whatever else a simulation might call for.

Another figure appeared, hovering before her. It was a bare-bones sim, little more than an international symbol for humanoid.

"!Xabbu? How are you feeling?"

"Very strange. It is different from the Harness Room. I feel much more as though I am . . . *in* something."

"I know what you mean. Let's try it out." She flashed a few hand-commands and created a darker gray plane beneath them that stretched to a putative horizon, giving the empty space an up and down. They settled onto the plane and felt it flat and hard beneath their feet.

"Is that the bottom of the tank?" asked !Xabbu.

"No, it's just the gel hardening where the processors tell it to harden. Here." She summoned up a ball the same color as the ground. It felt quite substantial beneath her fingers. She deliberately softened it to the consistency of rubber: the processors obliged. "Catch!"

!Xabbu reached up and plucked the ball from the air. "And this, too, is the gel, hardening where we are supposed to feel an object?"

"That's right. It may not even make a whole object, but just give us the correct tactile impressions on our hands."

"And when I throw it," he lobbed it underhand back to Renie, "it is analyzing the arc that it should make, then recreating that, first in my tank, then in yours?"

"Right. Just like what we did in school, except with better equipment. Your tank could be on the other side of the earth, but if I can see you here, the substance in these tanks will make the experience fit."

!Xabbu shook his rudimentary head in appreciation. "I have said it before, Renie, but your science can indeed do wonderful things."

She snorted. "It's not really my science. Besides, as we've already seen, it can do some pretty dreadful things, too."

They created and arranged a few more objects, checking the calibration of the tactor system and the various effects—temperature, gravity—not available on the Poly's more primitive harness system. Renie found herself wishing she had a more sophisticated simulation to work with, something that would give her a real idea of how the tanks could perform. Still, it had been a good first day. "I think we've done what we needed to," she said. "Anything else you want to try?"

"Yes, actually." !Xabbu—or his featureless sim—turned to face her. "Do not worry. I have something to share with you." He waved several hand-commands. The gray universe disappeared, dropping them into blackness.

"What are you doing?" she asked, alarmed.

"Please. I will show you."

Renie held herself still, fighting hard against the urge to thrash around, to demand answers. She did not like letting someone else control things.

Just when the wait seemed interminable, a glow began to spread before her. It started as a deep red, then broke into marbled patterns of white and gold and scarlet and a deep velvety purple. Broken by this glaring brilliance, the darkness formed itself into strange shapes; light and dark swirled and commingled. The light grew steadily brighter in one spot, coalescing at last into a disk so bright she could not look at it directly. The dark areas took on shape and depth as they settled to the bottom of her field of vision like sand poured into a glass of water.

She stood in the middle of a vast, flat landscape painted in harshly brilliant light, broken only by stunted trees and the humps of red rocks. Overhead the sun smoldered like a white-hot ingot.

"It's a desert," she said. "My God, !Xabbu, where did this come from?"

"I made it."

She turned and her surprise deepened. !Xabbu stood beside her, recognizably himself. Gone was the impersonal sim from the military lab's operating system, replaced by something very close to her friend's own small, slim form. Even the face, despite a certain smooth stiffness, was his own. !Xabbu's sim wore what she guessed was the traditional garb of his people, a loincloth made of hide, sandals, and a string of eggshell beads around the neck. A quiver and bow hung from one shoulder and he held a spear in his hand.

"You made this? All of this?"

He smiled. "It is not as much as it seems, Renie. Parts of it are borrowed from other modules on the Kalahari Desert. There is much free gear available. I found some academic simulations—ecological models, evolutionary biology projects—in the University of Natal databanks. This is my graduate project." His smile widened. "You have not looked at yourself yet."

She looked down. Her legs were bare, and she, too, wore a loincloth. She had more jewelry than !Xabbu, and a sort of shawl of hide that covered her upper body, tied at the waist with rough twine. Remembering that they were supposed to be testing the V-tanks, she fingered it. The cured skin felt slithery and a little tacky, not unlike the thing it was supposed to be.

"That is called a *kaross*." !Xabbu pointed to the place where the shawl gaped at the back. "The women of my people use it as much more than a garment. Nursing babies are carried there, and also forage discovered during the day."

"And this?" She held up the piece of wood clutched in her other hand.

"A digging stick."

She laughed. "This is astonishing, !Xabbu. Where did this come from? I mean, how did it get onto this system? You couldn't have done all this since we got here."

He shook his head, sim face grave. "I copied it from my storage at the Poly."

Renie felt a clutch of alarm. "!Xabbu!"

"I had Martine's help. Just to be safe, we shipped it through . . . what did she call it? An 'offshore router.' And I left you a message."

"What are you talking about?"

"While I was in the Poly's system, I left a message on your account there. I said that I had been trying to reach you, and hoped to speak to you soon about my studies and my graduate project."

Renie shook her head. She heard tinkling, and reached up to touch her dangling earrings. "I don't understand."

"I thought that if someone was looking for your contacts, it would be good if they thought I did not know where you were. Maybe then they would not persecute my landlady. She was not a pleasant person, but she did not deserve the sort of trouble we have had. But, Renie, I am unhappy."

She was finding it hard to keep up. "Why, !Xabbu?"

"Because I realized as I was leaving the message that I was deliberately telling a lie. I have never done that before. I fear that I am changing. It is no surprise that I have lost the song of the sun."

Even behind the mask of his simulation, Renie could see the small man's discomfort.

This is what I was afraid of. She could think of no comfort to give him. With any other friend, she would have argued the ethics of the useful lie, the self-projecting falsehood—but no other friend would feel a lie as a sort of physical corruption; she could not imagine anyone else in her life despairing because he could not hear the sun's voice.

"Show me more." It was all she could say. "Tell me about this place."

"It is only just begun." He reached out and touched her arm, as though to thank her for the distraction. "It is not enough to make something that looks like the home of my people—it must *feel* like it as well, and I am not yet skilled enough for that." He began to walk, and Renie fell in beside him. "But I have made a small piece, in part to learn the lessons that come from mistakes. Do you see that?" He pointed to the horizon. Above the desert pan, just visible beyond a stand of thorny acacias, loomed a cluster of dark shapes. "Those are the Tsodilo Hills, a very important place for my people, a sacred place you would call it. But I have made them too easily visible, too stark."

She stared. Despite his discontent, there was something compelling about the hills, the only tall things in this wide, flat land. If the real ones were even remotely similar, she could understand the power they must hold over the imaginations of !Xabbu's people.

Renie reached up and stroked her earrings again, then touched the eggshell necklaces at her throat. "How about me? Do I look as much like me as you look like yourself?"

He shook his head. "That would have been presumptuous. No, my own sim was concocted from an earlier project at the Poly. I added to it for this, but at the moment I have only two other sims, male and female. They are made to look like a man and woman of my people." His smile was sad and a little bitter. "In this place, anyway, I shall make sure no one comes onto Bushman land but Bushmen."

He led her down a sandy slope, deeper into the pan. Flies hummed lazily. The sun was so fierce that Renie found herself longing for a drink of water, despite the fact that they had surely been in the tanks less than half an hour. She almost wished they had hooked up the hydration system, despite her dislike of needles.

"Here," said !Xabbu. He squatted on his heels and began to dig with the butt of his spear. "Help me."

"What are we looking for?"

He did not answer, but concentrated on digging. The work was hard, and the heat of the sun made it even more tiring. For a moment, Renie completely forgot that they were in a simulation.

"There." !Xabbu leaned forward. Using his fingers, he unearthed something that looked like a small watermelon from the bottom of the hole. He lifted it triumphantly. "This is a *tsama*. These melons keep my people alive in the bush during the season of drought, when the springs have no more water." He took his knife and cut the melon's top off, then took the butt of his spear, wiped it clean of dirt, and pushed it into the melon. He worked it like a pestle until the fruit's contents were a liquified pulp. "Now you drink it," he said, smiling.

"But I can't drink—or at least I can't taste anything."

He nodded. "But when my simulation is complete, you will have to drink, whether you can taste it or not. No one can live like my people if they do not struggle to find water and food in this harsh land."

Renie took the *tsama* rind and upended it over her mouth. There was a curious absence of sensation around her face, but she could feel little splatters of wetness down her neck and belly. !Xabbu took it from her, said something she could not understand, full of clicks and trills, and drank from the melon himself.

"Come," he said. "There are other things I wish to show you."

She stood, troubled. "This is wonderful, but Jeremiah and my father will be worried about us if we're on too long. I didn't tell him how to monitor our conversation, and I doubt he'd be able to figure it out on his own. They might even try to pull us out."

"Knowing I would show you this place, I told them we might be longer than you had planned." !Xabbu looked at her for a moment, then nodded. "But you are right. I am being selfish."

"No, you're not. This is wonderful." She meant it. Even if he had cobbled it together from other modules, he had an incredible flair for virtual engineering. She could only pray that his association with her ended happily. After seeing even this small piece, she thought it would be a crime if his dream went unfulfilled. "It's truly wonderful. I hope to spend a lot more hours here someday soon, !Xabbu."

"Do we have time for something else? It is important to me."

"Of course."

"Then come with me a little way farther." He led her forward. Although they walked what seemed to be only a few hundred yards, the hills were suddenly much closer, looming overhead like stern parents. In their shadow stood a small circle of grass shelters.

"This is unnatural, to move so fast, but I know our time is short." !Xabbu took her wrist and drew her to an empty stretch of sandy soil before one of the shelters. A pile of small sticks was already laid out there. "I must also do one more unnatural thing." He gestured. The sun began to move swiftly; in moments it had completely disappeared behind the hills and the sky had darkened to violet. "Now I will build a fire."

!Xabbu took two sticks from his pouch. "Male stick, female stick," he said with a smile. "That is what we say." He placed one into an indentation in the other, then held the second to the ground with his feet while he rapidly spun the first between his palms. From time to time he plucked bits of dry grass from his pouch and pushed them into the indentation. Within moments, the grass was smoking.

The stars had burst into view in the night sky overhead and the temperature was dropping rapidly. Renie shivered. She hoped her friend would get the fire going soon, even if that meant stretching accuracy a little.

As !Xabbu transferred the smoldering grass to the pile of sticks, she leaned back, looking at the sky. It was so wide! Wider and deeper than it ever seemed over Durban. And the stars seemed so close—she almost felt she could reach up and touch them.

The fire was surprisingly small, but she could feel its warmth. However, !Xabbu did not give her much chance to enjoy it. He took two strings of what appeared to be dried cocoons from his pouch and tied one around each of his ankles. When he shook them, they made a soft buzzing rattle.

"Come." He rose and beckoned. "Now we will dance."

"Dance?"

"Do you see the moon?" He pointed. It floated in the blackness like a pearl in a pool of oil. "And the ring around it? Those are the marks that the spirits make when they dance around it, for they feel it to be a fire, a fire just like this." He reached out and took her hand. Although a part of her could not forget that they were in separate tanks, yards apart, she also felt his familiar presence. However physics might define it, he was definitely holding her hand, leading her into a strange hopping dance.

"I don't know anything about . . ."

"It is a healing dance. It is important. We have a journey ahead of us, and we have suffered much pain already. Just do as I do."

She did her best to follow his lead. At first she found it difficult, but then, when she stopped trying to think about it, she began to feel the rhythm. After a while, she felt nothing but the rhythm—*shake, step, shake, shake, step, head back, arms up*—and always there was the quiet whisper of !Xabbu's rattles and the soft slap of their feet on the sand.

They danced on beneath the ringed moon, before the hills that bulked black against the stars. For a while, Renie quite forgot everything else.

She pulled off her mask before she was all the way out of the gel, and for a moment found herself choking. Her father's hands were under her arms and he was pulling her out of the tank.

"No!" she said, fighting for breath. "Not yet." She cleared her throat. "I have to scrape the rest of this stuff off me and put it back in the tank—it's hard to replace, so there's no point dripping it all over the floor."

"You were down a long time," her father said angrily. "We thought the two of you gone brain-dead or something. That man said not to bring you up, that your friend say it's okay."

"I'm sorry, Papa." She looked over to !Xabbu, who was seated on the edge of his own tank scraping gel. Renie smiled at him. "It was amazing. You should see what !Xabbu's made. How long were we under?"

"Almost two hours," said Jeremiah disapprovingly.

"Two hours! My God!" Renie was shocked. *We must have spent at least an hour of that dancing.* "I'm so sorry! You must have been worried to death."

Jeremiah made a disgusted face. "We could see that your breathing and heart and whatnot were all normal. But we were waiting for you to come back and join us because that French woman's been wanting to talk to you. Important message, she said."

"What? What did Martine want? You should have brought us back out."

"We never know what you expect," said her father, scowling. "All this craziness—how someone supposed to know when he going to get shouted at? What he supposed to do?"

"All right, all right. I said I was sorry. What was the message?"

"She say call her when you come out."

Renie wrapped a military-issue bathrobe around her still-sticky form, then called Martine's exchange number. The mystery woman was on the line within moments.

"I am so glad you have called. Was the experiment a successful one?"

"Excellent, but I can tell you about that later. They said you had an urgent message."

"Yes, from Monsieur Singh. He said to tell you that he thinks he may have found a way to beat the Otherland security. But he also said levels of use have gone up dramatically in the past few days—the network is very busy, which may mean something important is about to happen. Perhaps that was the meaning of the hourglass, the calendar. The ten days are almost up, in any case. We dare not wait for another opportunity."

Renie's heart sped. "Which means?"

"Which means that Singh will go in tomorrow. What he cannot do by planning, he will trust to luck, he said. And if you are joining us, you will have to do it then—there may not be another chance."

CHAPTER 30

In the Emperor's Gardens

Hurley Brummond stood at the helm of the airboat, wheel clenched in one hand, his stern, bearded profile silhouetted by the light of Ullamar's two moons.

"We'll tweak their noses, Jonas!" he bellowed over the roar of the wind. "The greenskin priests will learn they can't go fiddling about with an Earthman's fiancée!"

Paul wanted to ask a question, but he didn't have the heart to shout. Brummond had returned to his figurehead pose, staring down on the lantern-lit towers of Tuktubim. Paul had wanted to find the winged woman again, but he was not entirely sure that this was the way he wanted to go about it.

"Hurley's got his blood up now," said Professor Bagwalter. "It really won't do any good to fret. But never fear—he's mad as a March hare, but if anyone can get the job done, he can."

The airboat abruptly lurched downward, making the ship's brass fittings rattle. Paul put out a hand to steady himself, then reached to make sure Gally had not been knocked over. The boy was wide-eyed, but seemed more excited than frightened.

The airboat's angle of descent steepened. With the ship plunging downward at such an angle that it was all Paul could do simply to hold on to the railing, Hurley Brummond left his position at the helm, dragging himself forward hand over hand along the railing, then tugged at a great metal handle on the back of the ship's cabin. All the ship's lanterns, on the bow, on the sailcloth wings, and along the hull, suddenly went dark. The airboat continued to plummet.

A towertop suddenly leaped up on one side of the ship and flashed upward past them. Another daggered up just beyond the rail on Paul's side, so close he felt he could touch it. A third sprouted beside the first. Terrified, Paul looked through the carved railing. The ship was hurtling down toward an entire forest of needle-sharp minarets.

"My God!" Paul jerked Gally toward him, although he knew there was nothing he could do to protect the boy. "We're going to . . ."

The ship suddenly bottomed out, throwing Paul and the others to the deck. A moment later it shuddered to a halt in midair, hovering in the midst of a thicket of pointed roofs. Brummond had scrambled back to the helm. "Sorry about the bump," he brayed. "Had to snuff the lanterns, though! We're going to *surprise* them."

As Paul helped Gally to his feet, Brummond was tipping a furled rope ladder over the railing. As it rustled down into darkness, he straightened with a satisfied smile on his face.

"Perfect. We're right over the Imperial Gardens, just as I thought. They'll never expect us to go that way. We'll be in and out with your fair lady in the blink of an eye, Jonas old man."

Professor Bagwalter was still kneeling on the deck, searching for his glasses. "I say, Hurley, that was a bit uncalled-for, wasn't it? I mean, couldn't we have made a bit more leisurely approach?"

Brummond shook his head with obvious fondness. "Bags, you old stick-in-the-mud! You know my motto: 'Move like the wind, strike like lightning.' We aren't going to give these ghastly priest chappies a chance to spirit our quarry away. Now, let's get cracking. Jonas, you'll come, of course. Bags, I know you're anxious for a little action, but perhaps you should stay here with the ship, be ready to take off. Besides, someone ought to keep an eye on the young lad."

"I want to go!" Gally's eyes were bright.

"No, against my rules." Brummond shook his head. "What do you say, Bags? I know it's hard cheese on you, but just this once perhaps you should give the adventure side a miss."

The professor did not seem unduly put out. In fact, Paul thought he seemed grateful for the excuse. "If you think it best, Hurley."

"That's settled, then. Let me just strap on old Betsy here . . ." Brummond opened the lid of a trunk beside the steering wheel and removed a sheathed cavalry saber, which he belted around his hips. He turned to Paul. "How about you, old man? Weapon of choice? I might have put a pistol or two in here, but you'll have to promise not to spark one off until I give the word." Brummond pulled out a pair of what to Paul seemed vaguely archaic sidearms and peered down their barrels. "Good. Both loaded." He passed them over to Paul, who shoved them in his belt. "After all, we don't want to let the priests know we're on our way any earlier than we have to, hmmmm?" Brummond continued to dig in the chest. "So you'll need something to start with, too. Ah, just the ticket."

He straightened up, holding an outlandishly ornate weapon that seemed part ax, part spear, and which stood two-thirds of Paul's height. "Here you go. It's a Vonari *saljak*. Surprisingly good for close-in work, and rather appropriate, since your fiancée's one of 'em. A Vonari, I mean."

As Paul stared at the strange, filigreed weapon, Brummond trotted to the railing and swung his leg over. "Come on, old man. Time to go." Feeling almost helpless, as though he moved through someone else's dream, Paul followed him over the railing.

"Be careful," said Gally, but Paul thought the boy looked like he was enjoying the prospect of violent danger more than he ought to be.

"Do try to keep Hurley from creating an interplanetary incident," added Bagwalter.

Paul found it difficult to climb with the *saljak* in one hand. A hundred feet below the ship—and still half that distance from the ground—Brummond stopped and waited impatiently for him.

"I say, old chap, you'd think it was someone else's sweetheart entirely that we were on our way to rescue. We're going to lose the element of surprise."

"I'm . . . I'm not really used to this sort of thing." Paul swayed, his free hand sweaty against the ladder's rungs.

"Here." Brummond reached up and took the *saljak* from him, then resumed his descent. Paul now found it easier to descend, and could even look around for the first time. They were surrounded still, but by oddly-shaped trees rather than towers. The garden seemed to stretch a great distance in all directions: the warm Martian night was full of the scent of growing things.

There was something about the thick greenery and the silence that tickled his memory. *Plants* . . . He struggled to remember. It seemed somehow important. *A forest surrounded by walls. . . .*

Brummond had stopped again, this time at the bottom of the ladder, a short jump from the ground. Paul slowed. Whatever memory the Imperial Gardens had called to now slid out of reach once more, replaced by a more recent concern. "You said that they would never expect us to come in this way, but I saw lots of airships tonight. Why will this surprise them?"

His companion slid his saber out of its sheath, then vaulted lightly to the ground. Huge, flesh-colored blossoms swayed in a breeze Paul could not feel. Some of the trees had thorns as long as a man's arm, and others bore flowers that looked like wet, hungry mouths. Paul shuddered and jumped down.

"Because of the *vormargs,* actually," Brummond said in a confidential whisper. He tossed over the *saljak;* Paul had to twist to avoid catching it by the razor-sharp blade. "Most people are scared to death of the things." He set off at a swift pace. Paul hurried after him.

"*Vormargs?* What are those?"

"Martian beasties. 'Snake-apes,' some people call 'em. Ugly bastards."

Paul had only a half-second to absorb this concept before something huge, shaggy, and stinking dropped from a tree into the middle of the path.

"Speak of the devil!" said Brummond, and swiped at the thing with his saber. Even as the creature snarled and shied back—Paul had a glimpse of slotted yellow eyes and a wide snout full of curving fangs— two more shapes dropped from a tree beside them. Paul only just managed to get the Vonari ax up in time to ward off a long-taloned paw lashing toward his face; even so, the blow loosened his grip on the weapon and nearly knocked him over.

"Don't drive them toward the palace," called Brummond. He had engaged two of the beasts simultaneously, and his saber was an almost invisible blur in the moonlight. "Keep them here in the dark part of the garden."

If Paul could have managed to drive them anywhere, he would have done so happily, but he was hard-pressed just to stay alive. The hairy thing in front of him seemed to have arms as long as buggy-whips; just blocking them as they slapped at his face and belly consumed every part of his strength and speed. He thought of the pistols, but realized he could not possibly draw one before the thing would be on him with its venom-dripping fangs at his neck.

Even Brummond was finding it difficult to talk now. From the corner of his eye Paul saw something stagger back. For a terrifying moment he thought it was his companion, but then he heard the other man's quiet chuckle of pleasure as one of the beasts fell and did not rise. Still, the second of the *vormargs* seemed quite capable of occupying Brummond until its comrade had finished with Paul.

Paul took a step backward and almost stumbled over an exposed tree root. As he regained his balance, his enemy leaped toward him. In desperation he flung the *saljak* in the snake-ape's face. The weapon was not balanced for throwing; it turned in midair, striking the creature heavily and knocking it off-balance, but doing little damage. During the moment's lull, Paul tugged one of the pistols from his belt, pushed it as close to the *vormarg*'s face as he could reach and pulled the trigger. The hammer fell. For a hideously long split-second nothing happened, and then the gun jerked and made a noise like a thunderclap as fire vomited from the end of the barrel. The snake-ape sat down, nothing left atop its shoulders but blood, tatters of burnt flesh, and fur.

"For heaven's sake, old chap, what are you doing?" Brummond was clearly irritated. He had braced his boot against the chest of the second *vormarg* he had killed so he could pull his saber out of its belly. "I told you not to touch that off until I said to."

Paul was too busy struggling for breath to argue.

"Well, if there are any more of these lovelies around, that'll bring 'em down on us like flies on a honey-wagon—not to mention that you've doubtless woken up the Soombar's Onyx Guard. We'd better leg it toward the Imperial Residence and make the best of a bad business. I must say, I'm disappointed in you, Jonas." Brummond wiped his saber on a leaf the size of a tea tray, then sheathed it with one thrust. "Come along." He turned and trotted away through the vegetation.

Paul picked up the *saljak* and stumbled after him. He tucked the pistol he had fired into his belt and pulled out the other one, just to be prepared. It was impossible to guess what ghastly death trap this idiot might lead him into next.

Brummond sprinted through the tangle of the Imperial Gardens as though he had been doing it all his life, with Paul pounding along doggedly behind. Within moments they reached a stone wall that rose dozens of feet, featureless but for a single window more than a man's height above the ground. Brummond vaulted up and caught at the sill, then pulled himself up. He reached down a hand and dragged Paul after him.

The room before them was empty but for a group of stone urns stacked in one corner, and was lit only by a candle guttering in an alcove. Brummond dropped down from the window and moved on noiseless feet toward the far door, listened there for a moment, then led them into the brighter, torchlit hallway outside.

The hall was also unoccupied, but sounds coming from one direction—harsh voices and the rattle of armor—suggested it would not be that way for long. Brummond snatched one of the row of torches from its sconce and touched it to the hem of a tapestry that filled the middle reaches of the wall as far in both directions as Paul could see, an endless and incomprehensible record of animal-headed people at work and play. Flames ran along the tapestry's bottom edge and began to climb upward.

"Com on, man." Brummond grabbed Paul's arm and dragged him away. "That's to slow the Onyx Guard down a jot. A quick sprint and we'll be in the temple precinct!"

Bits of burning tapestry had already fallen to the floor, where the carpet was beginning to smolder. Other flames were already pawing at the heavy wooden ceiling beams. The hallway was beginning to fill with smoke.

Taltors appeared in some of the doorways as Paul followed Hurley Brummond down the long hallway. Most appeared to have been sleeping. It was clearly hard to tell an Earthling complexion from the greenish skin of the Ullamari by torchlight: several of the palace residents shouted excited questions at them, thinking—more rightly than they knew—that these hurrying men might be privy to the nature of the emergency.

Not all were so passive. One huge taltor soldier whose black livery suggested he must be part of the Onyx Guard Brummond had mentioned stepped out of a crossing corridor to bar their path. Paul's companion, showing a slightly surprising degree of restraint, merely dealt him a swift uppercut to the jaw; Paul, a few paces behind, was forced to vault over the collapsed guardsman.

This is all like something out of an old film, he thought, *some Arabian Nights melodrama,* and for an instant that thought opened a whole vista of memory in his head, of countless things and names and ideas, as though someone had swung wide the doors of a great library. Then he slipped on the polished floor and nearly went headfirst onto the stone tiles. By the time he had regained his balance and was hurrying after Brummond again, the mental fog had returned. But he knew now that there was something behind it, that this murkiness was not his natural state. He felt a surge of hope.

Brummond skidded to a stop before a tall archway sealed by a heavy door. "This is it," he said. The noises of pursuit and the sounds of confused palace residents had merged into a single rising din behind them. "Don't believe everything you see in here, and don't lose your head. Also, don't kill anyone! The Soombar's priesthood has a deuced long memory!" Without waiting for a reply, he slammed his shoulder against the door. It rattled in its sockets but did not open. Brummond took a step back, then kicked at it. The door shivered and fell inward, the bolt broken off on the inside.

A few white-robed Martians who had apparently come to investigate the first assault on the door were standing just beyond the threshold. Brummond bowled them over like tenpins. As Paul followed him through, another who had been lurking behind the doorway leapt out. Paul stunned him with the handle of the *saljak.*

"Now you're in the spirit of the thing!" Brummond shouted. "Head for the inner sanctum."

They pelted down another long corridor lined with huge statues of the same beast-headed beings who had decorated the tapestry, then broke through another doorway, this one little more than a ceremonial screen, and were greeted by a blast of hot, foggy air. They were in a large chamber. An ornamental pool shrouded in steam filled the center of the room. Several more priests, these wearing golden beast masks, looked up in startlement at their sudden entrance.

Brummond sprinted around the edge of the pool, pausing only to

fling one of the masked priests into the water. The splash set the mists
eddying, and for a split-second Paul could see clearly to the far side of
the room. The winged woman was slumped on a bench, her chin on
her chest, her thick, dark hair falling forward so that it almost hid her
face—but it was her, Paul knew it beyond a doubt. Paul felt a thrill of
horror to see her so seemingly lifeless. All this lunatic adventure had
been to rescue her—but was he too late?

He sprinted forward. Two hissing priests rose up before him out of
the mist, waving long thin daggers. He lifted the *saljak* horizontally
before him and knocked them backward, stepping on one of them as
he hurtled past. Brummond was on the other side of the pool, keeping
three more robed assailants at bay with his saber. Paul ducked under
a priest's dagger stroke, dealt a backhand blow that sent another
sprawling to the tiles, then reached the stone bench in a few steps. He
reached out his hand and cupped the woman's face, lifting it. Her pale
blue skin was warm, her eyes half-open. She had been drugged in
some way—but she was alive. He was seized by an intense joy, a feeling as foreign as it was powerful. He had found someone who meant
something to him, who perhaps knew something of who he was,
where he came from.

"Oh, for heaven's sake, Jonas, what are you waiting for? Must I
keep swapping chops with these greenskins all night?"

Paul leaned forward to pick her up, but discovered that her hands
were manacled to the bench. Brummond was still holding the trio of
priests at the end of his sword, but several others had escaped and
were running for the door, doubtless to alert the guard. Paul stretched
the woman out on the bench, pulling her arms out straight above her
head, aimed carefully, and brought the *saljak* down as hard as he
could, sending links flying like popcorn. He lifted her, careful not to
crush her fine wings, and threw her over his shoulder.

"I've got her!"

"Then leg it, man, leg it!"

Paul staggered a little as he made his way back around the pool.
She did not weigh much—in fact, she was surprisingly light—but he
was running out of strength and the *saljak* was heavy. After only a
moment's consideration he let it fall, so he could wrap both arms
around his precious burden.

He and Brummond met on the far side of the pool and plunged
through the doorway. They had gone only a few steps when another
priest stepped into their path, this one robed in black; his golden mask
was a featureless disk with eyeholes. The priest raised his staff and

the air seemed to thicken. A moment later, a huge spiderlike beast appeared before them, entirely blocking the corridor. Paul took a step backward in horror.

"Run at it!" Brummond shouted. Paul looked at him with incomprehending despair. "I said run at it! It ain't real!" When Paul still did not move, Brummond shook his head in frustration and lunged forward. The spider-thing dropped down on him, appearing to enfold him in its clicking jaws. A moment later it faded like a shadow blasted by sunlight. Where it had crouched, Brummond stood over the supine form of the black-robed priest, whom he had just stunned with the pommel of his cavalry saber.

"We'll never make it out the way we came in," Brummond shouted, "but I think there's a door to the roof somewhere."

Overwhelmed, but determined to get the Vonari woman to safety, Paul hobbled behind Brummond as the adventurer led them through the twisting side-passages of the temple precinct. Brummond plucked a torch from the wall, and within moments they had left the lighted main halls behind. Paul could not help but be impressed by the way Brummond found his way through the dark and confusing maze. The journey lasted only minutes, but seemed much longer: Paul was again caught up in the feeling that he was living through someone else's dream. Only the tangible warmth and weight of the woman on his shoulder kept him anchored in reality.

At last Brummond found the stairwell. Paul was staggering as they made their way out onto the roof to stand, as he had doubted they ever would again, free beneath the twin moons.

"Of course, damn the luck, Bags is waiting over the Gardens," Brummond said. "And unless I'm hearing things, the Guard is going to be with us any moment." Paul could also hear the sounds of angry soldiers swarming up the stairwell. Brummond took his torch and flung it up in the air as hard as he could. It arched high and then fell, flame rippling behind it like the tail of a shooting star.

"Just pray old Bags is keeping his eyes open. Now you'd best put her down and help me lean on this door."

Paul gently set the winged woman on the rooftop—she murmured something, but did not awake—then added his flagging strength to Brummond's. Already there were people shouting and pushing at the door. Once it was nearly forced open, but Paul and Brummond got their feet under them and slowly shoved it back.

"Hurley!" The voice came from overhead. "Is that you, man?"

"Bags!" shouted Brummond joyfully. "Good old Bags! Drop us the ladder! We're having a spot of bother down here."

"It's there! In the middle of the roof!"

"Now, you go and hoist up your lady love quick as you can while I hold the door." Brummond spoke as calmly as if he were ordering port in the Ares Club. "Maybe Bags can give you a hand."

Paul hurried back to the Vonari woman and carried her to the ladder, then slowly began to make his way up, rung by painful rung, struggling to keep her swaying weight from overbalancing him.

"I can't hold them much longer," Brummond called. "Bags—cast off!"

"Not without you, Hurley!"

"I'm coming, damn it! Just cast off!"

As Paul clung to the ladder, less than two dozen feet above the rooftop, he felt the airship begin to rise. The bottom of the ladder lifted free. Brummond gave the door one last kick, then turned and sprinted toward the fast-rising ladder even as the door burst open and several angry Onyx Guardsmen spilled out. The airship had pulled the ladder up so high that Paul felt his heart sink—they had doomed Brummond, who, madman though he might be, had risked his life for Paul's sake. But Hurley Brummond took two great bouncing steps and leaped, higher than Paul could have believed possible, and caught the ladder's bottom rung in his hands. Grinning, he dangled at arm's length as the airship swept upward and the Soombar's enraged guardsmen grew ever smaller below.

"Well, old fellow," he called up to Paul, "that was an exciting evening, what?"

The mysterious woman lay sleeping on the bed in the captain's cabin; even folded, her diaphanous wings almost touched the walls.

"Come along, Mister Jonas." Professor Bagwalter patted him on the shoulder. "You could use some tending yourself—you've eaten nothing since you've been with us."

Paul had sat by her for most of the night, reluctant to leave for fear she should wake up in a strange place and be frightened, but whatever drugs the priests had given her were powerful, and it seemed certain now that she would sleep until they reached the expedition camp. He followed Bagwalter to the airship's small kitchen where the professor made him a meal of cold meat, cheese, and bread. He took it to be polite, although he did not feel hungry, then wandered up to the helm where Brummond was relating their adventures to Gally for what was doubtless the third or fourth time. Still, it was a tale worth telling more than once, and Paul had to admit to himself that Brummond did not exaggerate his own deeds.

"And how is your lady love?" Brummond interrupted the battle against the *vormargs* to inquire. Upon being assured that she still slept, he was quickly at sword-blows again. Paul moved down the deck, wanting quiet. He stood at the rail and moodily pushed the food around on his plate, watching the two moons, neither of them quite symmetrical, as they edged slowly across the sky above the speeding ship.

"She's a lovely craft, isn't she?" asked the professor, joining him at the rail. "I'm glad we didn't damage her. Brummond may have been the one who borrowed her, but I would have wound up explaining things to the owner. That's the way it always works." He smiled.

"Have you traveled with him a long time?"

"Off and on for many years. He's a good egg, and if you want adventure—well, there's no one like Hurley Brummond."

"I'm sure of that." Paul looked over the railing. The dark line of the Great Canal meandered back and forth beneath them, glinting here and there with the scattered lamps of settlements, and sometimes, when they passed over one of the larger cities, set aglimmer by an entire jewel box of sparkling lights.

"That's Al-Grashin, down there," Bagwalter said as they flew over an immense expanse of dwellings. Even at their great altitude, it was taking a long time to cross. "The center of the *turtuk*-ivory trade. Brummond and I were kidnapped by bandits there once. Magnificent city, second only to Tuktubim. Well, there's Noalva, too. They may have more people, but I've always found Noalva a little grim."

Paul shook his head in bemused wonderment. People knew so many things—there were so many things to know!—yet despite the moment of recollection in the Soombar's palace, he knew almost nothing. He was alone. He had no home—he could not remember if he had ever had one.

Paul closed his eyes. The stars in their teeming numbers across the black sky had seemed to mock his hopeless solitude. He gripped the railing hard in his frustration, and for a moment felt a temptation simply to tumble himself over the side, to resolve all his confusions in one dark plunge.

But the woman—she'll tell me something. Her gaze, her dark, somber gaze, had seemed like a kind of refuge. . . .

"You appear to be troubled, old man," said Bagwalter.

Startled, Paul opened his eyes to find the other man standing beside him. "It's . . . it's only that I wish I could remember."

"Ah." The professor was again eyeing him in that disconcertingly shrewd way of his. "Your head wound. Perhaps when we reach camp you will allow me to examine you. I have had some medical training, and even some experience as an alienist."

"If you think that might help." Paul was not entirely comfortable with the idea, but did not wish to be rude to someone who had given him so much assistance.

"In fact, there were some questions I was hoping to ask you. If you don't mind, that is. You see, I have been . . . well, I must confess, rather struck by your situation. I hope it does not seem rude, but you do not seem to belong here."

Paul looked up, struck by an obscure but insistent sense of alarm. The professor seemed very intent. "Belong here? I don't know that I belong anywhere."

"That is not what I mean. I express myself badly."

Before Bagwalter could try again, a shining something streaked past their heads, then was followed quickly by three more. The things, which glowed with their own light and seemed almost shapeless, pivoted in midair and flew alongside the airship, pacing the vessel at great speed.

"What are those?"

"I don't know." Bagwalter polished his spectacles and replaced them, then squinted at the streaking smears of light, which rolled and tumbled along through the air like dolphins in the wake of a sea-ship. "They are no creature or phenomenon I have seen on Mars."

"Ho!" shouted Brummond from the helm, "we are being taunted by some sort of otherworldly fireflies. Someone fetch me my rifle!"

"Oh, dear," sighed Professor Bagwalter. "You can see that Science has a difficult time with Hurley around."

The strange glowing objects followed the airship for almost an hour, then vanished as abruptly and inexplicably as they had arrived. By the time they had gone, Bagwalter appeared to have forgotten the questions he wished to ask. Paul was not displeased.

Dawn was smoldering along the horizon as the ship at last began to descend. It had been a long time since they had passed the last large settlement, and Paul could see no sign of humanoid life whatever in this barren section of the red desert. Gally, who had been sleeping in Paul's lap, woke up and clambered to the rail.

The airship banked, running parallel to a long wall of wind-carved hills. It slowed to ease through a pass, then began to sink at an even more deliberate pace. For the first time, Paul could make out details of the landscape, odd yellow trees with spiky branches and fluffy purplish plants like tall plumes of smoke.

"Look!" Gally pointed. "That must be the camp!"

A small circle of tents, perhaps half a dozen altogether, huddled at the bottom of the valley beside a dry gulley. Tethered beside them was another airship, even larger than the one on which they flew.

"That's my *Temperance!*" Brummond shouted from the helm. "The finest ship on Ullamar."

A group of nimbors digging in the center of the gulley looked up at the airship's approach. One of them went running back toward the tents.

Brummond brought the airship down beside *The Temperance* with expert smoothness, halting it just slightly more than a man's height from the ground, then letting it settle as softly as goosedown. He vaulted from the captain's deck and over the railing, kicking up a puff of red dust, then dashed off toward the tents. Paul, Bagwalter, and Gally clambered down a little more slowly.

The nimbors had ceased their digging, and now clustered around the new arrivals, tools still in their hands. Their glances were furtive and fleeting; their mouths sagged open, as though they could not get enough air to breathe. They were obviously curious, but it seemed a curiosity born of boredom rather than any real interest. Paul thought they looked much more bestial than Klooroo and his Fisher People neighbors.

"And here they are!" Brummond's voice rang from the crimson stones. He had appeared from one of the larger tents, his arm around a tall, handsome woman in a crisp white blouse and long skirt. Even the sun-helmet on her head seemed quite formal and stylish. "This is Joanna, my fiancée—and Bags' daughter, of course. The only really clever thing he's ever done."

"Welcome to our camp." Joanna smiled at Paul and shook his hand. Her eyes lit on Gally. "Oh! And this must be the moppet. But you're not a child at all—you're almost grown! What a pleasure it is to meet you, young master. I think I have some gingersnaps in my breadbox, but we should make certain." Gally positively glowed as she turned back to Paul. "But first we must see to your fiancée, for I hear she has been terribly treated by the Soombar's priests."

Paul did not bother to argue over the word "fiancée": if Joanna was anything like her intended, it would be useless. "Yes. I was hoping Hurley would help me carry her down."

"Of course he will. Meanwhile, I will set out some morning tea on the porch—we call it a porch, but of course it is really only a sort of cloth roof beside the tent to keep off this scorching Martian sun." She smiled at him again, then took a step forward to kiss Professor Bagwalter on the cheek. "And I have not even said a word to you, Father dear! How dreadful of me! I trust you haven't done yourself any injuries while you and Hurley have been off gallivanting."

Joanna ran the camp with almost terrifying efficiency. Within a few minutes of their arrival she had established the Vonari woman in a bed in one of the tents, made sure everyone had water and a place to wash, then introduced Paul and Gally to two other members of the expedition, a taltor named Xaaro who seemed to be a cartographer, and a fat little human named Crumley who was the foreman of the nimbor work gang. She then led Gally off to the kitchen to help her prepare breakfast.

His other responsibility removed, Paul returned to the winged woman's side. He sat on the tent floor beside her mattress and marveled afresh at the powerful effect her presence had on him.

Her eyes fluttered. He felt an answering flutter inside his chest. A moment later her lids slowly drew back. She stared at the ceiling for a long moment, expressionless, then her face registered alarm and she tried to sit up.

"You're safe." Paul moved closer and laid his hand on her wrist, marveling at the cool silkiness of her azure flesh. "You've been rescued from the priests."

She turned her huge eyes on him, wary as a caged animal. "You. I saw you on the island."

Her voice struck the same resonant chord as did everything else about her. For a moment Paul grew dizzy. He knew her—he did! There could be no other explanation. "Yes," he said when he could find the breath. He found it hard to speak. "Yes, I saw you there. I know you, but something has happened to my memory. Who are you? Do you know me?"

She stared at him for a long time without speaking. "I cannot say. Something about you . . ." She shook her head, and for the first time the wariness faded, replaced by something more uncertain. "I am Vaala of Twelve Rivers House. But how could I have seen you before that moment on the island? Have you been to Vonar, my home? For I never left that place until I was chosen to be the Soombar's Gift."

"I don't know. Damn it, I don't know anything!" Paul slapped at his knee in frustration. The sudden sound caused Vaala to flinch, her wings spread, rustling as they brushed against the tent walls. "All I know is my name, Paul Jonas. I don't know where I've been or where I come from. I hoped you could tell me."

She fixed him with her black eyes. "Pauljonas. The name is strange to my ears, but I feel something when I hear you speak it." She furled her wings and slid back down into the bed. "But it hurts my head to think. I am tired."

"Sleep, then." He reached out and took her cool hand in his. She did not resist. "I'll stay with you. You're safe, now, in any case."

She shook her head slowly, like a tired child. "No, I am not. But I cannot tell you why that is." She yawned. "How full of odd ideas we both are, Pauljonas!" The dark eyes closed. "Could it be . . ." she said, her speech beginning to stumble, "I think I remember . . . a place with many leaves, with trees and plants. But it is like an old dream."

Paul could see it, too. His pulse quickened. "Yes?"

"That is all. I do not know what it means. Perhaps it is a place I saw when I was a child. Perhaps we knew each other when we were children. . . ."

Her breathing grew slower. Within moments she was asleep again. Paul did not let go of her hand until Joanna came and dragged him to breakfast.

He was on his way back to Vaala's side, a mug of tea and a plate of buttered scones clutched precariously in his hands, when he was intercepted by Professor Bagwalter.

"Ah, there you are. I was hoping to catch you alone—didn't seem like breakfast table conversation, if you know what I mean."

"What's that?"

Bagwalter removed and nervously polished his spectacles. "I've been wanting to ask you a question. It's . . . well, I suppose it could be considered rather rude."

Paul was very conscious of the hot Martian sun. Drops of sweat trickled down the back of his neck. "Go on," he said at last.

"I was wondering . . ." Bagwalter was obviously uncomfortable. "Oh, dash it, there's no polite way to say it. Are you a Citizen?"

Paul was taken by surprise. He did not know what he had been fearing, but it was not this. "I don't know what you mean."

"A Citizen. Are you a Citizen or a Puppet?" Bagwalter's voice was a harsh whisper, as though he were being forced to repeat an overheard obscenity.

"I . . . I don't know what I am. I don't know what those words mean. Citizen? Of where?"

The professor stared at him intently, then took out his pocket handkerchief and wiped his brow. "Perhaps it is not required to tell here. I must confess that I have never asked anyone before. Or perhaps my English is not as good as I believed it was and I have not made myself understood." He looked around. The taltor Xaaro was walking toward them, but was still far away. "I am privileged to be a guest of Mister Jiun Bhao, a very important person—the most powerful man in the New China Enterprise. Perhaps you have heard of him? He is a close friend and associate of Mister Jongleur, whose creation this is, and so I have been permitted to come here."

Paul shook his head. It was all gibberish, or almost all: the last name had a faint resonance, like an arcane word from a nursery rhyme unheard since childhood.

The professor, who had been watching him carefully, clucked his tongue in sad resignation. "I thought . . . because you did not seem to fit here . . . I meant no offense, but there are so few other Citizens. One or two I have met in the Ares Club, but they are mostly out having adventures. Also, I feared that secretly they were laughing at my English. It is not surprising, perhaps—I was quite fluent once, but I have not used it since my university days at Norwich. In any case, I hoped to have someone real to talk to. I have been in this simulation for a month, and it is sometimes lonely."

Paul took a step backward, baffled and more than a little frightened. The professor was spouting incomprehensibilities, but some of them seemed as though they *should* mean something to him.

"Professor!" The cartographer had almost reached them. His jade-tinged skin was shiny with perspiration. He did not look as well suited to the climate as the nimbor laborers. "Gracious sir, forgive my interruption, but you are wanted for a conversation on the radiophonic device."

Bagwalter turned, his impatience obvious. "For God's sake, what is it? Who would be calling?"

"It is the Tellari Embassy in Tuktubim."

The professor turned back to Paul. "I'd better take care of this. Listen, old man, if I've said something offensive, it was unintentional. Please put the whole thing out of your mind." He tried to hold Paul's gaze as if searching for something, his expression almost yearning. For a moment, Paul thought he could sense a very different face looking out from behind the mask of the phlegmatic Englishman.

Troubled, Paul watched Bagwalter head back toward the main circle of tents.

Vaala was awake and sitting up in bed when he arrived, her wings partially unfurled. There was something both confusing and gloriously appropriate about the great feathered sweeps that extended on either side of her, but Paul was already full-fed with half-memories. As he told her the complete story of her rescue from the Soombar's palace, he gave her the tea, which was finally cool enough to drink. She took it in both hands and lifted it to her mouth for a tentative sip.

"It's good." She smiled. Her look of pleasure made his insides ache. "Strange, but I like it. Is it an Ullamari drink?"

"I think so." He sat down on the tent floor, his back against the stiff canvas. "There are a lot of things I don't remember, of course. So much that I don't know where to start thinking, sometimes."

She gave him a long, serious look. "You should not have taken me from the priests, you know. They will be angry. In any case, they will only choose another daughter of Vonar for the sacrifice."

"I don't care. That may sound terrible, but it's true. I have nothing but you, Vaala. Can you understand that? You are my only hope of finding out who I am, where I come from."

"But how can that be?" Her wings lifted and extended, then folded behind her once more. "Before I came here for Festival Season, I never left my world, and in all my life I have only met a few of you Tellari. I would remember you, surely."

"But you said you remembered something—a leafy place, trees, a garden, something like that. And you said my name sounded familiar."

She shrugged her slender shoulders. "It is strange, I admit."

Paul was becoming increasingly conscious of an odd grinding sound coming from outside, but he was unwilling to be distracted. "It's more than strange. And if I know anything in the world, it is that you and I have met before." He moved closer and took her hand in his. She resisted for only a moment, then allowed him to possess it. He felt as though he could draw strength from the mere contact. "Listen, Professor Bagwalter—he's one of the people who helped rescue you—he asked me some very strange questions. I felt they should mean something to me, but they didn't. He called this place a simulation, for one thing.''

''A simulation? Did he mean an illusion, like the trickery practiced by the Soombar's priests?''

''I don't know. And he mentioned names, lots of names. 'Shongloor' was one of them. The other was something like 'June Bough.' ''

There was a rustle at the tent door. Paul turned to see Gally pulling the flap aside. The harsh whining noise was markedly louder. ''Paul, come see! They're almost here. And it's the most wonderful machine!''

Paul was irritated, but it was hard to ignore the boy's excitement. He turned back to find that Vaala had pushed herself against the tent wall, her black eyes wide.

''What is it?''

''That name.'' She lifted her long-fingered hands as though to keep something away. ''I . . . I do not like it.''

''Which name?''

''Paul, come on!'' Gally was pulling at his arm. The grinding was very loud now, and there was a deeper noise beneath it that he could feel through the very sand beneath the tent floor. It was almost impossible to ignore.

''I'll be back in a moment,'' he told Vaala, then allowed Gally to lead him out the door of the tent, where he stopped in astonishment.

Waddling down the valley toward the camp was the strangest machine he had ever seen or could ever imagine seeing, a huge four-legged device almost a hundred feet long that looked like nothing so much as a mechanical crocodile made of metal beams and polished wooden panels. The head was as narrow as the prow of a ship; the back, except for three giant smokestacks belching steam, was covered with striped tenting. Flywheels turned, pistons plunged up and down, and steam whistled from the vents as the thing slowly made its way down the slope. Paul could just dimly see several tiny figures standing in a recessed space on the top of the head.

''Isn't it grand!'' shouted Gally over the racket.

Professor Bagwalter appeared around the corner of one of the tents and approached them. ''Frightfully sorry about all this!'' he bellowed. ''They just called on the radiophone. Apparently they're from the Tellari Embassy. Supposed to perform some kind of check on our arrangements before we leave for the back of beyond. Some little irritation devised by the Soombar's mandarins, I have no doubt. Our embassy wallahs are always trying to stay on the Soombar's good side, which usually means bad luck for the rest of us.''

"Do you think it has anything to do with rescuing Vaala?" Paul shouted, watching in helpless fascination as the monstrous vehicle crawled to a halt a few dozen yards outside the camp, shuddering and piping like a tea kettle as its boilers were vented. A golden sun was painted on its side, surrounded by four rings, the inner two and outermost white, the third bright green.

"Oh, I rather doubt that, old man. You saw how slow the thing is. They would have had to set out a couple of days ago."

As the clamor of the device died down, Paul heard Vaala's wings rustling behind him. He blindly reached out a hand; a moment later, he felt her fingers close around his.

"What is it?"

"Someone from the Embassy. But it might be a good idea if they didn't see you," he said.

The great mechanical head had settled to within only a few feet of the ground. Now the side of it opened up, tumbling outward in an array of hinged plates that formed a stairway. A pair of figures moved out of the shade of the awning toward the steps.

"I suppose I'd better make myself useful," said Bagwalter, starting toward the strange crocodile-machine.

Something about the men moving down the stairway struck Paul with a pang of unease. The first was thin and angular; something glinted on his face as though he wore spectacles like the professor's. The second, only now emerging from shadow, was so grotesquely fat that he seemed to be having a difficult time descending. Paul stared, his fear growing. There was something dreadful about this pair, something that radiated chill through his thoughts.

Vaala was moaning in his ear. As he turned toward her, she jerked her hand away and took a stumbling step back. Her eyes were so wide with horror that he could see white all the way around her dark pupils.

"No!" She shivered as though with a fever. "No! I will not let those two have me again!"

Paul grabbed at her, but she had already moved out of reach. He darted a glance back at the new arrivals, who were just reaching the bottom of the stairs. Hurley Brummond and Joanna were stepping forward to welcome them, and the professor was only a few yards behind.

"Come back," he called to Vaala. "I'll help you—"

She spread her wings, then took a few steps away from the tents and brought the great pinions down; they beat the air with an audible *crack*. They flapped again and again and her feet began to lift from the red sand.

"Vaala!" He sprinted after her, but she was already six feet off the ground and rising. Her wings spread wider, catching the thin desert breeze, and she vaulted higher still. "Vaala!" He jumped, reaching hopelessly, but she was already as small and far away as—the notion came to him without source or explanation—an angel atop a Christmas tree.

"Paul? Where is she going?" Gally seemed to think it was some kind of game.

Vaala was moving rapidly toward the hills, flying strongly now. As Paul watched her growing more distant, he could almost feel his heart turning to stone inside him. Below, the fat shape and the thin shape were in some kind of heated conversation with the professor. They radiated a terrible *wrongness*—even a quick glance at them now filled him with the terror that must have forced Vaala into flight. He turned and dashed down the slope toward the far side of the camp.

"Paul?" Gally's voice was growing faint behind him. He hesitated, then turned and ran back toward the boy.

"Come on!" he shouted. Every moment wasted seemed an eternity. His past, his entire history, was disappearing rapidly toward the hills, and something dreadful was waiting for him at the bottom of the valley. Gally stared, confused. Paul waved his arms frantically. As the boy finally began to trot toward him, Paul turned and bolted toward the anchored airships.

He had already scrambled onto the nearest ship, the one that had brought them, when Gally caught up. He leaned down and pulled the boy aboard, then raced toward the helm.

"What are you doing? Where did the lady go?"

Bagwalter and the others had finally noticed that something was amiss. Joanna, shielding her eyes with her other hand, was pointing at Vaala, now little more than a pale spot in the blue sky, but Hurley Brummond was pelting toward the airship at a great pace. Paul forced himself to examine the mahogany panel that contained the controls. There were a number of small brass levers. Paul flipped one. Deep inside the hull, a bell rang. Paul cursed and flipped the rest. Something began to throb beneath his feet.

"Damn it, man, what do you think you're doing?" Brummond shouted. He was only a few dozen yards away now, covering ground swiftly with his great tigerish strides. His look of irritated disbelief was hardening into fury, and he was already fumbling for the saber at his belt.

Paul pulled back on the wheel. The airship shuddered, then began to rise. Brummond reached the spot where it had been and jumped, but fell short and tumbled back to the ground in a cloud of dust. The two new arrivals were hurrying forward, arms waving.

"Don't be a fool, Jonas!" Professor Bagwalter shouted, his hands cupped around his mouth. "There's no need to . . ." His voice became too faint to hear as the airship rapidly gained altitude. Paul turned his eyes upward. Vaala was only a pinpoint on the horizon, already traveling above the sawtoothed hills.

The camp quickly fell away behind them. The ship rocked and pitched as Paul struggled to decipher the controls, then abruptly rolled sideways. Gally slid down the polished floor of the cockpit, only saving himself by a last-moment clutch at Paul's leg. Paul wrestled the ship back more or less level, but it was not stable, and they were receiving rough handling in the windier skies above the hills.

Vaala was a little closer now. Paul felt a moment's sense of satisfaction. They would catch her, and the three of them would flee together. Together, they would solve all the riddles.

"Vaala!" he called, but she was still too distant to hear him.

As they came across the crest of the hills a sudden gust of wind pushed them sideways once more. Despite Paul's straining hands on the wheel, the ship's nose dipped down. Another gust set them spinning and he lost control. Gally clung to his leg, shouting in terror. Paul pulled back on the wheel until his joints were aflame with agony, but the ship kept tumbling. First the ground leaped up at them, then they were falling into the sky, then the ground was springing at them once more. Paul had a brief, cracked glimpse of the Great Canal writhing below them like a dark serpent, then something smacked against his head and the world exploded into sparks.

CHAPTER 31

Bleak Spaces

NETFEED/MUSIC: Dangerous Sonics Banned
(visual: young woman in pressurized hospital tent)
VO: After a series of injuries and one death during the latest tour by the
power wig band Will You Still Love Me When My Head Comes Off, promoters
have banned the use of sound equipment that operates outside the range of
human hearing. The ban was prompted when American and European
insurance companies declared they would no longer insure events where
"dangerous sonics" are used.
(visual: clip from "Your Blazing Face Is My Burning Heart")
WYSTLMWMHCO and other power wig groups have in turn threatened to
boycott the US and Europe if necessary, saying they cannot allow bureaucrats
to interfere with their artistic expression.

Renie hated it when her father sulked, but this was one time she
had no intention of indulging him. "Papa, I have to do this. It's
for Stephen. Isn't that important to you?"

Long Joseph rubbed his face with knob-knuckled hands. "Of course
it's important, girl. Don't you be telling me I don't care about my boy.
But I think all this computer monkeyshines is foolishness. You going
to make your brother better with some kind of game?"

"It's not a game. I wish it was." She examined her father's face.

There was something different about him, but she couldn't quite decide what. "Are you worried about me at all?"

He snorted. "What? Worried that you going to drown in some bathtub full of jelly? Already told you what I think of that."

"Papa, I might be online for days—maybe a week. You could make things a little easier." Her patience was beginning to sift away. Why did she even try to talk to him? What did it ever bring her except aggravation and heartache?

"Worried about you." Her father scowled, then looked down. "I worry about you all the time. I worry about you since you were a little baby. I break my back to give you a home, put food in your mouth. When you get sick, I pay for the doctor. Your mama and me, we sat up nights praying for you when you had that bad fever."

She suddenly realized what was different. His eyes were clear, his words unslurred. The departing troops that had occupied this underground site had taken everything portable that was of value, which had included any stocks of alcohol. Her father had made the beer he'd bought on the way in last as long as he could, but he had finished it the day before yesterday. No wonder he was in a foul mood.

"I know you worked hard, Papa. Well, now it's my turn to do what I can for Stephen. So please don't make it any more difficult than it needs to be."

He finally turned back toward her, his eyes red-rimmed, his mouth curved in a petulant frown. "I'll be fine. Nothing for a man to do around here anyway. And you—don't you get yourself killed in that thing, girl. Don't let it fry your brain or some foolishness like that. And don't blame me if it do."

And that, Renie supposed, was the closest he was going to come to telling her he loved her.

"I'll try not to get my brain fried up, Papa. God knows, I'll try."

"I wish one of us had some medical training." She was examining with some distaste the IV cannula secured to her arm under a thin sheath of permeable latex membrane. "I'm not very happy about having to do this out of a manual. And a military manual at that."

Jeremiah shrugged as he fitted the same device onto !Xabbu's thin arm. "It's not so difficult. My mother was in a car accident and had a wound that needed to be drained. I did all that."

"We will be well, Renie," said !Xabbu. "You have done a good job preparing everything."

"I hope so. But it seems like something always gets missed." She carefully lowered herself into the gel. Once covered, she removed her undergarments and tossed them out over the side. She doubted that Jeremiah cared one way or the other, and her father was off poking around in the kitchen supplies, unwilling to watch the sealing of the sarcophagi, but she still felt uncomfortable being naked in the presence of her friends. !Xabbu, who had no such inhibitions, had removed his clothes long ago, and sat through Jeremiah's last-minute instructions in unperturbed nakedness.

Renie connected the IV tube to the shunt in her arm, then fixed the urinary catheter and solid waste hoses in place, repressing a shudder at their unpleasant, intrusive touch against her flesh. This was no time to be squeamish. She had to think of herself as a soldier going behind enemy lines. The mission was the most important thing—all other considerations must be secondary. She went over her mental checklist for the dozenth time, but there was nothing left undone. All the monitoring and adjustment would be done by the V-tank itself, through the plasmodal gel. She fitted the mask and signaled to Jeremiah to turn on the air. When she felt the slightly clammy rush of oxygen in the mouth-bubble, she slid down below the surface.

She floated in dark weightlessness, waiting for Jeremiah to put the system online. It seemed to take forever. She wondered if there could be a problem with !Xabbu's rig. Perhaps his machinery was faulty, and she would have to go by herself. The thought, and the depth of her own unhappiness in reaction, frightened her. She had come to depend on the small man, on his calm presence and good sense, more than she really liked to depend on anyone, but that did not change the fact of her dependency.

"Renie?" It was Jeremiah, talking to her through the hearplugs. *"Is everything okay?"*

"I'm fine. What are we waiting for?"

"Nothing. You're ready to go." For a long silent moment, she thought he'd gone offline. *"And good luck. Find out who did that to the doctor."*

"We'll do our best." Online gray suddenly surrounded her, a sea of staticky nothingness with no surface or bed. "!Xabbu? Can you hear me?"

"I am here. We have no bodies, Renie."

"Not yet. We need to make contact with Singh first."

She summoned up the military base's operating system, a typically unimaginative control panel full of view windows, simulated buttons, and switches, then keyed the preprogrammed connection Martine had sent them. The control panel blinked various waiting messages, then the panel and the surrounding gray disappeared, swallowed by blackness. After a few moments, she heard the French woman's familiar voice: "Renie?"

"Yes, it's me. !Xabbu?"

"I am here, too."

"All present, Martine. Why are there no visuals?"

Singh's voice rasped in her hearplugs. "Because I don't have the time or inclination to entertain you with pretty pictures. We'll have more visuals than we can stand if we can get into this system."

"Nevertheless," said Martine, "you will need to set some default standards for your simulated forms. Monsieur Singh says that many of the nodes on this network will automatically assign sims upon entry, but some will not. Some of those that do will be influenced by the user's own selections, so you should choose something comfortable."

"And not too goddamn conspicuous," added Singh.

"How can we do that? Whose system are we on, anyway?"

Martine did not answer, but a small holograph cube appeared from the darkness in front of her. Renie found that using standard VR manipulations she could build an image inside it.

"Hurry up," growled Singh. "I've got a window coming up in about fifteen minutes and I don't want to miss it."

Renie pondered. If this Otherland network was actually a huge VR playground for the rich and powerful, as Singh seemed to believe, then a sim that was too generic, too low-rent, would attract the wrong kind of attention. She would indulge herself for once and have something nice.

She wondered whether it would be best to costume herself as a man. After all, the alpha males of the human world hadn't changed much in the last two thousand years, and from what she knew, very few of them seemed to think very highly of women. But on the other hand, perhaps that in itself was a reason not to pretend to be something other than what she was. If your average crazed, want-to-rule-the-world multizillionaire tended not to think of a woman as an object of respect, especially a young African woman, perhaps there was no better way of being underestimated than to be herself.

"I had a dream last night." !Xabbu's disembodied voice startled her. "A very strange dream about Grandfather Mantis and the All-Devourer."

"Sorry?" She chose the basic human female armature, which appeared in the cube, impersonal as a wire sculpture.

"It comes from a story I learned as a young man, a very important story of my people."

Renie could feel herself frowning as she tried to concentrate on the image of the sim. She gave it her own dark skin and close-cropped hair, then stretched it until it more closely resembled her small-breasted, long-limbed frame. "Do you think you could tell me later, !Xabbu? I'm trying to make a sim for myself. Don't you have to do the same?"

"That is why the dream seemed important. Grandfather Mantis spoke to me in the dream—to me, Renie. He said, '*It is time for all the First People to join together.*' But I apologize. I am making it difficult for you. I will leave you alone."

"I am trying to concentrate, !Xabbu. Tell me later, please."

She magnified the face and quickly ran through a number of shapes until she found one close to her own. Noses, eyes, and mouths paraded past like claimants to Cinderella's glass slipper and were rejected in turn until she found a combination enough like her own face not to feel like an imposture. Renie hated people who made their sims impossibly more attractive than the real-life owners. It seemed like a weakness, an unwillingness to live with what you had been given.

She stared at the finished product, scanning the placid face. The sight of what could pass, under swift scrutiny, for her own corpse gave her pause. There was no sense making it too much of a self-portrait. The people whose system they were entering illegally were not the forgiving kind, as she already knew. Why make retaliation any easier?

Renie exaggerated the shape of the cheekbones and chin and chose a longer, narrower nose. She gave the eyes an upward slant. This, she reflected, was not that different from a game of dress-up dolls. The finished product now looked only a little like her, and much more resembled some desert princess from a sand-and-scimitars netflick. She smirked at her work and herself—now who was guilty of glamorizing a sim?

She outfitted her new body in the most sensible clothing she could think of, a kind of pilot's jumpsuit and boots: if the simulation was good enough, then suitability of outfit would be a factor. She then ran down a row of options for strength, endurance, and other physical traits, which in most simworlds was a zero-sum game in which every increase in fitness in one category had to be counterbalanced by decreases elsewhere. When she had jiggled the numbers until she felt satisfied, she locked in the choices. The simulation and its prisoning cube disappeared, leaving her in blackness once more.

Singh's strident voice cut through the emptiness. "Now, I'm going to say this once and once only. We're going in, but don't be surprised at anything—and that includes failure. This is the weirdest damn operating system I've ever run into, so I'm not making any promises. And don't ask me any stupid questions while I'm working."

"I thought you were one of the people who worked on it," Renie said. She was getting tired of Singh's bad temper.

"I didn't work on the OS itself," he said. "I worked on the snap-on components. The operating system was the biggest secret since the Manhattan Project—that was the first atomic bomb back in the twentieth century, for those of you who don't know your history."

"Please go ahead, Monsieur Singh," said Martine. "We know time is short."

"Damn right. Anyway, I've been running little forays on this system and observing it for a long time, and I still have questions. The thing has cycles, for one thing, and I'm not talking about usage. Usage stays pretty constant overall across all time-zones, although in general it's been picking up a great deal lately—but the operating system itself has some kind of internal cycle that I can't figure out. Sometimes it works much faster than other times. Overall, it seems to be on some kind of twenty-five-hour cycle, so it'll go about nineteen hours at high efficiency, then things kind of get gluey for about six hours or so and it's easier to get around some of the more obvious security precautions. Mind you, it's still twice as fast as anything else I've ever come into contact with, maybe more."

"Twenty-five-hour cycles?" Martine sounded shaken. "You are certain?"

"Of course I'm certain," Singh snapped. "Who's been monitoring this thing for almost a year, you or me? Now, the only way to get through, *and* to get you people inside as well, is for me to establish a beachhead. That means I have to get the system to open up and let me all the way in, then I have to get a fix so I can get us all off fiberlines and onto a randomizing resat. And you're not going to have any pictures until you're in—I don't have time for any of that kiddie crap—so you're going to have to listen to my voice and do what I tell you. Got it?"

Renie and !Xabbu assented.

"Good. Sit tight and shut up. First I have to get to the backdoor me and Melani and Sakata put in. Normally, that would be enough to get into any system, but they've done some crazy stuff to this one—levels of complexity I've never seen."

Then Singh was gone and there was only silence. Renie waited as patiently as she could, but without the sound of other voices it was impossible to measure time. It could have been ten minutes or an hour when the old hacker's voice buzzed in her hearplugs once more.

"I take it back." He sounded breathless and far less composed than usual. " 'Complexity' isn't the word. 'Insanity,' maybe—everything on the inner rings of this system has got some kind of weird random angle. I knew they were going to install a neural network at the center of this thing, but even those have rules. They learn, and eventually they do the *right* thing every time, which after a point means more or less the *same* thing every time. . . ."

It was hard to sit in the darkness and do nothing. For the first time she could remember, Renie yearned to be able to touch something, anything. Telepresence, they had called it in her ancient VR text-books—contact over a distance. "I don't understand," she said. "What's happening?"

Singh was so discomfited that he didn't seem to resent the interruption. "It's open—wide open. I popped in through the back door. Every time I've probed that before, there's been some weird nesting-code barrier on the other side. I worked up a solution for that, assuming that was just the first layer of defenses around the heart of the system—but it's not there. There's nothing to keep us out at all."

"What?" Martine, too, sounded alarmed. "But does that mean the entire system is undefended? I cannot believe that."

"No." Renie could hear Singh's frustration. "I wish it were—that would just mean a systems breakdown. As far as I can tell, the hole, if you want to call it that, is only in the last ring of defenses, on the other side of my entry point—the back door we built in to this particular bit of gear, decades ago. But it's never been undefended before."

"Forgive me for speaking of something that is unfamiliar to me," said !Xabbu. Renie was surprised by the pleasure she felt at hearing his voice through the darkness. "But does it not sound like a trap?"

"Of course it does!" Singh's bad temper had not stayed away long. "There's probably a dozen of that bastard Atasco's systems engineers sitting in some room right now, like polar bears at an ice hole, waiting to see what pokes its head through. But tell me what else we should do."

Detached from her body as she had never been, floating in a kind of negative space, Renie still felt her skin tingle. "They *want* us to try to get in?"

"I don't know," the old hacker said. "I told you, this operating system is unfathomable. By far the most complicated thing I've ever seen—I couldn't even guess how many trillions of instructions per second. Jesus! These people are really going top-of-the-line—I haven't even heard whispers of processing speeds like that." There was more than a little admiration in his voice. "But we can't just assume it's a trap. For one thing, that's a bit stupidly obvious, don't you think— they just turn off the security we were expecting to have to hack through? Maybe it's nothing to do with us at all—maybe the operating system's doing something critically important somewhere else and it's diverted some resources from the inner circle of security, figuring it can reestablish them if something gets past the outer circle. If we don't try to go in, we might discover later we'd been counting the white-and-pearlies of the world's biggest gift horse."

Renie pondered for only a moment. "This may be our best chance. I say we go in."

"Thank you, Ms. Shaka." Underneath the sarcasm, there was a discernible note of approval.

"I am troubled by what you tell us." Martine sounded more than just troubled: there was unhappiness in her voice that Renie had never heard before. "I wish I had more time to consider."

"If the operating system is diverting resources, they could be planning some big change," Singh replied. "I told you, there's *something* going on—usage is way up, and there seem to have been a lot of alterations. They might even be planning to shut the whole thing down, or cut off outside access completely."

"I told Renie that I had a dream," offered !Xabbu. "You may not understand, Mister Singh, but I have learned to trust such messages."

"You had a dream telling you today was the day to break into the network?"

"No, of course not. But I believe you are correct when you say this opportunity may not come again. I cannot explain why I believe it, but your words speak to me as my dream spoke to me. The time has come for all Grandfather Mantis' children to join together—that is what my dream said."

"Huh." Singh's laugh was brief and harsh. "So, that's what—one 'yes,' one 'not sure,' and one 'I had a dream about a bug'? I guess I'm a yes, too. So we give it a try. But don't be surprised if I blow the whole thing up right away—I don't think they can backtrace me, but

I'm not even going to give those bastards the satisfaction of trying if I can help it.''

With that, he was gone. The silence descended again.

This time the waiting seemed even more unnaturally long. The blackness was everywhere; Renie could almost feel it seeping inside her, too. What did she and the others think they were doing? Four people trying to break into the world's most sophisticated network, then—what? Sift through unimaginable complexity in search of answers that might not even be there? Finding a particular grain of sand on a beach would be easier.

What is he doing? Is he even going to be able to crack it?

"Martine? !Xabbu?"

There was no reply. Either through some quirk of Singh's system or some failure of her own, she was temporarily incommunicado. The knowledge only added to her claustrophobic anxiety. How long had she been in the darkness. Hours? Renie tried to bring up some kind of clock, but the system was unresponsive to any of her signals. For a moment, as she moved hands she could not see, to no discernible effect, she felt the beginnings of real panic. She forced herself to lie still again.

Calm down, you silly cow. You're not down a well, or buried under a cave-in. You're in a V-tank. !Xabbu and your father and Jeremiah are only a few feet away. You could sit up if you wanted to, just rip out all those tubes and push open the tank lid, but that would spoil everything. You've been waiting for this chance for a long time. Don't ruin it. Be strong.

To occupy herself—and to prove time was really passing—she began to count, bending her fingers in turn as she did so to remind herself that she had a body, that there was more than blackness and her own voice in her head. She had just passed three hundred when something crackled in her hearplugs.

". . . Think I'm through . . . some . . . interfering . . . routers will . . ." Singh's voice seemed very faint and far away, but even with his words coming in staticky bursts, his fear was unmistakable.

"This is Renie. Can you hear me?"

The hacker's voice was even fainter now. ". . . No reason to . . . crazy, but . . . being stalked . . ."

'Stalked'? Had he said 'stalked'? Or 'stopped'? Renie fought against her own rising terror. There was nothing to fear, really—nothing except discovery and reprisal, but at this point those were beginning to feel like old friends. *Only a superstitious idiot could be afraid of the net,* she told herself.

The serpentine arms of Kali arose from her memory, mocking her.

Another burst of static, but no words this time. She suddenly realized that she was very, very cold. *"!Xabbu! Martine! Are you out there?"*

Silence. The cold was growing deeper. Psychosomatic, surely. A reaction to the darkness, to the isolation and uncertainty. *Hang on, girl, hang on. Don't panic. No reason to be afraid. You're doing this for Stephen. You're doing this to help him.*

She was shivering. She could feel her teeth bouncing against each other, clicking and rattling her jawbone.

Blackness. Chill. Silence. She began to count again, but could not keep the numbers straight.

"Renie? Are you there?" The sound was thin, as though it came to her down a long tube. The sheer joy at hearing her name spoken told her how frightened she was. A long moment passed before she realized whose voice it was.

"Jeremiah?"

"The tank—your temperature readings are way down." His voice was only a little clearer than Singh's had been. *"Do you want . . ."* A hiss drowned him out.

"I couldn't hear you. Jeremiah? Can you reach !Xabbu in the other tank?"

". . . Such a big drop. Do you . . . want . . . pull out?"

She could tell him she did. It would be easy. With just those words, she would be released from these strange, bleak spaces. But how could she do that—how could she just give up? Out of the void, clearest of all the phantoms flickering in her thoughts, she saw Stephen's face behind the crinkled transparency of the oxygen tent. This—darkness, isolation, nothingness—was his reality every single day. Could she let a few moments of it frighten her away from what might be his only chance?

"Jeremiah, can you hear me? There's interference. Just say yes if you can."

A quietly crackling pause. Then a sibilance. *Yes.*

"Okay. Don't pull us out. Don't do *anything* unless our vital signs go completely wrong—unless we're in real medical trouble. Do you understand? *Don't pull us out.*"

She heard nothing but crackle.

Okay, she thought. *Now you've done it. You've sent him away. No one to step in and save you, even if . . . even if . . . Hysterical, girl, you are getting . . .* She tried to reach a calm center in herself, but was convulsed with shivering again. *Jesus Mercy, it's cold! What's going on? What's gone wrong. . . ?*

Something was growing in the darkness, so faint that she could not be sure that it was not a trick of her reeling mind. A few spots became brighter, glowing like luminescent fungus in a root cellar. Renie stared, all of her attention focused, as the spots became lines, then moving smears of white and gray, resolving at last into a living image, blasted inside out like a photographic negative.

"Singh?"

The figure hanging in the emptiness before her raised its hands, its jerky movements oddly out of phase. Its mouth worked, but there was no sound in her hearplugs except her own shallow breathing. The old man wore the same threadbare robe and pajamas she had seen before. But how could that be? Surely he would have constructed a sim for himself, something that would hide his identity.

The cold grew heavy, pushing down on her like a great hand, sending her into spasms of trembling. Singh's image expanded, stretching and distorting until it filled the entirety of her vision, reaching away into infinity at its corners. It opened a twisted mouth the size of a mountain and the face around it contorted in pain. The sound which scraped and roared through her hearplugs, loud as a jet engine, was only barely identifiable as speech.

"*. . . IT . . .*"

And now, even through the killing cold that was making her body shake itself to bits, she could feel something else, a presence that stood behind the bizarre, gigantic apparition of Singh as the endless vacuum of space stood behind the blue sky. She could feel it looming above her, a mind like a fist trembling over a table-crawling gnat, a thing of pure thought that was nevertheless idiot-empty, a presence colder than cold, sick and curious and powerful and completely insane.

Her thoughts were flying away like roof tiles in a hurricane. *Hyena!* a part of her shrieked, !Xabbu's stories and her dreams giving the fear a name. *The Burned One.* A moment later, as it blanketed her with darkness and the cold burrowed into her guts, something else !Xabbu had said heaved itself up from her memory.

All-Devourer.

It touched her idly then, nosing at her as a beast might nose someone pretending to be dead. An icy void, but something squirming at the heart of it like cancer. She felt certain her heart would stop.

Singh's voice again blasted in her ears, a gigantic howl of agony and horror. *"OH, GOD! IT'S . . . GOT ME . . ."* His image contorted, twisting itself inside out, and Renie shrieked in startled terror. A hideously distorted but indisputably real vision of the old man as he must be at this very moment filled the blackness—his turban askew and bathrobe rucked under his arms as he convulsed like a worm at the end of a cruel hook. His eyes rolled back until only white showed. His toothless mouth gaped. Renie could feel his pain almost as though it were her own, a terrible tension that ran through her like an electrified wire. It flared and then stopped. She felt Singh's heart burst. She felt him die.

The image vanished. The dark settled again, the cold clutched her and held her, and the inconceivable *something* brought her close.

Oh, God, she thought hopelessly, *I've been so stupid.* She could feel her brother and her father and so many others, crying out their anger at her. The cold grew deeper, impossibly complete, as if every sun in the universe had been extinguished. Her body was now too weak even to shiver. She felt strength whistling out of her, her mind floating, dying.

Something abruptly opened before her, a lessening of density dimly perceived. She felt herself falling into it as if from a great height. She was going through something—an opening? A gate? Had she passed through into . . . into wherever it had been that she had once wished to enter, eternities ago? Was she being allowed in?

Somewhere a memory. Teeth. Miles of gleaming teeth. A giant mouth, grinning.

No, she realized, a last flicker of reason in her dying mind. *I'm being swallowed.*

CHAPTER 32

The Dance

NETFEED/LINEAR.DOC: IEN, Hr. 23 (Eu. NAm)—"DEATH PARADE"
(visual: slow-motion of man being kicked and beaten by mob)
VO: Sepp Oswalt hosts a roundup of deaths, including a lynch-mob beating
caught on surveillance cameras, a rape/murder recorded by the murderer and
later used as evidence against him, and a live telecast from a beheading in
the Red Sea Free State. Winner of Name the Reaper Mascot contest to be
announced.

So you're having trouble breathing, are you?" The smiling, yellow-haired man pushed something made of cold metal into Orlando's mouth. It clicked against the back of his throat like someone had snapped him there with a weak rubber band. "Hmmm. Well, maybe I'd better have a listen, too." He placed a membranous probe against Orlando's chest, then watched the spikes on the wallscreen. "That doesn't sound good, I'm afraid."

Orlando had to hand it to the bastard. He'd never seen Orlando before, but he'd barely reacted at all, not even that funny look in the eyes Orlando had become used to seeing when people were working hard at treating him normally.

The yellow-haired man straightened up and turned to Vivien. "It's definitely pneumonia. We'll put him on some of the new contrabiotics,

but with his special circumstances—well, I'd recommend you bring
him in for a stay at our infirmary."

"No." Orlando shook his head emphatically. He hated the Crown
Heights infirmary, and didn't like this smooth-talking rich-people's
doctor either. He could also tell that the slick young medicine man
wasn't very comfortable with the "special circumstances"—the unig-
norable fact of Orlando's long-term condition—but much as he would
have liked to, Orlando couldn't really hold that against him. Nobody
else was comfortable with it either.

"We'll talk about it, Orlando." His mother's tone unmistakably told
him not to embarrass her by being a stubborn little bastard in front of
this nice young man. "Thank you, Doctor Doenitz."

The doctor smiled and bobbed his head, then sauntered out of the
examining room. Watching him go, Orlando wondered if he'd gone to
some special creepy suck-up-to-rich-patients school.

"If Doctor Doenitz thinks you belong in the imfirmary . . ." Vivien
began, but Orlando interrupted.

"What are they going to do? It's pneumonia. They're going to give
me contra-bees just like the other times. What difference does it make
where I am? Besides, I hate that place. It looks like they had some
horrible person come in and decorate it so the rich jerkies who come
here would feel like when *they* get sick it's not like normal people
getting sick."

A smile tugged at the corner of Vivien's mouth, but she did her best
to suppress it. "No one's saying you're supposed to like it. But this is
your health we're talking about . . ."

"No, it's whether I'm going to die from pneumonia this time, or
from something else next week or next month." The brutality of it
silenced her. He slid off the examining table and began pulling his
shirt on. Even that effort made him feel weak and short of breath. He
looked away, determined to hide how miserable he felt. Otherwise,
the whole thing would be too much like a bad flick.

When he turned, she was crying. "Don't talk like that, Orlando."

He put his arm around her, but at the same time he was angry. Why
should *he* be comforting *her?* Who was living under the death sentence, anyway?

"Just get me the drugs. The nice pharmacy woman will give them
to us and we'll add them onto my pile. Please, Vivien, let's just go
home. They say that making the patient feel comfortable is important.
I won't be any better off in that stupid infirmary."

Vivien wiped her eyes. "We'll talk to your father about it."

Orlando levered himself back into the wheelchair. He *did* feel pretty impacted, feverish and slow, bubbling a little at every breath, and he knew he didn't have the strength right now even to walk back across the Crown Heights Medical Center to the car, let alone to their house half a mile away across the complex. But he was damned if he was going to get stuck in their damned infirmary. For one thing, they might try to keep him off the net—nurses and doctors got some idiot ideas sometimes, and now of all times he couldn't afford that risk. He'd had pneumonia twice before and survived, although it had never been fun.

Still, as Vivien pushed him down the corridor toward the pharmaceutical department—the Patch Ranch, as Orlando called it—he couldn't help wondering whether this might not really be it. Perhaps he had already walked somewhere on his own for the last time. That was a horrible thought. There ought to be some way to tell when you were doing something for the last time so you could appreciate it. An announcement crawling along the bottom of your vision, like when you had the news ticker running on the net. *Fourteen-year-old Orlando Gardiner of San Mateo, California, has just eaten ice cream for the last time in his life. His last laugh is expected sometime next week.*

"What are you thinking about, Orlando?" his mother asked.

He shook his head.

The city stood before him, golden, thrilling, impossibly tall towers shimmering with their own inner light. The only thing he truly wanted waited for him within that thicket of brilliance. He took a step toward it, then another, but the gleaming spires wobbled and disappeared. Cold wet darkness was suddenly all around him. A reflection! He had lunged at a reflection in the water, and now he was drowning, choking, filling up with black fluids. . . .

He sat up, his breath rattling in his lungs. His head felt like a hot balloon.

"Boss?" Beezle whirred in the corner, detaching himself from the power outlet.

Orlando waved his hand, struggling to get air past the phlegm. He thumped himself on the chest, then coughed. He bent over, feeling the blood rush into his throbbing skull, and spat into the medical wastebasket.

"I'm okay," he wheezed when he got his breath back. "Don't want to talk." He pawed his t-jack off the bedside table and clicked it into the neurocannula.

"Are you sure you're okay? I could wake up your parents."

"Don't you dare. I just . . . I had a dream."

Beezle, who had very little in his programming about dreams other than the ability to access literary and scientific references, did not reply to this. *"You had a couple of calls. Do you want to hear the messages?"*

Orlando squinted at the time, superimposed on the upper right of his field of vision and glowing blue against the shadowy drapes beyond. *"It's almost four in the morning. Who called?"*

"Fredericks, both times."

"Tchi seen! Okay, return the call."

Fredericks' broad-faced sim appeared in the window, yawning broadly but still somehow looking nervous. "Jeez, Gardino, I figured I wasn't going to hear back from you tonight."

"Well, what is it? You aren't going to back out on me, are you?"

Fredericks hesitated. Orlando felt a stony weight in his stomach. "I . . . I was just talking to some people at school yesterday. And this guy they know, he got arrested for breaking into some local government system—it was a prank, basically, just tap-and-nap—but they threw him out of his academy and gave him three months in one of those juvenile re-edge holes."

"So?" Orlando turned down the gain on his voice line so he could cough up more phlegm. He didn't feel up to this. He didn't have the strength to keep pushing ahead by himself—didn't Fredericks see that?

"So . . . so the government and the big carriers are really cracking down right now. I mean, it's a bad time to be messing around with other people's systems, Orlando. I don't want to . . . See, my parents would . . ." Fredericks trailed off, oxlike face showing a sort of blank concern. For a moment, Orlando hated him or her.

"And when would be a good time? Let me guess—never?"

"What is this, Orlando? I asked you before—why is this city or whatever you saw so damned important? I mean, you signed up to go work for some gearhouse for *years,* just so you could try to get a little closer to this thing."

Orlando laughed sourly—Indigo Gear had as much chance of getting blood from a billiard ball as years out of him. Then the anger suddenly evaporated, leaving behind only a vacuum-like emptiness. Here, in his dark room, with his parents only yards away and his friend on the other end of the line, he suddenly felt completely and utterly alone.

"I can't explain," he said quietly. "Not really."

Fredericks stared. "Try."

"I . . ." He took a breath, grunted. When it came down to it, there *was* no way to explain, not really. "I have dreams. I dream about that city all the time. And . . . and in the dreams I know there's something there, something important that I have to find." He took another pinched breath. *"Have to."*

"But why? And even if you . . . if you do really have to find this place, what's the hurry? We just got thrown out of that TreeHouse network—shouldn't we wait for a little while."

"I can't wait." After he'd said it, he knew that if Fredericks asked, he would explain everything. The words hung in the air as though he could see them, as though they glowed in the night shadows like the clock numerals.

"Can't wait?" Fredericks said it slowly, sensing something.

"I'm . . . I'm not going to live very long." It was like taking off your clothes in public—frightening, but then a kind of chilly freedom. "I'm dying, basically." The silence stretched so long that if Orlando had not been able to see his friend's sim, he would have thought that Fredericks had clicked off. "Oh, come on, say *something."*

"Orlando, I'm . . . Oh, my God, really?"

"Really. It's not a big deal—I mean, I've known about it for a long time. I was born with . . . well, it's this genetic thing. Called Progeria. You might have heard about it, seen a documentary. . . ."

Fredericks said nothing.

Orlando had trouble getting his breath. The silence hung, an invisible and painful bond between two bedrooms three thousand miles apart. "Progeria," he said at last. "It means you get old when you're still young."

"Old? Like how?"

"Every way you can think of. Lose your hair, muscles shrink up, you get wrinkly and bony, and then you die of a heart attack, or pneumonia . . . or something else that kills old people. Most of us don't make it to eighteen." He tried to laugh. "Most of us—hah! There's only about two dozen people who have this in the whole world. I guess I should be proud."

"I . . . don't know what to say. Isn't there medicine?"

"There's not much you *can* say, Frederico old buddy. Medicine? Yeah, like there's medicine for growing old. Meaning they can slow it down a little bit, which is the only reason I'm still alive—hardly any Progeria cases even used to reach their teens." Orlando swallowed. There it was, all exposed. Too late to take back. "Well, now you know *my* dirty little secret."

"Do you look. . . ?"

"Yeah. As bad as you'd imagine. Let's not talk about it any more." His head was hurting worse than before, a throb like someone was squeezing it in a hot fist. He suddenly wanted to cry, but he wouldn't let himself, even though the intervening, normal-looking, no-Progeria sim would hide it from Fredericks. "Let's . . . let's just drop it, okay?"

"Orlando, I'm so sorry."

"Yeah, life's tough. I want to be a normal boy—and so do you, at least the online kind. I hope at least one of us gets a magic Christmas wish, Pinocchio."

"Don't talk like that, Orlando. You don't sound like yourself."

"Look, I'm tired and I don't feel good. I gotta take my medicine now. You know when those little kids are meeting me. If you want to be there, be there." He broke the connection.

Christabel waved her hand. The beam of light leaped up from the Official Uncle Jingle's Jungle Krew Klok, projecting the numbers on the ceiling. Christabel waved her hand in front of Uncle Jingle's eyes, hurrying before his recorded voice shouted out the time. She only wanted the quiet part of the clock right now.

00:13, the numbers read. Still a long time to go. Christabel sighed. It was like waiting for Christmas morning, except scarier. She waved her hand through the beam and the numbers disappeared, leaving her bedroom dark again.

She heard her mother's voice in the living room, saying something about the car. Her father answered, deep and grumbly so she couldn't understand any of the words. Christabel scrunched down and pulled the blanket up under her chin. Listening to her parents talking when she was in bed usually made her feel safe and warm and cozy, but right now it only made her feel frightened. What if they didn't go to sleep, even when it was 02:00? What would she do?

Her father said something else she couldn't hear and her mother replied. Christabel pulled the pillow over her head and tried to remember the words to Prince Pikapik's song in Ottertown.

For a moment she didn't know where she was. She had been having a dream that Uncle Jingle was chasing Prince Pikapik because the otter prince was supposed to be in school. Uncle Jingle had been smiling his big crazy smile, getting closer and closer to Pikapik, and Christabel had been running toward him, trying to tell him that Prince

Pikapik was an animal, so he didn't have to go to school. But no matter how fast she had run, she didn't get any closer, and Uncle Jingle's smile was so big and his teeth were so bright. . . .

It was very dark, then it wasn't. There was a light flashing on and off. Christabel rolled over in bed. The light was coming from her Storybook Sunglasses where they lay on the carpet next to her dresser. She watched the lenses blink, then go dark a couple of times, and then she remembered.

She sat up in bed with her heart beating really fast. She had fallen asleep! The one thing she hadn't wanted to do! She swiped her hand over the clock and the numbers sprang onto the ceiling: 02:43. Late! Christabel flung back her blankets and scrambled out of bed toward the Storybook Sunglasses.

"So you wanna know what time it is?" shouted Uncle Jingle. He was muffled by the blanket that had accidentally fallen in front of his mouth, but his voice still seemed like the loudest thing she had ever heard. Christabel squeaked and pulled the blanket away, then waved her hands in front of his eyes before he could yell out the time. She crouched in the darkness and listened, expecting any moment to hear her parents getting out of bed.

Silence.

She waited a little longer, just to make certain, then crept across the floor to her blinking glasses. She put them on and saw the words "CHRISTABEL I NEED YOU" sliding past, over and over again. She turned the sunglasses on and off, like Mister Sellars had told her to do last time, but the words "CHRISTABEL I NEED YOU" just kept going past.

When she had put on the clothes and shoes she had hidden under the bed, she took her coat from the closet, moving it slowly so the hangers didn't rattle, then opened the bedroom door and tiptoed out into the hallway. Her parents' door was a little bit open, so Christabel went past with the silentest tiptoe she could do. Her father was snoring, *snkkkk, hrrrwww, snkkkk, hrrrwww,* just like Mister Daddywhiner. Mommy wasn't making any noise, but Christabel was pretty sure she could see her, a sleeping lump just on the other side of her father.

It was funny how different the house looked at night with no lights on. It seemed bigger and much, much scarier, as though it turned into a whole other house after everyone went to bed. What if there were strangers who lived in her house, she suddenly wondered—a whole family, but they were night-time people who only came home after

Christabel and her mother and father were in bed? That was an awful thought.

Something made a noise, a kind of thump. So frightened she felt cold, Christabel held herself very still, like a rabbit she had seen on a nature show when a hawk went by overhead. For a moment, she even thought it might be the night-time people, that a big man, an angry daddy—but not *her* daddy—might suddenly jump out of one of the dark corners, yelling *Who's this bad little girl?* But then she heard the noise again and realized it was just the wind bumping the weather-blinds against the windows outside. She took a deep breath and hurried through the wide-open living room.

When she got to the kitchen, where the light from the streetlamp came in through the windows and made everything seem funny and stretched, she had to stop and think hard to remember the alarm number. Mommy had taught it to her so she could let herself in if there was A Nemergency. Christabel knew that letting herself out of the house at 02:43 in the morning was not the kind of A Nemergency her mother had meant—in fact, it was just about the worst Bad Thing that Christabel could imagine doing—but she had promised Mister Sellars, so she had to. But what if some bad men came while the alarm was off and got her parents and tied them up? It would be her fault.

She pressed the numbers in order, then put her hand on the plate. The light above it changed from red to green. Christabel opened the door, then decided to turn the alarm back on again to keep burglars out. She stepped outside into the cold wind.

The street was empty in a way it never was in the daytime. The trees were waving their branches like they were angry, and almost none of the houses had any lights on. She stood, hesitating. It was scary, but in a way it was wonderful, too, wonderful and exciting and big, like the whole Base was a toy meant only for her. She carefully buttoned her coat, then ran across the lawn, slipping a little on the wet grass.

Christabel ran up her street as fast as she could because she was already late. Her shadow was giant-sized as she went out from under the streetlamp, then it got fainter and fainter until it reappeared again, just as gigantic but behind her, when she reached the next light. She turned on Windicott, then onto Stillwell, her feet going *slap, slap, slap* on the pavement. A dog barked somewhere and she bounced down off the sidewalk and into the middle of the street, amazed that she could be there without having to watch out for cars. Everything was different at night!

From Stillwell she turned onto Redland. She was panting now, so she slowed down to a walk as she passed beneath Redland's old tall trees. There were no lights that she could see at Mister Sellars house, and for a moment she wondered if she had done something wrong, if she had forgotten something he had told her. Then she remembered the Storybook Sunglasses spelling out her name over and over and she was frightened. She started to run again.

It was dark on Mister Sellars porch, and his plants seemed bigger and thicker and stranger than ever. She knocked, but no one answered. For a minute she wanted to run home, but the door opened and Mister Sellars' scratchy voice came from inside. "Christabel? I was wondering if you'd be able to get away. Come in."

Mister Sellars was in his chair, but he had rolled it out of the living room into the hallway and he was holding out a shaking hand.

"I cannot tell you how grateful I am. Come here, stand next to the heater for a moment. Oh, and put these on, will you?" He produced a pair of thin, stretchy gloves and handed them to her. As she struggled to pull them on, he turned his chair back toward the living room. "No sense in leaving fingerprints. I've cleaned up everything else already. But listen to me babble. Are you freezing, little Christabel? It's a cold night out."

"I fell asleep. I tried not to, but I did."

"That's all right. We have plenty of time before it starts to get light. And we have only a few things left to do."

In the living room, sitting on the little table, was a glass of milk and three cookies on a plate. Mister Sellars pointed to them, smiling his funny, crooked smile.

"Go ahead. You're going to need your strength."

"Well, then," he said as she nibbled the last bite of the last cookie, "I think that's everything. Do you understand what you need to do? Really understand?"

Since her mouth was full, she only nodded.

"Now, you must do it just the way I said. This is *very dangerous*, Christabel, and if you were hurt I couldn't bear it. In fact, if there were any other way to do this, I would never have involved you at all."

"But I'm your friend," she said through the crumbs.

"Yes, and that's why. Friends don't take advantage of friendship. But this is really the most important thing, Christabel. If you could only understand how important it is . . ." He trailed off. For a moment, she thought he might be going to fall asleep, but his yellowish eyes popped open again. "Ah! I'd almost forgotten." He rummaged in a pocket of his bathrobe. "These are for you."

She stared at them, not sure what to say. "But I already *have* Storybook Sunglasses. You know that."

"But not like these. You must take these home with you when we've finished, and then you must be sure to get rid of the other pair—throw them somewhere no one will ever find them. Otherwise, your parents will want to know why you have two pairs."

"These are different?" They looked just the same, no matter how she turned them. She put them on, but they felt just like her other pair.

"You'll see later on. Tomorrow, in fact. Put them on after you get home from school—what time is that? Two o'clock?"

She nodded. "Fourteen hundred hours is what my daddy says."

"Good. Now, we need to get to work. But first, would you wash this glass and plate? Just a precaution—I know you have the gloves on, but we don't want to leave any other traces we don't need to."

When she'd finished, and had put the plate and glass back into the cupboard, Christabel found Mister Sellars in the hallway. Sitting so still, with his funny head and small body, he looked like a doll. "Ah," he said, "time to go. I'll miss this place, you know. It's a prison, but not an altogether uncongenial one."

She didn't know what the long word meant, so she just stood.

"Come along," he said. "It's in the back yard."

Christabel had to push away some branches that the wind had knocked down before she could help Mister Sellars down the ramp. There was just enough light from the streetlamp to see by, but it was still very dark. The plants were growing everywhere, even in the middle of the lawn and out of the cracks in the pavement—Christabel thought it looked like nobody had come to do any work in the garden for a long time. The wind was still blowing hard, and the wet grass slapped at her ankles as she pushed him across the lawn. They stopped at the far edge. A rope hung over the grass there, both ends dangling from a funny metal thing on the limb of the big oak tree.

"It's here," he said, pointing at the ground. "Just lift up the grass and push it back. Like this. Now you take the other side."

The grass at the edge of the lawn rolled up, just like her mother rolled up the dining room carpet before she set the floor polisher to work. In the middle of the dirt that was now showing was an old metal plate with two holes in it. Mister Sellars picked up a metal bar that was lying at the edge of the path and put it in one of the holes, then braced it against the handle of his wheelchair and pried up the plate, which fell over onto the lawn with a soft *thump* noise.

"Now," he said, "first me, then the chair. You're about to learn the principle of the pulley, Christabel. I've used it to lower a lot of things already, but it will be much easier with you to help me."

He heaved on the rope to lift his withered body from the chair, then looped part of it under his arms, and with Christabel's help maneuvered himself over the hole. She kept him from bumping against the side as he slowly let the rope slide through his fingers. He only went down a little way before the rope stopped moving.

"See? It's not far."

She leaned over the edge. A funny little square flashlight sat on the floor of the cement tunnel, splashing red light on everything. Mister Sellars sat beside it on the floor, his legs curled under him. If she'd had an umbrella, she could have reached down and poked him. He loosened the rope around his chest and pulled it off without untying the knot.

"We'll hope that I'm the only person who knows about this," he said, smiling his melted-looking smile. "These emergency tunnels haven't been used in fifty years. That's before even your mother and father were born. Now the chair," he said, tossing the loop of rope up to Christabel. "I'll tell you how to tie it."

When she had attached the rope, Mister Sellars pulled hard. The little metal thing in the tree squeaked, but at first the chair didn't move. Christabel pushed it, but that only made it move sideways. Mister Sellars pulled again, this time rising up off the floor so that all his weight was hanging on the rope. The tree branch bent, but the chair rose up just a little way off the ground. Christabel steered it over the hole, then Mister Sellars let the rope slide back gently through his fingers and the chair bumped to the bottom of the tunnel. Mister Sellars pulled himself up into the chair, then attached both ends of the rope to the chair's handles.

"Step back, Christabel," he said. When she did, he waggled his fingers over the armrest and the chair started forward. When the rope had pulled tight, the branch bent far down. Mister Sellars waggled his fingers a little faster. The treads on the bottom of his chair seemed to grab at the tunnel floor, and for the first time the chair made a quiet noise, like a cat purring. Something went *snap!* The branch sprang up and the rope flew down into the tunnel.

"Ah, good. The pulley came with it. That was the only thing I was still worrying about." Mister Sellars looked up at her. In the reddish light, he seemed like something in the Hallowe'en spookhouse at the PX. "I'll be fine from here," he said, smiling. He folded one of his arms in front of him and bowed his head to her like she was the Otter Queen. " '*We who still labour . . . Being weary of the world's empires, bow down to you . . .*' That's Yeats again. Now, don't forget to put on your new Storybook Sunglasses after school. And remember—be very careful with the car." He laughed. "I'm finally going to get some use out of that thing." His face went serious again and he lifted his finger. "Be very, *very* careful. Do everything just the way I said. Can you remember the whole rhyme?"

Christabel nodded. She said it all for him.

"Good. Don't forget to wait until the streetlight goes out." Mister Sellars shook his head. "To think that it has come to this—that I should be forced to such ends! You're my partner in crime, Christabel. I've been planning this for a long time, but I couldn't do it without you. Someday, I hope I can explain to you what an important thing you're doing." He lifted his crinkly hand. "Be good. Be careful!"

"Aren't you going to be scared down there?"

"No. I may not be going very far, but I'll be free, and that's more than I've been able to say in a long time. Go on now, little Christabel. You have to get home soon anyway."

She waved good-bye. Then, with Mister Sellars helping from underneath, she dragged the metal plate back over the hole, then rolled back the grass and patted it down.

> "*Here's the first thing you must think*
> *The bar goes back beneath the sink . . .*"

She took the pry bar with her into the house and put it under the sink, just like in the poem Mister Sellars had taught her. She kept saying the rhyme over and over—there was so much to think about, and she was scared she'd get some of it wrong.

The bundle of stiff, smelly cloth was in the can under the sink, just like the old man had told her. She took it, and the little plastic thing beside it, then walked out the other kitchen door into the garage. There was just enough light coming in through the window at the top of the door to make out the car, Mister Sellars' Cadillac, sitting in the shadows like a huge animal. She very badly wanted to turn on the light, just as she had wanted to turn on the kitchen light—with Mister Sellars gone, the house seemed darker and stranger than her own house had been—but the rhyme said not to:

". . . And leave off every single light."

She made up her mind to be brave and thought of the next part.

"Now wave to open the big garage door
A switch by the kitchen will do that chore . . ."

When she passed her hand in front of the sensor by the entrance from the kitchen, the garage door slid upward on silent runners. Beyond the shadowy bulk of the car, she could see all the way past the streetlamp to the end of Beekman Court.

Christabel walked around the car, reciting Mister Sellars' rhyme. As she passed the passenger door she saw something inside, slouching in the driver's seat. It startled her so much she almost screamed, even though she could see right away it was just a big plastic bag. But even if it was only a bag, she didn't like it. She hurried around to the back of the Cadillac.

". . . Next, find the little secret door
Hidden behind the number four . . ."

The number four was on the car's license plate. She pulled at the edge and the whole license tipped down. Behind it was the place where you put something in the car—it was an old-time car, Mister Sellars had once explained, and didn't work on electricity or steam. Even though he said the car had been in the garage when he moved to the house, Mister Sellars always acted like it belonged to him and he was proud of it.

She unscrewed the cap, then unrolled the thick cloth and pushed one end into the hole and shoved it down. As she was doing this, the streetlamp behind her suddenly went out. It got so dark so fast that it seemed like all the lights in the world had gone out at the same time.

Christabel held her breath. She could see the deep, deep blue sky and the stars through the open garage door, so it wasn't as scary as she'd thought at first. Besides, Mister Sellars had told her it would happen, and anyway she was nearly done with her special job.

She stepped away from the cloth, held up the little plastic tube, and pushed the button. A spark jumped up. Even though she had been expecting it, it surprised her and she dropped the plastic thing, which clattered on the garage floor and bounced away somewhere to one side. There was nothing but shadow on the floor, deep and black. She couldn't see anything.

Her heart went *bump, bump* in her chest like a bird was trapped inside her and trying to get out. What if she lost the plastic tube? Then Mister Sellars would get in trouble—he'd said it was very very important—and maybe *she* would get in trouble too, and her Mommy and Daddy would be so angry, plus maybe Mister Sellars would be put in jail. Christabel got down on her hands and knees to search. Right away she put her hands on something dry and crackly. She wanted to scream again, but even though she was really afraid of what might be down there (spiders, worms, snakes, more spiders, skeletons like in the spookhouse) she had to keep looking, she just had to. Mister Sellars had said to do it when the streetlamp went out. He had *said!* Christabel began to cry.

At last, after a very long time, she felt the smooth plastic beneath her fingers. Sniffling, she got to her feet, then felt her way to the back of the car again. She held the thing away from her so it wouldn't be so scary, then pushed the button. The spark jumped and turned into fire. She took the end of the cloth—carefully, just like Mister Sellars had said—and touched it to the fire. The cloth began to burn, not a big fire, just a blue edge that smoked. She crammed her gloves into the opening to keep the license plate from swinging shut, then stretched the burning end of the cloth as far from the car as it would go before dropping it onto the floor. She walked out of the garage quickly, saying the last part of the rhyme to herself, partly to make sure she remembered, partly because she was really scared. Outside, she pushed the button on the wall and the garage door hissed down.

Now, with almost everything done, Christabel turned and ran up Redland as fast as she could. All the houses were dark, but now all the streetlamps were dark too, so she ran with only the light of the stars to show her the way. As she turned the corner and hurried down Stillwell, she threw the plastic flame-maker into some bushes. Then, when she reached her own front lawn, all the streetlamps suddenly started to shine again. She hurried to her front door.

Christabel had forgotten about the alarm. When she pushed the door open, speakers all over the house began to buzz, startling her so much she almost wet her pants. Over the horrible noise, she heard her father begin to shout. Terrified, she ran as fast as she could and got through her bedroom door just before the door to her parents' room banged open. She threw off her coat and shoes and clothes, praying that they wouldn't come in. She had just got her jammies on when her mother hurried in.

"Christabel? Are you okay? Don't be scared—it's the door alarm, but I think it went off by accident."

"It's some kind of power outage, I think," her father shouted from down the hall. "The wallscreens are all off, and my watch is almost an hour different than the kitchen clock. Must have triggered the alarm when it came back on."

Christabel had just been tucked back in bed by her mother, and was scrunching down beneath the covers, feeling her heart begin to slow, when the flame at last reached the gas tank in Mister Sellars' Cadillac. It made a noise like God himself clapping His hands together, rattling windows for miles and waking up almost everyone on the Base. Christabel screamed.

Her mother came back into the bedroom, and this time sat beside her in the dark, rubbing her neck and telling her it was all right, it was a gas line or something, it was a long way away. Christabel clung to her mother's stomach, feeling like she was so full of secrets that she might blow up, too. Light flickered in the treetops outside as the fire trucks hurried past going *weeaaw, weeaaw, weeaaw* . . .

"**H**ey, Landogarner, you got sword-head house," Zunni commented.

Tiny yellow monkeys were busily rearranging the decor of Orlando's 'cot. Two of them were adding an exaggerated handlebar mustache to the severed head of the Black Elf Prince, and half-a-dozen others seemed to have changed the body of the Worm of Morsin Keep into a transparent chute; as Orlando watched, one little banana-colored simian was sliding on its belly through the innards of Thargor's prize beast.

"Sword-head? Oh, yeah. I used to spend a lot of time in the Middle Country. You know that?"

"Boring," pronounced Zunni. "Kill monster, find jewel, earn bonus points. Wibble-wobble-wubble."

Orlando couldn't really argue. He turned to watch another pair of monkeys altering the historical pictures of the Karagorum Tapestry into a procession of cartoon snails having sex. He scowled. It wasn't so much the exuberant vandalism that bothered him—he had gotten pretty sick of the old decor—as the seemingly effortless way the Wicked Tribe had penetrated his protected programming. It would have taken a team of engineers from some place like Indigo a whole afternoon to manage what these little lunatics had done in minutes. He suddenly understood how his parents must have felt when he tried to explain the things he did on the net.

Beezle appeared from a hole in the ceiling and was instantly swarmed by mini-apes. "If you don't get these things offa me," the agent warned, "I'm gonna drez 'em."

"Be my guest. I'd like to see you manage it."

Beezle knotted his legs tight to protect them from marauding monkeys. "Fredericks is requesting permission to enter."

Orlando felt something grow warmer inside him. "Yeah, sure. Let him . . . her . . . let him in." He would have to get this straightened out in his mind, it seemed. So, if Fredericks wanted to be treated like a guy, then she was a guy. Just like old times. Sort of.

Fredericks popped in and was immediately set upon by flying yellow creatures. As he waved his hands reflexively to clear his field of vision—he could have made them transparent if he had thought about it, since he knew the capacities of Orlando's 'cot almost as well as its creator did—Orlando looked him over. Fredericks' sim seemed a little less spectacularly muscle-bound than usual. Maybe after hearing about Orlando's disease, he thought that looking so healthy might be offensive.

"Los Monos Volandos!" shouted one of the Tribe, buzzing Fredericks' face. "We Supremo Bigdaddy culture club! Happy Flappy Trails!"

"Jesus, Orlando, this is fun," grumped Fredericks as he flicked away a tiny ape who had been swinging from his simulated earlobe. "I'm utterly glad I didn't miss this."

"Yeah. I'm glad you didn't miss it, too."

A moment of awkward silence—silence except for the chattering and aimless noisemaking of the Tribe—ended when Orlando clapped his hands. The yellow cloud split apart into simian particles which settled down on various virtual surfaces. "I wanted to ask you guys for a favor." He tried to look like the kind of person a flock of feral children should want to help. "I need help really badly."

"You cred us?" squealed some of the monkeys. "Spree-buy? Toyzn-gear?" But Kaspar—Orlando was beginning to recognize a few of their voices—shushed them.

"What favor you need?"

"I'm trying to find somebody. The name is Melchior, and it's something to do with TreeHouse. He or she—or maybe it's more than one person—did some software work, some gear, for a Red Gryphon in the Middle Country simworld."

"Melchior?" said Zunni, rising to hover in the air like a particularly homely little fairy. "Easy! Dog, Dog, Dog!"

"And Doggie-friends!" said another monkey.

"Wait a minute. What do you mean?"

"This is like talking to breakfast cereal," said Fredericks. "Give it up, Orlando."

"Hang on. Zunni, is 'Dog' a person?"

The tiny ape spun. "No, no, not person—old! Million years!"

Kaspar shushed some of the younger Tribesfolk again. "He is old person. We call him 'Dog.' He lives in Cobweb Corner."

"Older than rocks!" shouted one of the monkeys.

"Older than Uncle Jingle!" giggled another. "O-O-*Old.*"

Tortuously, Orlando managed to glean the information that some old person called something like "Blue Dog and Krite," or just "Dog," kept an elcot in Founder's Hill at TreeHouse, and along with some other people had once created gear under the name of Melchior.

"Made Blast-Up Button," Zunni remembered with pleasure. "Put it on someone head, push it—*boooooom!*"

Orlando hoped that she was talking about something that happened to sims, not real people. "Can you get us back into TreeHouse so we can talk to him?"

"Woof!" said Zunni. "Even better. You-view-he, he-view-you."

"We get him right now," Kasper explained. "Dog, he *love* Wicked Tribe. Always he says, 'just what I need!' when we visit him for fun games."

The monkeys rose in a sudden yellow cyclone, spun so rapidly they seemed to smear like melting butter, then disappeared.

Orlando sat appreciating the silence. His head was beginning to throb, a slight feverish ache. Fredericks rose and glided to the vandalized pyramid of trophies, stopping in front of the Black Elf Prince. "Dieter Cabo would love this."

"Don't blame me, blame the Tarzan Memorial Art Appreciation Society."

Fredericks glided back. "So you think these micro-scannies are going to help you find something you see in your dreams? Orlando, do you ever listen to yourself any more?"

"I'll follow whatever lead I can get."

"Yeah, I noticed." His friend hesitated. "How are you feeling?"

"Don't start. I shouldn't have told you anything."

Fredericks sighed, but before he could say anything else, one of the 'cot walls went permeable and a blizzard of monkeys blew through it.

"Come on!" one shouted. "Come now *fast-fast-fast!*"

"What is it?" Orlando couldn't make any sense out of the Tribal din. "What?"

"Found Dog." Zunni's voice purred in his ear. She was hovering just above his left shoulder. "He having big secret. Strongline, throughput plus, all kinds of colors! Come 'long!"

"Dog is doing something," elaborated Kaspar in his other ear. "Something he is trying to hide. Big secret, but no one fools the Wicked Tribe!"

Orlando could not help thinking of a cartoon he had once seen, a man with a devil hovering on one shoulder and an angel on the other, each trying to sway him to its own ends. But what if you had only voices of uncontrolled anarchy in both ears? "What are you talking about? What kind of secret? Throughput?"

"Big hole to somewhere. Come! We hook you up!" Zunni was buzzing at his ear like a bumblebee. "We surprise Dog! Laugh and shriek, laugh and shriek!"

"Wicked Tribe *mejor* net-riding Krew!" shouted another. "*Kilohana!* Fasten belts!"

"Slow down!" Orlando winced. The fever headache had suddenly gotten fierce, and he did not want to be rushed. But it was too late for any chance of consultation—the monkeys were in full-speed-ahead mode. Fredericks wavered and disappeared, sucked away to only the Wicked Tribe knew where. The entire 'cot began to swirl like several colors of paint poured down the drain.

"Damn it, wait a minute. . . !" Orlando shouted, but he was shouting into emptiness and a hiss like an empty signal as they took him, too.

Darkness washed over him. He was falling, flying, being pulled apart in several directions. The crackling in his ears grew louder until it roared like the jets of an interplanetary rocket.

"Hang on, 'Landogarner!" Zunni shouted happily above the noise, somewhere in the darkness. She sounded completely undisturbed; was this unsettling experience his alone, or were these mad children simply used to it? The sensation of being pulled grew stronger, as though he were being stretched thin and sucked through a straw. It was like being in some roller-coastering simulation, but surely they must be *between* simulations . . . Orlando could hardly think. He seemed to be going faster, ever faster. . . .

Then the universe collapsed.

Everything stopped, as though something had seized him with a giant hand. He heard distant shrieks, the thin voices of children, but not happy now. Faintly, as though from behind a thick door, those children were screeching in terror. Something had them . . . and it had Orlando, too.

The void began to tighten around him, a squeezing fist of nothingness that froze his thoughts and heart. He was helpless, suspended in an arc of slow electricity. The part of him that could still think struggled, but could not free itself. The darkness had weight, and it was crushing him. He could feel himself flattened, pressed, until his last remaining piece of self fluttered helplessly and ever more slowly, like a bird caught beneath a thick blanket.

I don't want to die! It was a meaningless thought, because there was nothing he could think or do to change what was happening, but it echoed over and over through a mind that was running down. All the death-trip simulations in the world could not have prepared him for this. *I don't want to die! I don't want . . . to die . . .*

Don't . . . want . . .

Astonishingly, the darkness was not infinite.

A tiny spark drew him up out of the unspeakable emptiness. He rose toward it helplessly and without volition, as though he were a corpse being dragged from the depths of a river. The spark became a blur of light. After the killing blackness, it seemed an impossible gift.

As he floated closer, the light grew, shooting out at all angles, scratching bright marks on the endless slate of night. Lines became a square; the square gained depth and was a cube, which then became something so mundane that for a moment he could not believe it. Floating in the void, becoming larger every moment, was an *office*—a simple room with desk and chairs. Whether he rose to it or it descended to him he could not tell, but it spread and surrounded him, and he felt the freezing numbness inside him shift and loosen a little.

This is a dream. I'm having a dream. He was certain—he had fallen asleep wearing his jack before and knew the sensation. *It's the pneumonia, must be—a fever dream. But why can't I wake up?*

The room was something like a medical examining room, but everything in it was made of gray concrete. The vast desk looked like a stone sarcophagus, something from a tomb. Behind the desk sat a man—or at least Orlando thought it was a man: where the face should be hung a radiant emptiness.

"I'm dreaming, aren't I?" he asked.

The being behind the desk did not seem to hear the question. "Why is it you wish to come and work for us?" The voice was high but soothing.

Never in a million years could he have anticipated such a conversation. "I . . . don't want to work for anyone. I mean, I'm just a kid."

A door in the wall behind the desk slowly swung open, revealing swirling, smoky blue light. Something moved inside this brilliance, a shadow with no discernible shape that nevertheless filled him with horror.

"*He* wants you," said the shining personage. "He'll take anyone— he's bored, you see. But on our side we have slightly higher standards. Our margin is very slim. Nothing personal."

"I can't have a job yet. I'm still in school, see . . ." This *was* a dream—it had to be. Or maybe it was something worse. Maybe he was dying, and his mind had cobbled together this last fantasy.

The thing in the room beyond moved, making the light waver. Orlando could hear it breathing, the deep, ragged inhalations coming a long time apart. It was waiting. It would wait as long as necessary.

"Well, then I suppose you might as well step through." The figure behind the desk gestured toward the open door and the terrible something beyond. "If you don't want the job, you shouldn't have wasted our precious office hours. Things are busy just now, what with the expansion *and* the merger."

The hoarse breathing became louder. Orlando knew that he did not ever want to see what made that noise.

"I've changed my mind," he said hurriedly. "I'm sorry. I want the job. Is it something to do with mathematics?" He knew he had good scores—wasn't that what grown-ups wanted? Good scores? He would have to ask his mother and father for permission to leave school, but when he told them about the thing in the other room, surely they would . . .

The shining person stood. Was that rejection in the set of shoulders, in the cold white fire of the faceless face? Had he argued too long?

"Come and give me your hand," it said.

Without knowing how it happened, he was standing before the

desk. The figure there put out a hand which burned like phosphorus, but without heat. At the same time, he could feel the cold air billowing out from the blue-lit room, air that made his skin shrink and his eyes water. Orlando reached out.

"You must remember to do your best." As the figure enveloped his hand with its own, he felt warmth flooding back into him so swiftly that it was almost painful. "Your scores were good. We'll take a chance."

"Don't forget Fredericks," he said, suddenly remembering. "I made him come—it's not his fault!"

The thing in the room beyond made a horrid noise, part bark, part wet sob. Its shadow moved forward, darkening the doorway and quenching the cube of light that was the office, blotting out even the brilliance of the thing that held Orlando's hand. He shouted in terror and stepped back, and then he was falling again.

Falling.

The setting sun, as it passed behind the haze that shrouded Calcutta, seemed to kindle the entire sky. An orange glow spread along the horizon, molten light against which the factory smokestacks stood in charcoal silhouette like the minarets of hell.

It has begun, he thought. *Even the skies reflect it. The Dance has begun.*

The holy man bent and lifted his single possession from the sand, then walked slowly down to the river to wash it clean. He was finished with it now, this last tie to the illusory world of Maya, but there were rituals to be observed. He must finish properly, as he had begun.

He squatted in the brown river, a delta finger of the mighty Ganges, and felt its sacred waters wash over him, thick with the effluvia of Calcutta's industrial and human waste. His skin itched and burned, but he did not hurry. He filled the bowl and then poured the water out again, rubbing and scraping with his long fingers in all the crannies until the bowl gleamed in the dying sunlight. He held it up before him with the teeth resting on his palm, and remembered the day he had come here to ready himself, a full two years before.

No one had troubled him as he picked through the ashes of the cremation ground. Even in the modern Indian Federation, where pulsingly new electronic nerves ran through the flesh of a nation as old and withered as humankind itself, there was still a superstitious respect for the Aghori. The cremation sites to which he and a few other devotees of Shiva the Destroyer still came as pilgrims, sinking themselves in filth and carrion in the search for purity, were ceded to them, the most untouchable of untouchables. Those who believed welcomed evidence that the old ways were not completely gone. Others, who had once believed, turned away with a guilty shudder. And those who did not believe at all had better things to do than worry what might go on in the festering bonepiles beside the great, filthy river.

On that day two years ago, when he had shed his city clothes as easily and completely as a snake sloughs its skin, he had carefully inspected every pile of human bones. Later, he would return to them in search of unconsumed flesh, for the servants of Shiva eat carrion as well as live with it, but on this first day he had been searching for something more durable. He had found it at last, complete but for a jawbone, sitting on the scorched remains of a rib cage. For an idle moment he had wondered upon what scenes the empty eye sockets had once looked, what tears they had shed, what thoughts, hopes, dreams had lived in the now-hollow braincase. Then he had reminded himself of the first lesson of the cremation ground: everything comes to this, but this, too, is illusion. Just as the death represented by the nameless skull was all death, so also was it no death, merely an illusion of the material world.

His mind refocused, he had taken the skull down to the riverside. As the sun, like this day's sun, had sunk down to disappear at last into the western haze, a torch doused in a basin of muddy water, he had found a sharp stone and begun to work. He had first placed the point of the stone in the middle of the forehead in the place where a living man placed a *pundara* mark, then scored the bone all the way around the skull's circumference, across frontal, temporal, occipital—words from his previous life that he now discarded as easily as he had put off his clothes. The circle delineated, he had taken the sharp edge of the stone—which was nevertheless not very sharp—and begun to saw.

For all his patience—he had spent that first night without a fire, in shivering nakedness, so as not to lose concentration—it had not been a simple task. Others of his kind, he knew, chose a skull which had already been weakened by fire, or which in some cases had already broken open, but, with some thought of the ultimate rigors before him, he had not allowed himself such luxury. Thus, it was not until the sun had reappeared in the east and turned the river to rosy copper that he lifted the top of the skull free and tossed it aside.

He had taken the rest of the skull down to the river then, his first time touching the holy waters since his arrival. Although he had been feeling a thirst like fire in his throat for hours, it was not until he had sanded down the edges of the hollow on a flat rock that he allowed himself to dip it into the river and drink. As Mother Ganges' polluted waters passed down his throat, replacing the thirst with another kind of fire, he had felt a great clarity transfix him.

Lord Shiva, he had thought, *I reject the coils of Maya. I await your music.*

Now, as he stared at the bowl for the last time, the Aghori began to speak. His voice, unused for months, was dry and faint, but he was not talking for anyone's benefit but his own.

"*It came to Lord Shiva's ears that there were living in the forest of Tāragam ten thousand heretical priests. These heretics taught that the universe is eternal, that souls have no lord, and that the performance of works alone is sufficient for salvation. Shiva determined to go among them and teach them the error of their ways.*

"*To Lord Vishnu the Preserver he said, 'Come, you will accompany me. I will put upon myself the seeming of a wandering yogi, and you will put upon yourself the appearance of the yogi's beautiful wife, and we will confound these heretical rishis.' So he and Vishnu disguised themselves and went among the priests in the forest of Tāragam.*

"*All the wives of the priests found themselves filled with painful longing for the powerful yogi who came to them, and all the rishis themselves were full of longing for the yogi's wife. All the business of that place was disrupted, and there was great unrest among the priesthood. At last they decided to set a curse upon the yogi and his wife, but all of their cursings were to no effect.*

"*So the priests prepared a sacrificial fire, and from it summoned a dreadful tiger, which rushed upon Lord Shiva to destroy him. But Shiva only smiled a tender smile, then pulled the skin from the tiger using only his little finger, and wrapped that skin about himself for a shawl.*

"*The furious rishis next evoked a terrible serpent, vast and poisonous, but Shiva smiled again and snatched it up, then hung it about his neck for a garland. The priests could not believe their eyes.*

"*Lastly, the priests brought forth a hideous black dwarf with a club that could shatter mountains, but Shiva only laughed and set his foot upon the dwarf's back and then began to dance. Shiva's dance is the source of all movement within the universe, and the vision of it, and the splendor of heaven's opening, filled the hearts of the heretical priests with awe and terror. They cast themselves down before him, crying for mercy. He danced for them his five acts, creation, preservation, destruction, embodiment, and release, and when they had seen Lord Shiva's dance, the priests were freed from illusion and became his devotees, and error was forever burned from their souls.*

"Thus it is that as the First Cause—sometimes called 'The Terror' and 'The Destroyer'—dances upon darkness, he contains in himself both the life and death of all things. So for this reason his servants dwell in the cremation ground, and the heart of his servant is like the cremation ground, wasted and desolate, where the self and its thoughts and deeds are burned away, and nothing remains but the Dancer himself."

When he had finished speaking, he bent his head and shut his eyes. After a few moments, he set his bowl down upon the sandy soil, then lifted a heavy stone and broke the bowl to pieces.

The sun had disappeared, leaving only a bloody ribbon of light stretched on the horizon behind the city. The Aghori stood up and walked through the ashes and smoke to the place among the reeds where he had left his briefcase twenty-four months earlier, protected by a plastic bag, nestled in a pile of rocks. He took it from the bag and placed his thumb against the lock, then opened it. The scent that rose from the case, to senses now used only to the smell of the charnel house, was that of another life, one that seemed impossibly different. For a moment he allowed his roughened fingers to indulge themselves against the almost unbelievable softness of the clothing that had awaited him there all this time, and marveled that he had once thoughtlessly worn such things. Then he lifted the silky bundle and took from beneath it a pad in an expensive leather case. He flipped open the lid and ran a finger across the touchscreen. It glowed into life, its spark-chip still charged. He uncapped his neurocannula and swabbed it with alcohol from the briefcase pocket—there were some things for which even the sacred water of Mother Ganges was not entirely suitable—then unspooled a fiberlink from the side of the pad and plugged it in.

Ten minutes later Nandi Paradivash unplugged the fiberlink and stood up. As he had anticipated, the message had been waiting. It was time to move on.

He pulled on the pants and shirt, helplessly conscious of their soft feel against his skin, then sat down on a rock to don his shoes. The cremation ground had prepared him, but for the next part of his journey he must return to the city. What he needed to do next would require access to serious bandwidth.

The Grail Brotherhood have taken up their instruments, and now we of the Circle take up ours. Others have been drawn to the music, too, as we guessed they would. And only Lord Shiva knows how it will end.

He closed the briefcase, then made his way up the sandy bank. It was evening now, and the lights of the city glimmered before him like a jeweled necklace upon the dark breast of Parvati, the Destroyer's wife.

It has begun, he told himself. *The dance has begun.*

Fourth:

THE CITY

. . . And he answered and said,
"Babylon is fallen, is fallen;
and all the graven images of her gods
he hath broken unto the ground . . ."

—Isaiah, 21:9

CHAPTER 33

Someone Else's Dream

NETFEED/SITCOM-LIVE: Come to Buy Some "Sprootie"!
(visual: Wengweng Cho's dining room)
CHO: What is this? I thought someone went to get Sprootie! This is a very
important meal! The regional governor is coming! You have all betrayed me!
(visual: Cho exits. Daughter Zia shoves Chen Shuo.)
ZIA: You are going to give my father a heart attack, Shuo!
SHUO: I hear that Sprootie is a good cure for that, too!
(audio over: laughter)
ZIA: He really believes there is such a thing! You are a very cruel man!
SHUO: Is that why you love me? Or is it just because I am so beautiful?
(audio over: laughter and applause)

For a long time she lay on her back, staring up at the feverish green of the trees and the random multicolored bits of flame that she at last identified as butterflies. Where she could see it through the puzzle of leaves, the sky was awesomely deep and blue. But she could not remember who she was, or where she was, or why she should be lying on her back, so empty of knowledge.

At last, as she idly watched a green bird making urgent little hooting noises on a green branch above her, a memory drifted up. There had been a shadow, a cold hand upon her. Darkness, terrible darkness.

Despite the moist warmth of the air and the strength of the sun beyond the filter of leaves, she shivered.

I have lost someone, she thought suddenly. She could feel the space where that person should be. *Someone dear to me is gone.* An incomplete picture flitted through her thoughts, a small body, slender, a brown-skinned face with bright eyes.

Brother? she wondered. *Son? Friend or lover?* She knew all the words, but could not say exactly what any of them meant.

She sat up. The wind in the trees made a long sighing noise, an exhalation that surrounded her, as the trees themselves did, on all sides. What was this place?

Then, tickling her thoughts like a cough gathering in a throat, she began to hear a word. It was only a sound at first, but in her thoughts she could hear a woman's voice saying it, a sharp sound, a sound meant to get her attention: *Irene! Irene!*

Irene. It was her mother's voice, playing back from her memory like an old recording. *Irene, put that down now. Girl, you tire me out sometimes. Irene. Irene Sulaweyo. Yes, Renie, I'm talking to you!*

Renie.

And with her name, everything else came flooding back as well—her father's angry scowl and Stephen's sweet face gone slack in endless sleep, Pinetown, the wreckage of Doctor Van Bleeck's laboratory. And then the dark thing, the terrible blackness, and old Singh shrieking without any sound.

!Xabbu!

"!Xabbu?" There was no answer but the hooting green bird. She raised her voice and tried again, then remembered Martine and called her, too.

But that's foolishness. She wouldn't be here with me—she's in France, wherever. And this was clearly not France, and not the military base beneath the mountain either. This was . . . someplace else.

Where in God's name am I? "!Xabbu! !Xabbu, can you hear me?"

The vibrant jungle swallowed her voice; it died almost without echo. Renie stood on shaky legs. The experiment had clearly failed in some terrible way, but how had it resulted in this? Her surroundings were nothing like the arid Drakensberg Mountains—this looked like someplace in the north, like one of the rain forests in the West African Federation.

A thought, an impossible thought, kindled in her mind.

It couldn't be. . . .

She reached up to touch her face. Something was there, something invisible that nevertheless had form and texture beneath her probing fingers—something that even covered her eyes, although the green world before her demonstrated that nothing could be impeding her vision. . . .

Unless none of this was real. . . .

Renie grew dizzy. She sank slowly to her knees, then sat down. There was thick, soft soil beneath her, hot and alive with its own cycle of life—she could feel it! She could feel the serrated edge of a fallen leaf against the edge of her hand. The thought was impossible—but so was this place. The world around her was too real. She closed her eyes and opened them. The jungle would not go away.

Overwhelmed, she began to weep.

It's impossible. She had been walking for half an hour, struggling through thick vegetation. *This quality of detail—and it goes on for miles! And there's no latency at all! It just can't be.*

An insect hummed past. Renie threw out her hand and felt the tiny body smack against her knuckle and bounce off. A moment later, the bright, winged thing had struggled back into flight and was zigzagging away.

No discernible latency, even at this level of complexity. What did Singh say— trillions upon trillions of instructions per second? I've never heard of anything like this. Suddenly, she realized why the golden city had looked the way it did. At this level of technology, almost anything was possible.

"!Xabbu!" she shouted again. "Martine! Hello!" Then, a little more quietly: "Jeremiah? Is the line still working? Can you hear me? Jeremiah?"

Nobody answered her except birds.

So now what? If she was indeed in the network called Otherland, and if it was as big as Singh had said, she might be as horrendously far from anything useful as someone at the Antarctic would be from an Egyptian coffee house. Where had Singh meant to start?

The weight of hopelessness threatened for a moment to immobilize her completely. She considered just dropping offline, but rejected the thought after only short consideration. Singh had died in that . . . darkness (which was as much thought as she dared to give to what had happened) to get them here. It would be a terrible betrayal to do anything but go on. But go on where?

She ran through a quick set of exploratory commands without result. None of the standard VR control languages seemed to be in operation, or else there were permissions necessary for users to manipulate the environment that she simply didn't have.

Someone's spent an unimaginable amount of time and money to build themselves a world. Maybe they like playing God—maybe no one else gets to do anything but visit this place and take what they get.

Renie looked up. The tree-shadows had taken on a new angle, and the sky seemed just perceptibly darker. *Everything else is just like RL,* she thought. *So maybe I better start thinking about a fire. Who knows what's going to be walking around here at night?*

The impossibility of her situation once more threatened to overcome her, but beneath the shock and confusion and despair, there was also a tiny trace of sour humor. Who would ever have guessed that her precious, hard-earned college education, the thing that everyone had said would make her an integral part of the twenty-first century, would instead have led to her building imaginary fires in imaginary jungles to keep imaginary beasts at bay.

Congratulations, Renie. You are now an official imaginary primitive.

It was hopeless. Even with the trick !Xabbu had showed her, she could not manufacture a single spark. The wood had been too long on the damp ground.

Whoever made this bastard place had to be a stickler for detail, didn't he? Couldn't have left a few dry sticks around. . . .

Something rustled in the bushes. Renie jerked upright and seized one of the branches, hoping it would make a better club than it had a bonfire.

What are you so afraid of? It's a simulation. So some big old leopard or something comes out of the dark and kills you, so what?

But that would probably throw her out of the network, game over. Which would be another way of failing Singh, Stephen, everyone.

And this whole place feels too goddamn real, anyway. I don't want to find out how they'd simulate me being something's dinner.

The clear place in which she had settled was scarcely three meters wide. The moonlight filtering down through the trees was strong, but it was still only moonlight: anything big enough to harm her would probably be on her before she could react. And she couldn't even prepare herself for possible dangers, because she had no idea where she was supposed to be. Africa? Prehistoric Asia? Something completely imaginary? Whoever could dream up a city like that could invent a whole lot of monsters, too.

The rattle grew louder. Renie tried to remember the things she had read in books. Most animals, she seemed to remember, were more scared of you than you were of them. Even the big ones like lions preferred to avoid humans.

Assuming we have anything like real animals here.

Dismissing this bleak thought, she decided that rather than crouching in fear, hoping not to be discovered, she would be better off announcing her presence. She took a breath and began singing loudly.

> *"Genome Warriors!*
> *Brave and strong*
> *Battle Mutarr's evil throng*
> *Separate the right from wrong*
> *Mighty Genome Warriors . . ."*

It was embarrassing, but at the moment the children's show theme—one of Stephen's great favorites—was the only thing that came to her mind.

> *"When the mutant mastermind*
> *Threatens all of humankind*
> *Tries to sneak up from behind*
> *And cut genetic ties that bind . . ."*

The rustling grew louder. Renie broke off her song and raised the club. A shaggy, strange-looking animal, somewhere between a rat and a pig in appearance and closer in size to the latter, pushed through into the clearing. Renie froze. The thing raised its snout for a moment and sniffed, but did not seem to see her. A moment later two smaller versions of the original bumbled out of the vegetation behind it. The mother made a quiet grunting noise and herded her offspring back into the shrubbery, leaving Renie shaken but relieved.

The creature had looked vaguely familiar, but she certainly could not say she had recognized it. She still did not have any idea where she was supposed to be.

> *"Genome Warriors. . . !"*

She sang again, louder this time. Apparently, at least judging by the pig-rat or whatever it was she had just met, the local fauna weren't aware that they were supposed to be afraid of humans.

". . . Bold and clean
With Chromoswords so sharp and keen
They'll fight the Muto-mix Machine
Mighty Genome Warriors!"

The moon had passed directly above her, and she had run through every song she could remember—pop tunes, themes from various net shows, nursery rhymes and tribal hymns—when she thought she heard a faint voice calling her name.

She stood, about to shout a reply, but stopped. She was no longer in her own world—she was very evidently trapped in someone else's dream—and she could not shake off the memory of the dark something that had killed Singh and handled Renie herself as though she were a toy. Perhaps this strange operating system, or whatever it was, had lost her when she slipped through, but was now looking for her. It sounded ridiculous, but the horrible living darkness followed by the overpowering realness of this place had shaken her badly.

Before she could decide what to do, something decided for her. The leaves rattled overhead, then something thumped down onto the floor of the clearing. The intruder had a head like a dog and yellow, moon-reflecting eyes. Renie tried to scream, but could not. Choking, she raised the thick branch. The thing skittered back and lifted surprisingly human forepaws.

"Renie! It is me! !Xabbu!"

"!Xabbu? What . . . is that really you?"

The baboon settled onto its haunches. "I promise you. Do you remember the people who sit on their heels? I am wearing their shape, but behind the shape is me."

"Oh, my God." There could be no mistaking the voice. Why would anything that could copy !Xabbu's speech so perfectly bother to send an imposter in such a confusing shape? "Oh, my God, it *is* you!"

She ran forward and lifted the hairy animal body in her arms, and hugged it, and wept.

"But why do you look like that? Is it something that happened when we passed through that . . . whatever that was?"

!Xabbu was using his nimble baboon fingers to apply himself to fire-making. By climbing he had found some dead branches, comparatively dry because they had not yet fallen to the ground; a tiny wisp of smoke was now rising from the piece braced between his long feet.

"I told you that I had a dream," he said. "That it was time for all the First People to join together once more. I dreamed that it was time to repay the debt that my family owes to the people who sit on their heels. For that reason—and others that you would think more practical—I chose this as my secondary sim after a more ordinary human shape. But when I came through to this place, this was the body I had been given. I cannot find any way to make things change, so even when I did not wish to frighten you, I still had to remain in this form."

Renie smiled. Just being reunited with !Xabbu had lifted her spirits, and the sight of a smoldering red spot in the hollowed-out branch was lifting them higher still. "You had practical reasons for choosing that sim? What exactly is practical about being a baboon?"

!Xabbu gave her a long look. There was something inherently comical in the bony overhanging brow and canine snout, but the little man's personality still made itself felt. "Many things, Renie. I can get to places you cannot—I was able to climb a tree to find these branches, remember. I have teeth," he briefly bared his impressive fangs, "that may be useful. And I can go places and not be remarked upon because city-people do not notice animals—even in a world as strange as this, I would guess. Considering how little we know of this network and its simulations, I think those are all valuable commodities."

The curls of leaves had now begun to burn. As !Xabbu used these small flames to ignite a larger blaze, Renie reached her hands toward the warmth. "Have you tried to talk to Jeremiah?"

!Xabbu nodded his head. "I am sure you and I have made the same discoveries."

Renie leaned back. "This is all so hard to believe. I mean, it feels incredibly real, doesn't it? Can you imagine if we had direct neural hookups?"

"I wish we did." The baboon squatted, poking at the blaze. "It is frustrating not to be able to smell more things. This sim desires nose information."

"I'm afraid the military didn't think smells were very important. The V-tank equipment has a pretty rudimentary scent palette. They probably just wanted users to be able to smell equipment fires and bad air and a few other things, but beyond that . . . What do you mean, anyway, 'nose information'?"

"Before entering into VR the first time, I had not realized how much I rely on my sense of smell, Renie. Also, perhaps because I am wearing an animal sim, the operating system of this network seems to give me slightly different . . . what words do you use? . . . sensory input. I feel I could do many things that I could never do in my other life."

A brief chill went through Renie at !Xabbu's mention of an "other life," but he distracted her by leaning close and snuffling at her with his long muzzle. The light touch tickled and she pushed him away. "What are you doing?"

"Memorizing your scent, or at least the scent our equipment gives you. If I had better tools, I would not even have to work at it. But now I think I will be able to find you even if you get lost again." He sounded pleased with himself.

"Finding me isn't the issue. Finding *us*, that's the difficult part. Where are we? Where do we go? We have to do something soon—I don't care about hourglasses and imaginary cities, but my brother's dying!"

"I know. We must find our way out of this jungle first, I think. Then we will be able to learn more." He rocked on his haunches, holding his tail in his hand. "I think I can tell you something about where we are, though. And *when* we are, too."

"You can't! How could you? What did you see before you met up with me, a road sign? A tourist information booth?"

He furrowed his brow, the very picture of cool simian indignation. "It is only a guess that I am making, Renie. Because there is so much we do not know about this network and its simulations, I may be wrong. But part of it is common sense. Look around us. This is a jungle, a rain forest like the Cameroon. But where are the animals?"

"I saw a few. And I'm sitting next to one."

He ignored this. "A few, indeed. And there are not as many birds as you would expect in such a place."

"So?"

"So I would guess that we are quite close to the edge of the forest, and that either there is a big city nearby or some kind of industry. I have seen it before, in the real world. Either one of those would have driven many of the animals away."

Renie nodded slowly. !Xabbu was emotionally perceptive, but he was also just plain clever. It had been easy to underestimate him sometimes because of his small stature and the quaintness of his clothes and speech. It would be even easier to make that mistake while he wore his present appearance. "Or, if this is an invented world, someone may just have made it this way," she pointed out.

"Perhaps. But I think there is a good chance we are not far from people."

"You said 'when,' as well."

"If the animals have been driven away, then I suspect that the technology of this . . . this world . . . is not too far behind our own, or even ahead. Also, there is a harsh scent in the air that I believe is part of this place, and not just an accidental product of our V-tanks. I only smelled it when the wind changed, just before I found you."

Renie, enjoying the surprisingly powerful comfort of the fire, was content to play Watson to the small man's Holmes. "And that scent is. . . ?"

"I cannot say for certain, but it is smoke more modern than that of a wood fire—I smell metal in it, and oil."

"We'll see. I hope you're right. If we've got a long search ahead of us, it would be nice if it took place somewhere with hot showers and warm beds."

They fell silent, listening to the crackle of the fire. A few birds and something that sounded like a monkey called in the trees above.

"What about Martine?" Renie asked suddenly. "Could you use this baboon nose of yours to find her?"

"Perhaps, if we were close enough, although I do not know what smell she has in this simulation. But there is nothing that smells like you do—which is the only measure I have for a human scent—anywhere nearby."

Renie looked past the fire into the darkness. Perhaps if she and !Xabbu had wound up reasonably close to each other, Martine would not be too far away. If she had survived.

"!Xabbu, what did you experience when we were coming through?"

His description brought back the gooseflesh, but told her nothing new.

". . . The last thing I heard Mister Singh say was that it was alive," he finished. "Then I had a sense of many other presences, as though I were surrounded by spirits. I woke up in the forest as you did, alone and confused."

"Do you have any idea what that . . . thing was? The thing that caught us and . . . and killed Singh? I can tell you, it wasn't like any security program *I've* ever heard of."

"It was the All-Devourer." He spoke with flat certainty.

"What are you talking about?"

"It is the thing that hates life because it is itself empty. There is a famous story my people tell, of the last days of Grandfather Mantis and how the All-Devourer came to his campfire." He shook his head. "But I will not tell it here, not now. It is an important story, but it is sad and frightening."

"Well, whatever that thing was, I never want to go near it again. It was worse than that Kali creature in Mister J.'s." Although, as she thought about it, there had been certain similarities between the two, especially the way they apparently managed to effect physical changes through virtual media. What connection might there be, and could contemplating the Kali and what had happened inside the club help her understand what !Xabbu called the All-Devourer? Could *anything* help them understand?

Renie yawned. It had been a long day. Her brain didn't want to work any more. She pushed herself back against a tree trunk. At least this tropical simulation wasn't too full of insects. Perhaps she'd actually be able to get some sleep.

"!Xabbu, come over here closer, will you? I'm getting tired and I don't know how much longer I can stay awake."

He looked at her for a silent moment, then walked on all fours across the small clearing. He crouched beside her for an awkward moment, then stretched out and lay his head across her thighs. She idly stroked his furry neck.

"I'm glad you're here. I know that you and my father and Jeremiah are really only a few meters away from me, but it still felt terribly lonely when I woke up by myself. It would have been much worse spending the whole night here alone."

!Xabbu did not say anything, but extended one long arm and patted her on the top of the head, then lightly touched her nose with his hairless monkey finger. Renie felt herself drifting into welcome sleep.

"I can see the edge of the forest," !Xabbu called, twenty meters up. "And there is a settlement."

Renie paced impatiently at the foot of the tree. "Settlement? What kind?"

"I cannot tell from here." He walked farther out onto the branch, which swayed in a way that made Renie nervous. "It is at least a couple of kilometers away. But there is smoke, and buildings, too. They look very simple."

He descended swiftly, then dropped to the spongy ground beside her. "I have seen what looks like a good path, but the jungle is very thick. I will have to climb up again soon and look some more or we will spend all day tearing our way through."

"You're enjoying this, aren't you? Just because we happened to wind up in a jungle, your baboon idea looks brilliant. But what if we'd wound up in the middle of an office building or something?"

"Come along. We have been in this place most of a day already."
He loped away. Renie followed a little more slowly, cursing the thick
vegetation.

Some path, she thought.

They stood, sheltering in the darkness of the forest's edge. Before
them lay a descending slope of reddish mud, pimpled with the stumps
of cut trees and scarred with the ruts of their removal.

"It's a logging camp," Renie whispered. "It looks modern. Sort of."

A number of large vehicles were parked in the cleared area below.
Small shapes moved among them, cleaning and adjusting them like
mahouts tending elephants. The machinery was large and impressive,
but from what Renie could see there were odd anachronisms as well.
None of them had the tanklike treads she was accustomed to seeing
on heavy construction equipment; instead, they had fat wheels covered with studs. Several of them also seemed to be powered by steam
boilers.

The row of huts beyond, however, clearly made from some prefabri-
cated material, were indistinguishable from things she had seen on
the outskirts of Durban. In fact, she knew people, some of them students of hers, who had lived their whole lives in such huts.

"Just remember, stay close to me," she said. "We don't know how
they feel about wild animals here, but if you hold my hand, they'll
probably accept that you're a pet."

!Xabbu was becoming quite adept at using the baboon face. His
expression clearly said that she should enjoy this small reversal of
fortune while she could.

As they made their way down the slippery hillside beneath the gray
morning sky, Renie for the first time had a view of the countryside.
Beyond the camp a wide dirt road cut through the jungle. The land
around it was largely flat; rising mist obscured the horizon and made
the trees seem to stretch endlessly.

The camp's inhabitants were dark-skinned, but not as dark as she
was, and most that she could see had straight black hair. Their clothing gave no clues as to time or place, since most of them wore only
pants, and their choice of footgear was hidden by red mud.

One of the nearest workers spotted her and shouted something to
the others. Many turned to stare. "Take my hand," she whispered to
!Xabbu. "Remember—baboons don't talk in most places."

One of the workmen had ambled off, perhaps to alert the authorities. Or maybe to get weapons, Renie thought. How isolated was this

place? What did it mean to be an unarmed woman in such a situation? It was frustrating to have so little knowledge—like being transported by surprise to another solar system and dumped off the starship with nothing but a picnic basket.

A silent half-circle of workers formed as Renie and !Xabbu approached, but remained at a distance that might have been respectful or superstitious. Renie stared boldly back at them. The men were mostly small and wiry, their features vaguely Asian, like pictures she remembered of the Mongols of steppe country. Some of them wore bracelets of a translucent, jadelike stone, or wore amulets of metal and mud-draggled feathers on thongs around their necks.

A man wearing a shirt and a wide-brimmed, conical straw hat bustled up from behind the gathering crowd of workers. He was thickly-muscled, with a long sharp nose, and had a paunch that hung over his colorful belt. Renie guessed he must be the foreman.

"Do you speak English?" she asked.

He paused, looked her up and down, then shook his head. "No. What is it?"

Renie's confusion passed in a moment. Apparently the simulation had built-in translation facilities, so she seemed to be speaking the foreman's language and he hers. As she continued the conversation, she saw that his mouth movements did not quite match his words, confirming her guess. She also noticed that he had a pierced lower lip with a small gold plug in it.

"I am sorry. We . . . I am lost. I have had an accident." Inwardly she cursed. In all the time they had spent struggling through the jungle, she had given no thought to a cover story. She decided to wing it. "I was with a group of hikers, but I got separated from them." Now she just had to hope the custom of walking for pleasure existed in this place.

Apparently, it did. "You are far from any towns," he said, looking at her with a certain shrewd good humor, as though he guessed she hadn't told him the truth but wasn't too bothered about it. "Still, it is bad to be lost and far from home. My name is Tok. Come with me."

As they walked across the encampment, !Xabbu still silent at Renie's side, uncommented-upon despite all the stares he received, she tried to get a better fix on what sort of place this was. The foreman looked as Asiatic or Middle Eastern as any of the laborers. On his belt was something that looked like a field telephone—it had a short antenna—but was cylindrical and covered with carvings. Something that very much resembled a satellite dish also stood atop one of the larger huts. It didn't add up to any recognizable pattern.

The satellite hut proved to be Tok's office and home. He sat Renie down in a chair in front of his metal desk and offered her a cup of something that did not fully translate, which she accepted. !Xabbu crouched beside her seat, wide-eyed.

The room in which they sat offered no more definitive clues. There were a few books on a shelf, but the writing on their spines was in strange glyphs she could not read: apparently the translation algorithms served only for speech. There was also a shrine of some sort, a boxlike affair with a frame of colorful feathers, which contained several small wooden figures of people with animal heads.

"I can't figure this place out at all," she whispered. !Xabbu's small fingers squeezed her hand, warning her that the foreman was returning.

Renie thanked him as she took the steaming cup, then lifted it to her face and sniffed it before remembering that, as !Xabbu had complained, the V-tank gave her a very limited sense of smell. But the mere fact that she had tried to smell it suggested that this place was already impairing her VR reflexes; if she didn't stay vigilant, she could easily forget that it wasn't real. She had to lift the cup carefully, feeling for her lips to make sure she was placing it correctly, since her mouth was the one spot where she had no sensitivity—it was like trying to drink after having been anesthetized at the dentist's office.

"What sort of monkey is that?" Tok squinted at !Xabbu. "I have not seen one like it before."

"I . . . I don't know. It was given to me by a friend who . . . who traveled a lot. It is a very faithful pet."

Tok nodded. Renie was relieved to see that the word seemed to translate. "How long have you been lost?" he asked.

Renie decided to stick close to the truth, which always made lying easier. "I spent one night in the jungle by myself."

"How many? How many of you were there?"

She hesitated, but her course had been set. "There were two of us—not including my pet monkey—who got separated from the rest. And then I lost her as well."

He nodded again, as though this jibed with some personal calculation. "And you are a Temilúni, of course?"

This was slightly deeper water, but Renie took a chance. "Yes, of course." She waited, but this also seemed to confirm the foreman's casual suspicions.

"You people, you townfolk, you think you can just walk in the jungle like it was (some name she could not quite grasp) Park. But the wild places are not like that. You should be more careful with your life and health. Still, the gods are sometimes good to fools and wanderers." He looked upward, then muttered something and made a sign on his breast. "I will show you something. Come." He stood up and walked around the desk, beckoning Renie toward the door at the back of the office.

On the other side was the foreman's living quarters, with a table, a chair, and a bed canopied by a curtain of mosquito netting. As he stepped toward the bed and pulled back the gauzy netting, Renie braced herself against the wall, wondering if he was expecting some kind of exchange of favors for her rescue—but there was already someone there. The sleeping woman was small and dark-haired and long-nosed like Tok, dressed in a simple white cotton dress. Renie did not recognize her. As she stood frozen, unsure of what to do, !Xabbu loped to the bed and jumped up beside the woman, then began to bounce up and down on the thin mattress. He was clearly trying to tell her something, but it took her a long moment to understand.

"Martine. . . ?" She hurried forward. The woman's eyes fluttered open, the pupils roving, unfixed.

"*. . . The way . . . blocked!*" Martine, if this was her, lifted her hands as though to ward off some looming danger. The voice was not familiar, and there was no French accent, but the next words dispelled any doubt. "*No, Singh, do not . . . Ah, my God, how terrible!*"

Renie's eyes stung with tears as she watched her companion thrashing on the bed, apparently still in the grip of the nightmare that had awaited them at Otherland's shadowy border. "Oh, Martine." She turned to the foreman, who was watching the reunion with grave self-satisfaction. "Where did you find her?"

Tok explained that a party of tree markers had discovered her wandering dazedly at the edge of the jungle a short distance from the camp. "The men are superstitious," he said. "They think her touched by the gods," again the reflexive gesture, "but I suspected it was hunger and cold and fear, perhaps even a blow on the head."

The foreman returned to his work, promising that they could have a ride back with the next convoy of logs, leaving at twilight. Renie, overwhelmed by events, neglected to ask where "back" might be. She and !Xabbu spent the dwindling afternoon sitting beside the bed, holding Martine's hands and speaking soft words to her when the nightmares seemed to pursue her too closely.

* * *

The foreman Tok helped Renie up into the back of the huge, gleaming, steam-powered truck. !Xabbu clambered up by himself and sat next to her atop the chained logs. Tok made her promise that she and her "mad Temilúni friends" would not wander around in the wild country any more. She did, and thanked him for his kindness as the convoy pulled out of the camp and onto the broad muddy road.

Renie could have ridden in one of the other truck cabs, but she wanted the privacy to talk to !Xabbu. Also, Martine was belted into the passenger seat of this truck—whose driver, Renie had noticed with interest, was a broad-faced, broad-shouldered woman—and Renie wanted to stay close to their ill companion.

". . . So that's not Martine's voice because she's delirious and she's speaking French, I suppose," she said as they bumped out of camp. "But why do you have your voice and I have mine? I mean, you sound like you, even though you look like something out of a zoo."

!Xabbu, who was standing upright, leaning into the wind and sniffing, did not answer.

"We must have all been piggybacked on Singh's index," she reasoned, "and that index was marked 'English-speaking.' Of course, that doesn't explain why I kept this body, but you got your second-choice sim." She looked down at her own copper-skinned hands. Just as !Xabbu had wound up with a good body for jungle wandering, she had chosen one that seemed physically very close to the local human norm. Of course, if they had landed in a Viking village or in World War Two Berlin, she wouldn't have fit in quite so well.

!Xabbu clambered down and crouched beside her again, his erect tail curved like a strung bow. "We have found Martine, but we still do not know what we are searching for," he said. "Or where we are going."

Renie looked out at the miles of thick green jungle lying behind them in the dying light, and the miles that the strip of red road still had to cross. "You had to remind me, didn't you?"

They drove through the night. The temperature was tropical, but Renie soon learned that virtual logs made no better a bed than real ones. What was particularly annoying was knowing that her real body was floating in a V-tank full of adjustable gel, which could have been made to simulate the softest goosedown, if she could only work the controls.

As the sun came up, ending a darkness that had brought Renie very little rest, the trucks reached a town. It was apparently the home of the sawmill and processing facilities, and something of a jungle metropolis; even at first light, there were scores of people on the muddy streets.

A handful of Landroverlike cars rolled past as they drove down the wide main thoroughfare, some clearly powered by steam, others more mysteriously. Renie also spotted more of the objects that looked like satellite dishes, which seemed restricted to the largest buildings, but in many other ways the town looked as though it might have been transplanted whole from the set of some saga of the American West. The wooden sidewalks were raised above the clinging muck, the long, town-bisecting main street seemed designed for gunfights, and there were as many horses as cars. A few men even seemed to be having an early-morning brawl outside one of the local taverns. These men, and the other people Renie could see, were better dressed than the jungle workers, but except for the fact that many wore shawls of brightly-dyed, woven wool, she still could not put her finger on anything definitive in their clothing styles.

The trucks rattled through town and lined up on the vast mud flat outside the sawmill. The driver of Renie's truck got out and, with a certain taciturn courtesy, suggested she and her sick friend and their pet monkey might as well stop here. As she helped Renie unload the semi-conscious Martine from the cab, the driver suggested they could find a bus in front of the town hall.

Renie was relieved to know there was somewhere else beyond this place. "A bus. That's wonderful. But we . . . I don't have any money."

The truck driver stared at her. "You need money for city buses now?" she said at last. "By all the lords of heaven, what shit will the Council think of next? The God-King ought to execute them all and start over."

As the driver's surprise had suggested, the buses were apparently free. Renie, with surreptitious assistance from !Xabbu, was able to help Martine stumble the short distance to the town hall, where they took a seat on the steps to wait. The Frenchwoman still seemed to be caught in those terrible moments when they had broken into the Otherland system and everything had gone so badly wrong, but she was able to move around almost normally when prompted, and once or twice Renie even felt a returned pressure when she squeezed Martine's hand, as though something inside was struggling toward the surface.

I hope so, Renie thought. *Without Singh, she's the only hope we've got of making any sense of this.* She looked out at the utterly foreign yet utterly realistic surroundings and felt almost ill. *Who am I kidding? Look at this place. Think of the sort of minds and money and facilities it took to make this—and we're going to put the ringleaders under citizen's arrest or something? This whole venture was ridiculous from the very beginning.*

The sensation of helplessness was so powerful that Renie could not summon the will to speak. She, !Xabbu, and Martine sat on the steps in silence, an oddly assorted trio that received its due in the covert stares and whispers of the local populace.

Renie thought the jungle might be thinning a little, but she wasn't positive. After watching an uncountable number of trees go by, hour upon hour, she was seeing the monotonous landscape slide past even when she closed her eyes.

The gold-toothed, feather-medallion-bedecked bus driver had not batted an eye at her two unusual companions, but when Renie had asked him where the bus went—whatever information was printed over the windscreen was illegible to her, like the foreman's books—he had stared as though she had asked him to make the battered old vehicle fly.

"Temilún, good woman," he had said, lowering his chunky sunglasses to examine her more closely, perhaps thinking that someone might ask him later to describe the escaped madwoman. "The city of the God-King—praise to his name—the Lord of Life and Death, He Who Is Favored Above All Others. Where else would it go?" He gestured to the single straight road leading out of the sawmill town. "Where else *could* it go?"

Now, with !Xabbu standing in her lap, his hands pressed against the window, and Martine sleeping against her shoulder, Renie tried to make sense of all she had learned. The place seemed to have nineteenth and twentieth century technologies mixed up together, so far as she could remember the differences between the two. The people looked something like Asians or Middle Easterners, although she had seen a few in the town who had fairer or darker appearances. The foreman hadn't heard of English, so that might indicate a great distance from English-speaking peoples, or a world in which there was no English at all, or just that the foreman was ignorant. They seemed to have at least one well-established religion and a God-King—but was that a person or a figure of speech?—and the truck driver had made it sound as if there were some kind of governing council.

Renie sighed miserably. Not much to go on at all. They were wasting time, precious, precious time, but she couldn't think of a single thing they could do differently. Now they were headed to Temilún, which apparently was an even larger town. And if nothing there brought them closer to their goal, then what? On to the next? Was this foray, for which Singh had paid with his life, going to be just bus trip after bus trip, one long bad holiday?

!Xabbu turned from the window and put his head next to her ear. He had been quiet during the journey so far, since there were passengers crammed into every possible space on all the seats and in the aisles, half-a-dozen at least just within a meter radius of Renie's cramped seat. Many of these passengers were also transporting chickens or small animals Renie couldn't quite identify, which explained the bus driver's disinterest in !Xabbu, but none of these creatures showed any inclination to talk, which was why the baboon in Renie's lap now whispered very quietly.

"I have been thinking and thinking what we must look for," he said. "If we are seeking the people who own this Otherland network, then we first must discover something of who wields the power in *this* world."

"And how do we do that?" Renie murmured. "Go to a library? I suppose they must have them, but we'll probably have to find a pretty large town."

!Xabbu spoke a bit louder now, because a woman seated in front of them had begun singing, a wordless chant that reminded Renie a little of the tribal odes her father and his friends sometimes sang when the beer had been flowing freely. "Or perhaps we will have to befriend someone who can tell us what we need to know."

Renie looked around, but no one was paying attention to either of them. Beyond the windows, she could see cleared farming land and a few houses, and thought they must be drawing close to the next town. "But how can we trust anyone? I mean, any single person on this bus could be wired right into the operating system. They're not real, !Xabbu—most of them can't be, anyway."

His reply was interrupted by a pressure on her arm. Martine was leaning toward her, clutching as though to save herself from falling. Her sim's eyes still wandered, unfocused, but the face showed a new alertness.

"Martine? It's Renie. Can you hear me?"

"The . . . darkness . . . is very thick." She sounded like a lost child, but for the first time the voice was recognizably hers.

"You're safe," Renie whispered urgently. "We've come through. We're in the Otherland network."

The face turned, but the eyes did not make contact. "Renie?"

"Yes, it's me. And !Xabbu's here, too. Did you understand what I just said? We've come through. We're in."

Martine's grip did not slacken, but the look of anxiety on her bony face softened. "So much," she said. "There is so much . . ." She struggled to collect herself. "There has been much darkness."

!Xabbu was squeezing Renie's other arm. She was beginning to feel like the mother of too many children. "Can't you see us, Martine? Your eyes aren't focusing."

The woman's face went slack for a moment, as if she had been dealt an unexpected blow. "I . . . something has happened to me. I am not yet myself." She turned her face toward Renie. "Tell me, what has happened to Singh?"

"He's dead, Martine. Whatever that thing was, it got him. I . . . I swear I felt it kill him."

Martine shook her head miserably. "Me also. I had hoped I dreamed it."

!Xabbu was squeezing harder. Renie reached down to lift his hand away, but saw that he was staring out the window. "!Xabbu?"

"Look, Renie, look!" He did not whisper. A moment later, she, too, forgot her caution.

The bus had turned in a wide bend, and for the first time she could see a horizon beyond the trees. A flat band of silver lay along the distant skyline, a span of shimmering reflection which could only be water, a bay or an ocean by the size of it. But it was what lay before it, silhouetted against its metallic sheen in complicated arcs and needles, glittering in the afternoon sun like the largest amusement park that ever was, that had riveted the disguised bushman and now brought Renie halfway out of her seat.

"Oh," she breathed. "Oh, look."

Martine stirred impatiently. "What is it?"

"It's the city. The golden city."

It took an hour to reach Temilún, crossing a great plain full of settlements—farming villages surrounded by fields of swaying grain at first, followed by thicker concentrations of suburban housing and ever-increasing modernity—shopping complexes and motorway overpasses and signs festooned with unreadable glyphs. And always the city grew larger on the horizon.

Renie made her way down the aisle toward the front of the bus so she could get a better look. She slid between a pair of pierce-lipped men who were joking with the driver, and hung swaying on the pole by the front door to watch a dream become reality.

It seemed in some ways a thing out of a story book, the tall buildings so completely different than the towerblocks and functional skyscrapers of Durban. Some were vast stepped pyramids, with gardens and hanging plants at every level. Others were filigreed towers of a type she had never seen, huge spires that nevertheless had been built to suggest piles of flowers or sheaves of grain. Others, as wildly uncategorizable as abstract sculpture, had angles and protrusions that seemed architecturally impossible. All were painted, the bright colors adding to the impression of floral profusion, but the single most common color was the flashing yellow of gold. Shining gold capped the tallest pyramids, and wound in barberpole stripes up the tall towers. Some of the buildings had been plated top to bottom, so even the darkest recesses, the most deeply gouged niches, still gleamed. It was everything the blurry captured image salvaged in Susan's lab had suggested and more. It was a city built by lunatics, but lunatics who had been touched by genius.

As the bus jounced through the outer rings of the metropolis, the tops of the tall buildings rose out of sight above the windows. Renie pushed through the crowding passengers and returned to her seat, breathless.

"It's incredible." She could not shake off what she knew to be a dangerous kind of exhilaration. "I can't believe we found it. We found it!"

Martine had been very quiet. Still without speaking, she reached out and took Renie's hand, pulling her thoughts in another direction. Here in the midst of the larger miracle was a small one: Martine, the mystery woman, the voice without a face, had become a real person. True, she was using a sim body in the way that a puppeteer used a marionette, and she was thousands of miles away from Renie's real body, and even farther away from this purely theoretical place, but she was here; Renie could feel her, could even tell something about her real physical self. It was as though Renie had finally met a treasured childhood pen pal.

Unable to express this odd happiness, she only squeezed Martine's hand.

The bus stopped at last, deep in the golden-shadowed canyons of the city. Martine could now walk fairly well under her own power. She and Renie and !Xabbu waited impatiently for the other passengers to file out before making their way down onto the tiled floor of the bus station, a vast, hollow pyramid braced with mammoth beams which rose level upon level like a kaleidoscopic spider web. They had only a few moments to appreciate its high-ceilinged magnificence before a pair of men in dark clothing stepped in front of them.

"Excuse me," one of them said. "You have just come on the bus from Aracatacá, yes?"

Renie's mind raced, but to no useful purpose. They wore overcoats with small ceremonial capes, and both had a look of hard-faced professionalism. Any hope that they might be particularly stern ticket takers slipped away when she looked at the oddly ceremonial-looking clubs at their belts and their polished black helmets shaped like the heads of snarling jungle cats.

"Yes, we were . . ."

"Then you will show me your identification, please."

Helplessly, Renie patted the pockets of her jumpsuit. Martine stared into space, her expression that of someone lost in a daydream.

"If the show is for our benefit, you may dispense with it." Beneath the high-crowned helmet, his head appeared to be shaved. "You are outsiders. We have been expecting you." He stepped forward and took Renie's arm. His partner hesitated for a moment, staring at !Xabbu. "The monkey will come with us, too, of course," the first policeman said. "I am sure none of you wish to delay any further, so let us go. Please, content yourself that you will be transported to the Great Palace with all dispatch. Those are our orders."

!Xabbu lowered his head, then took Renie's hand and followed docilely as the policeman walked them through the station toward the doors.

"What are you doing with us?" Renie did not feel there was much purpose in it, but she did not want to give in without trying. "We haven't done anything. We were hiking in the country and got lost. I have my papers at home."

The policeman threw the door open. Parked just outside was a large panel truck that vented steam like a sleeping dragon. The second policeman pulled open the doors at the back and helped Martine up into the shadowed interior.

"Please, good woman." The first policeman's voice was cold. "Everything will be better if you save your questions for our masters. We have been ordered days ago to wait for you. Besides, you should be honored. The Council seems to have special plans for all of you."

When Renie and !Xabbu had been ushered inside with Martine, the door was slammed shut. There were no windows. The darkness was complete.

"We've been here *hours*." Renie had paced the same figure eight across the small cell so many times that she was now doing it with her eyes closed as she struggled to make sense of things. All that she had seen, the jungle, the magnificent city, and now this bleak stone dungeon out of a bad horror story, swirled in front of her mind's eye, but she could make no sense of them. "Why all this show? If they're going to hypnotize us or whatever that Kali thing tried on me before, why not just do it? Aren't they afraid we'll just drop offline?"

"Perhaps we cannot," said !Xabbu. Soon after the policeman locked them in, he had climbed to the single high window, and after ascertaining that it was covered with a metal grate sufficiently fine to prevent a medium-sized monkey slipping through, had climbed back down and squatted in the corner. He had even slept there for a while, something that Renie found inexplicably annoying. "Perhaps they know something about it we do not. Do we dare to try?"

"Not yet," said Martine. "It might not work—they have already proved they can manipulate our minds in ways we do not understand—and even if we can, we will have admitted defeat."

"In any case, these are the people who we're looking for." Renie stopped and opened her eyes. Her friends looked up at her with what she felt sure was the near-indifference of the helpless, but she herself was struggling against mounting rage. "If I didn't know it already, I'd be able to guess just from the way those slick, self-satisfied policemen acted. These are the people who've tried to kill us, who *did* kill Doctor Van Bleeck and Singh and God knows how many others, and they're as proud of themselves as can be. Arrogant bastards."

"It will not help to be angry," Martine said gently.

"It won't? Well, what *will* help? Saying we're sorry? That we'll never interfere with their horrible goddamned games again, so please send us back with just a warning?" She balled her hands into fists and swung at the air. "Shit! I am so tired of being pushed and chased and scared and . . . and *manipulated* by these monsters!"

"Renie . . ." Martine began.

"Don't tell me not to get angry! Your brother isn't lying in a quarantined hospital. Your brother isn't a vegetable kept alive by machines, is he? Your brother who counted on you to protect him?"

"No, Renie. They have not hurt my family as they have yours."

She realized she was crying and wiped at her eyes with the back of her hand. "I'm sorry, Martine, but . . ."

The door to the cell clanked and then slid open. The same two policeman stood there, ominous black shapes in the shadowy corridor.

"Come along. He Who Is Favored Above All Others wants to see you."

"Why don't you run away?" Renie whispered fiercely. "You could hide somewhere and then help us break out. I can't believe you're not even going to try."

!Xabbu's look, even filtered through the baboon countenance, was pained. "I would not leave you, knowing as little as we do about this place. Besides, if it is our minds they seek to affect, then we are stronger together."

The first policeman looked over his shoulder at them, irritated by the whispering.

They climbed a long flight of stairs, then entered a wide hall with a polished stone floor. By the shape and the height of the roof, Renie guessed that they were inside another one of the pyramids she had seen from the bus. A crowd of dark-haired people in various kinds of ceremonial dress, most of which featured capes similar to those the police wore, bustled in all directions. This multitude, full of hurry and self-obsessed energy, paid no particular attention to the prisoners; the only ones who showed any real interest were the half-dozen armed guards standing before the doors at the far end of the hall. These bulky men had animal helmets even more garishly realistic than those of the police, long antique-looking rifles and very functional-looking clubs, and seemed like they might enjoy the chance to hurt someone.

As Renie and the others approached there was an anticipatory straightening of the ranks, but after examining the policemen's emblems with great care the guards reluctantly stepped aside and swung the doors open. Renie and her friends were pushed through, but their captors remained outside as the doors closed again.

They were alone in a chamber almost as large as the hall they had just left. The stone walls were painted with scenes of fantastical battles between men and monsters. At the center of the room, in the pool of light cast by an electrified chandelier of wide and grotesque design, stood a long table surrounded by empty chairs. The farthest chair was considerably higher than the others, and had a canopy of what looked to be solid gold in the form of the sun's disk blazing through clouds.

"The Council is not here. I thought you might be interested to see the meeting place, though."

A figure stepped from behind the massive chair, a tall youth with the same hawklike features as the rest of the inhabitants. He was naked above the waist except for a long cloak of feathers, a necklace of beads and sharp teeth, and a high crown of gold studded with blue stones.

"Normally I am surrounded by minions—'numberless as the sands' is how the priests put it, and they are nearly right." His accented English was softly spoken, but there was an unmistakable core of sharp, hard intelligence behind the cold eyes: if this man wanted something, he would get it. He was also clearly much older than he appeared. "But there are quite a few other guests expected, so we shall need our space—and anyway, I thought it best we have our conversation in private." He showed a wintry smile. "The priests would be apoplectic if they knew that the God-King was alone with strangers."

"Who . . . who are you?" Renie struggled to keep her voice steady, but the knowledge that she faced one of their persecutors made it impossible.

"The God-King of this place, as I told you. The Lord of Life and Death. But if it will make you more comfortable, let me introduce myself properly—you *are* guests, after all.

"My name is Bolivar Atasco."

CHAPTER 34

Butterfly and Emperor

NETFEED/NEWS: *Refugee Camp Given Nation Status*
(visual: refugee city on Mérida beach)
VO: *The Mexican refugee encampment called "the End of the Road" by its*
residents has been declared a country by the United Nations. Mérida, a small
city on the northern tip of Mexico's Yucatán Peninsula, has swollen to four
million residents because of a series of killer storms along the coast and
political instability in Honduras, Guatemala, and northeastern Mexico.
(visual: UN truck being driven through frenzied crowd)
The three-and-a-half million refugees are almost entirely without shelter,
and many are suffering from tuberculosis, typhoid, and Guantanamo fever.
By making Mérida a nation in its own right, the UN can now declare
martial law and bring the new country under its direct jurisdiction. . . .

"Dzang, Orlando, you were right! You were right!" Fredericks was leaping up and down on the beach, almost crazy with excitement and terror. "Where are we? What happened? That's *it!* You were right!"

Orlando could feel sand beneath the palms of his hand, hot and gritty and undeniable. He scooped up a handful and let it pour away again. It was real. It was all real. And the city, wilder and more wonderful than anything in a fairy tale, the golden city was real, too, stretching almost as far as he could see, reaching toward the sky in a profusion of towers and pyramids as ornate as Russian Easter eggs. The thing that had haunted him was now just a few miles away, separated from him only by an expanse of blue ocean. He was sitting on a beach, an inarguable beach, staring at his own dream.

And before that, he had passed through a nightmare. That darkness, and then that thing, that hungry, horrid thing. . . .

But it wasn't only a dream. There was something real behind it—like it was a puppet show. Like my mind was trying to make sense of something too big to understand. . . .

There was more wrong than just the nightmare. Wherever he was, he had not left the illnesses of his real body behind. The city stood in front of him—the couldn't-be city, the don't-dare-hope city—and yet he could barely force himself to care. He was melting like a candle, giving off too much heat. A big, hot something inside him was eating away at his thoughts, filling his head and pressing behind his eyes.

Where are we?

Fredericks was still jumping up and down in an ecstasy of uncertainty. As Orlando struggled to his feet, he realized that the Fredericks he was looking at was wearing the body of Pithlit, arch-thief of the Middle Country.

That's wrong, he thought, but could not pursue it any farther. Standing up had only made him feel worse. The golden-daubed city suddenly tilted, and Orlando tried to follow it, but instead the sand jumped up to meet him, slamming against him as though it were one solid thing.

Something in the dark touched me. . . .

The world was spinning, spinning. He closed his eyes and went away.

Pithlit the Thief was shaking him. Orlando's head felt like a rotten melon; at every wobble it seemed about to burst.

"Orlando?" Fredericks seemed to have no idea how much his voice was making Orlando's bones aches. "Are you okay?"

". . . Sick. Stop shaking . . ."

Fredericks let go. Orlando rolled onto his side, hugging himself. He could feel the bright sun beating down on his skin, but it was a weather report from another part of the country; deep inside him there was now a chill resistant to any sun, real or simulated. He felt the first shivers begin.

"You're shivering," Fredericks pointed out. Orlando gritted his teeth, lacking the strength even to be sarcastic. "Are you cold? But it's hot! No, what does that matter? Sorry, man. We need to put something over you—all you're wearing is that loin cloth." Fredericks looked around, scanning the empty tropical beach as though someone might have thoughtfully left a down comforter behind one of the lava rocks. He turned back to Orlando as another thought struck him. "Why are you in your Thargor sim? When did you put that on?"

Orlando could only groan.

Fredericks knelt beside him. His eyes were still wide, pupils pinned like a lab animal given too much of something strong, but he was struggling his way back to some kind of logic. "Here, you can have my cloak." He untied it and draped it around Orlando's shoulders. Beneath he was wearing his character's usual gray shirt and breeches. "But, hey, this is Pithlit's cloak! Am I Pithlit like you're Thargor?"

Orlando nodded weakly.

"But I never . . . this is scanny!" Fredericks paused. "Feel this. It feels real. Orlando, where are we? What happened? Is this somewhere on the net?"

"Nobody . . . on the net . . . has equipment like this." He struggled to keep his teeth from chattering: the clicking made his head hurt even more. "We're . . . I don't know where we are."

"But there's the city, just like you told me." Fredericks wore the look of a jaded child who has unexpectedly encountered the actual Santa Claus. "That *is* the city you meant, right?" He laughed, a little shrilly. "Of course it is. What else would it be? But where are we?"

Orlando was finding it difficult to keep track of Fredericks' overstressed chattering. He wrapped the cloak tighter and lay down to ride out another wave of shivers. "I think . . . I have to sleep . . . for a few minutes. . . ."

Blackness reached out for him again, gathering him in.

Orlando floated through fever dreams of stone tombs and Uncle Jingle singing and his mother searching through the halls of their house for something she had lost. Once he surfaced to feel Fredericks holding his hand.

". . . Think it's an island," his friend was saying. "There's a temple or something made out of stones, but I don't think anyone uses it anymore, and that's about it. I couldn't get all the way to the other side, because there's like an amazingly thick forest—well, more like a jungle—but I think because of the way the beaches curve . . ."

Orlando slid down again.

As he bobbed in the buffeting currents of his illness, he snatched at the few thoughts swimming past which seemed part of reality. The monkey-children had wanted to take him to someone . . . an animal? . . . an animal name? . . . who knew about the golden city. But instead they had all been seized by something that had shaken him almost to pieces, as a dog grabs and dispatches a rat.

A dog. Something about a dog.

And now he was somewhere else, and the city was there, so he must be dreaming, because the city was a dream-thing.

But Fredericks was in the dream, too.

Another thought, cold and hard as a stone, dropped into his fevered mind.

I'm dying. I'm in that horrible Crown Heights Medical Center, and I'm strapped onto a bunch of machines. The life is draining out of me, and all that's left is this one little part of my mind, making a whole world out of a few brain cells and a few memories. And Vivien and Conrad are probably sitting next to the bed practicing their coping-with-grief skills, but they don't know I'm still in here. I'm still in here! Trapped in the top floor of a burning building and the flames are climbing up, one story at a time, and all the firefighters are giving up and going home. . . .

I'm still in here!

"Orlando, wake up. You're having a bad dream or something. Wake up. I'm here."

He opened his eyes. A gummy smear of pink and brown slowly became Fredericks.

"I'm dying."

For a moment his friend looked frightened, but Orlando saw him push it down. "No, you're not, Gardiner. You've just got the flu or something."

Oddly, watching Fredericks decide to say something encouraging, despite the unlikeliness of it being true, made him feel better. Any hallucination in which Fredericks acted so much like Fredericks was pretty much as good as real life. Not that he seemed to have a lot of choice anyway.

The chills had subsided, at least for the moment. He sat up, still holding the cloak tightly around himself. His head felt like it had been boiled until his brains had turned to steam and hissed out. "Did you say something about an island?"

Relieved, Fredericks sat down next to him. With the oddly sharp focus of someone whose fever is in remission, Orlando noted the brisk, bearlike clumsiness of his friend's movements.

He certainly doesn't move like a girl. The actual fact of Fredericks' sex was beginning to recede into the distance. For a moment, he wondered about what Fredericks—Salome Fredericks—really looked like, then he pushed the thought aside. Here he looked like a boy, he moved like one, he said to treat him like one—who was Orlando to argue?

"I think this is. An island, I mean. I was looking in case there was some way to get a boat—I thought I could even steal one, since I seem to be Pithlit right now. But there's no one here but us." Fredericks had been staring out at the amusement-park intricacy of the city just across the water, but now he turned back to Orlando. "Why *am* I Pithlit anyway? What do you think is going on?"

Orlando shook his head. "I don't know. I wish I did. Those kids were going to take us to meet someone, then they said something about a 'big hole to somewhere,' and that they were going to 'hook us up.' " He shook his head again; it felt inordinately heavy. "I just don't know."

Pithlit waved his hand in front of his own face, frowning as he watched it. "I've never heard of anywhere on the net like this. Everything moves just like in real life. And there are smells! Everything! Look at the ocean."

"I know."

"So, what do we do now? I say we build a raft."

Orlando stared at the city. Seeing it so close, so . . . *actual* . . . he had misgivings. How could anything that solid-looking live up to all the dreams he had invested in it? "A raft? How are we going to do that? Did you bring your Mister Carpenter Tool Kit?"

Fredericks made a disgusted face. "There's palm trees and vines and stuff. Your sword's lying right over there. We can do it." He scrambled across the sand and picked up the blade. "Hey. This isn't Lifereaper."

Orlando stared at the simple hilt, the bare blade so naked compared to Lifereaper's rune-scribed length. His burst of energy was wearing off, his thoughts dulling at the edges. "It's my first sword—the one Thargor had when he first came into the Middle Country. He got Lifereaper just about a year before you came in." He looked down at his sandaled feet sticking out from beneath the cloak. "I bet there isn't any gray in my hair either, is there?"

Fredericks examined him. "No. I've never seen Thargor without a few streaks of gray. How did you know?"

He was feeling very tired again. "Because these sandals, the sword—I'm the young Thargor, when he first came down from the Borrikar Hills. He didn't get the gray hair until the first time he fought Dreyra Jahr, down in the Well of Souls."

"But why?"

Orlando shrugged and slowly lowered himself back to the ground, ready to surrender again to the soft tug of sleep. "I don't know, Frederico. I don't know anything. . . ."

He slid in and out of sleep as light turned into darkness. Once he was pulled almost completely to wakefulness by someone screaming, but the sound came from far away and might have been another dream. There was no sign of Fredericks. Orlando wondered dimly if his friend had gone off to investigate the noises, but his thoughts were clotted with fatigue and illness and nothing else seemed very important.

It was light again. Someone was crying, and this noise was close by. It made Orlando's head hurt. He groaned and tried to fold his pillow over his ears, but his grasping fingers were full of sand.

He pulled himself upright. Fredericks was kneeling a few feet away, face in hands, shoulders shaking. The morning was bright, the virtual beach and ocean made even sharper and more surreal by what was left of the night's fever.

"Fredericks? Are you all right?"

His friend looked up. Tears were streaming down the thief's face. The simulation had even reddened his cheeks, but most impressive of all was the haunted expression in his eyes. "Oh, Gardiner, we're so locked." Fredericks caught at a hitching breath. "We are in bad, bad trouble."

Orlando felt like a sack of wet cement. "What are you talking about?"

"We're trapped. We can't go offline!"

Orlando sighed and let himself slump back onto the ground. "We're not trapped."

Fredericks crawled swiftly across the intervening distance and grabbed his shoulder. "Damn it, don't give me that! I went off and it almost killed me!"

He had never heard his friend sound quite so upset. "Killed you?"

"I wanted to go offline. I was getting more and more worried about you, and I thought maybe your parents were out somewhere and didn't know you were sick—like, you might need an ambulance or something. But when I tried, I couldn't unplug. I couldn't make any of the usual commands work, and I couldn't feel anything that isn't part of this simulation—not my room, not anything!" He reached up to his neck again, but this time more carefully. "And there's no t-jack! Go on, you try!"

Orlando reached up to the spot where his own neurocannula had been implanted. He could feel nothing but Thargor's heavy musculature. "Yeah, you're right. But there are simulations like that—they just hide the control points and make the tactors lie. Didn't you go on Demon Playground with me once? You don't even have any *limbs* on that—you're just neural ganglia strapped into a rocket sled."

"Jesus, Gardiner, you're not listening. I'm not just guessing—I *went* offline. My parents pulled my jack out. And it *hurt,* Orlando. It hurt like nothing I've ever felt—like they'd pulled my spine out with it, like someone was sticking hot needles into my eyes, like . . . like . . . like I can't even tell you. And it didn't stop. I couldn't do anything but . . . but scream and scream . . ." Fredericks stopped, shuddering, and could not speak again for a few moments. "It didn't stop until my parents put the jack back in—I couldn't even talk to them!—and, *bang,* I was back here."

Orlando shook his head. "Are you sure it wasn't just . . . I don't know, a really bad migraine or something?"

Fredericks made a noise of angry disgust. "You don't know what you're talking about. And it happened again. Jesus, didn't you hear me screaming? They must have taken me to a hospital or something, because the next time it came out, there were all these people standing around. I could hardly see, it hurt so bad. But the pain was even worse than before—the hospital gave me a shot, I think, and I don't remember much after that for a while, but here I am again. They must have had to plug me back in." Fredericks leaned forward and gripped Orlando's arm, his voice raggedly desperate. "So you tell me, Mister Golden City—what the hell kind of simulation acts like that? *What have you gotten us into, Gardiner?"*

The hours of daylight and night that followed were the longest Orlando had ever spent. The fever returned in full strength. He lay thrashing in a shelter Fredericks had built from palm fronds, freezing and burning by turns.

He thought his subconscious must be acting out Frederick's story of escape and forced return, because at one point he heard his mother speaking to him, very clearly. She was telling him about something that had happened in the security estate—the "Community" as she called it—and what the other neighbors thought about it. She was prattling, he realized, in that very particular way she did when she was scared to death, and for a moment he wondered if he was dreaming at all. He could actually see her, very faintly, as though she stood behind a gauze curtain, her face leaning in so close that it seemed distorted. He had certainly seen her that way often enough to make it a feature of a dream.

She was saying something about what they were going to do when he got better. The desperation in her tone, the doubt behind the words, convinced him that dream or not, he should treat it as real. He tried to make himself speak, to bridge the impossible distance between them. Mired in whatever it was, hallucination or incomprehensible separation, he could barely force his throat to operate. How could he explain? And what could she do?

Beezle, he tried to tell her. *Bring Beezle. Bring Beezle.*

She fell away from him then, and whether it was only another phantasm of his febrile sleep or an actual moment of contact with his real life, it was gone.

"You're dreaming about that stupid bug," Fredericks growled, his own voice clumsy with sleep.

Bug. Dreaming about a bug. As he slid back into the dark waters of his illness, he remembered something he had read once about a butterfly dreaming it was an emperor, wondering if it were an emperor dreaming he was a butterfly . . . or something like that.

So which is real? he wondered groggily. *Which side of the line is the real one? A crippled, shriveled, dying kid in some hospital bed . . . or a . . . a made-up barbarian looking for an imaginary city? Or what if someone completely different is dreaming . . . both of them. . . ?*

All the children at school were talking about the house that burned down. It gave Christabel a funny feeling. Ophelia Weiner told her that a bunch of people got killed, which made her feel so sick she couldn't eat her lunch. Her teacher sent her home.

"No wonder you're feeling bad, honey," her mother said, a hand on Christabel's forehead, checking for a temperature. "Up all night like that, and then having to listen to all those kids telling stories about people dying." She turned to Christabel's father, who was on his way to the den. "She's such a sensitive child, I swear."

Daddy only grunted.

"No one got killed, honey," her mother assured her. "Only one house burned and I don't think there was anyone in it."

As her mother went off to wave her some soup, Christabel wandered into the den where her father was talking with his friend Captain Parkins. Her father told her to go outside and play—as if she hadn't been sent home from school sick! She sat down in the hall to play with her Prince Pikapik doll. Daddy seemed very grumbly. She wondered why he and Captain Parkins weren't at their office, and wondered if it had anything to do with the big bad secret thing that had happened last night. Would he find out what she had done? If he did, she would probably get punished *forever.*

She pulled Prince Pikapik out of the nest of pillows she had made him—the otter doll tended to scramble toward dark, shadowy places—and scooted closer to the door of the den. She put her ear against the crack to see if she could hear anything. Christabel had never done that before. She felt like she was in a cartoon show.

". . . A real goddamn mess," Daddy's friend was saying. "After all this time, though, who'd have guessed?"

"Yeah," said her father. "And that's one of the biggest questions, isn't it? Why now? Why not fifteen years ago when we moved him the last time? I just don't get it, Ron. You didn't turn him down for one of his weird requisitions, did you? Piss him off?"

Christabel didn't understand all the words, but she was pretty sure they were talking about what had happened at Mister Sellars' house, all right. She had heard her daddy on the phone in the morning before she went to school, talking about the explosion and fire.

". . . Gotta give the bastard credit, though." Captain Parkins laughed, but it was an angry laugh. "I don't know how he managed to pull it all off, but he damn near fooled us."

Christabel's hand tightened on Prince Pikapik. The doll let out a warning squeak.

"If the car had just burned a little longer," Captain Parkins went on, "we wouldn't have been able to tell the difference between the stuff he left on the seat and a genuine cremated Sellars. Ash, fat, organic wastes—he must have measured it out with a teaspoon to get the proportions right. Clever little bastard."

"We would have found the holes in the fences," said Christabel's daddy.

"Yeah, but later rather than sooner. He might have had an extra twenty-four hours' head start."

Christabel heard her father get up. For a second she was scared, but then she heard him begin to walk back and forth like he did when he was on the phone. "Maybe. But shit, Ron, that still doesn't explain how he got away from the base in the time he had. He was in a wheel-chair, for God's sake!"

"MPs are checking everything. Could be someone just felt sorry for him and gave him a lift. Or he might have just rolled down the hill and he's hiding out in that squatter town. Nobody who knows any-thing will keep their mouths shut once we finish rousting the place. Someone will come forward."

"Unless he had a confederate—someone who helped him get out of the area entirely."

"Where would he find someone like that? Inside the base? That's a court-martial offense, Mike. And he doesn't know anyone off the base. We monitor all his household contacts, outgoing calls—he doesn't even access the net! Everything else is harmless. We watched him real close. A chess-by-mail arrangement with some retired guy in Australia—yes, we checked it out carefully—a few catalog requests and magazine subscriptions, things like that."

"Well, I still don't believe he could have pulled it off without any outside assistance. Someone must have helped him. And when I find out who it is—well, that person's going to wish he was never born."

Something was making a thumping noise. Christabel looked up. Prince Pikapik had crawled away under the hall table and now the otter doll was bumping over and over against the table leg. The vase was going to fall over any second, and her Daddy would hear that for sure and come out really angry. As she scrambled after the runaway otter, eyes wide and heart beating fast, her mother came around the corner and almost tripped over her.

Christabel shrieked.

"Mike, I wish you'd take some time to talk with your daughter," her mother called through the closed door of the den. "Tell her that everything's all right. This poor little girl is a nervous wreck."

Christabel had her soup in bed.

In the middle of the night, Christabel woke up scared. Mister Sellars had told her to put on the new Storybook Sunglasses after school, but she hadn't done it! She had forgotten because she came home early.

She slid down onto the floor as quietly as she could and climbed under the bed where she had hid them. She had taken the old pair with her to school and thrown them into the trash door outside the classroom during recess, just like Mister Sellars had told her to.

Being under the bed was like being in the Cave of the Winds in Otterland. For a moment she wondered if there really was any place like that, but since there weren't any otters left that didn't live in zoos—her daddy had told her that—there probably wasn't a Cave of the Winds anymore.

The sunglasses weren't blinking or anything. She put them on, but there was no writing, which made her even more scared. Had something happened to Mister Sellars down there under the ground when the house blew up? Maybe he was hurt and lost down in those tunnels.

Her finger touched the switch. The sunglasses still did not turn on, but just as she was thinking they might be broken, someone said *"Christabel?"* very quiet in her ear. She jumped and banged her head against the underside of the bed. When she dared, she took off the sunglasses and stuck her head out, but even with the dark all over, she could tell that there was no one in the room. She put the glasses back on.

"Christabel," the voice said again, *"is that you?"* It was Mister Sellars, she suddenly realized, talking to her through the sunglasses.

"Yes, it's me," she whispered.

Suddenly she could see him, sitting in his chair. Light was shining on only one half of his runny-looking face, so he looked even more scary than usual, but she was happy to see that he wasn't hurt or dead.

"I'm sorry I didn't put them on before . . ." she began.

"Hush. Don't fret. Everything is all right. Now, from here on, when you want to talk to me, you must put the glasses on and say the word . . . oh, let me see . . ." He frowned. *"Why don't you pick a word, little Christabel. Any word you want, but not one that people say very often."*

She thought hard. "What was the name of that little man in the story?" she whispered. "The name the girl was supposed to guess."

Mister Sellars slowly began to smile. *"Rumpelstiltskin? That's very good, Christabel, very good. Say it yourself so I can code it in. There. And you can use it to call me every day after school, maybe on your way home when you're by yourself. I have some very difficult things to do now, Christabel. Maybe the most important things I've ever done."*

"Are you going to blow more things up?"

"Goodness, I hope not. Were you very frightened? I heard the noise. You did an excellent job, my dear. You are a very, very brave girl, and you would make a wonderful revolutionary." He smiled another of his raggedy smiles.

"No, nothing else is going to blow up. But I'll still need your help from time to time. A lot of people are going to be looking for me."

"I know. My daddy was talking about you with Captain Parkins." She told him what she could remember.

"Well, I have no complaints, then," said Mister Sellars. *"And you, young lady, should go back to sleep. Call me tomorrow. Remember, just put on the glasses and say 'Rumpelstiltskin'."*

When the funny old man was gone, Christabel took off the Storybook Sunglasses and crawled out from under the bed. Now that she knew Mister Sellars was okay, she suddenly felt very sleepy.

She was just climbing back under the covers when she saw the face peering in through her window.

"It was a face, Mommy! I saw it! Right there!"

Her mother pulled her close and rubbed her head. Mommy smelled of lotion, like she always did at night. "I think it was probably just a bad dream, baby. Your daddy checked and there's no one outside."

Christabel shook her head and buried her face against her mother's chest. Even though the curtains were drawn, she didn't want to look at the window any more.

"Maybe you'd better come and sleep with us." Christabel's mother sighed. "Poor little thing—that house burning down last night really frightened you, didn't it? Well, don't worry, honey. It's nothing to do with you and it's all over now."

The technicians wanted to make notes for the clean-up.

Dread was mildly irritated, since he had last-minute details to attend to and this was not the most convenient time to be forced out of the observation center, but he approved of their thoroughness. He took a small cigar from the humidor and went out onto the top floor balcony overlooking the bay.

The *Beinha y Beinha* technical crew had already broken down his office in the city. Now that the project had moved into the final phase, there was no longer a need for it, and once the operation was complete, there would be no time to go back and tie up loose ends, so the crew had emptied it completely, which included sandblasting the top level off all permanent surfaces, repainting, and replacing the carpets. Now the same men and women were busily examining the beach house which served as observation center. By the time Dread and his team were in the water heading for the target, the cleaning crew, like white-clad scavenger beetles, would be pulling the two-story house to pieces and destroying all clues as to who had inhabited it these past three days.

He really didn't mind at all being forced out to the balcony on a fine tropical night, he decided. He had not allowed himself a moment's recreation since the stewardess, and he had been working very, very hard.

Still, it was hard to forget business with the target literally in sight. The lights of the Isla de Santuario were barely visible across the expanse of black water, but the island's various security devices—the drone submarines, minisats, and hardened sites defended by armed guards—were not visible at all, yet each and every one had to be dealt with. Still, barring the kind of major miscalculation that Dread had never yet made. . . .

Confident, cocky, lazy, dead, he reminded himself.

. . . Barring miscalculation or criminally negligent intelligence gathering, all were known and prepared for. He only awaited the solution of a few minor loose ends and then the actual arrival of the rest of the team, slated in four hours. Dread had deliberately kept them away until this moment. There was nothing the actual site offered that could not be learned and mastered in simulation, and there was no sense doing anything that might alert the target. The clean-up crew were the one group that did not prepare in VR, but their van was parked in plain sight in the driveway, bearing the name of a well-known local carpet retailer, and of course the Beinhas had arranged for someone on their own payroll to be answering the phones at the carpet warehouse all week, in case someone on the island should spot the van and do that little extra conscientious bit.

So now, with all the leisurely pleasure of an actual householder enjoying the prospect of handsome new floor coverings, Dread turned up his internal music, then leaned back in a broadly striped canvas chair, lit his cigar, and put his feet up on the balcony railing.

He had smoked barely half the cigar, and was idly watching the island's perimeter spotlights reflecting on the water like amber stars, when a much smaller light began to blink at the corner of his vision. Dread cursed silently. The soaring Monteverdi madrigal—his favorite music when he was playing a contemplative scene—descended in volume to a sweet murmur. Antonio Heredia Celestino appeared in an open window superimposed on Dread's vision, his shaved head hover-

ing above the dark Caribbean as if he were treading water. Dread
would have preferred that Celestino actually *were* treading water.

"Yes?"

"I am sorry to disturb you, *Jefe.* I hope you have been having a
pleasant evening."

"What do you want, Celestino?" The man's attention to meaningless formalities was one of the things that did not sit well with Dread.
He was a more than competent gear man—the Beinhas would not
hire technical people who were second-rate—but his plodding humor-
lessness was annoying in itself as well as evidence of a lack of imagination.

"I am having a few doubts about the data tap. The defenses are
complicated, and there is a risk that the preliminary work itself may
have . . . consequences."

"What are you talking about?"

Celestino bobbed his head nervously and tried to form a winning
smile. Dread, a child of the ugliest tin-siding towns of the Australian
Outback, was torn between disgust and amusement. If the man had
a forelock, Dread decided, he would have tugged it. "I fear that these
preliminary inspections, the preparation work . . . well, I fear that they
may alert the . . . the designate."

"The 'designate'? Do you mean the target? What in hell are you
trying to say, Celestino?" His anger building, Dread turned the madrigal off completely. "Have you compromised the action somehow? Are
you calling me to say that, oops, you've accidentally scorched our mission?"

"No, no! Please, *Jefe,* I have done nothing!" The man seemed more
alarmed by Dread's sudden fury than by the implication of his incom-
petence. "No, that is why I wished to talk to you, sir. I would do
nothing to risk our security without consulting you." He hurriedly
outlined a series of concerns, most of which Dread found laughably
exaggerated. Dread decided, to his great irritation, that what was
going on was simple: Celestino had never cracked a system this tough
or this complicated, and he wanted to make sure that if anything went
wrong, he would have the excuse that he was following orders.

*The idiot seems to think that just because he's in an apartment a few miles
away from the exercise, he'd live through the failure of this action. He obviously
doesn't know the Old Man.*

"So what are you saying, Celestino? I've been listening for a long
time and I haven't heard anything new."

"I wished only to suggest . . ." He obviously found this too forward.

"I wondered if you had considered a narrow definition data bomb. We could introduce a hunter-killer into the system and immobilize their entire household net. If we properly code our own equip . . ."

"Stop." Dread closed his eyes, struggling to remain calm. Maddeningly, Celestino's pinch-faced image still haunted the blackness behind his eyelids. "Remind me—didn't you spend time in the military?"

"BIM," said Celestino with a touch of pride. "Brigada de Institutos Militares. Four years."

"Of course. Do you know when this operation begins? Do you know anything? We are less than eighteen hours away, and you come to me with this kind of shit. Data bomb? Of *course* you were in the military—if you're not sure about something, blow it up!" He scowled horribly, forgetting for a moment that Celestino, for security's sake, was only seeing a low-grade and largely expressionless Dread sim. "You miserable little poofter, what do you think we're going in for? Just to kill someone? If you had been a foot soldier, or a door-opener, or even the goddamned janitor, you might have an excuse for thinking that, but you are the Christ-save-us gear man! We are going to freeze and strip the entire system and any remote attachments. Data bomb! What if the thing's programmed to dump everything under assault?"

"I . . . but surely . . ." The sweat on the hacker's brow was clearly visible.

"Listen carefully. If we lose one particle of that data, *anything*, I am going to personally rip your heart out of your body and show it to you. Understand?"

Celestino nodded, swallowing hard. Dread cut the connection, then began to search through his files for music that might salvage his good mood.

". . . That man has a crack in him a mile wide."

The shapeless sim that was the Beinha on the left leaned forward slightly. "He is very good at his job."

"He's a nervous small-timer. I'm flying someone in to keep an eye on things. No arguments. I'm doing you the courtesy of letting you know."

There was a long silence. "It is your choice," one of them said at last.

"It is. Damn." The red light was blinking again, but this time in a recognizable rhythm. "Excuse me. I have to take a call."

The two sisters nodded and blinked off. They were replaced by one of the Old Man's functionaries—a Puppet as far as Dread could tell, dressed in the usual costume-bazaar Egyptian.

"The Lord of Life and Death, Mighty in Worship, Who is Crowned in the West, summons you to the presence."

Dread suppressed a groan. "Now? Can't he just talk to me?"

The functionary did not bat an eye. "You are summoned to Abydos," it said, then vanished. Dread sat for a long moment just breathing, then stood and stretched to release tension—it might prove a very painful mistake to take his frustration and anger to the Old Man—and looked with more than a little sorrow at the cigar, which was now mostly gray char in the bottom of the ceramic bowl he had been using as an ashtray. He sat down again and found a comfortable position, since the Old Man's caprice often extended to hour-long waits, and closed his eyes.

The massive hypostyle hall of Abydos-That-Was stretched before him, the swollen, skyscraper pillars made even more dramatic by the light of innumberable flickering lamps. He could see the god's chair on the dais at the far end of the hall, looming above the bent backs of a thousand priests like a volcanic island rising from the ocean. Dread grunted in disgust and made his way forward.

Even though he could not actually feel the jackal ears above his head or see the cur's muzzle he wore, even though the priests kept their faces to the floor as they made way for him and not a single one even stole a glance at him, he felt angry and humiliated. The action would begin in mere hours, but would the Old Man cut through some of his ridiculous ceremony and make things a little easier? Of course he wouldn't. Dread was his dog, summoned to hear His Master's Voice, and would never be allowed to forget it.

As he reached the front of the hall, and lowered himself to all fours in front of the throne, he harbored a brief but satisfying fantasy of putting a match to the old bastard's mummy wrappings.

"Arise, my servant."

Dread stood. Even had he been standing on the dais, he would have been dwarfed by the figure of his employer.

Always has to remind me who's on top.

"Tell me of the Sky God Project."

Dread took a breath, suppressing his fury, and delivered a status report on the final preparations. Osiris, the Lord of Life and Death, listened with apparent interest, but although his corpselike face was as immobile as ever, Dread thought the Old Man seemed vaguely distracted: his bandaged fingers moved ever so slightly on the arms of his throne, and once he asked Dread to repeat something that should have been perfectly comprehensible the first time.

"The responsibility for this idiot programmer is yours," Osiris pronounced when told about Celestino's call. "Take steps to make sure this is not a weak link in our chain."

Dread bristled at the assumption that he had to be told. With effort, he managed to keep his voice even. "A professional with whom I have already worked is on her way down. She will watch over Celestino."

Osiris waved his hand as though this were all perfectly obvious. "This must not fail. I have placed great trust in you despite your many lapses of behavior. This must not fail."

Despite his own simmering unhappiness, Dread was intrigued. The Old Man appeared to be worried—if not about this, then about something else. "When have I ever failed you, Grandfather?"

"Don't call me that!" Osiris lifted his arms from the throne and crossed them over his chest. "I have told you before I will not allow it from a mere servant."

Dread barely restrained a hiss of rage. No, let the old bastard say what he wished. There was a longer game—the Old Man himself had taught him to play it—and this might be the first crack in his master's defenses.

"I apologize, O Lord. All will be done as you say." He lowered his great black head, bumping his muzzle gently against the stone flags. "Have I done something new to make you angry?" He wondered briefly if the stewardess . . . No. Her body couldn't even have been found yet, and for once he had refrained from leaving his signature, art shackled by necessity.

The God of Upper and Lower Egypt tilted his head down. For a moment, Dread thought he could see the fierce intelligence glinting in the depths of the Old Man's eyes. "No," he said at last. "You have done nothing. I am over-quick in my anger, perhaps. I am very busy, and much of the business is unpleasant."

"I'm afraid I probably would not understand your problems, my Lord. Just managing a project like the one you've given me takes everything I've got—I can't imagine the complexity of what you must deal with."

Osiris sat back in his great throne, staring out across the hall. "No, you cannot. At this very moment—this moment!—my enemies are assembling in my council chamber. I must confront them. There is a plot against me, and I do not yet . . ." He trailed off, then twitched his huge head and leaned forward. "Has anyone approached you? Have you been asked about me, offered anything for information or assistance? I promise you, as terrible as my anger will be at anyone who betrays me, my generosity to my faithful servants is even greater."

Dread sat in silence for a long second, afraid to speak too swiftly. The old devil had never talked this openly before, never shown worry or vulnerability in front of him. He wished there was some way he could record the moment for later study, but instead he must commit every word and gesture to his own frail human memory.

"No one has approached me, Lord. I promise I would have told you immediately. But if there is something I can do to help you—information you need gathered, allies you are not sure of that you want to . . ."

"No, no, no." Osiris waved his flail impatiently, silencing his servant. "I will deal with it, as I always have. You will do your part by making sure that the Sky God project goes as planned."

"Of course, Lord."

"Go. I will speak to you again before the action is launched. Find someone to keep a close eye on that programmer."

"Yes, Lord."

The god waved his crook and Dread was expelled from the system.

He remained in the chair for a long time, ignoring three different incoming calls while he thought about what he had just seen and heard. At last he stood up. Downstairs, the cleaning team had finished their prep and were climbing into their van.

Dread flicked the cigar end off the balcony into the dark water, then went back into the house.

"**L**ook, we just have to tie the ends one more time, then we're done." Fredericks held up a handful of serpentine creepers and vines. "Those are waves out there, Orlando, and God only knows what else there is. Sharks—sea monsters, maybe. Come on, a little extra trouble now will make a big difference when we're on the water."

Orlando looked down at the raft. It was a decent-enough job, lengths of stiff, heavy reeds knotted together in long bundles, which had then been tied together to make one long rectangle. It would probably even float. He was just finding it hard to care very much.

"I need to sit down for a minute." He stumbled to the shade of the nearest palm tree and flopped to the sand.

"Fine. I'll do it. What else is new?" Fredericks bent to the task.

Orlando lifted a trembling hand to shade his eyes from the sun filtering down between the palm leaves. The city was different at noon; it changed throughout the day, colors and reflective metals mutating with the movement of light, shadows expanding and contracting. Just now it seemed a kind of giant mushroom patch, golden roofs springing from the loamy soil of their own shade.

He let his hand fall and leaned back against the palm trunk. He was very, very weak. It was easy to imagine burying himself in sand, like the roots of a tree, and never moving again. He was exhausted and sluggish because of his illness, and he could not conceive of how he would make it through another night like the last, a night of confusions and terrors and madness, none of it comprehensible and none of it in the least restful.

"Okay, I've double-tied everything. Are you at least going to help me carry it down to the water?"

Orlando stared at him for a long time, but still Fredericks' pink, unhappy face refused to disappear. He groaned. "Coming."

The raft did float, although parts of it remained resolutely below the waterline, so that there was nowhere dry to sit. Still, the warm weather did not make that too uncomfortable. Orlando was glad at least that he had prevailed on Fredericks to bring the wall of the palm-leaf shelter along, no matter how short a trip his friend expected. Orlando tilted it over them, letting it lean against his shoulders. It kept off the worst of the afternoon sun, but it did little to cool the heat in his head and his joints.

"I don't feel very good," he said quietly. "I told you, I've got pneumonia." It was about the only conversation he had to offer, but even he was growing tired of it. Fredericks, splashing obdurately with a makeshift paddle, did not reply.

Astonishingly—to Orlando, anyway—they were actually making a kind of slow progress toward the city. The cross-current was bearing them unmistakably to what Orlando guessed was the northern side of the shoreline, but the drift was slight; he thought they might very well make it to the far side before the current pulled them out into what were probably ocean waters. And if they didn't . . . well, Fredericks would be disappointed, but Orlando was having trouble seeing what the difference would be. He was adrift in some kind of limbo, his strength leaking away hourly, and what he had left behind (in what he still quaintly thought about from time to time as the "real" world) was no better.

"I know you're sick, but could you try to paddle for a little while?" Fredericks was working hard not to be resentful; as if from a distance, Orlando admired him/her for it. "My arms are really aching, but if we don't keep pushing, the current will take us away from the beach."

It was a tough call as to which would take more energy, arguing or paddling. Orlando went to work.

His arms felt as flabby and weak as noodles, but there was a certain soothing quality to the repetition of dipping his paddle, pulling, raising it, then dipping it again. After a while the monotony combined with the sun's rippling reflections and his fevered driftiness to lift him into a kind of reverie, so he didn't notice the water rising until Fredericks shouted out that they were sinking.

Alerted but still buffered by his dreamy detachment, Orlando looked down at the water, which was now up to the crotch of his loincloth. The middle of the raft had descended, or the sides had risen; in either case, most of the craft was now at least partially underneath the water.

"What do we do?" Fredericks sounded like someone who believed that things mattered.

"Do? Sink, I guess."

"Are you scanning out, Gardiner?" Clearly fighting back panic, Fredericks looked up at the horizon. "We might be able to swim the rest of the way."

Orlando followed his gaze, then laughed. "Are *you* scanned? I can barely paddle." He looked at the length of split reed in his hand. "Not that it's doing us any good, now." He tossed the paddle away. It splashed into the water and then popped up again, bobbing along far more convincingly than the raft.

Fredericks shouted in horror and stretched toward it, as though he could reverse physics and draw it back through the air. "I can't believe you just did that!" He looked down at the raft again, full of twitchy, terrified energy. "I have an idea. We'll get in the water, but we'll use the raft as a float—you know, like those rafts in swimming class."

Orlando had never been in a swimming class, or anything that his mother feared might be dangerous to his fragile bones, but he was not disposed to argue anyway. At his friend's urging he slid off the raft into the cool water. Fredericks splashed in beside him, then braced his chest against the trailing edge of the raft and began to kick in a manner that was a credit to his long-ago instructors.

"Can't you kick, too, at least a little?" he panted.

"I *am* kicking," Orlando said.

"Whatever happened," Fredericks gasped, "to all that Thargor strength? All that monster-ass-kicking muscle? Come on!"

It was an effort even to explain, and frequent mouthfuls of salt water didn't help. "I'm sick, Frederico. And maybe the gain isn't turned up as high on this system—I always had to crank the tactor outputs way up to make it work as well as it did for someone normal."

They had only dog-paddled for a few minutes when Orlando felt his strength finally desert him. His legs slowed, then stopped. He hung onto the back of the raft, but even that was difficult.

"Orlando? I need your help!"

The city, which once had waited squarely before them, had now shifted to the right. The blue water between the raft and the beach, however, had not narrowed appreciably. They were drifting out to sea, Orlando realized—as he himself was drifting. They would get farther and farther from land, until eventually the city would disappear entirely.

But that's not fair. The thoughts seemed to come in slow bumps, like the waves. *Fredericks wants to live. He wants to play soccer and do things—wants to be a real boy, just like Pinocchio. I'm just holding him back. I'm the Donkey Island kid.*

"Orlando?

No, not fair. He has to paddle hard enough to pull my weight, too. Not fair. . . .

He let go and slid under the water. It was surprisingly easy. The surface snapped shut over him like an eyelid closing, and for a moment he felt complete weightlessness, complete ease, and a certain dull smugness at his decision. Then something seized his hair, jerking him into fiery pain and a throatful of sea water. He was pulled to the surface, spluttering.

"Orlando!" Fredericks shrieked, "what the hell are you *doing?*"

He was clinging to the raft with one hand so he could maintain his grip on Orlando's—Thargor's—long black hair.

Now nobody's kicking, Orlando thought sadly. He spat out salty water and barely avoided a coughing spasm. *It isn't doing any good at all.*

"I'm . . . I just can't go any farther," he said aloud.

"Grab the raft," Fredericks directed. "Grab the raft!"

Orlando did, but Fredericks didn't relinquish his grip. For a moment they just floated, side by side. The raft rose and fell as the waves moved past. Except for the stinging pain in his scalp, nothing had changed.

Fredericks, too, had gotten a mouthful of seawater. His nose was running, his eyes red-rimmed. "You aren't going to quit. You're not going to!"

Orlando found enough strength to shake his head. "I can't. . . ."

"Can't? You impacted bastard, you've made my life a living hell about this stupid goddamned city! And there it is! And you're just going to give up?"

"I'm sick. . . ."

"So what? Yeah, yeah, it's really sad. You've got some weird disease. But *that's* the place you wanted to go. You've dreamed about it. It's the only thing you care about, practically. So either you're going to help me get to that beach, or I'm going to have to drag you like I learned in that stupid swimming class, and then we'll *both* drown, five hundred yards away from your goddamned city. You goddamned coward." Fredericks was breathing so hard he could barely finish his sentence. He clung to the bobbing raft, neck-deep in the water, and glared.

Orlando was faintly amused that anyone could muster so much emotion about a pointless thing like the difference between going on and going down, but he also felt a slight irritation that Fredericks—Fredericks!—should be calling him a coward.

"You want me to help you? Is that what you're saying?"

"No, I want you to do what was so important that you got me into this impacted, *fenfen* mess in the first place."

Again, it had become easier to paddle than to argue. Also, Fredericks was still gripping his hair, and Orlando's head was bent at an uncomfortable angle.

"Okay. Just let go."

"No tricks?"

Orlando wearily shook his head. *You try to do a guy a favor. . . .*

They edged forward until their chests were back on the raft and began kicking again.

The sun was very low in the sky and a cool wind was making the tips of the waves froth when they made it past the first breakwater and out of the cross-current. After a short celebratory rest, Fredericks let Orlando climb up onto the bowed raft and paddle with his hands while Fredericks continued his outboard-motor impersonation.

By the time they reached the second breakwater they were no longer alone, but merely the smallest of the waterway's travelers.

Other boats, some clearly equipped with engines, others with full-bellied sails, were beginning to make their way back from a day's work. The wakes of their passing made the raft rock alarmingly. Orlando climbed back into the water.

Above them and around them the city was beginning to turn on its lights.

They were debating whether or not to try to signal one of the passing boats when Orlando began to feel another wash of fever pass over him.

"We can't try to take this raft all the way in," Fredericks was arguing. "Some big ship will come through here and they won't even see us in the dark."

"I think all the . . . big ships come in the other . . . side," Orlando said. He was finding it hard to get enough breath to speak. "Look." On the far side of the harbor maze, beyond several jetties, two large vessels, one of them a tanker of some sort, were being hauled into the port by tugboats. Nearer, vastly smaller than the tanker but still fairly large and impressive, was a barge. Despite his exhaustion, Orlando couldn't help staring at it. The barge, covered in painted carvings and with something that looked like a sun with an eye in it painted on the bow, seemed to belong to a different age than the harbor's other ships. It had a single tall mast and a flat, square sail. Lanterns hung in the rigging and at the bow.

As Orlando stared at this strange apparition, the world seemed to pass into some greater shadow. The lanterns flared into blurry star shapes. He had a moment to wonder how twilight had become dark midnight so suddenly, and to feel sad that the city's residents had doused all their lights, then he felt the water slide up and over him again.

This time Orlando barely felt it when Fredericks pulled him out. The fever had gripped him again, and he was so exhausted that he could not imagine it ever letting go. A distant foghorn had become a smear of sound that rang in his ears, fading but never completely stopping. Fredericks was saying something urgent, but Orlando could not make sense of it. Then a light as bright as anything Orlando could imagine replaced the darkness with a whiteness far more painful and terrible.

The spotlight belonged to a small boat. The small boat belonged to the Harbor Police of the great city. They were not cruel, but they were briskly uninterested in what Fredericks had to say. It seemed that they were on the lookout for outsiders, and the two men treading water beside a handmade raft seemed to fit the description. As they hauled Orlando and Fredericks on board, they talked among themselves; Orlando heard the words "god king," and "council." It seemed that he and Fredericks were being arrested for some kind of crime, but he was finding it harder and harder to make sense out of what was happening around him.

The barge loomed above them, then the carved hull began to slide by as the patrol boat motored past it on the way to the dock of the Great Palace, but before they had reached the hull's far end, consciousness escaped Orlando's grasp.

CHAPTER 35

Lord of Temilún

NETFEED/NEWS: *Vat-Beef Poisoning Scare in Britain*
(visual: mob outside Derbyshire factory)
VO: A rash of fatal illnesses in Britain has caused chaos in the cultured meat
industry. One food product company, Artiflesh Ltd., has seen drivers attacked
and a factory burned to the ground.
(visual: Salmonella bacteria under microscopic enlargement)
The deaths are blamed on a Salmonella infection of a beef "mother," the
original flesh matrix from which up to a hundred generations of vat-grown
meat can be derived. One such "mother" can be the source of thousands of
tons of cultured meat. . . .

"**A**tasco!" Renie raised her hands to defend herself, but their captor only regarded her with faint irritation.

"You know my name? I am surprised."

"Why? Because we're just little people?" Confronted with the first real face—as real as any sim face could be—behind Otherland, she found she was not frightened. A cold anger filled her and made her feel she was standing apart from herself.

"No." Atasco seemed genuinely puzzled. "Because I did not think my name was commonly known, at least outside of certain circles. Who are you?"

Renie reached out and touched !Xabbu on the shoulder, as much for her own comfort as his. "If you don't know, I'm certainly not going to tell you."

The God-King shook his head. "You are a most impertinent young woman."

"Renie. . . ?" Martine began, but at that moment something slithered at high speed across the floor of the Council Chamber, an iridescent blur that skirted Renie and !Xabbu by a matter of inches before disappearing into the shadows.

"Ah!" As he followed the odd apparition with his gaze, the annoyance faded from Bolivar Atasco's face. "There it is again. Do you know what that is?"

Renie could not gauge his tone. "No. What?"

He shook his head. "I haven't the slightest idea. Well, that is not exactly true—I have an idea of what it represents, but not what it *is*. It's a phenomenon of complexity, the immense complexity of the system. Not the first, and I dare say not the last or the strangest." He stood for a moment, pondering, then turned back to Renie and her friends. "Perhaps we should cut this unsatisfying conversation short. There is still much to do."

"Torture?" Renie knew she should keep quiet, but months of frustration and rage could not be ignored; she felt hardened and sharpened like a knife blade. "Firebombing people's apartments and putting children into comas and beating old women to death not satisfying enough?"

"Renie . . ." Martine began again, but was interrupted by Atasco's angry shout.

"*Enough!*" His eyes had narrowed to slits. "Are you a madwoman? Who are you to come into my world and make such accusations?" He turned to Martine. "Are you her caretaker? If so, you have failed. The monkey has better manners."

"The monkey is perhaps more patient," Martine said quietly. "Renie, !Xabbu, I think we may have made a mistake."

"A mistake?" Renie was astonished. Perhaps Martine had developed some kind of amnesia because of her traumatic entry into this simworld, but she herself remembered Atasco's name only too well. In any case, she had only to look at the arrogant, aristocratic face that he had chosen to know everything about him. "I don't think there's any mistake except him thinking that we'll be polite about this."

!Xabbu clambered up onto one of the chairs, and from there onto the surface of the vast table. "A question, Mister Atasco. Why did you bring us here?"

He took in the talking monkey without comment. "I did not bring you here. You brought yourselves here, I would assume."

"But why?" !Xabbu persisted. "You are the ruler of this fantastical place. Why are you spending time speaking to us? What do you think that *we* want?"

Atasco raised an eyebrow. "You have been summoned here. I have let the person who summoned you use my city, my palace, for the sake of convenience—well, and because I share some of his fears." He shook his head as though it were all quite obvious; his high, feathered crown swayed. "Why am I speaking to you? You are guests. It is courtesy, of course—something you seem able to do without."

"Are you saying . . ." Renie had to stop for a moment to figure out just what he *was* saying. "Are you saying that you haven't brought us here to hurt us or threaten us? That you don't have anything to do with my brother being in a coma? With the people who killed Doctor Susan Van Bleeck?"

Atasco stared at her for a long moment. The handsome face was still imperially condescending, but she could sense a certain hesitation. "If the terrible acts you describe can be laid at the doorstep of the Grail Brotherhood, then I am not entirely without blame," he said at last. "It is because I fear I may have unwittingly contributed to that evil that I have made my beloved Temilún available as a gathering place. But I am not personally responsible for the things you suggest, for the love of God, no." He turned to look across the broad room. "Lord, these are odd times. Few strangers ever come here, and now there will be many. But, this is a time of change, I suppose." He turned back. "Do you know what tomorrow is? Four Movement. We inherited our dates from the Aztecs, you see. But that is a very significant day, the end of the Fifth Sun—the end of an age. Most of my people have forgotten the old superstitions, but of course that's because it's been a thousand years in their time."

Is he crazy? Renie wondered. *I'm talking about people killed and crippled, he's talking about Aztec calendars.*

"But you said we were 'summoned.' " !Xabbu spread his long arms. "Please, summoned by whom?"

"You must wait for the others. I am the host, but I am not the one who has chosen you."

Renie felt as though the world had abruptly reversed its spin. Were they just going to take this man's word for it that he was somehow

on their side? If that were true, why all this vagueness? She picked at
the knot, but could see no immediate solution. "So that's all you can
tell us, even though you're the big chief around here?" she asked at
last, earning a reproachful stare from !Xabbu.

Atasco had not conquered his initial dislike, but he made an effort
to answer her civilly. "The one who called you has labored long and
with great subtlety—even I do not know everything he has done or
thought."

Renie frowned. She was not going to be able to make herself like
the man, that seemed certain—he reminded her of some of the worst
South African whites, the rich ones, subtle, secretive heirs of the *an-
cien regime* who never had to assert their superiority because they just
assumed it was obvious—but she had to admit to herself that she
might have misjudged him.

"Okay. If I've been too quick to accuse, I apologize," she said.
"Please understand, after the attacks we've survived, and then to find
ourselves in this place, manhandled by police. . . ."

"Manhandled? Is this true?"

She shrugged. "Not violently. But they certainly didn't make us
think we were honored guests either."

"I will pass them a word. Gently, of course—they must have auton-
omy. If the God-King speaks too harshly, the whole system becomes
perturbed."

Martine had been looking as though she wished to speak for some
time. "You have . . . built this place, no? It is yours?"

"Grown it would perhaps be closer to the mark." His chilly expression softened. "You came in by bus, I understand. That is too bad—
you did not see the splendid canals or the harbor. Would you like me
to tell you something about Temilún?"

"Yes, very much," Martine said hurriedly. "But first something else.
I am having trouble filtering my input—the raw data is very strong.
Could you . . . is there a way you could adjust it? I am afraid it is
rather too much for me."

"I should think so." He paused, but it was more than a pause; his
body simply froze in place, with none of the small signs that a living
but still human body shows. !Xabbu looked at Renie, who shrugged:
she did not know what Atasco was doing, and wasn't quite sure what
Martine was talking about either. Then, with no warning, Atasco's
sim was alive again.

"It can be done, I believe," he said, "but not easily. You are receiving
the same quantity of information as the others, and since you are all

on the same line, I cannot change yours without lowering their input as well." He paused, then shook his head. "We must find some way to bring you back on a different line. You should not do it, though, until you have spoken to Sellars. I do not know how he plans for you, and you might not be able to enter the network again in time."

"Sellars?" Renie tried to keep her voice calm; this man obviously preferred his conversations politely formal. "Is he the one who . . . summoned us, as you said?"

"Yes. You will meet him soon. When the others arrive."

"Others? What. . . ?"

Martine cut her off. "I will not enter the network again. Not if it means I must pass through the security system."

Atasco inclined his head. "I could bring you in as my guest, of course—I could have brought you all in as my guests, and offered to do so—but Sellars was violently opposed to anything like that; it was something about the security system. You must speak to him about it, since I do not quite understand."

"What *was* that thing?" Renie asked. "That so-called security system killed our friend."

For the first time, Atasco seemed truly shocked. "What? What do you mean?"

Renie, with interpolations from !Xabbu and Martine, told him what had happened. By the time she was finished, Atasco had begun to pace. "This is dreadful. Are you sure? Could he not simply have had an attack of the heart?" Under stress his English was a little more heavily accented, a little less precise.

"It had us all," Renie said evenly. "Singh said that it was alive, and I don't know how else you could describe it. *What is it?*"

"It is the neural network—the thing that underlies the Grail network system. It was grown as the simulations were grown, I believe. I do not know much about it—that was not my role. But it was not meant to . . . that is terrible. If what you say is true, then Sellars is not a moment too soon! My God! Terrible, terrible." Atasco had stopped pacing, and now looked agitatedly around him. "You must hear what he says. I will only confuse things. It seems he is right, though—we have lived in our own isolated world too long."

"Tell us about this place you have . . . grown," said Martine.

Renie was irritated. She wanted to hear more about this mysterious Sellars, about the thing that !Xabbu had named the All-Devourer, but it seemed Martine preferred a hobby lecture from a rich crank. She looked to !Xabbu for support, but he was giving Atasco a soulful and

attentive look, particularly galling on the face of a baboon. She made
a quiet noise of disgust.

"Temilún?" Their host brightened a little. "Of course. You came
from Aracatacá, no? Down from the forests. What did you think of
the people you saw? Were they happy? Well-fed?"

Renie shrugged. "Yes. Seemed to be."

"And not a word of Spanish. No priests—well, a few these days
from overseas, but they have trouble finding people to come to their
strange and unfamiliar churches. But no Catholicism to speak of. And
all because of horses."

Renie looked at !Xabbu, who also looked confused. "Horses?" she
asked.

"Oh, it is most elementary, my dear . . . what is your name?"

Renie hesitated. *In for a penny, in for a pound,* she decided. *If he's
faking this whole thing, these people are even farther out of our league than we
guessed.* And if the Grail Brotherhood could burn down her flatblock
and freeze Jeremiah's credcards, her name wouldn't be news to anyone. "Irene Sulaweyo. Renie."

". . . Elementary, my dear Irene." Warming to what was obviously
a favorite subject, Atasco seemed to have totally forgotten his earlier
antipathy. "Horses. The one thing the Americas lacked. You see, the
ancestral horse died out here—well, in the 'here' that is my real-life
home, but *not* in the world of Temilún. When the great empires of the
Americas arose in the real world—the Toltec, Aztec, Mayan, Inca, our
own Muisca—they had several handicaps the civilizations of the Tigris
Valley or the Mediterranean did not have—slower communications,
no large wagons or sledges since there were no animals capable of
hauling them, less need for broad flat roads, hence less pressure to
develop the wheel, and so on." He began pacing again, but this time
with an air of happy energy. "In the real world, the Spanish came to
the Americas and discovered them ripe for plucking. Only a few hundred men with guns and horses subjugated two continents. Think of
that! So I built America again. But this time the horse did not die
out." He took off his feathered crown and set it on the table. "Everything was different here. In my invented world, Aztecs and others
developed much broader empires, and after receiving trading visits
from ancient Phoenicia, began reaching out down the sea-roads to
other civilizations. When gunpowder came from Asia into Western
Europe and the Middle East, the boats of the *Tlatoani*—the Aztec emperor, if you will—brought it back to the Americas as well."

"But . . . these people have *cellular phones!*" Against her better judgment, Renie found herself drawn into Atasco's fantasy. "How many years old is this civilization?"

"This simulation is now only a little behind the real world. If there were an actual Europe on the far side of the ocean outside this palace, it would be experiencing the early part of the twenty-first century. But Christ and the western calendar never came here, so even though the Aztec Empire fell long ago, we still call this day Four Movement, the Fifth Sun." He smiled with childlike pleasure.

"But that's what I don't understand. How could you have started back in the Ice Age or whatever and now be in the present day? Are you trying to tell me you've been watching this thing for like ten thousand years?"

"Ah, I see. Yes, I have." Another self-satisfied smile. "But not all at regular speed. There is a macro level where the centuries hurry past and I can only gather data in large, general clumps, but when I wish to really understand something, I can slow the simulation down to normal speed, or even stop it."

"You play God, in other words."

"But how could you create every one of these people?" !Xabbu asked. "Surely each one would take a long time." He sounded quite convincingly interested; Renie at first thought he might be trying to prevent her from further antagonizing their host, but then she remembered the Bushman's own cherished goal.

"You do not create separate individuals in a system like this," said Temilún's God-King. "Not one at a time, anyway. This simulation—and all the others in this entire network—are grown. The units of life begin as simple automata, organisms with very basic rules, but the more they are allowed to interact, adapt, and evolve, the more complex they become." His gesture encompassed himself and the other three. "As is true with Life itself. But when our automata get to a certain level of complexity, we can, as it were, file off the rough edges and have a sort of fractal seed for an artificial plant or animal—or even a human being—which will then grow as its own individual genetics and environment dictate."

"That's pretty much what they do already on the net," said Renie. "All the big VR setups are based on data ecologies, one way or the other."

"Yes, but they do not have the power that we have." He shook his head emphatically. "They do not have the potential for complexity, for sophisticated individuality. But you know this now, do you not? You have seen Temilún. Is it not as true, as authentic in its variety as any place you have visited in the real world? You cannot accomplish that on the net, no matter how much money and effort you put in. The platform will not support it."

"Yeah, but the security systems on the net don't kill people either."

Atasco's high-boned face flushed with fury, but it lasted for only a moment, then a more doleful expression took its place. "I cannot defend it. I have spent so long watching the results, I fear I may have overlooked the price being paid."

"But what is this place, really? Is it an art project, a science experiment—what?"

"All of those things, I suppose. . . ." Atasco broke off, staring over their shoulders. "Excuse me for a moment."

He walked past them around the table. The great doors at the chamber's far end had opened and the guards were ushering through three more people. Two of them wore female bodies similar to Martine's, dark-complected and black-haired like Temilún's native inhabitants. The other was a very tall figure dressed from head to foot in extravagant, showy black. Feathers, ruffles, and long pointed boots gave this newcomer the silhouette of some ancient court dandy; a skull-tight black leather hood covered all the stranger's head but for a bone white, sexually ambiguous face with blood-red lips.

Looks like someone out of some horrible Ganga Drone band, Renie decided.

Atasco greeted the new arrivals. Before he had finished, the apparition in black ostentatiously detached itself from the rest and sauntered to the room's far wall to examine the murals. Atasco showed the other two to chairs and returned to Renie and her friends.

"Temilún is both science and art, I suppose," he continued as though the interruption had not happened. "It is my life's work. I have always wondered what my native land would have been like if the Spaniards had not conquered. When I realized that for money, mere money, I could discover the answer, I did not hesitate. I have no children. My wife lives for the same dream. Have you met her?"

Renie shook her head, trying to keep up with him. "Your wife? No."

"She is around here somewhere. She is the genius with numbers. I can perceive a pattern, guess at an explanation, but she is the one who will tell me the hard facts, how many bushels of rice have been sold in the Temilún market, or what effect the drought is having on population emigration to the countryside."

Renie wanted to go and talk to the other guests—if "guests" was the right word—but she had belatedly realized that she could also learn things from Atasco, for all his eccentricity. "So you've made an entire world? I wouldn't think there were enough processors in the universe to do that, no matter what kind of fancy new network architecture you had."

He raised his hand, graciously condescending to point out what should have been obvious. "I have not created the entire world. Rather, what exists here," he spread his arms, "is the center of a greater world that exists only as data. The Aztecs, the Toltecs, they were only information that influenced Temilún in its growth, although for a while there were real Aztec overlords here." He shook his head in fond remembrance. "Even the Muiscas, who built this city during the height of their empire, largely existed outside the boundaries of the simulation—their capital and greatest city was at Bogotá, just as in the real world." He seemed to interpret Renie's look of general confusion as something specific. "The Muiscas? You may know them as the Chibchas, but that is the name of the language group rather than the people. No?" He sighed, a potter forced to work with faulty clay. "In any case, there are less than two million humanoid instruments in the simulation, and the rest of the world in which Temilún exists is only an extremely complicated system of algorithms without telemorphic representation." He frowned slightly. "You said you came from Aracataca, did you not? That, you see, is very close to the northern border of the world, as one might say. Not that you would see the edge of the simulation—it is not so primitive! You would see the water, of course, and some illusion of country beyond."

"So all this network—this Otherland—is made up of such places?" Martine asked. "The dreams and conceits of wealthy men?"

Atasco did not appear to take offense. "I suppose, although I have not traveled outside my own domain very often—not surprising when you consider how much of my blood and sweat I have put into this place. Some of the other domains are . . . well, I find them personally offensive, but as our homes should be bastions of privacy, so should our worlds. I would be very displeased if someone came here to tell me how to manage Temilún."

Renie was watching the stranger in black, who was very pointedly not paying attention to anyone else. Was this someone who had been summoned as she had? Why? What was the point of people being gathered in the irritatingly self-centered Atasco's virtual kingdom? And who in hell was Sellars?

Renie's pondering was interrupted by the doors thumping open to admit several more people. One appeared to be under police restraint, for a caped guard stood on either side of him, but after a moment

Renie saw that they were helping him to walk. He was tipped into a chair where he slumped like a sick child, odd because he wore the impossibly well-muscled body of an Olympic gymnast. A smaller friend huddled beside him, offering what looked like words of encouragement. These two, and a third who wore a shiny, robotic body, remained when the guards left. Bolivar Atasco left again to greet these latest arrivals.

Renie stared at the newcomers. There was something naggingly familiar about the muscular, black-haired sim. As she turned to consult !Xabbu, she felt a gentle touch on her arm. One of the previous group of guests, a small, round woman in a Temilúni sim, stood beside her.

"I am sorry to bother you. I am very confused. May I speak with you for a moment?"

Renie could not help looking the stranger over, but there was no way to deduce anything certain about anyone in VR. "Of course. Sit down." She led the woman to the chair beside Martine's.

"I . . . I do not understand where I am. That man said we are in his simulation, but I have never seen a simulation like this."

"None of us have," Renie assured her. "It's a whole new universe when you've got that kind of money, I guess."

The newcomer shook her head. "It is all so strange! I have been searching for help for my poor granddaughter, and thought I had discovered a source of information about what had harmed her. I have worked so hard to learn the truth! But now, instead of finding information, I find myself in . . . I do not know what it is."

!Xabbu popped up beside her. "Is your granddaughter ill?" he asked. "Is she asleep and will not wake up?"

The woman drew back, although Renie thought it was more from the startling suddenness of his question than !Xabbu's simian form. "Yes. She has been in the hospital for many months. The cleverest specialists in Hong Kong do not know what the problem is."

"The same thing is wrong with my brother." Renie described what had happened to Stephen, and how she and her friends had been led to Temilún. The woman listened avidly, making little noises of shock and unhappiness.

"I had thought I was the only one!" she said. "When my little dear one became sick, my flower, I felt sure it was something to do with the net. But my daughter and her husband, I think they believe I have lost my mind, although they are too kind to say so." Her shoulders trembled. Renie realized she was crying, although the sim did not show tears. "Forgive me. I have worried that I might indeed be going mad." She wiped at her eyes. "Oh! I have intruded on you, but have not even told you my name. I am so impolite! My name is Quan Li."

Renie introduced herself and her friends. "We're as surprised by all this as you are. We thought we were breaking into our enemies' personal playground. I suppose we did, in a way, but this man Atasco doesn't seem very much like an enemy." She looked over at their host, who was talking to the black-clad stranger. "Who is that with him— the one with the clown face? Did he come in with you?"

Quan Li nodded. "I do not know him—I am not even sure it *is* a him." She giggled, then lifted her hand to her mouth as though she had shocked herself. "He was waiting outside when the guards brought us—me and the other woman sitting there." She indicated the other Temilúni sim. "I do not know her name either. We all entered together."

"Perhaps he is Sellars," !Xabbu suggested.

"He is not," said Martine distractedly. She was staring at the high ceiling, her eyes still without focus. "He calls himself 'Sweet William.' He is from England."

Renie realized after a moment that her mouth was open. Even on a sim, that was not an attractive expression. She shut it. "How do you know?"

Before Martine could answer, the sound of chairs being scraped against the stone floor made them all turn. Atasco had seated himself at the head of the long table, where he had been joined by a coldly beautiful Temilúni woman dressed in a white cotton dress, her only ornament a magnificent necklace of blue stones. Renie had not seen her enter; she guessed it must be Atasco's number-crunching wife.

"Welcome to the Council Hall of Temilún." Atasco spread his arms in benediction as the rest of the guests seated themselves. "I know you have come from many places, and with many different purposes. I wish I had the leisure to speak with each one of you, but our time is short. Still, I hope you have had at least a brief opportunity to see something of this world. It has much to offer the interested sightseer."

"Oh, for God's sake," Renie murmured, "get on with it!"

Atasco paused as though he had heard her, but his expression was puzzled rather than irritated. He turned and whispered something to his wife, who whispered back. "I am not sure what to tell you," he said aloud. "The one who summoned you should have been here by now."

The shiny, robotic sim Renie had noted earlier stood. Its excessively

intricate armor had razor sharp points everywhere. "This far duppy,"
it said in a contemptuous Goggleboy drawl. "No clock for this. Flyin'
now." It made a series of gestures with its chrome-gleaming fingers,
then seemed taken aback when nothing happened. Before anyone else
could say anything, a yellowish light flared brightly beside the Atascos. Several of the guests cried out in surprise.

The figure that stood beside Bolivar Atasco when the flash subsided
was a featureless, humanoid splash of white, as though someone had
ripped away the substance of the council chamber.

Renie had been one of those who had shouted, but not because of
the apparition's startling entrance. *I've seen that thing before! In a dream?
No, in that club—in Mister J's.*

A memory that had been almost lost was coming back, her last
feeble moments in the depths of that horrible club. This thing had . . .
helped her? It was all very fuzzy. She turned to !Xabbu for confirmation, but the Bushman was watching the latest arrival with keen interest. Beside him, Martine looked completely overwhelmed, as
though she were lost in a dark forest.

Even Atasco seemed taken aback by the entrance. "Ah. It's . . . it's
you, Sellars."

The empty space at the top of the blank turned as it surveyed the
room. "So few," it said sadly. Renie felt the hair on her neck lift: she
had indeed heard those high, almost feminine tones in the trophy
garden at Mister J's. "We are so very few," it went on, "—only twelve
all told, including our hosts. But I am grateful that any are here at all.
You must have many questions. . . ."

"We certainly do," the one Martine had called Sweet William interrupted loudly. His accent was an impossibly exaggerated, theatrical
northern English. "Like who the friggin' hell are you and what the
friggin' hell is going on here?"

The empty face showed nothing, but Renie thought she heard a
smile in the soft voice. "My name is Sellars, as Mister Atasco has said.
Like many of the rest of you, I am in hiding now, but that name at
least is no longer a secret I need to keep. As to the rest of your question, young man . . ."

"Puh-leeeeze! Watch what you call a body, chuck."

". . . I will do my best to answer it. But it is not something I can do
quickly. I ask for your patience."

"Asking's not getting," Sweet William said, but waved for Sellars
to continue. !Xabbu, perhaps seeking a better vantage point, climbed
up out of his chair and crouched on the tabletop beside Renie.

"I am something of an expert on the movement of data from place to place," Sellars began. "Many people examine data for particular purposes—financial market data to make money, meteorological data to predict weather—but because of my own interests, I have always tended to study the patterns themselves as phenomena, rather than for what they represented."

Renie felt Martine stiffen in the chair beside her, but she could see nothing but the same confused look on her companion's face.

"In fact," Sellars continued, "at first, my interest in the patterns that have brought us to this place today were almost purely observational. Just as a poet may examine the way water runs and splashes and pools without the practical interest of a plumber or physicist, I have long been fascinated with the way information itself moves, collects, and moves again. But even a poet may notice when the drain is blocked and the sink is beginning to overflow. I came to see that there were certain very large patterns of dataflow that did not correspond to what I knew of the accepted map of the information sphere."

"What does all this have to do with us?" demanded the woman who had entered with Quan Li. Her English was blandly unaccented. Renie wondered if she was hearing the effects of translation software.

Sellars paused. "It is important you understand my journey or you will not understand the reasons for your own. Please, hear me out. After that, if you wish, you may walk away and never think of this again."

"You mean we're not prisoners?" the woman asked.

The blank space that was Sellars turned to Bolivar Atasco. "Prisoners? What have you told them?"

"Apparently some of the local police misunderstood my desire to have new arrivals brought here to the palace," the God-King said hurriedly. "I may have been a little unclear in my orders."

"What a surprise," said his wife.

"No, none of you are prisoners." Sellars was firm. "I know it cannot have been easy for any of you to come here. . . ."

"Except me," chirped Sweet William, fanning himself with his black-gloved hand.

Renie could not stand it any longer. "Will you *shut up!* Why can't anyone here just listen? People are dead, others are dying, and I want to hear what this Sellars has to say!" She slapped her hand on the table and glared at Sweet William, who curled up in his chair like a wet spider, plumes and points quivering.

"You win, Amazon Queen," he said, eyes wide in mock-horror. "I'll shut me gob."

"It cannot have been easy for any of you to come here," Sellars repeated. "It was certainly very difficult to gather you here. So, I hope you will hear me out before making up your minds." He stopped and took a deep, sighing breath. Renie was oddly touched. There was a living person behind the bizarre blank sim, somebody with fears and worries like anyone else. "As I said, I noticed unexplained patterns in the virtual universe some call the datasphere—excessive activity in certain areas, particularly in the wholesale accessing of technical libraries and the abrupt disappearance from their jobs of many top names in network and VR-related technologies. I began to examine these events more closely. Money, too, left its own trails as stocks were sold unexpectedly, businesses suddenly liquidated, and other businesses founded. I discovered after long research that most of these activities were being controlled by a single group of people, although they had shielded their transactions so well that only luck and a certain talent for pattern recognition allowed me to find them and learn their names.

"These people, wealthy and powerful men and women, were a consortium that called themselves the Grail Brotherhood."

"Kinda Christian thing," suggested the robot Goggleboy. "God-hoppers."

"I saw nothing particularly Christian in their activities," Sellars said. "They were spending incalculable amounts of money on technology, apparently building . . . *something*. What that something was I could not discover. But I had a great deal of time on my hands and my curiosity was aroused.

"I pursued this investigation for a number of years, growing ever more uneasy. It seemed unlikely that anyone would put as much effort and expense into something as the Brotherhood had and still keep it secret. At first I had assumed that the project was a long-term business being built from the ground up, but after a while the sheer amount of money and time dumped into this invisible resource began to make that seem unlikely. How could this Brotherhood spend uncountable billions on something—the resources of entire family fortunes or a lifetime's hoarding by many of the world's richest people poured down a metaphorical hole for two decades, earning nothing—and still hope to make a profit? What business could possibly be worth that sort of investment?

"I considered other goals the Brotherhood might have, some of them as extreme as any of the most lurid net entertainments. The overthrow of governments? These people *already* overthrew governments as easily as an average person might change jobs or wardrobes. World conquest? Why? These people already had everything a human could want—unimaginable luxury and power. One of the Brotherhood, the financier Jiun Bhao, ranked on his personal income is the fifteenth richest country in the world."

"Jiun Bhao!" Quan Li was horrified. "He is one of the men who has done this to my granddaughter?" She rocked fretfully in her chair. "They call him 'Emperor'—the Chinese government does nothing without his approval."

Sellars inclined his head. "Just so. But why would such people wish to do anything to upset the balance of world power, I asked myself? They *are* world power. So what were they doing and why were they doing it?"

"And?" asked Sweet William. "I'll do the drumroll, chuck. The answer is?"

"There are still more questions than answers, I fear. When I began to encounter rumors of something called the Otherland, supposedly the world's largest and most powerful simulation network, I understood the *what* at last. But the *why* . . . it is still a mystery."

"Saying this some tabnet-like conspiracy?" asked the chrome battle-robot. "Space aliens, something? *Far* scanning, you."

"It is indeed that," Sellars replied, "—a conspiracy. If it were not, why was such an immense exercise kept secret? But if you think I am merely an alarmist, consider the factor that I know has brought most of you here. The Brotherhood has an unusual interest in children."

He paused, but now the room was silent. Even Atasco and his wife were raptly attentive.

"Once I knew who to watch, once I began to discover the names of Otherland's secret masters, I could hunt for more specific kinds of information. I discovered that several of the organization's key members have an exceptional interest in children, but one that seems to go bizarrely farther than even pedophilia. Based on the quantities of medical and sociological research they have sponsored, the number of pediatric specialists who briefly occupied the payrolls of companies linked to the Brotherhood, the number of youth-oriented facilities—adoption agencies, sports clubs, interactive networks—which were founded or bought up by Brotherhood-related front organizations, this interest is clearly professional, all-encompassing, and frighteningly inexplicable."

"*Mister J's,*" Renie muttered. "The bastards."

"Exactly." Sellars nodded his uppermost blank space. "I apologize," he said. "I am taking longer than I wished to explain this." He rubbed at the place where his forehead would be. "I have thought about this so long, and now I find there is so much to tell."

"But what could they want with these children?" asked Quan Li. "I am sure that you are right, but what do they want?"

Sellars lifted his hands. "I wish I knew. The Grail Brotherhood has built the most powerful, sophisticated simulation network imaginable. At the same time, they have manipulated and injured the minds of thousands of children. I still have no idea why. In fact, I summoned you here, all of you, in hopes that together we might discover some answers."

"You put on a good show, ducky," said Sweet William cheerfully. "And I admire the little touches very much, although the preventing-me-from-going-offline bit is rapidly losing its charm. Why don't you just take your strange little story to the news nets instead of involving us in all this cloak and dagger?"

"I tried in the early days to do what you suggest. Two reporters and three researchers were killed. The news nets broadcast nothing. I am only here to speak to you because I had kept myself anonymous." Sellars paused for another long breath. "I am shamed by those deaths, but they taught me that this is not a mere obsession on my part. This is a war." He turned, surveying all the faces at the table. "The members of the Brotherhood are too powerful and too well-connected. But my attempt to interest others in an investigation did bring me one huge piece of luck. One of the researchers found and contacted Bolivar Atasco and his wife Silviana. Although they refused to answer the researcher's questions, the way in which they refused interested me, and I followed up on my own. I was not immediately successful."

"We thought you were a madman," said Silviana Atasco dryly. "I still think that is possible, Señor."

Sellars bowed his shapeless blank head. "Fortunately for us all, the Atascos, who were among the earliest members of the Grail Brotherhood, had fallen away from the central body and left the board of directors several years before. They retained their investment in the form of this simulation, Temilún, but otherwise had nothing to do with the day-to-day affairs of the consortium. Señor, Señora— perhaps you would like to tell a little of your experiences?"

Bolivar Atasco started; he seemed to have been thinking of something else. He looked helplessly to his wife, who rolled her eyes.

"It is simple," she said. "We needed a more sophisticated simulation engine for our work. We had gone as far as possible with existing technology. We were approached by a group of wealthy men—there were no women in the group then—who had heard of our early versions of Temilún, created with what was then the state-of-the-art technology. They were planning to build the most comprehensive simulation platform ever conceived, and they brought us in to help supervise the construction of that platform." She curled her lip. "I never liked them."

She might make a better God-King than her husband, Renie decided.

"They wouldn't let me do my job properly," Bolivar Atasco added. "I mean to say, there are totally unknown factors of complexity in something this large and rapid. But when I tried to ask questions, when I tried to find out why some things were being done in the peculiar way the Brotherhood had chosen, I was interfered with. So I gave them my resignation."

"That is all?" The woman with the translator accent sounded furious. "You just said, 'I don't approve' and resigned, but hung onto your big playground?"

"How dare you speak like that to us?" Silviana Atasco demanded.

"All of this . . . these things of which Sellars speaks," her husband waved his hands in vaguely all-encompassing circles, "we knew nothing of them. When Sellars came to us, that was the first time we heard."

"Please." Sellars gestured for quiet. "As the Atascos say, they were unaware. You can judge them harshly if you wish, but we are here by their permission, so perhaps it would be better to hold that judgment until you have all the facts."

The woman who had spoken sat back, tight-lipped.

"To hurry through what has already gone on too long for one sitting, I approached the Atascos," Sellars continued. "After much effort, I was able to convince them that there were things about the Grail Brotherhood and Otherland they did not know. Using their access to the network, I was able to do some further investigating—only a little, however, because I dared not attract attention either to the Atascos or myself. It quickly became clear to me that I could not hope to achieve anything working alone. Still, I could not bear to send more people to their deaths.

"I cannot overemphasize the power of the Brotherhood. They have immense holdings in all parts of the world. They control, or at least influence, armies and police forces and governmental bodies in all the world's states. They killed those researchers as swiftly as a man swats a fly, and paid no more penalty for it than that man would. Who would join me against such enemies, and how could I contact them?

"The answer came fairly easily, at least to the first question. Those who had suffered at these people's hands would wish to help—those who had lost friends and loved ones to the Brotherhood's inexplicble conspiracy. But I dared not put more innocents at risk, and I also needed people who would be able to bring skills to the struggle, because a shared concern alone would not be—will not be—enough. So I conceived of a sort of task, like something from an ancient folktale. Those who could find Temilún would be the ones who could help me unravel the schemes of the Brotherhood.

"I left clues, scattered seeds, floated out obscure messages in digital bottles. Many of you, for instance, received an image of the Atascos' virtual city. I put these significators in obscure places, but always at the periphery of the Brotherhood's activities, so that those who had chosen on their own to investigate might stumble on them there. But I was forced to make these hints temporary and vague, in part to protect the Atascos and myself. Those of you who have reached Temilún, whatever else you may decide about me and my hopes, be proud! You have solved a mystery where perhaps a thousand others have failed."

Sellars paused. Several of the listeners stirred.

"Why can't we go offline?" demanded the black-haired barbarian's friend. "That's the only mystery I want solved. I tried to unplug and it was like being electrocuted! My real body's in a hospital somewhere, but I'm still jacked in!"

"This is the first I have heard of it." Even over the murmuring of the guests, Sellars sounded surprised. "There are things at work in this place that none of us understand yet. I would never hold anyone against their will." He raised his shapeless white hands. "I will try to find a solution."

"You'd better!"

"And what was that *thing?*" Renie asked. "The thing that grabbed us—I don't know any other way to put it—when we were entering the simulation. It killed the man who got us here. Atasco says it's a neural network, but Singh said it was alive."

Others at the table whispered among themselves.

"I do not know the answer to that either," Sellars conceded. "There is a neural network at the center of Otherland, that much is true, but how it operates and what 'alive' might mean under the circumstances are more undiscovered secrets of this place. That is why I need your help."

"Help? You need help, all right." Sweet William stood, plumes wagging, and sketched an elaborate and mocking bow. "Darlings, my patience has just about gone. I am going bye-bye now. I shall climb into bed with something warm and do my best to forget I heard *any* of this nonsense."

"But you can't!" The brawny, long-haired man with the action-flick muscles got shakily to his feet. His voice was deep, but his way of speaking seemed incongruous. "Don't you understand? Don't any of you understand? This is . . . this is the Council of Elrond!"

The painted mouth pursed in a grimace. "What *are* you rattling on about?"

"Don't you know Tolkien? I mean, this is it! One ring to rule them all, one ring to find them!" The barbarian seemed to be getting worked up. Renie, who had been about to say something sharp to Sweet William herself, swallowed her annoyance and watched. There was something almost crazy in the man's excitement, and for a moment Renie wondered if he might be mentally unbalanced.

"Oh, one of *those* sort of stories," Sweet William said disdainfully. "I was wondering about that Mister Muscle look of yours."

"You are Orlando, yes?" Sellars sounded gently pleased. "Or should it be Thargor?"

The barbarian did a surprised double take. "Orlando, I guess. I didn't choose the Thargor body, really—not for this. It happened when . . . when we came here."

"That's where I've seen him!" Renie whispered to !Xabbu. "Tree-House! Remember? The Human Breakfast hated his sim."

"I am glad you are here, Orlando." Sellars again was grave. "I hope the others will come to share your beliefs."

"Share *scan*, that's truth," said the chrome-plated Goggleboy. "He crash, you crash, me def'ly flyin'." He stood up, spiky fists on spiky hips like a grumpy metal porcupine.

Orlando would not be discouraged. "Don't leave! This is how it always works! People who seem to have no hope, but each has something to give. Together they solve the mystery and conquer the enemy."

"A group of hopeless idiots all banding together to solve a seemingly impossible task, is that it?" Sweet William was scornfully amused. "Yes indeed, that sounds just like the kind of story you must like, sweetie—but it's just as good a description of a paranoid religious cult. 'Oh, no! Only we clever few understand that the world is coming to an end! But if we move into these storm drains and wear our special aluminum foil hats, we alone will be saved!' Spare me that sort of drama, please. I suppose now you'll all take turns telling your pathetic life stories." He drooped a hand across his brow as though it were all too much to bear. "Well, darlings, you can finish your little mad tea party without me. Will someone just shut off whatever bit of silliness is interfering with my command interface?"

Bolivar Atasco suddenly jerked upright in his seat, then stood and took a few staggering steps. Renie thought he had been offended by the foppish Sweet William, but Atasco froze in place, hands out as if to balance himself. There was a long instant of expectant silence.

"He seems to have dropped offline for a moment," Sellars said. "Perhaps . . ."

Martine began to shriek. She clapped her hands against her head and tumbled to her knees, keening like a toxic spill alarm.

"What is it?" Renie cried. "Martine, what's wrong?"

Silviana Atasco had gone as motionless as her husband. Sellars stared at her, then at Martine, then vanished like a popped bubble.

With !Xabbu's help, Renie hauled the Frenchwoman up into a chair, trying to find out what had gone wrong. Martine stopped shrieking, but could only moan as she swayed from side to side.

The gathering had flown apart into anxious confusion. !Xabbu was speaking rapidly but quietly into Martine's ear. Quan Li was asking Renie if she could help. The Goggleboy and Sweet William were arguing violently. Sellars was gone. The motionless forms of the Atascos still stood at the head of the table.

Except now Bolivar Atasco was moving.

"Look!" Renie cried, pointing.

The feather-crowned figure stretched its arms out to their full extension, fingers flexing convulsively. It took a staggering step, then braced itself against the table as awkwardly as a blind man. The head sank onto the chest. The guests fell silent as everyone turned to watch Atasco. The head came up again.

"I hope none of you think you're going anywhere." It was not Atasco's voice but someone else's entirely, the vowels broad and flat, the words without warmth. Even the facial expression was subtly different. *"Trying to leave would be a very bad idea."*

The thing wearing Atasco's sim turned to the frozen form of Silviana Atasco. It gave a casual shove and her sim tumbled out of the chair and landed on the stone floor, still stiffly holding its sitting position.

"I'm afraid the Atascos have left early," said the cold voice. *"But don't worry. We'll think of ways to keep the party entertaining."*

CHAPTER 36

The Singing Harp

NETFEED/PERSONALS: Wanted: Conversation
(visual: advertiser, M.J., standard asex sim)
M.J.: "Hey, just wanted to know if there's anyone out there. Anyone want to
talk? I'm just feeling kinda, you know, lonely. Just thought there might be
someone else out there feeling lonely, too. . . ."

He had hit his head, which made it hard to think of anything else. He was falling, the Great Canal heaving and spinning upward toward him. Then, through the pain and sparkling darkness, Paul felt things move *sideways,* a vast spasm that seemed to ripple through him and whipcrack him into fragments.

For an instant, everything halted. Everything. The universe lay tipped at an impossible angle, the sky below him like a bowl of blue nothing, the red land and the water tilting away above his head. Gally hung frozen in the middle of the air with his small body contorted and his hands outflung, one of them touching Paul's own fingers. Paul's other arm stretched above him toward the motionless canal, sunk to the wrist in the glassy water, a cuff of rigid splash stretching back along his forearm.

It's . . . all . . . stopped, Paul thought. Suddenly a great light burned through everything he could see, scorching it to nothingness, and he was falling again.

One instant of darkness, another of fiery brilliance—darkness, brilliance, darkness, becoming an ever-speeding stroboscopic alternation. He was falling through something—falling *between*. He could sense Gally somewhere just beyond reach, could feel the boy's terror but was helpless to relieve it in any way.

Then he was abruptly stationary again, down on his hands and knees on cold, hard stone.

Paul looked up. A white wall stretched before him, empty but for a huge banner of red, black, and gold. A chalice sprouted twining roses. A crown hovered above them, the legend *"Ad Aeternum"* written below it in ornate characters.

"I've . . . been here before." Although he only murmured, the slow, astonished words found little echoes up in the high ceiling. His eyes filled with tears.

It was more than the banner, more than the growing sense of familiarity. There were other thoughts crowding in, images, sensations, things that fell onto the parched earth of his memory like a renewing rain.

I'm . . . Paul Jonas. I was . . . I was born in Surrey. My father's name is Andrew. My mother's name is Nell, and she's very sick.

Remembrance was taking root in what had been empty places, sprouting and flowering. A walk with his grandmother, young Paul out of primary for the day and pretending to be a growling bear behind a hedge. His first bicycle, tire flat and rim bent, and the awful feeling of shame at having damaged it. His mother with her chemical respirator and her look of tired resignation. The way the moon hung framed in the branches of a budding plum tree outside his flat in London.

Where am I? He examined the stark white walls, the banner with its strangely shifting colors. A new set of memories filtered up, sharp and bright and jagged as pieces of a broken mirror. A war that seemed to last for centuries. Mud and fear and a flight through strange lands, among strange people. And this place, too. He had been here before.

Where have I been? How did I get here?

Old memories and new were growing together, but in the midst there lay a scar, a barren place they could not cover. The confusion in his head was terrible, but most terrible of all was this blankness.

He crouched and raised his hands to his face, covering his eyes as he struggled for clarity. What could have happened? His life . . . his life had been *ordinary*. School, a few love affairs, too much time spent hanging about with friends who had more money than he did and could better afford the long drunken lunches and late nights. A not-very-hard-earned degree in . . . it took a moment . . . art history. A job as a bottom-level assistant curator at the Tate, sober suit, wired collar, tour groups wanting to cluck over the New Genocide installation. Nothing unusual. He was Paul Robert Jonas, he was all that he had, but that still didn't make him anything special. He was nobody.

Why this?

Insanity? A head injury? Could there be a madness this detailed, this placid? Not that all of it had been so quiet. He had seen monsters, horrible things—he remembered them just as clearly as he remembered the clothesline on the roof outside his university residence window. Monsters . . .

. . . *Clanking, gnashing, steaming* . . .

Paul stood up, suddenly frightened. He had been in this place before, and something terrible lived here. Unless he was locked in some incomprehensible kind of false memory, a déjà vu with teeth in it, he had been *here* and this was not a safe place.

"Paul!" The voice was faint, far away, and thin with desperation, but he knew it even before he knew which part of his life it came from.

"Gally?" The boy! The boy had been with him when they had fallen from that flying ship, but Paul had let that knowledge slip away in the rush of returning memory. And now? Was the child being stalked by that huge, impossible thing, the machine-giant? "Gally! Where are you?"

No answer. He forced himself to his feet and hurried toward the door at the far end of the hall. On the far side another imposition of reality and memory, almost painfully potent. Dusty plants stretched out in all directions, reaching toward the roofbeams, all but covering the high windows. He was lost in an indoor jungle. Beyond—he knew, he remembered—there was a giant . . .

. . . And a *woman,* a heartbreakingly beautiful woman with wings . . .

"Paul! Help!"

He lurched toward the boy's voice, pushing at the dry, rubbery branches. Leaves came apart in his hands, turning to powder and joining the dust that drifted and swirled at his every movement. The thicket parted before him, the branches falling back, dropping away, some disintegrating at his touch, to reveal a cage of slender golden bars. The bars were mottled with black and gray smears, and dark tendrils wound through them. The cage was empty.

Despite his fear for the boy, Paul felt a shock of disappointment.

This was the place *she* had been. He remembered her vividly, the shimmer of her wings, her eyes. But now the cage was empty.

No, almost empty. In the middle, nearly covered by a tangle of vines and roots and the mulch of fallen leaves, something glimmered. Paul crouched and pushed his arm through the tarnished bars, straining to reach the center. His hand closed around something smooth and cool and heavy. As he lifted it and pulled it back through the bars, a string of chiming notes sounded in the air.

It was a harp, a curving golden loop with golden strings. As he held it before him and stared, it warmed beneath his fingers, then began to shrink, curling like a leaf on a bonfire. Within a few moments it had become as tiny as a twenty-pence coin.

"Paul! I can't . . ." The cry of pain that followed was sharp and sudden in its ending. He stood, startled into trembling, then curled the golden thing in his fist and began to smash his way through the crumbling vegetation. He had gone only a few steps when a door loomed before him, five times his own height. He touched it and it swung inward.

The massive, hangar-sized room beyond had timbered beams and walls of piled, undressed stone. Huge wheels turned slowly; great levers pumped up and down. Gears the size of a double-decker bus chewed their way around the circuit of even larger gears whose full extent was hidden, but whose toothed rims pushed in through vast slots in the walls. The place smelled like oil and lightning and rust, and sounded like slow destruction. The noise, the deep, steady ratcheting that vibrated the massive walls, the monotonous hammerthump of great weights falling, was the song of an incomprehensible, unceasing hunger, of machinery that could gnaw away even the foundations of Time and Space.

Gally stood in the one clear space at the center of the room. Two figures flanked him, one thin, the other immensely fat.

A despairing darkness settled behind Paul's eyes as he walked forward. Gally struggled, but the two held him without effort. The slender one was all shiny metal, claw-handed, inhuman, with an eyeless head like a piston. Its companion was so fat that his oily skin was stretched almost to transparency, glowing with a suety yellow-gray light of its own, like a massive bruise.

The big one's broken-tusked mouth spread in a smile whose corners disappeared into the doughy cheeks. "You've come back to us! All the way back—and of your own free will!" It laughed and the cheeks jiggled. "Imagine that, Nickelplate. How he must have missed us! It's too bad the Old Man isn't here to enjoy this moment."

"Only right that the Jonas should come back," the metallic one said, an inner door opening and shutting in its rectangular mouth. "He should be sorry, too, after all the considerable bother he's given us, the naughty fellow. He should beg us to forgive him. Beg us."

"Let the boy go." Paul had never seen the pair before, but he knew them as well and hated them as powerfully as the cancer that had slowly killed his mother. "It's me you want."

"Oh, goodness, it's not just you we want anymore," the metal creature said. "Is it, Butterball?"

The fat one shook its head. "First give us what's in your hand. We'll trade that for the boy."

Paul felt the hard edges of the harp against the skin of his fingers. Why did they want to bargain? Here, in this place of their power, why should they bother?'

"Don't do it!" Gally shouted. "They can't . . ." The thing called Butterball tightened sluglike fingers on his arm and the boy began to writhe and shriek, twitching as though he had fallen onto an electrified rail track.

"Give it to us," said Nickelplate. "And then perhaps the Old Man will be kind. Things were good for you once, Paul Jonas. They could be good again."

Paul could not bear to look at Gally's gaping mouth, agonized eyes. "Where's the woman? There was a woman in that cage."

Nickelplate turned a near-featureless face to regard Butterball for a long, silent moment, then turned back. "Gone. Flown—but not far, not for long. Do you want to see her again? That can be arranged."

Paul shook his head. He knew these things could never be trusted. "Just let the boy go."

"Not until you give us what's in your hand." Butterball made Gally convulse again. Horrified, Paul held out the harp. Both faces, chrome and candlewax, turned greedily toward it.

The room shuddered. For a moment Paul thought the massive machinery had begun to break down. Then, as the walls themselves seemed to shred, he had a sudden and greater fear.

The Old Man. . . ?

But Nickelplate and Butterball were also staring, mouths open, as the very planes of geometric form began to slide apart around them. Paul was still standing with his hand outstretched, and Nickelplate abruptly took an impossibly long stride toward him, shining claw scrabbling for the harp. Gally, who had slumped to the floor, curled his arms around Nickelplate's shiny legs and the creature stumbled and fell with a sound of metal scraping on stone.

The room and Paul and everything shuddered again, then fell apart and curled in on itself.

He was frozen in midair above the sky once more, and the Great Canal and red desert again arched above his head—but the air was now empty where Gally had hung beside him. Where Gally had touched his outstretched fingers, his own hand was now closed in a fist.

Even as his bedeviled mind tried to grasp the abrupt transition from the giant's gearhouse back to this perfect stasis, the world surged into life. Colors came unstuck and ran. Solids became air and the air became water, swallowing Paul with a great, cold slurp.

He floundered, his lungs full to bursting but beginning to ache. The wet blackness around him was chill and heavy. He could make no sense of up or down. He saw a dim glow, a yellow that might be sunlight, and heaved toward it, wriggling like an eel. For a moment the light surrounded him, then he was in blackness again, but this time the cold was murderous. He saw light again, a cooler blue, and fought toward it. As he rose he could see the slender tips of dark trees and gray, clouded sky. Then his hand struck and bounced back. He kicked, thrusting his face up toward the light, scrabbling with his fingers, but something solid lay between him and the air, prisoning him in the freezing water.

Ice! He smashed at it with his fists, but could not make even a crack. His lungs were filled with burning coals, his head with smothering shadows.

Drowning. Somewhere, somehow, and never to know why.

The knowledge will die with me. About the grail. The meaningless thought flitted through his deepening personal darkness like a shiny fish.

The water was sucking all heat from his body. He could not feel his legs. He pressed his face up against the ice, praying for a pocket of air, but a tiny breath brought him only more wet coldness. It was useless to fight any longer. He opened his mouth to take in the water that would end his pain, then paused for a last instant to try to focus on the glimpse of sky. Something dark covered the hole, and in that same moment the ice and the sky and the clouds crashed down at him, shoving him back and startling the air out of his straining body. He gasped reflexively and water rushed in, filling him, choking him, obliterating him.

A curtain wavered, a fluttering screen of orange and yellow. He tried to focus on it but could not. No matter how intently he stared, it would not take on resolution, but remained soft and without texture. He closed his eyes, resting for a moment, then opened them and tried again.

He could sense something touching him, but it was an oddly detached feeling, as though his body were impossibly long and the ministrations were being performed on a very distant section. He wondered if he had been . . . he could not remember the word, but found instead an image of a hospital room, the smell of alcohol, a sharp small pain like an insect sting.

Anesthetized. But why would they. . . ? He had been . . .

The river. He tried to sit up, but could not. The delicate ministrations, so soft, so distant, continued. He focused his eyes again and realized at last that he was staring at the shifting flames of a fire. His head seemed to be connected to his body by only a few nerves: he could feel something beneath him, and could tell that the surface was rough and uncomfortable, but his body was numb and the discomfort was purely speculative. He tried to speak, but could only make a faint gasping noise.

As if summoned, a face floated into view, perpendicular to his line of sight. It was bearded and heavy-browed. The brown eyes deep in the shadowed sockets were round as an owl's.

"You are cold," the face said, the voice deep and calm. "Dying cold. We will warm you." The face slid out of his sight once more.

Paul collected what thoughts he could. He had survived again, so far anyway. He remembered his name and everything that had returned to him as he knelt before the rose and chalice banner. But where he had been was still missing from his mind, and where he was now had become a fresh mystery.

He tried to sit up and could not, but managed to roll onto his side. Feeling was beginning to return to his body, sprays of needle-pricklings up and down his legs that were rapidly growing worse—he was alternately racked by shivers and spasms of pain. At least he could finally see beyond the curtain of fire, though it took a moment before he could make sense of what was before him.

The one who had spoken and half a dozen other bearded, shadow-eyed men were crouched in a semicircle around the fire. A roof of stone stretched above them, but they were not in a cave so much as a deep overhang of rock in the side of a hill. Beyond the opening lay a world of almost perfect whiteness, a world of deep snow that stretched all the way to a line of sawtoothed mountains in the distance. At the base of the hillside, perhaps a half-mile away, he could see the thin gray shape of the frozen river and the black hole out of which these men had pulled him.

He looked down. The one who had spoken was cutting Paul's wet clothes away with a piece of black stone that had been chipped into the shape of a leaf. He was powerfully built, with broad hands and flat fingers. His own clothing was a ragtag assortment of animal skins, tied in place with cords of sinew.

Neanderthals, Paul thought. *They're cave men, and this is the Ice Age or something. It's like a bloody museum exhibit, except I'm living in it. Fifty thousand years away from anything I know.* A horrible ache coursed through him. He was alive, but somehow he had lost his life, his real life, and was apparently doomed to wander permanently through some horrible labyrinth without ever knowing why. Tears welled up in his eyes and ran down his cheeks. Even the shivering and the pain in his awakening nerves fell away, overmatched by the anguish of total loss.

Gally is gone. Vaala is gone. My family, my world, everything gone.

He rolled his face against the stone, brought up one hand to hide himself from the eyes of the staring, bearded men, and wept.

By the time the stone knife tore through the last piece of his shirt, Paul could sit up. He dragged himself a few inches nearer to the fire. Another of his rescuers handed him a great fur-covered skin that stank of fat and smoke, and he gratefully wrapped himself in it. His shivering gradually subsided to a faint but continuous tremor.

The one with the knife picked up Paul's ruined clothing, which was stiff with ice, and set the pile to one side with a certain anxious care. As he did, something clicked against the stone and rolled free, glinting. Paul stared, then picked it up, turning it over in his hand, watching firelight spark from the golden facets.

"We saw you in the water," the knife wielder said. "We thought you were an animal, but Birdcatcher saw you were not an animal. We pulled you from the water."

Paul closed his fingers around the gemlike object. It warmed, then a gentle voice filled the cavern, making him jump.

"If you have found this, then you have escaped," it said. Paul looked around, afraid his rescuers would be terrified, but they were still looking at him with the same slightly worried reserve. After a moment, he realized they could not hear the voice, that it spoke to him alone. *"Know this,"* it said. *"You were a prisoner. You are not in the world in which you were born. Nothing around you is true, and yet the things you see can hurt you or kill you. You are free, but you will be pursued, and I can help you only in your dreams. You must remain uncaptured until you find the others I am sending. They will look for you on the river. They will know you if you tell them the golden harp has spoken to you."*

The voice went silent. When Paul opened his hand, the shining thing was gone.

"Are you a spirit of the river?" the knife wielder asked. "Birdcatcher thinks you are a drowned man returned from the land of the dead."

"The land of the dead?" Paul let his head sink to his chest. He felt exhaustion pressing on him, heavy as the stony hillside above them. His sudden laughter had a cracked sound, and the men shied back, grunting and whispering. More tears made his vision blur. "Land of the dead. That sounds about right."

CHAPTER 37

Johnny's Twist

NETFEED/SPORTS: TMX Makes Olympic "Goodwill Gesture"
(visual: TMX/Olympic flag rippling over Athenaeum, Bucharest)
VO: Telemorphix, Inc. has made what it calls a "goodwill gesture" to resolve
its dispute with the International Olympic Committee and the government
of the Wallachian Republic. Instead of "The Telemorphix Bucharest Olympic
Games," as the corporation had initially insisted the event be known, the
official name will be "The Bucharest Olympic Games, Sponsored by
Telemorphix."
(visual: TMX VPPR, Natasja Sissensen)
SISSENSEN: "We respect the Olympic tradition of peaceful compromise, and
we feel we've held out a major olive branch. However, the IOC should
remember that nobody ever gets something for nothing. Not that I've heard
about anyway."

The moon was only a fingernail sliver above the black Bahía de Barbacoas. The island, hedged by orange spotlights, glowed more brightly than anything in the sky. Dread smiled. It was a nest full of jeweled eggs, and he was the predator. He would take those lights in his jaws and crush them into darkness.

Dread brought up the *Exsultate Jubilate*, a piece of ancient music that throbbed like electricity and rang with joyful transcendence. He regretted using a piece of preprogrammed music, but he had too many things to do, and tonight there would be no time to build his own soundtrack as he acted out his starring role. Mozart would do well enough.

He fingered his t-jack, wolfishly happy to be off the fiberlink leash. He lowered his hands to his knees, intensely aware of the resistant neoprene of his suit and the tiny grains of sand adhering to his palms, then closed his eyes so he could see the important things.

"Track one, report."

A window containing a view of the choppy water from high above appeared against the blackness. *"Listo,"* declared Track One's foreman. "Ready."

"Track two."

. . . Another window, filled by a dim shape which he recognized as a reflection-resistant boat only because he had purchased it himself. Before it, a group of shadowy figures lying prone on the sand. One of the figures moved slightly: night-goggles glinted. "Ready, *jefe.*"

"Track three."

. . . A stack of equipment against the bad-paint wall of a rented apartment, each box finished in the irritating matte-black that was experiencing a revival among trendy wareheads. Nothing else.

What the hell. . . ?

The pause lasted several seconds before a shaved head appeared and Celestino's voice reverberated in the bones of Dread's skull. "I was making a last second adjustment, *jefe.* I am now ready."

Having a last-second-terror piss, more likely. Dread sent a closed sidebar call to the room next to the gear lab. A woman's face appeared, round and pale beneath flaming red hair.

"Dulcy, what's up? Is he going to get it done?"

"He's an idiot, but he's competent, if you know what I mean. I'm here. Go ahead and light it up."

He was glad he had brought her in. Dulcinea Anwin was expensive, but not without reason. She was smart and efficient and could have walked right through the Battle of Waterloo without blinking. For a brief moment, he wondered what kind of quarry she'd make. An interesting thought.

"Track Four."

The observation center balcony, which he had occupied himself only a few hours ago, appeared against his closed eyelids. This man, unlike Celestino, was waiting for the call. "Ready to spike."

Dread nodded, although neither the heads in the data windows or the dozen other men with him on the dark beach could see his face. He opened his eyes and summoned up the site map, allowing it to spread itself in a neon grid on top of the real Isla del Santuario looming just a few kilometers away. Perfect. Everything in place.

Action.

He brought up the *Exsultate,* and for a moment he was alone in the Caribbean night with the moon, the water, and the soprano's silvery voice.

"Track Four—spike it."

The man in the beach house keyed up a security code, then spoke a word into his throat mike. At this signal, Dread's contact at ENT-Inravisión injected the program he had been supplied into the Cartagena telecom net, a simple—although criminal—action for which the employee would receive Cr.S. fifteen thousand and an offshore bank account to go with it.

The code sought out and connected with an unobtrusive resident parasite in the Isla de Santuario house system, a lurker which had been deposited for the sum of forty thousand by a disaffected employee of the previous security company during her last night on the job. Acting in concert, the two created a temporary data tap into the island's information system. Either the system itself or human oversight would be bound to spot the tap within ten minutes or so, but Dread did not need any longer than that.

"This is Four. Spike is in."

The Mozart lifted him. Pleasure ran through him like cool fire, but he kept his elation to himself.

"Good. Track Three, start pumping."

Celestino bobbed his head. "My pleasure, *jefe.*" The gear man closed his eyes and swirled his fingers in a complicated pattern as he began to make the input/output connections.

Dread kept his voice calm. "Give me a link and arrays as soon as you have them." He was developing what might be an irrational hatred of this poofting ex-military idiot. That was almost as bad as being too trusting.

He closed his eyes again and watched the seconds tick off on the time display. Except for Celestino conducting his invisible orchestra of data, seeming to Dread's jaundiced eye to mock the sublimity of the *Exsultate,* the other windows were static, awaiting his orders. He took a moment to enjoy the sensation. On the rare occasions when they spoke about their work, some of the others in his very small field of expertise referred to what they did as "art." Dread thought that was self-aggrandizing bullshit. It was just work, although at times like this it was exciting, satisfying, challenging work. But nothing this orderly and preplanned could be called art.

Now the chase—that was art. It was art of the moment, art of opportunity, art of courage and terror and the blind razoring edge of things. There was no comparison between the two. One was a job, the other was sex. You could be good at your job, and proud of it, but no one would ever mistake the best of one for the transcendence of the other.

Celestino was in the bones of his ears again. "The pumping station is up and running, *jefe*. Do you want a line into the security net?"

"Of course I bloody well do. Jesus. Track One, report."

Track One's window showed more black water, this time from higher up. "Fifteen kilometers away and closing."

"Stand by for my call."

A moment more and the music began to swell toward crescendo. An array of tiny windows blinked on at the periphery of his vision.

"Track Three, which one's the broadcasting channel?"

"Second from the left," Celestino answered. "Currently quiet."

Dread brought it up and checked, not because he thought the gear man was *that* incompetent, but because he was in that singular, high-flying and godlike mode—he wanted every spark, every falling leaf, at his fingertips and under his control. As Celestino had said, there was only silence on the channel.

"Track One, go."

The silence lasted for a few more moments. Then, he heard the crackle of a radio in his ear. To make sure, he shut off the volume of his own line to Track One, but he could still hear it coming in over the Isla del Santuario's security channel. He was listening with the target's own ears.

"Mayday! Santuario, can you hear me!" There was a brief lag between the supposed pilot's Spanish and Dread's system's translation, but he was already pleased—under a professionally macho veneer, the actor sounded quite believably panicky. The Beinhas had made a good choice. *"Santuario, can you read me? This is XA1339 out of Sincelejo. Mayday! Can you hear me?"*

"This is Santuario, XA1339. We have you on radar. You are too close. Please turn east and move out of our exclusion zone."

Dread nodded. Polite, but fast and firm. The island's new security firm was worth the money.

"We have lost our tail rotor. Santuario, can you hear me? We have lost our tail rotor. Requesting permission to land."

The pause was only a brief one. *"Not possible. This is an exclusion zone, approved under the UN Aviation Act. Suggest you try for Cartagena, either the civil or heliport. It's only about five kilometers."*

The captain's scream of rage was most convincing. Dread could not help laughing. *"You bastards! I'm going down! I can't make Cartagena! I have four passengers and two crew, and I can barely keep this thing in the air."*

The Isla del Santuario continued not to live up to its name. *"I apologize, XA1339, but that is against my express orders, repeat, against my express orders. Suggest again you try for Cartagena. If you attempt to land here, we will be forced to treat you as an attacking force. Do you copy?"*

The pilot's voice, when it came again, was flat and bitter. The loud noises that squelched some of his words sounded quite distinctly like a turboprop helicopter shaking itself apart. *"I can't fight . . . damn rotor . . . can't any longer. We're going down. I'll try not . . . crash on your precious island. I hope . . . rot in hell."*

Another urgent Spanish-speaking voice came on. Dread checked the blinking lights, assuring himself that this was one of island security's sidebar channels.

"Visual contact, sir. The rear rotor is damaged, just like he said. It's getting very near the water, moving erratically. They may go down on the rocks . . . Oh, my God, there they go."

From a great distance away across the dark water came a dull clank like a mallet striking a held gong. Dread smiled.

"They've gone down within our perimeter, sir. The helicopter didn't catch fire, so there may be survivors, but the destroyer subs will be on them in a couple of minutes."

"Shit. Are you sure they're in our zone, Ojeda?" The commanding officer of island security obviously didn't like being put in this situation.

"I can see the helicopter, sir. It's still hanging on the rocks, but with the waves it won't stay there long.

The officer brought up the first pictures from the camera drones, and when he saw his observer's words confirmed, cursed again. Dread thought he knew just what was going through the man's mind: there had been security on this island for twenty years, even though his own employers had only gained the contract recently. Twenty years, and nothing more dangerous than a few local fishermen threatening to stray into the exclusion zone had ever happened. He had just denied landing rights, however legally, to an aircraft in distress. Could he

stretch that legality to the screaming point and let any of the helicopter's survivors be killed by the submarine security drones as well?
And, probably more tellingly, could he do it in front of his men and
hope to keep their respect for a real security emergency?

"Son of a whore!" He had wrestled it almost to the point where action
would be too late. *"Blind the subs—shut down the whole marine hunter-
killer grid. Yapé, get a boat out there as quick as possible to look for survivors.
I'll call the boss and tell him what we're doing."*

Hook, line, and sinker. Dread jumped up. "Track Two, launch." He
waved to his own half of the invasionary force, a dozen men in neoprene commando suits. By the time he had finished his gesture, they
were already running the boat into the water. He sprinted after them.
His own work had just begun.

The boat slid silently across the bay, slithering carefully through the
dormant mines. Their search-and-destroy responses had been turned
off, but that didn't mean one might not explode on accidental contact.
Dread sat in the back, happy for once to let someone else take charge.
He had more important things to do than steer a boat.

Where is it? He closed his eyes and turned off the music. The feed
from the spike into the island's security system was still open: he
could hear the security commander talking to the rescue boat, which
was just now setting out from the far side of the island. No one had
noticed the data tap yet, but that would shortly become academic,
anyway: the security forces would reach the downed helicopter in only
a few minutes. Unless it was very badly damaged, they would quickly
recognize that it had been wired for remote operation. They would
know they had been suckered.

Where? He let himself fall backward into his own thoughts, searching for the elusive first grasp—for that pulse, that electronic heartbeat,
that would show him where to grip.

He had discovered his ability to *twist,* as he thought of it, in his first
foster home. Actually, the twist was really the second miracle: the first
was that he had been fostered out at all. At seven years of age he had
already killed three people, all of them children about his own age.
Only one of the murders had been acknowledged, although ascribed
to a tragic but momentary loss of self-control; the other two deaths
had been blamed on an accident. This was all nonsense, of course. On
both occasions, Dread—who had not yet chosen that melodramatic
name—had carried a hammer in the waistband of his pants for days,

waiting. Pushing the pair of victims in the second attack down an iron stairwell after beating in their heads had been a last bit of anger rather than a precocious attempt to disguise his work.

Even without death in his background, the Queensland Juvenile Authority would not have found it easy to place the child. Just the fact of his parentage (his alcoholic, prostitute mother an Aborigine, his father a Filipino pirate who would be captured and summarily executed not long after the transaction that resulted in baby Dread) ensured that the Authority had to offer prospective foster parents cash on the side—a rebate, as it were. But moving young Johnny Wulgaru, the agency bureaucrats had quickly decided, was worth juggling the budget. Johnny was a disaster waiting to happen.

The moments leading up to the first time he *twisted* something had been surprisingly ordinary. His foster mother, infuriated by his cruel treatment of the family cat, had called him a little black bastard. He had knocked something off a table and she had grabbed him, intent on locking him in his room. As she dragged him aross the living room, he had reached a crescendo of screaming anger and the wallscreen had abruptly wavered and gone blank.

Much to his guardians' unhappiness, the damage to the internal electronics proved irreparable, and they had gone almost a month without a link to the normal world until they could afford to replace it.

They had not connected the occurrence with their ward, although they knew him to be capable of other, far more prosaic acts of destruction. But Johnny had noted it himself and wondered if it might be magic. A few experiments had proved that it was—or just as good as magic anyway—and it was apparently his alone. A single day in his dark room with his stepfather's pad had taught him that he could do it even without being angry, if he just thought the right things in the right way.

He had not used the ability for much of anything—minor vandalism, spiteful reprisals—for several years, and through several more foster homes. Even as his secrets grew deeper and more terrible, he never thought of using his ability to *twist* things for anything grander than blanking security cameras at the site of one of his robberies—or one of his chases, for those had begun even before he reached sexual maturity. It was not until the Old Man, at massive expense, had maneuvered him out of young offenders' prison, and then into a succession of mental institutions, the last one of which the Old Man more

or less owned, that Dread understood he could use the twist for bigger
things. . . .

The boat bounced, and for a moment he was jolted back into the
real world. Dread pushed away the sky, the water, the men crouched
silently beside him. *Where is it? Get it back. Hold it, now.*

But this kind of use was much harder than the simple destruction
he had practiced in the earliest days, or the later tactic of simply freezing electronic components. Tonight's sort of trick required skills he
still had not completely mastered, despite almost a year spent in one
of the Old Man's labs, going through exercise after exhausting exercise while white-coated scientists offered cheerful encouragement—a
supportiveness belied by the fear of him they could never quite hide.
It would have been hard to say which growing power he had enjoyed
more.

Find it, then reach. He grasped the data tap at last, seized it with his
mind, letting his thoughts slide around it and into it as he took its
measure. The mechanical intrusion into the island's electronic nerve
system accomplished by his gear team had been a crucial first step: he
needed to be as far into the security system as possible before beginning his own work. Already, the fine control required was making his
head ache. When he used his ability for more than a few moments,
he thought he could feel the twist itself glowing hot and sore in his
brain like an inflamed gland.

Like a hunting hound nosing for a scent, he searched through the
inexplicable inner darkness of the twist until he found just the kind
of electronic surges he needed, then followed their path backward,
tracking the data stream to its source in the security system's main
processors and memory. Processors were only electronic artifacts, not
really that much different than simpler things like surveillance cameras or car ignitions—just electrical impulses controlling mechanical
artifacts. Dread knew it would be easy to twist them hard, to give
them a jolt so strong that the system would shut down, but if that
had been all he wanted, he would have let that jackass Celestino have
his data bomb. He needed to wade through his own pain to achieve
something far more subtle, more useful: he needed to find the system's soul and make it his.

The system was complex, but its structural logic was no different
than any other. He found the desired set of electronic gates and gave
them each a little push. They resisted, but even the resistance told him
something. He had lost everything but the data stream now—even the

meaningless noises on the security radio and from the night and waves that surrounded his physical body were gone. He pushed the gates again, only one at a time now, doing his best to gauge the effect of each change before he made it. He worked delicately, even though his head was throbbing so hard he felt like screaming. The last thing he wanted to do was crash the system.

At last, in a blackness shot with blood-red migrainous lightning, he found the right sequence. As the metaphorical door swung wide, a dark joy swelled inside him, almost stronger than the pain. He had constructed an indescribable *something* out of his own will, a skeleton key to open an invisible, unreachable lock, and now the Isla del Santuario's entire system was opening to him like a ten-credit whore, ready to surrender its secrets. Exhausted, Dread struggled back toward the other world—the world outside the twist.

"Track Three," he said hoarsely. "I'm into the mother lode. Hook it up and sort it."

Celestino grunted a nervous affirmative and began making order out of the streams of raw data. Dread opened his eyes, leaned over the railing, and vomited.

The boat was only a half-kilometer off the island when he could think coherently again. He closed his eyes—the sight of the data windows superimposed on the choppy waters was making him feel sick again—and inspected the results of his infiltration, the naked workings of Santuario's infrastructure.

The security machinery's various scanners and checkpoints lured him for a moment, but after the obsessive way he had mapped out what to turn off and when in the planning stages of the action, he doubted even Celestino could mess it up. He also glanced at the standard programs which regulated the estate's physical being, but none of that was important at the moment. There was only one thing out of the ordinary, but that was exactly what he was looking for. Someone—some two, actually, judging by the paired input sites—was hooked up to a LEOS, a low orbit communication satellite, and a huge amount of data was moving through it both ways.

Our target is on the net, I guess. But what the hell is he doing there that he has to move so many gigs?

Dread pondered for a moment. He had everything he needed already. Still, it didn't seem like a good idea to let such high-intensity usage go unexamined. Besides, if this busy little bee really was the target, maybe Dread would get some kind of idea about why the Old Man wanted Sky God dead. A little information never went amiss.

"Track Three, spike me into one of those hot spots there—I think it's the target's lab. If what he's receiving is VR, don't give me the full wraparound, just a POV window and audio."

"Certainly, *jefe.*"

Dread waited for a long moment, then another window opened up against the blackness of his inner eyelids. In it, a table lined with faces that looked vaguely Indian stretched before him. There was a monkey sitting on the tabletop halfway down, and the target's gaze kept flicking to it. Dread felt an almost childlike glee. He was sitting unnoticed on his prey's shoulder like an invisible demon—like Death itself.

"*. . . Most of these activities were being controlled by a single group of people,*" someone was saying next to him. The quiet, earnest voice was not his target's. One of *El Patrón's* academic friends, perhaps. A group of self-satisfied scientists having a little virtual symposium of some kind.

He contemplated tuning out, but the next words jumped out at him as though they had been screamed. "*. . . These people, wealthy and powerful men and women, were a consortium that called themselves the Grail Brotherhood . . .*"

Dread watched and listened with rapidly increasing interest.

'Track Three," he said after a few moments, "keep this open. Are we recording this?"

"Just what you are seeing, *jefe.* I can try to copy everything going in and out, but I don't think we have that much memory, not to mention bandwidth."

Dread opened his eyes. The boat was almost within range of the perimeter lights. There were other things to worry about now; he could pick up most of the details once they had secured the target. "Don't worry about it, then. But there are a lot of other people at that gathering. Find out if they're sims, and if so, where they're coming in from. But first, be ready to initiate defenses shutdown, on my order." He checked on Track Two, who were waiting about the same distance off the island on the southeastern side. The reports coming in over the island's security band told him that the rescue team was just about to discover the helicopter trick.

"Track Three—shutdown."

The perimeter lights winked out. There was a squall of indignant protest over the security band, but with the shutdown sequence now

begun, none of the radio locations were talking to anyone but themselves—and Dread.

"Track Two, here we go."

He signaled to the pilot of his own boat, who gunned the engine
and sent them skidding across the bumpy surf toward the beach. As
they hit the shallows, his men were already rolling over the side, the
first to land sweeping the beach and house walls with ELF weapons.
Those of the island's guards not wearing counterfrequency gear
dropped, shaken into jelly, without ever knowing what had hit them.

As he followed his men onto the sand, Dread turned off all but the
necessary pictures, but he kept the voices from the target's virtual
conference going in his head. Already an idea was beginning to form.

The island was so dark that Dread did not even bother to crawl up
from the beach. Three more sentries in anti-ELF suits appeared on the
catwalk outside the nearest guardhouse, one of them holding a high-
powered flashlight—probably on his way to find out what had happened to the island's generators. Dread gestured. The silenced Trohn-
ers sounded like a stick being dragged along a picket fence as the
sentries fell. The flashlight bounced from the catwalk and blinked
end-over-end down to the beach.

Resistance was stiff at the front portico of the main house, but
Dread was not in such a hurry now. His target was still locked into his
simulation, and since Celestino had remotely sealed the doorlocks and
thrown a data blanket over the target to prevent incoming calls from
security, Sky God had no idea that his castle had been stormed.

If nothing else, Dread admired Atasco's new security service for
honoring their contract. They were fighting fiercely—the half-dozen
pouring fire out of the hardened guardhouse beside the front door
seemed capable of holding off an army far larger than Dread's. However, good security work required more than bravery: foresight was
important, too. One of the assault team managed to jam an incendiary
grenade through a gun port, although he sustained a fatal wound in
the process. When it exploded a moment later, the heat was so fierce
that even the steelplex windows softened and bulged outward.

The Track Two team, which had come in through the back of the
complex to attack the main security office, was going to be a little
while getting free, but Dread was quite satisfied. Out of two fifteen-
man assault teams, he had only three units down that he knew of,
and only one of those three killed, with the action 75 percent done.
Against the kind of security package a rich bastard like Atasco could

afford, that was more than acceptable. As his two bang men wired hemispheres of Anvax hammer gel to the massive front door, he allowed himself a few moments with his unsuspecting target.

". . . *Brotherhood has built the most powerful, sophisticated simulation network imaginable.*" It was the calm, high voice again, coming from someone standing near Atasco. "*At the same time, they have manipulated and injured the minds of thousands of children. I still have no idea why. In fact, I summoned you here, all of you, in hopes that together we might discover some answers.*"

Dread was getting more and more intrigued. If Atasco wasn't leading this little conspiracy, who was? Did the Old Man know things had gone so far?

The explosive gel was triggered. A flash of fire briefly illuminated the bodies scattered on the porch as the main door sagged and fell inward. Dread turned off the window feeding him the target's visuals; the audio channel was briefly usurped by an announcement of Track Two's successful conquest of the security office.

"This is it, gentlemen," he said cheerfully. "We forgot our invitations, so we'll just have to let ourselves in."

Once through the scorched doorframe, he stopped for a moment to inspect the piles of rubble and powder that had been a collection of Mayan stonework, installed by sad chance too near the front door. He detailed most of his crew to look for stray security and to round up the household staff, then took a bang man and two commandos and headed for the basement lab.

As the explosives man knelt in front of the lab door, Dread tuned in again to what had become a confusing welter of voices.

"Track Three," he said, "in just about a minute the target's line is going to be free. I want you to keep it open, whatever it takes, and to hold the rest of the guests in the simulation if possible while we figure out who they are. Is that clear?"

"Yes, I understand." Celestino sounded tensely excited, which gave Dread a brief moment of unease, but the Colombian was doing all right so far. It was the rare and exceptional person who didn't get at least a little worked up while participating in a large-scale armed criminal assault.

Dread and the others retreated back down the hallway, then the bang man thumbed his transmitter. The walls trembled only a little as the hammer gel bent the heavy security door into a curl like stale bread. They kicked it aside and entered. The white-haired man, who had been reclining in a pillowy chair, had apparently felt the vibration of the controlled blast and was struggling to his feet. His wife, on the far side of the lab in her own chair, was still submerged in VR, twitching gently.

Bolivar Atasco stumbled a little, still not completely separated from the simulation and its override on his exterior physical responses. He paused, swaying, and stared at Dread as though he felt he should recognize him.

You have just met the Angel of Death and he's a stranger. He is always a stranger. The line from some obscure interactive popped into Dread's mind and made him grin. As Atasco opened his mouth to speak, Dread flicked a finger and the nearest commando shot the anthropologist between the eyes. Dread stepped forward and pulled the jack out of Atasco's neurocannula, then gestured at the woman. The other soldier did not move toward her, but thumbed his Trohner to auto-fire and sprayed her down, blowing the cable out of her neck and sending her to the floor in a bloody heap. Mission accomplished.

Dread surveyed the two bodies briefly, then sent the two commandos upstairs to rejoin the others. He checked back in on the simulation in time to hear a new voice.

"Trying to leave would be a very bad idea."

It was an unfamiliar voice, processed through a translator. It took him several moments to realize it was Celestino's.

"I'm afraid the Atascos have left early," the gear man was saying through Atasco's usurped sim. *"But don't worry. We'll think of ways to keep the party entertaining."*

"You shit!" Dread screamed, "you bloody idiot, get out of there!" There was no response: Celestino was not listening to the command channel. Dread felt rage expanding inside him like scalding steam. "Dulcy! Are you there?"

"I am."

"Have you got a gun?"

"Uh . . . yes." Her voice suggested she always carried one, but didn't use it.

"Go in and shoot that little bastard. Right now."

"Shoot. . . ?"

"Now! He may have just blown the most important part of this whole thing sky-high. Do it. You know I'll take care of you."

Already high in Dread's estimation, Dulcinea Anwin rose even higher. He did not hear another sound from her until after something had exploded loudly on the Track Three audio channel.

"Now what?" She was back on the line, breathing hard. "Christ, I've never done that before."

"Then don't look at it. Go back to the other room—you can override from there. I want to know who's in that simulation. Find the outside lines. Most importantly, I want one of those lines—just one—that we can spike."

She took a ragged breath, then steadied. "Got it."

While he waited, Dread examined the Atascos' lab. Expensive stuff. In other circumstances, he wouldn't have minded taking some of it with him, although it would have been strictly against the Old Man's orders. But he smelled a bigger prize. He gestured to the bang man, who was standing in the hallway smoking a skinny black cigar.

"Wire it up."

The man ground the cigar out on the floor, then began attaching nodules of Anvax gel to various points around the room. Once Dread and Dulcy had emptied out the contents of Atasco's hard storage, he would trigger the explosives remotely.

As he was making his way back up the stairs, Dulcy Anwin came back online. "I've got good news and bad news. Which first?"

His grin was reflexive, hunger rather than humor. "I can take the bad news. There hasn't been much so far tonight."

"Can't get a fix on most of these folks. There seem to be several different setups, but most of them are trace-proof. They're not Puppets, I don't think, but they're using some kind of blind relay system—at least a couple of anonymous routers involved, plus some other even weirder stuff. If I had them all in one place for a couple of days, I might break something down, but otherwise, forget it."

"They're already starting to scatter. They'll probably be offline in a few minutes. But you said 'most.' Is that the good news?"

"I've got one of them in the crosshairs. Guested in by the target. No relay, no weird runaround. Spike's already in place."

Dread took a deep breath. "Great. That's perfect. I want you to do a quick trace, then pull up the user's index. Can you do that?"

"When do you want it?"

"Right now. I want you to use that spike to override and bump the user offline, then you hold the sim yourself. Browse the index—just quickly, we'll work up a better version later—and learn what you can. Whoever he or she is, that's who *you* are. Got it?"

"You want me to pretend to be this person? What about all the data work we have to do?"

"I'll do it myself. I need to do it myself. Don't worry, I'll get someone to relieve you in a little while. Hell, after I get the data squared away, I'll probably take that spike from you myself, too." The pain in his head, the residue of the twist, was almost completely gone now. Dread suddenly felt the need for music, and conjured up a swelling, martial air. He had something the Old Man didn't, had it firmly in his jaws, and he was going to hang onto it until Doomsday. "If any of the others at the conference or whatever it is stay in the simulation, you stay too. Keep your mouth shut. Record everything." He was already busily making plans. As soon as he knew where this user lived, he would have him or her investigated and sanctioned, not necessarily in that order. He now had a front-row seat—Christ, he exulted, a leading role—in some mysterious conspiracy that had the Old Man scared to death. Also, the conspirators seemed to know a lot more about what the Old Man and his friends were up to than Dread did himself. It was impossible to guess how valuable this little sleight-of-hand might turn out to be.

My time has come around at last. He laughed.

But he needed everything to be crystal clear, foolproof. Even the efficient Ms. Anwin could make a mistake in all this confusion. "Are you sure you got it?" he asked her. "You keep that sim working at all costs until I relieve you. You *are* that user. Don't worry about the overtime—I'll make it worth your while, Dulcy baby." He laughed again. His early thoughts about Dulcinea as quarry had been super-seded by a chase more glorious than anything he could have antici-pated. "Get on it. I'll be back as soon as I finish up some loose ends here."

He strode up the stairs and into the huge entry hall. There was data to sift, and a lot of it. He would have to take care of that before follow-ing up on the sim, monitor as much of it as he could before it went to the Old Man and his Brotherhood. He suddenly very much wanted to know what Atasco had been doing, as well as what Atasco had known. It would mean another night without sleep, but it would surely be worth it.

At the foot of the main staircase a stone statue of a jaguar, blocky and expressionistic, crouched on a pedestal. He patted its snarling jaws for luck, then made a mental note to add Celestino's body to the cleanup squad's list of things to do.

CHAPTER 38

A New Day

NETFEED/NEWS: *Krittapong USA Demands More Seats*
(visual: US Capitol Building, Washington, Cm.)
VO: *Krittapong Electronics, USA, is threatening to filibuster the US Senate
unless it receives more representation.*
(visual: Krittapong VPPR, Porfirio Vasques-Lowell, at press conference)
VASQUES-LOWELL: *"The House of Representatives allots seats based on
population, and the biggest states get the most House seats. The Senate is
business-based. Krittapong's gross worth has at least quintupled in the decade
since the Industrial Senate Amendment was passed, so we deserve more seats.
Simple. And we'd like to have a little chat with our colleagues in Britain's
House of Enterprise, too."*

Things had gone from strange to stranger. Orlando, who had roused himself for a few moments to try to make the others understand, now could only sit staring as the room erupted into madness.

Their hosts had vanished—the Atascos from their virtual bodies, Sellars completely. A woman across the table was screaming, a continuous wail of pain that was both heartbreaking and terrifying. Some of the sim-wearing guests sat like Orlando, in stunned silence. Others were shouting at each other like asylum inmates.

"Fredericks?" He turned his throbbing head, looking for his friend. Another wave of the fever was crawling over him, and despite the amazing chaos, he was suddenly fighting the pull of sleep. "Fredericks? Where are you?" He hated the plaintive sound of his voice.

His friend popped up from behind the table, hands over his ears. "This whole thing impacts *plus,* Orlando—we have to get out of here."

The shrieking stopped, but the excited babble continued. Orlando pulled himself upright. "How? You told me we can't go offline. Besides, didn't you hear what that guy Sellars was saying?"

Fredericks shook his head emphatically. "I heard, but I'm not listening. Come on." As he pulled at Orlando's arm, the room suddenly quieted. Over Fredericks' shoulder, Orlando saw Atasco moving again.

"I hope none of you think you're going anywhere." The sim was inhabited, but the voice was not Atasco's. *"Trying to leave would be a very bad idea."*

"Oh, no. Oh, Jesus," moaned Fredericks. "This is . . . we're . . ."

Something happened at the head of the table, something swift and violent that Orlando couldn't quite make out, but Atasco's wife disappeared from his line of sight. *"I'm afraid the Atascos have left early,"* continued the new voice, sounding as pleased with its own evil as any cartoon villain. *"But don't worry. We'll think of ways to keep the party entertaining."*

For a long moment, nobody moved. A rustle of frightened murmurs ran through the guests as Atasco, or what had been Atasco, turned to survey them each in turn. *"Now, why don't you tell me your names, and if you cooperate maybe I will be kind."*

The exotic woman Orlando had noted earlier, the tall, hawk-nosed one that he thought of as Nefertiti, shouted "You go to hell!" Through a haze of fever, Orlando admired her spirit. With just a little effort, he could almost imagine this as a particularly complicated and inventive game. If so, Nefertiti was clearly the Warrior Princess. She even had a sidekick, if the talking monkey was with her.

And me? Is there a category for Dying Hero?

Fredericks was clutching the arm of Orlando's sim so tightly that he could actually feel pain even through sickness and machinery. He tried again to shake off his friend's grip. It was time to stand up. It was time to die on his feet in the final battle. Thargor would have wanted to go that way, even if he was only an imaginary character.

Orlando rose, trembling. The false Atasco's eyes flicked toward him, then suddenly the feather-crowned head snapped forward as if struck a blow by an invisible club. The God-King body froze again, then top-

pled swiftly to the floor. The terrified babble of the guests rose once
more. Orlando took a few light-headed, staggering steps, then righted
himself and headed across the room toward Nefertiti and her monkey
friend. He had to push past the black-clad clown who called himself
Sweet William, who was arguing with the shiny robot warrior sim;
Sweet William shot Orlando a scornful look as they bumped shoulders.

That idiot would love the Palace of Shadows, Orlando thought. *Hell, they'd
probably make him the pope.*

As he reached Nefertiti, Fredericks caught up with him, clearly unwilling to be left on his own in the middle of this madness. The dark-
skinned woman was crouching beside the woman who had been
screaming, holding her hand and trying to soothe her.

"Do you have any idea what's going on here?" Orlando asked.

Nefertiti shook her head. "But something has obviously gone
wrong. I think we must find a way out." He wasn't sure, but he
thought her accent sounded African or Caribbean.

"Finally, somebody who makes sense!" Fredericks said angrily.
"I've been . . ."

He was interrupted by a shout of surprise. All turned to the front of
the room, where the white specter of Sellars' sim had reappeared. It
raised its formless hands in the air, and the people nearest it drew
back in fear.

"Please! Listen to me!" To Orlando's relief, it sounded very much
like Sellars. "Please, we do not have much time!"

The sims crowded forward, already calling out questions. Nefertiti
banged her fists on the table and shouted for silence. A couple of
others joined her—including Sweet William, Orlando was surprised
to see. After a few moments the room quieted.

"I do not know how, but we seem to have been discovered." Sellars
was laboring to sound calm and just barely succeeding. "The island—
the Atascos' real-world estate—is under attack. Our hosts are both
dead."

The robot wearer cursed in floridly fluent Goggleboy. Someone else
shouted out in surprise and fear. Orlando could feel hysteria rising
around him. If he had felt like his normal Thargor self, it would be
time to start slapping some quiet common sense into some of these
ninnies. But not only didn't he feel like Thargor, he was pretty terrified himself.

Sellars was riding the panic, holding it down. "Please. Remember,
the attack is happening in Cartagena, Colombia—in the real world,

not here. You are in no immediate danger. But we cannot be found out, or the danger will be very, very real. I will assume that this attack is the work of The Grail Brotherhood, and that they know what they are looking for. If so, we only have minutes before they will be upon us."

"So what should we do?" It was the monkey, his lilting voice calmer than anyone else's. "We have barely begun to speak of Otherland."

"Otherland? What the hell are you babbling about?" shouted the woman who had earlier railed at Atasco. "We have to get out of here! How do we go offline?" She scrabbled at her neck as though attacked by invisible insects, but plainly could not find her neurocannula.

There was another eruption; clearly no one else could leave the simulation either. "Silence!" Sellars raised his hands. "We have moments, only. If your identities are to be protected, I must do my work. I cannot stay here and neither can you. Temilún will not be a sanctuary—the Brotherhood will tear it to pieces. You must get out and into Otherland. I will work to keep you hidden until you can find a way to escape the network entirely."

"But how will we even get out of *this* place?" Nefertiti, like her four-legged familiar, was doing a good job of controlling her emotions, but Orlando could hear the crack threatening to widen. "This Temilún is as big as a small country. Are we going to run to the border? And how do you go from one simulation to another here, anyway?"

"The river is the boundary," Sellars said, "but it is also a route from one simulation to the next." He paused for a moment, thinking, then bent to Atasco's sim where it lay on the flagstones. He came up a moment later with something in his hand. "Take this—it's Atasco's signet ring. There is a royal barge, I think, down at the port."

"I've seen it," Orlando called out. "It's big."

"Remember, Atasco is the God-King here, the master. If you command it with his ring, they will take you onto the river." Sellars handed the ring to Nefertiti. Orlando felt another wave of stifling, muzzy warmth roll through his body. His eyes sagged halfway closed.

"Just sail on the river?" Sweet William demanded. "What is this, *Huckleberry* friggin' *Finn?* Where are we going? You got us into this, you bloody little man—how are you going to get us out of it?"

Sellars held out his hands, seeming to offer a benediction more than to plead for silence. "There is no more time for talk. Already, our enemies are trying to breach the defenses I have thrown together. There is much I still need to tell you. I will do my best to find you again."

"Find us?" Fredericks took a step forward. "You're not going to know where we are?"

"There is no time!" For the first time Sellars' voice rose to a shout. "I must go. I *must* go."

Orlando forced himself to speak. "Is there anything we can do to stop these people—or at least find out what they're doing? We can't . . . can't have a quest without something to quest for."

"I was not prepared for this." Sellars took a ragged breath; his shapeless form seemed to sag. "There is a man named Jonas. He was a prisoner of The Grail Brotherhood, his mind held captive in a simulation. I was able to reach him when he dreamed. I helped him to escape. Look for him."

"We supposed to sniff for some *sayee lo* net-knocker?" The battle-robot waved its arms, flashing the razor-sharp blades at its joints. "While someone try to six us? You *far* far crash!"

"I can't believe I have something in common with Bangbang the Metal Boy here," said Sweet William, a thin edge of panic in his voice, "but I agree. What *are* you talking about?"

Sellars raised his arms. "Jonas knows something—he must! The Brotherhood would have killed him already if he weren't important. Find him! Now go!"

The chorus of questions began again, but Sellars' sim abruptly flared and then disappeared.

Fredericks shook his head miserably. "This is horrible—like some kind of story where everything ends wrong!"

"We have to get going." Orlando grabbed his friend's arm. "Come on—what choice do we have?" He saw that Nefertiti and the monkey were helping their friend to her feet. "We're going with them." He stood, taking a moment to be sure he had his balance. The fever had receded a little; he felt weak, but more clearheaded. "We're going to the ship, just like Sellars said." Orlando made his voice louder. "The rest of you can do what you want. But *I* wouldn't stay here until they managed to trace me. So if you're coming, follow me."

Sweet William swept his cloak back over his shoulder. "Oy, sunshine, who died and made *you* Mister Happy?"

The monkey had climbed back onto the table. "The time for arguing is over," it said. "This man is right—go or stay."

"We can't just go charging out of here." Nefertiti was frowning. "If we do that, someone will come in to investigate."

"Investigate?" The woman on the other side of the table had a slightly hysterical sound. "They're already investigating—he just said so!"

"I'm talking about *here,*" said Nefertiti. "Outside, in the real world, the Brotherhood or whoever has shut Atasco down. But in here, the people of Temilún don't know they're not real, and they don't care a bit about what's happening in RL. They think we're here having a meeting with their king or whatever. If we go thundering out like something's worng, we'll never make it to the docks."

Orlando nodded slowly, revising his earlier high estimation upward. "Hide the body," he said. "Both the bodies."

It took more than a few minutes, since within the simulation the deserted sims had the weight and heft of corpses—corpses in advanced rigor mortis, as Orlando noticed while helping to trundle the unwieldy, seated form of Mrs. Atasco, which made their task even more difficult. What little strength he had was waning quickly in the struggle with the bodies, and he had no idea of how far they would have to travel. He surrendered to Fredericks his position as impromptu pallbearer and joined the search for a hiding place instead. The baboon discovered a small anteroom hidden behind a screen and the rest gratefully bundled the Atascos' sims into it.

Despite Sweet William's obvious discontent, the party then fell into line behind Orlando and Nefertiti. "Now, act calm!" the tall woman said as she reached for the door.

The guards stepped back as the guests filed out. Orlando saw with approval that Fredericks, though unhappy, was maintaining a stiff but impenetrable expression. Some of the others, however, were not hiding their anxiety quite so well, and the sharp-eyed proximity of the guards was not helping matters. Someone behind Orlando was trying to choke back a sob; the guards heard it, too, judging by the way their heads were swiveling to find the source of the noise.

Orlando stepped toward what he guessed was the captain, the guard with the highest helmet and longest and most brilliant feathered cape. He searched his game-playing lexicon for words that sounded properly melodramatic.

"Our requests were refused," he said. "The great and holy one, in his wisdom, has told us the time is not yet correct." He hoped he sounded both disappointed and yet honored belief even to have been granted an audience. "Blessed is he."

The guard captain cocked an eyebrow. Sweet William stepped forward, all tassels and points, and the captain's other eyebrow went up as well, while Orlando's heart traveled in the opposite direction. "Yes, blessed is he," said the apparition in black, with a fairly convincing stab at humility. "In fact, our poor embassy has angered him, and while he has kindly restrained his wrath so that we may return to our country and tell our masters the God-King's will, his displeasure with our masters is great. He commands that he will not be disturbed until sunset."

Mentally, Orlando put a check beside Sweet William's name. The guy was quick and smooth when he wanted to be, you had to give him that.

The captain did not seem entirely convinced. He fingered the stone blade of an ax that despite evidence of more modern technologies all around, did not look at all ceremonial. "But it is already sunset."

"Ah," said Sweet William, momentarily nonplussed. "Sunset."

Orlando jumped in. "Our command of your tongue is very poor. Doubtless the God-King meant 'sunrise.' In any case, he did not wish to be disturbed." Orlando leaned closer, in best conspiratorial fashion. "A word to the wise. He was very, *very* unhappy. I would not want to be the man who interrupted his thoughts and made him even more unhappy."

The captain nodded slightly, still frowning. Orlando rejoined the line at the back, just behind Sweet William.

"Not bad, chuck," William stage-whispered over his shoulder when they were out of earshot. "We could be a team—end of the pier, leave 'em laughing. You sing?"

"Keep walking," said Orlando.

When they reached the rotunda just inside the front doors, Orlando hurried forward. The tall woman was clearly chafing at the slow pace of her disabled friend, but was doing her best to maintain an air of deliberate dignity.

"Do you know where we're going from here?" Orlando asked in a whisper.

"Not a clue." She looked at him briefly. "What is your name? You said, but I've forgotten."

"Orlando. What's yours?"

She hesitated, then said: "Oh, God, what difference does it make now? Renie."

Orlando nodded. "I've been calling you Nefertiti. Renie is easier."

She gave him a strange look, then after a moment looked down at her long-fingered hand. "Ah. The sim. Right." She glanced up. The huge doors loomed. "Now what? Do we just mill around in front trying to figure out where the docks are? But even if we find out, how do we get there? I know they have buses—I rode on one—but somehow it seems like a strange idea trying to escape for your life by bus."

Orlando pushed at the doors, but could not get them open. Fredericks added his weight and they swung wide, revealing a mall lined with streetlamps stretching out from the bottom of the wide staircase.

Orlando was already feeling a little short of breath. "Escaping by bus won't be the strangest thing that's happened to us so far," he said.

"And it probably won't be the worst either," noted Fredericks.

Felix Jongleur, these days more frequently known as Osiris, Lord of Life and Death, was trying to decide where he was.

This was not the confusion of someone stupefied or geographically confused, but rather a fairly difficult philosophical proposition; in fact, it was a question with which he often wrestled in idle moments.

What he saw all around him was the stark grandeur of the Western Palace, its looming windows filled with eternal twilight. Flanking the table before him stretched the double line of animal faces that represented his collaborators, the Ennead. But even as he took a deep, contemplative breath in the Western Palace, his actual flesh-and-blood lungs were doing their work in a sealed hyperbaric chamber within the highest tower of his secluded Louisiana estate, along with the rest of his body. (The lungs were aided in their labors by some of the finest medical equipment that money could buy, for the god's lungs were very, very old, but that was the crux of an entirely different metaphysical enquiry.) So as always, the question remained this: where was *he,* Felix Jongleur—that which observed, the hot white point at the center of the candle flame?

To the extent that his actual body was located in the real world, he was in the southernmost part of the United States. But his mind lived almost entirely in virtual worlds, mostly within his favorite, an imaginary Egypt, complete with a pantheon of gods over which he reigned. So where was he, truly? On the shores of Louisiana's Lake Borgne, in a Gothic fantasy castle built on reclaimed swampland? On an electronic network, in an even more fantastic castle in Egypt's mythical West? Or in some other place more difficult to name or locate?

Jongleur stifled a small sigh. On this day, such maundering was a sign of nearly unforgivable weakness. He was a little anxious, although that was scarcely surprising: what happened in this gathering would affect not only his own life's ambition, but quite possibly the very history of humankind. The Grail Project, when completed, would have almost unbelievable ramifications, so it was critical he retain control: his own determined vision had prevailed for so long that the Project might well fail without him.

He wondered if some of the resistance to his long rule over the Brotherhood might be nothing more than the craving for novelty. For all their wealth and immense personal power, the Ennead had proven themselves to possess many other quite human frailties, and it was difficult to retain patience for a project that had stretched over so many years.

Perhaps he hadn't given them enough showmanship lately.

He was distracted by a movement down the table. A grotesque form with the shining head of a beetle rose and coughed politely. "If we may begin?"

Jongleur was again Osiris. The Lord of Life and Death inclined his head.

"First of all," the beetle-man said, "it is a pleasure to be in your company once more—to be among equals." The round brown head turned to make a careful survey. The god could barely refrain from laughing out loud at the attempts at political dignity, seriously undercut by goggling opaque eyes and quivering mandibles. Osiris had chosen Ricardo Klement's god-persona well: the beetle Khepera was an aspect of the solar deity, but for all that, he was still a dung-beetle—a creature that spent its life rolling little balls of shit, which described the Argentinian perfectly. "We have much to discuss today, so I will not take up time with unnecessary talk." Klement bobbed like a shop-keeping insect out of a children's book—a particularly apt simile, since his immense fortune had come out of black market organ-farming.

"Then don't." Sekhmet shot her claws and daintily scratched her chin. "What is your business?"

If the beetle had possessed recognizable facial features, the look he gave her might have been more effective. "I would like to ask the chairman for a progress report on the Sky God Project."

Osiris swallowed another chuckle. The Argentinian had made a complete nuisance of himself about Sky God on the grounds that it was in his own territory, offering bad advice and useless personal recommendations. Osiris had made a deliberate effort to seem grateful for all this help, though. A vote was a vote, after all.

"Thanks in large part to you, Ricardo, things are going very well indeed. I expect to have an update before the meeting is over, so if you will allow me to postpone any deeper discussion until then. . . ?"

"Of course, Chairman." The beetle-man bowed and settled back into his chair.

Osiris watched Ptah and Horus, who were very still. He suspected that the Americans were engaged in a little sidebar communication, and wondered what exactly had made them so eager to push forward the date of this month's meeting.

The normal business went swiftly—a consortium to be organized, the better to bypass certain UN restrictions on the transshipment of precious metals; a newly-privatized power grid in West Africa to be bought at an advantageous price; a few witnesses in an Indian court case to be bribed or removed. Osiris was beginning to think he might have overestimated his American rivals. He expected good results from Colombia at any time, and was considering how best to orchestrate the announcement when yellow-faced Ptah abruptly stood.

"Before we finish, Chairman, there is one thing more."

The god stiffened for a practically imperceptible moment. "Yes?"

"Last meeting, we had some conversation about the lost subject, if you recall—the one who somehow disappeared within the Grail system. Some information has developed in-house at TMX, so we thought it would be a good time for you to tell us how your *own* investigation of the incident is going." His smile was tight-lipped but wide. "That way, the Brotherhood will be updated and we can share necessary information."

So. The wire was now visible, which meant that Wells and Yacoubian must think that the snare was unavoidable. Osiris let his mind run quickly through the latest developments, which were few. What was their angle?

"I have agents operating within the system, as you know," he said. "They have made a few incomplete identifications—none of which, unfortunately, has been good enough to trigger a retrieval. It's likely that they were just spikes of statistical similarity." He turned to focus his remarks on Thoth, Sekhmet, and the rest of the Asian contingent: Osiris knew that the Asians liked personal guarantees. "Still, I have every confidence—*every* confidence—we will have results before too long." He turned back to Ptah, spreading his hands like a father teasing his young and overeager sons. "Now, what have you to add to this?"

"During a TMX security check—about a totally unrelated matter, as it happens—we ran into some anomalies in the access records for the Grail Project. To put it simply, there has been improper access." Ptah said it gravely, and was rewarded by appropriate noises of concern from around the table. "Please note I said 'improper' rather than 'un-authorized.' Yes, of course you're all shocked. You should be. Our chairman will agree that the energy and resources put into protecting the integrity of the Grail Project, not to mention its secrecy, have been immense—and, we thought, unbeatable."

Osiris remained silent. He did not like the direction this was going. For Wells to admit a security breach in his own operation in front of the assembled elite of the Brotherhood meant he thought he had something he could turn to his advantage—otherwise, he would simply have buried it. The escaped subject mattered little to anyone but Osiris.

"This is very bad." Sobek's crocodile head thrust forward. "Very bad. How could this happen?"

"There is only one way to get access to the system," explained Ptah. "And that is with command permission from myself or the chairman." He sketched a gently mocking bow toward Osiris. "Even those employees of mine or the chairman's who work with the Project every day must still receive permission before they begin their shift, and again if they come back after logging off for a break. This permission is in the form of a perpetually-changing code key, generated by sealed black box code generators. There are only two. I have one. The chairman has the other."

Sobek was nodding his long head up and down. The ruler of a West African nation, which he and his family had wrung dry of gold and blood for decades, he understood the concept of centralization of authority very well. "Get to the point. What does this have to do with someone interfering with our project?"

"Just as access to the system is carefully limited, so any adjustment to the system must also come with code authorization from one of the two of us." Ptah was speaking carefully for the benefit of those like Sobek whose place in the Brotherhood had less to do with technical expertise than with available resources. "If the escape of the subject was not a freak accident, then it had to have been directed. If directed, the action itself would have needed approval. The system will allow *no* outside modification that does not come with approval."

Osiris was still mystified, but he could feel Ptah moving closer to what he seemed to think was some kind of mortal blow. "I think we all have the gist now," he said out loud. "Perhaps you could move from the general to the specific. What exactly have you discovered?"

Horus now stood, golden eyes glinting. "We discovered anomalies, that's what we discovered. Actions taken by two different TMX employees in the week before the subject—or whatever you want to call him—escaped." The American general had all the subtlety of a cattle stampede; Osiris decided that Wells must feel fairly confident if he was going to let his crony handle part of the attack, especially if Wells' own employees were somehow to blame. "Although we can't figure out yet exactly how these two helped to drop the subject off our radar and lose him in the system, we're pretty damn confident that that's what happened. There is no other explanation for the actions they took, no other discernible results, and we can't find any reason for them to have taken those actions, either. Well, that's not strictly true. Actually, there was quite a good reason for them to do what they did."

The Lord of Life and Death was not going to let any upstart garner the benefit of dramatic pauses. "We are all fascinated, I assure you. Go on."

"They were both acting under coded orders from the chairman." Horus turned from the table at large to focus on Osiris. "From you."

Osiris remained absolutely still. Blustering would do nothing to silence the whispers or still the doubts. "What are you suggesting?"

"You tell us, Chairman." This was Ptah, with more than a hint of satisfaction. "You tell us how a subject—a subject that *you* wanted in the system in the first place, although you didn't bother to share your reasons with us—was cut free and released from surveillance by coded orders that only *you* can generate."

"Yeah," said Horus, unable to resist grinding the point home, "let us know, would you? An awful lot of people have invested an awful lot of money in this project. They might want to know if you've decided to make it your personal playground."

Osiris could feel the shock at the table, the rising anger and unhappiness, much of it directed at himself. Even Thoth, usually placid to the point of near-invisibility, was shifting in his chair.

"Am I to understand you are accusing *me* of this? Of engineering the escape of this subject? And you expect me to react to this dangerous nonsense with no evidence for it but your own words?"

"Let's not be hasty," said Ptah silkily. Osiris thought he might already be regretting the slack in Yacoubian's leash. "We have not formally accused you of anything. But we freely make our investigation records available to the Brotherhood, and they do raise some grave questions." He gestured, and a small glowing dot appeared before each of the participants, indicating the available files. "I think the burden of proof is on you, Chairman, at least to explain how your code wound up on orders that have no other visible purpose than to facilitate the subject's escape."

Underneath the permanent half-smile of his mask, Osiris employed the long pause to quickly range through the reports Wells had just made available. The details were uncomfortable.

"There is more here than simply concern over this subject," he said at last. He would have a far better chance if he could inject a note of the personal into things—the Americans were not terribly popular. "Am I wrong in thinking that you feel my leadership is somehow lacking?" He turned to the table at large. "Surely you have all seen our comrade's impatience with my direction. Ptah the Artificer was the cleverest of Egypt's gods, and our own version is equally clever. Certainly, he must often feel that he could do a better job, that if he could only dislodge me, he and bold Horus could bring a certain vigor to the Brotherhood's leadership." He let his voice drop a bitter degree. "He is a fool, of course."

"Please, Chairman." Wells sounded amused. "This is rhetoric. We need answers."

"I am never in as much of a hurry as you are." Osiris assumed his calmest tones. "However, sometimes I arrive at the same positions as you do, even if my pace brings me there more slowly. This is one of those times."

"What are you talking about?" Now Ptah was the one to sound off-balance.

"Simply this. If what you say is correct, then I do not deserve the confidence of the Brotherhood. We agree on that. Neither can the Project go forward without solidarity among us. So I propose that we examine the matter as fully as we can, examining *all* the evidence, and then put the matter to a vote. Today. If the Brotherhood votes against me, I will step down immediately. Agreed?"

Horus nodded briskly. "Sounds fair." Ptah also agreed, but a little more slowly, sniffing for a trap. Osiris had no trap to set—he was still rather dumbfounded by the revelations of the last few minutes—but he had decided a long time ago that it was better to die with your teeth in your enemy's throat than to slink away. As yet, he had never had to do either.

"First," he said, "while your report seems admirably thorough, I'm sure that the Brotherhood would like to hear from the two employees in person." He received nods from his other guests, which he accepted with a courtly inclintation of his own masked head. "You have detained them, of course."

"Of course." Ptah was confident now, a bad sign. Osiris had half-hoped that TMX's earlier, in-house interrogations had been too vigorous. It was hard to convict on the evidence of dead witnesses, even with hologrammatic records—data could be so easily manipulated these days. Not that real-time VR was immune from manipulation, but the process was much more difficult.

"Well, bring them in, will you? Isolated from each other, of course. And since you have brought what is tantamount to an accusation against me, you will permit *me* to do the interrogation, will you not?"

"Of course," Ptah agreed, but now it was his falcon-headed crony who did not seem pleased. Osiris took some small pleasure from this sign that, at some level, they still feared him, worried about his legendary craftiness. He would do his best to justify that unease.

The Lord of Life and Death waved his hand and the table vanished; the Ennead were now seated in a circle, each in his or her own throne-like chair. A moment later two figures blinked into existence at the circle's center, one stocky and one slender, both immobile as statues. They appeared quite human, and thus seemed strangely out of place amid the avid beast-faces. As befitted mortals in the land of the gods, they were only half the size of the smallest of the Ennead.

"My employees, Shoemaker and Miller," said Ptah. "You have all their personal details in our submission."

Osiris leaned forward and extended a mummy-wrapped finger. The older-looking of the two, bearded and strongly-built, twitched as though awakening from slumber.

"David Shoemaker," the god intoned, "your only hope is to answer all questions with complete honesty. Is that understood?" The man's eyes widened. He had undoubtedly gone directly from his last interrogation to the blackness of enforced sleep. Waking up to this, Osiris thought, must be disorienting to say the least. "I said, is that understood?"

"Where . . . where am I?"

The Lord of the Two Lands gestured. The man writhed, his eyes squeezed shut and his teeth bared in a rictus of agony. After the brief burst of induced pain ended, Osiris watched the convulsive bunching of the man's muscles, knowing that the other members of the Brotherhood were also watching. It never hurt to remind them what he could do. He *was* a god here, with powers that the others did not possess, not even in their own domains. It never hurt to remind them.

"I will try again. Your only hope is to answer all questions with complete honesty. Do you understand?"

The bearded man nodded. His sim, generated by the holocell in which he was restrained, was already white-faced with dread.

"Good. Please also understand that what I can do to you is not like normal pain. It will not damage your body. You will not die from it. That means I can subject you to it for as long as I like." He paused to let this sink in. "Now, you will tell us everything about the events that led up to your interfering in the normal workings of the Grail system."

Through the course of the next hour, Osiris led Shoemaker through a minute examination of his and Glen Miller's work as systems engineers on the Otherland network. Slow answers, even hesitations while the prisoner tried to remember some small detail, were met with immediate activation of the pain reflex, which Osiris often held like an orchestral note, judging what duration should most promote quick and honest responses. Despite the continual razor slashes of agony, Shoemaker stuck to the story he had already told TMX Security. He had received what seemed a legitimate order to modify the tracking elements that sent back data on the subject's whereabouts within the system, but had no way of knowing that the changes would eventually make tracking impossible. The order had appeared to come through legitimate management channels—although TMX security had proved afterward that the management approvals were fairly obvious forgeries—and, most critically, had contained the Chairman's own inimitable authorization.

The Chairman, the living Master of the Two Lands, was not pleased to hear himself indicted again. "Of course, if you were a spy within the system, you might say the very same thing. And if you had a high enough pain threshold, you might continue to say it no matter what kind of messages I pump into your central nervous system." He frowned at the panting, shivering simulation. "You might even have received some kind of post-hypnotic block or neural modification." He turned to Ptah. "I suppose you scanned both of these men?"

The yellow face smiled. "It's in the records. No detectable mods."

"Hmmm." Osiris gestured again. An array of glittering metallic arms sprouted from the floor, spread-eagling the prisoner. "Perhaps a more subtle approach is called for." Another gesture brought forth more jointed arms, each of these veined in transparent tubing and barbed at the end with a huge needle. "I understand from your employee profile that you have an aversion to medical procedure and pharmaceuticals. Some bad experience in your childhood, perhaps?" He pointed; one by one, the arms tilted down like the jaws of some strange, venomous insect, the needles plunging into different soft parts of the prisoner's body. "Perhaps this will help you to rethink your story, which I find woefully inadequate."

The prisoner, who had been struggling to find his voice, found it. As different colored liquids began to pulse through the tubing, oozing inexorably toward him, he let loose a bone-rattling scream. As black-and-green stains blossomed around the needle entries and began to spread out beneath his skin, Shoemaker's ear-piercing shriek jumped to a newer, higher level of madness.

Osiris shook his head. He dulled the man's ragged cries to a faint piping, then flicked the second prisoner into life. "I'm not going to tell you where you are, so don't bother to ask." The god was beginning to feel quite cross. "You are going to tell *me* things instead. Do you see your friend?"

The second man, whose thick black hair and high cheekbones suggested an Asian heritage, nodded, eyes wide with anticipatory terror.

"Well, Miller, the two of you have been very naughty fellows indeed. You have interfered with the proper functioning of the Grail Project, and worst of all, you have done so without authorization."

"But we were authorized!" Miller shouted. "Oh, Christ, why won't anyone believe us?"

"Because it is easy to lie." Osiris spread his fingers and Miller was suddenly surrounded by a glassy cube three times his height. Several of the Ennead leaned forward, spectators at an evening's entertainment. "But it is not easy to lie when you are fighting to maintain your very sanity. Your records indicate you have a morbid fear of drowning. So, while you think about who put you up to this little prank, I will give you a chance to explore that fear at first hand."

The cube began to fill with water. The prisoner, who must have known that his physical body was still in restraint somewhere in the Telemorphix offices while only his mind was being tortured, but could not enjoy the distinction, began to pound on the transparent walls.

"We can hear you. Tell us what you know. Look, the water is already at your knees."

As the brackish water rose to his waist, his chest, his neck, Miller babbled shrilly about the order he had received to turn on the thalamic splitter for what he had thought was some kind of testing. He had never imagined for a moment that the splitter was still enchained, and that his action would complete the subject's release. Even as he was forced to leap to keep his mouth above water, he swore that he knew nothing beyond what he had been directed to do.

The cube was filling faster. The prisoner swam in rapid, dog-paddle style, but each moment brought him closer to the roof of the cube and diminished the pocket of air. Osiris suppressed a sigh. This Miller's terror was so palpable it almost made him uncomfortable, but the man showed no sign of changing his story. More importantly, the Lord of Life and Death was rapidly losing the confidence of the assembled Brotherhood.

The cube was now completely filled. The prisoner's desperate thrashings, which had reached their peak, suddenly stopped as Miller took a great gulp of the greenish water, trying to hasten the end. A moment later he took another. The look of frenzied panic on his face abruptly grew even more acute.

"No, you won't die. Your lungs will burn, you will choke, you will struggle, but you will not die. You will continue to drown as long as I wish it." Osiris could not keep the frustration out of his voice. He looked to the other prisoner, a swollen lump of blackened, pustulent flesh now barely recognizable as human, still spiked beneath a dozen needles, still screaming through a ragged spiracle that had once been a mouth. This was all sideshow, now. These men knew nothing.

Sensing victory, Ptah stood. "If the Chairman has no further questions for these two unfortunates, perhaps he would like the chance to offer an explanation to the rest of the Brotherhood?"

"In a moment." He pretended an interest in the maddened struggles of the two TMX employees, while quickly reviewing the report Wells and Yacoubian had submitted. His expert systems had been combing the material for anomalies, and had compiled a short list of things that needed clarification. As the superimposed information flickered across his vision, a heaviness settled on him. The expert systems had turned up nothing but noise, discrepancies in testimony that indicated little but human sloppiness and imprecision. Everything else fitted Wells' interpretation. Within moments, control of the Brotherhood, and over the Grail Project, would slip from the chief god's hands. In its cocoon of metal and expensive liquids, Felix Jongleur's real body stirred, his heart seemed to labor. Osiris the immortal god suddenly felt his age.

His colleagues were murmuring, their patience exhausted. He scanned the report again listlessly, trying to think of something that could be done to save the situation. Adamant denial? Worthless. Delay? He himself had demanded speed, hoping to catch Wells and Yacoubian unprepared for a real showdown. He could not renege on that demand without ensuring a loss of control. Could he hold the project itself hostage? The others might have difficulty finishing it without his expertise, and most importantly his control over the Other, but an aborted Grail Project did him no good, and without the resources of the Brotherhood he could never duplicate the work that had gone into it. Not in time.

Desperately, he called back up the actual authorizations, hoping against logic to spot something his expert systems had not. The embedded dates were correct, the authorizations-for-work were real, and the authorization code had clearly been generated from his own machines.

"Chairman? We are waiting." Ptah was in a good humor. Comparatively speaking, he had all the time in the world.

"Just a moment." Osiris stared at the data before him, realizing absently that none of the Brotherhood could tell what he was doing, that they would only see him sitting motionless. Did they wonder if he were having some kind of breakdown? He called for some other records and compared them with the fire-bright numbers before him. Somewhere—it might have been another universe—his heart began to beat faster, like an ancient beast awakening from slumber.

Even the best expert systems could make assumptions.

Osiris began to laugh.

"Chairman?"

It was too perfect. He paused for a silent moment of exultation. "I would like to direct the Brotherhood's attention to the code sequences in question." He waved his hand. Line after line of numbers appeared on the council chamber's nearest roof column, carved into the very stone like the other names of power etched on the walls and doors of the Western Palace. It was appropriate: these strings of numerals were the incantations that would preserve Jongleur's most magnificent and audacious dream. "Please check to make sure they are the sequences you have submitted, the sequences that authorized action and allowed the subject's escape."

Ptah and Horus exchanged glances. Ibis-headed Thoth answered. "They are the same, Chairman."

"Good. As you see in the report, embedded between the larger random sections are other nonrandom sequences. These sequences indicate the kind of order it is, the date and time, the person who authorized it, and so on."

"But we've already established that this code came from your own generator. You admitted it!" Horus could not restrain his impatient anger.

If his funeral mask had permitted it, he would have grinned at him.

"But you do not know all the sequences and what they import. You see, this *is* an authorization for action, and it *did* come from me—but it did not go to either of . . . those creatures." He indicated the perpetually drowning man and the puddle of twitching slime, then turned back to Horus. "It went to you, Daniel."

"What the hell are you talking about?"

"All the orders generated from me carry a short sequence that indicates where they are bound. These were sent to the military arm of the Brotherhood, not to TMX. Someone has penetrated your system, Daniel. They intercepted what were probably fairly unimportant orders—likely something to do with that business in New Reno, the dates would be about right—modified them slightly, then used the coded authorizations to issue quite different orders of their own to the TMX engineering department."

"That's preposterous!" Horus groped in empty air, looking for a cigar on his RL desk.

Ptah was a little more cautious. "But we have never known that about your authorizations, Chairman. Isn't that . . . isn't that a little convenient?"

Osiris laughed again. "Bring up all the records you want. Let us have a really good look at prior authorizations. Then tell me I'm wrong."

Ptah and Horus glanced at each other. At the long table in the Western Palace they were silent, but the Lord of the Two Lands felt quite sure that conversation on the sidebar channel had suddenly become white-hot.

When they finally took the vote an hour later, it was unanimous: even Ptah and Horus displayed the good grace—or political savvy—to vote for his retention as chairman. Osiris was well pleased. Both Americans had received heavy blows to their ambition, and would be on the defensive for some time. First their own systems had apparently been penetrated, then they had been seen to blame that on their venerable chairman.

He particularly enjoyed ordering Horus to shore up his security, and to get to work locating and defining the incursion. "And while you're at it, excise those two." He indicated Miller and Shoemaker, neither of whom was now capable of making anything but bubbling noises. "I suggest a car accident. A couple of work chums on their way to some dreadful TMX morale-raising picnic. You know the sort of thing."

Ptah acceded with stiff grace, passing a message to his security service. The two sims disappeared, which gave the room a far more pleasant aspect.

As Khepera rose to his hind legs and began delivering the first of what promised to be a string of testimonials to the reelected chairman—establishing to the best of his dung-rolling ability that *he* had never once doubted, that *he* had been astonished by the charges, and so on—the god received a signal on a designated outside line. His priestly minion, forced to dispense with honorifics after the first few singsong phrases, announced that Anubis had an urgent message for him.

His absent attention unnoticed by the others, Osiris received his underling's report while the beetle-man droned on. His young minion seemed strangely calm, which troubled Osiris slightly. After such a triumph, Dread should have been at his strutting worst. Had he come across something in Atasco's records which had given him ideas?

There was also the issue of the actual adversary, the person who had so cleverly subverted TMX security and freed Paul Jonas. That would have to be the subject of many hours contemplation all by itself. Still, Osiris had known there was an enemy out there somewhere, and in a way was glad of it. The Americans had certainly proved an insufficient challenge.

When Anubis had finished his report and signed off, Osiris raised his gauze-shrouded hand for silence. Khepera stopped, his tribute uncompleted; he stood awkwardly for a moment, then lowered himself back into his chair.

"Thank you, my dear friend, for those inspiring words," the god said. "I will never forget them. But now I have an announcement to make. I have just received word that the Sky God Project has come to a successful conclusion. 'Shu' has been neutralized, along with his intimate circle, and we have possession of his system. Losses—of information—were negligible, and cleanup is finished. In short, a complete success."

The Western Palace echoed with cheers and congratulations, some of them sincere.

"I think today is an auspicious day to declare that we have begun the final phase of the Grail Project." He raised his other hand. The walls of the Western Palace fell away. The Ennead were now seated in the midst of an endless, twilit plain. "In only a matter of weeks our work will be completed and the fruits of our long labor available at last. The Grail system is about to become operational. Now we are *truly* become gods!'"

A red shimmer appeared along the far horizon. Osiris spread his arms as if he had summoned it into being—as, in fact, he had. There was a dramatic rumble of tympanis, a thundering crescendo of percussion.

"*Rejoice, Brotherhood. Our day has come!*"

The great disk of the rising sun edged upward into the heavens, bleaching the sky, scattering gold across the plains, and bathing the hungry, upraised animal faces in fire.

The docks were only a short distance from the broad front steps of the palace, perhaps less than half a mile judging by the rigging lights that glimmered between the buildings. Orlando and his new allies did their best to form a coherent group before setting off on foot.

"*This scans utterly!*" Orlando fumed. "*This is a VR simulation, the most powerful one anyone's ever heard of—and we're going to walk!* But any loopholes for instantaneous travel or other useful reality-molding tricks that might be built into the structure of Temilún were lost to Orlando and his new allies. *If we only had one of the Atascos with us.* . . .

They marched as quickly as they could, just beneath the threshold at which their anxious haste would be obvious. The city was busy at this early evening hour, the streets full of traffic, motorized and pedal-driven, the stone sidewalks crowded with Temilúni citizens on their way home from work. But even in this crush of pseudo-humanity, the band of travelers attracted attention. It wasn't that surprising, Orlando decided—there were few cities, virtual or otherwise, where someone as flamboyantly outrageous as Sweet William would not at least briefly draw the eye.

Tall Renie fell in beside him again. "Do you think Sellars meant that as soon as we get on the water we'll cross over into another simulation? Or are we going to have to sail for days?"

Orlando shook his head. "I can't even guess."

"What's to keep them from catching us on the river?" Fredericks asked, leaning in at Orlando's shoulder. "I mean, they're not going to leave that throne room alone forever, and when they go looking . . ."

He stopped, his eyes widening. "*Fenfen!* For that matter, what happens if we get killed here?"

"You drop offline," Renie began, then paused. The baboon, loping along beside her on all fours, looked up.

"You are thinking that if we cannot go offline now, there is no guarantee that dying a virtual death will change that?" he asked. "Or are you considering something worse?"

She shook her head violently. "It's just not possible. It can't be. Pain is one thing—that could just be hypnotic suggestion—even induced comas I will believe, but I really don't want to believe that something happening to you in VR could kill you. . . ." She stopped again. "No," she said firmly, as if putting something in a drawer and shutting it. "We'll have time to talk about everything later. None of this is useful now."

They hurried on in silence. Since the tall downtown buildings were now blocking the view of the water, Fredericks ran ahead to scout. Surfing along on the surreality of the moment, Orlando found that he was staring at Renie's baboon friend.

"What's your name?" he asked the simulated monkey.

"!Xabbu." There was a click and then a swallowing sound at the beginning. Orlando couldn't tell whether the first letter was supposed to be a G, an H, or a K. "And you are Orlando." The look on his face might have been a baboon smile. Orlando nodded. He was sure the person behind the monkey had an interesting story to tell, but he didn't have the strength to wonder about it very much. Later, as Renie had said. Later there would be time to talk.

If there is a later.

Fredericks was hurrying back toward them. "It's just around the corner," he said. "The boat's all lit up. What if it's not ready to go, Orlando?"

"It's ready to go," he said curtly. He had no idea, but he was damned if he was going to give these people anything else to worry about. "I saw it when they were bringing us in."

Fredericks gave him a doubtful look but kept silent.

"*Tchi seen, tchi seen,* man," muttered the robot sim dolefully, fingering his own anodized neck in search of his 'can. "They gonna catch us, do some harm. This dire, man, this far dire."

The barge was moored at its own dock, a single bright flower of pomp and colorful decoration amid the brutal functionalism of the working side of the harbor. Looking at the graceful ship, Orlando felt the weakness in his limbs recede a little, the dull pain in his head abate. The barge would take them away where their enemies couldn't find them. There would be time to rest, to recover his strength.

Renie was looking back over Orlando's shoulder, her finger wagging in the air as though she were conducting a very small orchestra.

"What are you doing?" Fredericks asked.

"Counting. There are nine of us. Is that right, or were there more when we left the palace?"

Fredericks shook his head. "I don't know. I didn't think about it."

"We should have." Renie was clearly angry, but it seemed to be at herself. "We may have lost people along the way."

"Can't worry about it," Orlando said flatly. "Let's just hope there's someone on board who knows how to make the thing go."

As if in answer, a group of figures began gathering at the top of the ramp that led onto the barge from the dockside stairs. As Renie gathered the travelers at the ramp's base, two of the figures on the ship detached themselves from the rest and came down the gangway toward them. One looked like a reasonably high muckamuck, his cape thatched in silver fish scales. Orlando wondered for a moment if he were the captain, but decided that no one could spend a life at sea and have such unweathered skin. The other man, a noncom in a small plain cape who was clearly the Temilúni navy's equivalent of a bone-breaker, had another of those large and unpleasant stone axes in his belt and some kind of pearl-handled pistol sheathed on the other hip. Renie held up the ring. "We have been sent by the God-King. He gave us this and commanded that you take us where we want to go."

The official leaned forward to inspect the ring while keeping his hands respectfully at his side. "It certainly looks like the signet of He Who Is Favored Above All Others. And who, may I ask, are you?"

"We are a delegation from . . ." Renie hesitated.

"The Banana Republic," said Orlando hastily. "Sent to request a boon from He Who Is Favored Above All Others." He looked up. At the top of the gangway, the dozen waiting sailors were managing simultaneously to stand at rigid attention and to watch the proceedings with interest. "Now we are being sent back with a message for our masters."

"The Ba . . ." The official shook his head as though it were all too much for him. "Still, it is very strange we have not been warned."

"The God-King—I mean, He Who Is Favored Above All Others— only made the decision a very short while ago. . ." Renie began.

"Of course." The official bowed. "I will contact the palace to receive my clearance. Please forgive me—I cannot allow you on board until that has been done. I apologize deeply and abjectly for the inconvenience."

Renie looked helplessly down at !Xabbu, then to Orlando.

Orlando shrugged, fighting a great and depressing weariness. He had half-known something like this would happen—that he could not wear the Thargor sim without inheriting certain responsibilities. He leaned a little closer toward the bonebreaker. The pistol was on the man's other hip, out of reach. Regretfully, Orlando curled his fingers around the stone ax and snatched it out of the belt even as he shouldered the startled noncom off the gangplank.

"Grab him," he said, shoving the official toward Renie and the others. The sailors at the top of the gangway, bellowing in surprise, had drawn their own sidearms. Orlando was gambling that they would not shoot for fear of harming this obviously important man. However, he couldn't afford to let them start thinking about alternative methods of capture. "Follow me," he called, already sprinting up the ramp.

"What are you *doing?*" Fredericks shouted.

Orlando didn't answer. If there was anything he knew about, it was virtual combat, and his own personal Lesson One was "Avoid Unnecessary Chitchat." Now he just had to pray that some of the Thargor sim's designated strength and speed remained despite his own illness and the strictures of an unfamiliar system.

"Help him!" Fredericks was shouting down below. "They'll kill him!"

Orlando leaped from the top end of the gangway and hit the deck rolling, upending the first two sailors. He brought the ax around in a swift arc and felt the sickening give of blade on bone as he shattered another sailor's kneecap, but he could already feel stickiness in his own usually fluid reflexes. The three bodies writhing on the deck around him gave him a moment's desperately-needed cover. What little strength he had, and it was less than he was used to in this sim, was draining fast; already his breath was stinging in his lungs. As he got to his knees, someone jumped onto his back, bearing him down so hard that his forehead cracked against the deck. For a moment he felt his limbs go uncontrollably limp, but he forced himself to pull his legs under him once more and rise to a crouch.

The man on his back was trying to snake an arm around his neck. As Orlando fought to hold him off, a hand with a gun in it swung down close to his face. Orlando smashed at it with the ax and was rewarded with a howl of pain; the gun skittered away, under the railing and into the water. He ducked his head, throwing the man on his back to the deck, then grabbed at the belt of the man he'd kneecapped a few moments before and tugged his pistol out of its holster.

Shadows were all around him, closing in. The urge to start firing, to clear away these threatening figures, was very powerful, but they were so much more convincingly human than his usual foes that he found himself almost fatally reluctant. He tossed the gun down the ramp.

"Grab it!" he gasped, hoping one of his companions would see it lying on the dark gangway. He didn't know if he'd been loud enough to be heard; his head was filling with echoes.

Several more men seized the chance and grabbed at his legs and arms. Another fell on top of him, jabbing a knee into his back and closing strong fingers on his throat. Struggling, he managed to throw off a few of his attackers, but more crashed down on top of him in their place. He fought wildly to rise, but only managed to turn over, face to the sky as he sucked desperately for air. The lights in the barge's rigging stretched and wavered as the blackness in his head grew, as though they were stars sending their dying flare into the eternal night of space.

It's funny, he thought. *Stars, lights . . . none real . . . all real . . .*

Something was hammering on his head, a dull, rhythmic thump that seemed to rattle his whole skull. Each pounding beat sent a splash of blackness through his thoughts, the tidal mark higher each time. He heard someone shouting—the woman, what was her name? It didn't matter. The breath, the life was being pressed out of him, and he was glad to let it go. He had been so tired, so very tired.

He thought he heard Fredericks calling him, but he could not answer. That at least was a little sad. Fredericks would have loved the lights—stars, they were stars, weren't they?—would have loved how bravely they burned in the darkness. He would miss Fredericks. . . .

He was in a place—a between-place, it seemed. A waiting-place, maybe. He couldn't really think about the whole thing very well, and it didn't matter just now anyway.

He was lying down, he knew that, but he was also standing, looking out across a great canyon. A massive slope of shiny blackness dropped sheerly away below him, its bottom edge invisible in a sea of swirling fog. On the far side of the canyon, dimly visible through the tendrils of rising mist, was the golden city. But somehow it was not the same city he had seen before—this city's buildings were taller and stranger than anything he could have imagined, and tiny radiant shapes flitted back and forth among the spiraling towers, brilliant specks of light that might have been fireflies. Or angels.

It's another dream, he thought, and was startled to hear he had said it aloud. Surely he should not speak here—someone was listening, he knew, someone or something who was looking for him, someone he did not want to meet.

It's not a dream, a voice said in his ear.

He looked around, startled. Sitting on a glossy outcrop of the smooth black substance was an insect the size of a small dog. It was made entirely of glittering silver wires, but was somehow completely alive.

It's me, boss, it said. *I've been trying to reach you for hours. I've got you amplified all the way and I can barely hear you.*

What's . . . It was so hard to think. The cottony fog had somehow got inside his head as well. *Where . . .*

Hurry up, boss, tell me what you want. If anyone comes in and catches me sitting on your chest, they're gonna throw me into the recycler.

A thought, small and fluttery as the distant lights, moved through his mind. *Beezle?*

Tell me. What's going on?

He fought to remember. *I'm . . . I'm trapped somewhere. I can't get out.*

I can't get back.

Where, boss?

He struggled against the waves of numbness, of darkness. The distant city was gone now and the fog was rising. He was having trouble seeing even the insect, though it sat only an arm's length away. *The place I was looking for.* He wanted to remember a name, a man's name, something with an A . . . ?

Atasco, he said. The effort was overwhelming. A moment later the insect had faded. Orlando was left alone with the mist and the mountainside and the growing dark.

CHAPTER 39

Blue Fire

T he coastline gliding past, thick jungle greenery and long-rooted trees drinking at the edges of sandbars, was not entirely strange to her—Renie had seen places along the African coast that looked only a little different. What troubled her now, as she watched a flock of flamingoes descending to a salt marsh like an air squadron returning to base, their brilliant pinks dulled by twilight, was the knowledge that none of it was real.

It's simply too much to accept. It's . . . seductive, that's what it is. She leaned over the rail. The fresh wind cooled all of her but the parts of her face covered by her V-tank mask. Even this curious numbness—a kind of tactile blind spot, dead to the world she saw all around her—was beginning to recede, as though her brain were beginning to fill in the experiences, just as with a real ocular blind spot. At certain moments, she could swear she *did* feel wind on her face.

It was difficult not to admire the completeness of this dream, the incredible skill and effort that had gone into it. She had to remind herself that Atasco, the man who had caused this wonder to be built, was perhaps the best of Otherland's feudal barons. He, arrogant and self-involved though he was, had at least had the basic humanity not to harm anyone in pursuit of his own satisfaction. The others . . . She thought of Stephen's beautiful brown legs atrophied, his arms now like slender sticks; she remembered Susan's shattered body. The others who had built this place were monsters. They were ogres living in castles built from the bones of their victims.

"I have a terrible confession, Renie."

"iXabbu! You startled me."

"I am sorry." He clambered onto the railing beside her. "Do you wish to hear my shameful thought?"

She put a hand on his shoulder. Resisting the impulse to pet him, she simply let it lie there in his thick fur. "Of course."

"Since I first came to this place, I have of course been worried for our safety, and frightened of the larger evil that the Sellars man described. But almost as strong in me, all this time, there has been a great joy."

Renie was suddenly unsure where this was going. "Joy?"

He pivoted on his rear end and stretched a long arm toward the darkening coastline, a curiously un-baboonlike gesture. "Because I have seen now that I can make my dream real. Whatever evil these people have done, or intend to do—and my heart tells me it is a very great evil indeed—they have also caused an amazing thing to be created. With such power, I think I could truly keep my people alive."

Renie nodded slowly. "That's not a shameful thought. But this kind of power—well, people who have something like this aren't going to give it away. They keep it for themselves. Just like they always have."

iXabbu did not reply. As the last daylight vanished they remained at the railing together, watching the river and the coast become one inseparable shadow beneath the stars.

Sweet William appeared to be taking a perverse pleasure in his role. "Just like Johnny Iceptick, me." He waved the gun menacingly at the captain and the God-King's Naval Adjutant, the official who had met them at the gangway. The two cringed. "It's not my normal line, dearies, but I could develop a taste for it."

Renie wondered which scared the Temilúni more, the gun or William's death-clown appearance. "How far are we from the end of the waters you know?" she asked the captain.

He shook his head. He was a small man, beardless as all the others, but his face was covered with black tattoos and he wore an impressively large stone lip-plug. "Over and over you ask that. There is no end. On the far side of these waters is the Land of Pale Men. If we continue along the coast as we are doing, we will cross the Caribbean," Renie heard her translation software pause for a split-instant before supplying the name, "and come to the empire of the Mexica. There is no end."

Renie sighed. If, as Atasco had said, there was a finite edge to the simulation, then the puppets themselves must not know it. Perhaps they simply ceased to be, then reappeared on their "return voyage," filled with suitable memories.

Of course, the same thing could be true for me. And how would I ever know?

As difficult as it was to look at the coastline and believe it a purely digital reality, it was even harder to imagine the captain and the king's adjutant as artificial. A coastline, even one filled with exuberant vegetable life, could be created fractally, although this level of sophistication beggared anything she had ever seen. But people? How could even the most sophisticated programming, the most strenuously evolutionary A-life environments create such diversity, such seeming authenticity? The captain had bad teeth, stained from chewing some leafy herb. He wore what was obviously a favored knickknack, a fish vertebra, on a chain around his thick neck. The adjutant had a port wine birthmark just behind his ear and smelled of licorice water.

"Are you married?" she asked the captain.

He blinked. "I was. Retired because she wanted me to, stayed ashore for three years in Quibdó. Couldn't take it, so I reenlisted. She left me."

Renie shook her head. A sailor's tale, so common as to be almost a cliché. But by the slight bitterness in his voice, like scar tissue around an old wound, he clearly believed it. And *every single person* in this simulation—in all the unguessable number of simulations that made up this Otherland—would have his or her own tale. Each one would believe himself to be alive and singular.

It was too much to comprehend.

"Do you have any idea how to make this ship work?" she asked Sweet William.

"Dead simple, really." He smiled lazily and stretched. Hidden bells jingled. "It's got a bit of a handle. Push, pull, forward, back—could do it in me sleep."

"Then we'll put these two and the rest of the crew overboard." She was startled by the adjutant's violent reaction for a moment, then realized the misunderstanding. "In the lifeboats. There seem to be plenty."

"Aye, aye." William saluted jauntily. "Whenever you're ready, Admiral."

The bed in He Who Is Favored Above All Others' massive stateroom was of a size commensurate with celestial royalty. Martine and Orlando lay at either edge where they could be reached by those caring for them, with a dozen-foot expanse of silken sheets between them. Orlando was sleeping, but Renie didn't think it was a healthy sleep. The big man's breath rasped in and out through his gaping mouth and the muscles in his fingers and face twitched. She laid her palm against his broad forehead, but felt nothing any more unusual than the mere fact of virtual tactility.

!Xabbu clambered up onto the bed and touched the man's face, but he seemed to have a different purpose in mind than Renie had, for he left his delicate simian hand there for a long time.

"He looks very sick," Renie said.

"He is." The slender man named Fredericks looked up from his seat by Orlando's side. "He's real sick."

"What is it? Is it something he caught outside—in RL, I mean? Or is it some effect from coming into the network?"

Fredericks shook his head morosely. "He's got something bad. In real life. It's a disease where you get old too soon—he told me the name, but I forgot." He rubbed at his eyes; when he spoke again, his voice was faint. "I think right now he's got pneumonia. He said . . . he said he was dying."

Renie stared at the sleeping man's almost cartoonish face, the square jaw and long black hair. Even after only a short acquaintance, the thought of his death was painful; she turned away, helpless and miserable. Too many victims, too many suffering innocents, not enough strength to save any of them.

Quan Li, who had been holding Martine's hand, stood up as Renie walked around the perimeter of the huge bed. "I wish there was something more I could do for your friend. She is a little quieter now. I thought of offering her some water . . .'' She trailed off. There was no need to finish. Martine, like everyone else, must be receiving nourishment and hydration in the real world. If not, nothing the Chinese woman or anyone else could do would help.

Renie sat on the edge of the bed and wrapped her hand around Martine's. The Frenchwoman had not spoken a word all the way to the ship, and after Sweet William had snatched up the gun which Orlando had tossed away, and pressed it against the adjutant's head to secure their passage on the barge, Martine had collapsed. Renie had carried her on board with Quan Li's help—it had taken three of the sailors to carry bulky Orlando—but there was nothing else she could think of to do. Whatever was afflicting Martine was even more mysterious than the young man's ailment.

"We're going to put the captain and crew into boats and set them free," Renie said after a while.

"Are there enough of us to run the ship?" Quan Li asked.

"William says it pretty much sails itself, but I suppose we need enough people to keep watch." Frowning, she thought for a moment. "What did I say we were? Nine?" She turned. !Xabbu was still crouched beside Orlando, his hands splayed on the big man's chest. His patient seemed to be resting a little more easily. "Well, there's the six of us in here. There's William, although he almost counts for two." She smiled wearily, for Quan Li's benefit as much as her own. "The robot man—what did he call himself, T-Four-B or something? And the woman who went up the rigging to keep watch. Yes, nine. Besides, having a full crew would matter more if we had some idea where we were going . . ."

She broke off as she realized that the gentle pressure on her fingers was becoming stronger. Martine's eyes were open, but still unfixed.

"Renie . . . ?"

"I'm here. We're on the ship. We're hoping to be out of this Temilún simulation soon."

"I'm . . . I'm blind, Renie." She forced the words out with great effort.

"I know, Martine. We'll do our best to find a way to . . .'' She was stopped by a very hard squeeze.

"No, you do not understand. I am blind. Not just here. I have been blind for a very long time."

"You mean . . . in your real life?"

Martine nodded slowly. "But I have . . . there are modifications on my system that allow me to read my way through the net. I see the data in my own way," She paused; speaking was obviously difficult. "In some ways, it has made me better at what I do than if I had sight, do you understand? But now everything is very bad."

"Because of the information rate, like you said?"

"Yes, I . . . since I have come here, it is like people screaming in both my ears, like I am being blown in a great wind. I cannot . . ." She brought trembling hands up to her face. "I am going mad. Ah, may the good Lord save me, I am going mad." Her face contorted, although no tears came to the sim eyes. Her shoulders began to shake.

Renie could only hold her as she wept.

Two large lifeboats held the ship's three dozen crew fairly comfortably. Renie stood on the deck, feeling the shudder of the engine beneath her feet, and watched the last sailor drop from the ladder into the boat, black pigtail flying.

"Are you sure you don't want another lifeboat?" she called down to the captain. "You'd be less crowded."

He looked up at her, plainly unable to comprehend this kind of soft-hearted piracy. "It is not far to shore. We will be fine." He mumbled his lip plug for a moment, contemplating an indiscretion. "You know, the patrol boats have only remained at a distance to protect the lives of the crew. They will stop you and board you within minutes after we are safe."

"We're not worried." Renie tried to sound confident, but of all their company only iXabbu seemed truly calm. The small man had found a long piece of twine in the captain's cabin and was blithely constructing one of his intricate string-figures.

Renie's intention to release the hostages before the ship reached the simulation's edge had been the subject of long discussion, but she had been adamant. She would not risk taking the Temilúni out of their world. Perhaps the Otherland machinery would not compensate for them in this peculiar circumstance, and they would then cease to exist. It would be no better than mass murder.

The captain shrugged and sat down. He signaled to one of his men to start the engine. The boat glided forward and then began to pick up speed, chugging along after the adjutant's boat, which was already only a white dot against the darkness.

A beam of light cut through the fog from the far side of the barge, flicking across the undraped mast.

"Well, there they are, chuck," said William. He held up his confiscated pistol and looked at it sadly. "This won't be much use against the Royal Featherhead Navy, now will it?"

More lights appeared, these fixed like low-slung stars. Several large vessels were coming up fast behind them. One of them blew a long deep note on a steam-whistle, a sound that vibrated in Renie's bones. !Xabbu had put down his string. "Perhaps we should consider . . ."

He never had a chance to finish his suggestion. Something whistled past them and splashed into the water off the bow. A moment later a globe of fire bloomed in the deeps, fountaining the coastal waters and releasing a sullen thump as the sound reached the surface.

"They're shooting at us," shouted Fredericks from one of the hatchways. Renie was silently commending him for obviousness under combat conditions when she noticed that the exploding shell had left some kind of unexpected aftereffect in the depths before them. The waters sparkled with glittering points of neon blue.

Renie caught her breath. She struggled to remember the name of the robot Goggleboy currently in the barge's wheelhouse, but could not. "Tell what's-his-name full speed ahead!" she screamed. "I think we're there!"

Another shell arched overhead and slashed into the water, nearer this time. The impact made the barge rock so that Renie and William had to grab at the railing. Slowly, though, she could feel the ship picking up speed.

She leaned over, squinting at the dark swells. Surely the sparkling blue light was brighter now. It looked like an entire school of some exotic bioluminescent fishes had surrounded the royal barge.

Something exploded directly beneath them. The entire front end of the barge lifted up, as though shoved from beneath by a giant hand. Renie fell to the deck and slid. The barge tipped sideways; then, like a living creature, it seemed to find its center of balance, and dropped back down into a trough between waves. The water rising around them seemed pulsingly alive with blue light.

It *was* alive, it was electrically active, radiant and throbbingly, brilliantly, vital. . . .

All the sounds of sea and ship and exploding shells abruptly stopped. In perfect silence and an absolute blue glow, they passed through.

Renie's first thought was that they were caught in the timeless instant of an explosion, stuck in the dreary heart of a quantum event that would never end. The bright light, more white than blue now, dazzled her so that she had to shut her eyes against the pain.

When she carefully opened them a moment later, the light was still there, but she realized it was only the brilliance of an ordinary daytime sky. They had left the night behind them in Temilún.

Her second thought was that the last explosion had blown the entire top off the barge. They still bobbed on the water, and the coastline—now revealed in crystal-clear daylight and full of startlingly huge trees as wide and tall as skyscrapers—was very visible, but there was no longer a railing to look over.

Renie realized she was on her knees, clutching at something curving and fibrous and as thick as her arm that stretched where the railing had been. She dragged herself around so she could look back at where the rest of the barge had been, the wheelhouse, the royal apartment. . . .

Her companions were lying in the center of something that was large and flat, but otherwise nothing like a barge—something ribbed and dimpled like a giant piece of modern sculpture, something that curled at the edges and was as stiffly yielding as crocodile hide beneath Renie's hand.

"!Xabbu?" she said. "Are you all right?"

"We have all survived." He still wore his baboon body. "But we . . ."

Renie lost the rest of his sentence in a growing drone from somewhere above. She stared at the flat expanse upon which they all lay, at the almost ragged shape of its edges where they curled up from the water, and realized what the thing they were floating on looked like.

Not a boat at all, but . . .

"A . . . *leaf?*"

The droning was growing louder and louder, making it hard to think. The huge trees on the distant shoreline . . . It made a sort of sense, then—they were not a trick of distortion and distance. But was the place itself too large, or were she and her companions . . . ?

The sound rattled in her ears. Renie looked up to see something the size of a single-engine airplane glide overhead, hover for a moment so that the wind almost knocked her flat, and then speed away again, wings glinting like stained glass in the bright, bright sun.

It was a dragonfly.

Jeremiah found him going through the cabinets in the kitchen for perhaps the dozenth time, looking for something that both of them knew was not there.

"Mr. Sulaweyo?"

Renie's father tugged open another door and began shoving industrial-sized cans and heat-sealed ration packs out of his way, working with ragged intensity. When he had cleared a hole, he reached in until his armpit was pressing into the front of the shelf and groped in the darkness at the back of the cabinet.

"Mr. Sulaweyo. Joseph."

He turned to stare at Jeremiah, his eyes red-rimmed. "What you want?"

"I want a little help. I've been sitting at the console for hours. If you'll take a turn, I can make us something to eat."

"Don't want nothing to eat." Long Joseph turned back to his search. After a moment he cursed, retracted his arm, then began the same process on the next shelf down.

"You don't have to eat, then, but I do. In any case, that's your daughter in that tank, not mine."

A canister of soy meal tipped off the shelf and thumped onto the floor. Long Joseph continued to scrabble in the space at the back of the shelf. "Don't you tell me about my daughter. I know who's in that tank."

Jeremiah Dako made a noise of angry frustration and turned to go. He stopped in the doorway. "I'm not going to sit there forever staring at those screens. I can't. And when I fall asleep, nobody will be checking their heart rates, nobody will be watching in case the tanks go wrong."

"God *damn!*" A line of plastic sacks slid off the shelf and toppled. One broke, puffing a sulfurous spray of powdered egg across the cement floor. "God damn this place!" Long Joseph swept more sacks from the shelf, then muscled a can up over his head and flung it down so hard it bounced before coming to rest against the rear wall. An ooze of syrup trickled from beneath the crumpled lid. "What the hell kind of place is this?" he shouted. "How someone supposed to live like this, in some goddamn cave in the ground?" Long Joseph lifted another can as though to throw it and Jeremiah flinched, but instead he lowered it again, staring at it as though it had just been handed to him by a visitor from outer space.

"Look at this craziness," he said, holding it out for Jeremiah to examine. Jeremiah did not move. "Look, it say 'Corn Porridge.' They got goddamn *mielie pap* in ten gallon cans! Enough porridge to choke an elephant, but they don't got even one beer." He laughed harshly

and dropped the can on the floor. It rolled ponderously against a cabinet door. "Shit. I want a drink. I am so dry."

Wide-eyed, Jeremiah shook his head. "There's nothing here."

"I know that. I know. But sometimes a man just have to look."

Long Joseph looked up from the mess on the floor. He seemed on the
verge of tears. "You say you want to sleep, go sleep. Show me what to
do with that goddamn machine."

". . . That's all. Heartbeat and body temperature are really the important things. You can bring them out just by pushing this—it lifts
the tank covers—but your daughter said not to do it unless they were
really in trouble."

Long Joseph stared at the two cable-draped sarcophagi, both now
standing upright. "I can't take this," he said at last.

"What do you mean?" There was an edge of irritation in Jeremiah's
voice. "You said you'd watch for me—I am exhausted."

The other man didn't seem to hear him. "It's just like Stephen. Just
like my boy. She right there, but I can't touch her, can't help her, can't
do anything." He scowled. "She right there, but I can't do anything."

Jeremiah stared at him for a moment. His face softened. He put his
hand gently on Long Joseph's shoulder. "Your daughter is trying to
help. She's very brave."

Joseph Sulaweyo shrugged the hand away, his eyes fixed on the
tanks as though he could see through the dense fibramic shells. "She
one damn fool, what she is. She think just because she go to the
university she know everything. But I tried to tell her these weren't
people to mess about with. She wouldn't listen. None of them listen,
they never do."

His face suddenly crumpled and he blinked at tears. "All the children gone. All the children gone away."

Jeremiah started to reach out again, then pulled back his hand.
After a long silence, he turned and made his way to the elevator, leaving the other man alone with the silent tanks and the bright screens.

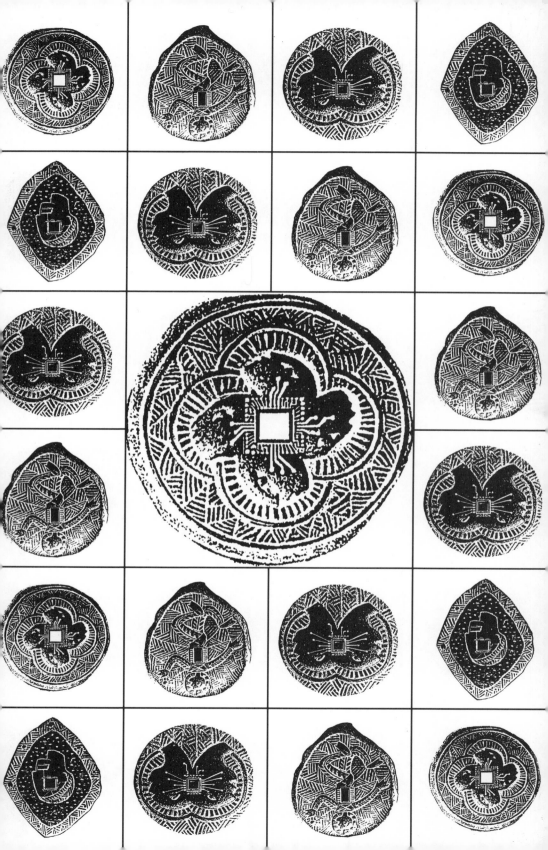